DANGEROUS GROUND
THE SERIES

VELLICHOR BOOKS

An imprint of JustJoshin Publishing, Inc.

DANGEROUS GROUND
March 2020
Copyright (c) 2012 by Josh Lanyon
Cover by Ron Perry for Ron Perry Graphic Design
Book design by Kevin Burton Smith
Edited by Judith David & Keren Reed
All rights reserved

ISBN: 978-1-945802-75-1
Published in the United States of America

JustJoshin Publishing, Inc.
3053 Rancho Vista Blvd.
Suite 116
Palmdale, CA 93551
www.joshlanyon.com

This is a work of fiction. Any resemblance to persons living or dead is entirely coincidental.

TABLE OF CONTENTS

DANGEROUS GROUND

BOOK ONE

CHAPTER ONE

The nose of the red and white twin engine Baron 58 was crunched deep into the bottom of the wooded ravine. Mud and debris covered the cockpit windows. One wing had been sheared off when the plane crashed through the surrounding pines, knocking three of them over. The other wing was partially buckled beneath the craft. The tail of the plane had broken off and lay several yards down the ravine.

Taylor mopped his face on the flannel sleeve of his shirt. Ten thousand feet up in the High Sierras, the sun was still plenty warm despite the chill spring air.

Behind him, Will said, "Either the pilot was unfamiliar with the terrain or he didn't have a lot of experience with mountain flying. Out here, avoiding box canyons is one of the first things you learn."

"Take a look at this," Taylor said, and Will made his way to him across the rocky, uneven slope. Taylor pointed to the fuselage. "You see those registration numbers?"

"N81BH." Will's blue eyes met Taylor's. "Now why does that sound so familiar?"

Taylor grinned. "It's the plane used in that Tahoe casino heist last year."

Will whistled, long and low.

"Yeah," agreed Taylor. Just for a moment he let his gaze linger on the other man's lean, square-jawed features. Will's hair, brown and shining in the sun, fell boyishly into his eyes. He hadn't shaved in three days, and the dark stubble gave him a rugged, sexy look—very different from the normal nine to five Will. Not that they exactly worked nine to five at the Bureau of Diplomatic Security.

Will's gaze held his for a moment, and Taylor looked away, focusing on the plane's registration numbers again.

"What'd they get away with again?" Will asked in a making conversation kind of voice. "Something in the neighborhood of 2.3 million, was it?"

"That and murder," Taylor said grimly. "They shot two sheriff's deputies making their getaway." These days he was touchy about law enforcement officers getting gunned down.

"Doesn't look like they got away far." Will moved toward the open door of the plane. He hopped lightly up onto the broken wing, and for a moment Taylor felt a twinge of envy. He was still moving slowly after his own shooting six weeks ago; sometimes he felt like he was never going to get it all back: the strength, the speed—the confidence—he had always taken for granted. He felt old at thirty-one.

He walked toward the broken off tail piece, and Will—only half-joking—called, "Watch out for snakes, MacAllister."

"You had to say that, didn't you, Brandt?" Taylor threw back. He studied the rim of the ravine. It had been winter when three masked men with automatic weapons robbed the Black Wolf Casino on the Nevada border of Lake Tahoe. They had fled to the nearby airport, hijacked a plane, and disappeared into the snowy December night.

Local law enforcement had theorized the Beechcraft Baron crashed in the High Sierras, but the weather and the terrain had inhibited searchers. It was clear to Taylor now that even under the best conditions, it would have been just about impossible to spot the little plane tucked away in the crevice of this mountainside.

He glanced back, but Will had vanished inside the wrecked plane. He could hear the eerie creak and groan of the aircraft as Will moved around inside.

Taylor worked his way around the crash site. Not their area of expertise, of course, but he knew what to look for.

Scattered engine parts and broken glass were strewn everywhere. A couple of seats had been thrown clear and were relatively intact. There was a weathered plank of wood that must have originally been a table or a desk, and some broken light fixtures and vinyl parts of storage bins. The plane could have carried five passengers in addition to the pilot. The casino had been hit by three bandits; the fourth had been driving the getaway car that sped them to Truckee Tahoe Airport. Four people would have inevitably left DNA evidence, but the crash site was four months old and contaminated by the elements and wildlife. He glanced around at the sound of Will's boots on the loose rock.

Will said, "The pilot's inside. No one else."

That was no surprise. The initial investigation had cleared the pilot of involvement in the robbery; if he'd been alive, he would have contacted the authorities. Taylor thought it over. "No sign there were any passengers on board when she went down."

"What about an incriminating black tie?" Will referred to the famous narrow black necktie that legendary hijacker D.B. Cooper left on the Boeing 727 he jumped out of way back in 1971.

"Not so much as a stray sock."

"Then I guess they weren't doing laundry up there," Will remarked, and Taylor drew a blank.

"You know how one sock always gets lost—forget it." It was a lame joke, but once Taylor would have known instantly what Will meant. Once Taylor would have laughed. "Parachutes?" Will asked.

"No parachutes."

"None?"

"Doesn't look like it," Taylor said.

"Interesting. The pilot's got a bullet through his skull."

"Ah," said Taylor.

"Yep."

Their eyes met.

"Come take a look," Will invited, and Taylor followed him back to the front section of the plane.

Will sprang onto the wing, reaching a hand down for Taylor, and with a grimace, Taylor accepted his help, vaulting up beside him. The wing bobbed beneath their weight, and Will steadied him, hands on Taylor's waist for an instant.

Taylor moved away. Not that he minded Will's hands on him—there was nothing he'd have liked more than Will's hands on him—but this had nothing to do with attraction and everything to do with lack of confidence. A lack of confidence in Taylor being able to look after himself. Not that Will had said so, but it was clear to Taylor—and maybe it was clear to Will too, which might explain what the hell they were doing up in the High Sierras one week before Taylor was officially due to start back at work.

Because if they couldn't figure this out—get past it—they were through as a team. Regardless of the fact that so far no one had admitted there was even a problem.

"After you," Will said, waving him into the gloomy and rotting interior of the plane with exaggerated courtesy. Taylor gave him a wry smile and ducked inside.

"Jesus. Something's made itself right at home in here."

"Yeah. Maybe a marmot. Or a weasel. Something relatively small." Will's breath was warm against the back of Taylor's neck.

"Relatively small is good," Taylor muttered, and Will laughed.

"Unless it's a skunk."

Almost four years they'd been together: partners and friends—good friends—but maybe that was over now. Taylor didn't want to think so, but —

His boot turned on a broken door lever, and Will's hand shot out, steadying him. Taylor pulled away, just managing to control his impatience.

Yeah, that was the problem. Will didn't think Taylor was capable of taking two steps without Will there to keep an eye on him.

And that was guilt. Pure and simple. Not friendship, not one partner watching another partner's back, not even the normal overprotectiveness of one partner for his injured-in-the-line-of-duty opposite number. No, this was guilt because of the way Taylor felt about Will—because Will didn't feel the same. And somehow Will had managed to convince himself that that was part of the reason Taylor had stopped a bullet.

He clambered across the empty copilot's seat and studied the remains of the dead pilot slumped over the instrument dashboard control panel. The pilot's clothes were in rags, deteriorated and torn. Bacteria, insects, and animals had reduced the body to a mostly skeletal state. Not entirely skeletal, unfortunately, but Taylor had seen worse as a special agent posted in

Afghanistan. He examined the corpse dispassionately, noting position, even while recognizing that animals had been at it. Some of the smaller bones of the hands and feet were missing.

"One bullet to the back of the head," he said.

"Yep," Will replied. "While the plane was still in flight."

Taylor glanced down at the jammed throttle. "And then the hijackers bailed out," he agreed. This part at least still worked between them. They still could work a crime scene with that single-mindedness that had earned the attention and approval of their superiors.

Not that they investigated many homicides at the Bureau of Diplomatic Security. Mostly they helped in the extradition of fugitives who fled the country, or ran interference for local law enforcement agencies with foreign police departments. But now and then they got to...get their feet wet. Some times were a little wetter than others. Taylor rubbed his chest absently.

"In the middle of the night and in the middle of nowhere," Will said. "Hard to believe all four of them made it out of these mountains safely. FBI and the local law were all over these woods within twenty-four hours."

"Yeah, but it was snowing, remember."

"Those guys are trained."

"They missed the plane."

"The plane wasn't making for the main highway."

"Maybe the bad guys were local," Taylor said. "Maybe they knew the terrain."

"Wasn't the prevailing theory, was it?"

"No." He backed out of the cockpit, and Will did it again—rested his hand on Taylor's back to stabilize him—although Taylor's balance was fine, physically and emotionally.

He gritted his jaw, biting back anything that would widen the rift between them. Will's friendship was better than nothing, right? And there had been a brief and truly hellish period when he thought he'd lost that, so...shut up and be grateful, yeah?

Yeah.

Will jumped down to the ground and reached up a hand. Taylor ignored the hand, and dropped down beside him—which jarred his rib cage and hurt like fuck. He did his best to hide the fact.

"More likely what's left of 'em is scattered through these woods," Will commented, and Taylor grimaced.

"There's a thought."

"Imagine jumping out of a plane into freezing rain and whatever that headwind was? Eighteen knots. Maybe more."

"Maybe someone was waiting for them on the ground."

Will nodded thoughtfully. "Two and an almost-half million divides nicely between five."

Taylor grunted. Didn't it just? Kneeling by his pack, he unzipped it, dug through his clothes and supplies, searching for something on which he could note the crash site coordinates. It was sheer luck they'd stumbled on it this time. He found the small notebook he'd tossed in, fished further and found a pen, pulling the cap off with his teeth. He squinted up at the anvil-shaped cliff to the right of the canyon. The sun was starting to sink in the sky. He rose.

Will moved next to him, looking over his shoulder, and just that much proximity unsettled Taylor. It took effort not to move away, turn his back. Will smelled like sunshine and flannel and his own clean sweat as he brushed against Taylor's arm, frowning down at Taylor's diagram.

"What's that supposed to be? A chafing dish?"

Taylor pointed the pen. "It's that…thing. Dome or whatever you call it."

"If you say so, Picasso." Will unfolded his map. "Let me borrow your pen."

Taylor handed his pen over, and Will circled a spot on the map, before folding it up again, and shoving it in the back pocket of his desert camo pants.

"Well, hell," he said, "I guess we should start back down, notify the authorities we found their missing aircraft."

Will looked at him inquiringly, and Taylor nodded. That was the logical thing to do, after all. But he wasn't happy about it. Three days into their "vacation" they weren't any closer to bridging the distance yawning between them—and it would be a long time before they had this kind of opportunity again. By then it might be too late. Whereas this plane had been sitting here for over four months; would another four days really make a difference?

"Right. We'll rest up tonight and head back tomorrow then," Will added, after a moment.

Taylor directed a narrow look his way, but the truth was he *was* fatigued, and climbing in the dark would have been stupid even if he wasn't. So he nodded again, curtly, and tossed the notebook and diagram back into his pack.

* * * * *

Will was tired. Pleasantly tired. Taylor was exhausted. Not that he'd admit it, but Will could tell by the way he dropped down by the campfire while Will finished pitching their two-man tent.

One eye on Taylor, Will stowed their sleeping bags inside the Eureka Apex XT. He pulled Taylor's Therm-a-Rest sleeping pad out of his own backpack where he'd managed to stash it that morning without Taylor noticing, and spread it out on the floor of the tent. He opened the valve and left the pad inflating while he went to join Taylor at the fire.

"Hungry?"

"Always." Taylor's grin was wry—and so was Will's meeting it. Taylor ate like a horse—even in the hospital—although where he put it was anyone's guess. He was all whippy muscle and fine bones that seemed to be made out of titanium. It was easy to look at him and dismiss him as a threat, but anyone who'd ever tangled with him didn't make that mistake twice.

He was too thin now, though, which was why Will was carrying about three pounds more food in his pack than they probably needed. He watched Taylor feeding wood into the flames. In the firelight his face was all sharps and angles. His eyes looked almost black with fatigue—they weren't black, though, they were a kind of burnished green—an indefinable shade of bronze that reminded Will of old armor. Very striking with his black hair— Will's gaze lingered on Taylor's hair, on that odd single streak of silver since the shooting.

He didn't want to think about the shooting. Didn't want to think about finding Taylor in a dingy storeroom with his shirt and blazer soaked in blood—Taylor struggling for each anguished breath. He still had nightmares about that.

He said, talking himself away from the memory, "Well, monsieur, tonight zee specials are zee beef stroganoff, zee Mexican-style chicken, or zee lasagna with meat sauce."

"What won't they freeze-dry next?" Taylor marveled.

"Nothing. You name it, they'll freeze-dry it. We've got Neapolitan ice cream for dessert."

"You're kidding."

"Just like the astronauts eat."

"We pay astronauts to sit around drinking Tang and eating freeze-dried ice cream?"

"Your tax dollars at work." Will's eyes assessed Taylor. "Here." He shifted, pulled his flask out of his hip pocket, unscrewed the cap, and handed it to Taylor. "Before dinner cocktails."

"Cheers." Taylor took a swig and shuddered.

"Hey," Will protested. "That's Sam Houston bourbon. You know how hard that it is to find?"

"Yeah, I know. I bought you a bottle for Christmas year before last."

"That's right. Then you know just how good this is."

"Not if you don't like it." But Taylor was smiling—which was good to see. Not too many smiles between them since that last night at Will's house. And he wanted to think about that even less than he wanted to think about Taylor getting shot.

"Son, that bourbon will put hair on your chest," he said.

"Yeah, well, unlike you I prefer my bears in the woods."

There was a brief uncomfortable pause while they both remembered a certain naval officer, and then Taylor took another swig and handed the flask back to Will.

"Thanks."

Will grunted acknowledgment.

He thought about telling Taylor he hadn't seen Bradley since that god-awful night, but that was liable to make things worse—it would certainly confuse the issue, because regardless of what Taylor believed, the issue had never been Lieutenant Commander David Bradley.

Taylor put a hand to the small of his back, arching a little, wincing—and Will watched him, chewing the inside of his cheek, thinking it over. It was taking a while to get back into sync, that was all. It was just going to take a little time. Sure, Taylor was moody, a little distant, but he still wasn't 100 percent.

He was getting there, though. Getting there fast—because once Taylor put his mind to a thing, it was as good as done. Usually. When he started back at work he'd be stuck on desk duty for a couple of weeks, maybe even a month or so, but he'd be back in the field before long, and Will was counting the days. He missed Taylor like he'd miss his right arm. Maybe more.

Even now he was afraid—but there was no point thinking like that. They were okay. They just needed time to work through it. And the best way to do that was to leave the past alone.

"Warm enough?" he asked.

Taylor gave him a long, unfriendly look.

"Hey, just asking." Will rose. "I was going to get a sweater out of my bag for myself."

Taylor relaxed. "Yeah. Can you grab my fleece vest?"

Will nodded, and passing Taylor, took a swipe at the back of his head, which Taylor neatly ducked.

* * * * *

They had instant black bean soup and the Mexican-style chicken for dinner, and followed it up with the freeze-dried ice cream and coffee.

"It's not bad," Taylor offered, breaking off a piece of ice cream and popping it into his mouth.

Actually the ice cream wasn't that bad. It crunched when you put it into your mouth, then dissolved immediately, but Will said, "What do you know? You'll eat anything. If I didn't watch out you'd be eating poison mushrooms or poison berries or poison oak."

Taylor grinned. It was true; he was a city boy through and through. Will was the outdoors guy. He was the one who thought a week of camping and hiking was what they needed to get back on track; Taylor was humoring him by coming along on this trip. In fact, Will was still a little surprised Taylor had agreed. Taylor's idea of vacation time well spent was on the water and in the sun: renting a house boat—like they had last summer—or deep sea fishing—which Taylor had done on his own the year before.

"They never did arrest anyone in connection with that heist, did they?" Taylor said thoughtfully, after a few more minutes of companionable chewing.

"What heist?"

Taylor threw him an impatient look. "The robbery at the Black Wolf Casino."

"Oh. Not that I heard. I wasn't really following it." Taylor had a brain like a computer when it came to crimes and unsolved mysteries. When Will wasn't working, which, granted, was rarely, the last thing he wanted to do was think about crooks and crime—especially the ones that had nothing to do with them.

But Taylor was shaking his head like Will was truly a lost cause, so he volunteered, "There was something about the croupier, right? She was questioned a couple of times."

"Yeah. Questioned but never charged." He shivered.

Will frowned. "You all right?"

"*Jesus*, Brandt, will you give it a fucking *rest*!" And just like that, Taylor was unsmiling, stone-faced and hostile.

There was a short, sharp silence. "Christ, you can be an unpleasant bastard," Will said finally, evenly. He threw the last of his foil-wrapped ice cream into the fire, and the flames jumped, sparks shooting up with bits of blackened metal.

Taylor said tersely, "You want a more pleasant bastard for a partner, say the word."

The instant aggression caught Will off guard. Where the hell had it come from? "No, I don't want someone more pleasant," he said. "I don't want a new partner."

Taylor stared at the fire. "Maybe I do," he said quietly.

Will stared at him. He felt like he'd been sucker punched. Dopey and… off-kilter.

"Why'd you say that?" he asked finally into the raw silence between them.

He saw Taylor's throat move, saw him swallowing hard, and he understood that although Taylor had spoken on impulse, he meant it—and that he was absorbing that truth even as Will was.

"We're good together," Will said, not giving Taylor time to answer—afraid that if Taylor put it into words they wouldn't be able to go back from it. "We're…the best. Partners and friends."

He realized he was gripping his coffee cup so hard he was about to snap the plastic handle.

Taylor said, his voice low but steady, "Yeah. We are. But…it might be better for both of us if we were reteamed."

"Better for you, you mean?"

Taylor met his eyes. "Yeah. Better for me."

And now Will was getting angry. It took him a moment to recognize the symptoms because he wasn't a guy who got mad easily or often—and never at Taylor. Exasperated, maybe. Disapproving sometimes, yeah. But angry? Not with Taylor. Not even for getting himself shot like a goddamned wet-behind-the-ears recruit. But that prickling flush beneath his skin, that pounding in his temples, that rush of adrenaline—that was anger. And it was all for Taylor.

Will threw his cup away and stood up—aware that Taylor tensed. Which made him even madder—and Will was plenty mad already. "Oh, I get it," he said. "This is payback. This is you getting your own back—holding the partnership hostage to your hurt ego. This is all because I won't sleep with you, isn't it? That's what it's really about."

And Taylor said in that same infuriatingly even tone, "If that's what you want to think, go ahead."

Right. Taylor—the guy who jumped first and thought second, if at all; who couldn't stop shooting his mouth off if his life depended on it; who thought three months equaled the love of a lifetime—suddenly *he* was Mr.

Cool and Reasonable. What a goddamn laugh. Mr. Wounded Dignity sitting there staring at Will with those wide, bleak eyes.

"What am I supposed to think?" Will asked, and it took effort to keep his voice as level as Taylor's. "That you're in love? We both know what this is about, and it ain't love, buddy boy. You just can't handle the fact that anyone could turn you down."

"Fuck you," Taylor said, abandoning the cool and reasonable thing.

"My point exactly," Will shot back. "And you know what? Fine. If that's what I have to do to hold this team together, fine. Let's fuck. Let's get it out of the way once and for all. If that's your price, then okay. I'm more than willing to take one for the team—or am I supposed to do you? Whichever is fine by me because unlike you, MacAllister, I —"

With an inarticulate sound, Taylor launched himself at Will, and Will, unprepared, fell back over the log he'd been sitting on, head ringing from Taylor's fist connecting with his jaw. This was rage, not passion, although for one bewildered instant Will's body processed the feel of Taylor's hard, thin, muscular length landing on top of his own body as a good thing—a very good thing.

This was followed by the very bad thing of Taylor trying to knee him in the guts—which sent a new and clearer message to Will's mind and body.

And there was nothing Will would have loved more than to let go and pulverize Taylor, to take him apart, piece by piece, but he didn't forget for an instant—even if Taylor did—how physically vulnerable Taylor still was; so his efforts went into keeping Taylor from injuring himself—which was not easy to do wriggling and rolling around on the uneven ground. Even at 75 percent, Taylor was a significant threat, and Will took a few hits before he managed to wind his arms around the other man's torso, yanking him into a sitting position facing Will, and immobilizing him in a butterfly lock.

Taylor tried a couple of heaves, but he had tired fast. Will was the better wrestler anyway, being taller, broader, and heavier. Taylor relied on speed and surprise; he went in for all kinds of esoteric martial arts, which was fine unless someone like Will got him on the ground. Taylor was usually too smart to let that happen, which just went to show how furious he was.

Will could feel that fury still shaking Taylor—locked in this ugly parody of a lover's embrace. He shook with exhaustion too, breath shuddering in his lungs as he panted into Will's shoulder. His wind was shit these days, his heart banging frantically against Will's. These marks of physical distress undermined Will's own anger, reminding him how recently he had almost lost Taylor for good.

Taylor's moist breath against Will's ear was sending a confusingly erotic message, his body hot and sweaty—but Christ, he was thin. Will could feel—could practically count—ribs, the hard links of spine, the ridges of scapula in Taylor's fleshless back. And it scared him; his hold changed instinctively from lock to hug.

"You crazy bastard," he muttered into Taylor's hair.

Taylor struggled again, and this time Will let him go. Taylor got up, not looking at Will, not speaking, walking unsteadily, but with a peculiar dignity, over to the tent.

Watching him, Will opened his mouth, then shut it. Why the hell would he apologize? Taylor had jumped *him*. He watched, scowling, as Taylor crawled inside the tent, rolled out his sleeping bag onto the air mattress Will had remembered to set up for him, pulled his boots off, and climbed into the bag, pulling the flap over his head—like something going back into its shell.

This is stupid, Will thought. We neither of us want this. But what he said was, "Sweet dreams to you too."

Taylor said nothing.

CHAPTER TWO

Will looked like hell. Eyes red-rimmed, hair ruffled. There was a black-and-blue bruise on his jaw, which Taylor tried to feel sorry about—but Will looked sorry enough for himself for both of them.

Taylor watched him pour a shot of bourbon into his coffee without comment. Yep, Will was definitely having a bad day, and it was only seven o'clock in the morning.

As though reading his thoughts, Will looked up and met his eyes. Taylor, feeling weirdly self-conscious, looked away.

"So I guess we're still not speaking this morning?" Will asked.

And despite the fact that he didn't want to fight with Will, that he wanted to find some way to step back from the precipice he teetered on, Taylor shrugged and said coolly, "What did you want to talk about?"

And Will just gave a kind of disgusted half-laugh, and turned back to his spiked coffee.

So that was that.

They moved around camp, neither of them speaking, moving efficiently and swiftly as they breakfasted and then packed up—like the day before and the day before that, only this morning the silence between them was not the easy silence of a long and comfortable partnership; it was as heavy and ominous as the rain clouds to the north.

It was still early in the season—and the weather poor enough—that they met no one as they started down the steep trail, stepping carefully on the gravel and small stones. It was a strenuous descent, requiring attention, and Taylor was glad to concentrate on something besides Will. He'd been thinking about Will way too much lately. For the last year, really.

The view was spectacular: huge clouds rolling in from the north, snow-covered mountains all around them, and a long, green valley way below, moody sunlight glinting off the surface of a slate blue lake. The scent of sagebrush was in the air—and the hum of bees. The sun felt good on his face after weeks of being indoors in bed.

Will, the experienced hiker, went first down the trail. The set of his wide shoulders was uncompromising, his back ramrod straight as though he could feel Taylor's stare resting between his shoulder blades—which he probably could. They'd got pretty good at reading each other's thoughts, and half the time they communicated with no more than a glance.

Back when they used to communicate.

The bulky sweater and comfortable fatigues couldn't conceal the lithe beauty of that tall, strong male body. Will was the most naturally gorgeous guy Taylor had ever known. And no little part of his attractiveness had to do with the fact that he was pretty much unaware of just how good-looking he was. Taylor's gaze dropped automatically to Will's taut ass. Yep, gorgeous.

Will's boot slipped on shale, and Taylor's hand shot out, grabbing him, steadying him.

Will grunted thanks, not looking at him. Taylor let go reluctantly.

It was weird the way his body craved contact with Will's. Any contact. A nudge in the ribs or a pat on the ass. It was like an addiction. In the hospital he'd lived every day waiting for Will to drop by—and to give Will credit, he'd managed to visit almost every single day, even if it was just for a few minutes. It had been strange, though, with Will so gentle and careful with him; at the time Taylor had been too ill to question it.

Even when Will didn't touch him, when he just stood next to him, Taylor could feel his nearness in every cell, his skin anticipating Will's touch—longing for the lover's touch that never came. Was *never* going to come, because Will didn't feel that way about him.

They couldn't go on like this. Even Will had to see that—although Will was pretty good at not seeing what he didn't want to see.

They stopped midmorning for water and granola bars, still not looking at each other, still not talking. Will consulted his map. Checked his compass. High overhead, a pair of golden eagles threw insults at each other.

"Are they mating?" Taylor asked, suddenly tired of the stand off. He missed Will, missed their old companionship. He'd been missing him for six weeks—and he was liable to be missing him from now on. It seemed worth making an effort for whatever was left of their trip.

Will glanced skyward briefly. His eyes were very blue in his tanned face. They held Taylor's gaze gravely. "That's your idea of romance?"

He was partly kidding, but partly not, and Taylor felt himself coloring.

"Hey." He lifted a shoulder. Not exactly sparkling repartee, but he didn't want to fight anymore, didn't know what Will wanted. He couldn't not feel what he felt; he'd tried that—had tried for well over a year to talk himself out of feeling what was obviously unwanted and unwelcome.

Will snorted, but he was smiling. Sort of. "You're a nut, MacAllister. Did I ever tell you that?"

"A girl never gets tired of hearing it," Taylor deadpanned, and Will did laugh then. He shoved the map back into his pocket, shrugged on his backpack.

* * * * *

They reached the meadow a little after one o'clock. The clouds roiling overhead were thunderous and black. The pine and fir trees were singing and swaying in the wind; the lake was choppy and dark. The gray green grass rippled like the earth was breathing beneath their feet.

"Let's get under the trees," Will said. "We'll pitch the tent and have lunch. Wait it out."

Taylor could see he was worried about the worsening weather conditions; Taylor was just grateful for flat terrain. He'd wanted to call for a rest an hour earlier, but he'd have died first. He could feel the ache of coming rain in his chest, and told himself to get used to it. The doctors had said the broken ribs were going to hurt forever—especially when it rained. The bullet had torn through skin, muscles, and a couple of ribs. Following the shock of impact—like a land mine going off inside his chest—the pain had been unbelievable. Unimaginable.

The miracle had been that no major blood vessels had been hit while the bullet ricocheted around his chest cavity. But it hadn't felt like a miracle at the time. His right lung had begun to squeeze, he'd had to struggle for each short breath, and it had been agony—like getting stabbed over and over. His vision had grayed out, he hadn't been able to call out or move, feeling the warm spill of his own blood on his chilled skin—and the blood had felt good, that's how cold he'd been. Cold to the core.

And then Will had been there. And he'd been glad. Glad for the chance to see him one last time, to say good-bye, even if it was just inside his own head because he sure wasn't capable of speech. And the expression on Will's face had been comforting. At least at the time. Now he knew it for what it was. Guilt. But at the time it had looked like something else, something it had been worth dying to see.

He glanced at Will, walking beside him as they tramped across the long meadow. Will appeared a million miles away, but he felt Taylor's gaze and looked over at him. He opened his mouth, and then closed it, and Taylor knew he had been about to ask if Taylor was all right.

And as tired as he was of Will asking if he was okay, he realized he preferred that to this new awkwardness. And he sure as hell preferred it to Will no longer giving a damn.

He started to say so, but something in the brush caught his attention: the sheen of black material.

"Hey," he said, stopping and nodding.

Will glanced at him, tracked his gaze, and saw exactly what Taylor had. He followed as Taylor waded into the currant bushes dragging what at first glance appeared to be a black seat cushion from out of the bush.

"It's a parachute," Will said, taking it from Taylor and turning it over.

Taylor nodded. "Still packed."

They met each other's gaze, and Taylor raised an eyebrow.

"Let's have a little look-see," Will drawled.

"I'll take the right."

They separated, fanning out across the meadow. It took less than half an hour to locate the other three parachutes—two still packed, one torn wide open by something with claws and a lot of optimism. It seemed clear to Taylor that all four parachutes had been jettisoned at the same time. The speed of the plane and the headwind had resulted in several yards between each landing, but not nearly the distance which would have resulted from dropping them out the plane door at deliberate intervals.

"That's it," Taylor said as Will rejoined him. "The fifth chute will have gone with the hijacker."

"Then it won't have gone far." Will's face was grim. He was staring past Taylor, and Taylor turned. Near the lake the trees grew in a thick wall of white firs, Jeffrey pines, and incense cedars. And there, dangling from a twenty-feet tall cedar like a dreadful Christmas tree ornament, was what remained of the missing parachutist.

* * * * *

"He's carrying a knapsack," Taylor commented, as they stood gazing up at the macabre thing swinging gently in the wind.

"Christ," Will said.

"I'll go up." Taylor started forward, but Will caught his arm.

"Uh, no, you sure won't."

That of course was a big mistake; Taylor freed himself, his face hard again. "Is that so?"

Will said calmly, "Yep, MacAllister, that is so." Even if he had to knock Taylor on his ass to make it so.

"I'm lighter, I'm faster —"

"You're sure as hell not faster these days."

Which was true, but not guaranteed to win points. But Will wasn't interested in winning points; he was interested in keeping Taylor in one piece, whatever it took, and maybe Taylor read that resolve in Will's eyes because after a pause, he shrugged. Said tersely, "Hey, suit yourself. You always do."

The injustice of that stung, and although Will had told himself he was not going to lose his temper again, that he could be patient, that Taylor and their partnership was worth working this through—whatever the hell *this* was and however much work it took—all the same he bit right back, "Christ, that's rich coming from *you*."

And instantly Taylor was cool, his body deceptively relaxed—a fighter poised for action. Oh, yes, Will had seen that loose, easy stance a hundred times. "What's that supposed to mean?"

"Forget it."

Taylor got in front of him. "I don't want to forget it."

Un-fucking-believable. In fact, if he didn't know better he'd have suspected Taylor had been shot in his goddamn head. Who was this stranger who had taken over Taylor's body?

Will planted both hands on Taylor's chest and pushed him back a step. "What, are we supposed to have another wrestling match now?"

The physical aggression caught Taylor off guard, and Will pressed his advantage. "You're self-centered, MacAllister. You do whatever you want whenever you feel like it, and to hell with everybody else. This is a perfect example."

"This?" Another time and place Taylor's indignation might have been funny. "I didn't even want to come on this goddamned trip. I did it for you. And what the hell you wanted out of it beats me since you obviously —" He broke off, and to their mutual horror, for an instant appeared to be choked with emotion.

Anger, Will could deal with. Arrogance, aggression, he knew what to do. This? No.

Before he had time to rethink, he reached out—and just in time stopped himself from pulling Taylor into his arms. He settled for squeezing those rigid shoulders. "Look, Taylor, all I meant was…you don't always think things through." He offered a tentative smile. "Come on, I've known you three years. We both know your track record. When it comes to relationships you think with your dick and damn the torpedoes. And yes, for the record, I…find you attractive too. You know that. But there's more at stake here. I don't want to screw up our friendship or our partnership because we sleep together."

"Why would it screw anything up?" Taylor was looking at him so seriously. So…earnestly. It cut him up inside. The last thing he wanted to do was hurt Taylor. Ever. But Taylor just wouldn't stay down. He kept getting up and coming back for more. And what the hell was Will supposed to do?

He said, struggling for patience, "It's already screwing everything up and we haven't even done it!"

"Why couldn't we give it a real shot?"

"What are you talking about? Give it a real shot? Give *what* a real shot?" Will let go of him, and gestured to the scene before them. "Here's why. Because we're in the middle of a crime scene and we're arguing about our goddamned *romance*."

He couldn't stand the look on Taylor's face, so he turned away. What they needed was a climbing harness but...what the hell. He jumped for the lowest limb, wrapped his legs partway around the thick trunk, and hauled himself up a couple of feet. Blowing out, he reached up for the next branch. He swung himself up, stretched for another tree limb—and began to climb.

At first it was like crawling through undergrowth, but then the branches spread out, and he was able to see what he was doing and move more freely. He had a good head for heights, and the tree had thick, dark, irregular bark, making it easier for his boots to find purchase. The limbs were plentiful. Yellow cones rained down as he swarmed up through the cinnamon-scented branches.

The tree groaned, swaying in the wind. Will looked up, and the feet of the dead parachutist were hanging an arm's length away.

Pausing to pull the knife from his ankle sheath, he looked down, surprised to see how small and faraway Taylor looked.

"Lightning to the north," Taylor called, batting away another hurtling cone. And then... "Brandt—maybe this wasn't such a good idea."

"Now you tell me," Will muttered. He called back, "Simmer down, buddy boy. It's under control."

Knife in hand, he studied the tangle of parachute and parachutist. Wind and weather had reduced the chute to ribbons, and the body wasn't in much better shape. A tree limb thrust from the hijacker's waist like a spear; he must have been impaled as he crashed through the branches. Crime really didn't pay.

His own position wasn't quite right...

Will transferred the knife to his mouth, and edged around the trunk, feeling cautiously for footholds. It was hard to see... He pulled himself up to another branch, balancing, and edged closer to the sack of rotting clothes, flesh, and bones.

And all the fresh pine scent in the world wasn't helping...

"That is definitely lightning," Taylor said from below. He had that irritable sound he got when he was nervous. "You mind not taking all day, Brandt?"

"Yeah, I mind. It's my vacation; I'll spend it any damn way I please."

"Asshole." But he could hear the unwilling laugh in Taylor's voice.

Will steeled himself and felt over the dead man's rags, seeking a wallet or any kind of identification. He didn't expect to find any, and he wasn't disappointed. That done, he began to saw with his free hand at the straps of the knapsack. He tried to be careful, but he was in a hurry now, and the clothes and corpse began to come apart with his tugging. One of the black boots fell.

Fuck. *Fuck.* He wiped his face on his shoulder. Called down, "Stand back, MacAllister. It's raining men."

"Are you *kidding* me?"

His tone was priceless. Will bit back a ferocious grin, and went back to hacking at the knapsack straps. A few more slices and he had it. The backpack tumbled down a few feet, knocking needles and cones and twigs loose—along with the corpse's other boot.

Will lowered himself down swiftly, pursuing the knapsack. He found it lodged in the V of the trunk and a branch.

Grabbing it by the severed straps, he swung it once, twice, out beyond the span of the branches—and let it fly. "MacAllister, heads up!"

The pack went sailing and then dropped to earth like a stone.

Will let himself down fast, ignoring the scrape of rough bark on his hands. A few feet from the ground he balanced on a thick limb.

Taylor had retrieved the bag. He knelt in the mud and pine needles, knapsack wide open, staring up at Will. "You sure you don't want to run away to Mexico with me?" He held up a neatly bound stack of greenbacks.

"Nah." Will jumped down, landing lightly on the soft wet earth. "Salsa gives you indigestion."

"True." Taylor tossed the stack of dollars to Will.

The money felt damp, sinister to his touch. He thumbed through it. Benjamin Franklin's skeptical expression flashed by over and over.

The rain began to fall.

CHAPTER THREE

"You warm enough?"

Taylor didn't bother to respond, staring out the mesh window of the tent at the rain sheeting down the sides.

Of course he was cold. He was freezing his ass off. Will had told him not to wear Levi's. He'd told him to dress in layers. Wool socks, long underwear, lightweight wool sweater or acrylic sweatshirt, military surplus pants or jungle fatigues. But no, Mr. Know-It-All had chosen flannel shirts and Levi's and a leather jacket. He'd changed his soaked clothes for dry, but he was still chilled, fine tremors rippling through his body every few minutes.

It had taken them a few minutes to set up the tent after the skies opened up. Now the rain beat down on the plastic and sheeted off the sides, puddling on the ground outside. Inside the tent it smelled of rubber, damp wool, and something dank and moldering.

The money and backpack sat in the far corner. They had been through the backpack. No ID there either. No clue at all as to who the dead man was, but Taylor thought he fit the general description of Jon Jackson, one of the suspects in the Black Wolf Casino robbery. As a former employee of the casino, Jackson had come under investigation despite—or maybe partly because of—the fact that he'd left town two days before the robbery and hadn't been heard from since.

Will opened his mouth to tell—suggest—that Taylor change into his own spare fatigue pants, but Taylor said abruptly, "Only one hijacker got on that plane."

"Looks that way."

"One robber gets on the hijacked plane. The others split and go their separate ways."

"Maybe."

"Maybe. Either way, they go prop up their alibis—maybe they *are* each other's alibis."

Will scratched his bristling jaw, considering. Taylor was a natural at this kind of doublethink. In fact, he was a little too good. Some of his scenarios were straight out of Agatha Christie, in Will's opinion. But this one sounded reasonable: Wile E. Coyote leading the hounds off the trail of the foxes. Still, there were problems with it.

He said, "You think they trusted him to get on that plane and fly away with all that money? What happened to the 'no honor among thieves' rule?"

"I think it's more of a guideline. Anyway, it was a risk, sure. But it's not like they weren't the gambling kind."

Will acknowledged that.

Taylor said, "Getting that money out of town was one way of protecting it—and maybe protecting them—assuming they were local."

Will turned it over, nodded. "Maybe. Yeah, they couldn't take the risk of being stopped with the money, and they sure wouldn't want it turning up in any subsequent searches. They couldn't know how much time they'd have to stash it." He wished he could read Taylor's face, but Taylor was mostly staring out at the rain—and it was the first time Will had ever felt lonely in his company.

"They've probably spent every weekend up here since the snow started melting searching for that plane." He gave another of those little shivers.

Will said, "Maybe. Maybe they figure he double-crossed them."

Taylor finally glanced Will's way, his eyes oddly colorless—almost gray—in the dim light. "Maybe. But say they did some checking around. It probably wouldn't take long to figure out that no one ever saw Jackson after that night in December."

"If it was Jackson."

"They'd know the plane went down. I think they'd figure Jackson—yeah, if it was Jackson—and the money went down with it."

"It fits," Will agreed slowly.

He studied Taylor's sharply etched profile. It was hard to see in the fading light, but little details struck him: the black stubble on Taylor's jaw, the length of his eyelashes, the soft dark hair growing over his collar, the set line of his mouth. It was kind of a sexy mouth. Sensual, even a little pouty, though Taylor was not the pouty kind, and his mouth spent a lot more time laughing and shooting itself off at the wrong moment than it did pouting.

Taylor had his faults, God knew, but he was smart, savvy, and tough. He was good company most of the time; the best partner—the best friend—Will had ever had. He'd missed him badly these last six weeks. Hospital visits, even stopping by Taylor's place once he'd been released, hadn't been enough; in fact, it felt like he'd barely seen Taylor since the shooting.

The shooting.

It had been a routine op. Scratch that. It hadn't even officially been an op. They'd received a tip-off that a passport counterfeit ring was operating out of the back of a nail salon in Orange County's Little Saigon. A nail salon fronting a ring of counterfeiters? How dangerous could they be?

Will had been up front chatting pleasantly with the teenaged pink-haired receptionist, and sizing things up. Taylor was supposed to be out back scoping the alley and neighboring businesses—just getting the lay of the land. They had nothing to move on at that point; it was just intelligence gathering. But Taylor had wandered around to the back of the salon and slipped in through the delivery door, apparently deciding all on his own to take a look around. And whatever he'd spotted amidst the boxes of acrylic powders and foam rubber toe separators had encouraged him to poke around a little more in the stock room—which is where two juvenile members of the local Phu Fighters gang had found him.

The first clue Will had was the sound of shots from a back room in the salon. Two shots—and neither of them the familiar and distinct bang of Taylor's .357 SIG—and he'd known. Known instantly that Taylor had been shot.

He'd mown through the screaming, hysterical women, racing for the stockroom, and finding it—for one bewildered moment—empty. Then his gaze moved past the wall of boxes and metal shelving units and he'd spotted Taylor slumped on his side, blood spilling out of his chest, pooling on the cement floor. Taylor's face had been bone white with shock, his eyes huge and black and stunned. Will had knelt down beside him, kneeling in the puddle of Taylor's blood, and for one instant of sheer blind terror, he couldn't think beyond the fact that Taylor was dying. That any one of those shuddering, faint breaths might be his last.

It had never crossed his mind to go after the shooters. Not until later.

"Hang on, Taylor," he'd said, and he'd yelled at the terrified faces grouped in the doorway of the stockroom to call 911. His voice shook when he said, "Stay with me, Taylor. Stay." The words had seemed laden, charged with fears and feelings he'd never considered—never allowed himself to consider. And he'd shrugged out of his sports coat, putting it around Taylor, shouting at the women to bring him towels, clean towels to try to stanch the bleeding. And the frightened women had scattered, a couple of them returning with freshly laundered towels that he jammed up against the bullet wound in Taylor's chest.

Taylor's lashes had flickered. His colorless lips parted but no words came out, and Will didn't even know if Taylor could hear him or not. Taylor's eyes were open, pupils huge and black, but there was no other sign of consciousness in his chalky face, no response to Will. Will had taken Taylor's icy hand in his and chafed it, feeling the long, lax fingers twitch feebly; maybe it was response, maybe it was just...a dying nervous system shutting down for good. And it was the worst day, the worst hour, the worst moments of Will's life waiting for the paramedics—waiting for Taylor to stop breathing, for his eyes to fix and glaze before help could reach them.

But then, afterward, when it was clear that Taylor was going to live—and recover fully—Will had been...angry. Why not admit it? He had been angry. About as angry as he'd been terrified—which was about as terrified as he'd been in his life.

Because the truth was Taylor had brought it on himself. His ego hurt, he'd gone looking for trouble, and when he found it, he'd charged right into it without following procedure or using common sense. He hadn't waited for backup, and he sure as hell hadn't waited for Will. Taylor was a little headstrong and he was a little arrogant, but he wasn't stupid and he wasn't reckless—why had he done such a reckless, stupid, *stupid*, potentially fatally stupid thing?

And Will knew why. Because of David Bradley. Because Taylor found out Will was seeing David Bradley, and he'd been...jealous. Which didn't make a lick of sense. Taylor knew Will dated. Taylor dated. It was one of the first bonds between them: the fact that they were both gay. Not a lot of gay special agents in DSS. They'd have been a good team in any case, and they'd probably have been good friends—they shared a similar jaded worldview and sarcastic sense of humor—but the fact that they also shared the same sexual orientation… Yeah, it forged that bond between them into reinforced steel. They were practically brothers. Brothers-in-arms.

Less than two months ago Will would have said no one knew him better—no one was closer to him—than Taylor. That was assuming he'd have been willing to talk about his feelings—which he wouldn't have, of course. They didn't talk about that kind of thing.

Will glanced over at Taylor. Profile hard, he was staring out the tent window at the rain thundering down.

The last thing he'd ever meant to do was hurt Taylor.

He still wasn't clear exactly where he'd gone wrong.

He'd mentioned David in passing a few times, mentioned that he was seeing him. Taylor had seemed—well, he hadn't seemed anything in particular. Why would he? But that last afternoon, Will had mentioned he had seen David the night before, and Taylor had got kind of quiet and weird.

"You're seeing a lot of him," he'd said, bringing it up a couple of hours later when they stopped for lunch.

"Yeah? So?" Will had known immediately who Taylor meant; he knew Taylor too well to have missed that odd moment in the car earlier.

"You…getting serious?" And Taylor's face had been—well, frankly, Will still couldn't quite describe what Taylor's face had been. Troubled? Uncomfortable? Hurt? All of the above? It had been a weird expression, and it had been weirder yet because he could tell Taylor was trying not to show anything.

"Nah." But then he had made the fatal mistake of being honest. "I don't know."

And Taylor had gone white.

White.

Like Will had stabbed him. He looked stricken.

"What's the matter?" Will had said. "What's wrong?" Because something sure as hell was wrong.

But Taylor had laughed, closing up instantly—which wasn't how they were together. "Nothing's wrong. Bradley's a great guy." And he'd shrugged—like a guilty little kid caught in a lie. And then he'd changed the subject.

What. The. Hell.

But Will had let it drop—not like he had a choice. Taylor was talking himself away from the moment, whatever that moment had been. And, truth to tell, Will couldn't get away from that moment fast enough himself.

They'd been okay by the end of the day though, back in sync, back in step, and after their shift they'd gone for drinks at their favorite watering hole. Will should have realized then: Taylor was knocking back Rusty Nails like they were going out of style. His usual drink was beer. In fact, Taylor had a thing about trying every obscure import or microbrew out there. Whenever and wherever they traveled, Taylor had to try the local brew. The only time he ordered the hard stuff was when he was stressed—or people had done their best to maim or kill him.

But that night Taylor was putting the booze away like he had hollow legs. By the time Will had been ready to call it a day, Taylor was blasted: tie loosened, hair disheveled, giggling. *Giggling*, for chrissake. And, yeah, it was mildly cute: that boyish little gurgle, and those under-lashed looks Taylor was throwing him—like he was flirting with Will.

"Last call for you, buddy boy," Will had said, shaking his head, trying not to laugh when Taylor—leaning toward him—nearly fell off his stool.

And Taylor had draped an arm around Will's shoulders and drawled, "Take me to bed, William, or lose me forever!"

Will had laughed, although that kind of thing was risky as shit in what amounted to their local hangout. It was one thing to be gay; it was another to be openly gay. The last thing they needed was to buck for Federal GLOBE poster boys.

But Taylor was an affectionate drunk, no problems there, and he'd let Will steer him to Will's car, let Will drive him to Will's house, let Will walk him to the spare bedroom and help him undress—like they'd done for each other plenty of times in the past three years.

But then...then it had gotten hinky.

Taylor had put his arms around Will and said a lot of stupid things—drunken shit that Will had tried to ignore, tried to joke away—but Taylor had been insistent, if incoherent. They had wrestled around a little, Will losing patience maybe faster than he should have.

Because…he was tempted. He could admit that now. Sure, he'd been tempted—what with Taylor trying to nibble on his ear and all.

And it turned ugly fast—with the end result of Taylor grabbing his clothes and departing into the night.

The next day, for the first time in three years, they had nothing to say to each other. Maybe it would have worked itself out, but by lunchtime Taylor was in surgery with a bullet in his right lung, fighting for his life.

"It's letting up," he said, jolting Will out of his thoughts. "The rain," Taylor said, meeting Will's blank gaze.

"We could make camp here tonight," Will heard himself say. It made sense. He and Taylor had to get things straight between them, and that wasn't going to happen once they got back to civilization.

But Taylor was already crawling out of the tent. "May as well keep moving," he said. "We've got a lot of ground to cover."

* * * * *

The light was amazing. Those crepuscular rays—golden shafts of illumination—penetrating the snowy rafters of clouds. What did they call those? Jacob's ladder? The fields around them were bathed in amber, the trees glinting and flashing in the dueling sun and shade. The surrounding mountains looked purple and blue.

With cold, probably.

Taylor put that thought away. As long as he kept moving he was warm enough, and it looked like they would be moving till nightfall. But that had been his choice. All he had to do was say the word and Will would be fussing over him like a hen with one chick. And the sad thing was, there was a part of him that would have almost enjoyed that.

He glanced at Will walking a little ahead. His face was flushed with sun and exertion, his eyes sparkled—despite everything, he was enjoying himself. Will was totally in his element out here. He liked the silence, the emptiness, the loneliness. He'd have been perfectly happy on his own, whereas nothing but Will would have dragged Taylor out to this wilderness—beautiful as it was.

He shivered as a gust of wind—tasting of snow and distant mountain-tops—hit him. Will glanced his way, but said nothing.

* * * * *

"I think we should stash the money," Taylor said, breaking the silence of nearly an hour. He was trailing two or three yards behind Will, and Will was glad to have a reason to stop and take a look at him. He looked beat, and it pissed Will off, made his voice sharper than it needed to be.

"What are you talking about?"

"I don't know if waltzing into a sheriff's station with two million dollars is a good idea."

Will stared, trying to see it from whatever angle Taylor was viewing this. "You think someone in the sheriff's department was involved?"

"I don't know." Even Taylor's voice was tired. "I just know it's a small town, a lot of money, and the sheriffs didn't seem to make a lot of headway on the case."

"Well, hell, neither did the FBI."

Taylor didn't say anything. Will's dad had been a small town sheriff in Oregon, and Will knew what Taylor thought: that Will was on defense because of that—and maybe Taylor was right.

"Okay. What's your idea?" he asked grudgingly.

"We could leave the money in one of these bear boxes, contact the feds —"

Will spluttered, "Leave two million dollars in a *bear box*?"

"Just hear me out."

Blue eyes met green.

"We could put the money in my pack. I don't have a dry change of clothes left and you're carrying half my gear anyway —"

Will had opened his mouth but he shut it at that.

"Whatever else I need—my pistol—I can carry."

"And what if someone steals your backpack?"

"The kind of people who hike back into these mountains aren't even the same species as the sewer rats we deal with. Besides, we've seen…what?

Two hikers and one park ranger since we set out? I don't think anyone's going to rip off my pack. But…I'll leave my ID."

"What?"

Taylor sighed. "Just listen a minute. It's only for about forty-eight hours, and we're basically alone on this mountain. But say some lowlife does go through my gear. My ID acts as a kind of hands-off. You've gotta be pretty hard-core to tangle with the federal government—which is what my ID amounts to."

"That is the dumbest damn idea I've ever heard." But even as Will was saying it, he was thinking that Taylor did have a point. Leaving his ID in his backpack was about as clear a staking of claim, a warning, as there was—and he was also right about the unlikelihood of their running into anyone. Even so…

He said, "And then the feds have to hike up here to retrieve the cash?"

"Come off it, Brandt. They have to anyway. There's the crash site, the body—this hill is going to be crawling with law enforcement in seventy-two hours. There won't be any possibility of the money slipping through the cracks."

"That would have to be a pretty big crack for two million dollars to slip through."

"Yeah, well, sorry if I don't feel like taking a chance when it's your name and mine attached."

"You are one paranoid sonofabitch." But Will was grinning, amused, and in a weird way, pleased by these nutty Machiavellian maneuverings. It was so…Taylor.

And Taylor gave him a little sideways grin, acknowledging the compliment like a pretty girl accepting roses.

* * * * *

The bear box was a long and low metal trunk painted a particularly ugly shade of brown. The campground was deserted, and Taylor's pack was on its own as he stowed it, and locked the lid.

Will was shaking his head, but he had decided it didn't hurt taking this extra precaution—and, frankly, they could move faster if Taylor didn't have to lug a fifty-five pound backpack.

"Did you want to camp here tonight?" he asked. The shadows were lengthening, the air growing chillier. They were going to have to call it a day shortly anyway.

"Let's keep moving." Taylor was already heading for the trail.

And Will couldn't help the edge that crept into his voice. "I didn't realize you were in such a big hurry to get back."

Taylor just gave him one of those long looks, aloof and wronged at the same time. It aggravated Will—but then Taylor seemed to do that without any effort these days. It didn't make sense. He and Taylor had always got along well; even in the ways that they were unalike they used to complement each other. It was just since the shooting that everything was different. Will didn't *want* it to be different. He wanted things to go back to the way they had been.

His eyes rested a moment on Taylor's wide shoulders, moved down to his narrow hips and long legs.

Damn Taylor for ever opening this Pandora's box because while it was true Will had refused to ever consider sleeping with his partner and friend—the best partner and the best friend he'd ever had—it wasn't like he had failed to notice how…hot…Taylor was. He'd have to have been blind to have missed it. Taylor was sexy as sin. Sexy, funny, smart, capable—all the things Will wanted in a lover. But besides being Will's partner and best friend, he was commitment-shy and had the mating instincts of a young gazelle. He was a bad relationship risk for anyone, but in particular he was a bad risk for Will.

Will liked stability, reliability, predictability. He needed those things.

All the same, turning Taylor down that night at his house had been one of the hardest things Will had ever done—and if Taylor hadn't been definitely the worse for alcohol, Will wasn't totally confident he'd have managed it.

He'd put the thought out of his mind during the long weeks of Taylor's recuperation, but now that Taylor was looking and acting more like his old self—and continuing to put himself on offer—Will was starting to have trouble.

Like…in his dreams at night.

The visuals were bad enough, but in his dreams it was the smell, the taste, the *feel* of callused hands sliding over ridged abdominals, cut pectorals, taut nipples—smooth skin and soft hair—the damp tangle of groin, fingers wrapping around a hot, rigid shaft. In the dream he was initiating and experiencing at the same time, as if there were no division, no separation between where he ended and Taylor began.

That wasn't a dream; that was a nightmare.

And a bigger nightmare was the fact that even in broad daylight it was a struggle keeping his mind off the thought of having Taylor—or, for that matter, Taylor having him. And how weird was that? Will didn't enjoy bottoming for anyone, but the idea of *Taylor*…imagining the exquisite shock of that full body contact, of strength equal to his pleasuring him, owning him. It made him half-hard just thinking about it, his face heating up in a way that made him grateful that Taylor had turned away again.

* * * * *

The terrain had changed quite a bit from that morning: sunbaked bluffs and stony slopes giving way to chinquapin shrubs and manzanita which yielded in turn to hillsides of oaks and conifers leading to a series of meadows and lakes.

After leaving the junction campsite, they followed a trail which descended the north wall of East Hancock Gorge. The drop was moderate at first but ended with a series of steep, rocky switchbacks.

Taylor's legs were shaking by the time they reached the bottom of a long trench where a green and sparkling tributary tumbled in a suicidal fall off the mountainside. They still had that mountainside to get down, and he was glad he wasn't carrying his pack—in fact, it seemed worth two million dollars to have unloaded it. He was cold, he was hungry, and he was depressed.

Even the thought of having recovered the money from the Black Wolf Casino heist didn't particularly cheer him up; maybe Will had a point if recovering a couple of million dollars felt less important than the rift in their partnership. Maybe his priorities were getting screwed up. At this point he was too tired to care.

He followed Will down a narrow, deeply shaded trail to a clearing where white steam rose in the rain-swept air from what looked like a rough, rock-ringed pool. Will stopped and lowered his pack, so apparently they were taking another break, and thank Jesus for that. At this point, a few weeks of being stuck on desk duty sounded like paradise.

"Junction Hot Springs," Will said. "There used to be a hotel a few miles down the mountain. I think it's a private lodge now. If it's still there at all."

"A hotel *here?*"

"It was a health resort. People used to come up here for the fresh air and massage and the miracle waters."

Taylor was rolling his head from side to side on his shoulders, trying to work out a crick. "I wouldn't mind a massage." He heard the echo of his voice, and just managed to avoid looking at Will.

After a minute, Will said, "Well, how about a hot bath anyway? Get you nice and warmed up, take the ache out of your muscles."

Will was already pulling his olive drab sweater over his head, followed by his thermal top, and then his snowy white T-shirt. Beneath all the layers, his chest was brown and smooth, the soft dark hair bisecting his taut, muscular torso and disappearing beneath the band of his camo pants.

"Are you serious?"

"Yeah. We could both use it." Unself-consciously—and why should he be self-conscious? They'd dressed and undressed in front of each other plenty of times—Will stepped out of his pants and boxers, lowering cautiously to the man-made cement bench inside the pool.

Hands propped on his hips, Taylor studied him, but Will just sighed and closed his eyes, putting his head back. "Come on, MacAllister," he murmured. "Relax for five minutes."

Swearing under his breath, Taylor peeled off his vest, flannel shirt, T-shirt and wriggled out of his Levi's. Will ignored him, still soaking, face skyward while the steam drifted up around him.

Taylor slid into the water and yelped, standing up and preparing to jump right back out. "Jesus, it's boiling!"

Will's eyes opened. "It's about one hundred and fifteen degrees." Will was a stickler for accuracy. He always insisted on looking over Taylor's reports before he handed them in—not that Taylor was any less accurate— but Will was a little bit of a control freak. "Stay still," he advised. He was flushed and perspiring, but on him it looked good. Sexy. But then Will looked sexy whether he was staring down the barrel of an M4 or eating a sloppy joe.

Taylor leveled him a look but held motionless, giving his body time to adjust to the heat. Finally, he eased the rest of the way down on the stone bench and sank back, the water level rising as he did, sloshing gently back against Will, who stretched his arms out along the back of the tub.

The steam settled on Taylor's face, and his forehead broke out in sweat. He breathed in deeply, hot moisture invading his nostrils.

Will smiled lazily.

Taylor spread his legs, the water rippling gently with his motion, and let the wet heat suffuse every part of his body. Yeah, that was better. The water was silky soft, and now the heat felt caressing, sinking into every pore, every cavity. Startling, but good. In fact, it was the first time he'd felt really warm in days.

He glanced over and Will was staring. He looked down. His chest was still a mess of scars beneath the soft dusting of returning hair. The scars would fade in time but they were ugly now. He let himself slip lower into the water, hiding the ugliness from Will.

Will's eyes moved to his face, and Taylor said, "This was a good idea."

Will nodded.

"Finally," Taylor added, and Will chuckled and kicked water his way. And because Taylor was lying so low, he took a wave of hot mineral water in the face—which couldn't go without retaliation.

A second later Will was the one with his hair plastered down his face. He whipped his hair back and laughed. Water sparkled on the tips of his eyelashes and his teeth were very white.

"You're living dangerously, buddy boy."

Taylor lazily flipped his foot, spattering Will with smoky wet.

"Bring it on, cowboy," he drawled.

Will dived for him and they grappled amiably, hands slipping on slick bodies, tussling and twisting in the steaming water. They stepped on each other's feet, but avoided kneeing anything vital, the rough stone scraping their backs and butts—panting and laughing.

Finally, Taylor managed to wriggle free, and half-lunged, half-waded over to the other side of the tub. Will turned his head to spit out the water he'd swallowed. "Hey," he said. "Do you have any protection?"

Taylor bit back a grin, scissoring his legs through the water. "You think I'll need more than the SIG to keep you back?"

"Funny," Will said. "I mean, do you have a condom with you?"

He was serious. Taylor stilled. All at once his heart was pounding very fast. He managed to keep his tone lazy as he asked, "Is this a trick question?"

Will said slowly, "Well, we could get it out of our system."

It took Taylor a moment to absorb that one.

Finally he managed, "Gee, and they say romance is dead."

"You want to, right? That's what you said. That's what it was all about, right?"

Taylor's eyes narrowed. "It wasn't just about fucking."

"No?" Will's smile was cynical.

"No."

Will moved next to Taylor on the rock bench, put a wet hand on Taylor's shoulder, tugging him over. A warm, possessive handprint breaking apart in tiny drops, rolling down Taylor's skin; it had no power over him—yet he let himself be drawn into Will's arms.

CHAPTER FOUR

"I don't know about this," Taylor said gruffly.

Which was kind of funny considering how hard he'd pushed for it on one notable occasion.

And even funnier considering how his body was already reacting to the proximity of Will's.

Will's muscular arms felt good about him; the last time he had held Taylor this tight they had been fighting for real, and Taylor had wanted to kill him. But now Will's arms felt friendly, familiar, and although he was asking for something Taylor wasn't sure he could give, he felt no need to fight, to force his release.

Will asked, "You want it, don't you?"

The words came out a little aggressively, and Taylor considered him for a moment. "Yeah."

"Well?"

"Well, what? This is kind of a sudden change of heart, isn't it?"

"I never said I didn't find you attractive. In fact, I said I *did* find you attractive. I just didn't think it was a good idea for us."

"Because we partners. And because we're friends."

"That's right." Will's gaze was cool and a little hard. "But you dis-agree. And who am I to argue? Maybe you're right."

Taylor's brows drew together.

"I'll tell you one thing," Will said. "Ever since that night I haven't been able to get the idea out of my head. I want you." His big hand slid over Taylor's flat belly, fingertips reaching. Taylor's cock was already stiff and swollen, anticipating that touch. "And you sure as hell want me."

Yeah, there was no hiding that fact. Taylor bit his lip as Will's hand fastened around his cock, trying to withhold the revealing groan threatening to tear out of his chest. Just...*that* felt so good. Just Will's hand on him. But he forced himself to try to think.

"And what happens afterward? Are you going to regret it? Maybe blame me?"

As though in answer, Will's hand pumped him—just once—down and up, fist brushing Taylor's belly and then sliding up to the sensitive glans. Taylor shuddered all over. *"Will..."*

Will's hands were moving over him, and instinctively Taylor cooperated, rising and letting himself be positioned between Will's powerful thighs. He could feel Will's half-erect cock nudging his backside as Will's arms around his waist drew him back. And the sad thing was it felt...good having this taken out of his hands. What did that say about him? But he'd been wanting it—yearning for it—for *so* long...

"Listen," Will said, his breath warm and steamy against Taylor's ear, "we already know each other, care about each other. This isn't going to change that, but I think it might settle something once and for all. For both of us."

Taylor was silent. He could feel Will watching him, waiting.

"You really think I'm just curious about what it would be like with you?" he asked finally.

"I think you want me. I think we've established I want you too," Will said. "But, sure, I think there's an element of curiosity in it, and I think if we take care of that...we'll be able to get back to business."

Taylor chuckled, although there wasn't a lot of humor in it. "Either you don't have a lot of faith in yourself or you're seriously underestimating my charms." He put his hands over Will's wrists, feeling the muscles move in Will's forearms.

Will said soberly, as though he were paying Taylor a compliment, "I know the partnership, the friendship means more to you than...this."

"That's easy to say when we haven't done *this* yet."

Will chuckled, his breath tickling the back of Taylor's neck. "But we're going to," he said. Beneath Taylor's hands, Will's arms were hard, muscular bands around Taylor's waist, holding him close, but Taylor knew if he wanted free he could have it in a minute. Will was crowding him, yeah, but he wasn't going to force him. Taylor could still say no. And if he had any sense at all, that's what he'd do because Will really had no clue what he was talking about.

But Taylor didn't push away. Instead he leaned back into Will's arms, resting his head against Will's broad shoulder and tipping his face up at the sullen sky. He could feel Will's surprise, feel his grip change instantly to support, automatically offering Taylor harbor. And it was surprisingly relaxing to…acquiesce just this much. To yield to the combined pressure of Will's desire and his own. Will's arms cradled him, his strength reassuring rather than challenging, while Taylor tried to decide whether he wanted to take this to the next level.

Oh, there was no question that he wanted to. But he didn't want to take this at the expense of further damaging his relationship with Will. And that could so easily happen, regardless of what Will said now—because Will wasn't looking at this realistically. Which was kind of funny, considering the fact that Will believed himself to be the practical, hardheaded one. But right now he was letting his other head rule.

"I didn't bring a condom," Taylor lied at last, reluctantly—and started to sit up.

Will's voice was unexpectedly harsh. "I did."

Taylor jerked around, water swirling, and Will let him go.

"Is that so?" He couldn't help the edge that came into his voice. "You always carry one?"

Will shrugged. "I noticed it in my pack last night."

Taylor absorbed this, trying to remember the last time Will had gone camping and who he'd gone with; he decided he'd be happier not thinking about it.

"Always prepared, huh?"

"Something like that." Will's gaze challenged him in some indefinable way.

The idea of Will with someone else settled it for Taylor. Sexual jealousy was the wrong reason to fuck your best friend and closest colleague, but —

He turned his back, pushing against the prod of Will's erection, instinctively encouraging that stiffening swell, forgetting all about the fact that this was probably a bad idea. Pushing away the thought that this wasn't even like Will really—and that Will was probably going to regret it—and that was going to hurt worse than not doing it at all. Will's cock scraped lightly down the crack of Taylor's ass, probing or maybe just moving with the water.

"Is that what you want?" Will's breath was cool compared to the steam.

He wanted—well, there wasn't one single thing he wanted. He'd have liked to bury himself up to his balls in Will's taut tanned ass, but Will returning the favor would be as good in a different way—maybe even better because Will might like it more like that, might remember it—and want to do it again sometime. Besides, just for one hour, he'd like to feel like he belonged to Will. He already knew Will didn't belong to him, but to belong to Will—would be good. Even if just for a little while.

"Yeah," he said huskily. "That's what I want."

"I want it too," Will grated. "I want to fuck you. Hard."

Taylor dipped his head, swallowed. He'd always pictured Will as a gentle lover, playful—teasing. There was a hint of anger in Will's tone that he didn't get, but he nodded his agreement anyway. The idea of Will taking him hard was weirdly exciting.

"Yeah, fuck me," he whispered. "Hard."

He jerked in surprise as Will bit his shoulder. It hurt. But then Will kissed the bite mark so sweetly. He shivered. He didn't want Will kissing him—that was liable to break his heart.

The smart thing would be to pull away, get himself on the other side of this tub, and laugh it off. But Will's arm was locked around him again—he wasn't going anywhere easily. Instead he lifted his hips as Will's free hand arrowed down the hard curve of Taylor's butt cheek, a friendly sweep of caress that ended with one finger poked right up into Taylor's pursed little hole.

Surprise.

He couldn't help his body's instinctive arch and the little guttural moan of stung pleasure.

"Jesus, Will…you could've…" But he was suddenly out of oxygen. The stroking motion of Will's finger made a funny suction with the water, and set the sphincter muscle fluttering in time to the butterfly beat of Taylor's heart. *"Oh…"* He closed his eyes. That wash of hot water and knowing press on spongy tissue. Will had big hands. Hard hands. Thick fingers and callused palms, and he was probing Taylor deeply, his touch possessive, knowing.

Too knowing. And abruptly Taylor wanted to fight that exquisite invasion. He didn't let anyone do this to him. Not ever. He was always the one in charge, the one who called the shots. He was the predator, not the prey. What the hell was he doing giving in to this?

He tried to pull back a little, but Will held him in place and thrust his finger in and out of Taylor's hole, delicately and ruthlessly finger fucking him. Taylor groaned, trying to angle his body, telling himself he was pulling away, but helplessly pushing back on Will's hand.

What was happening to him? Will was making him feel too much, too intensely. He was giving up control—no, admit it, control was being taken from him. That finger shoving even deeper in his body, forcing him to feel and respond. He bit his lip, trying not to cry out, to beg for more.

Will was going to make him come—just like that, and despite the dizzy pleasure, Taylor began to get mad. This wasn't what he'd wanted. He hadn't surrendered his will for this impersonal manipulation. He wanted Will's cock inside his body, not his hand. He wanted Will feeling it too, helpless with it, not playing him. He grabbed his dick and began to work himself, needing to control his body's reaction, to at least control his own orgasm.

"Next time I'm doing *you,*" he warned roughly. He focused on his own hands, what he was doing to himself, fighting to bring himself back under control.

Will's other arm let him go; he felt Will twisting, groping outside the pool, and then the tear of foil but it was distant because he just couldn't seem to think beyond that finger—two fingers now—pushing knowledgably inside his body, stroking and massaging him. Well, he'd said he wanted a massage, hadn't he? Not quite what he'd pictured. His hands rested weak and heavy on his groin.

"I don't want —" His breath caught raggedly, and against his best intentions he was shoving back, craving that touch buried in his body.

"Yeah, you do. You're desperate for it. You don't fool me," Will murmured. "If you were a cat you'd be purring." He wriggled his fingers, and Taylor, still trying to preserve the illusion of self-command, snarled. Will chuckled, but the joke was on Taylor because Will deliberately changed his angle and the pressure, and Taylor's voice cut off on a sound that was embarrassingly kittenish.

To distract himself he began to pump his cock again, water splashing, forcing himself to action.

"No you don't. Not without me you don't." Will heaved up, giving him a little bounce to break his concentration. "Wait for me."

Taylor groaned in frustration as Will moved around some more, and then suddenly Will half picked him up, one powerful arm clamped around Taylor's waist, shifting Taylor's slick, buoyant body. A few errant pokes at balls and cheeks, and without more warning than that, Will's cock pushed inside.

Taylor froze at the shock of it. Never. Never before had he let this happen. He had another guy's cock crammed in his ass. He was letting another guy take him. He shook with the pain and confusion of it.

Will was groaning. "Christ God almighty, Taylor…" His voice sounded desperate. On the edge of tears. Will was more shocked than Taylor was—and Taylor calmed a little, listening, absorbing the truth of that.

Will trembled with the effort of holding motionless, but Taylor could feel his heart thundering behind his own, and any fear that he was alone in this, that he had relinquished too much for too little, faded. He winced—wriggled, trying to accommodate that thick rigidity. Water was not enough of a lubricant. What had they been thinking?

"Are you okay?" Will sounded hoarse. He rocked against Taylor—stopped himself—then rocked again like he just couldn't help it. "Say… something."

To his astonishment, Taylor heard himself whimper. A helpless little submissive sound—and he nudged his ass against Will's groin in clear invitation.

WTF? *Literally* WTF.

And Will responded instantly, unleashed, thrusting in fierce, deep strokes into Taylor's tight channel, grunting softly like it was a fight, like he was taking body blows.

And Taylor responded by humping back, making those helpless little encouraging cries. Pushing, shoving, insisting.

Well, he'd asked for it, and now he was getting it, impaled on Will's cock and getting fucked hard and thoroughly. And there wasn't a damn thing he could do about it, mostly because he didn't want to do a damn thing about it. Will slammed into him, setting the pace—hard and fast—and Taylor raced to catch up, begging for more, just about wild with it. But at least it was mutual now. Both of them out of control with pleasure and pain and longing and bewilderment. This was *them*. And everything Taylor believed he knew about their partnership was taking a beating.

Splish, splash, he was pounding my ass...

He giggled a little hysterically and Will laughed too, a breathless huff. "You...crazy...bastard..."

And now Taylor had the rhythm, sliding up and down the length of Will's cock while he grabbed himself hard and jerked off under water, making a little turbulence like the struggles of a ship going down or a drowning sailor sinking under for the last time.

Their sweat hit the water in glistening droplets, steam rising. It was moist and hot and sexy as all get out although they were probably alarming the hell out of the local wildlife.

Taylor was bumping and grinding, trying not to lose the pace, wrestling Will for control. And Will fighting every step of the way, insisting on command. It was frenetic. Sensation started at the base of his cock and spine and sparkled up through nerves and muscle.

Will cursed under his breath and bit the vulnerable join of Taylor's neck and shoulder. Taylor choked back another gasp of something between a laugh and a sob, and then Will's hand covered his, pumping him frantically.

He was a little surprised when Will's face nudged his, Will's mouth latching on, sweet and hot and hungry. Oh, God. Kisses from Will. His chest tightened in crazy emotional response.

He'd known it would be sweet, but this was almost unbearable, his heart swelling with so much...*feeling* for Will. Such a terrible tenderness and longing and...love.

And then Will cried out, something broken and inarticulate that Taylor swallowed. He could feel the throb of Will's orgasm thrumming through his own body, hot water and rubber pushing into him and spilling right out again, and he was sorry it wasn't just their bodies, silk-skinned steel, but it was still so good —

Flagging, Will thrust against him again, sharply, once...twice...

He began to come himself, spurting into the water, a milky cloud that evaporated as if it had never been.

It was over so quickly. Not fair at all considering how long he'd waited for it.

But his own erection was wilting fast, shriveling down to nothing in the water, and after a few moments he felt Will's rigid length soften and then slip out of his body.

Will was turning him, pulling him into his arms, holding him tightly, burying his flushed, perspiring face in Taylor's throat.

"Yeah, you're right," Taylor said shakily, locking his arms around Will's shoulders, hugging him back tightly. "No big deal."

"Christ, shut up," Will said unsteadily.

"Thank God we did this. Now we don't have to ever think about it again."

"If you don't want me to drown you, shut up," Will said. He was laughing, but his laugh cracked.

* * * * *

It was twilight when they reached the bottom of the trail descending to the next canyon.

"We'll make camp here tonight," Will said as though expecting an argument, but Taylor just nodded. What was there to argue about? He was worn out, and Will's silence since they had left Junction Hot Springs unnerved him.

He'd known it would be a mistake to give in to that sexual hunger, but he'd sort of hoped it would take Will longer than three minutes to regret it. Apparently not.

They set up the tent in silence, and Will got the campfire going while Taylor collected loose firewood. The smell of wood smoke and coffee was sweet in the evening air and the stars were already faintly glimmering in the indigo and pink sky. He brought an armload of wood back, dumping it with relief.

"Coffee ready?"

"Not yet." Will handed Taylor his flask. "Here. Have a slug of this." He was watching Taylor in a way that made him self-conscious. Taylor raised his brows and Will turned away abruptly.

Great.

Taylor handed back the flask, but Will had already moved away—the line of his back unencouraging. Taylor put the flask in the breast pocket of his shirt.

It took effort not to say *I told you so.* Maybe that was funny coming from him because he had been the one originally pushing for this—except he had never been pushing for sex as a goal in itself. That was the thing Will had never understood about him.

"What'd you want tonight?" Will asked a short time later, rifling through the contents of his pack.

Taylor opened his mouth, then caught Will's expression and decided a joke would be a mistake. Will was just waiting for him to say something—the wrong thing.

"Whatever you want. I'm not particular." He was serious—and he was talking about their freeze-dried menu—but Will's face tightened.

"Right. We need to talk," he said grimly.

Words every man dreaded hearing—even when they came from another man.

Taylor said desperately, "How much can there be to say about dehydrated turkey tetrazzini, Brandt?"

"That's not what I mean."

Shit. There was no kidding around when Will got in this mood. He gave up fighting the inevitable, folded his arms on his knees, waiting.

"Shoot." He couldn't help adding, "But not literally, okay?"

That was just nerves talking, but there wasn't a glimmer of a smile from Will. "We can't go on like this, MacAllister."

A little irritably—wasn't this what he'd been saying all along?—he said, "Yeah, I know."

"Okay, maybe sex wasn't the point. Maybe you were right about that much."

"Well, no kidding."

"Do you really want to break up the team?"

Taylor exhaled a long breath, staring at his hands. He said finally, reluctantly, "I think it would be for the best."

Was that really what he thought? Because saying it felt like the end of the world. And the silence that followed didn't make it any easier.

Finally, Will said, "Is that really what you think or is this some kind of—I don't know. An ultimatum?"

Taylor searched inside himself. Tried to put aside his own feelings and figure out what he expected of Will. He was forced to conclude that he did not expect anything. He had always understood that Will did not want to get involved—not with his partner—not at the expense of their team. If they had met under other circumstances...well, probably not then, either, because Will was convinced that Taylor was incapable of a relationship that lasted longer than fifteen minutes. Will just did not believe that Taylor was his type, and who would know better? So Taylor knew what he wanted was unrealistic. It was really out of curiosity that he asked, "If it was an ultimatum, what would your answer be?"

Will groaned, put his head in his hands. "What kind of fucking question is that?" Lowering his hands, he sighed. It was a long, weary sound. "I don't know. Maybe you *are* right. I was hoping this afternoon might settle some things..."

"Did it settle something for you?" Taylor asked, and he couldn't help the note that crept into his voice because he thought if Will said yes he was totally bullshitting himself. It had been crazy, but it had also been fantastic between them, and Taylor was certainly experienced enough to know the feelings hadn't been all on his side.

But Will didn't answer that. He just said, "If you still feel like…you want out…"

He opened his mouth to deny that it was what he wanted, but that was what it amounted to. As painful as the idea of breaking the partnership was, he couldn't go on working side by side with Will feeling the way he did. The idea of watching the David Bradleys come and go in Will's life, or worse, watching Will settle down with someone like David Bradley—who, in fairness, was a perfectly decent guy—was more than he could take.

It wasn't reasonable or logical on his part, but…

Maybe he *was* as self-centered and egotistical as Will thought. As embarrassing as that was to admit.

And maybe fucking in a hot tub had settled everything nicely for Will, but it had just confirmed for Taylor what he already knew. He wasn't getting over this anytime soon.

He said carefully, "This way we walk away friends. Which matters to me. A lot. The way we were going… I don't know that we would."

The truth of that was in Will's eyes. After a very long moment, he nodded.

Which settled that.

They moved about the camp getting ready for the night, and every time Taylor looked at Will's closed expression his chest ached in a way that had nothing to do with cold air in his healing lung.

"Did you really want the turkey tetrazzini?" Will asked politely when the water had boiled.

"I was just kidding," Taylor returned, equally polite.

They ate beef stew in silence. They had cleared the air, but there didn't seem to be much to say any more. Taylor couldn't even work up enough enthusiasm to discuss their dead hijacker and casino heist.

The stars came out: incredibly huge and bright in the black skies. It got colder. They were both tired, and Taylor knew he wasn't alone in not wanting to squeeze into that little tent and lie there listening to each other pretend to sleep.

"Anything else you want out of my pack?" Will asked finally. "Tooth-paste? Soap? Anything else to eat?"

"No, I'm fine."

"I guess I'll bear bag everything."

Taylor nodded, but Will made no move to get up and hang the food and items that might attract bears. He poked the campfire with a stick, his grim face half in shadow, half in rosy light. He could have been a million miles away, sitting on that distant pockmarked moon rising over the serrated tips of the mountains.

Taylor shivered—and for once Will didn't notice. Taylor rose. Will didn't look up. He opened his mouth, but he didn't know what to say. In-stead, he went to get his jacket out of the tent. It was colder tonight, and the air was damp. The night air, spicy with pines and wood smoke, smelled like more rain was on the way. Looking at their sleeping bags lying there side by side gave him a funny feeling in the pit of his stomach.

His SIG was lying on his bag, and he remembered his joke about using it to keep Will back.

Shrugging on his jacket, Taylor crawled back out of the tent.

Will was watching him. He said suddenly, "Look, Taylor. What if we… tried to…I don't know. Take it one day at a time?"

He looked like a stranger, bearded, his eyes shining with a mystery emotion. He looked intense, urgent.

Bushes to the side of Taylor rustled, and something twittering flew up and winged away into the night. When he looked back, Will was on his feet—waiting for his answer, apparently. He wasn't even sure what the ques-tion was.

As he stared, Will shrugged. Said offhandedly, "We could try, right? It would be worth trying."

Taylor opened his mouth to ask what they were going to try, exactly, but there was motion to his left and—and then to the right—and a couple of shadows detached themselves from the darkness and walked into the ring of campfire light.

CHAPTER FIVE

There were three of them. Two men and a woman—although it took Taylor a moment to identify her as such beneath the shapeless clothing. They wore hunting caps, heavy plaid jackets, and they carried rifles. Taylor didn't know much about it, but he was pretty sure hunting was not allowed in a national park.

He barely caught himself from reaching for his missing shoulder holster, instead throwing Will a look, and what he read in Will's face confirmed that they were in trouble—even before the trio moved across the open space of the campsite, cutting him off from his partner.

"Evening," said one of the men. He was older than his companions, sixty or so, but he looked trim and fit—and very alert. "We saw your campfire."

The second man was tall, six-three, maybe six-four. Big. He had long blond curls beneath the duck-billed hunting cap. He stepped toward Taylor, staring at his boots.

"It's him. I'm bettin' it's him."

"You mind?" the older man said to Taylor.

"Do I mind what?" Taylor asked warily.

"The sole of your boot. Let's see it."

Taylor thought of the .357 SIG lying on his sleeping bag in the tent. Three short steps away.

But they'd still be outgunned. Will's 9mm was probably in his backpack, and although these were close quarters for rifles, all three were handling their weapons with the ease of long practice. Taylor counted two suppressed .22 rifles and one semiautomatic with a scope.

He lifted his leg, offering them a gander at the mountain grip outsole of his Adidas Badpak GTX, balancing for a moment in a way that felt way too *Karate Kid* for comfort.

"It's him!" the younger man exclaimed. "That's the boot that made the tracks around the plane."

"Nice job, Cinderella," Will said calmly, and Taylor understood that Will was letting him know that he understood the situation as Taylor did, that he was ready and waiting for opportunity to present itself.

"Hands on the back of your head, son," instructed the older man—clearly the leader—to Taylor. Taylor clasped his hands behind his head. "Search him, Stitch."

The woman kept her rifle trained on Will while the younger man yanked Taylor around, searching him roughly.

"We've been tracking you two most of the day," the older man said, watching this procedure closely. "You were making pretty good time until you decided to go skinny-dipping."

The woman laughed.

At that moment Taylor was glad he couldn't see Will's face.

"It's not on him," Stitch said, and he emphasized his disappointment by shoving Taylor down.

Taylor rolled with it, coming up on his knee. Ready, but too far away to do anything—especially with a rifle trained on Will.

"Well, well," the older man said, observing this. "What circus did you escape from?"

"Where's the money?" Stitch yelled, and he kicked at Taylor, who grabbed his foot and twisted, throwing the other man flat. He didn't have opportunity to follow up, though, because the other two rifles cocked simultaneously—one pointed at him and one pointed at Will's head.

"Stitch, would you stop fooling around," the older man said wearily. "Is he carrying any ID?"

"Nothin'," Stitch said, climbing to his feet. "Not a damn thing." He reached down, fastening his massive hands in Taylor's coat, dragging him up and punching him in the belly.

Taylor doubled over, beef stew and bile rising in his throat. He managed to stay on his feet, although that was partly because Stitch still had hold of his jacket.

Through the pain he heard the older man saying, "Here's the problem. We believe you two have something that belongs to us."

"I don't know what the hell it would be," Will said, his voice tight with anger.

"Put your hands behind your head! That plane that you walked round and around and climbed into and walked around some more yesterday? That plane was carrying something that belonged to us, and we want it back."

"If you mean the pilot, he's right where you left him," Taylor got out, muffled. His head was down so he didn't see the punch that caught him under the ribs. He cried out, the pain catching him by surprise; it hurt much worse than the slug to the gut, thanks to his damaged ribs. He remembered the doctor's warning about his healing lung being vulnerable to detaching from his rib cage again, and he thought he'd shut up for a bit. He coughed a couple of times and tried not to throw up.

"Look," Will said, "whatever you think —"

"Son, you move another muscle and I'll blow your goddamned head off," the older man interrupted. "Search him."

The woman went quickly, clumsily through the layers of Will's clothes. She pulled out a baggie—Will's ID carefully water and weatherproofed— dangled it in the firelight, and then nearly dropped it.

"Orrin," she called.

The older man backed up, still keeping his rifle trained on Will. Taylor was grateful for that unobstructed view of Will. Will was watching Orrin and the woman, but his eyes slid sideways, meeting Taylor's, and just that went a long way to calming Taylor.

The woman was hissing—like Will and Taylor shouldn't hear this?— "He's a *cop*. A *fed*. Special Agent Will Brandt. He's with the Bureau of Diplomatic Security."

"What the hell is Diplomatic Security?" Stitch asked. "They supposed to be diplomats or something?"

"Yeah, we're diplomats," Taylor muttered, forgetting his resolve to keep his mouth shut.

"Oh yeah, where's your embassy?"

"Oh, for chrissake," the woman said. *"Orrin."*

Orrin said to Taylor, "You're a fed too, I guess."

Taylor said nothing.

"That's quite a coincidence. Two federal agents just happen to be up here camping off-season?"

"We're on vacation," Will said. "It's a national park. A lot of people are camping here."

"Not here, they're not."

Unfortunately, he was right about that.

"Search the tent, Stitch." Orrin trained his rifle on Taylor, who was still leaning over, hands braced on his thighs, practicing breathing.

Feeling Will's gaze, Taylor looked up again, tried to reassure him with his eyes that he was okay, and ready to back Will up on whatever he wanted to try.

"So here's how it shapes up," Orrin said. "We want the money that was on the plane. We don't have time or inclination to sweet talk it out of you. You understand? If you want to walk out of this alive, hand it over."

"There was no money on the plane," Will said without hesitation.

And Taylor thought Will had called it right. No matter what they said or did, these bandits had no intention of letting them walk away alive.

"It's your funeral." Orrin nodded at the woman, who tightened her finger on the trigger. The blast tore through the night—drowning out Taylor's scream of protest—but amazingly Will was standing there, shocked and furious but still unharmed.

And Taylor, who had jumped forward instinctively, stopped dead, sick with relief—not even hearing Orrin's grim, "Don't do it, son!" Not noticing the semiautomatic aimed at him.

Stitch was poking his head out of the tent. He held Taylor's SIG. "Hey, look at this." He smiled a big, goofy smile. "Sweet!" He shoved the pistol into his belt, and crawled out of the tent. "There's nothing in there."

He picked up Will's backpack and began to go through it.

"The next one goes through your belly," Orrin said to Will. "It's your choice."

"There was no money," Taylor said desperately, and his fear for Will lent his tone a certain credibility that sounded misleadingly like truth.

"Maybe someone else took your money," Will said. "You ever think about that?"

Which was about as close as he could come to reminding them of their own missing confederate. Not that they would have forgotten, but they obviously weren't convinced of the way the skyjacking had gone, so they were eliminating possibilities. Taylor could follow their logic. And of course, while they couldn't know it, they were quite right about Will and himself—if for all the wrong reasons.

But then, that was the confusing thing: how couldn't they know it? How had they missed the body in the meadow? Or had they?

Yes, they had to have missed it, because if they'd found the body, there wouldn't be any question about who had that money—and Taylor knew they were uncertain. Not that their uncertainty would keep them from clipping either himself or Will—but he didn't let himself dwell on that.

If they'd been watching him and Will in the hot spring through binoculars they could have been miles back—still on the mountainside—which would have left them crossing that meadow in the dusk.

That was the only thing that made sense because if they'd been close enough to see them in the meadow, they'd have surely seen them stashing Taylor's pack in the bear box. And they wouldn't all be enjoying this little get-together.

"No money," Stitch said disgustedly, pulling Will's SIG P228 out of his backpack. He stuck that into his waistband too, and then turned the pack upside down, dumping all the packs of freeze-dried meals and desserts into the grass. "They got a helluva lotta food, that's for sure."

Silence.

"That *is* a lot of cheesecake," Orrin drawled thoughtfully. "I think maybe I'm inclined to believe you," he said to Taylor.

And Taylor knew Orrin was going to kill them.

Will must have drawn the same conclusion at the same instant. He said, "You're out of your fucking mind if you think you can murder two federal officers in cold blood and walk away."

Orrin said, "You'd be surprised at what people walk away with—when they're willing to take a few chances."

Now there was irony, and he hoped Will appreciated it; Taylor was pretty damn sure Orrin was a cop. The way he spoke, the way he handled himself: it all spelled law enforcement—maybe retired, given his age.

Will opened his mouth, and Taylor knew he was going to try and use the money as a bargaining chip. Waste of time. Any way you looked at it, they didn't need both him and Will, and they could ensure that the one left alive started talking just by blowing off a kneecap.

Orrin confirmed this the next moment by saying coolly, "All the same, I think we'll hang on to one of you for insurance. Just in case."

He looked from one to the other of them, and reading that expression, Taylor went for him. Because if it was coming down to him or Will, it had to be Will. Taylor couldn't see Will die and go on living. It was that simple.

But Stitch was there first, tackling him around the waist and throwing him back a few feet into the grass and weeds. Taylor landed awkwardly, only making it halfway to his feet before Stitch landed on him. It was like having a piano dropped on his chest, but it didn't matter; he already knew this was a lost cause. The point was to make the choice easy for Orrin— and to go down fighting—but as he delivered a few satisfying punches to Stitch's head, sending his hat flying, it occurred to Taylor to roll away from the campsite, to move toward the cliffside.

It was more instinct than sense, but he rolled again, managing to flip Stitch with him, and Stitch kept the momentum going, slugging in raw fury at Taylor. Somewhere in the background—behind Stitch's cursing and grunts—Taylor could hear Orrin shouting at them, and the woman's shrill tones.

And then a rifle butt slammed into his head, and all the fight drained out of him. Through the sick pain he could see Orrin standing over him, ready to strike again. And through the blur of tears and blood he saw Will edging forward, crowding the woman. She backed up, yelling for Orrin, bringing her rifle up to fire.

Orrin stepped away and turned his own rifle back on Will, who stopped in his tracks.

Stitch scrambled up, grabbed Taylor's jacket collar, dragging him to his knees. The barrel of his gun knocked against Taylor's face. He didn't care, didn't notice, all his focus on Orrin.

Orrin stared at Will. It felt like forever before he nodded at Taylor. "Yeah. He'd be less trouble. Kill him."

"Well, that doesn't make sense," the woman objected. "Why don't we kill *him*?" She nodded at Will, who stared stonily back at her.

Orrin said reasonably, "Because if you kill *him*, you'll have to kill pretty boy anyway. And we need to hang on to one of them in case we need a hostage."

Taylor heard his death sentence with something like relief, just making out the words over his own pained gulps for air and the distant thunder of the river crashing over the boulders down the mountainside behind them.

The woman and Stitch began to debate Orrin's decision. Taylor brought his head up for one last look at Will.

"My God, do I have to do everything myself?" Orrin inquired rhetorically, and the bullet slammed into Taylor's chest, left side—for a change—knocking him back. He went with it, letting himself topple right over the side of the mountain.

He nearly blacked out with the pain.

He slid and slithered a few feet, stones showering down around him, the momentum of his fall carrying him several yards down the slope. He rolled, trying to protect his head from trees and boulders, trying to absorb how badly he'd been hit, listening to the sound of the shot reverberating off the mountains—and the echo of Will's cry.

Will sounded... There were no words to describe that cry. Horror, grief—he'd sounded mortally wounded.

And after that one outcry, he sounded mad enough to kill—beyond rage, beyond sanity. Taylor, snatching frantically for handholds, anything to slow his descent, could hear him over the roar of the river below, ranting, swearing, threatening.

And then silence.

Jesus. Jesus, Will…

Let him be okay. Don't let them have changed their minds, don't let them have killed him…

He managed to grab onto a tangle of tree roots. A boulder, loosened by his brush against it, crashed on down the slope and plunged into the tumbling water below with a loud splash.

There had been no second shot, right? He hadn't heard a second shot.

The vegetation he was holding on to loosened in the wet soil above him, and Taylor refocused on his own peril: legs dangling over an outcrop of rocks and nothing but the cold night air and a couple hundred feet of falling beneath him. He shifted his grip, hauled himself up a foot, onto firmer ground. Dug his fingers and boot tips into the soggy earth.

He could hear voices drifting above him.

"He went into the river," Stitch called. "I heard his body hit the water."

Taylor, a couple of yards to the left, jammed his face into his arm and smothered his whimpers in his coat sleeve. He had to stay motionless, had to stay quiet, but the pain from being shot—again—was stupefying. Almost impossible to get beyond it.

But after a few moments of relative calm—of no longer falling down the slope and no more rocks raining down on him—and no more shooting at him—he did manage to think; and he began to wonder why he wasn't soaked in blood. There had been a hell of a lot of blood the other time; his body had begun to shut down immediately. That wasn't happening. Excruciating though the pain was, it was just…pain.

He reached up, feeling the hole in his jacket. He poked his finger through the leather, felt the hole in his shirt pocket—and there was dampness there, but not nearly enough—and then his fingertip touched metal. Dented metal. The stainless steel of Will's flask gently leaking bourbon around the lodged bullet in its face.

And for one crazy moment he almost laughed.

Jesus Christ. Saved by the bourbon. He struggled against the hysterical giggles threatening to burst out of his throat. It wasn't that funny, for God's sake, and he was still in a hell of a lot of trouble, but the relief of not being really shot again outweighed the extreme pain of being…well, shot again.

Let's hear a round of applause for the man upstairs...

He pulled himself up a few inches, trying for a more secure position, then rested, gathering himself, listening for what was happening topside. He couldn't hear much over the river's boom. But then he heard voices—and froze.

He knew that Stitch had been joined by the others, that they were all looking over the edge of the cliff, trying to spot his body in the water below—or on the slope.

He could just make out snatches of their discussion.

"He went in the river...splash was too heavy to be anything else..."

"What's that? There on the left?"

He stopped breathing, waiting, eyes staring into the darkness. He could just make out the dim outline of figures on the ledge above him but the moon was behind them, acting like a spotlight. He, on the other hand, lay in the deep shadows of the hillside. He could barely see his arm curled an inch or so in front of his nose.

Someone turned a flashlight on. The circle of light picked out a fallen tree, moved slowly across the hillside toward him...

He lay very still, trying not to breathe, praying the darkness and the scraggly vegetation concealed him. Every shallow, bruised breath was a reminder of how vulnerable he was, and the terror of being shot again was paralyzing—it hadn't been so bad when he didn't have time to think about it, but he was thinking about it now, thinking that he'd already had two close calls, and a third time was liable to be seriously unlucky. For the first time in his life he was too scared to move.

Fuck.

Please God...

"I'm telling you, he went in the river. I heard him hit the water."

"I don't see any blood." That was the woman. Taylor felt a surge of hatred for her. Why couldn't she mind her own business? Busybody bitch.

The flashlight beam swept past his boots and he tensed.

"Even if Orrin missed, there's no way he survived that drop."

"I'm just wondering why there's no blood."

And from further away: "That was point-blank range. One way or the other, he's history."

He couldn't hear Will. But then Will wouldn't have a lot to say now. Will was smart. Will knew when to shut up and what to do to stay alive. Will would be okay.

The flashlight switched off. The figures at the top of the hillside drew back.

Taylor closed his eyes. His chest hurt like he'd been kicked by a mule. Or a Transformer. He'd bought his nephew a couple of those for his birthday last week. Yeah, one of those red-eyed evil autobot dudes like Megatron or Starscream.

"If the river carries his body down…"

"…no ID on the body…"

Their voices were moving off.

A few moments later he nearly gave himself away when a couple of heavy items went smashing down the hillside past him—and he realized they had thrown Will's pack and the tent into the river.

CHAPTER SIX

"I didn't even want to come on this goddamned trip. I did it for you."

Taylor was dead. And he'd stood there and let it happen. Will felt dead himself; numb, empty—words didn't begin to cover it.

Taylor was dead. Confirming the almost superstitious dread that Will had felt for weeks—ever since Taylor had been hit—that they were on borrowed time, that Taylor's recovery had been nothing more than a temporary reprieve, that he had lost Taylor the night he'd turned him down. Told him he didn't love him.

Didn't love him?

And now it was too late.

"Are we going to walk all night?" the blond ape inquired. "Aren't we ever going to make camp?"

Orrin walked ahead carrying a high-powered flashlight, the beam catching stark glimpses of tree trunks, rocks, the crooked trail winding up through the hillside. Will's boot caught on a tree root; he stumbled over a rivulet in the trail, but caught himself.

"Don't even think about it, asshole." The woman nudged the base of Will's spine with the barrel of her rifle. He ignored her. He didn't give a damn if they shot him now. He should have jumped them when they killed Taylor. Why hadn't he? Why had he stood there? Why had he let the rifle pointed at his head stop him? What was wrong with him that he'd chosen to stay alive when they'd killed Taylor? Because Taylor wouldn't have; the gray-haired fucker had that right. Taylor would have gone for them; they'd have had to put him down to stop him. Taylor would have rather died—and so would Will, but yet Will had let them knock him down and tie his hands. He'd let them kill Taylor.

But what he wouldn't do was let them get away with it.

They were going to pay. He was going to stay alive that long. All three of them were going to pay—he wasn't sure how yet—for murdering Taylor. His eyes rested on Orrin's back, picturing with grim pleasure blowing a hole in its retreat.

"Hey, he's carrying a map or something in his pocket," Stitch reported suddenly. He reached forward and grabbed the map out of Will's back pocket.

Their weary procession stopped. Orrin plucked the map out of Stitch's hands, unfolding it and turning the flashlight on it.

"How'd you miss that, Bonnie?" Stitch said, and the woman's face—gargoyle-like in the ring of flashlights—twisted into a sneer.

"I had other things on my mind, moron. Like the fact that he's a god-damned fed!"

"Knock it off, you two." That was Orrin. He looked at Will and then down at the map. "Well, well. What's this?" He pointed at the circled point on the map.

Will stared at him without speaking.

Bonnie and Stitch glared at him. Orrin smiled. He had nice, even white teeth. "This is where the plane went down." The circle of flashlight beam moved across the map to the second circled point. "So what's so important here?"

"Figure it out," Will said.

"Oh, we will," Orrin said. "We will." He nodded to the others, and Bonnie prodded Will with her rifle again.

* * * * *

It had to be true love. Because if Taylor's only incentive for getting himself off that mountainside was his own health and welfare, he'd have been happy to spend the rest of his—few—days right where he was. But Will's only hope was Taylor, so he tried to work up a little enthusiasm.

But for chrissake…he'd already put in a full day's hike before he'd got punched a few times, got slammed in the head with a rifle butt, got shot, and then dived off a cliff. And lying here in the cold earth with a gentle mist coming down wasn't helping his recovery time.

On the positive side, he wasn't afraid of heights, and that was very good because when he looked down and saw nothing beneath him but the tumbling shine of the river and the swaying treetops, he felt a little...tired.

After all, technically he was still convalescent.

And while that bullet hadn't penetrated anything more vital than Will's flask, the impact had left bruises and contusions down the left side of his chest. The pain was draining, especially once the adrenaline that had numbed him to the worst of it faded away during the long, long minutes while he waited for the bandits to leave.

Even once he was sure it was safe to move, it was difficult to force himself to action. If he hadn't been afraid he'd fall off the mountainside he'd have closed his eyes for a few moments. As it was, he began to inch his way up, groping for handholds, feeling for something to brace his feet on.

The recent rains made it worse, causing the soft ground to slide out from under him, for plants to pull out by their roots when he tugged on them. It was slow—and nerve-wracking—going.

It took him forty-five minutes to crawl six yards, and by then Taylor was beginning to panic about Will. He was not going to be able to track these assholes through the woods; he couldn't afford to let them get too far ahead of him. He wasn't sure how long they planned on keeping Will alive. He wasn't sure why they felt they might need a hostage.

There was no guarantee that his worst nightmare wasn't waiting for him at the top—but he couldn't let himself think like that or he might as well let go and drop into the river.

He continued on his wet and muddy way, clambering up a few inches at a time, refusing to look down—and eventually refusing to look beyond his next handhold because his progress was too demoralizing. But then, finally, he was dragging himself over the embankment, lungs burning, muscles screaming, body soaked in sweat. He crawled away from the edge, scanning the now empty campsite, verifying—and re-verifying—that Will was not lying there dead. He let himself collapse, resting his head on his forearms, closing his eyes.

His heart was racketing around his chest like it was trying to find an escape route.

He only allowed himself a few minutes before he pushed up and began trying to figure which way Orrin and his pals had taken Will. It would have been nice if Will had left some sign or some clue, but Will, of course, believed Taylor was dead.

At first studying the ground seemed hopeless. As far as Taylor was concerned a herd of wildebeests could have been milling around the clearing, but after a time the moon rose above the trees and he began to discern the mess of footprints into separate tracks.

They were using the trail heading back toward the meadow and lake, retracing the path that Will and Taylor had taken that afternoon. Obviously they weren't worried about being followed—or even running into other hikers or park rangers.

Every so often Taylor got a faraway glimpse of light through the trees—the stray beam of a flashlight. And once he heard the sharp clatter of rock on rock—miles ahead and outdistancing him fast.

He didn't allow himself to think about anything but getting to Will in time. If he stopped to consider his own situation…well, forgetting about his various aches and pains for a moment—which wasn't all that easy to do the longer the night wore on—he'd never felt quite this isolated or lost. Not in any of his foreign postings, but then he'd never been so far out of his own element.

Not even in an Afghan embassy compound surrounded by a desert full of hostiles.

He wasn't sure how long he followed Orrin and the others, but he was headed back through one of the meadows he and Will had crossed earlier that day when he saw motion in the darkness ahead.

Not far enough ahead, unfortunately—as an indescribable heavy oily scent of wet fur, fish, and grass resolved itself into an enormous black bulk that suddenly rose up on its hind legs.

A bear.

Taylor stopped dead, hand reaching automatically for his shoulder holster—which was not there.

The bear, a weaving shadow in the darkness, made a heavy blowing out sound and then a strange wooden clicking noise.

Jesus. What was he supposed to do—besides not run? That much he knew. You didn't run from a bear. And you didn't try to climb a tree. What the hell had Will said about this? Play dead with grizzlies and fight back with black bears. And there were no grizzlies in the High Sierras so…yell, make noise, clap hands—and if he started yelling and screaming he was liable to alert Orrin and his pals that he was alive and on their trail.

Taylor took a careful sliding step backward. The bear was still blowing and making those clacking sounds. It had to be six feet tall and about three hundred pounds. It looked like it was all claws and teeth to Taylor.

Funny. They looked so cute in the zoo.

"Get the hell out of here, you sonofabitch," Taylor growled, trying to look and sound aggressive. He bent down, hands skittering over pine cones, rejecting them—he didn't want to merely annoy the thing—and caught up a stone, pelting it hard at the bear. It bounced off its head. The bear made more exhalations and chomping sounds, and Taylor, scrabbling for more stones, wasn't sure if he was merely pissing it off. He pitched another couple of hard balls—putting everything he had into his throw—and to his relief the bear dropped back on all fours and lumbered away, crashing through the brush and bushes.

For a few seconds Taylor stood there panting; he hadn't thought he had that much adrenaline left. He mopped his wet forehead with his sleeve.

"I *hate* camping," he said softly, just for the record.

* * * * *

He was weaving with exhaustion when he gave in to the need for sleep. Even after he decided to rest, it took him time to find a safe and suitable place. Safe and suitable being relative. Finally he took shelter in a small cavity in the hillside. It wasn't large or deep enough to be a cave, but that was fine by Taylor. A cave was likely to be already inhabited, and he'd had all the close encounters with local wildlife he could handle for one night. He tucked himself in the little vault made by a couple of precariously balanced boulders, huddling, arms wrapped around his bent knees, head resting on folded arms. The rocks weren't warm, but they protected him from the wind and the night air, and at least it was relatively dry.

He closed his eyes.

The night seemed alive with sound. Far noisier than the city ever had.

He let himself dream of Will. Only half dream really—and half confused memory. Memories of when they had first been partnered. Nothing dramatic. Not like TV shows where the partners hate each other on sight but then come to like and eventually trust each other. The fact was, he'd liked Will right away. Liked his seriousness, his professionalism. Will was relaxed and experienced, and his calm approach to the job was a good balance for Taylor's own more…intense work style. He'd liked Will's sense of humor, and when he'd realized Will was gay…

For the first time ever in DSS he'd felt completely at ease, completely comfortable…understood and appreciated. Up until this week, he couldn't have conceived of voluntarily seeking another partner.

He tried to picture that: getting used to someone who wasn't Will. Maybe someone who took his coffee black, who didn't like overpriced bourbon or dumb action films, who dated girls from the Computer Investigations Branch, and didn't own a beer-drinking dog or listen to Emmylou Harris. Someone who wasn't allergic to penicillin or who wasn't an expert marksman. Someone who might not be there the next time he got his ass into a jam.

He thought of waking up in the hospital with Will sitting right there. His eyes had been bluer than summer skies, and his smile had been sort of quizzical. "Welcome back," he'd said in that gentle voice he'd used for the first few days after Taylor recovered consciousness. And Taylor had managed a smile because it was Will—despite the fact that he'd never been in so much pain in his entire life.

And all the other times Will had shown up bearing magazines and fruit and CDs—sometimes only managing to squeak in about five minutes before visiting hours were over.

A million memories. A million moments. Will's laugh, the way his eyes tilted when he was teasing, the way he bit his lip when he was worried, that discreet tattoo of a griffin on his right shoulder—the way his skin had tasted this afternoon. The way his mouth had tasted…

* * * * *

It was still dark when Taylor woke. He was freezing. He was starving. He could hear the high-pitched yapping hysteria of coyotes. They sounded close by. Too close. But he knew enough to know it was unlikely coyotes were going to attack a full-grown man. He pressed the dial of his wristwatch and studied the luminous face. Two-thirty in the morning. Still a couple of hours of darkness. He needed to get moving again.

But as he crawled outside his shelter, he was seized with doubt. Was he making a mistake following Will and his captors? What if he couldn't catch up with them in time? He had no idea how long they would keep Will alive. Would the smarter move be to go for help? Get off the mountain and get down to the nearest ranger station?

For a moment he was torn. If he got this wrong, it meant Will's life.

* * * * *

"So what was it? You didn't like the retirement package?" Will asked conversationally as Orrin settled across from him, rifle across his lap, when they finally stopped for the night.

"Can we have a fire?" Bonnie asked.

"Nope. We don't want to attract any more goddamn rangers." Then Orrin nodded at Will as though acknowledging a point scored. "Yeah, it's always the quiet ones you've got to watch. I pegged you for trouble right off the bat."

Will ignored that. He wasn't going to be distracted by the pain of remembering Orrin playing God. He couldn't let himself think about Taylor, couldn't let himself grieve until he'd done what he needed to do—starting with surviving this night.

"You're a cop?"

"Deputy sheriff. Used to be." Orrin watched Bonnie huddling down in her sleeping bag. Just for a moment something softened in his weathered face. Bonnie didn't fit Will's idea of a femme fatale, but to each his own.

"Let me guess. The line got blurry watching all those bad guys get away with it year after year," he mocked.

Orrin shrugged genially. "Something like that. Anyway, it's not like we robbed a mom and pop store. We hit a casino."

"And killed two sheriff's deputies and the pilot of the plane you hijacked."

"And your partner," Orrin said evenly.

Will said very quietly, "And my partner."

For a moment Orrin's gaze held his. He said softly, "You're not going to get the chance, son."

Will smiled—and had the satisfaction of seeing Orrin's eyes narrow.

"Was it really just a coincidence you were up here?" Bonnie asked suddenly, opening her eyes.

Will turned his head her way. She had a hard, plain face, drab blonde hair. Maybe she looked different when she wasn't cold, miserable, and had fixed herself up, put a little makeup on. Or maybe she had nothing to do with it; maybe she was just one of the perks for Orrin.

"It was just a coincidence," he replied.

"I don't believe in coincidence," she said. "I don't even believe in luck."

"The house always wins?" Will said.

"That's right."

"Stop jabbering and let me get to sleep," Stitch complained, lying a few feet away.

Will stared across at Orrin. Orrin stared back.

* * * * *

He thought about the days after Taylor had been shot—days spent prowling Little Saigon looking for the two punks that the restaurant owner next door had seen screeching away from the parking lot behind the nail salon.

With the help of the Orange County Sheriff's Department he'd tracked Daniel Nguyen and Le Loi Roy to their favorite noodle shop where the teenage gangstas were scarfing down pigskin-filled rice paper wraps. Nguyen had surrendered without trouble, but Le Loi Roy had gone for a shoot-out at the bok choy corral and wound up with a shattered hip and a couple of missing fingers. He was fifteen. Nguyen was thirteen.

When questioned about the nail salon incident, according to Nguyen, the FBI guy—who was Taylor, apparently—had drawn his gun but had hesitated—and Le Loi had shot him. To Nguyen's way of looking at it that made it self-defense.

Le Loi's story—when he was well enough to offer one—was that the FBI guy had waited too long—obviously thinking they were a couple of dumb little kids. Too bad for him. Le Loi had been chagrined to hear that he had not actually killed the FBI guy as this was seriously going to damage his own newly-minted street cred.

The couple of times Will had tried to talk to Taylor about it, Taylor claimed he didn't remember much of anything. He didn't want to discuss it—didn't want to hear about the fate of Daniel Nguyen and Le Loi Roy, and Will – reprimanded and removed from the case himself—let it drop. The trial was scheduled for May, still two months away. Moot now with Taylor dead.

* * * * *

Once, Will thought Orrin might just be drifting toward sleep, but he sat up, shifting the rifle abruptly, and pinning his gaze on Will's watchful face.

"If I were you, son, I'd grab some shut-eye."

"You're not me," Will said pleasantly. "And I'm not your son."

Orrin laughed. Glanced at his confederates, who were soundly sleeping. Stitch's snores were loud enough to echo off the mountains.

"What was his name? Your partner."

"MacAllister. Taylor MacAllister."

"Partners a long time?"

"Four years in June."

"That's a long time in law enforcement. How'd that work? You and him being...?" Orrin made a seesawing hand gesture.

Will opened his mouth and then recognized that sorrowful inevitable truth for what it was, and changed what he had been about to say. "It worked fine till you killed him."

"I had a partner for a few years. Meanest sonofabitch you'd ever want to meet."

"That's quite a compliment coming from you," Will said.

Orrin laughed. Then he called to Bonnie and Stitch. They came awake immediately, rolling over and sitting up. Will noted that Bonnie reached for her rifle first thing. Stitch went for his boots. Good to know.

"Orrin, can we please have a fire? I'm freezing my butt off," Bonnie complained through chattering teeth, pulling her boots on.

"Yeah. Stitch, collect some firewood and we'll have some coffee and breakfast. We got a long day ahead of us." Orrin pulled out Will's map and studied it by the light of his flashlight.

"How long are we —?" Bonnie nodded toward Will.

"We'll see how useful he makes himself," Orrin replied.

"I've gotta pee," Bonnie announced, and wandered off into the bushes.

She wandered back a short time later and took Orrin's place while Orrin vanished to relieve himself. He left his rifle propped against a rock, but Will knew he was carrying Taylor's SIG. He had taken it from Stitch; spoils of war, apparently. All the same, this was probably as good a chance as he was going to get. He studied Bonnie. Rifle aimed at him, she stood poised and ready for him to try something—dangerous with nerves and fatigue.

"Quit staring at me," she said shortly, though it was too dark for either of them to really see what the other was looking at.

"It's not too late to get yourself out of this," Will said. "You're not the one who shot a federal agent. If you help me —"

"Orrin!" she yelled.

Orrin came back fast, zipping up his pants. "What's going on?"

"He's trying to work me! He's going to try and play us off against each other!"

"Of course he is," Orrin said reasonably. "Wouldn't you?"

"Yeah, well, it just might work on that moron Stitch."

"Where *is* Stitch?" Orrin said abruptly, looking around the clearing.

"He's gathering wood for the fire," Bonnie said.

"We're not building a bonfire, for God's sake." Orrin walked out a little way, yelling for Stitch.

The silence that followed his call was eerie.

"Stitch!" shrieked Bonnie. Her voice seemed to echo off the distant mountains and come rolling back louder than before.

Orrin shushed her impatiently. They listened intently. "Okay, keep an eye on him." He added as Will moved to stand up, "No, you don't. Stay where you are, son."

"No!" Bonnie said. "We need to stay together."

A tall shadow stepped out of the trees: Orrin's flashlight gleamed off the rifle barrel pointed straight at him.

"Together is good," Taylor said.

CHAPTER SEVEN

For one very strange moment Will thought he might—for the first time in his entire life—faint. He could actually hear the blood surging in his head, drowning out coherent thought. The shock was enough to send him rocking back on his heels, staring in disbelief at the slender shadow that resolved itself into a tense and familiar outline.

"Where's Stitch?" Orrin asked evenly, gaze on the rifle Taylor held. And aside from that pregnant pause before he spoke, he seemed to take Taylor's return from the dead without batting an eyelash.

"Unavailable."

Taylor's voice. Taylor. Alive.

Taylor said, "Will?"

"Right here."

"Are you okay?"

"I am now."

Orrin chuckled, and the sound was jarring. "Son, you can't take both of us. Even if you do shoot me before I get to my rifle —"

"He's got your SIG," Will interrupted.

Orrin chuckled again. "Even if you did hit me at this distance and in this light, Bonnie will blow a hole through lover boy over there. No way you can take us both in time."

"You're right," Taylor said. "But I guarantee I can—and will—take *you*." And they could all hear the easy confidence in his voice.

Bonnie was shaking, but she knew better than to take her eyes off Will for one second. "Orrin?" she said worriedly.

Orrin didn't say anything, his hand still resting on the rifle stock, but making no move to pick it up.

"All it takes is one .22 plowing right between your eyes and into that lizard brain of yours, and that's it for you, Orrin," Taylor said. "I won't make the same mistake you did."

"Okay," Orrin said. "So what do you think you have to bargain with?"

"Your life." Taylor barely tilted his head in Will's direction. "The only reason you're not already dead is I want him."

"You do seem sorta sweet on each other," Orrin remarked. He barely twitched his fingers and Taylor took two fast steps forward, his finger caressing the trigger but somehow managing not to pull. "Okay, okay. Keep your hair on!" Orrin said, holding very still. "So what's your plan, son? Him for me, is that the deal?"

"That's the deal."

The inability to read anyone's face made the moment all the more fraught. Taylor's outline was poised, ready. But despite his hard calm, Will felt his tension, and he suddenly knew what Taylor was afraid of. Stitch must not be dead, and wherever he was, Taylor was afraid he wasn't going to stay there long enough.

"Mexican standoff." Orrin sounded amused.

The woman said, "Orrin…" as Will used his back against the tree trunk behind him to lever to his feet. He took a slow step away from her, aiming for the shadows of the trees.

His hands were still tied behind his back, which meant he was going to have trouble running. But they needed to go because the minute Stitch turned up, armed or unarmed, the balance tipped out of their favor.

Will passed Taylor, reaching the fingertips of the shadows. Taylor took a slow, careful step backward, his bead on Orrin never wavering.

"Orrin —" Bonnie moved, trying to keep Will in her sights

"It's okay," Orin said calmly. "They're not going far."

Will reached the safety of the thicket, and a moment later Taylor was beside him—and a moment after that Bonnie and Orrin opened fire.

Taylor dived to the side, taking Will with him. The air was alive with gunfire, and they stayed low, moving fast, plastered to the ground as they crawled for cover. Or Taylor crawled. With his hands behind his back, Will was reduced to trying to hump along with Taylor tugging at him, half-dragging him.

They weren't going to get far like this, but apparently Taylor wasn't trying to get far, just get them into concealment. They plowed right into a stand of thick vegetation, flattening themselves to the ground. Will opened his mouth to ask what Taylor had in mind, but Taylor reached out and scooped up some wet earth, smearing it over Will's face. The cold of the mud silenced Will. He watched Taylor camouflage his own face.

The shooting had stopped and the silence was nerve-wrenching.

Bushes rustled noisily down the path. A tall shadow staggered drunkenly out of the trees. Taylor breathed an obscenity. Before Will had a chance to work it out, he spotted muzzle flash to the left. A rifle opened fire and the second rifle joined in a moment later. There was an animal scream as bullets tore apart the shrubs and low-hanging tree limbs.

Will tried to get lower, but molded to the ground was about as low as it got.

Silence. They could hear Bonnie and Orrin thrashing about in the bushes.

"Oh my God," screeched the woman. "It's Stitch!"

Will picked up the lower murmur of Orrin speaking too, but his voice didn't carry as well.

"Well, what was he *doing* here?"

More muted words from Orrin.

"Christ," Will breathed. He glanced at Taylor. He could only make out the shine of his eyes.

"I thought I hit him harder than that," Taylor said almost inaudibly. He didn't seem particularly distressed as he glanced at Will. "One down, two to go," and Will saw the glimmer of his smile.

Abruptly, Orrin and Bonnie started firing again, startling Taylor into immobility. A lot of firepower raking through the brush—you had to respect that—but the shooting seemed to be moving in the wrong direction— away from them, and it began to seem that Orrin and Bonnie were just taking their frustrations out in ammo.

Taylor cracked open the barrel of the .22, checked the magazine and swore very softly. "Three cartridges," he mouthed to Will.

Not good.

Under the barrage of rifle shots, Taylor nudged Will back into motion, guiding him with one hand locked on his arm. They wove their way through the ferns and bushes, hunched down, stopping every few feet to listen.

Taylor pulled him down, and Will knelt, trying not to lose his balance. Taylor's hands felt over him, covering Will's for a fleeting moment, as Taylor groped for the cords binding his wrists. Will could hear the grin in his whispered, "So…did you miss me?"

"I thought you were dead," Will said simply. He couldn't joke, couldn't cover, couldn't pretend it had been anything but what it seemed: the end of everything he cared about—made all the worse by the realization that he hadn't accepted how important Taylor was to him until it was too late.

Taylor said calmly, "Yeah, sorry about that." And from his tone Will knew that Taylor at least partly understood what he wasn't saying. "Are you okay? They didn't rough you up too much?"

For a minute Will couldn't manage his voice. "You shouldn't have come back for me," he got out finally.

"You have the car keys." Taylor was working the knots frantically. Thin, strong fingers wriggling and tugging—apparently without luck. *"Fuck."*

"I can run like this if I have to," he reassured softly.

Bullshit with which Taylor didn't even bother to argue.

He did more picking and pulling and plucking and prying, and finally Will felt the cords around his wrists loosen and fall away. He shook his hands free, and Taylor grabbed up the rope and stuffed it into his jacket pocket, which was good thinking since it was hard to know what might come in handy later.

Clenching his jaw against the torture of blood rushing back into his arms and fingers, Will was dimly aware of Taylor's hands rubbing, trying to aid circulation. He was astonished when Taylor suddenly pulled him into his arms, lowering his head to Will's. For a moment he was held fiercely. He felt Taylor's lips graze his cheekbone, and then Taylor had let him go again, turned away.

Will yanked him back, running his hands over him until he found the bullet hole in his jacket.

"I knew it. You *were* hit." His probing fingers found the punctured flask. "Taylor... Christ."

"It's okay. I'm fine. A couple of bruises." And he freed himself, crawling out of the thicket, moving slowly, stealthily. Will followed—shaky with an emotion that had nothing to do with their peril or the pain in his arms and hands.

Since Taylor now seemed to have a plan, Will kept silent until they found the place where the trail branched off.

In the opposite direction they could hear the crack of sticks and twigs, the echo of voices. Every so often a light flashed through the trees.

"It's not going to take them long to figure out we doubled back," he warned.

Taylor nodded, and started down the sharply descending path.

The crack of a rifle split the night.

The echo ringing off the mountains made it hard to judge direction. It was possible that they had been spotted, or that Orrin and company were shooting at something else.

To the left there was a clatter of falling stones, a small slide maybe—hard to identify in the darkness. Taylor started running—Will right on his heels.

They sprinted down the crooked trail like deer outracing brush fire, flying—sometimes literally—over the dips and rocks and fallen tree limbs, feet pounding the muddy trail. Taylor slithered once, and Will's hand shot out, steadying him. Will tripped a few yards further on and Taylor grabbed him by the collar before he went tumbling. Both times they barely slowed their headlong rush.

The miracle was they didn't break their necks or at the least a leg in the first three minutes. The stars were fading in the sky but there was no light to speak of, and even if there had been, the trail was mostly in the shadow of the mountainside, which was to their advantage in one way—and not at all in another.

But it had a kind of amusement park ride charm to it, Will thought vaguely, barely catching himself from turning into a human avalanche yet again. That time he saved himself by jumping and landing, still running, on the trail winding below.

Somehow they made it down to the bottom without killing themselves. Taylor dropped down on all fours, gulping for air. Will walked a loose circle, giving his burning muscles a chance to recover, trying to catch his breath, listening for sounds of chase.

Throwing a look at the face of the craggy mountainside just beginning to materialize in the dawn, he was belatedly stricken at what they had attempted. It was a good thing he hadn't realized it before they started running.

At muffled sounds of distress, he turned his head. Next to a small rivulet splashing down into a rocky pool, Taylor was on his knees, being quietly sick. Will didn't blame him. That trail had to have dropped five hundred feet in less than a mile. Will thought he might have left his own stomach somewhere around the last bend.

Kneeling, Will put a hand on his shoulder. "You okay?"

Taylor nodded, scooped a hand in the water and splashed his face, further smearing the mud and sweat.

Will gave him a moment, rising and scanning the mountainside for the flashlights, for motion, for anything indicating pursuit.

Nothing.

That didn't mean they weren't being followed. The tiny waterfall rushing down into the pool at the foot of the path effectively drowned out the most immediate of the night sounds.

"We've got to keep moving," he said, and Taylor nodded, got one knee under and shoved himself back to his feet.

They staggered their way down the canyon, finally taking shelter behind a series of sandy rock formations as the blackness of night began to dull to gray. From this vantage point they'd be able to see in all directions once it turned daylight. But once it turned daylight, they needed to be moving again. Will lay on his belly, watching.

There was nothing.

Taylor was on his back, his head leaning against the edge of Will's shoulder. Will listened to him struggle to catch his breath. He thought Taylor's inhalations sounded funky: sort of squeaky…wheezy; was the injured lung holding up to the strain?

"Okay?" he asked, undervoiced.

Taylor nodded. Then shook his head. "Need a…minute."

Yeah. They both needed a minute. But Taylor sounded winded. And Will could feel him shaking with exhaustion. Not that Will wasn't shaky himself, but he was in better shape than Taylor. He turned it over in his mind. He didn't like being on defense, but Taylor's fatigue made any kind of offense impossible for now.

Assuming Orrin and Bonnie didn't give up and go home—and he couldn't see how they could afford to do that—they'd expect him and Taylor to continue down to safety and civilization, and they'd attempt to cut them off. That's what he'd do in their position. Will shifted, and Taylor rolled away, swallowing hard.

"What do you want to do?" he whispered.

"We rest for a minute. Then we move to higher ground."

Taylor's face turned toward him. "We could split up. Make it harder for them."

"We're not splitting up." Will held Taylor's eyes with his own. "Never again."

Taylor laughed.

"Something funny?"

"The whole goddamned thing is funny." It sounded like he had recovered his breath, anyway. Will took care of that by covering Taylor's mouth with his own in a quick, hard kiss.

* * * * *

The sky was turning a peachy pink when they started up the slope, sticking to rock as much as possible in an effort to hide their tracks.

Without his map it was hard to be sure, but Will thought they were on the west side of Elk Pass. This was confirmed when they later came upon an old, half-tumbled down mining shack.

There had been no sign of any pursuit since they'd made their escape down the cliff the night before. Will thought they could risk going to ground for a few hours. It wasn't like they had a choice, really. Taylor was moving on willpower alone, and he needed time to figure out how they were going to get to help before Orrin and Bonnie got to them.

Will kicked the door, and half the wall fell in. Taylor began to laugh. And soft though it was, it echoed off the rocks and bounced around the canyon, a ghostly chuckle in the crisp, cold dawn.

"Shhh. *Shit*," Will hissed, but he started to laugh too. "Be quiet, for God's sake." He grabbed Taylor and pushed him through the broken door—and wall—realizing how glad he was to have an excuse to hold him.

"Jesus, there could be snakes…spiders…" Taylor was letting Will guide him under the half-fallen logs which made a kind of lean-to. He got down on his hands and knees. "Are you sure this is safe?"

His muffled complaint nearly started Will laughing again.

"You mean is it up to code? Probably not." Will shoved him, not ungently, hands lingering. "Get in there."

And Taylor handed him the rifle and crawled the rest of the way beneath the makeshift shelter. He drew his long legs up, and Will wriggled in beside him. The smell of damp earth and moldering wood and leather and perspiration was warm and strangely reassuring. Taylor was scrunched up against him, shoulder to shoulder, hip to hip.

"Comfortable?" he asked, and Taylor started that wheezy laughing again. "Will you shut up?" But he couldn't get any heat into it.

After a few moments, Taylor quieted. "I don't see why they would come after us. It makes more sense for them to give up on the money and get out while they can."

Will didn't answer.

"Don't you think?"

"No," said Will. "And neither do you."

Taylor sighed and shifted. They sat for a time…listening.

Taylor's head dropped forward, and he jerked awake. He swore quietly.

Will whispered, "Put your head on my shoulder."

"I'm awake."

"Put your head on my shoulder. I'll take first watch."

There was something wary in Taylor's silence. At last, he adjusted position, lowering his head to Will's shoulder. They sat there stiffly for a moment or two, but then Taylor settled more comfortably; his breath was warm against Will's throat.

"Hold on," Will mumbled. He wriggled, got his arm free, and slid it around Taylor's back, pulling him close and offering a little more support. "You can stretch out if you want to."

"There's no room."

"Yeah, there is. Stretch out to the side of me." Will tried to shift more, and Taylor inched down a little. A board slid from above them, clattering loudly in the crisp morning.

They both froze. Then Will said grimly, "Careful. Don't knock down our happy home."

Taylor's laugh was a breath of sound, then he swore again, and Will guided him down the length of his own body, hands moving over Taylor's jean-clad legs, his hips, his torso. He just managed to avoid Taylor head-butting him, and then Taylor's hand landed on his crotch.

Will was a little surprised at his body's instant reaction, but that was adrenaline for you. His cock pressed uncomfortably against the canvas pants.

"Ow," Taylor said.

"Whaddya mean, 'ow'? You're the one doing all the banging."

There was an astonished silence, then Taylor muttered, his knee just missing a vital part of Will's expanding anatomy, "I'm pleading the fifth."

He finally got himself positioned to his satisfaction, the heat of his body pressed down the length of Will's, his head resting once more on Will's shoulder. He put his arm around Will's waist, and Will put his arm around Taylor's shoulders.

"Comfortable?" He was grinning, although there wasn't much to smile at.

"Oh, yeah. You didn't forget to put out the Do Not Disturb sign, did you?"

"Nah. And room service at seven."

Taylor expelled a long breath that sounded mostly like a moan.

Will patted him absently. Seconds later he could tell by Taylor's breathing he was asleep.

CHAPTER EIGHT

He came awake to shivery darkness, and he couldn't remember for a moment where he was or what had happened. But he was lying with someone—on the cold, very hard ground it seemed—and he was being undressed, warmed. Warm hands undoing his shirt, sliding inside and stroking him. Part caress, part reassurance, part…salvage effort. Comfort and joy—and he…knew those hands. Knew that touch.

He parted his lips and to his delight, a warm mouth covered his own. And he knew that taste too.

Taylor opened his eyes and Will was a warm bulk lying against him, Will's hands moved over him, and Will was undressed too, heated skin, soft hair, hot mouth licking Taylor's nipples into taut little points.

"We'll be warmer like this," he whispered.

Yes, it was definitely warmer like this. Taylor slipped his hands beneath Will's arms for a moment, enjoying being held, treasuring the flush of heat between them, his own shivers easing in the wake of excitement and pleasant sleepy surprise. He remembered now. Remembered where they were—and why—that waking up at all was a miracle, let alone waking up in each other's arms—which they most definitely were.

"Morning…"

Will's mouth found his own again—hungry, calescent—and traveled a slow, lazy trail down Taylor's jaw…throat…collarbone…gentling over the puckered scar on Taylor's chest. Taylor sucked in his breath.

"Does that hurt?"

He shook his head, although the scars were still sensitive, still felt weird being touched; he wouldn't want anyone to see them, let alone touch them—but it was different with Will.

This felt healing. The moist trace of lips, the delineation of tongue. He nipped Will's ear, and Will caught his breath, nudged Taylor's face, finding his mouth again for a hard, sweet kiss. A lover's kiss—while Will's fingertips dusted lightly over the whorls of damaged tissue. A little more to the left and the bullet would have hit Taylor's heart, but there it was thumping away, fast and strong against Will's fingertips, and desire buzzed through his nervous system, and he had never felt more alive than he felt right now.

Will's hands slid down, fastening on Taylor's waist, holding on, lips moving over Taylor's. Hot and soft, Will's tongue pushing inside Taylor's mouth, and Taylor mewled, wriggling closer.

The roughness of their jaws rubbing against each other, eyelashes flickering against each other, noses rubbing against each other.

Taylor tore his mouth away and said breathlessly, "You must not think we're going to make it."

"We're going to make it."

"Yeah? What's this supposed to be? A mercy fuck?" Taylor was smiling—he could feel Will's surprise.

Will shut him up the best way he knew, slipping his tongue back inside Taylor's mouth, teasing and sweet, playful like they had all the time in the world—like they should have done a long time ago.

Taylor's newly warmed hands slid eagerly over Will's body, moving to the fastening of his pants, and Will reciprocated, undoing Taylor's jeans and working his hand inside Taylor's boxers as they humped against each other, pressing close, hips grinding, cocks stiff and shoving against each other.

Palming one hard ass cheek, Will pinched. Taylor bucked. Will smoothed away the sting, smiling against Taylor's mouth, and their kiss went deeper, hotter, tongues twining.

Will thrust up, Taylor arched back, and they were struggling desperately to find the rhythm, pushing into each other's touch, frantic with need to be together in this, burning up with it.

Will was panting against his ear, hot moist gusts. Taylor pulled him closer, bit his throat, groaning pleasurably when Will nipped back. Bodies writhing, cocks rubbing, chests pushing against each other—it was feverish and fast and all too fleeting. Will reached down and took Taylor's wet-tipped cock in his hand, and Taylor rocked up against him, hands reaching up blindly, sliding down his biceps, hips pushing frantically into Will's grasp.

"You're purring again," Will said unsteadily, starting to laugh. "That is…beautiful…"

He was working both their cocks together, and Taylor struggled not to thrash around, to keep his movements tiny and tight because he didn't want to knock down the entire building. He fastened his mouth over Will's, smothering the yell he knew was coming.

And sure enough, Will's body bowed and then released in blazing hot pulse beats, slick heat spilling over Taylor's hand while he tried to hush Will's cries against his own.

Will shuddered all over, his hands faltering for a moment, going soft. He tore his mouth away, gasping for air. Taylor jerked against him, frustrated, and then Will's hands tightened again, and he set Taylor free with a couple of hard strokes, and bright release crackled through his body like raw electric current. He was coming hard, and he felt Will's hand slip, regain its grip, and milk him of the last sweet splashes of liquid heat.

They rested together then, warm and drowsy while the birds in the meadow sang good morning.

* * * * *

Will stroked Taylor's hair, fingering the little streak of silver that had appeared after the shooting. "It's light. We should get moving."

Taylor nodded. "They've got your map?"

"I don't think they'll go for the money now. They'll figure they have to stop us first."

"But they've gotta know they're running out of time. What are they going to do about Stitch's body?"

"There are all kinds of places they can stash that body. It could be months—years—before anyone discovers it."

"If it was me, I'd go for the money."

Will grinned reluctantly. "Yeah, but you've got nerves of steel. Nothing distracts you from what you want."

"You oughta talk," Taylor said. "Anyway, I've been known to…cut my losses." A little muscle moved in his jaw. "I know not everything I want is possible."

"What do you want?" Will asked. His fingers brushed Taylor's cheek, feeling the softness of beard over the hard planes of jaw. "Besides getting out of here alive."

Taylor didn't speak for a moment. "I want you," he said at last. Sunlight filtering through a chink in the lean-to illuminated his face. He looked tired and unexpectedly vulnerable. "I know what you think. And I know I don't have a great record when it comes to relationships, but —"

"Four years," Will interrupted. "Or close enough. That's how long we've been partners—that's the longest relationship I've ever had, and it's been with you."

To his surprise, Taylor's face quivered. He closed his eyes, hiding his feelings from Will, and Will absently noted how long his eyelashes were. He'd noticed that in the hospital too, sitting by Taylor's bedside waiting for him to wake up. Those long, black eyelashes…

"Hey," he said softly, "are you falling asleep in the middle of my big romantic speech?"

Taylor's lashes lifted. "Did you mean it? What you said before about taking it one day at a time?"

"Yeah, I meant it. Of course I did. I'm not letting you go without a fight."

Taylor said carefully, "As your partner or —?"

"As my friend, my lover, my partner. All of it. One day at a time," Will said. "Starting with today." And this time his kiss was a promise.

* * * * *

"Watch for rock slides here," Will warned.

It was late afternoon. It had taken the larger part of the day to cut back over the bluffs and they were working their way down the back of the mountainside. There was no trail to speak of, and they had to focus on their footing. Far below was a long valley with what appeared to be the scattered buildings of a ranch.

"What is that?" Taylor asked, sliding to a stop beside Will.

"I think that's the health resort I was telling you about." Will shaded his eyes, studying the empty corrals and tumbled down buildings. "It looks abandoned."

"We could burn the buildings down." And at Will's expression, Taylor said, "We've got to get the attention of someone: other hikers, rangers, campers. We can't keep this up forever."

Will's gaze was measuring, and Taylor said, "That's not what I mean. I'm okay, but we can't play hide and seek on this mountain all day."

"Yeah, you're great. We both are. Tired, hungry, thirsty —" He brushed the edge of his thumb against Taylor's cheekbone. "Sunburned. Next time, you pick the vacation spot."

"Now *that* I'm holding you to." Taylor smothered a yawn. "Maybe they did go after the money."

Will shook his head. "Even if they went to that meadow and found Jackson's body, they know we were there first. It's just going to confirm their suspicion that we found the money and hid it. And they're right."

"If they did use your map to find the meadow, how long would it take them?"

Will did some calculations. "If they started last night they'd have reached the meadow by midmorning."

"They'd look around to see if we hid the money. They were tracking us with binoculars from the time we stopped at the mineral springs."

"We'd already hidden the money by then—and if they knew where we'd stashed it, they wouldn't have bothered tracking us down last night."

"Do you think there's any chance they could follow our tracks to the bear box?"

"One of that group has a fair amount of tracking experience. I'm guessing it's Orrin." Will's eyes met Taylor's. "But I think they'll come straight after us. They know we eventually have to make our way down. They'll try to intercept."

"Then we better keep moving." Taylor rose and reached down a hand to Will.

* * * * *

The wind made a mournful sound through the broken boards of the old lodge. Shafts of sunlight, fading with the dimming daylight, highlighted floating motes—and striped the body lying facedown in the dust. The bullet hole in the back of the uniform jacket was crusted with blood several days old.

"Jesus." Taylor buried his nose in the crook of his arm as he approached the corpse. "That's why they thought they might need an insurance policy. They killed a ranger."

He glanced back; Will was standing in the open doorway watching the hills behind them.

"Everything okay?"

Will nodded—but absently. "I'm not sure. I thought I saw a flash on that hillside."

Taylor joined him and they watched for a moment.

Nothing moved. Nothing but the ripple of winter grass in the fields.

"Why hasn't anyone noticed they're missing a park ranger?"

Will shook his head. "Maybe they have." His eyes never left the pine-studded hillside.

"Are you thinking what I'm thinking?" Taylor asked.

Will turned his head and grinned slowly. "Probably."

* * * * *

"Actually, what I'm thinking is I'm going to have to take away one of your merit badges," Taylor remarked forty-five minutes later.

Will grimaced between gentle puffs of breath on the pile of smoking pocket lint and dried leaves. "The approved Firecrafter method is a bow and drill." He tilted the purpling broken glass to better catch the sun's rays. "I don't know if it's bright enough or hot enough," he muttered. "You've got wood stacked up inside if I can get this going?"

"It's all ready to go. We just have to transfer the blaze from here to there."

"The blaze…?" Will said ruefully.

They were silent, watching.

Minutes passed.

Taylor made a sharp exclamation as the pocket lint suddenly ignited. "Beautiful!"

"We're in business." Will used the glass to scoop up his tiny fire, protecting it with his hand as he stepped carefully through the broken door and put the fire to the stack of dried boards and timber Taylor had piled in the center of the lodge floor.

They stared in silent satisfaction as the flames caught.

"There's the cheese," Taylor said. "Now we just wait for mice to show up." He smiled at Will, who reached a hand behind his neck, drawing him close and kissing him.

Will was smiling, but the smile didn't reach his eyes. "You watch your back, Taylor. Understand me? Twice is all I can take."

Taylor kissed him in return, a quick, distracted press of mouths—then turned back as Will caught his arm. "You're doing it again, Will," he said softly.

"For the record, this isn't about not trusting you."

"You sure? Because that's how it feels."

Will said, "You want the truth? There's no one I'd rather have beside me in a fight than you. There's no one I trust more to watch my back."

Taylor grinned. "And your faith is well-placed, my son. I'm the best there is."

Will's hand tightened on Taylor's thinly-muscled arm. "No. Don't joke around. And don't get cocky. If something happens to you now—I don't think I'd get over it."

"That's fine," Taylor said, "because nothing is going to happen to me. And I'll tell you something else. You were afraid we couldn't do our job if we let ourselves care too much. That was one reason you didn't want to get involved. But you said it yourself this morning. We've been involved a long time—regardless of what we call ourselves: friends, lovers, partners. We're a team, Will. We always have been. We always will be."

He freed himself, catching Will's hand briefly in his own before slipping away. Frowning, Will watched him lift himself up and out through the broken window frame.

Taylor paused, balanced in the window for a moment. "And when this is over, you owe me a real vacation," he said. "We'll call it a honeymoon." The next moment he was gone, disappearing into the twilight.

Will waited, watching the fire shadow dance over the dead ranger's body.

* * * * *

They would come. Taylor had no doubt on that score. He lay in the tall grass behind the well, watching the meadow, waiting for their approach. A glance back at the lodge showed empty windows orange with firelight. Yeah, they would come, expecting to find Taylor and Will inside—maybe even sleeping.

The moon turned the waves of grass to silver. Somewhere on the other side of the building Will was lying in wait with the rifle. The thought cheered him. There was no better shot than Will. He smiled a little, thinking of Will's words before they'd separated.

Funny how he'd resented Will's overprotective streak before. Now it just felt reassuring.

If unnecessary.

The hours passed.

Taylor began to wonder if they were wrong. Maybe Bonnie and Orrin had decided to cut their losses and head for the hills.

And then he heard the rumbling in the distance—raising his head he saw lights in the distant sky. A helicopter—with search lights.

Too far away—checking the next valley over. Interesting, though. He wondered what it meant; would have liked to ask Will what he made of it.

He resisted the temptation to look for his partner. He knew he was there. He could feel him out there—hunting—just as Taylor was, and it was crucial to their survival both as a team and a couple that they prove to themselves that they could still do this. That they could still operate.

All the same, he'd have liked to know where Will was right now.

An owl hooted somewhere over on the other side of the corral: a low, raspy *who-o-o, who-o-o.*

It sounded so natural that it took Taylor a moment to recognize that call for what it was: Will checking in, letting him know where he was positioned. He grinned in the darkness, and cupped his hands, mimicking a whippoorwill—which was the only birdcall he could make that sounded halfway realistic.

As far as he knew there were no whippoorwills in the High Sierras, and he could just imagine Will shaking his head over it.

More time passed. His stomach growled. Too much longer and he'd be willing to sample the berries growing by the side of the house. He was beginning to feel his assorted aches and pains with a vengeance, his muscles stiffening up. That was liable to slow him down when the moment came.

Taylor was still mulling this over when a rifle fired, cracking the silence. He scooted out from behind the well and Orrin was striding up the meadow, firing steadily at a clump of chinquapin. He made no attempt at concealment, so he had to believe he had them cornered—which meant he already knew they weren't inside the building.

And Will wasn't firing back.

For a split second Taylor was afraid, and then he put it out of his mind, trusting Will to know what he was doing as he expected Will to trust him. He crawled forward along the outside corral, and as he did a bullet slammed into the wooden fence a few inches above his head. Bonnie—coming up from behind the lodge.

He had to give them credit; that was a smarter move than he had expected, but Orrin and Bonnie weren't taking any chances this time. Taylor dived behind a small shed. He could hear the *whup, whup, whup* of the helicopter, the searchlight skimming over the trees and fields heading down the valley—moving toward them.

Orrin was still blazing away. As Taylor watched, Will rose up out of the grass—nowhere near that chinquapin shrub.

"Drop it."

Orrin froze.

"I said drop the rifle, Orrin," Will called.

Orrin didn't move—and didn't throw the rifle away—and Taylor immediately understood. He began to look for Bonnie.

"Not going to tell you again," Will said calmly, trusting Taylor to take care of business.

Sure enough, there Bonnie was, stepping out from behind the smoke shack, drawing a bead on Will. Taylor launched himself at her, tackling her around the waist. He felt one bullet burn past his cheek—she went down firing—and he felt another bullet hit the ground next to his foot.

He slammed Bonnie against the ground—wanting it to end there, wanting to not have to punch her—and wrested the rifle from her.

She was screaming and swearing, doing her best to kick him in the balls, and then, in the distance, Taylor heard another rifle shot.

And even though he trusted Will to look after himself, for one very long second his heart forgot how to beat.

He cuffed Bonnie on the head, and she stopped fighting, sobbing with fury and frustration. Scrambling to his feet, he searched for Will, and became aware of the thrum of helicopter rotor blades drowning out everything else. Pale light bathed the yard like a spotlight. He couldn't see anything.

"Brandt?" he yelled.

"This is the California Department of Fish and Game. Put down your weapons."

Taylor stared across the blanched white yard, the tall grass whipping in the wind created by the helicopter blades.

He opened his mouth to call for Will again, but Will shouted back, "Right here, MacAllister."

"We repeat. This is California Department of Fish and Game. Put down your weapons."

Saved by the Department of Fish and Game? They were never going to live that one down. Filing that one away for future amusement, Taylor threw aside Bonnie's rifle.

"You *bastard*," Bonnie said. "I wish we'd killed you."

Taylor made a kissing sound to her, moving forward to pat her down quickly, and then stepping back.

She continued to swear a steady stream of invective as the helicopter landed, dust blowing toward them in a wave. Taylor ignored her, ignored the Fish and Game wardens piling out of the copter. He gazed across the sea of grass and spotted Orrin standing there, swaying, one arm cradling the other—and a few feet to his left, Will.

And Taylor relaxed. At last.

Feeling Taylor's gaze, Will looked across to him. He nodded. Taylor nodded back. And then Will's face broke into a grin. Taylor returned his grin.

Yeah, they were back. Back on solid ground.

OLD POISON

CHAPTER ONE

That prickle between his shoulder blades meant he was being watched.

One hand on the mailbox, Taylor glanced around. There was a woman pushing a kid in a stroller down the long, shady street. She was moving in the opposite direction. There was a guy in a parked Chevy reading a newspaper. Old Mrs. Wills was in her garden. She was shading her eyes, staring at him.

Taylor raised his hand in greeting.

She fluttered a hand back in hello.

The guy in the Chevy turned the page of his newspaper, remaining mostly concealed behind the tall pages.

A comfortable, quiet street in a small beach community. Old houses beneath old shade trees. But it was a neighborhood in flux. Old residents dying off, new residents not staying longer than a couple of years.

Taylor pulled the mail out of his box. The usual circulars and catalogs of junk he never bought and didn't want. And a birthday card. From Will.

Taylor studied the pale green envelope for a long moment. He was aware of a tightness in his chest, a confused rush of emotions. Amusement, sure, but uppermost…a sort of…a feeling he couldn't begin to describe.

That neat, careful cursive with which Will had spelled out Taylor's name and address. Not like Will's usual hand. Not that Will's usual hand was sloppy; Taylor was the one who had to translate his hieroglyphics for the front-office staff. But there was something painstaking and self-conscious about the writing on the envelope.

There was something else in the mail slot. Taylor pulled out a slip informing him that he had a package in the side locker of the mailbox stand.

He unlocked the long cabinet, and sure enough there was a rectangular parcel addressed to him. He tucked it under his arm, slammed the metal door shut, and crossed the street.

The guy in the Chevy remained well buried behind his newspaper.

Taylor cut across the patchy, threadbare lawn of his house, took the three front porch steps in one, and let himself into the house.

He locked the door behind him, looking down at the green envelope. Just the fact that Will had mailed him a birthday card. They'd be seeing each other that night—barring Will getting delayed on his current case—but Will had taken the time to pick a card and mail it. It was so…

It touched Taylor more than he wanted to admit. Of course this was a special birthday. Not one of the "0" birthdays; Taylor was thirty-two years old as of four o'clock that morning. It was special because ten weeks earlier Taylor had been shot in the chest and had nearly died.

It had been very close. The closest he'd ever come to checking out. He was still stuck on desk duty, although—thank Christ—this was the last week of that. He'd passed his fitness exam that very afternoon and Monday he'd be back in the field, partnered with Will again. Life would finally be getting back to normal. The new normal. The normal of him and Will as a… well, couple.

Partners and friends for four years, and lovers for not quite two months. Taylor was still afraid to trust it. It seemed dangerous to be this happy, like it was tempting fate. He couldn't quite forget that Will hadn't wanted this change in their relationship, that love had taken him unwilling and off guard.

He tore open the envelope.

It was the usual kind of thing. Sailboats, smooth water, and cloudless blue sky. *Happy Birthday to My Sweetheart* in sunshine yellow script.

His throat tightened. Hell. He'd never been anyone's sweetheart before. No one had ever sent him a card like this. Will had even signed the inside *Love, Will.*

There was a parcel too. A brown cardboard box. The kind of thing wine was shipped in—or good booze. The label was typed. Taylor used his pocketknife to slice through the tape sealing the box shut. Inside was a Styrofoam shell to protect the glass contents. He pried it out, and sure enough it was a bottle. A wine bottle with a yellow seal. He nearly dropped it.

There was a cobra inside the wine bottle.

Black-brown hood flared, fangs bared, the coiled cobra stared blindly through the clear rice wine.

What the fuck?

It was dead, of course. Dead and pickled. Asian snake wine was an authentic Asian beverage supposedly valuable for treating everything from rheumatism to night sweats. It was also supposed to be a natural aphrodisiac with mystical sexual properties, although what the hell was natural about a cobra in a wine bottle?

Feeling slightly queasy, Taylor set the bottle on the kitchen table.

No way had Will sent that. He searched through the box's packing materials to see if there was a card or a note. *Nada.*

Weird.

A joke maybe. Probably. He had a few friends at the Bureau of Diplomatic Security who would find this kind of thing amusing. Except it was an expensive joke. These specialty wines weren't cheap. And most of his pals at the DSS were.

He contemplated the bottle for another second or two, but he had things to get ready before Will arrived. He wanted this to be a very good weekend.

* * * * *

Taylor was not going to be happy.

Will tried to tell himself that Taylor's happiness was beside the point. Not that it didn't matter to him, but it couldn't be Will's first consideration when it came to work. Taylor was a professional. He needed to understand that this was (a) not Will's choice, (b) all part of the job, (c) no big deal, (d) all of the above.

The long red snake of taillights slithered to another halt in front of him. Will sighed and tapped the brakes, rolling to a stop. He turned up Emmylou Harris on the CD player. On the seat next to him, Riley, his German shepherd, licked his chops nervously. Riley liked traffic even less than Will did.

Traffic on the 101 was always a bitch these days, and it was especially a bitch on Friday evenings when half the Valley residents seemed to be pouring out every side street and crevice of the smoggy basin for a weekend in the mountains or at the beach.

It could take an exasperating hour just to travel from his Woodland Hills home to Ventura. Lately Taylor had been hinting that they should move in together. Will had ignored the hints.

Not that he didn't like Ventura. He did. Living that near the beach would be great, in fact. And not like he and Taylor didn't get along well. They had always got along well, even before they moved the relationship from best friends and partners to lovers.

Lovers.

Not a word Will would typically have used to describe one of his relationships. But then he wouldn't generally describe his relationships as... relationships.

The cars in front of him began to move again, brake lights flicking off, turn signals flicking on. The sea of traffic rolling forward once more.

And then...stop.

"Goddamn traffic," Will growled, and Riley flicked his ears.

Will closed his eyes, picturing his eventual arrival, savoring it, momentarily shutting out the smog and exhaust and noise of Friday evening on the 101, seeing Taylor's face in his mind: that weirdly exotic bone structure; wide green eyes that looked almost bronze; a wicked angel's full, sensual mouth; the soft, dark hair with that new—since the shooting—streak of silver.

He did not want to fight with Taylor over this thing with Bradley. He especially did not want to fight with him tonight when he had been looking forward to this evening—this weekend—all day.

They needed this time together. It had been a rough couple of weeks with Will working late most nights and Taylor increasingly frustrated with desk duty. Taylor wasn't the most patient guy in the world at the best of times. And this had not been the best of times for him.

Will had planned on a long weekend of spoiling him rotten, starting with dinner at Taylor's favorite Japanese restaurant. But now...

So did he tell Taylor the bad news up front or did he wait till Taylor was properly fed and fucked?

Emmylou sang, "I'm riding a big blue ball, I never do dream I may fall…"

"What do you think?" he asked Riley.

Riley flicked his ears and stared out the window, panting softly.

"You're no help," Will grumbled.

* * * * *

Will parked behind Taylor's silver Acura MDX in the narrow side driveway and got out of his own Toyota Land Cruiser. Evenings were damp this close to the beach. The air smelled of salt and old seaweed—corrupt yet invigorating.

He let Riley out of the passenger side of the SUV. Riley trotted down the driveway to the large, overgrown backyard, barking a warning to the neighborhood cats.

Will slid the gate shut. The house was an original Craftsman bungalow. It had been in terrible shape when Taylor bought it two years previously. Actually, it was still in terrible shape, but Taylor was renovating it, one room at a time, in his spare hours.

Will got his duffel bag from the backseat and the heavy, blue-and-gold-wrapped birthday present. He felt self-conscious about that present; he'd spent a lot of time and a fair amount of money on Taylor this year.

Hard to forget that Taylor nearly hadn't lived to see this birthday.

Speak of the devil. The side door opened, and Taylor came down the steps, an unguarded grin breaking the remote beauty of his face. There was a funny catch in Will's throat as he saw him alive and strong and smiling again.

"How was traffic?"

Will opened his mouth, but the next instant Taylor was in his arms, his mouth covering Will's in unaffected hunger. They were safe here. The cinder-block wall was high, and the bougainvillea draping over the edge of the roof neatly blocked out the view of this driveway from the street.

"Man, I missed you," Taylor said when they surfaced for air.

"You saw me this morning."

"For three minutes in front of Varga, Jabowitz, and Cooper. It's not the same."

"No," agreed Will, "it's not the same." His gaze rested on Taylor's face; his heart seemed to swell with a quiet joy. "Happy birthday."

"Thanks." Taylor's smile widened. "Hey, I got your card."

"Oh." Will was a little embarrassed about that card. *To My Sweetheart* or whatever it said. Kind of over-the-top. He'd bought it on impulse. Taylor was smiling, though, and with no sign of mockery, so maybe it was okay.

"Is that for me?" Taylor asked as Will retrieved the tote bag and parcel he'd dropped when Taylor landed in his arms.

"Nah. I'm heading over to another party after I get done here." Will shoved the blue-and-gold present into his hands. "Of course it's for you."

"Okay if I open it now?"

"You're the most impatient guy I ever met." Will was amused, though.

"Hey, I waited four years for you," Taylor threw over his shoulder, heading up the stairs into the house.

"Yeah, remind me again how you whiled away the hours in that lonely monastery?"

Taylor's chuckle drifted back.

Will heeled the side door shut and followed Taylor through the mud porch and into the kitchen.

This was one of the first rooms Taylor had renovated: a cozy breakfast nook with built-in window benches, gleaming mahogany cabinets and drawers with patinated copper fixtures, green granite counters, and gray-green slate floor. The numerous cabinets were well designed and well organized. The care and priority given the kitchen might have deceived someone into thinking cooking played a role in Taylor's life. In fact, the kitchen had been designed to please Will—the only person who had ever cooked a meal in that house.

There was a German chocolate cake on the table in the breakfast nook. Will's card was propped next to it with a couple of others: *To Our Son, To My Son, To My Brother, What is a Brother? Happy Birthday, Uncle.* Greetings from the whole tribe. To the side of these was a wine bottle-shaped science experiment gone awry.

"What the hell is that?" Will peered more closely at the pickled contents of the wine bottle. What it was, was a fucking *cobra*. The cobra stared back sightlessly at him, fangs bared.

"It's my snake. I've been waiting all day to show it to you." Taylor wiggled his eyebrows salaciously.

"Funny," said Will, glancing at him. "Where did you get it?"

"It came in the mail."

"Who sent it?"

Taylor shrugged.

"You don't know?"

"The card must have got lost."

They both studied the bottle.

"What is the liquid?"

"Rice wine."

"Is it poison?"

"It's not supposed to be. In fact, it's supposed to be a cure-all—and an aphrodisiac."

"I bet bourbon works just as well, and you don't have that nasty cobra aftertaste."

Taylor's smile was preoccupied. Will gave him a closer look.

"You don't have any idea who would have sent something like this?"

Taylor shook his head. Will laughed and threw an arm around his wide, bony shoulders.

"Spooked?"

"Nah." But Taylor's brows were drawn together as he continued to gaze at the bottle. "Weird, though, isn't it?"

"Yeah."

Taylor had some weird friends. And weirder acquaintances. He had been in the DSS longer than Will, signing on right out of college, and he'd been posted to Tokyo, Afghanistan, and briefly, Haiti. The next time he was posted overseas it would be as a regional security officer responsible for managing security operations for an embassy or for a number of diplomatic posts within an assigned area. That was one reason Will was hesitant to move in with him. Not a lot of point in setting up house when one or both of them could be stationed overseas within a year or so.

Taylor didn't see it this way, of course. Taylor's idea was they should move in together immediately and they'd deal with the threat of a future separation when—if—it happened. He'd always had a tendency to leave tomorrow to take care of itself, but getting shot had cemented his determination to live every day as though it were his last.

Will understood that. He even agreed with it, in principle, but what happened to him when Taylor was posted overseas for three-or-so years? Things weren't as simple as Taylor liked to pretend.

He glanced at Taylor's profile. He was frowning, and Will did not want him frowning on his birthday.

"Hey," he said softly. Taylor's head turned his way. "Want to open your present?"

"Sure." Taylor started to pull the gold ribbon on the parcel he was carrying. Will put his hand over his.

"Your other present," he said meaningfully, and Taylor started to laugh.

* * * * *

Will stretched out on Taylor's wide bed in the cool, dark room that looked out onto the overgrown garden with the broken birdbath and the tumbledown garden shed, and he rested his face on his hands and spread his legs.

So gorgeous. So casually, unconsciously gorgeous. Wide shoulders, strong, lithe torso, long legs. There was a tiny velvet mole above his left butt cheek and, on his right shoulder, a small griffin tattoo that he'd acquired the night before he went into the Marine Corps. Will, his brother, Grant, and their three cousins all sported those griffin tattoos on their right shoulders. Some kind of male-ritual, family-bonding thing.

Taylor had heard this from Will. He'd never met Will's family. Never met the brother or the cousins or Will's dad, who had been a sheriff in a small town in Oregon. Maybe one of these days.

He stroked a slow hand down the long, sleek line of Will's back, and Will shivered. Taylor bent his head and kissed Will right over the tiny velvet mole. Will shivered again.

Anticipation or something else?

Taylor enjoyed being fucked.

In fact, he enjoyed it so much, it made him uneasy. He'd never told Will that, but Will probably knew. Will was scrupulous about keeping the scales perfectly balanced, because they always took turns. However, though that particular evening was Taylor's turn to be fucked, Will—in honor of Taylor's birthday—offered his own taut, tanned ass up for Taylor's pleasure.

And it *was* Taylor's pleasure. Doubly so because he sensed that Will didn't enjoy being fucked nearly as much as he did, and he was humbled to receive this gift. Taylor had never let anyone shove his cock in his ass besides Will; Will was more fair-minded and had probably taken turns with his other lovers.

Taylor didn't like thinking about Will's other lovers.

He took his time preparing, squirting the exotic oil he'd purchased— ginger, jasmine, rose, black pepper, sandalwood, and ylang-ylang in a slick, silvery liquid that warmed his fingers. A sweet scent like spicy flowers.

"What's that?" Will asked, glancing over his shoulder.

"Passion oil. You'll like it."

Will resettled his chin on his folded arms. "You're into some strange shit, MacAllister."

True enough. He'd done some wild things when he was younger. Will didn't know the half of it. But in other ways he'd been very conservative. In fact, the first time he'd let Will fuck him, something had seemed to snap in his brain; made him fear he was having some kind of psychotic break. Alerted him to the fact that he probably had one or two sexual hang-ups after all. Before Will, it was unthinkable that he'd let anyone take him. Occasionally one of his lovers would ask to fuck him, and if they pushed it, that was usually Taylor's cue to end the relationship. His relationships never lasted long anyway.

Will was the exception. In every way. Though Taylor had always tried to be an inventive and skilled lover, he took special pains that everything be good for Will.

He slipped his fingers down the crevice between Will's butt cheeks, seeking the tight pink bud of his anus. *Splitting the peach*: that's what the Chinese Taoists called this. Such romantic terms for everything: *blowing the flute* and *clouds and rain* and *jade stalk*. Funny stuff but…maybe sort of nice, too.

Ever so delicately he circled Will's opening, then slipped the tip of one oily finger inside, careful and slow.

Will held very still, goose bumps rising over his smooth, tanned skin.

Taylor pushed inside, closing his eyes at the dark-felt grip around his finger. His heart pounded hard, his own cock lifted—*arisen, angry*, those old Chinese would have said, but Taylor was anything but angry. Happy, excited…he stroked and pressed…satiny inside and satiny out.

"Does that feel good?" he murmured.

"Sure." Will sounded a little winded.

Taylor silently cued Will to move onto his knees; even here they could communicate deftly without words. He guided his cock, already pearling and damp, and pushed slowly, inch by inch, into Will. "Are you —"

"Go," Will jerked out. "Do it."

Was Will loving it or just wanting it over with? Taylor was never quite sure, but he couldn't stop himself at this point. Will was pushing back against him, rocking into him. Taylor thrust back, and they settled into a quick, efficient rhythm.

Oh yes. More. More of this. Harder. Deeper. Faster. Taylor's eyes shut tight. Just feeling, feeling that gorgeous drag on the thick, pulsing shaft of his cock, feeling the heat and snug darkness, feeling everything.

Will grunted as Taylor changed angle, tried to hit the sweet spot just right.

"Good, Will?" gasped Taylor.

"Yeah. Good."

So good—but it was good all the ways they did it. And they had done it nearly every conceivable way. At least all the ways that Taylor figured wouldn't shock or dismay Will. Very much a meat-and-potatoes man, Will.

Will's harsh breaths were coming in counterpoint to his own. The rich, rolling sweetness tingled through Taylor, and he cried out as Will's body

seemed to spasm around his own and he began to come in hard, hot jets
clouds and rain, firing the cannon, surrender, and die...

CHAPTER TWO

"**S**omething on your mind?" Taylor asked as they were leaving for dinner.

"Who me?"

"Nah. The monster in your pants. Yeah, you. You seem kind of quiet tonight."

"Nope." But Will made an effort to snap out of his reflections.

They chatted about Will's case as they drove over to the restaurant. Taylor didn't ask about Monday, didn't mention it, so Will didn't have to evade or lie; he wouldn't have been able to lie, anyway. Even if he had a hope of getting away with it.

Which he didn't. He glanced at Taylor's profile and smiled inwardly.

To look at Taylor MacAllister, you would never think he was a dangerous man.

Correction. If you knew enough to recognize that easy, sure-footed way Taylor moved, the confidence with which he carried himself, the cool, direct way he met your eyes, you'd recognize that here was a guy who could handle himself in any situation. But that required being someone of experience yourself, someone who wasn't fooled by the fact that Taylor looked deceptively slender and graceful—almost pretty. The truth was, he was all wiry muscle and bones harder than unalloyed titanium. He was tough and relentless and utterly fearless.

He frightened Will. He frightened him because even after being shot—twice, if someone wanted to get technical about it—Taylor seemed to have no sense of his own vulnerability. Or he just didn't care.

When they arrived at the Red Dragon restaurant at nine o'clock that evening there was an altercation going on in the parking lot. Three Hispanic youths—baby faces and gang tattoos—appeared to be hassling a young black woman. One of the punks was sitting on the hood of the woman's Sebring convertible. Another was lounging in the backseat, drinking a can of Tecate beer—and that was the woman's mistake for leaving the top down and the car unattended while she went inside to get her carryout. This was not a nice neighborhood.

The third asshole was blocking the girl's retreat. He didn't look too dangerous to Will, although the girl—young woman—was plainly upset. She was trying to escape to the safety of the restaurant, and the punk jumped in front of her, grabbing his crotch and flicking his tongue in and out lizardlike. He was still keeping a hands-off distance from her, though, and the posturing seemed mostly about amusing his compadres in the convertible. He was probably not more than eighteen. The other two looked of a similar age.

Just pulling into the parking lot signaled the end of playtime, and if more was called for —

Taylor swung sharply next to the convertible and was out of the Land Cruiser before Will had his seat belt unbuckled.

Will heard Taylor's flat, hard, "What's going on here?" which promptly changed the entire dynamic of the situation.

It might have changed for the worse anyway, of course, but Taylor, sleek and deceptively slight in his tight jeans and green silk shirt—with the expensive car and pugnacious attitude—triggered all their cholo insecurities and hostilities.

Will scrambled out quickly, cursing the fact that neither of them was armed because they were going out to dinner and alcoholic beverages were sure to be consumed, and they shouldn't have to carry when they were just going out to eat, for chrissake.

"What's *goin' on here* is none of your business, *culeros*," the punk hassling the girl said, drawing himself up to all his compact, muscular five-eight. The kid on the hood of the car rolled off and started for Taylor. The kid in the back raised his arm as though threatening to throw his beer can.

Will was closer. He grabbed the kid's arm, yanked it back hard, surprising a yowl of pain out of him. "*Don't* be a litterbug," Will warned.

The kid snatched his arm to his chest, rubbing it and glaring. The one who had previously been lounging on the convertible hood stopped midtrack, eyeing Will warily.

"What are you supposed to be, cops?"

"Something like that," Taylor said. "What are you supposed to be, gangbangers?"

"Something like that."

Taylor laughed. The kid opened his mouth, then read something in Taylor's face that shut him up, already backing down, looking for a way out.

"Out of the car," Will instructed the kid in the backseat.

The kid climbed awkwardly, one-handed, joining his glaring, resentful cohort. "Come on, Jorge," he called to the third gangbanger.

Jorge, the kid who had been hassling the girl—who had remained wide-eyed and silent, clutching her carryout bags throughout this intervention—was a different animal.

"You're no cop!" Face twisted in a sneer, he advanced on Taylor. That put him in Will's path. Will planted his hand in the kid's chest, shoving him back a step.

Furious, Jorge looked from him to Taylor. "What is this? What are you? Two *jotos*, eh? Yeah, I bet you are."

"Want to find out the hard way?" Taylor inquired.

"No, you *don't*," Will answered as Jorge opened his mouth. "Believe me, you don't."

After a trembling pause, Jorge flung away, hands raised in the air in a grand "don't touch me!" gesture. He started walking, furious, head down, and his minions raced down the street after him, shouting back obscenities at Taylor and Will.

Game over. But what if they'd been carrying? What if Larry, Moe, and Curly had whipped an arsenal out of their falling-down pants and opened fire at Taylor? It gave Will chills to think about it.

The girl launched into tearful thanks and explanation, and it was a few more minutes before they were finally in the restaurant, apologizing for being late for their reservation.

"You really pushed that, you know," Will said from behind his menu once they were seated and the waiter had departed with their drink order.

Silence on the other side of the table. Finally Taylor lowered his menu. "You think we should have stood by and watched them carjack her?"

"Of course not." Will couldn't help adding, "They weren't going to carjack her."

"You don't know that."

True. Will's instinct was that they were just having fun hassling her, but it could have turned ugly fast—it nearly had. Jorge had turned out to be harder and more reckless than Will had initially reckoned. If Jorge had been packing, he probably would have pulled his weapon.

Into Will's silence, Taylor said carefully, "You think I mishandled the situation?"

"Of course not. I don't have a problem with what you did. I have a problem with the way you did it."

Taylor's brows were drawn together in a narrow black line. His eyes glinted like old jade in the soft lighting. "How's that?"

"You didn't talk to me. You didn't wait to see if I was with you. You didn't —"

"Since when do we need to discuss our every move?"

It was Will's turn to be nonplussed. There was truth to what Taylor was saying. They usually knew exactly what the other was going to do without discussing it—half the time with no more than a glance between them. They had been reading each other's thoughts for years. That was part of what made them such an effective team.

Taylor had always been a little quick off the mark, a little hot tempered. Will had taken a tolerant view of it and watched for Taylor's cues so he could back his play.

Watching Will, apparently reading his surprised recognition, Taylor said quietly, "You know what? I haven't changed, Will. You have."

* * * * *

The mai tais came in small red urns carved with dragon heads. Taylor rarely drank hard liquor, and then he stuck to Rusty Nails, but Will seemed to think the evening called for the Red Dragon mai tais, and who was Taylor to argue? The mai tais were sweet and citrusy and very cold. Under their influence, Will finally relaxed and forgot about the incident in the restaurant parking lot.

Something was going on with Will. Something more than the usual thing going on with Will—which was confusing enough. Taylor watched for the visual cues of Will's eyes, his hands, his mouth. Will was the stoic type, so every little gesture, every microexpression, meant something.

From the point that they had moved from being partners to lovers, Will had had problems. Initially Taylor had put it down to the old thing about Will feeling guilty for Taylor getting shot. He'd been convinced that Taylor had stopped a bullet because he didn't love him—not the same way Taylor did Will.

Taylor had been shot because he was careless. End of story.

They'd worked through that, for the most part, during the now-famous camping trip from hell. A week in the High Sierras—in freeze-your-ass-off April, of all times—where they'd managed to fall afoul of murderous hijackers looking for the ruins of a crashed plane—and two million dollars.

They'd survived that, come out of it stronger than ever, come out of it lovers as well as friends. Will had stopped feeling guilty, and he trusted Taylor to be able to handle himself again—and yet something *had* changed.

"How's the tea-smoked duck?" Will inquired.

Taylor picked up a bite with his chopsticks. "Great. Excellent."

And it was. The best Japanese food in town. Will had taken the trouble to call ahead so that Taylor could have his favorite tea-smoked duck, which had to be prepared the night before. Taylor was particular about his Japanese food, having lived in Tokyo for two years.

He preferred not to think about Tokyo, though.

"You want another drink?"

Taylor hesitated, and Will said, "Go ahead. I'll drive home."

Home. That sounded good. Taylor wished… Whatever. This was good too.

He nodded yes to another drink. Refocused on Will. Yeah. Whatever was going on with Will tonight wasn't just the dustup in the parking lot. "Did you get a call about testifying in the Black Wolf hijacking case?"

"Yep." Will met his eyes, smiled faintly.

"Don't ask me to go camping again," Taylor warned him.

"Good things come to those who camp." Will batted his eyelashes. There was nothing remotely camp about Will, and Taylor nearly choked on his duck.

"Ha," he managed. "Anyway, next vacation it's my turn to pick where we go."

"Well, this wouldn't be a vacation, MacAllister. We'd be testifying in a federal case."

"I'm going to remind you of that when you start packing the fishing poles."

Will grinned, conceding the point, and returned to his wild salmon. He was not much of a fan of Japanese food.

Taylor bit back a smile, watching him. "How's the fish?"

"Fine." Will gave him one of those looks that turned Taylor's bones to jelly. "I'm looking forward to dessert."

Taylor said blandly, to cover the fact that his cock was instantly hard and aching, "I hear the green-tea ice cream is something else."

"Maybe we can get it to go."

Taylor smiled into his mai tai.

* * * * *

When they got back to Taylor's house, Will fed Riley, and Taylor cut the birthday cake.

"We're not singing 'Happy Birthday'?" Will asked, accepting the paper plate with the generous slice of cake Taylor handed over.

"Go right ahead," Taylor invited. Taylor couldn't carry a tune to save his life, but Will liked to sing, and Riley—after a couple of beers—was known to howl along.

"Maybe later," Will promised. He was anxious to see Taylor open his birthday present. Anxious and nervous both. He'd never bought anything this expensive for anyone, and this particular item was pretty far out of his realm of expertise.

He was relying on this gift to go a ways toward fixing the damage when Taylor heard what Will kept putting off telling him.

Taylor got a glass of iced water, took the wrapped parcel into the den, and sat down on the long sofa beside Will. He gave an experimental tug to the golden coil of ribbon and gave Will a half smile that seemed to flutter in Will's chest like a butterfly.

"Well, go on," he said.

Taylor held the box up and shook it gently. "Emmylou Harris's greatest hits?" he guessed.

"You must think I'm pretty cheap. That would be her entire collection. And all her collaborations."

Taylor raised his brows. Guessed again. "Porter Cable Speed-Bloc sander."

Now that was a very good guess. That was the gift Will had originally planned to give him. In fact, that was the gift Taylor had admitted he'd like when Will dropped a couple of casual hints about upcoming birthday requests.

But this was a special birthday.

Will kept his expression blank.

Taylor smirked. Mr. Know-It-All was in for a surprise. He pulled the gold ribbon off the box, tore the cobalt blue paper away, opened the oversize, unmarked cardboard box, and lifted out the flat wooden box.

He shot Will a puzzled glance, opened the box, and stared.

Will waited tensely, watching Taylor's profile. He saw Taylor's Adam's apple jump as he swallowed.

He said at last, almost inaudibly, "Will."

Will relaxed, pleased with himself. He could see Taylor struggling to stay stoic and knew he'd scored big-time.

Inside the box was a Japanese percussion pistol. The black wood grip was carved in the shape of a dragon head with a gleaming brass eye. The dragon had a large pearl in its fangs. The long, narrow brass barrel was ornately engraved with kanji on a textured background.

Taylor said disbelievingly, "Where did you did find this?"

"I've got a few contacts. You like it?"

Taylor nodded. He still hadn't faced Will, so Will made it easy on him by hooking an arm around Taylor's neck and pulling him over. Taylor grabbed him fiercely, didn't say a word—pretty much a first.

Will's heart seemed to light up. He'd hoped this was the right thing. Taylor had a small but pricey collection of vintage Japanese weapons. A couple of samurai swords, a pistol—but nothing as nice as this.

"You shouldn't have," Taylor said, voice stifled by Will's shoulder. "Must have cost you a fortune."

Nearly three thousand bucks, as a matter of fact. And worth every penny to see Taylor MacAllister finally at a loss for words.

Will kissed Taylor's ear, which was all he could reach. "Happy birthday, sweetheart," he said, and he was astonished to find his own voice husky, choked.

Taylor sat up, swiftly dipping his head to his forearm, then studying the pistol with awe. "How old is it?"

"Eighteenth century. The details are on the bottom of the box." Will turned his attention to his cake, which was moist and delicious and lavishly frosted with gooey pecans and coconut.

"Beautiful," Taylor murmured, and Will tended to agree.

* * * * *

It was even better the second time.

They weren't in any hurry now. They had the whole weekend ahead of them, and they'd already taken the edge off their urgency before they'd gone to dinner.

"What would you like?" Will asked, clearly still in a generous mood.

Taylor said the truth. "I want you to fuck me."

"Fucking. A present you give yourself," Will deliberately misquoted, and a giggle—borne of one too many mai tais—escaped Taylor.

He'd have been happy to be taken on the sofa in the den, or the kitchen table, or even the freshly sanded floor in the hallway, but Will opted for the bedroom and all its comforts, including the mysterious bottle of passion oil.

Taylor lay on his back, shivering enjoyably as Will's blunt, oily finger slowly traced the crack of his ass.

"I like that." He was more vocal than Will, offering feedback whether solicited or otherwise. But Will had never seemed to mind.

"Yeah?" There was a smile in Will's voice as his fingers pierced Taylor, slowly, sweetly, slipping the warm, flowery oil into his tight little hole. "And this?"

"That too." Taylor closed his eyes tight, savoring that slippery-fingered invasion. Will was good at this, good at making a sensual delight of preparation, and Taylor wanted that stroking touch to never end. It made him feel like he was melting inside, all the walls, all the barriers dissolving in a wet, hot thaw.

"More," he whispered as Will's fingers gently withdrew. "More."

Will settled over him and Taylor spread his thighs, wriggling and shifting to accommodate Will's muscular length. Taylor smiled up at Will, and Will smiled back. He sang softly, "They say it's your birthday."

Taylor obligingly did the guitar riff in his cracked tenor.

"It's my birthday too, yeah."

Another riff from Taylor as his restless hands caressed Will's buttocks in air guitar, drawing Will down. His hips raised to meet the frustrating, tantalizing prod of the blunt head of Will's cock as it grazed the entrance of his body.

"I'm glad it's your birthday," Will growled. "Happy birthday to you."

His cock finally rifted Taylor, shoved deep inside, stretching him wide open and then filling him up with a sweet, fierce throbbing. Taylor arched up to meet it, gave a deep, groan of pleasured pain. Will's muscular body pressed Taylor deep into the bed, pushing deep inside him, and Will's warm breath tickled Taylor's ear as they began the old rock and roll, slow, sensual strokes in the push-pull argument over whether it was better to give or receive.

Energetic, forceful, but affectionate. This thrust-and-parry debate of cock and ass was no longer about winning or control. It was now teamwork to make it last as long as possible—unfortunately, in Taylor's opinion, never quite long enough.

He gave a shout as that hot tingle began in his groin, that wild electricity in the base of his cock, that fluttering in his chest like there was too much sensation, too much emotion to contain in one body. His balls drew tight, his entire body clenched tight, his fingers sank into Will's broad back, and he began to come in great straining pulses.

He smothered his yell against Will's shoulder.

A few sweating, spent seconds later he felt Will shoot into him, deep inside him.

Afterward, they watched the 1932 film *The Mistress of Atlantis* about two best friends and foreign legionnaires who fall victim to the evil queen of the lost city. For a time they amused each other commenting on the movie. Then Will dozed off and Taylor ate some of his birthday cake while his eyelids grew heavier and heavier.

The last thing he remembered was hearing Lt. Saint-Avit running through the streets of Atlantis shouting for his missing comrade...

CHAPTER THREE

"**W**hat on God's earth is this?"

Will stepped out of Taylor's bathroom holding a blue bottle of oil labeled *UP*. He read aloud, "'Australia's Number One Erectile Performance Oil. Take control of your erection today.'"

"Hey!" Taylor yelped, casting his Levi's aside. "Put my UP down." He was in the bathroom in two long-legged steps.

"My my. I've never noticed you having any problem keeping your up, up."

"I don't. It's just a-a performance enhancer."

Will scrutinized him. This was a new side of Taylor. Not that Taylor didn't go in for some screwball things.

He was blushing now—and rightly so—as he snatched at the bottle Will held. They wrestled briefly; then Taylor grabbed the bottle and tossed it under the sink.

"I was looking for shaving cream," Will told him mildly. "I forgot mine."

"I use an electric razor; you know that."

He did know that. He knew pretty much everything about Taylor, but every so often Taylor surprised him. Like with the UP oil. The funny thing was, the idea of that oil vaguely excited him too. *Firmer, fuller, harder. More responsive erections.* That all sounded pretty good. The idea of Taylor, damp from his shower, massaging that oil into the shaft and head of his penis every morning; his hard, thin hands moving briskly on himself—or no, moving slowly, languidly on himself —

Will gulped. For chrissake! They'd just spent the night and the morning fooling around. It was like being seventeen again. He asked briskly, "Anyway, where do you want to go for breakfast? Or lunch?"

Taylor, still uncharacteristically rattled, was squeezing past him out of the bathroom, muttering about coffee mugs and soap foam. It was, well, endearing.

Will caught him by the arm. "Hey. MacAllister."

Taylor stopped. Faced him.

Will opened his mouth, but he lost his nerve. Couldn't say it.

"What?"

You know I…

Taylor raised his brows.

Will shook his head and turned back to the mirror. He gave his reflection a sheepish look.

* * * * *

They had brunch at Café Verve, eating out on the crowded sidewalk patio beneath the yellow umbrellas.

Verve was their favorite place for breakfast, as they did biscuits with milk gravy, something Will was partial to. Taylor opted for a veggie omelet and black coffee.

It was a sunny, pleasant morning. The sun was shining, the sky had that extra blue tint to it that spring brought. They talked leisurely of this and that, and then Taylor brought up work and the following week.

Will had put all thought of that aside—or mostly aside—so as to not spoil Taylor's birthday, but he had known he was going to have to bring it up at some point that day. Now the moment was on them; there was no putting it off, as much as he hated to spoil this lovely morning.

He waited till Taylor paused, and then he said, "Listen, I have to tell you something."

Maybe the bad news was written in his face, or maybe it was something in the tone of his voice. The line of Taylor's body stayed relaxed and easy, but Will could feel his tension like a fine wire drawn tight between them. "Yeah?"

"On Monday"—Will took a deep breath—"you're working with Varga."

For a second he thought Taylor hadn't heard him or hadn't understood. He continued to stare at Will, narrow-eyed, as though a pirate ship had appeared on the horizon. Then he said flatly, "Was that your idea?"

"My idea? No, it wasn't my idea." Will was both taken aback and indignant. "Of course it wasn't my idea."

Taylor didn't say a word, just stared at him with those wide green eyes. Such an odd color. Like old, oxidized pennies.

"Why the hell would you think it was my idea?"

"You said from the first that it would be a bad idea to try and balance being lovers with being partners."

"That's right, but we went ahead with it, didn't we." It wasn't a question.

"But you're not happy about it."

Will kept his voice down, but it wasn't easy. "What are you talking about?"

Taylor bit out, "You're not happy with it. You wish it hadn't happened. You'd have preferred that things stay the way they were."

Startled, because there was truth to that, Will didn't have an immediate answer.

Taylor's face grew tighter, all stark bones and shadowed planes in the bright Ventura sunlight.

"Yeah, but it did happen," Will said in a low voice. "And there's no going back from it."

Taylor hadn't moved. In fact, he was so still, he barely seemed to breathe. No reaction at all. And that wasn't like him.

Suddenly awkward, Will said, "Anyway, the reteaming is just temporary."

"Who are you partnered with?"

Fuck. Well, there was no getting around it. It was just that Taylor was taking it even worse than Will had imagined he would—and Will hadn't even got to the really bad part yet. Bad from Taylor's point of view, anyway.

"I'm not—I'm working a visa fraud case. Illegal aliens using forged docs to unlawfully gain employment to naval bases in the region."

"Naval bases," Taylor said slowly. And then, dangerously, "Who are you working it with?"

Will said, careful to keep any inflection from his voice, "I'm acting in liaison with the navy. With David Bradley."

For one taut second Taylor didn't move, and then he was up and out of his seat, striding for the gate that led from the patio to the sidewalk.

"Taylor!"

Uncomfortably aware that they now had the attention of most of the diners on the patio, Will threw a bunch of bills down and took off after Taylor.

Instead of heading for the car, Taylor was cannoning down the pavement, head down like a bull—yeah, like the bullhead he was. Will, unwilling to bowl right through people, lost valuable seconds trying to catch him. No way in hell was he going to *run* after Taylor.

He couldn't believe this. Where the hell did Taylor think he was going? Was he planning to walk home? Catch a taxi? Who the hell knew? Did he?

Will's gut was churning. It was partly anger, largely directed at himself for not finding a better way to break it to Taylor, but most of it was that sick feeling that came anytime he knew he'd hurt Taylor. Taylor had a rep for being a tough bastard, and he was, but...

God only knew what he made of something like this, and Will couldn't help but remember the last time Taylor had thought Will was getting serious about David Bradley.

He darted around two middle-aged women with piles of shopping bags between them, dodged a kid on a skateboard—illegal here, by the way—and sidestepped a couple of guys on cell phones who sounded like they were talking to each other.

Taylor was still flying down the street, charging along in his white-faced fury. Will put on a burst of speed as Taylor reached the corner of the sidewalk, pausing—amazingly—the few seconds before the crossing light turned green.

The light turned, the perky pedestrian symbol glowing white-green, and Taylor stepped out ahead of the rest of the people milling on the corner. At the same time, a battered Chevy pulling away from the curb accelerated, tires squealing as the driver tried too late to make the light.

A woman on the corner screamed in warning. Will saw Taylor's head jerk up, too late, to see the car bearing down on him.

* * * * *

Oh yeah. *That.* Speeding cars coming his way.

Taylor had barely time to recognize his serious miscalculation when something significantly big and muscular hurtled full bodied into him, knocking him halfway across the intersection. He landed hard and unprepared, the breath knocked out of him, hands and knees burning as asphalt scraped away skin.

He felt the hot breath of the car rushing past, tires squealing, the smell of rubber and exhaust and roasting tar.

Sluggishly, he was aware of people screaming. But I had the right-of-way, he thought. That was shock, though, not logic. Will was beside him, getting to his knees, which took care of Taylor's immediate concerns. He'd known the minute that solid mass of bone and muscle had crashed into him that it had to be Will.

"The sonofabitch didn't stop." Will swore bitterly, examining his bloody elbow.

"Why should he? He didn't hit us." Taylor staggered to his feet, offered a hand to Will, who took it and let himself be pulled up.

They examined each other quickly, awkwardly—it was hard to forget what had precipitated that close call. Wincing at more than scrapes and bruises, Taylor considered his own grazed hands. Will must have noticed, because he reached out, catching Taylor's wrists and studying his palms.

After what seemed a smoldering sort of moment, he released Taylor, saying curtly, "You'll live."

"Thanks to you," Taylor admitted. No point in pretending otherwise. He owed Will that one.

Will was apparently too pissed to want to take credit. He turned away, heading back across the intersection, asking whether anyone had managed to get a license-plate number. The witnesses—those who had stuck around—were already disagreeing about whether Taylor had stepped out before the light turned green.

This was not the place to conduct an inquiry, and Taylor couldn't understand Will's insistence on trying. As there were no longer any pedestrians sprawled in the intersection, the opposite street traffic was now trying to make its left-hand turn and impatient motorists were laying on the horn. He followed Will to the curbside, frowning, as Will tried to insist on someone supplying a make on the car or some kind of ID on the driver.

A brown Chevy, according to Will. Why did that ring a bell?

Either nobody could or would volunteer any part of a license-plate number. The crowd had already dispersed as people remembered they had places to be and things to do. It wasn't as though there had actually been an accident; it was just another close call, and they happened every day.

Within a matter of seconds it was just Taylor and Will standing on the sidewalk while pedestrians streamed like ants around the obstruction they created.

"Are you okay? Are we done here?" Taylor asked, seeing that Will was still quietly fuming. He knew what Will wanted, of course. What Will wanted was to yell at *him*, for nearly getting himself flattened like Wile E. Coyote. Taylor understood that impulse perfectly well because he felt the same way anytime Will had a close call on the job. Ordinarily Will would fire off a few well-chosen volleys, but they had been arguing when Taylor stepped in front of the car, and Will was restraining himself at the expense of his blood pressure.

Taylor understood all this in a matter of seconds. That's how it was with him and Will. They always knew what the other was thinking. Except Taylor hadn't known about David Bradley or the fact that he and Will weren't going to be working together, and the memory of that left him bewildered and off balance. How long had Will known? Why hadn't he told him? And how did he just happen to be working with David Bradley of all people?

"Let's go," Will said curtly, wiping again at the blood on his elbow.

He led the way in a forbidding silence down the crowded street to where they had parked earlier that morning. Somberly aware that he could have got them both injured or even killed—and in such a *stupid* way—Taylor followed docilely, unspeaking.

A few feet from the SUV, Will pressed the key fob to unlock the car. They both got in. The leather was warm from sitting in the sun. Emmylou Harris jerked into "Together Again" as though she had never been rudely interrupted.

Will didn't start the engine.

"You want me to drive?" Taylor asked. His hands were in worse shape than Will's, but Will seemed more shaken by their near miss.

"No." Still Will made no move.

Taylor was painfully conscious of Will's nearness, his still-not-quite-even breathing—although that was emotion, not physical stress. He said, "Why didn't you tell me about Bradley?"

"I did. What do you think that was?"

In Taylor's opinion, Will's terse tone was defensive. He tried to keep the accusation out of his own. "How long have you known?"

"End of day yesterday." Will gave him a hard look, which Taylor turned to meet. "I didn't tell you last night because I was afraid you'd react exactly like you did, and I didn't want to ruin your birthday."

Taylor nodded curtly. He deserved that for flipping out, but it had shaken him badly, the entire conversation. Including the part where Will admitted he'd have been happier if they'd never become lovers. That still hurt too much to examine, so he put it aside to enjoy later.

"How long are we working apart?"

Will shook his head.

Taylor stared out the window at the shady street, the shop windows full of overpriced junk.

Will said, "It won't be for that long. They've got you and Varga doing protection detail on the wife of some East African minister." He added, "Cooper plans on filling you in himself, so don't let on I told you."

Taylor nodded absently. "Maybe it's the first step to splitting us up permanently. Maybe he knows about us."

Will shook his head.

"You don't know that for a fact."

"He doesn't know." Will's eyes met his. "I haven't told him. You haven't told him. No one else knows."

"Come off it," Taylor scoffed. "We work for one of the largest and most efficient security agencies in the world. You think they don't occasionally run a check on their own employees when something flags? And we've sent plenty of flags up in the last few months."

Will was silent. At last he said, "I don't think so. I can read him pretty well. I didn't get any impression this was anything but expediency. Bradley and I have worked together—and well—in the past."

Taylor didn't want to hear the answer, but he asked anyway. "Did you ask for this assignment?"

"Absolutely not." Will turned to face him. "Tay. No. I did not ask to work with Bradley. I don't want to work with anyone but you. I don't want to *be* with anyone but you. Why don't you believe me?"

Tay. The only time William called him that was in bed. Hearing it in this context was disconcerting but reassuring.

"If you tell me, I believe you."

But Will was still not over being angry. "Why would I *have* to tell you this? It ought to be obvious by now. We're practically living together."

"Yeah, but we're not living together," Taylor said. "And you don't want to live together. And you said yourself you'd be happier if we had left things alone."

Will groaned and dropped his head back, staring at the roof of the car. "I don't believe this. You're acting like a —"

"Like a what?" Taylor kept his voice even, but now he was getting mad all over again.

Will had the smarts to correct quickly, although he was still blunt. "You're acting jealous and insecure and irrational."

Taylor weighed his words, but he had gone this far, he might as well shoot his wad. Will apparently thought he was acting like a queen as it was. He said, "That's because I've got more invested in this relationship than you. We both know the bottom line is I care more for you than you do for me."

Will's profile could have been cut from stone. "I'm not even going to answer that." He jammed the key into the ignition and turned it. The engine roared into life.

* * * * *

It was okay once they were back at Taylor's. Taylor, apparently realizing he had gone too far, was low-key and nonconfrontational. They took turns in the shower, took turns squirting each other with disinfectant and taping on Band-Aids. Taking care of each other, that's what it was about.

Will's shirt was torn, so he borrowed one of Taylor's. It was too tight, which suited the general atmosphere pretty well.

Not that it was that different from usual. They generally worked on the house or watched a game on TV and had a few beers, fucked, napped, caught up on the newspapers, maybe rented a movie. They would have talked or not as they felt like it. Their weekdays were action-packed enough; on the weekends they liked to unwind and rest. There was no one Will wanted to unwind and rest with more than Taylor.

This was not turning out to be the most restful weekend they'd spent, but it wasn't bad. They worked at sanding the built-in shelves and counters, the fireplace, the tapered columns that divided the living room from the dining room. It was slow going, because Taylor liked everything to be perfect, but one day it was going to be a very valuable property with the gleaming resanded hardwood floors and funky art tiles and big stone fireplace—all in walking distance of the beach. As they worked they recovered some of their usual harmony.

When they finished in the front room, uncovering what appeared to be genuine oak beneath layers of navy, green, and finally white paint, they showered again and then ate their leftovers from the night before.

A framed Japanese print of a samurai on horseback had been propped in the doorway for safekeeping while they worked in the front room. Looking at it, and seeking a neutral subject for dinnertime discourse, Will asked, "What was it like, being in Tokyo? You never talk about it."

Taylor, whose own attention had been on the bottle of Asian snake wine sitting on the kitchen counter, gave him a blank look. He raised a shoulder. "Nothing to tell."

Now that was odd. Taylor *always* had something to say. About every-thing. How could he possibly have spent two years in Japan and not have anything to recount. *Nothing?*

"Did you like it?"

"I liked the country, yeah."

He hadn't liked the assignment. Interesting.

"Well, I know you like the food. Is it true they have octopus pizza?"

Taylor snorted, expertly wielded his chopsticks to take a bite of rice-crusted duck. Will considered the chopsticks. Taylor was…prone to en-thusiasms.

He had liked Japan. He collected Japanese weapons, watched Japanese movies, had a couple of Japanese art books and a couple of Japanese prints on the walls. Japan had been important to Taylor. But he never talked about it.

Never.

"Are there really over fifteen hundred earthquakes a year?"

"They have a lot of earthquakes. A lot of volcanoes too."

"Is the sun really red?"

Taylor smiled faintly. "They paint it that way."

"What about the gay samurai? Is that true?"

Taylor's face changed. He scowled, selecting another bite of duck. "What's with all the questions, Brandt?"

"I'm just making…just curious. It's a part of your life I don't know anything about."

"You don't need to know anything about it."

That took Will a second to absorb. "Okay," he said evenly.

Taylor flicked him a look under his lashes. "Sorry."

Will nodded coolly. He was used to Taylor's ratty temper—and more curious than ever now.

Taylor sighed. "It wasn't a great time for me, okay? I was twenty-four, it was my first overseas posting and I was homesick and lonely. Japan is… different."

As opposed to Afghanistan? Or Haiti? Taylor didn't mind discussing either of those postings.

He said slowly, "Sure." It was weird thinking of Taylor as homesick and lonely. But he'd been in the DSS ten years; safe to say he hadn't started out a worldly, all-knowing sonofabitch. Will had taken a different career path. College, then the marines, then the DSS. So far he'd had one overseas posting—Afghanistan, though years after Taylor had been there. When he'd returned to the States, he'd been partnered with Taylor.

He opened his mouth to ask, well, he wasn't even sure what he was going to ask, but he never got the chance because Taylor rose abruptly, saying, "You feel like watching TV?"

Not waiting for Will's reply, he took his plate in the den and turned on the news; they generally avoided the news on the weekends. They got enough bad news about the world in their day jobs. Will listened to the blast of international bad news from down the hall.

"What do you think?" Will asked Riley. Riley cocked his head, tongue lolling.

"Me too," Will said.

* * * * *

In bed that night it was complicated. And quiet.

They were being too polite with each other, but better that than the alternative.

By now they were comfortable enough that they knew where the other wanted to go without having to read a road map. Will wanted to fuck Taylor, but he was afraid it would be a mistake to ask that tonight. He'd said a couple of things he regretted earlier that day, implying that Taylor was behaving like a jealous teenager. Taylor was always very generous in the bedroom, and Will didn't want to be viewed as taking advantage of that tonight.

The fact was, he did enjoy topping more than bottoming. Not a big deal, just a personal preference. In particular he enjoyed topping Taylor. Having Taylor submit to him was the sweetest thing in the world because it was entirely voluntary. Taylor matched him strength for strength, so that willing capitulation seemed so tender, so generous, so *loving*.

He wanted—needed—Taylor to offer, but Taylor didn't. Neither did he ask for a repeat of the night before. Instead, they settled for some energetic rubbing and stroking. Friction. It's a good thing. And it *was* good; it was a very enjoyable substitute for the real thing. The other thing. Through the net of his eyelashes Will watched Taylor's mobile, exquisitely pained face; it never ceased to thrill and amaze him that it was Taylor on the other end of this. Taylor. Beautiful and intense in sex as he was with everything.

Did Taylor honestly believe he had more invested in this relationship than Will? Because that was funny. Sometimes it scared Will how much he felt for Taylor. Nobody should need anyone that much.

It wasn't safe.

CHAPTER FOUR

"**W**hat do you think I should do with this?" Taylor asked, holding up the bottle of snake wine.

It was Monday morning—and all too soon. They'd managed to fall back into sync on Sunday, and they'd spent the remainder of their weekend companionably working on stripping and sanding the last of the front room woodwork.

Will studied the cobra weaving gently in the bottle as Taylor tilted it. "Mix it with orange juice?"

"Funny."

"Probably chock-full of vitamin C and antioxidants."

"I'll stick to my Flintstones Plus."

"You mentioned something about it being an aphrodisiac."

Taylor extended the bottle. "Feeling insecure?"

"You complaining?"

Taylor's sexy mouth quirked. "No way." He added thoughtfully, "I was thinking maybe I could call the bottling company and see if they can tell me who ordered it."

Will's grin faded. "Are you worried about this?"

"Nah."

But now Will was frowning, his investigatory instincts roused. "How much is something like this bottle worth?"

Taylor bridled. "How would I know? It's not like I hand these out every Christmas to friends and family."

"Take a guess. You prowl around Chinatown and places like that."

"I don't know. Sixty bucks. A hundred bucks?"

His hand hovered over the trash bin; then he set the bottle on the counter. "This probably qualifies as toxic waste."

* * * * *

They left the house at the same time, Will opening the side door of the SUV for Riley to jump in. He was stopping by his house in Woodland Hills to drop the dog off and then heading down to San Diego. San Diego and David Bradley. Taylor was determined to be practical about that; he believed Will when Will said he hadn't volunteered for the assignment with Bradley.

Granted, Will hadn't refused the assignment either. But Will never refused assignments.

Either way, this was good-bye, probably for what was going to be a long and stressful week. It was a five-hour drive to San Diego, and Will would be working late most nights, so it was unlikely they'd spend any real time together before next weekend.

Taylor was determined not to be an asshole about it. He'd already been there and done that on Saturday.

"Bye," he said briskly, leaning in to kiss Will. "Talk to you later."

Will's mouth was firm, his kiss a statement that everything was good and normal between them. Taylor turned away, going to his Acura and unlocking the door, sliding behind the wheel.

He spotted a folded sheet of white paper beneath the wiper blades, and he leaned out, tugging it free.

Japanese kanji. Precise black characters on a field of white.

He stared at it for a long time.

Vaguely, he was aware of Will getting back out of his vehicle, the scrape of boots on cement.

"What's up?"

Taylor looked up blankly. How the hell did Will know there was a problem? He did, though.

Without speaking he handed the folded sheet to Will.

Will scanned it. "What do you make of it?"

Taylor shook his head.

"Do you know what it says?"

Another shake. His oral Japanese wasn't great; his written, even worse. He'd learned the necessary minimum to find his way around the city and work efficiently within the confines of the American embassy; that was about it.

"Advertising flyer from the Red Dragon?" Will suggested.

"We took your car."

Will considered this and shrugged.

Well, he had a point. The alternative was too bizarre to consider. Taylor got out of the Acura, circled it, checking his vehicle to see if someone had backed into him or scratched his paint job on Friday while he'd been out shopping, and maybe he hadn't noticed.

Everything looked fine.

Riley poked his nose out the window of Will's Land Cruiser, snuffling at him.

"Hey, Riley," Taylor murmured absently. He returned to Will, who was watching him curiously. He retrieved the note from Will's hand—Will letting go reluctantly.

"Everything okay?" Will asked.

"Of course." Taylor opened the Acura door, climbed in, shoved the note into his glove compartment. In his rearview he watched Will walk back, get inside the navy blue Land Cruiser. Taylor pressed the automatic opener, and the security gate slid slowly open across the driveway.

Will nodded to him in his rearview before putting his vehicle into gear. Taylor nodded back.

It was weird, though. If that note hadn't been there on Friday afternoon—and Taylor was pretty sure it hadn't—someone had climbed over the gate and bypassed Will's Land Cruiser to tuck this note on Taylor's windshield.

Why?

* * * * *

Denise Varga was small, dark, and bellicose. She had probably had to fight—and fight hard—be taken seriously in the mostly all-male world of international security, and it had left a sizable chip on the shoulder of her Anne Klein onyx suit. She made a point of never making the simple, courteous gestures of one coworker to another in case anyone mistook her for a woman. She charged out of doors first, letting them slam in her male coworkers' faces, she never made or bought anyone coffee when she got her own, she interrupted and talked over and contradicted. It was hard working with her. It felt like penance.

Taylor would have preferred to work on his own, but that idea was shot down instantly by Assistant Field Office Director Greg Cooper, who welcomed Taylor back to active duty and informed him he'd be working with Special Agent Varga until further notice.

"Further notice?" Taylor had repeated woodenly.

"We'll see how it goes," Cooper said, shuffling papers.

Taylor was smart enough to nod and keep silent. If Cooper did suspect that Will and Taylor's relationship had changed, and that that change might ultimately conflict with their loyalties to the DSS, any objection would hammer the last nail into the coffin of their partnership.

He listened unemotionally to their briefing, let Varga do all the bitching about the fact they were being landed with a low-profile babysitting job. Varga was taking it personally, as she did pretty much everything. She didn't actually accuse Cooper of sexism, but she wasn't far from it. Taylor closed his eyes at one point, anticipating the explosion.

When he opened them again, Cooper was watching him, and he had the impression the AD was trying to keep a straight face. Cooper wasn't too bad a guy, even if he did play it—every play you could think of—strictly by the book. He heard Varga out unemotionally, was not swayed an iota, and sent them on their merry way.

In the car—Varga's car, which Varga insisted on driving—she announced, "I know you don't want to work with me, MacAllister. For the record, I don't want to work with you either."

"Who do you want to work with?" Taylor asked out of curiosity. That seemed to take Varga by surprise.

She said shortly, "I'd prefer to work alone."

Taylor nodded politely and settled in for what was sure to be a long, long week.

They had been assigned to protect Madame Sabine Kasambala, the very young and very lovely wife of a cabinet minister of the African island nation of Comoros. Comoros had about as screwed up a political situation as could be imagined, and it seemed to have revolutions about every fifteen minutes as far as Taylor could make out. Death threats were routine, even de rigueur, and Madame was far less interested in arrangements for her safety than possible diplomatic discounts the DS might be able to arrange for her with Beverly Hills boutiques.

Varga's stony professionalism scored zero points with their charge, and it was left to Taylor to try and charm Madame into cooperating. He was not particularly good at working the charm; that was generally Will's forte. In fact, Taylor had the uncomfortable feeling that one reason he didn't like Varga was she reminded him a little too much of himself.

He did his best, though, and by eleven o'clock they were trotting Madame in and out of the famous shops along Rodeo Drive, a three-block obstacle course of palm trees, lampposts, flower urns, expensive cars, and self-absorbed people.

* * * * *

In or out of uniform, Lieutenant Commander David Bradley was a big, handsome bear of a man. He did look exceptionally handsome in his naval uniform. He had a silky dark beard, warm brown eyes, and a sexy growl of a voice.

"Good to see you, Will," he said when Will was shown into his office at Naval Base San Diego just before lunch on Monday morning.

They shook hands, and Bradley's grip lingered just a fraction of a second longer than strictly necessary. His smile was white in his tanned face, his gaze friendly if rueful.

"It's great to see you, David," Will said. He meant it. He was grateful that Bradley wasn't being difficult about the awkward way things had ended between them. It wouldn't have been unreasonable if he'd held maybe a bit of a grudge.

Will had broken their budding relationship off at the stem after Taylor had been shot. As much as he liked Bradley—and Will liked him very much—he had been guilt stricken at the knowledge that one reason Taylor had been shot had almost certainly been because he was distracted and upset over Will's relationship with the other man.

The idea of ever doing anything to upset Taylor again had been unthinkable in those first few days when his life had been hanging by a thread. Then later Will had been preoccupied with hunting down the men (boys, as it turned out) who had shot his partner—and keeping up the spirits of that same partner while he was stuck in the hospital.

So he'd called Bradley and apologetically told him he just wasn't at a place in his life where he could focus on a relationship, blaming the pressures of work and a sidelined partner. Bradley had been understanding, accepting Will's decision with maturity and dignity. It had been excruciating, because Will really had thought he and Bradley might have something together. But by then Taylor was recovering, and Will's attention and focus were on getting his partner back.

He had wanted Taylor back with a ferocity that surprised even himself. To this day the depth and power of his feelings for Taylor took him aback.

But seeing Bradley again, he couldn't help thinking what an easy natural match they would have been. He and Bradley were a lot alike.

"How've you been?" Bradley asked as they took chairs on either side of his well-organized desk.

"Very good," Will said. "You?"

He was disconcerted at the way Bradley was smiling at him. There seemed to be such a wealth of liking and understanding there.

"Good. Great. Busy time for us right now." There was a twinkle in Bradley's eyes as he added, "I never did get around to camping on Catalina."

Will's face felt warm. He and Bradley had planned a camping trip at Black Jack campground on Santa Catalina Island. Unlike Taylor, Bradley loved camping as much as Will, and they'd had nearly as good a time planning their trip to the pines and eucalyptus trees of Mt. Orizaba as they would have had making that trip.

If they *had* made that trip, Will was pretty sure their relationship would have reached a turning point, moved into deeper waters. But it was not to be. And Will had no real regrets.

Bradley continued to smile at him in the old open way. "Why don't we grab some lunch and talk the case over?" he suggested.

Bradley drove them to an off-base steak house for lunch. They ordered prime rib sandwiches and got down to brass tacks.

Naval Station San Diego provided shore support and berthing facilities to the operating forces of the US Pacific Fleet. Over fifty ships called NAVSTA home, with more than fifty tenant commands at the NAVSTA. The base population exceeded thirty-five thousand military personnel and in excess of seven thousand civilians. Needless to say, security was an issue for a naval station that had grown to be one of the largest surface-force support installations in the world.

Will pounded ketchup out of the bottle onto his fries and said, "Okay, so to cut through the bullshit, we think we're looking at illegal Mexican nationals using forged documents to gain access to the Thirty-second Street Naval Station?"

Bradley agreed. "Originally we thought illegal aliens were using fraudulent passports to get other documents like drivers' licenses, ID cards, car registrations, and the like in order to unlawfully gain employment in San Diego's concrete construction industry."

"But the passports aren't fraudulent."

"According to your people."

Will grinned. David's return smile was reluctant.

"The passports aren't fraudulent," Will said. "However, we've got a line on the guy some of these nationals were going to for these additional documents. Jose Valz runs a side business helping Hispanic immigrants obtain legal documents so they can work in the concrete construction industry—where he's also employed."

Bradley's eyes lit with interest. "You're after Valz?"

Will nodded. "We want Valz. He's made false statements regarding his status on I-9 forms. He claimed to be a United States citizen. He claimed he was a lawful permanent resident. And he provided documentation that concealed his true immigration status as an alien in temporary protected status."

Bradley held up his empty beer bottle in question.

Will shook his head. "Valz's false statements not only allowed him to fraudulently obtain employment but also allowed him to obtain a US Navy badge that grants him access to all the naval bases in the region."

"We're going after Valz," Bradley said grimly.

Somebody had to. But it was going to be a long and probably dull week. Will wondered how Taylor was faring his first day back on active duty. Then he had to bite back an inward grin at the idea of Taylor partnered with Varga. Talk about two peas in a pod.

As though reading his mind, Bradley said suddenly, "Your partner never made it back, I take it?"

Will was startled at the stab of emotion that went through him at the idea of Taylor not making it back. He wasn't sure he was ever going to get over the memory of seeing Taylor shot and dying on that stockroom floor. Will couldn't understand it. He had been in the marines; he'd seen men die. He'd lost friends. It had been ugly, painful, but none of it shook him to the marrow the way seeing Taylor shot had. He wasn't given much to praying, but he'd prayed then. It wasn't very often your prayers were answered; he knew to count his blessings.

"He's back on active duty now," he said calmly. "We're just working different cases at the moment."

The old unease about what was happening with Taylor when Will wasn't there to watch his back returned. Not that Taylor wasn't very good at taking care of himself—with one notable exception. Will's separation anxiety made no sense.

"Are you seeing anyone?" Bradley asked casually.

The stock answer, the safe answer, was *no*. If the higher-ups discovered that he and Taylor were lovers, they'd be repartnered faster than you could say *nonfraternization policy*. But lying to Bradley was difficult.

"Sort of."

Bradley raised his eyebrows.

"It's complicated," Will admitted.

"Someone you work with," Bradley guessed.

Will nodded apologetically.

Bradley sighed. "Oldest story in the world." His smile was wry. He glanced at his watch. "We should get back."

* * * * *

By the time Taylor got back to the office on Temple Street, his feet ached. So did his head.

He wasn't one of those guys who made a drama out of hating to shop, but even he couldn't figure out how the hell anyone could shop for nine hours. *Nine hours.* And almost straight through, because no one could seriously consider the stop for herbes de Provence french fries and pomegranate-blackberry iced tea at Café Rodeo a legitimate break.

Madame Kasambala had spent the probable equivalent of her nation's defense budget between Gucci, Chanel, Dior, Valentino, Versace, and Tiffany's. Varga was in an even worse mood than Taylor—which was some comfort. Of course, she had a point. If they had dispensed with the pleasures of Rodeo Drive in one day, what fresh hell was Madame going to drag them through tomorrow—and beyond?

Still, as boring as the day had been, and despite the fact that he had not been working with Will, Taylor felt almost cheerful. He was back in the field, back on active duty—and he felt fine.

There had been a time when both those things had seemed unobtainable goals.

He hung around the office for a time in the hope that Will might get back early from San Diego, but no dice. He hadn't really expected it.

He was the last person out of the office, and it was dark when he reached home.

He parked in the side drive, walked down to the corner to pick up his mail from the stand of metal boxes. Walking back up the quiet, shady street, moon shining like a newly minted dime above the treetops, he remembered the Chevy that had been parked curbside on Friday when he'd gone to get the mail.

That was why Will's description of the car that had nearly run them down on Saturday had rung a bell. Not to overreact. There were one hell of a lot of Chevrolets driving around Southern California. And a lot of motorists could use a driver's ed refresher course.

Taylor reached his own overgrown patch of yard, reflected he needed to hire some kid to mow the grass once in a while, and went up the steps to his porch.

He stopped.

One of those bright plastic phone-book bags hung from the front door handle. He reached for it, but the plastic straps were knotted around the handle and in the amber porch light he caught a glimpse of white string.

A fuse.

His fingers froze on the cool plastic. After a couple of seconds of frantic thought, he decided he hadn't touched or tugged anything. He delicately let go, retreated a few steps, and then jumped off the porch and sprinted for the relative shelter of the nearest car parked along the street.

Nothing happened.

He gave it a few more seconds. Feeling silly, Taylor returned to the steps and from that distance studied the yellow plastic bag. Now that it had his full attention, he realized that whatever the plastic bag contained was not square or even shaped like a phone book. It was round. Like an old-fashioned bomb. Like a cartoon bomb.

As hard as it was to believe, it looked to Taylor like someone had booby-trapped his front door.

CHAPTER FIVE

Will's phone rang as he was negotiating the intricacies of the 405/101 inter-change. He reached inside his sports coat, extracted his cell, noted the photo of a sunburned Taylor on a chartered fishing trip, and flipped the cell open, hastily refocusing on the freeway traffic merging in front of him.

"Hey," said the two-year-old photo of Taylor.

"Hey." Will opened his mouth to ask how Taylor's first day back had gone; it had been in the back of his mind all day. But Taylor interrupted; there was a note in his voice that Will couldn't quite pinpoint. "Are you still in San Diego?"

He was now sure something was up. Taylor was perfectly calm, but it was his on-the-job voice. "No. I'm stuck on the 101. Why? What's up? Where are you?"

"I'm at the Red Dragon."

"You're where?" Will glanced at the dashboard lights. Tea-smoked duck at ten o'clock at night? It seemed unlikely.

"I'm having something translated."

Weirder and weirder. "Like what?"

"Like the note that was left on my windshield this morning. Apparent-ly it's connected to the bomb on my front door."

"*What?*" Will narrowly missed plowing into the BMW that swerved into his lane without signaling—and apparently without looking.

"Yeah. Someone hung a *shaku* ball in a plastic bag on my front door."

"What the hell is a shaku ball?"

"You want the short answer or the long answer?"

"Short."

"*Hanabi*. Japanese fireworks."

"That's too short."

"That pretty much covers it, though. They're these big spherical balls. They call them *flowers of fire*."

Will cut through the "flowers of fire" crap. "Someone tried to kill you?" he demanded.

"Doubtful. I might have lost a hand or my eyesight, but I wouldn't have been killed."

"That's comforting. For the record, I like your hands. I like your eyes. I'd prefer nothing happened to them."

"Me too. Anyway, it was just wishful thinking on someone's part, because the fuse was fucked-up. Even if I hadn't noticed the bomb in time, it wouldn't have gone off."

Will turned on his signal and started inching over traffic lanes, whether his fellow motorists liked it or not, moving into the far lane bound for Ventura. "Did you get LAPD and the bomb-disposal unit over there?"

"Yeah, they're on it, but essentially this amounts to someone leaving a bag of dud fireworks on my porch."

"Bullshit!"

"Cool it, Will," Taylor warned.

Will cooled it. "What did the note on your windshield say?" That much he had already figured out. A note in Japanese writing turned up on Taylor's vehicle the same day someone tried to booby-trap his front door with fires of flower or whatever the hell it was? Taylor had made someone very angry, and Will thought he knew who.

"Mama-san says it's a death threat."

"Say again," Will ordered tersely.

"It might be a threat. It reads 'Old poison slays as swiftly as new.'"

"Stay right there," Will said. "I'm coming to meet you."

"No."

"The hell I'm not."

"For chrissake, Will." Taylor sounded exasperated. "First of all, they're trying to close for the night here. Secondly, there's no reason I can't go home. Nobody broke in. There isn't even any property damage, let alone damage to me."

"That place is as secure as a cardboard box. I'll meet you at my place."

"Oh for God's sake." Taylor sighed. "All right, Mom. Whatever. I'll meet you at your house."

* * * * *

"Just for the sake of argument, let's consider the punks from the Red Dragon parking lot," Will said, pouring a short glass of bourbon. He held the bottle of bourbon up in offer. Taylor shook his head. He was sticking to iced water tonight.

They were sitting in the comfortable den of Will's Woodland Hills ranch-style home. It was a small room—the entire house was small, though more than big enough for one guy who was never there anyway. The walls were oak paneled, and the furniture was upholstered in funky blue and black plaid. There were a couple of rifles over the fireplace and a couple of marksman trophies on the mantel below.

Riley was snoring softly on Taylor's feet. A rare honor. He said, "Nah. Why would they leave me a note in Japanese? *How* would they leave me a note in Japanese? It's gotta tie in to the cobra in the wine bottle."

"You said you had no idea who sent the cobra in the rice wine."

"I don't."

Will gave him a skeptical look before proceeding with his own line of reasoning. "They would leave you a note in Japanese to throw suspicion off themselves. If they left you a note in Spanish—assuming the morons can even write—it would lead directly back to them. As for how: one of them could have a Japanese girlfriend. Who knows?"

"Why not leave me a note in English? That would be easier. Plus, there would be more chance of me understanding the threat."

"They wanted you to know it was about what happened in the parking lot of the Red Dragon."

Taylor said reasonably, "Then that cancels out what you said about them not wanting me to know it was them."

Will's easy smile took him aback. "Good, then we can eliminate that bullshit before you ever think about using it as a smoke screen. Who, besides the cholos in the Red Dragon parking lot, have you had a run-in with?"

Sometimes Will really did annoy the hell out him. Irritably, Taylor shook his head.

"Not good enough."

Taylor gave him a narrow look. "Maybe not, but it's the truth."

"What about Japan?"

Taylor tensed. "What about it?"

"Someone sends you a cobra in a bottle, a note in Japanese, and a Japanese firework bomb? I'd say we have to consider Japan."

"There's nothing to consider. Japan was eight years ago. I worked in the embassy. That's it." He was trying, but he must not have been too successful at hiding his anger. His muscles were locked so tight, Riley half woke, blinking up sleepily.

Will's brow knitted. "Hey, it's me. Remember me? I'm on your side. Who's got it in for you?"

"No one." Taylor took a deep breath, forced himself to think objectively about this. Will was wrong. This could not have to do with Japan, so it had to be something else. *One of these things is not the same...* He answered honestly, "Well, not lately. Not since before I was shot."

Their eyes met. "The Phu Fighters," Will said.

Taylor nodded. Old poison, for sure.

They'd been in Orange County following a lead on a possible counterfeiting ring, when he'd been shot by a juvenile member of the Phu Fighters, a Vietnamese street gang. While Taylor had been in the hospital, Will prowled Little Saigon, eventually tracking down the two punks involved in the shooting, and—according to the reports Taylor had read—pretty much prodded them into a fight. One kid had surrendered without trouble. The other had gone for his gun and ended up with a shattered hip and missing fingers.

It was still hard to believe that Will—patient, easygoing, teasing Will—had gone hunting with vengeance in his heart. But reading between the lines of the police report and the DSS's own internal investigation, that's exactly what Will had done.

The official verdict was that Will had been under extreme emotional stress; cops and DSS alike understood the bond between law-enforcement partners. And Will had been careful to let Le Loi Roy get off the first shot. Even so, Will was lucky to slide out of it with nothing more than an official reprimand and his picture in the paper. He'd been more riled about the newspaper photo than the reprimand.

"The Asian snake wine was bottled in the Mekong Delta," Taylor said slowly.

"Did you phone the manufacturer?"

Taylor shook his head. "I never had a chance."

Will finished his bourbon and set the empty glass on the table. "Well, tomorrow you're going to call the Asian snake people, and I'm going to see what Le Loi Roy is up to these days."

Later, brushing his teeth, Taylor stuck his head out of the bathroom to say, "If it was revenge, I don't see why anyone would come after me. They already shot me. *You*'re the guy who crippled Roy."

Will was lying on the bed, staring moodily up at the ceiling. "Who knows? They're kids. They're nuts. Roy was counting you as a kill. He was disappointed when he found out you didn't buy it. Maybe he's trying to re-establish his street cred?"

It seemed shaky to Taylor, but he didn't have a better theory. He spit the toothpaste out, rinsed his mouth, rinsed the sink, and turned out the bathroom light.

He threw himself down on the bed beside Will.

"Why Japanese and not Vietnamese, though? The note, I mean."

Will shook his head, raised up to shut off the bedside lamp. "You're the one who insists it's nothing to do with Japan."

Taylor didn't really have a response for that. But how the hell *could* it be anything to do with Japan? He didn't believe in ghosts.

For a few seconds they lay not touching, not speaking in the darkness. It was unexpectedly lonely. "How was San Diego?" he inquired politely into the silence between them.

"Sunny, with a high of seventy-six."

"Ha."

Will was silent. Taylor thought he might be falling asleep, but he said suddenly, "If you could live anywhere, where would it be?"

With you. Taylor knew better than to say that aloud. "The beach. I like the beach."

Will was silent.

"What about you?" Taylor asked.

"The mountains."

Taylor rolled over on his side and set about falling asleep. After a couple of minutes of slow, easy breaths, Will's arm slipped around him, pulling him close.

* * * * *

Will woke to the unmistakable nudge of Taylor's cock trying to elbow its way into his dreams. Taylor was still sleeping, as evidenced by the warm gusts against the back of Will's neck, but his body was waking up and taking an interest. Will was faintly amused by that heat and hardness pushing against him, that unconscious urgency. Taylor was the randiest guy Will had ever met—well, who actually possessed a brain to go with the balls.

It seemed sort of a shame to waste this. He shifted around, gathering Taylor close, interrupting but not rejecting. Taylor started awake, blinking dazedly into Will's eyes, his mouth soft and young looking—he rarely looked that vulnerable.

"Hey, wanna fuck?" Will whispered hopefully, and Taylor started laughing.

"Beat the clock?"

Will nodded, and they shifted around some more, trying to accommodate legs and arms and cocks.

"We don't have any passion oil here," Taylor regretted.

"Use the homemade brand," Will suggested.

Taylor did, his fingers slick with his own slippery urgency. He was inclined to be overly conscientious about this part, and Will shoved back against him. "Let's go. Move it or lose it."

Taylor chose to move it. He shoved his cock into Will's body, sank into him pedal to metal, and began to drive. He thrust into Will's tight heat in a steady rocking motion, and Will moved to match that smooth, steady rhythm. Taylor timed it expertly, like a driver taking a winding mountain road, decelerating in and accelerating out, long, smooth strokes, whipping around the curves, drawing his cock all the way out to the rim of tight muscle, then pushing back hard.

Will closed his eyes tight, just focusing on that pumping rhythm as Taylor sped up, pushed them both harder, faster…they were going to break the odometer this morning…and there it was. The finish line. Blazing sensation peaking, overloading…

Taylor's hands were going to leave bruises, and Will didn't mind, because that warm glow was spreading through every cell of his body in the wake of those pulses of shocking delight.

They could only spare a few minutes to hang on to each other, damp and flushed and muscles trembling in their own tracks. Will kissed the bridge of Taylor's cheek, and Taylor kissed his jaw, and then they were rolling free of each other, up and running.

Taylor had taken him with gentle, relentless strength, and for the first time Will had stopped struggling against it—mentally, that was—and just enjoyed the fact that Taylor was taking control, driving them. Part of what Will loved about him was that rough and reckless strength. Maybe because he looked like the kind of guy who should be going to art museums and babbling about postmodernism, but he was a hard-nosed, hard-ass cop at heart. Taylor's tenderness always took him by surprise.

* * * * *

The fourteen-hour time difference between Vietnam and Los Angeles created a slight problem for Taylor. He arrived later at the office than he'd planned. That had been Will's fault. Will woke up horny and happy. It was just his nature.

Not that Taylor was complaining.

Even without the time difference, there was no way Taylor was going to find time to squeeze in a call during a day spent bargain hunting and babysitting.

Madame Kasambala had decided to hit the garment district, in particular Santee Alley, famous for its bargains and carnival-like atmosphere.

Carnival-like was putting it mildly, and the security nightmare presented by Santee Alley made Taylor homesick for dear old Rodeo Drive, with its snooty shopkeepers and private security.

"I'm going to kill her myself," Varga muttered as they watched their charge pawing scornfully through piles of knockoff Prada bags.

"I'm thinking homicide, double-suicide pact," Taylor said.

Varga giggled, surprising him. She had a very endearing giggle.

Slowly but surely they were beginning to figure out how to work together. It wasn't like with Will; it was never going to be like it was with Will, but it wasn't the rather-work-for-the-postal-service torture of the first day either.

A major corner seemed to have been turned when Taylor brought Varga a caramel macchiato that morning. Initially she had eyed the coffee as though suspecting poison and had actually said stiffly, awkwardly, "I like to keep things strictly business, MacAllister. I don't screw around with co-workers."

Did she honestly think…?! Taylor had done a double take, spluttered, "Relax, Varga. I'm gay."

Varga had laughed.

Taylor had laughed too, but he said, "Hey, I'm not kidding."

Her jaw had dropped. "You're shitting me."

"No."

Well, that was the point of GLIFAA, right? Gays and Lesbians in Foreign Affairs Agencies. This wasn't the bad old days when foreign service employees were fired for "moral weakness." Not that he and Will went around advertising, but they didn't hide it either. That had been one of the initial bonds between them when they'd first been partnered.

"I had no idea," Varga said.

"Why should you? It's not relevant to the job."

"But I mean, we've worked in the same field office for eighteen months." She'd thought it over. "Does Brandt know?"

"I think he suspects," Taylor said gravely.

So whether because he'd won her heart with chain-store coffee or by removing himself from the potential-sexual-predator list, today had been much easier. Which meant he had more time to brood over Will in San Diego with David Bradley.

Not that he was really brooding over Will and Bradley. Will was genetically incapable of cheating, even if Taylor didn't already know Will loved him. The ongoing problem—for Taylor—was that he was convinced that Will didn't *want* to love him. That Will believed loving him was a bad idea. That Will was now focused on all the ways they weren't compatible instead of all the ways they were: Like that question about where Taylor would live if he had a choice. What was that about?

Whatever it was about, it was depressing as hell.

Taylor hated thinking about this stuff. It wasn't even like him to worry about things like this. He wasn't that kind of guy. He had never fretted as to whether his feelings were returned, because previously his feelings were always returned. More than returned. *He* was the one other guys worried about.

So he was experiencing some kind of karmic romantic backlash, and he probably deserved every miserable minute of it, but it was still unsettling and messing with his focus.

Not that he needed a lot of focus on this detail. If the enemies of Comoros had any brains at all, they'd just leave Madame Kashandcarry to go on spending like there was no tomorrow, and the government would soon be bankrupt and out of business.

It was a long, boring day. They didn't get back to the office until after six. Varga couldn't wait to take off. She bade Taylor a quick good night, and he waved her off, sitting down at his desk to have another try at calling the Asian Snake Winery.

He was surprised when he actually got through. Finessing his way through the language barrier was harder, but he finally managed to make himself clear without resorting to calling in local law enforcement—an absolute last resort.

Unfortunately, according to the company's records, they had not shipped any wine to him. This meant someone else had purchased a bottle and shipped it to Taylor from within the States.

Taylor tried to remember the shipping label and wrapping paper on the box. Nothing distinctive, that he recalled. A plain, sealed cardboard box with a computer-printed label? Had there been a return address? A postmark? He thought not. He'd have surely noticed.

Trash pickup was Tuesday morning, so it was —

No, it wasn't too late, because he had spent the night at Will's and not put his trash out for pickup. So somewhere in the trash barrel were the box and label that might or might not offer some clue to the identity of the person who had sent the snake wine.

Taylor was pretty sure the wine had to be connected to the threatening note and the firecracker bomb. A cobra in a bottle was about as creepy an illustration of old poison as anyone could ask for.

* * * * *

"Thanks for dinner," Bradley said as they walked out of the seafood restaurant. The indigo-orange sunset turned the water bronze. The crimson-tinged sails of the boats along the docks whipped musically in the evening breeze.

"My pleasure," Will said.

"Do you feel like working some more tonight?"

"I need to start back. It's a long drive," Will said regretfully. They'd made some good progress, even with Will spending part of the morning on the phone to the Orange County Sheriff's Department, following up on Le Loi Roy.

The information they'd dug up on Jose Valz had led them to other suspects, all employed by construction companies with questionable residency or work-eligibility permits. A little more digging had uncovered the fact that those companies employed at least five people who had presented false resident-alien cards to their employers.

Will was feeling satisfied.

"You know," Bradley said lazily, "we can put you up at the base if your expense account won't stretch to a hotel room for the night. It would save some time in the morning."

"I know. And thanks for the offer. But I've got some things to take care of at home. Feed the mutt, put out the milk bottles, you know." The briny, astringent sea-breeze smell reminded him of Taylor.

"Your choice." Bradley was smiling. Will thought again how much he liked him. How if things were different —

But they weren't different, and he wanted to get back and talk to Taylor. Wanted to reassure himself that Taylor was fine. It was not a lack of confidence in Taylor; it was just…he didn't trust anyone to watch Taylor's back as diligently as he would. Nobody else had quite the investment in Taylor's well-being, did they?

Besides, that morning had been mind shatteringly good, and his body had been aching pleasantly with the memories all day long. He was craving Taylor. He wasn't even sure why. It wasn't anything they hadn't done before, but somehow that morning everything had just…fallen into place.

Will told Bradley good night and set off for home. Emmylou was singing about the train in the Tulsa night. He felt good; the flow of traffic was with him. He had his case to preoccupy his thoughts, and before he knew it he was pulling onto his own street.

Only to find his house dark and the driveway empty.

Taylor was not there.

CHAPTER SIX

The phone clattered off the hook and Taylor's sleep-husky voice said, "MacAllister."

"Where are you?" Will asked.

The answer was evident, of course, but Taylor replied anyway. "Home."

"What are you doing there?"

"Uh… I live here?" Taylor suggested.

"You know what I mean. What the hell are you doing there? Is that what you'd tell a client who was being stalked? *Go home?*"

"I'm not being *stalked.*" His derision at the very idea was loud and clear. "Even if I was, I'm not exactly a civilian. We do this stuff for a living. If I can't handle one nutcase, I need to find another line of work."

"You know damn well you should not be there on your own."

There was an instant smile in Taylor's voice as he drawled, "Come and keep me company."

"I don't really feel like making that drive at one thirty in the morning." Despite himself, some of Will's annoyance—disappointment—crept through.

Taylor smothered a yawn, not entirely successfully. "Did you just get in?"

"Yeah."

"Burning the midnight oil, huh?"

"I had dinner with Bradley before driving back."

Will wanted to get that out of the way fast. No way was it ever coming back to bite him in the ass. But there was no hesitation, no pause. Taylor said calmly, "How's the case coming?"

"It's coming. Listen, I talked to the OC sheriff's department, and Le Loi Roy is still incarcerated at the Lacy Juvenile Annex."

Taylor seemed to be considering this.

"Did you hear me?"

"Yes. I guess we can rule him out."

"Him, yes. But maybe someone's acting on his behalf."

"Maybe." Taylor's tone was noncommittal.

"Did you think of something else?"

"No. It's just..."

"Just what?" *Old ghosts?* Will was suddenly convinced that Taylor was hiding something from him.

Meanwhile, Taylor was reporting, "I called the wine manufacturer. According to their records, they didn't ship the bottle to me. So someone else must have purchased it and then sent it. I dug the box and wrapping out of the trash. It was mailed last Tuesday from Ventura County. I'm going to have it analyzed."

"Good thinking," Will approved.

There was a short silence.

"I thought you'd be here," Will said. He was a little embarrassed at the reproachful note that crept into his voice, but it was true. He'd expected to find the lights on and Taylor home and was still unsettled at how let down he'd been to be proved wrong.

"I wasn't sure you were coming back to LA tonight." Taylor sighed. "Anyway, I can't hide out at your house."

"Who said anything about hiding out? I just... I was looking forward to you being here."

"Yeah?"

"Yeah."

Taylor said slowly, "Are you driving back tomorrow night?"

"Sure."

"Maybe I could stay over tomorrow night."

"That'd be good. I might be late, but I'll be here. How's it going with Varga?"

"We've reached détente."

"Ever think about trying out for the diplomatic service, my son?"

Taylor chuckled.

Will wrapped his hand absently around his cock. "Talk to me," he said suddenly, urgently.

"What would you like me to say?" Taylor sounded amused, but then his voice sharpened. "Hey, are you —"

"Yeah. I am."

Taylor laughed, a husky, naughty, full-throated laugh that closed Will's own throat. Desire. That was what he felt. More than lust. It was the longing, yearning to be together. To be one.

"Oooh, Brandt," Taylor cooed. "Oh God, what you *do* to me."

Will laughed breathlessly, kept his hand moving.

Taylor moaned, mocking them both probably, but certainly mocking himself, that keening sound that escaped him when Will was fucking him hard. Those little cries that drove Will insane with lust.

"Bastard," Will gulped out.

Taylor chuckled again. Then he said huskily, deliberately, "No one's ever made me feel what you do, Will. When you push that big, hot cock inside my body. I never let anyone do that to me before. It...scares me, it's so good. I want it so much. But there's always this moment of panic when I think, No, he's too big. I can't take him. Not just my body but my mind. Like you're taking me over. Pounding my ass and pounding my brain."

Will started to laugh, breathlessly.

Taylor's voice dropped lower. "And it feels so *good*. In a dark, dirty way to let you do that to me...to shove right inside my body, right inside my skin. The friction...the way it feels for you to move inside me. It kind of burns and it kind of scrapes and I feel it in my belly and my chest..."

Will bit his lip hard, hand moving frantically.

* * * * *

On Wednesday they had their first viable threat against Madame.

Well, at least it looked that way for the first few seconds.

They were shopping—what else?—in the Beverly Center, located at the edge of Beverly Hills and West Hollywood. Madame had already chewed them out once that day for hovering too closely. Did she suspect that in the guise of protecting her they were going to snatch a great bargain from under her nose?

A woman with a stroller was passing to the side of Taylor; he was absently tracking her out of his peripheral vision because she was a little closer than he liked. The kid suddenly screamed. There was no mistaking that sound, it was raw pain, and Taylor turned instinctively. It turned out to be nothing more serious than pinched fingers, and he was relaxing as Varga suddenly shouted, "Gun!"

Taylor ducked and spun, pulling his own weapon, and there in his sights stood a beanpole of a kid in dreadlocks holding up one of those little goofy autograph books. His hand was shaking, the color draining out of his face.

He opened his mouth, and no words came out.

Plenty of words, however, were coming out of Madame Kasambala. Varga had knocked her to the department-store floor and was using her own body to shield Madame. Madame was less than grateful and making it clear.

Loud and clear.

"Identify yourself," Taylor ordered the half-fainting autograph hound. It was already clear to him they had got it wrong and it was probably going to be on the news—not to mention YouTube—in a matter of hours, judging by the cell phones clicking from around the store displays where other customers and staff were hiding.

"Norman Piggot. Little Piggy," the kid quavered. "I just wanted to get Krista Kross's a-autograph."

"Who the hell is Krista Kross?"

Little Piggy barely inclined his head toward the tangle of Varga and Madame Kasambala. Madame was rejecting Varga's protective embrace for all she was worth, and in another time and place, Taylor would be laughing his ass off at the picture they made. At the moment, not so funny. Pulling their weapons in this kind of a crowd situation? He and Varga would be lucky if they didn't wind up with an official reprimand.

A voice from behind a display of lady's hosiery—a chorus line of mannequin feet and shapely, stocking-clad shins—volunteered, "She's a female rap artist."

"You've got the wrong lady," Taylor informed Little Piggy.

Little Piggy nodded, eager to show himself cooperative.

It took a few minutes to sort it out: reassure the public that all was well, reassure Madame that they were truly sorry, reassure Little Piggy that he wasn't going to jail.

"I misread it," Varga said, chagrined, when they had moved on to Bloomingdale's.

"Better safe than sorry."

He knew Will would have been amused to hear him say it.

* * * * *

Jose Valz lived with his wife, parents, brother, sister-in-law, and assorted rug rats in an older Spanish-style apartment in downtown San Diego. Had he lived alone, it would have simplified everything.

The plan was to interview Valz. They weren't ready to make an arrest yet, and when they did scoop him up, they planned on catching as many of the little fish in their nets as possible.

In fact, Will wanted to do the interview on his own; he suspected—and he turned out to be correct—that Valz was liable to panic when he spotted Bradley's uniform. But Bradley was adamant that Will was not walking in there on his own, not when they didn't know exactly what they were dealing with.

So they waited till suppertime, when the odds were in their favor that Valz would be home from a hard day's work ripping off the US government. Señora Valz opened the door to their knock. Good smells issued forth, along with a babble of non-Spanish.

Nahua, identified Will, who had spent some time in San Salvador. So there was another strike against Valz, who claimed in a couple of documents to be a lawful citizen of Mexico—those would be in the documents where he didn't claim to be a United States citizen.

A roomful of wary black eyes turned their way, and silence fell.

Bradley began to explain their business in painstaking Spanish. There was the squeak of floorboards behind them. Will turned, and there was Valz rabbiting down the apartment hallway toward the staircase.

Will was after him, shouting a warning for Valz to stop. He wasn't going to shoot the guy in front of his kids—wasn't going to shoot him at all. Nothing in Valz's profile indicated he was dangerous or warranted shooting. In any case, Valz paid no attention.

Will jumped over the railing and gained a flight, dropped over another metal railing, and hit the ground floor the same time as Valz. He could hear the pound of Bradley's feet behind him—slower and heavier than Taylor, who would have passed Will up by now.

Valz burst out through the side entrance that led to the pool courtyard.

Will shot through the doors a few seconds behind him.

The courtyard was empty. It was too cold for swimming this time of year, even in San Diego, but there was some kind of pool maintenance going on and the deck was wet. A large gray hose was stretched across from a rumbling truck in the parking lot, and it sounded like the pool was being vacuumed.

Though small and portly, Valz was fast. Or very scared. He went through the obstacle course of lounge chairs and tables like a steeplechaser. Will was gaining on him, though, until he slipped in a puddle. He knew an instant of chagrined surprise before his foot shot out from under him and he plunged headfirst into the pool, his skull grazing the cement lip of the edge. His last thought was the hope that they weren't draining the damn thing…

CHAPTER SEVEN

"**W**ill?"

A hand was patting his cheek. Annoying.

"Will?"

He twitched his eyebrows in irritation. His head was pounding sickeningly, like someone was kicking an oil drum next to him. He was wet and cold and starting to shiver…

"Come on, Marine. Talk to me."

And if that fucking voice and fucking hand slapping his cheek did not go away, Will was going to punch someone. His eyes snapped open.

David Bradley was leaning over him, his handsome face grim and worried. In fact, his face was quite close to Will's, his mouth a couple of inches away, his breath warm on Will's chilled skin.

Seeing that Will was conscious, he drew back in relief. "How do you feel?"

Now that he thought about it…not good. In fact…

A wave of nausea rose inside him. Salty saliva filled his mouth; his stomach lurched. He rolled onto his side, away from Bradley, and was sick on the pavement.

"Great," he got out.

"I see that." Bradley's big hand was on his shoulder, squeezing in support.

"I'm okay," Will assured him hoarsely. "That's just reaction." He pushed up from the mess.

Bradley grabbed his hand, pulling him to his feet. "More like concussion."

"Nah. Where's our guy?"

He was upright now, weaving a little in the mild evening breeze. Bradley steadied him and chuckled. "He ran straight into the arms of a pair of sheriff's deputies here to collect a deadbeat dad."

Will laughed shakily, put a hand to his throbbing head.

"Let's get you back to the base," Bradley said with quick concern. "They've got it under control here. It'll do Valz good to wait a little before we question him."

* * * * *

The base medic pronounced mild concussion, recommended a couple of days of bed rest, and sent them on their way. When they got back to Bradley's office, Will accepted a change of clothes and declined the offer of a bunk.

"I'm serious. You can stay at my place," Bradley said. "You should not try driving tonight. I've got plenty of room. I'd like to have you."

No kidding. And Will would like to have Bradley too. But that was not going to happen. Will might be suffering from mild concussion, but he'd have to have major brain damage to go along with that idea. He tried to imagine breaking it to Taylor he was having a slumber party at David Bradley's house. Not going to happen.

Bad enough that he wasn't going to be able to drive back home tonight. He wanted to, but he knew better. He was just groggy and exhausted enough to make that unwise.

"I appreciate it," he said, "but I think I probably better get a hotel room."

"Now I'm insulted," Bradley said, and he did look pretty formidable. Definitely not a guy to jerk around. "I sort of thought, regardless of the rest of it, we were friends."

"We are friends," Will said.

"But what?"

"There *is* the rest of it. I'm not going to pretend I don't still want you. But I've got someone now."

"So you said." Bradley was watching him closely, speculatively. "Is it this partner of yours?"

Will hesitated. He felt he owed Bradley this honesty. "Yes."

"I wondered. I knew you were close. When he was shot, it was pretty clear your world narrowed down to him."

What could Will say? It was the truth.

"I've never been partnered with anyone, so I wasn't sure if it was like that for everyone. I had a feeling it might be unique to the two of you." Bradley asked tentatively, "Does he feel the same?"

Will nodded. He had a sudden sense of how very lucky he was. He could see it on Bradley's face.

"Well, hell." Bradley grimaced. "I guess I made a mistake backing off when I did. I was kind of hoping you'd see the light. Unfortunately it turned out to be a different light."

"I'm sorry," Will said. "It…caught me by surprise too."

"I believe that. I thought we had something pretty special ourselves."

Will didn't want to hear this; what was the point? "We had something good," he acknowledged.

Bradley was still eyeing him in that steadfast, measuring way. "And you don't have any doubts about this partner of yours? I thought he was kind of a wild card?"

"I don't have any doubts about him." End of discussion.

Bradley nodded, mostly to himself. His eyes met Will's, and there was a wicked gleam in the brown depths. "Okay if I kiss you good-bye?"

Will laughed uneasily. His heart started thumping. It was ridiculous and stagy, but easier to get it over with than make a fuss. "Sure."

Bradley put his arms around him, and Will thought what a crazy thing it was that for all Bradley's greater size and obvious strength, it was only when Taylor held him in that bony, fierce grip that Will felt helpless. Then Bradley's mouth was on his, and Will stopped thinking, because he'd forgotten how good this was. And Bradley was applying his considerable talents to this moment.

Dazedly, Will was aware of a surge of sexual hunger, of fierce physical desire, his body responding to the expert pressure of the hot mouth on his own. It was startling because it wasn't like he was doing without these days, and it was alarming because it would be very easy to give into this. Sex had always been good between him and Bradley.

But what he had with Taylor went way beyond this.

He drew back—not without effort—and said, "And this is why spending the night at your place would not be a good idea."

Bradley looked slightly dazed himself. "Will —"

"I'll stop by tomorrow on my way out of town," Will said, and he got himself out of there.

* * * * *

The generic hotel was mostly clean and mostly quiet. Will used the complimentary toothbrush, took a couple of painkillers, climbed into bed, and phoned Taylor.

Taylor's voice had that edgy, on-the-job note when he answered, and Will said, "Everything okay?"

"Sure."

Will could hear the conscious effort to ease up. Something had happened; Taylor was definitely wound tight. Tighter than usual. Will silently cursed the fact he wasn't driving back. "Any more weird gifts or notes?"

"Nah." He sounded relaxed about that, so it was probably just the stress of working with Varga. Taylor confirmed that a second later. "Varga and I are in the doghouse. I'll tell you when you get here."

"Well, I've got bad news," Will admitted. "I'm not going to make it back tonight after all."

"Ah." Neutral.

"It's... Well, I had a slight mishap."

"What's that mean?"

"I was in pursuit of a suspect, and I —" Will broke off to cough. He hadn't swallowed a lot of water, but enough that his lungs were still a bit foggy.

"And you *what*?"

"Fell in a swimming pool and knocked myself out."

"You've got to be—Are you all right?" Taylor's voice was hard and terse.

Will reassured quickly. "I'm fine. But I don't think driving back tonight is a good idea. Much as I want to."

The edge was noticeably sharper as Taylor questioned, "Where the fuck was Lt. Commander Bradley during all this?"

"He was right there. He pulled me out of the pool."

"If he'd been doing his job, you'd never have fallen *into* the pool."

"Come on, MacAllister."

"Don't 'come on, MacAllister' me, Brandt. He was supposed to be watching your back."

"Nobody failed in their duty, nobody made any mistakes—except me slipping in the pool water."

"It shouldn't have happened."

This was touchy. The few times he'd tried to address this with Taylor, Taylor had shut him down fast. Will gentled his voice. "Shit happens, Tay. No one should know that better than you."

Silence.

Taylor changed the subject. "You sure you're okay?"

"I'm okay. Swear to God." Will added softly, "I'm disappointed too."

Taylor let out a pent-up, irritable breath. "It's not that. Well, yeah, it is partly that, but…you could have been killed, Brandt, and here I am stuck babysitting East Africa's answer to Paris Hilton."

"That bad?"

"Yes. And don't change the subject. Did you actually see a doctor, or did you just decide all on your own you didn't have a concussion?"

"Yes. I saw the base doctor. I just stunned myself for a few seconds. If I hadn't fallen into a swimming pool, it wouldn't have been worth mentioning."

Taylor made a huffy sound that made Will's lips twitch into a grin he'd never dare have shown.

"On the bright side, we've wrapped our case up," he offered.

"Yes?" Taylor sounded slightly mollified.

"Yep. I'm driving back first thing tomorrow morning, and we can spend tomorrow night together. Your place or mine, you can choose." He planned on stopping off in Orange County and doing some more checking into the recent activities and general attitude of the Phu Fighters, but he wasn't going to mention that right now. Taylor was edgy enough.

"We've got one more day escorting Miss Congeniality around LA. Then they fly her off to San Francisco, and the gang on Pine Street get to amuse her for the next forty-eight hours."

"So, tomorrow night. My house or yours?"

"Mine. I…want to show you something."

"Oh yes?" Will said hopefully, suggestively.

There was a smile in Taylor's voice, but he sounded absent. "Will?"

"Right here."

There was a pause. "When I was shot —"

Will's heart quickened; he wasn't even sure why. "Yeah?"

"It wasn't because of you…turning me down. It wasn't because my mind wasn't on the job."

"No?"

"No. I know—at least, I think I do—that you thought you were somehow to blame for me getting nailed. It wasn't anything to do with you." He heard Taylor sigh. "It was when I saw how young they were. Kids. And I hesitated. I hesitated a couple of seconds too long. That's all."

Something inside Will relaxed, like the clutch of a child's hand on a balloon. The balloon went sailing free and happy. "Yeah?"

"Yeah. So if you're, you know—you don't have to."

"Huh?"

Taylor said carefully, painstakingly, "So, if you're *you know* —"

Will burst out laughing. He couldn't help it—not to save his life. "You are fucking insane, do you know that?"

"I beg your pardon?" Taylor said in outrage.

The formal words and indignant tone made it all the worse, and Will was already having a very hard time not roaring. He couldn't even explain why he felt so happy. "You think I'm with you out of guilt?"

"No, you ass. Of course not. I just mean —"

"You're a nut, MacAllister. I'm with you because I love you."

There it was, out. Three little words. Three of the most common words in the world, but string them together and they were more powerful than any warrant, any extradition papers, or even treaty. Stronger than any magical spell. Had he really never said them aloud to Taylor? Something in the ringing silence that followed made him think he maybe hadn't.

It was a relief when Taylor said, at last, in that irritable voice that always signified nerves or great emotion, "That's fine. I just thought you should know."

"I love you," Will repeated firmly, having got the hang of it. "I'll see you tomorrow night, you lunatic."

"Love you," Taylor said tersely and hung up.

* * * * *

Taylor stared at the receiver in its cradle and then got ready for bed.

If he was spending the night by himself, he'd have preferred to be between his own sheets. Somehow it felt lonelier in Will's bed without Will. And it was hotter and smoggier here than in Ventura, and the street outside Will's place was noisier than his own neighborhood.

He left his .357 SIG on the nightstand within grabbing distance.

Even Riley seemed uneasy without Will, jumping up and growling at phantom shadows a couple of times during the long night.

"Easy, Riley," Taylor muttered, and each time the dog curled up next to the bed, grumbling under his breath. He lay, head raised, panting softly in the gloom, ears twitching at every sound.

Taylor wasn't much better. He wasn't nervous, but every time he started to relax into sleep, he'd remember something and jerk back to full consciousness. At first the memories were good: Will saying he loved him. Not that he didn't already know this, but if Will was saying it out loud, saying it so casually, acceptingly, they had turned some corner.

The laughter, the affectionate exasperation in Will's voice was…well, the best birthday present he could have received.

But then the memories grew darker. Things he had forgotten, tried to forget, came back to him. His shooting. The subsequent trip to the High Sierras when Will had been taken hostage. When he'd feared Will was dead. Other memories, older memories. Other friends, other losses and failures.

Japan.

A long time since he'd let himself think about Japan, let himself remember. No point to it. Nothing productive was going to come out of raking over those memories. Better, healthier, to forget.

Not that there weren't good memories too. A lot of good memories. Even if he wasn't ready to face them yet.

It was the cobra in the bottle that had started him remembering. Old poison.

Weird.

There couldn't be a connection. It was nearly a decade ago.

But equally he had trouble believing that the Orange County Phu Fighters were still gunning for him. He couldn't even picture them coming after Will, let alone him.

And that note: *Old poison slays as swiftly as new.* Vietnamese gangbangers were not going to leave notes in Japanese kanji. If they wrote anything at all, which would be doubtful, it would be in their own Romanized national language—or English. But the fact was, they wouldn't leave notes; they wouldn't send cobras pickled in rice wine or try to set booby traps with Japanese fireworks. They'd shoot him when he walked out his door one morning.

By the same logic, he dismissed the idea of the punks in the Red Dragon parking lot. To start with, the cobra in the bottle had been sent before the altercation in the parking lot. And that little dustup couldn't have been staged, because no one but Will knew where they were headed that night. Secondly, Mexican gangstas were even less likely to leave notes in Japanese than Vietnamese gangs. Thirdly, this whole complicated threat scenario was out of character. Out of character for both the Latino and the Vietnamese gangs. Wine with cobras? Cryptic notes? Bombs made out of fireworks? It was just too involved.

Convoluted.

Personal.

Granted, he and Will pissed people off in the normal course of their duties, but Taylor just couldn't see the forgers and counterfeiters they typically went after lashing back with this kind of scenario.

It was sort of, well, theatrical. Like those Noh dramas Inori had dragged him to see.

Taylor was tempted to dismiss it as a joke, but there was no reason anyone would be joking about Japan to him. Ninety bucks for a giant firecracker and another ninety bucks for a bottle of imported rice-and-cobra wine was a fairly expensive joke.

No, there was something not right.

Nothing he couldn't handle, but maybe he did need to talk to Will about Japan. He didn't want to. He could think of few conversations he wanted to have less. But Will had brought it up, and he deserved to hear the truth.

CHAPTER EIGHT

Taylor woke early—very early—and was momentarily confused to find himself in Will's bed—minus Will.

He dealt briskly with missing Will. A hot shower and hotter coffee helped chase away the remaining fog. He fed Riley, put the dog out in the backyard, to Riley's evident disappointment.

He borrowed a pair of Will's briefs—every single pair pristine and conservative white—and one of his clean shirts and dressed listening to the suburban birds in Will's well-kept backyard. He was still well ahead of schedule when he went out to try his car and found it dead.

It had been fine the day before, but that didn't necessarily mean anything. The Acura MDX wasn't new. It wasn't the battery, though, because he'd replaced that the previous month, and the lights and CD player were operating just fine.

Taylor thought it over, went inside, and phoned Varga.

"My car won't start. You mind picking me up this morning?"

She did not sound pleased. "In *Ventura*?"

"I'm not in Ventura. I'm in Woodland Hills."

"What are you doing in Woodland Hills?"

"We could talk about this on the way," he pointed out.

She sighed. "All right. What's the address?"

He gave her the address, and she hung up.

Shortly before eight o'clock, Varga rang his cell to say her ETA was two minutes out—clearly expecting him to be on the sidewalk waiting.

Taylor rinsed his coffee cup, set it in the sink, locked Will's front door, and walked out to meet her, surprised to see a battered brown Chevy in the driveway, blocking his own disabled Acura.

Brown Chevy...

He registered this, registered that Riley was snarling and throwing himself at the chain-link gate, and instinctively Taylor's hand went to his shoulder holster, even as he opened his mouth to calm the dog. A woman was getting out of the driver's side. He didn't recognize her, but he recognized the nightmare expression on her face—so white she looked like she was painted for Kabuki theater: black holes for eyes, a slash of mouth, and ghost white skin. She had a gun in her hand, and it was pointed at him.

Too slow this time, MacAllister. His main regret was Will; that this was happening on Will's home turf. Will was going to think he should have been here, should have stopped it. Shoulda, woulda, coulda.

At the same instant, someone walked up behind him, someone who must have been waiting along the side of the house. Taylor felt the prod of something hard and cylindrical beneath his ribs. His hand froze, fingertips brushing the butt of his pistol.

"Drop it."

"You've got to be kidding me," Taylor said. "Do you know I'm a federal officer?"

"We know who you are."

Okay. If he wasn't already dead, the odds in his favor were improving. He gingerly drew his weapon and dropped it to the grass.

"Walk," a man's voice ordered. A toneless, empty voice. Accented? Seeing that there was a chance he might survive this, Taylor started taking mental notes.

The woman was scrambling to throw open the trunk of the Chevy. Brown hair, Caucasian, five-six or -seven, medium build, mid to late forties. He didn't know her. Did he? "Hurry!" she urged. "For God's sake, hurry up!"

A motor gunned from down the street. Varga's blue sedan roared up behind the Chevy, blocking it in. She must have seen what was happening, because she jumped out, drawing her weapon on the man who held Taylor.

"Halt. Fed —"

Before she could finish identifying herself, the woman by the rear bumper of the car opened fire. The bullets hit Varga squarely in her chest, the white silk of her blouse turning red as she dropped to her knees. She discharged her weapon harmlessly into Will's lawn and sagged forward onto her face.

Taylor saw it out of the corner of his eye, and it was the last thing he saw; he had whipped around, grabbing for the gun, trying to disarm the man behind him, when there was an explosion in his head.

Hanabi. A brilliant chrysanthemum burst of purple and red lights. Bloodred stars like chrysanthemum petals drifted, twinkling through the night. The lights went dark.

* * * * *

Will was in Orange County talking to Deputy Brown about the recent suspicious movements of the Phu Fighter gang leadership when the call came through.

Assistant Director Cooper came up as the Incredible Hulk on Will's phone screen.

Will made a face and stepped outside to take the call.

"Where are you?" Cooper bit out.

Sure he was about to get his ass reamed for taking time off to pursue his own investigation, Will hedged, "On my way back to LA."

"There's been a shooting at your residence."

The phone nearly dropped from Will's nerveless hand. "Who?" a weird, flat voice asked on his behalf.

"Denise Varga. She was shot to death in the street outside your house a few minutes after eight. Apparently she was on the way to pick up your partner."

"MacAllister?" Will managed the force the question from his locked-tight throat.

"Missing. From a neighbor's account, it sounds like he may have been abducted."

"Abducted?"

"His disabled vehicle is sitting in your driveway. Any idea what he was doing at your place?"

"He spent the night."

"Something wrong with his house?"

Frost crackled in Cooper's voice. And no wonder. One agent dead. Another—*Jesus.* Let him be okay.

Will thought rapidly. "I told him to stay at my place while Ventura PD investigated the bomb threat he received. Did my neighbor say if Ta—MacAllister—was injured?"

"She believed he was knocked unconscious and thrown in the trunk of a brown Chevy. I thought it had been determined that there was no bomb threat, that it was just a practical joke?"

"I never bought the practical-joke theory. I think this bears me out."

"Report back here. Out."

* * * * *

"Why didn't you tell me the truth?" Will demanded. His face was white with fury, his eyes almost black. He looked at Taylor with condemnation, dislike. Never, not once in the four years of their partnership, had Will looked at him like that. Like Taylor was a stranger.

Not even when they had been strangers to each other.

"I...tried."

"You didn't try. You never said a word about it. You let me believe that you were different. That you were good. Someone I could care about."

"I am. I am those things."

Dread welled in Taylor. If Will stopped believing in him, if Will didn't care about him anymore—it was like losing his compass, having his mooring torn away, like being lost at sea and no star to guide him.

"You disgust me," Will said.

Taylor was shaking his head, childishly insisting this wasn't true. "You know me, Will. You're just like me."

"I'm not like you," Will said scornfully. He was glaring at the thing Taylor held in his hand. Taylor looked down. He was holding a percussion pistol. Some of his fear lightened. Will had given him this. A magnificent gift. Smooth black wood grip carved in a snarling dragon head. A large pearl glowed in the dragon's jaws. The pearl beyond price. No, not a pearl. An eye. A brown eye. It stared at him maliciously—and winked.

"You're so fucking lame, MacAllister," Will exclaimed. "You're so fucking useless."

He snatched the pistol out of Taylor's hand and held the long, engraved barrel to his temple. "Here's what you do," he said and pulled the trigger.

A blast of dust and exhaust filtered through the cracks in the car trunk, blew in Taylor's face, waking him. He began to choke.

CHAPTER NINE

Yellow crime-scene tape cordoned Will's yard and lawn from the rest of the neighborhood and the spectators who had gathered. There was a horrifying red-brown stain at the end of the drive, where Varga had died.

The doors of Taylor's MDX stood open, and LAPD's crime-scene investigators were collecting and documenting evidence.

"Our theory is the perps damaged the MDX's starter coil at some point during the night and then left the scene," Lt. Wray said.

She was a tall, lanky redhead in an ill-fitting suit. Other than the suit, she seemed to know what she was doing. Time would tell.

"Why would they leave the scene?"

"We don't think these were professionals. There's every indication the shooter was panicked into opening fire. Plus, you've got a pretty active neighborhood watch here. We're speculating that the perps didn't want to draw attention to themselves by parking on the street or loitering near your domicile. We think your partner came out early this morning, earlier than the perps were anticipating. He couldn't start his vehicle and went back inside to call Agent Varga. Varga showed up, your partner walked outside, and this time they were waiting for him."

"Quiet, Riley," Will threw back at the dog, who had been barking ever since his arrival. To the cop, he said, "You have a partial on the Chevy's license plate?"

"Yes. We're running it now. So far we're not coming up with any matches. They may have switched plates with another car." Wray hesitated. "If you're right about this being the same car that nearly hit Special Agent MacAllister on Saturday, they've been tracking him for some time."

Why the hell hadn't Taylor listened to him? Why the hell did he always have to be such a damn bullhead? Except…Taylor *had* listened to Will last night. He'd stayed at Will's place like Will wanted. Will was the one who failed. If he'd been here…

He shoved it aside, questioned, "ID on the perps?"

"Two. Male and female. The witness didn't get a clear look at the male. She thought he might have been Asian. Midtwenties. Possible gang tattoos. A little shorter than your partner and a little heavier. She thought he hit MacAllister with some kind of karate chop or martial arts move."

"And the woman?"

"The woman is described as older, maybe even early fifties. Tall, athletic, Caucasian, brown hair. Our witness got a good look at her; she's going through mug shots now."

Will nodded. If Taylor's attackers were not professional criminals, how useful were mug shots going to be?

"Any chance this is tied to a case he's working?" Wray asked.

"Doubtful. MacAllister was on sick leave for eight weeks and then desk duty for another month. He was only cleared for active duty this week, and it's a routine protection detail."

"Then it's something personal."

Reluctantly, Will said, "It looks that way."

"Did your partner have any recent run-ins with anyone?"

Will filled Wray in on the altercation at the Red Dragon restaurant.

She heard him out but seemed unconvinced. "Doesn't really sound like the MO of any Latino gang I ever heard of."

"I agree. And for what it's worth, that was MacAllister's take too." Will knew he was going to have to tell her about the snake wine, the threatening note, and the dud bomb. He disliked cracking open the shell of Taylor's close-guarded privacy, but privacy meant little compared to getting Taylor back alive and in one piece.

When he'd filled Lt. Wray in on everything he could remember, she said thoughtfully, "Did he have a theory about who was harassing him?"

"If he did, he didn't share it." Will admitted, "He was resistant to the idea."

"Maybe so, but on the surface it sounds like someone was stalking him, all right."

Old poison, thought Will. "He was stationed in Japan about eight years ago."

"You believe there's a tie-in?"

"Maybe. Not necessarily, though. He's always been interested in Japan. He's studied martial arts. He's got a collection of Japanese weapons." Will thought about the pistol he'd bought for Taylor's birthday. It was a nice piece, an antique, but three thousand dollars wasn't incentive for abduction or murder. Besides, if someone wanted that pistol, or any of Taylor's collection, they'd have had the perfect opportunity to break into his house while he was staying at Will's. No, this was about Taylor himself.

He added, as they walked toward Taylor's MDX, "He could have pissed someone off at his dojo or when he was hanging around Little Tokyo. He can be…abrasive."

"How abrasive?"

"I like him," Will said evenly.

"Plus you have an alibi." He must have looked unamused. Wray said, "Any chance he was snatched as a means of leverage in a case you're working?"

"We're not working the same case right now. We've been temporarily reassigned."

"That's not what I asked."

Will stopped walking. "What *are* you asking?"

Her eyes were hazel and direct. "I was partnered with a guy for six years. I understand the bond. Is it possible your partner was taken in an attempt to put pressure on you?"

"No."

"What's the full extent of your relationship with Special Agent MacAllister?"

Funny thing being on this side of a criminal investigation. Will found he didn't like it at all. "We're partners, and we're best friends."

"You're both gay."

Well, he had to give LAPD credit; they had done one hell of a lot of background work in less than four hours.

"That's right." He looked past her to the crime-scene investigator and asked if there were wrappings from the wine shipping box in the MDX.

Negative from the crime-scene personnel.

Will questioned, "What about a note? Japanese writing on plain white paper?"

Another negative.

Wray observed this interchange silently. When Will had finished, she said calmly, "Like I said, I understand the bond between partners, Special Agent Brandt, but this is an LAPD investigation—at least until the Feds yank it away from us. I'll keep you up-to-date on any developments, but I expect your full cooperation."

Will nodded tightly.

"And I'm going to have to insist that you leave the investigating to us."

If Will's nod had been any tighter, his neck would have snapped.

Untroubled, Wray moved forward, pointing to the tire tracks across Will's lawn. "Agent Varga had them boxed in. You can see where they pulled forward and drove across your front yard and out your other neighbor's driveway..."

* * * * *

It was hard to breathe. There was more dust than air permeating the hood seal of the trunk, and the combination of exhaust fumes and burned pollen was making him sick. Or maybe that was the *taiko* drum banging in his skull.

Boom, boom, boom, with every labored beat of his heart.

Something had happened...

He tried to piece together the picture of the last thing he remembered. Had Will been with him? He didn't think so. It was confused...

The car hit another pothole or a dip in the dirt road and slammed down. Nausea rose in Taylor's throat, and he fought it back.

"Will?" he asked the stuffy darkness. But there wasn't enough room for both Will and him in this crowded compartment. There wasn't enough room for him on his own. Woozily, he began to feel around for something he could use as a weapon. But there was nothing. No tire iron, no jack, no handy crowbar or two-by-four.

The car banged down on another dip in the road, and this time the struggle to control his stomach failed. Sickness swept over him in a humiliating tide, wrenching his muscles. His head pounded more fiercely with each gasped retch.

* * * * *

"This is a goddamned, unbelievable screwup of near-*mythic* proportions," Assistant Director Cooper snarled.

It was the most pleasant thing Cooper had said so far, and it indicated he was finally cooling down.

Will nodded curtly. That had been the extent of his participation for most of his meeting with Cooper.

"If MacAllister believed himself to be in some kind of danger —"

"He didn't."

At Cooper's look of irritable inquiry, Will said, "He'd have told me, yes, but more to the point, Taylor wouldn't ever believe there was a threat he couldn't handle."

Cooper snorted, but he couldn't argue with that.

"Well, he obviously perceived there was some threat, because he sent off a sheet of Japanese writing and a cardboard box with wrapping paper to the FBI lab."

Will swallowed and managed to say unemotionally, "Did they come up with anything?"

"It wasn't a high-priority request at the time." Cooper sighed. "We should know something soon."

"Would it be possible for me to see MacAllister's file as it relates to his posting in Japan?"

Cooper was scowling again. "Certainly not. Anyway, LAPD is taking point on this for now."

"Until the G-men take it over?"

"Don't remind me." Cooper scrutinized Will. "You think this ties back to MacAllister's first posting?"

"I think it's possible. There's certainly a Japanese theme to these threats."

"That was, what? Ten years ago?"

"Eight, I think." Will apologized silently to his missing partner. "He doesn't talk about it, but I can't think of any other connection. He likes Japanese food, but I doubt if that's the key."

"I can't grant you access to your partner's personnel file, Brandt."

Will nodded.

"I'll look at the file myself. If I find anything…" Cooper let it trail. "Meantime, I'm instructing you to give your full cooperation to LAPD. And I mean that, Brandt. *Full* cooperation."

* * * * *

Wake up."

Bright pain beneath his ribs. His right side. He needed to be careful of his right side —

Taylor bit off a groan. A firework display seemed to be going on inside his head. His brain pounded sickeningly with each pulse of flashing bright light. He pried his eyes open. An indistinct figure stood over him. Was the light bad or was it his vision? Or both?

"Wake up."

The voice was cold, level. It was followed by another spike of pain in his side as a foot landed solidly beneath the ribs. He bit off his cry and rolled away—tried to, anyway. There was a rope around his ankles and another around his wrists.

He was on the ground. No, a floor. A cement floor. An interior. It was chilly, and it smelled weird. Like fish. Like the ocean.

Taylor began to remember. He had been at Will's. His car wouldn't start. Then it came to him: Varga getting hit. Jesus. In the chest.

"Varga?" His voice sounded like gravel.

"She's dead. Thanks to you."

No. It wasn't—that couldn't... He shook his head. A very bad idea.

"Why the hell did you have to choose today to ride together?"

A woman's voice from down a long, echoing tunnel. She seemed to expect an answer. Taylor mumbled, "Car wouldn't start."

"Of course your goddamned car wouldn't start," ranted the voice. "That was the point. If you'd just walked out the door at the time you always do, everything would have been fine. But you had to try and play tricks. And now another person has died *because of you.*"

He tried to place her. She seemed to know him, so he must know her, right? Nothing was familiar about her. The voice wasn't familiar. He tried to peer up at her through his sticky eyelashes. Nothing. Nothing she said made any sense. She went rambling on about Varga and how he'd caused her death. He tried to assess the situation, but so far nothing was making sense.

Maybe his bewilderment was too obvious to miss. "You don't know who I am, do you?" she asked finally.

He shook his head.

"I'm Alexandra Sugimori. The wife of the man you murdered."

CHAPTER TEN

"**S**ugimori," Taylor echoed.

"Are you going to pretend you don't remember, you lying sack of shit?"

"I remember."

"Yes," she said with bitter satisfaction. "You could hardly forget."

No, he could hardly forget. And now the pieces clicked into place like a Japanese puzzle box. Except it still didn't make sense.

"You destroyed him. You destroyed our life."

He shook his head, and she kicked him again. He began to worry about his right lung, the one that had been shot three months earlier. The doctors had warned him that it would always be vulnerable, especially to tearing loose from his rib cage again. He was pretty sure getting repeatedly kicked in the ribs would be discouraged.

"Murderer!"

"I don't know what you're talking about," he protested. "I didn't kill Inori. I wasn't even in Japan when he —" Taylor stopped. Over the past few days the memories had returned, and though the pain had faded through the years, it still hurt. It always would.

"When he killed himself?" she asked.

Taylor nodded. He pulled surreptitiously at the rope binding his wrists. A lot of rope. Hopefully that meant they didn't know what they were doing.

"The suicide that you drove him to."

He tried to deny it, moving his head in negation—not easy lying on the floor.

"Liar."

She kicked at him again, but this time he rolled to protect his lung and ribs. Her foot caught him over the kidneys. Not a huge improvement, as these things went.

"I'm not lying," he gasped. "I don't know who you are or what you think happened —"

"I told you who I am." She turned to someone else. "Lift him up. I want him to see my face. I want to see his."

Someone bent over him, hands grabbing his shirt, dragging him up. He was half lifted, half thrown against a wall. Taylor struggled to stay vertical, to face his abductors.

It was hard to discern them in the gloom, but the man was Japanese. Young, early twenties, neck and hands covered in the intricate tattoos of the Yakuza. Terrific. Taylor turned his attention to the woman. He still didn't remember her except for the few seconds before he'd been knocked out. He'd seen her shoot Varga. He wasn't about to forget that.

She was saying to him, "Are you pretending you didn't know Inori was married?"

Taylor swallowed. "I…"

She came toward him again, and he burst out with the truth. "I knew. It wasn't real to me."

That stopped her. "Wasn't *real*?"

"You weren't there. You were just a photo on his desk. I knew you were in the States. I thought you were separated or something." The woman standing over him, trembling, fists clenched, bore no resemblance to that long-ago smiling portrait.

"Bullshit. You wanted to think that. You seduced my husband, a good and honorable man, and you drove him to suicide."

"I didn't seduce anyone." This was insane. He couldn't believe it was happening. Where the hell had this madwoman been for eight years? Why was she was doing this? And why now?

The man said something quietly to her. Alexandra listened to him, but her fierce pale eyes never left Taylor's face.

She nodded. "You abandoned my husband and left him to face the disgrace alone. You're a coward as well as a murderer."

"It wasn't like that. I was reassigned. I didn't have a choice about leaving. And Inori broke it off with me before I left, before I started my second tour in Afghanistan. It wasn't a question of leaving him to face…disgrace."

He knew he was wasting his breath, but somehow he had to try and reach her. The kid…no way. Taylor recognized those empty eyes, eyes like a gun barrel. There was no mercy in him. The woman was his only hope. And it wasn't much of a hope.

"Listen to me. It was my first foreign posting at an embassy. I was young and inexperienced. Your husband was kind to me, and eventually we did become friends. It was…not my intention to hurt anyone."

"You used my husband. You seduced him. You perverted him."

Taylor shook his head.

"My husband kept a safe-deposit box. Did you know that?"

"No."

She was smiling eerily at him. "I didn't know either. Yuki found out about the box after the death of Otou-sama."

Otou-sama. The respectful honorific for one's father. The woman was Western, so she must be referring to her father-in-law, Inori's father. But who the hell was Yuki?

The young thug next to Alexandra folded his arms, staring at Taylor with his bold black eyes. *Yuki, I presume?*

One thing for sure, if they were introducing themselves, they had no intention of letting Taylor leave there alive.

* * * * *

Will was on the phone to a contact in Little Tokyo when Cooper stepped inside his office and closed the door.

"Later," Will said to Noriyori Arai and replaced the receiver.

Cooper said, "MacAllister spent two years in Japan. If his annual evaluations are anything to go by, he was a choirboy. A smart, efficient, ambitious choirboy."

"I never thought otherwise."

"No? Well, maybe I'm more cynical than you. There's nothing here that suggests grounds for a grudge match eight years later."

Will's heart sank. There had to be some lead, some clue, some*thing* that would help him find Taylor, but every turn seemed to be a dead end. According to Lt. Wray, the license plate belonged to a Dodge Pinto that had hit the scrap heap six months earlier. And Will's neighbor Linda Schnell had been unable to pick the female shooter out of any mug-shot books. Linda was working with an LAPD sketch artist, trying to come up with a composite of the female abductor.

"There's only one very small indication of a potential lead. MacAllister was friends with a Japanese American contractor, Inori Sugimori, at the embassy. Sugimori was a political specialist. He committed suicide two weeks after MacAllister was reassigned to Afghanistan."

"Is there anything suspicious about Sugimori's death?"

"Other than the fact it was suicide?" Cooper asked drily.

"*Was* it suicide?"

"Yes. It was certainly never questioned. It was pretty gruesome, and the physical evidence seems to have been conclusive."

Reluctantly, Will asked, "How did he do it?"

"He used a family sword dipped in poison to run himself through the belly."

Will clenched his jaw lest any unwise words escape.

"The family on Sugimori's father's side was very old and very respectable samurai stock. The rumor—and this is only rumor—is that Sugimori killed himself as a matter of honor."

"I don't see what this could do with MacAllister."

"No?" Cooper looked grimmer than ever. "The other rumor was that Sugimori and MacAllister were sexually involved. As you know, eight years ago the State Department took a very different view of homosexuality within the ranks."

The State Department was very proud of its new and enlightened views. Will didn't bother to tell Cooper that gay employees still faced discrimination and harassment from coworkers both at home and abroad. No point. Progress *had* been made since the days MacAllister had been posted in Japan; after all, Rome wasn't burned in a day.

"Okay," Will said. "Any proof MacAllister and this Sugimori were actually involved?"

"No. But there seems to have been no other reason for Sugimori to have killed himself. And there was the little problem of him being married, you see."

"If this is some kind of revenge thing, why would anyone wait eight years?"

"Sugimori's father recently passed away. At a guess? I'd say some special information the old man had came to light after his death, and it triggered a sequence of events..."

* * * * *

"I want him to suffer..."

He could hear them arguing from the other room. Alexandra was still crying, still ranting. Yuki had dragged her from the room to spare her that final loss of face. She'd come unglued as she started describing the contents of Inori's safe-deposit box. The cracks had already been there—had probably always been there, barely plastered over. Taylor had no way of knowing. Inori had barely spoken of his wife in the States.

One thing for sure, Alexandra had never been meant to see the contents of that fucking box. No wonder she was coming apart in pieces; even Taylor wasn't finding it easy to hold it together. Why had Inori kept that junk? Why hadn't he destroyed it before he'd destroyed himself? What could he have been thinking? He was such a fastidious, meticulous man. To have kept those items... Had a part of him wanted them found?

Christ. Blindfolds and cock rings were the least of it. The Japanese were a highly inventive race. And Taylor... Well, he'd had a wild streak, no doubt about it. He had prided himself on being willing to do anything once. Granted, they had played those games more than once. But for Taylor it had always been a test of his manhood, of himself, of his limits. Inori... No question it had been different for Inori. Those pretty, pretty needles. The butterfly board. No wife was meant to see those. Hell, he wouldn't want Will to see those things.

No, he definitely didn't want Will to know about that stuff.

Taylor listened with half an ear while he took stock of his surroundings and tried to figure his options. They were, at best, limited.

He had worked out that he was in a house. An abandoned house. Even the carpet had been torn up and removed. They'd dumped him in a large empty room with vaulted ceilings and tall windows. A dining room, maybe? He could see shadows moving across the distant white ceiling. Water. He was sure he was very near the ocean. Right on the beach. He could feel the pound of the surf beneath the floor like a sluggish heartbeat. The smell of fish and tide pools permeated. The sound of surf and mewling gulls drifted through a broken window high overhead.

The gulls and waves were the only sounds he heard.

There were no sounds of cars, no hum of traffic, no voices, telephones, televisions. Wherever he was, he was not near people.

"With this knife, I'm going to cut off his balls. With this knife, I'm going to chop off his dick —"

Yeah, that would be not counting Alexandra and Yuki, who were still discussing what to do with him in a passionate spate of mixed Japanese and English. Yuki was all in favor of a bullet between Taylor's eyes and getting the hell out of Dodge. Alexandra kept stressing the importance of making Taylor suffer for his past sins. Making Taylor pay was her theme song, and it was easy enough to see who was the mastermind—using the term loosely—behind the tokens of disaffection over the past week.

She had mentioned castration several times, and Taylor was fervently hoping Yuki's sense of self-preservation would prevail. It wasn't just fear for himself—although that was considerable. Taylor didn't want Will having to face the horror of a mutilated lover. A dead lover would be bad enough. There was always that risk in their profession, and they both accepted it. But the kind of thing Alexandra was talking about? No. Taylor did not want Will struggling to come to terms with that. Will would find a way to blame himself. Taylor knew only too well how painful—well, he knew how it had felt when he'd learned Inori had killed himself.

But he couldn't think about that now. He'd avoided thinking about it too closely for eight years. Now was definitely not the time to confront those memories.

The sea air gusted in, brisk and salty, catching his attention. He looked up to where the small round window had been broken. Way too high to climb, unfortunately, even if his hands and feet were free, but there might still be some glass around. He studied the filthy floor for the sparkle of anything bright and shiny and useful.

He saw nothing. It was just a broken window, and it would be cold when evening came—assuming he was still alive when evening came.

* * * * *

"Is the wife still around?" Will asked.

Cooper nodded and handed a sheet over. "Here's her LKA. She's based out of Los Angeles."

If Cooper had bothered rounding up a Last Known Address, his mind was working the same way as Will's. Not that it was any great leap to want to speak to the surviving spouse or lover. Spouses and lovers always ranked high both for doing in loved ones and avenging them. Feeling the way he did about Taylor, Will understood why—on both counts.

Cooper said, "She wasn't in Japan when Sugimori died. In fact, she wasn't in Japan for the two years MacAllister worked at the Tokyo embassy. Some problem with her visa. At least that's how it looks on paper."

"You think they might have been estranged?"

"Hard to say. It's difficult to get a handle on Sugimori. Professionally he was well regarded, highly respected. His private life—well, that's harder to read. He was the product of a mixed marriage. His mother was an American. She worked as an interpreter for the UN, which is where she met Sugimori's father. He was a wealthy Japanese businessman, and she was his second wife. She died giving birth to Sugimori, and he married his third wife, a Japanese national, shortly after. So what you've got there is this half-American kid born into a very traditional, conservative Japanese family. There's an older son and daughter by the first wife, then Sugimori, then a younger son eventually born to the third wife."

Taylor's lover. Okay. So why hadn't Taylor told him about Sugimori when Will asked about Japan? That was the part Will was having trouble wrapping his mind around. Not like they didn't know they'd each had other lovers, Taylor in particular. In fact, that was one of the reasons Will had been hesitant to ever start with Taylor.

Oh.

Maybe he'd just answered his own question. Maybe Taylor was guilty about this relationship? Thought Will would disapprove? He was funny that way. Took Will's occasional criticisms to heart in a way that Will never intended—nor reciprocated.

"Sugimori was educated in Japan but went to university in the States, which is where he met the wife, Alexandra Burton. They married right after college, and Sugimori worked for the State Department. Eventually he applied for the posting to Japan, got it, and moved back to Tokyo."

"And Alexandra didn't follow?"

"Apparently not. Now it might have been bureaucratic red tape, or it might have been something else. If MacAllister and Sugimori were having a sexual relationship, it was probably something else."

"Why don't I go find out?" Will suggested.

"Why don't you? But bring LAPD along. We don't want any accusations of coercion or improper use of force."

Will raised his brows. "Me?"

* * * * *

He needed to piss quite desperately by now. Maybe it was weird to worry about that, seeing that there was a good chance he might end up with his balls or dick cut off—never mind dead—but there was something especially humiliating about being forced to wet himself. It made him furious.

Taylor opened his mouth to let loose a string of invective, but they were back, and the look on Alexandra's face shut him up. Not that he had ever imagined he was going to make her understand, see things from his point of view, but he thought she would string it out, want to keep talking to him, make him listen.

Give Will a chance to find him.

Maybe she would have, but there was Yuki to consider. Whatever Yuki's role in all this—besides discoverer of his older brother's box of secrets and bearer of bad news—was hard to say. Clearly he was the more practical of the two. He was observing Taylor with those cold, unwavering eyes, already thinking about how to dispose of the body.

"Here's what we're going to do," Alexandra announced. She sounded relatively cheerful, so she was getting her way about whatever this was. She carefully set down a white sake bottle a few feet from Taylor and straightened up.

The bottle reminded him how thirsty he was. That he hadn't eaten since lunchtime the day before. The bottle scared him.

"This is laced with rat poison. When you become desperate, you can drink it."

"Gee, thanks." Taylor looked past her to Yuki, who stood in the doorway, arms folded and impassive. "You think of everything."

"Oh, you *will* drink it," Alexandra informed him. "Even though you'll have to struggle to get to it. You see, we're going to leave you here to die. To die of thirst and hunger. Like you, this house is condemned. Abandoned. No one ever comes here. It's private property in the middle of nowhere, so you can scream and yell all you like. No one will ever hear you. No one will ever find you."

Taylor said nothing. What on earth could he say? It was all he could do to hide his relief. He'd been thinking the jar was to keep his private parts in after she surgically removed them. Or that maybe it contained a baby cobra or scorpions or black widows. Or that it contained battery acid. Rat poison was pretty mild unless they were going to force it down his throat themselves, and apparently that was not the plan.

Alexandra smiled. "You don't believe me. You think someone will find you, but there's nothing to connect us to this house, so even if the police do figure out I'm involved, they'll never find this place. I'll never tell them. It doesn't matter what they do to me."

That much he believed. She was as committed as any martyr lashed to the burning stake. Even Will would have trouble getting this chick to talk, and Will was very good at getting people to talk.

"I'm glad you don't believe me," she added. "I'm glad you're hopeful, because I want you to take a long time to die. I want you to suffer as much as I did. As much as Nori did. I want you to stay hopeful, to keep believing someone will find you, until you can't stastand the thirst and hunger and loneliness anymore and you drink the poison."

He knew he should try to talk to her, try to appeal to her, try to make her empathize with him, but somehow he couldn't seem to find the energy. He knew it was useless, could read it in her cold, crazy eyes. There was no going back for her. She had killed Varga, and even if she was unbalanced enough to forget that, Yuki wasn't.

Taylor glanced at Yuki again, and a chill ran down his spine. No, Yuki wasn't crazy or stupid, and regardless of what Alexandra thought, Yuki was not going to leave Taylor here and trust that he'd get despondent enough to drink rat poison. Yuki wasn't going to leave him alive one minute longer than he had to.

As though he read Taylor's thoughts, Yuki offered the first glimmer of emotion he'd yet revealed. He smiled.

CHAPTER ELEVEN

The house felt weirdly empty after Alexandra and Yuki left. It felt as though Taylor were already dead. As though it were already far too late for him.

He had to hurry. He knew that. Yuki was going to come back just as soon as he unloaded Alexandra, and he was going to kill Taylor. No doubt about that; Taylor had seen it in the other man's eyes.

He had no idea of how much time he had; he had to act based on the assumption that it was very little. He inched and scooted around, crawling toward the sake bottle. When he was within range, he drew his legs up and gave it good hard kick. The bottle went flying, hit the wall, and shattered into pieces, poisoned sake splashing against the wall and dripping down to the cement floor.

Taylor rolled over to the broken pieces and tried to kick a couple of the larger ones out of the pool of poisoned wine and line them up so that he could lean against the wall and saw the ropes without having to lie on the thick glass.

His bladder now felt in danger of bursting, and he knew he was going to have to give in to the indignity of peeing his pants. It added to his general fury—and discomfort—but once that was out of the way he was better able to concentrate on the task at hand.

Literally, at hand.

And now was the time to be grateful for his martial arts training. All that stretching and bending and limbering made it possible for him to move his arms out far enough from his back in order to saw awkwardly, frantically, against the dull chunk of broken earthenware.

Even so, that position quickly grew tiring and then painful and then agonizing. His shoulders and back ached with the strain, his muscles burned. Unable to see behind himself, he was unsure he was making progress.

Every minute or so he had to stop to rest his shaking arms. He used that time trying to free his legs, wiggling his ankles to loosen the ropes binding his lower limbs together. Alexandra and Yuki had not been taking any chances. The rope was looped around his ankles four times, but the excess of rope length actually meant there was play in the line, if he could just…

After a time he had to stop and rest. Had to. Getting slammed across the head, kicked in the ribs a few times, took it out of a guy. He rested, gulping, on the cool cement, willing the world to stop spinning, his guts to stop churning. Looking up at the faraway ceiling, he tried to calculate the time. He could tell by the reflected shadows that the sun was moving across the sky. How the hell long had it been now?

It felt like hours, but that was probably wrong.

Even so, Yuki might be on his way back to the house.

He wondered what Will was doing, tried to guess what steps Will would be taking to find him. He had no doubt that Will was hunting for him. No doubt that Will would find him—Taylor just wanted to make sure Will found him in time.

He heaved himself up and started sawing at the ropes around his wrists again.

* * * * *

Elegant brows raised, Alexandra Sugimori studied their badges for a very long moment.

She raised her milky blue gaze to Will's. "Bureau of Diplomatic Security? It's a long time since I've heard from the State Department."

Mrs. Sugimori was a tall, slender woman in an elegant navy silk housecoat. Her dark hair was pulled back in a sleek chignon. She could not have looked more different from the description of the woman who had shot Denise Varga and helped to abduct Taylor, but as Will gazed into her pale gaze, he got that telltale prickle at the back of his scalp.

"Your name came up in connection with a case we're investigating."

"Oh yes?"

She sounded uninterested. Too uninterested. She smiled a chilly smile at Lt. Wray, who was—after some debate—letting Will take point on this, and said, "Well, we may as well be comfortable."

She led them into a formal living room furnished with expensive Asian objets d'art. "Can I offer you something in the way of refreshment?"

"No, thank you," Lt. Wray said. She looked around with the innocent interest of a tourist in a museum. She nodded to the credenza, where a silver-framed picture of a young Japanese man and a boy sat. "Is that your husband?"

"That's Nori, yes. He died seven years ago. Seven years ago exactly, as of tomorrow." She added into the awkward silence, "The boy is Yukishige, his younger brother."

Will asked, "You've stayed in touch with your husband's family?"

"I've stayed in touch with Yuki. He chose to attend school in the States."

"Where does he go?" Wray asked.

The pale gaze rested on her. "Stanford University. The same as my husband."

"When was the last time you saw your brother-in-law?" Wray asked at the exact moment Will opened his mouth.

He contained his impatience. He and Taylor had this kind of thing down to a science. There was no talking over each other, no waste of time or energy. Still, Wray was a smart cop, and he thought she was right there on the same wavelength.

Mrs. Sugimori didn't hesitate. Her eyes slanted right as she said thoughtfully, "We met for dinner two weeks ago."

The right-eye movement was a cue that she was visually remembering an actual event. Taylor put a lot of stock in these visual access cues; he was very good at reading them. Will was less sold on body language and eye movement, but he observed that their suspect was holding herself stiffly as she tucked a nonexistent strand of hair behind her ear. All supposedly indicators for lying.

Lying by omission?

He deduced that Mrs. Sugimori had had dinner with her brother-in-law two weeks ago but had seen him more recently. "Where could we get in touch with Yukishige?"

Her eyes slanted left as she said, "Through the university, I suppose. I would call his dorm. Forgive me for asking, but why would you need to speak to him?"

Instead of answering, Will said, "We apologize for having to bring up what are undoubtedly painful memories, but we wanted to ask you one or two questions about your husband's death."

"Why?"

Seven years later it was clearly as raw as if it had just happened.

Wray said, "A federal agent has been killed and another abducted. We believe these crimes may be somehow connected to your husband's death."

"That's ridiculous!" Sugimori was on her feet and walking agitatedly around the room, keeping tables and sofas in between herself and them, Will noted. That could be an indication that she was lying—or that she was going to try and pull a weapon out of that big flower arrangement. "That's insane. And you think Yuki is part of this?"

Wray asked, "Was he very close to his brother?"

"Yes. They were close. But what you're suggesting is ridiculous." She stood still. "Why would Yuki wait seven years to avenge his brother?"

Avenge.

Will said, "Your father-in-law recently passed away, I believe. We thought that perhaps some new information might have come to light at that time. Families often have secrets."

"I don't care for what you're implying."

"We're not implying anything, ma'am," Wray said. "We're just trying to get to the truth. It's nothing personal."

Maybe not for Wray. As far as Will was concerned it was time to take the kid gloves off. They needed to break Sugimori and break her fast, because if they walked out of this house without the answers they needed, she was going to make two phone calls: one to a lawyer and one to Yukishige Sugimori. There was a more-than-good chance that the first thing she told little brother would be to kill Taylor—assuming he was not already dead.

Will refused to consider that. If they'd wanted Taylor dead outright, they'd have executed him in Will's front yard when they shot Varga.

"Why do you think your husband killed himself, Mrs. Sugimori?" Will inquired.

For an instant the pale mouth seemed unable to form words. "He was... depressed."

"I'd say that goes without saying."

She blinked at him, nonplussed by the sudden, blatant aggression.

"Marital problems?" Will pressed. "That's the usual thing, isn't it?"

"No!"

He could feel Wray watching him, but she didn't try to intervene. "You weren't with him in Japan. That could have made a difference. Why weren't you there with your husband?"

Her lips were parted, but no words were spoken.

Wray interjected, equally cool, "Do you happen to own a brown Chevy, Mrs. Sugimori?"

The pale eyes widened like an animal at bay.

"Mrs. Sugimori, do you own a gun?" Will asked.

* * * * *

The broken edge of the earthenware jug had to be fairly dull, because his hand slipped several times but he didn't cut himself—maybe a good thing, if the contents of the bottle had been laced with rat poison. Not so good for cutting through these fucking ropes.

Jesus, he was tired. If he could just rest a few minutes.

But he was making progress. He'd kicked his legs free of the ropes a short while earlier.

He just needed...a few more...minutes...

A door slammed, the bang as loud as a shot in the empty building. Taylor's head jerked up. Time. He rolled onto his knees, tucked his feet, and stood. Thank you God for the use of his legs, because he'd be a sitting duck otherwise. He leaned back against the wall, fighting his dizziness, trying to contain his breathing.

Footsteps approached briskly. Yu-Gi-Oh! was going to make this fast.

Taylor hit him coming through the door, a shoulder ramming into the other man. Yuki slammed into the opposite wall and dropped the gun he held. It clattered on the cement floor. After a fleeting second of astonished realization, Yuki dived for it. Taylor kicked him in the jaw, and Yuki went flying. He landed on his back and was back on his feet in a reasonably steady kip-up.

Terrific.

Taylor gave a hard, despairing yank on the rope around his wrists and felt it give. Not enough, though, and Yuki was coming at him *Fists of Fury*-style, throwing kicks and chops like a crazy windmill. Taylor ducked away, kicked the pistol through the door into the other room, away from their area of combat. He delivered a couple of roundhouse strikes.

Yuki staggered back and laughed. "You think you're Chuck Norris, dude?"

Taylor didn't have the breath to spare. Sweat stung his eyes, soaked the back of his shirt. This had to be fast, because he didn't have the strength left for extended combat.

Yuki flew at him again; this time Taylor turned aside and let the kid hit the wall. He smashed into it but was up again, fists and feet flying, *laughing*.

Oh, to be twenty and a fucking psycho again.

Taylor was only too conscious of the fact that if one of those strikes connected, it was all over for him. He kept moving, ducking, weaving, managing to deliver a few good kicks. His basic strategy was to wear Yuki down a little. The problem was he was wearing down too.

He kept working at the rope around his wrist, tugging and rubbing at it, ignoring the pain of his flesh being scraped raw.

Yuki came hurtling at him again, delivering a succession of showy tornado and 720 kicks. Exhibition stuff. The prick was playing with him, cat and mouse. Taylor faked a retreat toward the doorway and, when Yuki charged after him, dropped him in his tracks with a jackknife kick to the head. Unfortunately, unable to use his arms for balance, it landed Taylor too. Hard.

It was like flipping a turtle on its back. Taylor rolled over, trying to get his feet under him. Yuki, stunned for a few seconds, was getting up again, and the look in his eyes said he was through playing games. He rushed at Taylor.

Taylor gave one last desperate yank to the restraints around his wrists and felt the rope give. He dived through the doorway, scrambling for the gun.

* * * * *

"You have no right to insinuate these things!" Alexandra Sugimori cried. There was color in her face now; her eyes seemed to glitter.

"Have you heard of the Federal Death Penalty Act of 1994?" Will inquired. He felt Wray's double take, but he had no time for that. Time was running out for Taylor. He knew it; call it instinct or intuition or gut feeling. He knew it as sure as he was standing there. It was now or never. It was *now*. He was not standing by while Taylor died.

"No," Sugimori said defiantly. "No doubt you'll tell me."

"It means if you're responsible for the death of Federal Agent Varga, you get the death penalty too. But if you help us save the life of the remaining agent, that could go a long way toward making a difference to what happens to you." That wasn't exactly accurate, but it was close enough for their purposes.

Sugimori seemed to struggle internally. Her face worked. She said, "I have *nothing* to do with anyone's death."

"Bullshit."

"How *dare* you? How *dare* you come into my home and accuse me of these things?"

"There's an easy way to solve this," Wray said, a voice of calm in the high seas. "Mrs. Sugimori, we'd like to ask you to voluntarily come downtown to take part in a lineup."

Sugimori froze. She said finally, "I'm not going anywhere with you people. I'm calling my lawyer!"

* * * * *

Taylor's fingers brushed the butt of the pistol as Yuki landed on top of him, knocking the wind out of his lungs, sending the pistol skittering. He heaved the younger man off, crawled for the gun. They were in a large open room and not far from away was a sliding glass door. And beyond the sliding glass door was…nothing. Empty sky and then the vast blue stretch of ocean.

The house perched precariously on a hillside that was being steadily eaten away by the waves below. The yard, the deck, the steps—all gone into the ocean.

No wonder Alexandra had been so confident no one would ever find him.

Yuki tackled him around the waist, and they both rolled away from the gun. Taylor head butted Yuki, and as Yuki's grip relaxed, he wriggled free and stretched for the pistol again.

Yuki grabbed his waistband, dragging him back, and Taylor flipped over and kicked him in the chest as hard as he could. Yuki stumbled back and crashed through the glass doors, dropping from sight with a scream.

Trembling, gulping for breath, Taylor lay on the floor, staring at the man-sized hole in the shattered glass, at the gaping hole in the sky. He half expected Yuki's bloody hands to appear over the jagged glass in the door track, see Yuki drag himself back, invincible like those villains in movies.

Nothing happened. He could hear the thunder of the surf, feel the pound of it hitting the rocks below. The chill, salty air gusted in through the broken door and cooled his sweating face. He could hear the cries of the gulls wheeling outside the glass door.

He rested his forehead on the cement.

At last he pushed to his feet, picked up the fallen pistol, and went over to the broken door. He looked down at a dizzying sheer drop of rocks and swirling water. There was no sign of Yuki. If he'd missed the rocks and knew how to swim, he might have survived the fall. Probably not. Taylor hoped not. That one had been for Varga.

Far out on the blue, diamond-dazzled water, he could see sailboats beneath the bright yellow sun. He remembered the card Will had given him for his birthday. Abruptly all the strength seemed to drain out of him. He sat down slowly, carefully, as though he were a thousand years old.

* * * * *

Alexandra Sugimori was tougher than she looked. From some hidden reserve of strength, she found the will to ignore their threats and reject their bargains. Finally she refused to answer at all, sitting and staring into space, her face as remote as one of those Shinto goddesses.

"We can't continue to deny her access to her lawyer," Wray warned Will in an undervoice as they took a break from hammering at their suspect's walls. "Even if you are the federal government."

"No way does that bitch phone anyone without us knowing exactly who and what instructions she's giving."

Wray opened her mouth, but her phone rang. She moved away to answer it. Will glanced at her and then glanced at Sugimori. She was staring at him with cold hatred. He stared back.

Wray suddenly let out a disconcertingly girlie squeal. "You got a partial print from the fuse? Yeah?" Her eyes met Will's. "Yukishige Sugimori. The brother."

At the same time Will's phone rang. He grabbed it. *Unknown Caller.* If this was some moron trying to sell him something, he was going to be slapped with a federal charge so fast, his head would spin.

"Brandt."

"It's me," Taylor's faraway voice said.

Will's heart seemed to stop cold, then bounded like a deer. "Are you all right? *Christ.* I thought—Where are you?"

"I'm not sure." Taylor's voice was muffled as he turned away to speak to someone. An equally muffled voice answered. Taylor came back on the line. "I'm on the coast road between Surf Beach and Casmalia. At an abandoned roadhouse called Richardson's. You can't miss it. It's the one surrounded by cop cars." He sounded very tired. "I'm okay, Brandt. Can you come and get me?"

"I'm on the way."

Taylor said quickly, "Brandt? Swear out a warrant for Alexandra Sugimori."

"Done." His voice softened; he couldn't help it. "Hold on, MacAllister."

"I'm holding," Taylor said and disconnected.

CHAPTER TWELVE

The sun was setting when Will pulled up in front of Richardson's Road-house.

There were cop cars parked by the rusted gas pumps, a red peeling sign with the words RICH…R…AD… The roadhouse itself was boarded up. The faded paint had an appropriately queasy green cast to it.

Taylor walked out from between the gas pumps, and Will got out of his car. He went around the front and didn't care who was watching as Taylor walked into his arms.

They hugged, drew apart, and Will said, "Whoa. You *have* been through the wars."

"I know. I stink."

"I'm not complaining."

"That's because you haven't been shut up in a car with me for a couple of hours. Wait till we head back to LA."

Will glanced at the official buzz of cars and personnel, radios squawking and people talking. "Are we going back to LA tonight?"

"Eventually." Taylor said, "Is Sugimori under arrest?"

"Yes."

Will watched him brace to ask, "She said Varga was dead."

Will nodded. "I'm sorry."

Taylor's eyes shut. He opened them and said, "Yeah. If you don't mind, I'm going to sit in your car and wait for them to clear us to leave."

"I don't mind."

A faint smile touched Taylor's colorless mouth. "Not yet, you don't. You will."

But Will didn't. Not all the long drive back to LA. Taylor slept, mouth ajar and face lined and unlovely with strain and exhaustion. Will drove and used his cell phone to fill in Lt. Wray and Assistant Director Cooper. He talked while he kept one eye on his partner. Despite efforts to clean himself off in at a rest-stop men's room, Taylor was indeed more than a little on the pungent side, but Will had no complaint.

* * * * *

Taylor woke when Will stopped for coffee, and he explained in what was clearly the abridged version how he had managed to get free.

"It was like those convoluted schemes the villains in *Batman* came up with." He was trying to joke, but it wasn't quite coming off.

"She's insane," Will said. "I don't know about the legal definition, but she's deranged."

Taylor nodded without energy. He described knocking Sugimori Junior. into the ocean.

"They haven't found him yet," Will replied in answer to the question Taylor hadn't asked.

"Good," Taylor replied. "I hope the fish are having him for supper." He told Will about leaving the wrecked and derelict house on the cliff, hot-wiring Sugimori's car and driving into Casmalia to phone the cops and Will. "That's pretty much it."

He made it sound simple. Will tried to keep it low-key too. "Lucky you found it. You could have blinked and missed it. Population less than two hundred. The town's a toxic dump," he said. "I mean literally."

"No wonder I headed straight for it."

They both smiled, but it took effort.

* * * * *

Taylor sat grimly through the medical exam and brusquely declined the amenities of an overnight hospital stay. Will couldn't argue, since he'd done the same thing the day before—was it only the day before?

The doctor and Will exchanged a look, and then the doctor gave Will a list of signs and symptoms to look for in case of concussion and sent them on their way—which was straight to a debriefing with Cooper.

When Cooper had finally tired of the pleasure of their company, or maybe just the sound of his own voice, Will had driven home—to Taylor's house—and Taylor had showered and was dressed in the softest, most comfortable jeans and T-shirt he owned, resting on the sofa in the den drinking the hot coffee Will had prepared. His head still hurt, his ribs ached, but he felt okay. Wrung out but okay. He was alive, and that counted for a lot.

Will sat down on the sofa and put an arm around him. Taylor relaxed, closed his eyes, and let his head fall back against Will's shoulder, relinquishing himself to Will's care. "I guess you have a few questions."

"If you want to tell me."

"No." Taylor smiled faintly. "Yeah."

Will kissed his forehead and didn't say anything.

Taylor opened his eyes and watched Will's three-quarter profile as he said, "He wasn't my first or anything." Taylor had been fourteen the first time he and Bobby Machek had jacked off together behind the broken-down concession stand at Sandoval Baseball Field. He could still remember the ghostly silhouettes of the painted players on the peeling red wood wall. Those guilty, giddy minutes with Bobby had been the launch of a long and occasionally wild journey of sexual exploration that had really only ended when he found harbor with Will.

He closed his eyes and admitted, "But it was the first time I thought maybe I was in love."

In the silence that followed, Taylor raised his lashes. There was so much affection and understanding in Will's blue eyes, he had to close his own again.

"Not like us," he clarified, although he was sure Will already understood that. "We had to be careful, obviously. It would have meant the end of both our careers. You know how it was back then." Eight years. Amazing what a difference a decade—or near decade—could make.

"I know," Will said, and he seemed to be speaking about more than the State Department's historic attitude regarding same-sex relations.

"Inori was married. Separated, I thought. That's what he told me, and I had no reason to believe otherwise. Even so, he was—it was hard for him. After the first rush of finding each other, he was terrified all the time that we were being watched, that we would be discovered. The idea of failing, of disgrace, was unthinkable. His family—his father—was old-school. Samurai. We're talking something straight out of a Kurosawa film. Inori already felt like an outcast because his mother was Caucasian. There was always this standard he was trying to live up to. Being gay just made it worse for him."

"How was it for you?"

Taylor grimaced. "I took my career just as seriously, but being younger, I didn't think we'd get caught. You know how it is. I felt bulletproof back then. Anyway." Taylor swallowed hard. "Anyway, after about ten months he…broke it off with me. Said that as much as he loved me, the risk to both of us was too great." He could still taste the bitterness of that, knew Will could read it in his face. "So I requested a transfer, and I got one. Faster than I expected." Taylor opened his eyes, his expression wry. "They sent me to Afghanistan."

"Hell."

"It was, yeah. Anyway, at least I knew I wouldn't have time to brood. For Inori, though… I don't think he'd expected me to go. I'm not sure what he expected, to tell you the truth. I guess he thought he'd failed me too. I don't know, Will."

Will said calmly, firmly, "What he did was not your fault, Tay. Don't take responsibility for Sugimori's decisions."

"No, it's just —"

"No."

"No." Taylor flicked him a smile. "Thanks." He sighed. "Anyway. I found out a few months later than he killed himself not long after I left Japan. The word was, he'd left some note about family honor and not wishing to live with disgrace, but that was all I heard. If my name had been mentioned —"

"Your name was never mentioned in connection with Sugimori's suicide." Will said carefully, "There were rumors about the two of you, but no one chose to investigate them."

"Jesus."

"It doesn't matter now."

Taylor pinched the bridge of his nose, hard. "I guess not. It's just… It was true about the old poison. All that time that hurt and betrayal were festering."

"You could have told me, you know. I wouldn't have thought any less of you," Will said slowly.

"You wouldn't have thought any more of me." Taylor was kidding. Only not really.

Into Will's silence, he said, "I should have told you. It's just…sometimes…" He didn't finish it, and Will didn't push.

Taylor let his eyes drift closed again. Neither of them spoke. Taylor felt Will take the coffee mug from his hand and set it on the table.

"I'm awake," he murmured. And he mostly was. It was very pleasant lying there with Will's strong arm around him and his head on Will's broad shoulder. He listened to the peaceful, steady beat of Will's heart.

"I've been thinking," Will said eventually.

"Yeah?"

"It really doesn't make sense keeping two separate houses. It's not very practical."

Taylor's heart jumped. He said carefully, "What about Cooper? No way is he going to believe we're just roommates."

"He might let it go. Or he might decide to reteam us. I guess we deal with it when it happens. The bottom line is, I want to wake up beside you every morning, and I want to go to bed with you every night. I don't care who knows. And I don't care what we have to do to make that happen. I like my job, but I love you. There's no question of what takes priority here."

Taylor stared at him. Will stared back at him, steady as a rock.

"You're sure." It wasn't a real question; the certainty was right there on Will's face.

"I'm sure." Will smiled. "Partner."

BLOOD
HEAT

CHAPTER ONE

Lightning flickered in the blue-black distance. Somewhere in the sultry, moonless night, a coyote yipped. Still farther away, another answered. There was no movement in the barren, walled yard. A single light burned in the second story of the pueblo-style house.

"I don't like it," Will muttered, ducking back from the gate to land against the thick adobe wall next to his partner.

Taylor shot him a quick look and laughed, a ghost of a sound. Taylor hadn't liked this setup since they'd arrived in Denver to find their prisoner, suspected terrorist Kelila Hedwig, had somehow charmed her way out of police custody and was once more on the run.

Hedwig was the prime suspect in the death of Los Angeles Field Office Director Henry Torres, which was why DSS Special Agents Will Brandt and Taylor MacAllister had been tasked with escorting her back to the City of Angels. Technically, pursuing and *re*apprehending her was a job for the US Marshals, not the law enforcement branch of the Bureau of Diplomatic Security. But Taylor, ever a cynical and suspicious son of a bitch, had suggested that the cowboys on Nineteenth Street had already had their shot and blown it—in his opinion, a little too conveniently. From the first, there had been an ugly rumor that Hedwig was getting help from the inside.

Will doubted it. He'd seen a couple of photos of Hedwig. She was a frail slip of a girl behind oversize spectacles. True, he was no expert, but he thought it unlikely she'd seduced anyone. He figured Denver PD had underestimated her resourcefulness—and desperation. It happened. It didn't automatically follow that there was a conspiracy afoot.

If she was getting help, it wasn't very expert help because, after fleeing Colorado, she'd headed straight back to the mountains of New Mexico and an ex-boyfriend, Reuben Ramirez.

Ramirez was Hedwig's high school sweetheart. Not that either of them had attended high school on a regular basis. He was an ex-con currently on probation for drug-related charges. Apparently Hedwig wasn't too much of a bad-girl superstar to forget the little people.

"It's too quiet," Will said.

"Nah. Ramirez is a punk. Strictly small-time. It's not like he can afford to keep a standing army."

Taylor's eyes looked silver in the gloom as they met Will's. His broad but bony shoulder was hard warmth pressing against Will's, and Will felt a disconcerting stirring in his groin. It caught him at unexpected times, this distracting awareness of Taylor. They'd been partners and best friends for four years, but lovers for only three months. They were still adjusting.

Some parts needed more adjusting than others. He shifted uncomfortably against the still-warm adobe bricks.

"Are we doing this?" Taylor asked when Will didn't say anything else.

Were they? It had seemed like a good idea at the time, but now as they waited outside the mud walls of Ramirez's hacienda, listening to the crickets, the hot wind skipping across the rocks and sand, and the distant rumble of thunder, Will wondered if they shouldn't maybe have requested backup from at least the Ruidoso Downs Police Department.

Taylor's view, unsurprisingly, had been that local law enforcement was likely to get underfoot and complicate things. Taylor had a refreshingly direct approach to such matters. He was also, for such a deceptively graceful-looking guy, a little on the forceful side.

The thought brought a faint, self-conscious smile to Will's face.

It was too dark to read each other's expressions, but Taylor must have sensed the smile, because he whispered, "What?"

"Nothing. Are you sure you don't want to bring in some support on this?"

"I don't like the fact that it took the feebs nearly a year to track her down, and then twenty-one hours after she's finally incarcerated, she manages to slip through the cracks again."

That bothered Will as well. "All right. We'll do it the old-fashioned way."

"Rape and pillage?"

"And people say you're the sensitive one."

Taylor's grin was a glimmer of white in the darkness. He turned from Will, slapping his hands against the dusty brick. "Give me a boost."

No. Let me go first.

Will caught the words back in time. Technically Taylor was the senior member of the team. Besides, lighter and faster than Will, Taylor had always taken point on this kind of op. But four—no, nearly five—months ago on a routine investigation, Taylor had been shot in the chest and nearly died. He'd recovered and was back to full field agent status, but Will was never going to be able to erase the memory of Taylor slumped on his side, scarlet spreading across his chest as his life's blood pumped out…

He was smart enough to keep that worry to himself, though. He linked his hands together. Taylor planted his boot squarely in the stirrup and vaulted lightly up, balancing briefly on the wall before dropping down.

Diplomacy in action. Like the slogan said.

Will heard the dull impact of his landing. A few seconds later, the wooden entrance gate was swinging creakily open.

Will slipped through the gap, the soles of his boots whispering on sand.

In the kennels behind the house, dogs were going crazy. Not guard dogs, fortunately. Ramirez fancied himself as some kind of hot-shit breeder. Over the past thirty-six hours, Will had observed that no matter how much noise the dogs made, no one from the house came out to investigate. Being a dog lover, he found himself irked by that on a number of levels—though it was a plus for their immediate purposes.

A minus was the long empty stretch of unlandscaped yard around the house. There was nowhere to hide once they were out of the deep shadow of the surrounding walls. No way to reach the house without running across several very exposed lengths of dirt and rock.

On the bright side—or, actually the not so bright side—the moon was down and there was a heavy indigo cloud cover pierced only by the occasional fork of faraway lightning. Taylor was a swift shade zigzagging through the darkness toward the garage.

Will went left, jogging for the main entrance in the portico beneath the exposed wooden beams. The familiar surge of adrenaline lent him speed, feet pounding the hard-packed earth, pebbles skittering as he ran, ears attuned to the night sounds.

He reached the heavy front door without incident and spared a quick look over his shoulder. There was no sign of Taylor. He would be in position by now—or nearly.

Will wiped his forehead with his arm—the moist air was surprisingly warm—and knocked on the door.

He waited.

Will's official knock was not easy to ignore, but there was no response from within.

He rapped again, and a dog began to bark inside the house.

Will swore under his breath. He could get a lot louder and a lot more vehement, but he and Taylor had discussed this, and their idea was to attract as little attention as possible since they were, in a manner of speaking, out of their jurisdiction.

Seeing movement out of the corner of his eye, he turned to spot Taylor sprinting across the flat top of the garage.

Now what the hell was that about? Taylor was supposed to be watching the back entrance, not playing one-man assault team. No way was he going inside without Will to back him up. Will took a couple of steps in brief retreat and sized up the front door. Kicking any door down was nowhere as easy as movies made it look, and this was a massive and rustic structure. But as far as Will was concerned, that door was kindling. He launched himself at it.

Light flared behind the downstairs windows. Will stumbled to a halt as the front door opened a crack and two suspicious black eyes peered out at him. One eye—a bleary, red-rimmed eye—was human. The other was canine and belonged to some breed of shepherd with a black rectangular muzzle and a lot of sharp white teeth.

"Who are you? What are you doing here?" growled the human.

The dog was less articulate but more convincing.

Will kept his voice low. The last thing he wanted to do was spook Ramirez's houseguest. "Special Agent William Brandt. I'm with the DSS."

"What's the DSS?"

"Diplomatic Security Service. We're a branch of the Bureau of Diplomatic Security." He held his badge up so there could be no mistake. "You better hear what I have to say."

The dog made another lunge through the opening between door and frame. Will took a hasty step back. "Hang on to that mutt if you don't want me to shoot it."

"He's not a mutt. He's a purebred Anatolian shepherd."

It didn't really seem like the time or place for semantics. Will opened his mouth to make himself heard over the snarling dog, but the sound of a shotgun blast from overhead ripped through the night.

A woman started screaming.

The shotgun wasn't Taylor's. Taylor and Will were carrying their roscoes and wearing underarmor, but that was the extent of their regulation equipment. Which meant Taylor was under fire.

Will grabbed the edge of the door. Ramirez, if it was Ramirez, let go of the dog, which lunged through the doorway, nails scrabbling on brick as it tried to get to Will.

"*Shit!*" Will twisted left, then right, like a bullfighter dodging a set of razor-sharp horns. He flung himself forward, bursting through the entrance in the opposite direction of the charging dog, almost simultaneously slamming the door behind him. His heart drummed in his chest as he slumped back against the uneven wooden surface. *Shit, shit, shit.* Their plan, such as it was, was already crumbling away like sandstone.

The snarling dog threw itself against the door. It sounded like a bear clawing the timbers.

Will had other, more immediate concerns. There was another blast from overhead. The shotgun's second barrel—definitely not Taylor's .357

SIG. Taylor was not firing back. There were plenty of reasons for that and none of them meant Taylor was in trouble, but Will still had to fight that instinctive and all-consuming rush of fear.

Ramirez had already fled the tile entryway and was running barefoot for the wooden staircase. His feet slapped the tiles, the tiny, desperate sound carrying oddly down the hallway. Will tore after the man and managed to tackle him three stairs up. Ramirez fell back, and they tumbled down the steps to the tile floor below.

Will's forehead grazed the edge of one step; his elbow and knee connected sharply with the floor. A goddamned *disaster* was what this was. He grunted and wrestled his way on top of Ramirez, who was short but muscular, compact and pumped up on adrenaline and possibly other things.

Ramirez flailed with arms and legs. He jabbed at Will's throat with a move unapproved by the WWF. Will blocked and grabbed Ramirez's hand, bending it back in a maneuver also frowned on by most wrestling associations. He followed it up with a knee in the groin that would have ended the fight then and there if it had connected as intended.

It didn't.

Ramirez screeched and began kicking with renewed energy—if not accuracy.

Upstairs the woman was still screaming, which Will distractedly registered as a positive sign. If she was screaming, chances were Taylor was still a threat to her, and that meant he was likely unhurt. In fact, over Ramirez's gasps and curses, Will could just make out Taylor's muffled tones.

Will got his handcuffs out and half dragged, half wrangled Ramirez over onto his front side. Straddling his quarry awkwardly, he snapped the cuffs around thick tattooed wrists.

Ramirez yelled. "What the fuck do you want?"

"I tried to tell you. You're harboring a fugitive, asshole."

"You're no cop!"

"If you don't stop resisting arrest, you'll find out how much of a cop I am."

Ramirez tried to rear up and throw Will off. "I'll fucking kill you if you hurt her."

"Nobody's going to get hurt if you shut up and settle down." Will checked the cuffs and jumped up from Ramirez, avoiding one of his wilder kicks.

"You're dead. You're a dead man!"

Ramirez's curses and the barking of the Anatolian shepherd outside followed Will as he took the stairs two at a time. His footsteps pounded on wood, the staircase shaking beneath him.

He reached the second story and scanned the unlit hallway. At the end of it, light pooled from an open bedroom door. The woman had stopped screaming. The sudden absence of sound was nearly as jarring as the shrieking had been.

Will heard Taylor say quite clearly, "Oh *fuck*."

Will drew his weapon, holding it at low ready. "MacAllister?" Something in the tone of Taylor's voice had raised the hair on Will's nape. It brought to mind too many alarming—though as yet unrealized—images: Taylor looking down to see he'd been mortally wounded, Taylor realizing he'd just pulled the pin on a grenade, Taylor—

"Brandt, you'd better get in here." Taylor's voice interrupted Will's alarmed speculations.

Will was already on his way down the hall.

Taylor blocked the doorway. He was holding a shotgun in one hand and his weapon in the other, but neither was trained on the room's occupant.

There was no noise from within the room at all. Jesus. Was it not Hedwig? Had Hedwig been shot in the altercation? Or worse, had someone who was *not* Hedwig been injured in the altercation?

Will came up behind Taylor, trying to see past him into the room. "What is it? What's wrong?"

Taylor retreated another inch—actually stepping on Will's toes. Will manfully managed not to yell. In their entire four years of partnership, he had never known Taylor to retreat so much as a centimeter. From anything.

He put a steadying hand on Taylor's back. "What's the matter?"

Taylor jerked his head as though it should be obvious what the matter was. Will stared past him. There was a chunk of plaster on the floor where one of the shotgun blasts had taken out a section of the ceiling. The woman was not dead. She didn't even appear to be injured. She was sitting on the foot of the bed. At first glimpse, Will thought it was not Hedwig. She'd dyed her long, lank hair blonde again, but that was her only effort at disguise. She looked older, her face was a little fuller, and she was not wearing her glasses, but it was unmistakably Kelila Hedwig.

Will threw Taylor a quick, questioning look. Taylor's profile was grim.

Will turned back to their prisoner. Studied her more closely. She was wearing a big, white, voluminous nightgown, and her skinny arms were wrapped protectively around her midriff. Around her basketball-sized midriff.

"Oh shit." Will turned back to Taylor. Taylor was shaking his head, repudiating what was only too obvious. "She's *pregnant*?"

CHAPTER TWO

"That's just great," Will said. He sounded uncharacteristically put out. "How the hell did *that* happen?"

"Don't look at me."

Will muttered something that could have been, "Dumb question."

Taylor acknowledged the words absently. Now what? In his envisioning of possible scenarios, this one had not occurred. He glanced doubtfully at Will, who was looking unusually ruffled, dark brown hair standing up in tufts like someone had tried to grab fistfuls of it out by the roots. Beneath the navy bulletproof vest, the sleeve of his yellow T-shirt was torn, revealing a hard brown bicep. He had a scrape over one blue eye. Otherwise he looked unharmed. He was still breathing hard, but no wonder if the sounds from downstairs had been anything to go by.

Their prisoner seemed to pick up on Taylor's thoughts. "What have you done to Reuben?" She had a light, girlish voice. It was more like the voice of a hair salon receptionist than a terrorist. She peered nearsightedly at them with wide, pale eyes that reminded Taylor of a frightened white rabbit.

"Nothing too serious from the sound of it." From the way Ramirez was shouting threats and obscenities, he sounded pretty healthy to Taylor. Hedwig looked unconvinced.

She licked pale lips. "You're really marshals?"

"DSS. Diplomatic Security Service. We're a branch of the Bureau of Diplomatic Security." The law enforcement arm of the State Department, if someone wanted to get technical.

Hedwig shrugged as though it were all the same thing. Had it been all the same thing when she'd gunned down Henry Torres in that underground parking lot?

"It's just the two of you?" She watched them warily.

"That's right. But don't get any ideas." Taylor handed Hedwig's shotgun to Will. Some girls had a thing for shoes; some girls had a thing for double gauge. His was not to reason why.

Will's gaze held his for a moment, his eyes dark with emotion. That would be Will fretting over the idea of Taylor nearly coming down with a case of lead poisoning. Taylor sighed inwardly. Will needed to get over it. Especially if he wasn't going to be around to watch Taylor's back anymore. He holstered his own weapon.

"Were you followed?" Hedwig looked from Taylor to Will.

"Why would we be?" He drew his handcuffs and approached the bed. Hedwig awkwardly levered herself up, her expression defiant.

Taylor stopped. "Seriously? Didn't we just do this?"

In answer, she tucked her hands behind her back.

"Oh for—" He looked at Will. Will, damn him, looked like he was trying not to laugh. Like this was funny? Well, maybe one day. Not at the moment. "Feel free to jump in here anytime, Brandt."

"Why? You're doing fine."

Taylor looked back at Hedwig. She bared her teeth at him. No shit. Bared her tiny white teeth like Monty Python's Rabbit of Caerbannog. Like something raised in an underground den—which was probably not far from the truth.

"Listen, little girl. We can do this the civilized way, or I can knock you on your ass and do it the other way. Why don't you think about that kid you're carrying?"

"I *am* thinking about him!"

The dark side of Planned Parenthood.

"We need to call for backup," Will said.

He was right, as much as Taylor hated to admit it. This was already way more complicated than he'd anticipated, and transporting a pregnant female prisoner from New Mexico to Los Angeles...

"*No.*" Astonishingly, Hedwig caught his arm. "Please no."

Taylor took advantage of her distraction to grab her right arm, turning her to snap the cuff on her wrist. She began to struggle. "Front or back?" he asked Will.

Will looked blank. "Front or back what?"

"*Cuffing her.* Do I cuff her in front or in back?"

"How should I know? You're the one with the nieces and nephews."

"So far I haven't had to arrest any of them."

William grimaced. "There's protocol on this, right?"

"I assume." He'd also assumed Will would be familiar with the protocol. Will was generally better at dealing with the gentler sex. Not that their prisoner exactly qualified.

Taylor stepped forward, using a standing leg sweep to knock Hedwig's feet out from under her. She overbalanced and dropped down on the bed again, bouncing a little, puffing angrily. She glared up at him as he snapped the second cuff on her.

It had to be the pregnancy thing, because no way should he be feeling anything but cold contempt for this murdering bitch.

"How far along are you?" Will joined them bedside.

She tossed her hair out of her face. "Eight months."

Taylor met Will's eyes. Will shook his head. Taylor sighed. "I'll call for backup," Will said again, and Taylor nodded.

"No. Please no." Hedwig held up her cuffed hands in supplication. "I'll make a deal with you."

"This ought to be good."

"Save your breath," Will told her.

"But I didn't kill that man. You have to believe me. I didn't have anything to do with it. I *swear.*"

"Yeah, yeah," Taylor said. "You weren't even in LA at the time."

"I *wasn't* in LA at the time."

Will already had his cell phone out and was dialing.

Hedwig said desperately, "If you call the police, they'll hand me straight over to the FBI and I'll be killed. And my baby too."

"Someone's been watching the *X-Files* again," Taylor told Will.

Will snorted.

"Anyway, you won't be handed over to the FBI. You'll be handed over to the Marshal Service, who may or may not hand you back to us."

It worried him, though. That…teary-eyed intensity as she gazed up at them. Not that he hadn't known his share of bold-faced liars. Enough so he thought he was pretty good at telling truth from fiction. Believed he had an instinct for it. And it was a silly lie—not being in LA at the time—easily disproved, right? So she'd probably come up with something better if she was alibiing herself. She'd had enough time to think of a stronger story. Seven months.

Hedwig was still pleading, still insisting. "It's the truth. I'm telling you the truth. If you're not going to listen to me, if you're going to drag me back to LA, then at least do yourself a favor and take me in on your own. If you're halfway good at your job, we all might even make it alive." Even with her hands cuffed, she unconsciously, protectively cradled her belly.

It wasn't science, but…

"Brandt, wait."

Will paused, his look watchful.

"We've got her in custody. We don't need local support now. Let's take her back on our own."

Will's expression was pained. "Come on. You don't believe that bullshit about the police and the FBI trying to kill her?"

"No." Taylor said more firmly, "No way. But it won't hurt to be on the safe side."

"Yeah, well I don't think you and me trying to transport her back to LA is on the safe side."

"If she cooperates—"

Will's jaw dropped. He recovered immediately. "Uh, buddy boy…" He glanced at their prisoner, who was tensely following their exchange. "If anything goes wrong…"

"What could go wrong? We're just going to drive up to Sierra Blanca, board a plane with her, and fly back in to Los Angeles."

"Like she goes into labor."

Taylor chewed his lip.

"It'll be our heads on Popsicle sticks."

Taylor nodded. "But what if, just on the off chance, there *is* something to what she's saying?"

"What is she saying? So far all I've heard is the usual *I been framed!*"

"I *was* framed," Hedwig put in.

Will raised his eyebrows.

"Who framed you?" Taylor asked.

"I don't know."

"Oh! Well!" Will gave Taylor an exasperated look.

"If I knew, I'd have given the name up a long time ago," Hedwig protested. "But it's someone at the DEA. I know that for sure."

"Why's that?" asked Will. "Why couldn't it be the FBI? Or the CIA? Or the PTA?"

"Because I was working with the DEA as an informant, and some of the information I had implicated agents at a high level."

The pause that followed her words was filled in by the dogs baying in the kennel behind the house and Ramirez's continuing, though increasingly hoarse, rants from downstairs.

"You're saying there's a mole in the DEA?" Taylor headed off Will's questions.

But Will had another question in mind. "Who were you informing on? Who was the target?"

Hedwig hesitated.

Will's gaze met Taylor's. "Who?" they questioned at the same time.

"Mikhail Bashnakov."

"Who?" Taylor could feel Will's stare.

He said carefully, colorlessly, "Mikhail Bashnakov. The Technician."

"Yes," Hedwig said softly.

There was a flash of white outside the bedroom window, followed by a long rolling boom of thunder. Perfect timing. Pretty funny, in fact. Except...

not. Taylor had the horrifying sensation of having reached his hand into a cookie jar, only to find a coiled rattlesnake.

"Who's Mikhail Bashnakov?" Unlike Taylor, Will made it a policy not to concern himself with crimes that were unrelated to the DS. It was Will's view that their game preserve was stocked with all the bad guys they could ever require—and that was certainly true.

"He's a kingpin in one of the Russian drug cartels," Taylor told him.

Hedwig nodded confirmation.

"Oh. Good." The mildness of that made Taylor's lips twitch. Yeah. No wonder he loved Will.

"Let me see if I have this straight," Will stated. "You were framed for killing a DS director by someone within the DEA who was afraid that your information would implicate him—or her—in the Russian drug trade?"

"Yes. That's what I believe."

"And I believe this is total bullshit."

"What if it's not?" Taylor intervened.

"You keep saying that. What if it *is*?"

"Well, what does it matter in that case? I'm not saying we turn her loose. I'm saying we take her back to LA ourselves. That was the original plan, right? Escort her back to LA?"

"Yes."

"So?"

When Will had no immediate response, Taylor pressed, "So that's what we do. Except we don't advertise the fact that we've picked her up. We just…take her back."

"*Yes*," Hedwig pleaded. "That's all I'm asking. That you take me in yourselves."

"See. I don't trust that." Will nodded at Hedwig's strained face.

"I don't trust it either. That just means we're prepared for anything she might try."

He could see Will struggling with it, but it made sense. Right? This *had* been the plan from the beginning—before Denver PD lost Hedwig in the system. Whatever the hell system that had been. True, the original plan would have supplied them with backup and resources they didn't current-ly have, but if there was a chance that what Hedwig was telling them was true—and Taylor followed the news enough to know there was more than a chance that it was—the best chance of all of them reaching home safe and sound was to slide in under the radar. To make it back to California before anyone knew they'd even located their quarry.

"This is the way you want to play it?" Will asked finally.

Taylor nodded.

"Okay." Will's smile was sour. "Your call. For the record, I think it's a lousy idea."

Will went downstairs to have a friendly chat with Ramirez while Taylor gave Hedwig five minutes to dress and pack an overnight bag. He had no idea what essentials a pregnant woman might need. He'd been overseas during his sister's pregnancies—not that the circumstances were similar, and not that he would have paid attention even if they had been. If their prisoner wanted anything very complicated, she was going to have to do without. Anyway, it was a little over an hour to the airport, and then a short, hope-fully direct flight to Los Angeles. A toothbrush and her spectacles ought to do her, in his opinion.

He kept the door half-open while she dressed, observing impersonally while offering the illusion of privacy.

Downstairs he could hear Ramirez bellowing at Will and Will's qui-et responses. It took a lot to get Will really worked up. Like Will, Taylor wasn't concerned with Ramirez. If he needed persuading to go along with the change in plans, Taylor had no doubt that Hedwig could handle it. She seemed like a resourceful girl, appearances to the contrary. Either that or unbelievably lucky.

The door to the bedroom swung open. Hedwig had changed into jeans and a loose green and white-checked smock thingie. Her hair was tied back in a lank ponytail, and she wore her glasses. She carried a white denim jack-et draped over one arm, and she held a small flat overnight case. She looked like a timid kindergarten teacher. Taylor took the jacket and the overnight case, setting them aside to examine at his leisure.

Hedwig made a scornful sound at this display of suspiciousness.

"Hands behind your head."

"How stupid do you think I am?" she demanded as he briskly patted her down.

"I don't know. How stupid do you think *I* am?"

"*Totally* stupid."

He laughed. "Ask a silly question." He sort of liked the sheer outrageous balls of her. Anyway, he was making double sure, knowing Will would expect this, but he didn't expect—nor did he find—that she'd tried to arm herself while he was looking on. "Sorry, but I have to cuff you again."

"That's not necessary."

"Maybe not, but that's the way we're doing it."

Taylor snapped the cuffs on her wrists again, retrieved her bag and jacket, and nodded for her to precede him down the hall, watching critically as she moved. She didn't have that ungainly pregnant-lady waddle, but no way was she going to be outrunning them. That didn't mean she wouldn't try any other means that presented itself to get rid of them. He would. Anyone would. Yep, it was better to keep her cuffed.

"Did you search her?" Will asked when they reached downstairs.

Taylor assented.

Ramirez was still cuffed. He sat on the floor, glaring out of a puffy eye. Blood crusted his nostrils.

"You okay, *chiquita*?" he asked Hedwig.

She nodded. "I'm so sorry, Reuben. Did they hurt you?"

Ramirez shook his head. "It's my fault. I should have shot this pig when I had the chance. I should have turned the dog on him. I should have—"

"Don't blame yourself, Reuben."

"Cute couple." That was Will.

"Yeah. Reuben and Juliet. You better explain the facts of life to your boyfriend," Taylor told Hedwig.

"He's not my boyfriend."

Will's gaze rolled to meet Taylor's; Taylor could practically hear the casters clicking. "This could take all night."

Taylor ignored that. "Well, whatever Senor Ramirez is, we'd prefer to turn him loose, but if he comes trailing after us, things are going to get messy. If what you've told us is true, the less attention we attract, the better."

Hedwig scowled over this, then rattled off a string of Spanish.

"In English," Will interrupted.

"It's better if I go with them," Hedwig told Ramirez. "Better for everyone."

"They're not cops, chiquita. You can't trust them. They're Feds."

"I know. They're Diplomatic Security."

"Who? What's this Diplomatic Security? I never heard of them."

"I think our PR machine is broken," Taylor told Will.

"If they were part of it, we'd be dead now," Hedwig said. "They're going to take me in themselves."

"Bullshit. Don't trust them, Kelila."

"The trust is all on this side." Will was losing patience. "In fact, if I had my way, you'd be on your way to jail and we'd be handing your girlfriend over to anyone who'd take her."

Taylor couldn't tell if he meant it or not. If Will *really* was dead set against this—well, there was more at stake here than the honor of the DSS or their own professional reputations. More at stake for Will, certainly. But if Will *was* dead set against taking her back themselves, he'd say so. He wasn't one for beating around the bush.

Ramirez was stubbornly shaking his head. Taylor's unease increased. "We can't waste any more time here. Make up your mind."

"Reuben...*please.*"

"Here's what we're going to do," Will said. "I'm going to take the cuffs off you." He was talking to Ramirez. "You're going to get hold of Cujo out there, and then the three of us are walking out of here. If it all goes smoothly, that'll be the end of it. Your part of it, anyway. If you do anything stupid, I'm arresting you and handing you over to the Ruidoso cops for aiding and abetting a fugitive."

Ramirez looked at Hedwig. "It's okay," she said. "Really. Just do what they tell you. Please."

Ramirez was still shaking his head as he rose. He stood sullenly while Will uncuffed him. He didn't like it, but that made it unanimous. So long as he followed orders...

He did. He went to the door and shouted for the dog. It trotted inside, nails ticking on tile, woofing aggressively. Ramirez grabbed its collar and held tight, muttering what he apparently imagined were soothing noises.

Dog and man watched in silence as Will, followed by Hedwig and then Taylor, moved briskly across the exposed yard. The night air smelled of distant pines and approaching rain. The Sierra Blanca Mountains stood silent and silver beneath the scaffolding of clouds and stars.

Man and dog were still silhouetted in the lighted doorway when they reached the road.

Will closed the heavy wooden gate behind them, and they started, still single file, down the dirt road lined with the twisted, tortured forms of Joshua trees. They'd parked the rental car about a mile from the house. It felt like the middle of nowhere, nothing to see but sagebrush and cactus. Lightning flashed overhead like a failing light behind a lavender veil. Thunder boomed and rolled away into the forest-covered mountains.

Beautiful if you liked that kind of thing. Taylor didn't particularly. He was a city boy through and through.

Fortunately it wasn't cold. In fact, despite the threat of rain, it was unseasonably warm for this time of year in the Lincoln National Forest.

The girl, Kelila—no, better to think of her as Hedwig—was breathing fast as they hurried her along the deeply rutted road. Were they pushing her too hard? Speaking for himself, Taylor felt they couldn't get to the car a minute too soon. The vast panorama of the desert, however majestic, made him feel too exposed. Vulnerable.

He was relieved to spot the gleam of the car roof a few yards ahead.

The moon had been out when they'd parked earlier that evening. Now it was too dark to see past the brush and cactus. Still, everything seemed undisturbed.

Several feet from the car, Will swore and stopped in his tracks.

Taylor tensed, his hand automatically rising toward his shoulder holster. "What's wrong?"

"We've got a flat."

Taylor moved past the girl. Sure enough, the right side of the sedan slumped to the side. The front tire was completely flat.

"Hell." He quickly scanned the surrounding landscape. Between the razor-sharp rocks dotting the sand and the wickedly spiked cactus, a flat wasn't impossible, but his disquiet ratcheted up another notch.

Will gave voice to his own thought. "This just keeps getting better and better."

Hedwig laughed, the sound startling in the still night.

Taylor rounded on her. "Why don't we have you change it?"

Will made a faint sound. Something between calming and disapproving.

They returned to studying the tire as though there might be some trick of the light. "Rock, paper, scissors?" suggested Taylor.

"No way. It's your turn to change it."

"That's not how I remember it. Come on, Brandt."

Will sighed, long suffering, and scissored his arm three times. Taylor followed suit.

They both came up with fists.

"I may kill you before the night is over," Will said. "Just so you know."

Taylor laughed.

Once again they sliced the air three times.

Taylor came up rock again, but this time Will chose paper. He laughed at Taylor's chagrin and grazed his chin with a friendly fist. "You're getting predictable, sweetheart."

"Sweetheart?" Hedwig repeated curiously. Taylor had nearly forgotten about her. She leaned against the fender, catching her breath and watching them.

Will tossed the car keys. Taylor caught them one-handed and walked around to the trunk.

"What do you want to bet there's no jack in here?"

He didn't catch Will's muttered response. If there wasn't a jack in the trunk, they were going to have to walk back up the road and borrow

Ramirez's pickup. He could just imagine how well that would go over with all concerned parties, but standing out here waiting for the AAA was not an option.

He unlocked the trunk and raised it. It took his eyes a second to discern what he was seeing in the dark interior—and his brain a few seconds after that to make sense of it.

For the second time that night he was staring down the barrel of a shotgun.

CHAPTER THREE

"**S**o are you *gay*?" Hedwig asked.

The raised hood of the trunk blocked Taylor from Will's view. He half turned, surveyed the mutable shadows ringing them: the jagged outline of mountains, the pale shifts of sand, the black outline of Joshua tree and yucca.

Hedwig's question refocused Will's attention on her. "Because I called him 'sweetheart'?" He infused his tone with amusement, although he wasn't amused. His and Taylor's sexual preferences were not a secret from Uncle Sam. His and Taylor's relationship was. That was to protect their working partnership. Early in their…er…romance, they'd agreed they wanted to keep working together for as long as possible.

Of course, that might be moot now. If he took the posting in Paris.

It was a big *if.*

Wet flicked his face. The first fat drops splattered the hood of the car. It was starting to rain. Naturally. Because a downpour was all that was keeping this from being the perfect evening. The drops came faster, plopping down, dimpling the dust at their feet.

"Because of the way you are together," the girl answered.

Will shrugged. "We've been partners a long time."

She briefly weighed it. "If you weren't together, you'd have just said so. You wouldn't try to explain."

It was the first indication Will had that she might be smarter than the average bimbo.

Motion behind the car caught his attention. Taylor stepped back from behind the slant of the raised lid. His hands were locked behind his head, and even in the poor light, Will could see enough of his profile to know they were in trouble.

"Get down," Will told Hedwig, drawing his pistol.

She dropped into an awkward squat behind the fender.

Will was already scrambling around to the far side of the car, watching as the figure unfolding from behind the trunk door kept getting taller.

Jesus fucking Christ. Taylor was tall, but this guy was a monster. A giant of a man with a Mohawk and a sawed-off shotgun. Will could see his pitted profile in what little hazy light there was. His profile and Taylor's.

Taylor's jaw could have been cut from stone as he said in a flat voice, "You're making a big mistake."

"Shut up." The guy had a very deep voice, distinctive even on those two chopped syllables. Maybe an accent?

The lid of the trunk blocked Will's view of the giant's body. He could try for a head shot, but what he could see of the shotgun barrel was aimed directly at Taylor's forehead. If the guy's finger tightened on the trigger…

Will's palms felt damp. Not a chance he was willing to take if he didn't have to.

Without turning his head, the giant called, "Come around the other side, hombre, if you do not want your partner's brains splattered all over those cactus. And you, *milaya moyna*. You can quit hyperventilating behind the fender and get your skinny ass over here."

"Don't do it," Taylor said.

Will watched the shotgun barrel. It never wavered. The giant said, "You do *not* want to fuck with me."

Definitely an accent. Eastern European? Surely not *Russian*? The guy had one of those basso profundo voices all these oversize dudes seemed to possess. Was that anatomy or showmanship?

"We're federal agents, asshole."

Taylor's voice was cold and clear. Would it kill him to soft-pedal once in a while? As dearly as Will loved his toughness, his sheer grit, sometimes he wondered whether Taylor secretly had a death wish.

"I know. I know you are Feds. I am a Fugitive Recovery Agent."

"You're a what?"

"Bounty hunter," Will supplied automatically.

"That is right. Ioakim Nemov. Licensed by the Colorado Insurance Division of the Department of Regulatory Agencies."

"Colorado? You've been following us since Colorado?"

"That is right. That is exactly right. I followed you, and you led me straight to little Kelila."

Little Kelila sounded like she was getting ready to give birth any second.

"Show some ID," Will said.

"I don't care if you're licensed by the Better Business Bureau," Taylor cut in. "You're going to be under arrest yourself in a minute for interfering in a federal—"

"No. I do not think so," Nemov interrupted. "I have been watching you two hombres. I have been wondering why there are no cops around. No FBI. No one but you two. You know what I think? I think this is a black op."

For the life of him, Will couldn't think of an answer. For once, even Taylor seemed to choose discretion over valor.

Nemov laughed. "I am right! I knew it. When I watched you scale the perimeter wall of the Ramirez property, I knew. Very smooth, that was. Textbook."

"You're Russian mob," Taylor guessed.

"No. Certainly not. What interest would the *bratva* have in this little girl? I have told you who and what I am. Here. I have identification." After a moment, ID was proffered, a wallet being shown to first Taylor, then flashed in Will's direction.

Not that Will could make a damn thing out at this distance, and not that it mattered anyway. ID or not, this guy was flirting with charges for everything from interfering with law enforcement officers to kidnapping. "If you're legitimate, what the hell do you think you're doing?"

Taylor said slowly, "He's after the RFJ."

The Rewards for Justice Program. That's what Taylor meant. Nemov was after the five million dollar reward the Bureau of Diplomatic Security offered to those with information leading to the arrest or conviction of anyone who planned, committed, or attempted terrorist acts against US persons or property.

One problem with that plan: the RFJ program was designed to prevent international attacks. Not domestic.

Maybe not the best time to bring that up.

"That's only for international terrorist acts, dumb shit," Taylor said.

"But Kelila is married to a Russian national," Nemov said, unperturbed. "Her strike against the DSS was masterminded by none other than Mikhail Bashnakov."

"That's not true!" Hedwig said shrilly. "That's insane. None of it is true."

Will turned on her. "You're not married to Bashnakov?"

"Yes. All right, that part is correct, but—"

"That's something you left off the CV." He hadn't thought that drug lords bothered with polite conventions like marriage.

"No way are you collecting that reward," Taylor said. "She's already in federal custody."

"She was. Now she's in my custody. Get over here, milaya moyna. I won't ask so nicely again."

If only the bastard would look away from Taylor long enough for Taylor to make a move for cover. But Nemov was too experienced.

"Don't let him…take me," Hedwig panted, clinging to the front bumper like an old-fashioned suffragette.

"He's not taking you anywhere," Taylor said.

He had to speak up to be heard over the rain now rattling loudly off the surface of the car and pouring to the ground. At this rate, they were going to be mired in mud.

"Let me explain your options," Nemov said. "Or rather my options. Option one. I give up and go home. That is not going to happen. Option two—"

"My partner blows your head off while we're standing here shooting the breeze."

That was Will's order to shoot. That was Taylor telling him as clearly as he could to *take the shot*. And Will could do it. He had about as clear a shot as he was going to get, and he was an excellent marksman. But there was still the chance that Nemov's dying reflex would be to blow Taylor's head off.

Nemov laughed. "I think your partner is not so reckless as you, little man. He knows it will be very hard to explain away two bodies—especially if one of them is yours. I think he will wait to hear option three."

Will said, "Which is?"

Taylor was apparently still trying to absorb "little man."

"I take the girl and deliver her safely to Los Angeles, and we all forget about this unpleasantness. No good can come to any of us if word of tonight's showdown gets out. True?"

"You've got to be kidding me," Taylor said. "You think we're going to hand her over and let you walk away?"

"Yes. Why not?"

"No. Way."

But Will was already convinced. They had to end this standoff. Get themselves into strategic position. Let Nemov take Hedwig. Worst-case scenario, they'd have the cops pick them both up at Sierra Blanca. But better yet, they'd overtake them on the way to the airport, retrieve Hedwig, and continue on to LA. If it was true that he and Taylor couldn't afford to let anyone know about this evening's activities, it was equally true Nemov couldn't.

"Deal," Will said.

Hedwig cried out. Taylor looked his way in disbelief.

Nemov laughed. "What did I tell you? Your partner is a practical man."

"Brandt—"

"He's got a fucking gun to your head, MacAllister. Now is not the time."

Nemov said, "Throw your weapon away, Agent Brent."

Will tossed his weapon to the sand.

Nemov made a sound of disgust. "Now kick it away where you cannot grab it quickly."

Will kicked his piece farther away.

"Now clasp your hands behind your head and stand up slowly."

"You can't let him just take me!" Hedwig cried as Will complied.

Will spared her a look. He'd lost whatever sympathy he had for her—pretty much nil—at the news that she'd been married to the Technician, but she was his prisoner and he had a sworn duty to protect her. He reassured himself he was only temporarily relinquishing custody, but he didn't like what he was doing. He was furious at being placed in the position of having to choose between her and his partner, but there was no question in his mind whose life was more important.

"Just calm down and do what he says. You'll be fine."

"I *won't* be fine. He's been sent to kill me."

"If that was the case, I'd have shot this agent when he opened the trunk," Nemov pointed out. "Then I'd have shot Agent Brent, and then I'd have shot you."

Was that option four? Judging by the way he trotted out the scenario, Nemov had clearly been considering wholesale slaughter as a possible game plan.

Of course, if Nemov believed Will and Taylor would be willing to sacrifice one terrorist skank to preserve their careers, he might plan on executing Hedwig once he had her on his own. That saved him a potential gun battle and the risk of the DS coming after him following the inevitable full-scale manhunt that would result from the murder of two agents.

"Now you," Nemov told Taylor. "Slowly."

Taylor obeyed, unspeaking. The fact that he was unspeaking was a very bad sign, but there was nothing Will could do about that now. In some ways Taylor was as direct as an arrow to the heart. It was possible he was never going to understand—Will wasn't sure *he* understood—the choice Will had just made. But Will couldn't stand by and see Taylor die. Not if there was any chance in hell of avoiding it.

"Get your cuffs out."

"They're on the girl."

"Oh? Agent Brent. Take your cuffs out and walk over here. The right side of the car, please."

"My right or yours?"

Nemov chuckled. "I like you, Agent Brent. You are of a pragmatic nature. As is Nemov."

Will walked around the front of the car, passing Hedwig, who was crying quietly. He joined Taylor in front of the sawed-off shotgun.

Taylor didn't look at him. Will clenched his jaw against the protest, the explanations. In the end there was nothing to say, no excuse, and—for him—no choice.

"Cuff yourself to your partner."

Still not looking at Will, Taylor shoved his arm forward, offering the lower part of his forearm.

Good thinking, MacAllister.

But it was a no-go. Nemov said, "Uh-uh. I know that trick. He has skinny arms, your partner. Make sure the cuff is tight around the wrist."

In stony silence, Will snapped the cuff around Taylor's bony wrist. Will clicked the metal circlet around his own wrist, joining them.

"Keys to the handcuffs?"

Will handed them over.

Nemov smiled at Taylor. With tight, quick movements, Taylor used his free hand to pull his ID out and awkwardly remove the key from behind his badge.

"You are the wily one, yes? Not so wily as Nemov, though." Nemov took the key with every appearance of good humor. "Throw the car keys as far as you can. And do not throw like a little girl."

Taylor gave Nemov a baleful look, felt around for the keys in his Levi's, dangled them fleetingly in front of Nemov's long nose, and then hurled them with ferocious energy across the yucca and Spanish bayonet. They glinted as they fell like a shooting star.

"Nice. You play baseball, I bet. All right, milaya moyna. Time to go."

Footsteps dragging, Hedwig came slowly around the car.

"Just do what he says," Will told her. "You'll be okay." He felt he was speaking as much to Taylor as Hedwig.

"Listen to Agent Brent. He is a smart man."

Will couldn't seem to tear his gaze from Taylor's averted face.

"Start walking," Nemov ordered. "I will be right behind you."

Hedwig stumbled past them and started up the increasingly muddy dirt trail.

Nemov said quietly, "Now, my young friends, you find out what teamwork is really about. Take my advice. Forget about Kelila Hedwig. If anyone asks, tell them you followed a cold trail. She was gone by the time you found Ramirez's. No need to wreck your careers over this, you will agree."

A pulse jumped in Taylor's temple, but to Will's relief, he restrained himself.

Nemov backed away, keeping the shotgun trained on them until his tall figure dissolved into the darkness. They could hear his quick stride down the road as he followed Hedwig.

Taylor swung on Will. "What the hell were you thinking?" he half whispered. "For God's sake, Will. You *surrendered* your weapon—"

"I know what I did."

"You let him take our prisoner."

"I know."

"You allowed him to take you hostage."

"I know."

Will's quiet response seemed to confuse Taylor. He peered at Will through the rain-swept gloom. "I don't get it. Help me understand. *How* could you do that?"

Will shook his head.

Taylor's voice rose again. "Goddamn it. It's not only against agency policy and training, it's against common sense."

"I don't need to hear this from you. Not right now."

"Will…" Will could practically see the wheels turning. Taylor said, "He was *not* going to shoot me."

Despite Will's determination not to defend his decision, he heard himself arguing, "You don't know that. My instinct is he *would* have shot you. Maybe he wouldn't have killed you, but he was ready to shoot you."

"Then you'd have shot him, right?"

It took a second to work past the sweeping obliviousness of that. "Right. You'd *still* be dead."

"Your way, we *both* could have been dead. And the girl too. It's totally against policy, and you damn well know it."

"Don't *you* throw policy at me."

"Anyway, there's no way he'd have shot a federal officer."

"Of course not. That *never* happens."

"For Christ sake, Will. The fact that I got shot once—"

"*Twice.*" Will said fiercely, "I've seen you take a bullet *twice.*"

"You didn't even see it the first time!"

"What the…? Like that makes a difference? I saw the *result*, Taylor. I saw you lying there in what looked like a lake of your own blood. I saw you choking, trying to breathe with a hole in your lung."

The anger drained out of Taylor. "Will," he said helplessly. "You've got to let it go. We've talked about this. You can't make decisions in the field based on my safety."

He was right. About all of it. Which was one reason Will had never wanted their relationship to move from friends to lovers. But that was ancient history. They *were* lovers, and there was no going back from it. Not for Will. Not now.

"Like you wouldn't have done the same goddamned thing?"

Taylor's expression—what Will could see of it—was decidedly weird. "No. I wouldn't have."

He could hear the rain pattering off the stiff material of their vests. "You don't—" Will stopped. "Look. This *isn't* the time."

The rumble of a car's engine drifted across the distance.

"Come on." Will started to move in the direction Taylor had thrown the car keys. "I hope you took time to pick a landmark."

Taylor didn't budge, and the steel tether yanked Will back. He whipped around, his temper suddenly soaring. Maybe it was true that there was nothing he feared as much as losing Taylor, but for one blazing instant, he was ready to kill his partner himself.

If Taylor saw his anger, he gave no sign. He said mildly, "I didn't throw the car keys."

"What? I saw you."

"I threw my own keys, not the rental car keys."

Will stared at him and then, surprising himself, started to laugh. "You're kidding."

Taylor shook his head. He reached into his pocket, dragging Will's hand along as he wiggled his fingers, feeling for the rental keys. The denim was stiff and already wet through from the rain, making the body beneath seem warmer than ever. Warm. Alive. No, Will could not regret any decision that kept Taylor living and breathing. Even if that decision ultimately cost him Taylor.

"Got 'em." Taylor held the plastic fob up triumphantly.

"Nice going." Will meant it.

"Thanks. You can pay for the rekey of my house."

Will ignored that. "Now we just need to get rid of the bracelets. I've got an extra set of handcuff keys in my luggage."

"Back at the hotel? How's that's going to help?"

"Hey, I'm open to suggestion. Unless the suggestion is you want to shoot the cuffs off."

"It works in the movies." Taylor was moving along the road, searching for his pistol. Will was forced to follow.

"I hope you're kidding."

Taylor grunted. He squatted down to retrieve his pistol, and Will was forced to squat too, watching as Taylor dusted off the clumping sand.

"Nice of him to leave us these. We'd have a hell of a time explaining how we *both* lost our pieces." Taylor shoved the pistol into his shoulder holster.

"No kidding." Will met Taylor's eyes. "Hey."

Taylor was silent.

"Just so you know, if I have to be shackled to someone, I'd choose you. Every time."

He saw the glimmer of Taylor's teeth as he curled his lip in something that was not exactly a smile. "Just a wild and crazy romantic, aren't you, Agent Brent?"

"Yep, little man, I am."

Taylor gave him a friendly shove, and they both nearly overbalanced.

Maybe the camaraderie was a little forced, but it helped ease the strain between them. Dusting off their hands, they went to retrieve Will's weapon.

He found his SIG Sauer P229 a few feet from the car. Wincing at the thought of grit working its way into the mechanism, he wiped away as much wet and sand as he could with the tail of his T-shirt. He reholstered the pistol with a feeling of relief.

"I lost my pen," Taylor said. "Do you have yours?"

Will felt around, handed his pen over.

Taylor held it up. "I can't *see* anything."

"What is it you need to see? Because unless you're planning on writing your resignation, we need to get out of here pronto."

"I know. Let's get in the car."

"Uh, don't we need to change the tire first?"

"First we need to get out of these cuffs, but I have to be able to see what I'm doing."

"What *are* you doing?" Will inquired as they unlocked the car. Taylor crawled in first, followed by Will, who slid beneath the wheel. The pine tree-shaped deodorizer swayed gently, its artificial scent mingling with that of wet clothes and desert rain.

"I'm going to make a shim and pick this lock." With his free hand, Taylor reached up and turned on the dome lamp. Pallid light illuminated his face. For a second, Will stared at him, stared at a face he knew as well as his own: the wide, long-lashed green eyes, the full, sensual mouth, the silver streak in the dark hair starting to curl with the damp.

Unaware of his scrutiny, Taylor was busily taking the pen apart, prying the silver clip from the body. "Hold your wrist up."

"I don't recall lock picking as part of my FLETC training."

Taylor grinned faintly as he slid the piece of dismantled pen between the teeth and the mechanism of the cuffs. There were goose bumps on his brown, thinly muscled forearms. The tip of his tongue touched his upper lip. Will felt an inappropriate longing to pull him into his arms and hold him for a moment.

Possibly more than a moment. And possibly do more than just hold Taylor. But definitely inappropriate.

Taylor levered the shim, wiggled it, pushed, and the teeth of the lock, thrown out of alignment, clicked over. The cuff opened. He smiled broadly.

Will rubbed his wrist. "Nice job, MacGyver."

"Thanks. Now me." He frowned, trying to crane his head to see the lock mechanism properly.

"Someday you're going to have to tell me where you learned some of these esoteric skills of yours."

"Boy Scouts."

"You weren't in the Boy Scouts."

"True. I knew one or two, though." He spared a wink for Will. "Hold that cuff out of the way."

Will obeyed.

It took a little longer, but in another minute or so, Taylor too was free.

Will expelled a long sigh of relief. They were back in action. Hopefully not too late to fix this fucked-up operation. "Let's get that tire changed."

Taylor tossed the broken pen into the cup holder. "Roger that."

"And then," said Will, yanking open the car door again, "we're going to knock that goddamned giant off his goddamned beanstalk."

CHAPTER FOUR

The rain lashing out of the darkness and streaming in rivulets down the windshield looked white-blue in the artificial glare of the headlights. The wipers could barely keep up. Ahead of them, the narrow road was a winding, slick ribbon of night. The hills around them were shapeless black bulk.

Eyes intent on the muddy road ahead, Taylor was glad Will had elected to drive. He'd rarely seen worse weather conditions outside of Japan. "God almighty. What is with this rain? It's summer."

The car lagged as Will shifted into a lower gear. "We're in the mountains. And July is the rainy season."

"Great. On the upside, they can't be making much better time than we are."

Will, his attention on the winding road ahead, grunted.

Taylor glanced at the dashboard: 3:18. It was beginning to feel like the longest night in his life. He refocused on the screen of his BlackBerry GPS—essentially useless at the moment thanks to the lack of steady signal. Happily he could still read a map, and the BlackBerry was at least serving as a light for his navigating.

"Sierra Blanca Regional Airport is northwest of here. It looks like it's just over an hour."

"Okay. What am I looking for?"

"West Smokey Bear Boulevard." He looked up from the map to stare at the nightmare landscape swinging past as Will sped along the canyon road. "Jesus, I believe it. It's like the Black Forest through here."

"City boy."

Taylor acknowledged it without resentment. "You know, no way is Nemov going to try and drag her on a plane. He can't depend on us not going for help."

Will threw him a somber look. "No?"

"Okay. Maybe he can. But I still don't think he's going to make for the airport. Not the local airport anyway. I think he'll go for one of the larger, busier airports. Somewhere he's guaranteed a direct flight to Los Angeles."

Will mulled it over. "Agreed."

"So…Albuquerque? He's going to travel back roads for as long as possible. At least till he's sure he's lost us."

"*If* he's taking her to LA. He could have been lying about that. Maybe he'll take her back to Denver."

"True." Taylor hadn't considered that possibility and wasn't any happier for having it pointed out.

Will's jaw clenched still tighter, but he didn't respond. Watching him, Taylor said, "Listen…if this all goes south—or further south—I'll take full responsibility."

"Why would you?"

"Snatching her from Ramirez was my call, and it was a bad call. We should have sent for backup the minute we located her. You would have if you'd been on your own. I fucked up."

"You didn't hold a gun to my head. We both fucked up. Now we've got to fix it. Fast."

"Right. I just…want you to know that whatever happens, I won't let it mess up your promotion."

Will looked away from the road long enough to offer a disbelieving face. "Not this again. I already told you—"

"That you're not sure you'll accept the Paris tour. I know."

"I haven't decided anything."

Taylor nodded. Realizing Will probably couldn't see that gesture, he said again, "I know."

"Really? Because every time this comes up, you make it sound like a foregone conclusion that I'm going."

"No."

"I *haven't* made my mind up either way."

"Yeah. Well…"

"Well what?"

He couldn't tell him, but that was part of what hurt: the fact that Will was seriously weighing taking this overseas assignment.

"It's just…ironic. I guess. We knew one of us would get marching orders, but—"

"We thought it would be you."

"Yeah."

Taylor was the senior agent and due for promotion, and he'd been back in the States longer than Will. Four years now. But in June, Will had been part of a protection detail for the French president's wife during her stay in Southern California. Apparently he'd made such a favorable impression that a request had come through the highest channels that he be invited to fill a vacancy at the embassy in Paris.

Taylor summoned his energy and hoped any lack of enthusiasm would be put down to natural fatigue. "It's a big honor, and it's an incredible opportunity. A *hell* of an opportunity."

"So you keep saying."

"And I'm proud of you. Happy for you."

Except…

Except it would mean Will would be posted in Paris for a minimum of two years.

Two years apart.

"But?"

"There is no *but*. I'm happy for you. I'm proud of you." The more he insisted, the less sincere he sounded, and he was afraid Will could hear it.

There was an uncomfortable pause.

"Right. *But* if you'd been offered the assignment, you'd have refused it."

The bitterness of Will's tone shocked Taylor silent for an instant. And then he was angry.

"Yeah. I would've." No question in his mind. Taylor had already thought it through, and he'd decided that if he couldn't avoid another overseas tour, he'd resign. Leaving a job he loved was obviously the final recourse. He was pretty sure that with his excellent record and history of foreign service, he'd be able to postpone another overseas assignment for a couple more years, until he and Will were on more stable ground.

"Bullshit."

The fierceness of Will's denial shut him up. He shouldn't have brought it up in any case, least of all now. But the unfairness still rankled. That *was* the way Taylor would have played it, whether Will wanted to believe it or not. Taylor was trying very hard to be supportive of Will—which meant fighting his own worst instincts. It'd be nice to get a little credit.

"Fine. Forget I said anything."

"Sure. No problem."

He could hear the controlled anger vibrating in Will's voice. Unlike Taylor, it took a lot to rile Will, so he was obviously feeling self-righteous. Maybe Taylor really was in the wrong here. The promotion was Will's, and Will wanted it. Of course he did. Taylor couldn't blame him for that. It was a plum assignment, and there was no telling where it might ultimately lead. In fact, if it wasn't for his relationship with Taylor, Will would probably have accepted the minute he'd been offered the tour.

Nor had Will been with the service long enough to be as sure declining an overseas posting wouldn't have a detrimental effect on his career.

There was every reason to accept—and only one to decline. And Taylor knew he was a selfish bastard for even thinking Will should put their still-tentative relationship first. At least he hadn't committed the cardinal sin of asking. Not in so many words, anyway.

He said, trying to undo some of the damage, "Look, I don't know how we got off on this. All I meant to say was…I don't want your choices to be limited because of what we did here tonight."

"Don't worry about it. I make my own decisions." Will scowled, concentrating on the storm-swept road.

True enough, but Taylor knew he'd dragged Will along on this New Mexico detour. Left to his own recognizance, Will would have played this by the book and Kelila Hedwig would now be safely in custody and on her way back to Los Angeles.

For a few minutes, the only sound was the *hiss* of tires on wet road and the beat of the windshield wipers. There was no sign of taillights anywhere in the darkness stretching ahead.

"I believed her," Taylor said, thinking aloud. "Believed her…fear that she wouldn't make it back to LA alive. I read genuine terror there."

It was satisfying, even reassuring, the way Will instantly returned to business as though their earlier argument had never occurred. "That could have been fear of what she's facing in LA."

"Yeah. Fair enough."

And if Hedwig had been telling the truth, maybe Nemov was tasked with making sure she never reached her destination.

He felt rather than saw Will look his way again. "Hey. I trust your instincts, MacAllister." There was an apology of sorts in there.

Taylor nodded.

"Although you've got to get over this notion that you're bulletproof."

Taylor snorted.

Will reached over, found his hand, and squeezed briefly before steadying the wheel once more. "It'll be okay. We got into this together. We'll get out of it together."

Taylor nodded, already missing that hard, warm hold. Will had been making more of these physical gestures lately. It was one reason Taylor was pretty sure Will was taking the Paris job, even if he didn't know it himself yet.

"Any sign of that sonofabitch ahead of us?"

They crested another rise in the road. Taylor scanned the ink-washed world. "No." He returned to studying the map by the light of his BlackBerry. "If he avoids the main highways—and he will because he thinks we'll be looking for him to take the fastest route possible—it should take him over four hours to get to Albuquerque. Probably more in this weather."

"Assuming he thinks as logically as you."

They were both silent as the car seemed to sway, buffeted by a gust of rain, before Will corrected. Visibility was increasingly bad.

Taylor said evenly, "So once we find West Smokey Bear Boulevard, we'll follow it for about twenty miles."

"Jesus Christ."

Taylor's head jerked up. He stared out the windshield, trying to make sense of what he was seeing. A tree seemed to be flying out of the darkness and down the road toward them. The next instant, he realized the uprooted tree was in front of a wall of brown water rushing their way.

Flash flood. He'd read about them, seen their aftermath on the nightly news, but he'd never witnessed that sheer destructive capability firsthand. The little he knew was enough to freeze his brain.

In what felt like slow motion, he watched Will wrench the wheel to send the car skating off the road and sliding across the shoulder, heading for the tree-studded hillside. The earth was soft and muddy on the shoulder, and Taylor felt the front tires sink, felt them spinning. Will swore, cut the gas, gunned the motor, then took his foot off the accelerator again. Miraculously, through that alternating on and off of gas and neutral position, they gained traction.

Where the hell were they going?

The car shot forward, bumping and grinding up the grassy slope, ripping out saplings and brush as they went.

They were traveling at a diagonal, the hillside grade too sharp to permit a straight approach.

"Come on, baby." Will gritted the words out as they plowed through a dense thicket of coarse shrubbery.

Taylor realized he hadn't taken a breath since they'd left the main highway. He looked past Will and saw a brown river tumbling just a few feet below them—where no river had previously existed.

The car's chassis slammed down on what felt like solid rock. The transmission screeched. The tires spun. They dragged forward another yard and lurched to a stop. The car balanced precariously, the left side tilting downhill. A pine cone hit the windshield and bounced away. It was followed by a tree branch.

"That's not good."

Taylor wasn't aware of speaking until Will, staring down the hillside at the rapidly rising water, released a startled choke of laughter and turned back to him. "You think? We've got to get to higher ground."

"You can't drive any farther up this slope." It seemed to Taylor that Will had defied gravity to get this far.

"No. We'll have to climb. Move it." Will pointed. "Your side."

Taylor shoved the door open against the wind and rain beating down. He crawled out, then held the door, reaching back for Will. Will scooted gingerly across the gearbox and then froze, his knee planted in the passenger seat.

Did the car slide a few inches? Taylor couldn't tell, but it was only too likely. "Hurry the hell up, Brandt." His hand locked on Will's, and he hauled with all his strength. Will scrabbled out to stand beside him, breathing hard.

The muddy water was steadily rising. Taylor could make out the murky tide through the pelting rain. He stared, fascinated, as the water crept still higher. How could it move so fast?

"Climb." Will punched him on the shoulder.

Taylor obeyed, turning to climb.

His boots slipped in the pine needles and mud. He grabbed for a low-hanging branch, used it to support himself till he could wrap an arm around a narrow tree trunk. Will was right on his heels.

They left the trees and clambered up a few unsheltered feet. Taylor leaned into the wind and half crawled, half staggered forward. The wet stung his face and knocked the breath out of him. This was July? It felt like December.

A tree branch slapped him in the cheek as they reached another stand. His skin was so numb he barely felt it. What had happened to all that sultry, sodden heat?

Another branch hit him, and he swore. The wind snatched his words away.

Taylor trudged on, slithering every few feet, clutching boulders, branches, jutting roots, anything to keep moving. A quick glance over his shoulder showed the paved road below submerged beneath maybe sixteen feet of water that seemed to boil through the canyon curves like a soup of boulders and tree trunks and pieces of house siding.

Their car had slid back a few feet and was leaning still more alarmingly. It wouldn't take much to send it toppling down into that flood.

Vaguely, he wondered if Will had bothered to take out insurance on the rental. It seemed a trivial concern at the moment, merely a point of curiosity.

"Keep moving." Will threw the words at him.

Unnecessarily. Taylor might be a city boy, but he was survivalist enough to know that even six inches of water could knock a man off his feet. A foot of water could float a car. The water he saw below them? That much water could wash a small town away.

He continued up the wet hillside, grateful as the trees grew denser, offering a little respite from the wind and wet at last. By then his muscles were burning and he was drenched in sweat, a sobering reminder that if they weren't in peak physical condition, they'd probably be dead.

After what felt like an eternity, Taylor reached the top of the hill, huddling beneath the dripping branches. He dropped back against the rough trunk of a pine tree and closed his eyes.

Will, shaking with cold and exertion, crawled beside him. Taylor opened his eyes, acknowledging Will's presence, then closed them again and concentrated on catching his breath.

"Too close," Will huffed, sounding equally out of breath. "That was too...damned close. You okay?"

Taylor coughed, nodded, and wearily raised his eyelashes. "You?"

Will nodded.

"That was..." Words failed him. He stared at what he could see of Will's face. "Among other things, that was the best goddamned driving I ever saw in my life."

Will laughed shakily, acknowledging what a close call they'd had. Not like their jobs weren't plenty dangerous enough without Mother Nature getting into the act.

He reached out, hauled Taylor awkwardly into his arms. For a few seconds, the world narrowed down to the hard breaths, to the hard, shaken pound of their hearts through wet clothes, to the hard grip of arms.

Taylor's wet face was pressed to Will's; their breath warmed each other's faces. "It could have been worse."

"I'll say."

"It could have been my car we left on that mountain."

Will gave a half laugh. They moved apart enough to study each other.

The night was fading. It was too early to be called dawn yet, but Taylor could just make out the outline of Will's weary, unshaven face. His deep blue eyes were the only color in the gray world of rain and shadows.

Will leaned in, and his mouth covered Taylor's, rough but sweet, his tongue seeking Taylor's. Taylor opened willingly to that kiss, forgetting for a second his scratched, scraped hands and the rain running down the back of his neck. They kissed a lot these days, especially for men who had never been much for kissing. Taylor had become expert in all Will's kisses, from the hungry, lustful kisses that always made his own cock rise so fast it hurt, to the tender, almost cherishing kisses that Will generally saved for when he thought Taylor was sleeping. That dawn kiss beneath the pine trees rippled through him like an electric shock, a reminder that, tired, wet, and lost as they might be, so long as they were together, they were all right.

Better than all right. Much better.

CHAPTER FIVE

They parted reluctantly.

"Now what?" Taylor asked.

"Now we try to find someone with a working phone."

"Well, that shouldn't take long. Ranger Rick is probably on his way to pick us up right this minute."

Will recognized that little sarcastic note as a sure sign Taylor's nerves were fraying fast. Not that he blamed him. Taylor didn't like the great outdoors when everything was going beautifully.

Things were not going beautifully.

"There are homes and campsites sprinkled all through these mountains," he reassured Taylor. "We'll find someone. Worst-case scenario, we wait till we run into the emergency vehicles and rescue teams that'll be combing the area before long."

Taylor shivered. "There were pieces of broken houses in that flood."

"I know. It channeled right through the canyon, though. And a lot of those structures are vacation homes, not permanent residences. It could have been a lot worse. Especially at a different time of night."

"Do you think Nemov got caught in that?" It was a pointless question since Will had no more way of knowing the answer to that than did Taylor. But he understood Taylor's anxiety. The knowedge that Kelila Hedwig and her unborn child might have died as an indirect result of their failure to report her whereabouts the minute they discovered where she was holed up...

That was something Will didn't want to contemplate.

He said quietly, "I don't know. We don't know for sure they even came this way."

"True."

Will gazed up through the tree branches at the gray flannel skies. He looked back at Taylor, who was chewing at a ragged thumbnail and scowling. Will smiled faintly. For all his pale weariness, the little lines of stress and worry, Taylor alive and in one piece was still the most beautiful thing Will had ever seen.

"Good news," Will told him.

Taylor directed a skeptical look his way.

"It's stopped raining."

* * * * *

According to Taylor's watch, it was after six in the morning by the time they started down the far side of the mountain and found the black SUV mired in mud up to its custom rims.

By then the rain had stopped and the water had receded considerably. The canyon road was a knee-high swamp of debris and water, but the danger was past.

"It could be anyone's vehicle," Will called as Taylor splashed through the water to peer through the tinted side windows.

"Sure," Taylor said. "Who doesn't go on vacation without taking their leg irons?"

Will joined him in the water-filled ruts at the side of the road, making a frame for his face and trying to see inside. "Are you sure?" He could just make out a baseball bat, what looked like a military utility bag, and, yes, metallic links that appeared to be leg shackles. "Hmm. You just might be right."

"I guess someone could have kinky tastes."

"You ought to know."

Taylor grimaced.

"Which is one of the things I like best about you," Will added.

"Just a born diplomat, aren't you? No wonder you're climbing through the ranks."

Will had no reply to that. They sloshed through the water and clambered back to the relatively dry area of the hillside.

A flash of blue caught Will's eye. A blue jay landed on the branch of a pine tree and greeted the morning with its harsh song. The sun was rising, and it was already growing warm. The receding floodwater had a dank, unhealthy smell to it.

Taylor wiped his forehead. "Which way do you think they went?"

"Assuming they aren't lost or didn't get swept away, they'll be heading the same direction we are. They need food, water, and shelter, the same as us."

"Hedwig couldn't climb these mountains. Could she?"

Will shrugged. "I guess if she had to, she would. I've seen pregnant weight lifters. In magazines."

"She didn't look like the athletic type to me."

"Maybe Nemov carried her. He looked like he could."

"He looked like he could carry his SUV. I don't know why he didn't." Taylor had his BlackBerry out and was clicking away and frowning at the results. Or lack of same.

"You're not going to get any reception down here."

Taylor muttered something uncomplimentary, though whether to the national forest or Will was unclear.

They began to walk, continuing at a brisk pace until the sun appeared over the trees. There wasn't a cloud in the sky. Pine needles glistened and sparkled in the pure sunlight.

"You have to admit this is beautiful country," Will said, shading his eyes and gazing up at the distant snowcapped mountains.

Taylor opened his mouth—though it was unlikely he was going to admit anything of the kind—when something big, mottled brown and gray burst out of the brush and took wing, gobbling in fright.

He jumped a foot and gazed openmouthed at Will. *"Jesus.* What was *that?"*

Will dropped against a tree trunk and tried not to laugh. He didn't really have the breath to spare, but Taylor's half-alarmed, half-offended expression struck him as hysterically funny.

"Wild turkey. A hen, I think. You should see the size of the toms."

"No thanks. I prefer my turkeys on a Thanksgiving platter."

Again, Will had to struggle not to laugh.

They resumed their hike, having found what looked like an old track. Possibly a former stagecoach route. It paralleled the highway for a time and then led up into the hills. It was Will who spotted the two sets of footprints in the mud. One large, one smaller.

"That answers one question. They both made it out of the flash flood."

Taylor nodded. He looked as relieved as Will felt. "They'll have holed up somewhere ahead of us on the trail. No way did he drag a pregnant woman up and down a mountainside in the middle of a rainstorm at night—even if he wanted to. She'd never have made it."

"Maybe he doesn't need her to make it."

Taylor stared at him, thinking it over. He shook his head. "In that case, I think he'd have taken advantage of the flood to arrange a fatal accident. Plenty of opportunity. Especially if he left her handcuffed. Get her halfway up the slope and then give her a little push. Oops."

"You worry me sometimes."

"Good." Taylor grinned a brief and dangerous grin.

"I think you're right. If he got this far, he must have been working like hell to do it."

They continued to work their way up the rough track, keeping an eye out for signs that they might be closing in on Nemov.

"I didn't think turkeys could fly," Taylor said suddenly, seemingly still brooding over his close encounter with the local inhabitants. "You don't think there are bears or anything out here?"

"No way," said Will, who did absolutely think this state forest had bears, mountain lions, rattlesnakes, and a whole lot of other critters Taylor didn't need to know about.

He bit back a smile, thinking of their one and only camping trip in April. He'd heard Taylor's story about his run-in with a bear a couple of times. He loved that story. It was classic Taylor.

He studied Taylor's wide shoulders and trim Levi's-clad butt as he scrambled agilely up a natural staircase of lichen-covered boulders. Watching him, Will was hit by a wave of affection—hell, of tenderness—that almost brought him to a halt.

He moved quickly to catch up to Taylor, falling into step beside him.

"Hey."

Taylor shot him a sidewise look. "Hey."

"You know…I mean, I *know* you know this, but I just want to say it in case… If I do take the assignment in Paris, it doesn't mean that we're not still together."

"Other than the six thousand miles between us."

"Five thousand six hundred and sixty-one miles."

"But who's counting."

"MacAllister…Taylor…I'm not leaving *you*. I still want everything we talked about. I just…we're just talking about postponing it for a little while."

"Two years. Minimum."

Will caught Taylor's arm, bringing him to a halt. "I want this. I've worked hard for it."

Taylor sucked in a sharp breath and then let it out slowly. "I know you do. I know you have."

"It's not about us. I haven't changed my mind about us. I never will."

The difficult part was watching how hard Taylor worked to hide his feelings, how hard he was trying to be fair about this. Will wasn't sure he'd be that noble. He wanted to think he would, but he'd wondered how they— how *he*—would adjust when Taylor got his next overseas posting. It shook him that Taylor seemed so sure he'd turn such a posting down. How could he be sure when he had no idea what the assignment would be? And yet Will believed him. One thing he'd learned through the years: if Taylor said he would do something, it was as good as done.

"I…just don't see why I can't have both these things. We're not the first couple to have to deal with a long-distance relationship."

"I know."

"It's only two years. Look how fast the last five months have gone by."

"I know."

"We'll spend our vacations together."

"Yep."

"We'll spend every possible minute together. I promise you that."

"Yep. You know it."

"We'll…work it out."

"We will." Taylor nodded. His mouth was firm and smiling, his eyes miserable.

Abruptly, Will let him go and turned to lead the way down the path.

* * * * *

It was Taylor who noticed the thin white trail of smoke drifting from the ruins of what had once been Hoskin's Store.

A quarter of a mile back, they had passed through the remnant of an old graveyard, silvered wooden markers with names faded out by sun and rain, so, even before they spotted the first crumbling adobe structure, they'd known they were close to one of the ghost towns that dotted these mountains.

After the discovery of the graveyard, they'd stuck mostly to cover where they could find it. The sun was up by then, and the mist had cleared. They'd spotted helicopters in the blue distance, but nothing within signaling range. The National Guard and FEMA would have their hands full with the more populated areas, at least for the next couple of hours.

Taylor, who was in the lead again, raised his hand, gesturing to Will. Will acknowledged with a curt nod, and they split up, each taking a side of the wide, weedy dirt lane that was all that remained of Main Street.

There was nothing left of the majority of the buildings but gaping holes in the ground and rubble. Antique timber and genuine adobe had a way of disappearing from abandoned towns like this, only to turn up on trendy new construction sites.

Hoskin's Store was the tallest remaining structure, and it was mostly just a foundation and three walls of white-painted brick. Not much of a shelter, but any port in a storm, Will supposed.

They moved quickly through the wreckage of the few broken buildings until they had positioned themselves outside the foundation of the store.

In the intersecting far corner of the two standing walls, Nemov knelt over a small fire. His trusty shotgun leaned against the wall within reach. A bedraggled Hedwig was huddled close to the feeble flames. She wore a jacket that was too big to belong to anyone but Nemov.

Taylor signaled to Will. Will signaled back and drew his weapon. He trained it on Nemov, who was busily throwing handfuls of what looked like bird's nests into the fire.

"Morning," Will said laconically, stepping out from behind the wall.

Hedwig gasped. Nemov lunged for his shotgun.

"Hold it right there." Taylor appeared behind the waist-high wall.

Nemov froze.

"Not a good feeling, is it?" Taylor said as Nemov gazed down the barrel of his SIG.

"No."

Will started toward the fire and Hedwig.

"In fact, it's pretty sickening thinking about what a bullet can do to you. Especially a .357 cartridge. Have you ever been shot?"

Nemov swallowed. "No."

"I have. I don't recommend it."

Will listened to this exchange with half an ear. His attention was on Hedwig, who had her eye on Nemov's shotgun. He didn't like her expression.

"Let us make a deal," Nemov said.

"Let us not," Taylor returned, "and say we did."

Hedwig sprang for the shotgun, but Will was faster. He dived, grabbed her by her ponytail, and dragged her back. She let out a squeal of pain and fury but stopped struggling, folding her arms protectively around her middle.

"Down, girl."

Hedwig let off a stream of invectives that might have made a Russian drug lord blink. If he wasn't already used to her winning ways. She finished inexplicably with, "You have no right!"

"You see," Nemov said. "You should leave her with me. I will split the reward money with you."

"What have I told you two about eating juniper berries for breakfast?" Will confiscated Nemov's shotgun. "Why'd you uncuff her? It seems rash."

"She could not climb in handcuffs."

"Well, we'll give her a helping hand with that." Will reached for his handcuffs.

Hedwig gave a vicious but inaccurate kick at his legs. He jumped aside. Nemov laughed nastily.

"I'm really getting tired of you two," Taylor commented. "You, the Mad Russian, take your—actually *my*—handcuffs out. Good. Now siddown, hands behind your head."

Nemov slowly complied. Taylor reached across the wall, took the cuffs, and locked one end around Nemov's hairy right wrist, looped the other through one of the rusted rods partially sticking out of the bricks, and locked it around Nemov's left wrist.

"That ought to hold you for a bit."

Hands fastened behind his head, Nemov glared up at him. "This is not legal."

"Isn't it?"

Taylor looked at Will in surprise. Will said, "Uh, you really want to leave him like that?"

"What I'd really like to do is shoot him, but I was thinking you'd probably object."

Will hoped—assumed—he was kidding. He looked at Hedwig, who was still glowering up at him. "My partner's not in a great mood. I'd advise you to start cooperating. If you don't, the first thing we're doing after we drag your ass off this mountain is call the marshals and let them deal with getting you back to charm school."

She bared her teeth at him.

"I'm sure I can find a stake to chain her to," Taylor said.

"You'd like that," Hedwig said. "You don't care about me. I'd be safer with *him*." She jerked her head at Nemov.

Nemov nodded approvingly.

"Yeah, but who'll protect him from you?" Will knelt and got Hedwig handcuffed. For all her quivering fury, she didn't put up any resistance. If she was half as tired as Will felt, she had to be ready to drop. Weren't pregnant women supposed to sleep a lot anyway? Maybe Hedwig hadn't gotten the memo.

Will helped her to her feet. "Do we leave the fire or not?" he asked Taylor.

"What do you think?"

Will considered. "There's nothing for it to burn in here, but while it's going it'll keep off predators and act as a beacon for the choppers." To Nemov he said, "The first phone we get to, we'll contact the sheriffs and have them send someone for you."

"I will not be here."

"That would be my suggestion, but if you come after us, you'll wish you'd waited for the sheriffs."

CHAPTER SIX

The Mountain Inn in Carrizozo was like a lot of motor courts built back in the thirties and forties. At night its blue and pink neon lights beckoned the weary traveler. By day it offered adobe-style cabins with royal blue doors, paintings of Southwest Indian designs on the stucco facade, and shady, juniper-lined walkways. The pool was bone-dry, aqua paint flecking away in the white-hot sunlight, but the ice machine still worked. Taylor could hear it thumping and rattling outside their cabin window. It was the closest thing to air conditioning the Mountain Inn offered.

Inside the cabin, the red and brown furnishings were ugly and worn. The furniture was battered, but the rooms were clean and the beds looked comfortable. Of course, anything short of a slab in a morgue looked comfortable to Taylor at that point.

It had taken them two hours to get down the mountain to a fire road. By then Hedwig had been out on her feet. Rescue had come in the unexpected form of a bumblebee yellow Hummer driven by a self-described "rock hound."

Apparently flash floods were the equivalent of Christmas for lapidaries. When the waters dried, all kinds of goodies could be discovered in the silt. Crowded in the backseat, shoulder and thigh pressed against Will's, Taylor had listened in a kind of dream state to their bewhiskered savior drone on about fire agates, Mexican opals, Apache jasper, and petrified wood. When Will had asked about flood damage in the surrounding area, the Good Samaritan had been vague but professed a belief that there had been no loss of life.

He'd dropped them off in Carrizozo, population one thousand (give or take), a per capita income of slightly over twelve grand, and an open invitation to any and all renewable energy companies looking to invest. Welcome to hell, in other words.

It did have an airport, but it sounded too small for their purposes.

After checking in to the Mountain Inn, Will had handcuffed Hedwig to the bed in the adjoining room of their cabin—probably unnecessary as she was asleep before her head hit the pillow—and he and Taylor had spent the next hour calling rental car companies, ranger stations, and just about anyone they could think of.

"Who calls Cooper?" Will asked.

Cooper as in Assistant Field Office Director Cooper. Their boss. The man who would have a few things to say about a pair of special agents who took it upon themselves to go hunting a fugitive suspected terrorist when their assignment was merely to escort her to LA.

"I will," Taylor said. "It was my idea."

"For the last time. You didn't force me into this. We came up with this plan together."

"Do you think it makes it better or worse that it took two of us to come up with this scheme?"

"I think we should hold off talking to Cooper."

"You mean because of the supposed leak to the DEA?"

Will shrugged. "I'm just saying."

"We can't stay off the radar indefinitely."

"I know. But—"

"I'll tell him we're following up a lead."

Will's mouth opened in objection.

Taylor added, "And I'll call the office while he's at lunch, instead of calling his cell."

"Good thought."

"Easier to ask forgiveness..."

Will was nodding. His own cell rang, and he reached for it, frowning as he listened. "Right. Thanks. Appreciate it." He disconnected.

"Nemov?" Taylor asked.

"Long gone by the time they got there."

"We knew that would happen."

"True." Will went to the adjoining room and looked in at their prisoner. "She's still out for the count," he told Taylor, leaving the door open a crack. "I didn't know women could snore that loud."

Will's mother had passed away when he was six. He'd grown up in an all-male household, which, in Taylor's opinion, was one reason Will retained such chivalrous ideas about women.

Taylor tugged his remaining boot off and let himself fall back on the Indian-patterned bedspread with a groan.

It was going to be a scorcher of a day. The noon breeze was desert dry and scented with the burgers frying in the coffee shop next door to the motel.

"I don't think I could move if my life depended on it," he muttered as the mattress sank beneath Will's weight.

He managed not to jerk as Will's hand rested on his brow. Will slowly stroked the hair back from his forehead. Taylor kept his eyes closed. That uncharacteristically open tenderness made his heart ache.

"You get some sleep." Will's voice was low. "We've got a couple of hours before we need to leave for the airport. I'll call Cooper when I'm sure he's left for lunch."

Taylor snorted; it was more of a tired sniff. His eyelashes felt too heavy to lift, and he didn't want to see what was in Will's face anyway. Regret? Apology? Good-bye? Sometimes he was so angry with Will it was all he could do to control himself. How could Will do this to them?

Other times he was just...sad.

Will's warm lips nuzzled his temple. Taylor's eyes flew open. Will's eyes crinkled at the corners.

"Save me a place in those dreams."

Taylor summoned a weary grin. "Front row. Always." He let his lids fall shut, closing out Will's smile.

* * * * *

He must have slept deeply, because when Will stretched beside him, Taylor had no idea how long he'd been out. It could have been five minutes or five hours. The curtains were closed against the harsh daylight, thin plaid fabric rustling in the occasional gusts of hot wind.

"Time?" he mumbled.

"We're good. We're flying out of Ruidoso at five. We'll have to take the back way because of flood damage, but we've got time for a little siesta."

Taylor yawned. Rubbed his eyes. "I thought that *was* the back way?" He let himself be tugged over to Will, although it was really too hot for cuddling. Too hot for anything—except maybe a cold shower.

Cold showers seemed to be the last thing on Will's mind. They embraced, and Taylor buried his head in the strong curve of Will's shoulder.

"You're beautiful." Will's voice was rough, uneven. "You know that?"

Face hidden against Will, Taylor shook his head.

"Yeah, you do. And yeah, you are."

Taylor pulled himself together. He nipped the fleshy part of Will's shoulder and drew back. "You're not so bad yourself."

Will's blue eyes were solemn. He'd showered and shaved. Taylor didn't remember that, so he must really have been out.

Will continued to study Taylor like he was trying to memorize his face. "I love you."

Taylor moved his head in assent. His mouth tingled as Will traced his lower lip with the pad of his thumb. He lightly bit the finger.

"You think Patty Hearst is liable to wake up?"

Will shook his head, his gaze sharpening.

"In that case…let's save the siesta for the plane."

Will groaned soft accord, moving to undo the buttons of Taylor's shirt. He laid the khaki cotton wide and bent his head, his lips warm on Taylor's already flushed skin.

Taylor's breath caught as Will's mouth trailed, tasting, kissing from his collarbone to his chest. The combination of soft lips and sharp teeth was maddening in the best possible way. He ran his fingers through the damp, dark silk of Will's hair, raised his head to kiss Will's ear, which was all he could reach. He groaned and dropped back as Will's mouth closed around one of his nipples. Excitement and pleasure arrowed straight to his groin. He gasped, arched up, pushing the hard, sensitive nub of flesh into Will's mouth.

"I like that."

"I know you do." Will was smiling indulgently. He didn't find having his breasts touched nearly as arousing as Taylor did. In fact, Taylor suspected it made Will a little uncomfortable, but he seemed happy to oblige this kink of Taylor's. He nibbled and licked his way to Taylor's other nipple and then sucked hard.

"God. *Will.*"

Will bit him gently.

Taylor whimpered. He was already erect and aching, his cock bobbing over his flat belly.

"I know, sweetheart." Will gave Taylor's taut nipple a final wet lick. He lifted up, straddled Taylor, trapping his cock between Will's buttocks. Will clenched his muscles around the shaft while leaning forward to claim Taylor's mouth again.

"Nice…large muscle control," Taylor gulped out when he could breathe again.

"Wait'll you see my fine muscle control."

Taylor shivered and then laughed. He slipped his hand down between the hot, moist press of their bodies and began to stroke his belly, slowly, deliberately stimulating himself for their mutual enjoyment. Will teased him about being an exhibitionist, but Will definitely liked to watch. And Taylor liked to be watched by Will.

Will's eyes were so dark they looked black as Taylor stretched his spine, arching. His own gaze lingered on Will's lean, tanned, muscular body. Will's cock thrust up out of the black, silky thatch of his pubic hair.

Reaching out, Taylor feathered his fingers down Will's cock, stroking the thick, hot shaft. He could feel the pulse of blood throbbing beneath the satiny skin. You wouldn't think it could possibly feel good to have something that big and stiff shove into your ass, but it did. It was the best feeling on earth.

"What do you want?" Will whispered, as though reading his mind. "Want me to fuck you?"

Taylor nodded urgently.

"I love it when you say it."

"Please, Will. God. *Please* fuck me. I need it." Taylor had no inhibitions about asking for what he wanted. He had few inhibitions, period. Not being afraid to face what he liked gave him control, even power in this delicately balanced relationship of theirs.

He could see the effect of those words on Will, see Will's expression transform into a revealing composite of desire and vulnerability. "Oh yeah—" Will's face fell. "Oh *hell*. Hold on!"

He was off the bed and heading for the bathroom.

"Was it something I said?"

Will's strangled laugh came from the bathroom. Taylor, absently stroking himself, watched as Will reappeared. He was back on the bed in a leap and a bounce.

The bounce nearly sent them both through the mattress. Taylor started to laugh.

"What the hell was all that about?"

Will held up a small bottle of complimentary hand cream.

"Ah." Taylor nodded approval. "Good thinking."

"Assume the position," Will told him, and Taylor wriggled more comfortably into the disarranged bedding and lifted his legs.

Will squirted some pale, scented lotion into his hand and lazily stroked Taylor. The liquid felt cool and slick on heated skin. Taylor murmured approval.

"Hedonist." Will tickled his balls, which began to tighten. Taylor sucked in a breath as Will's fingers grazed the crevice beneath his cheeks.

Will squirted more lotion into his palm. He traced up and down the moist curve of Taylor's buttocks. Taylor groaned, gazing dizzily up into Will's gravely smiling face. "Oh God. Yes. Do it to me, Will."

Will slipped his fingers inside, making Taylor cry out sharply and toss his head against the flat pillows.

"Shhh." Will threw a guilty look at the door dividing their room from their prisoner's.

Taylor acknowledged the warning, but the feel of Will's fingers moving inside him was exquisite. He stretched and pushed down, aiding Will in that quest to find the spongy nub of his prostate.

"Good?" Will watched his face.

Taylor swallowed. Nodded. Hard to find words in the face of pleasure that intense. He closed his eyes and simply *felt*. The scent of musk and flowery lotion, the prickle of hair and fingernails…

As always there was the little regret when Will's fingers gently withdrew. But the next moment, Will's thick cock was pressing into him, pushing, piercing him slowly, deeply.

"*Tay*," Will breathed.

There was a brief pang of resistance, the alarming, stretching pull of skin and muscle, the almost unbearable pressure, and then the instant overwhelming pleasure.

Taylor wrapped his legs around Will's lean waist. His hands rested on Will's broad shoulders, smoothing, absently urging him on. Will began to move into a more powerful rhythm, and Taylor pushed back into it, the blood-hot clutch of flesh on flesh. Fevered, damp, restless…he rode the tiger, absorbed the pounding flash fire inside himself, both their bodies slick and shining with sweat, incalescent…

The pleasure of his coming was almost painful, so ferocious it racked him. The sun seemed to fill the room with light, brighter and brighter, burning him up—and then pinched out.

* * * * *

"You're right," Will said sometime later. "I did screw up out there last night. With the Mad Russian. I could have got us all killed."

Taylor turned his head on the pancake pillow. There were lines in Will's face he only remembered seeing once before. That had been the afternoon he'd thought he was dying. The afternoon they'd both believed he was dying.

"Sometimes it does get in the way. My feelings for you. I can't…"

"I can't either," Taylor said. "But we agreed that it was better to take our chances together than apart. We knew it would be hard sometimes."

Will's jaw worked. Taylor brushed his knuckles against the tight, smooth skin. "That why you feel you need five thousand miles between us?"

Will shook his head. "That's not fair. You know why I want this job."

Taylor turned his face away. Stared at the dark, scarred paneling. "I know."

"I'm not running from *us*. I'm not running *from* anything. You said yourself it's a huge opportunity for me. It's the chance of a lifetime. I can't turn it down. It would be stupid to turn it down."

Taylor closed his eyes against Will's pain—and his own. "I know. Sorry. I'm being a jerk."

"Taylor, you *know* I love you."

Taylor opened his eyes, turned his head, and Will's face was for once unguarded, all his feelings there to be read. His own throat closed. He nodded.

"I know you don't believe it, but it's just the same for me. It's *exactly* the same for me. The thought of these two years is killing me. But if I don't take the posting, I'm afraid of what it will do to us. I'm afraid I'll resent that decision later on."

Taylor nodded. "I know. I'm afraid of that too. You need to go."

But two years? *Two?* He missed Will when they were working apart just for a couple of days.

It would be a mistake to cry, not least because he'd never get over the humiliation, but he was about as close to tears as he'd ever been in his life. It was a real struggle, and he wasn't totally sure he wouldn't drown in all that backwash of dammed-up emotion. He kept his eyes screwed tight, but for expediency's sake, he had to open his mouth and drag in a soggy breath.

Will groaned. "Don't. God. Don't." He gathered Taylor tight, burying his face in Taylor's shoulder. He could feel Will shaking with the same effort at control.

Paris seemed a long way away.

CHAPTER SEVEN

The heat shimmered off the cracked asphalt and seemed to settle on the drooping leaves of the pecan trees along the wide street as they went into the coffee shop next to the Mountain Inn motor court.

"I don't understand why we're flying out of Ruidoso," Hedwig said once they had been seated. "There's an airport here."

"Because if anyone is following us, they'll expect us to fly out of the airport here," Will told her. "Besides, if we'd waited for a flight out of here, we wouldn't have been able to get a connecting flight to Los Angeles from Albuquerque this evening."

She gave him a long unreadable look from behind her glasses and picked up her menu.

Will shook his head inwardly. Through the coffee shop's plate-glass windows, he spotted Taylor, wearing a new pair of aviator sunglasses, walking from the parking lot.

A moment later, the glass door pushed open. Will's heart skipped in that funny way it had a habit of doing these days at the sight of Taylor's lean, rangy figure.

He raised his hand, and Taylor crossed over to them and sat down in the crescent-shaped booth across from Will. "We're all checked out at the motel, and the rental car is in the parking lot behind this place."

"Good."

Taylor's face was unreadable behind the shades, but Will had the sense that Taylor wanted to tell him something.

He raised his brows. Taylor gave a slight shake of his head.

Will asked, "Do we have time for lunch?"

Hedwig looked up in surprise.

"Why not?" Taylor picked up a menu.

The waitress arrived, and Hedwig, presumably eating for two, ordered a Monte Cristo sandwich, a strawberry milkshake, onion rings, and fried shrimp. Even Taylor, who most often had an appetite like a young wolf, seemed in awe over the fried shrimp. He opted for the Santa Fe salad with chicken, black beans, and tortilla chips. Will ordered a burger and fries.

The business of ordering taken care of, Hedwig folded her arms on the table and scrutinized Taylor and then Will. "Do you two live together?"

"Not your business, is it?" Taylor said, checking e-mail messages on his BlackBerry.

That was the correct answer, so Will was startled to hear his own voice simultaneously answer, "Yes."

"*Yes?*" Taylor questioned, looking up as though someone else had answered.

"Half my stuff is at your place. My dog is at your place."

"That's not the same as living together."

"According to Riley it is." Will was trying to joke, but Taylor was unsmiling.

"You have to hide your relationship," Hedwig deduced.

"Not anymore," said Taylor.

Apparently the truce Will thought they'd reached earlier that day was already at an end. "Wait a minute."

Taylor's gaze was cool. "Our relationship won't be a problem once we're not partnered."

That was true. Will hadn't thought about it before. He said staunchly, against the sinking sensation in his belly, "That's one of the positives then."

"Yeah." Taylor returned to studying his e-mail. "I know I'm thrilled."

Will folded his lips against all the things he wanted to say. He needed to be sensitive to Taylor or this long-distance thing was going to rip them apart, and he had no intention—regardless of what Taylor believed—of letting that happen. So he would bite his tongue and keep biting his tongue, and eventually Taylor would get over his insecurity and they'd be okay again.

"How'd you get involved with Bashnakov?" He thought Hedwig looked mildly disappointed at his change of subject.

"I met him when I was an exchange student in Moscow. I was friends with his son Alexi. Mikhail and I...there was an instant...connection. The age difference meant nothing."

"How long ago was that?"

"I was in high school. When I came home, I wrote him. He wrote back." She shrugged. "One thing led to another."

"Those must have been some postcards."

"Then, when I was at Barnard, Mikhail bought an estate in New York—"

"You went to Barnard?" Taylor interrupted.

"Yes. Why not? *Oh.* Because I don't fit your preconceived notion of what a Seven Sisters graduate is like?"

"You don't fit my preconceived notion of what a junior college graduate is like. Or a normal high school graduate."

"Okay," Will said. "Don't make me separate you two."

Hedwig gave Taylor her bared-teeth expression. Fortunately, their lunches arrived, ending further civilities. Hedwig tore into her plate of shrimp with the savage satisfaction of a great white.

When the meal was over, Will went to pay the bill. He was replacing his credit card into his wallet when he spotted a familiar figure heading in to the Mountain Inn next door.

Of course it was possible there was a dog show in town, but somehow Will suspected Reuben Ramirez might have another reason to be wandering around Carrizozo. He returned to the dining room.

As he reached the table, Taylor, apparently reading his expression, hooked a hand around Hedwig's arm and drew her to her feet.

"I have to use the ladies' room."

"You're going to have to hold it," Will told her.

"I can't hold it!"

"Make it snappy."

She yanked her arm away from Taylor and sailed off to the restrooms.

"We should have left her handcuffed," Taylor said.

"The idea was to avoid attracting attention. That might be academic now. I just saw Reuben Ramirez go in to the Mountain Inn lobby."

"That's quite a coincidence. Here's another one. There's an automotive repair shop next to the car rental place. Guess who I spotted getting a tire replaced on his SUV?"

"Our friend with the Mohawk?"

"Da."

"Great. The sooner we get out of town, the better. Hopefully Ramirez and Nemov will stake out the airport. Or each other."

"I'll go watch the rear in case Mother Russia decides to climb out the bathroom window."

Will nodded. Taylor disappeared through the crowded tables of diners and exited through the glass door.

A few minutes later, Hedwig pushed out through the bathroom door.

Will hustled her to the parking lot. Taylor joined them, and they piled into the rental SUV.

Nobody appeared to be following them as they left Carrizozo in the red dust and started the drive to Sierra Blanca. Nor did anyone have much to say. To fill the silence, Will turned on the radio, and they listened to weather and traffic reports. There was an update on the flash flood cleanup efforts. It seemed that their rescuer in the Hummer had been correct. No lives had been lost, though property damage had been considerable. That section of the national forest was currently closed to visitors.

"Have you ever been with a woman?" Hedwig asked suddenly from the backseat.

Pop goes the weasel. She had to be doing it on purpose, Will decided. Either because she liked mixing things up or because she believed she could gain some advantage by keeping them distracted and on edge.

"What is it with you?" Taylor asked, possibly reaching the same conclusion.

"I'm curious. In the *Mafiya*, it's one of the four unforgivable transgressions. It carries a death penalty."

Taylor made a sound of amused disgust.

"Anyway, how do you know you wouldn't like sex with a woman if you've never tried?"

Will said, "I have tried."

The words just…popped out. Seeing Taylor's astonishment, Will wished he'd kept his mouth shut.

"You have?" Taylor was frowning. "When?"

"Back in high school."

"High school? You never mentioned it before."

Will shrugged. That was one thing that had always surprised him about Taylor. For all Taylor's sexual adventures, one thing he'd never tried was intercourse with a woman.

Hedwig asked, "You didn't like it?"

"I liked it fine." Will was a little irritated at the way Taylor was staring at him—as though Will had confessed to having an extramarital affair. It was kind of ironic coming from a guy who'd had intimate acquaintance with such items as butterfly boards and piercing needles.

"Did you only try once?"

"Mind your own business," Taylor told Hedwig. To Will he said, "How many times?"

Will sincerely wished he'd kept his mouth shut. "I don't know. A few. I had a girlfriend."

"A girlfriend? A steady girlfriend?"

Will nodded. Why the hell was this a big deal? For the life of him, he couldn't imagine, but he could feel Taylor's shock like an electromagnetic field.

"Why've you never mentioned this?"

"I have." Will knew he hadn't, actually, but not because it was some deep, dark secret. It was just a long time ago and…well, a little painful.

"No you haven't. I'd have remembered."

Will glanced in his rearview mirror. Hedwig was staring out the window as they wound higher up into the trees and hills. Apparently she'd lost interest in the conversation. Nice. Had her only purpose been to wind Taylor up? If so, she'd succeeded.

Seeing that Taylor was still waiting for a reply, he said mildly, "Why would you? It's not a big deal."

"What was her name?"

"Madonna."

"Madonna? What kind of a name is that?"

"Catholic, I guess. Her family was Catholic. You're acting kind of weird about this, in case you haven't noticed."

Taylor sat back in his seat. He was still eyeing Will narrowly.

"So…you consider yourself bisexual?"

"No, I don't consider myself bisexual. What are you talking about? Because I had a girlfriend in high school? A lot of people have girlfriends in high school and college."

"*And* college? Were you still seeing her in college?"

Will could happily have bitten his tongue out. "It's just a…an example."

"Were you still together in college?"

Goddamn that persistent, ruthless investigative streak of Taylor's.

"For a little while," Will admitted.

"Well." Taylor had that huffy, irritable tone he got when he was edgy or nervous. "This is certainly an interesting development."

Will looked away from the road to throw him an exasperated look. "Why would it be? It's nothing. It was a million years ago. A lifetime ago. I can't figure out why the hell we're even still discussing it."

"So this is why I've never met your family?"

The sheer breathtaking illogic of that jump was only secondary to the deadly intuitive accuracy of it. Until Taylor had put it into words, it had never occurred to Will that it was one thing to admit to your all-American, red-blooded, manly man family you were gay. It was another to bring your male lover home to meet the folks. And maybe that difference was one reason he'd always managed to arrange visits to his family when Taylor couldn't go.

"That's the most fucking ridiculous thing I ever heard!"

Taylor said with infuriating calm, "Okay, okay. Just asking."

From the backseat, Hedwig suddenly sucked in a sharp breath.

"Now what?" Will growled.

Her wide bespectacled gaze met his in the rearview. She swallowed. "I-I think… I'm not sure… Could you stop the car?"

"*No,*" Taylor and Will answered in unison.

"But I think the baby is coming!"

* * * * *

The middle of nowhere. That's about as close as Taylor's trusty GPS seemed to be able to narrow their location down to. A small grassy knoll in the middle of nowhere. On either side they were surrounded by hills and trees. Behind them, the clearing fell away to a long series of steep slopes covered in more rocks and trees.

Hedwig was walking a big circle around the glade, hand pressed to her bulging belly, taking deep, distressed breaths.

Standing by the car, watching her, Will said, "Maybe she's just carsick. Considering what she put away at lunch…"

Taylor was scowling at his BlackBerry. "I *still* can't get a signal."

"If she *is* in labor, we could have hours, right? It can take hours."

Taylor shook his BlackBerry. In a minute, he'd be knocking it against a boulder.

"Don't you think?" Will persisted. "It's not like in the movies."

"True. I guess." Taylor scowled across the clearing at Hedwig, who continued to make her big slow loop. "She's got to be faking."

"I know. But for the sake of argument, let's say she's not."

Taylor shook his head. "I don't know."

"We've had training on this."

"Good. You can deal with it."

"I can't remember anything about it except how to tie off the umbilical cord."

Taylor looked horrified. "Her…uh…water has to break, right? I don't think it did."

"How would you know?"

"She'd have said."

Will nodded, relieved. That made sense. "Should we head back to Carrizozo or try to make it to Sierra Blanca?"

"I say we try to make it to the airport."

"The airport?" Will was doubtful about that.

"Maybe not the airport itself, but Ruidoso. She's *got* to be faking."

"Okay. They'll have more extensive medical facilities, anyway. It's—" He broke off as a long black sedan with tinted windows pulled off the road, tires shelling rock as it drew into the turnout.

"I don't like this," Taylor remarked, planting himself squarely in line with Will. "Is this somebody we know?"

Will cast a quick look back at Hedwig. She had stopped circling the mini meadow and was standing in a pose that conveyed a creature at bay. At his quick gesture, she moved toward the stand of trees. One thing he couldn't fault was her instinct for survival.

The passenger door of the sedan opened. A short, slender form emerged. A man with cropped, fair hair. He wore dark sunglasses and a black tailored suit.

"Is everything all right? Can we offer assistance?" Not a man. A woman. It wasn't just the voice. Unless Will was very much mistaken, there were small breasts beneath that sexless suit.

Will politely waved her off.

"Does she look familiar?" Taylor inquired out of the side of his mouth.

"The car does."

"It does?"

"Classic movie villain wheels."

"True. So are the threads. They scream 'Hit Person.'"

Will grunted a laugh. He sobered as the driver's door of the car swung open. "Here we go."

A man got out, blond counterpart of the woman.

"They could be feebs." Taylor looked back at where Hedwig was hiding, then looked at Will.

"I don't think so. They'd have identified themselves by now." Will called to the woman, "Thanks again. It's under control." Under his breath, he said to Taylor, "Shit. They're not going to buy it. Move."

He was aware of the man reaching beneath his blazer. Hip holster, probably. He was aware of Taylor leaping for a cairn of rocks. That was all there was time for; Will himself was already moving. He raced for the edge of the hillside to his right, throwing himself down behind a shoulder of rock and grass, drawing his weapon. What he wouldn't give for one of the standard issue Colt SMGs or even a Remington 870.

"We just want the girl," the woman yelled.

"We're federal agents," Will shouted back.

"Give us the girl, and no one has to get hurt."

"You're not getting the girl."

A granite splinter just missed the tip of his nose, and he heard the familiar whine of a bullet ricocheting off stone. In reply came the brisk, untroubled *bang* of Taylor's SIG.

Will rolled over and risked a quick look. The female shooter was situated behind a boulder near the edge of the road. The male shooter was behind his vehicle, wasting ammunition like it grew on trees. He was focusing his firepower on Taylor's position, but Taylor was safely dug in and not easily flustered.

Will fired a succession of rounds at the car to give Taylor a little breathing space. He hit the gas tank twice, but of course it was only in movies that cars conveniently exploded. He nailed the front right tire and, with grim satisfaction, watched the front half of the vehicle sag.

Dropping back, Will ejected the SIG's magazine, replaced the empty clip with a full one, slapped the magazine back into place.

Taylor was conserving ammo, laying down just enough fire to keep the other two from advancing toward the copse where Hedwig hid. The female shooter was equally conservative, biding her time, watching closely for a clear shot.

Two on two. Well, they'd certainly had worse odds. With the road in front of them and the downside of the knoll to their rear, they were in pretty good position. If they had to fall back, the trees and vegetation supplied plenty of camouflage. Yes, it could definitely be worse.

And it could definitely be better. Will was disgusted with himself for missing the fact that they'd picked up a tail. Even if they had been keeping well back—a big black sedan? It didn't get more in-your-face than that. How long had he and Taylor been followed? He'd been so preoccupied with Taylor and keeping an eye out for Nemov, he'd missed the obvious. And what was Taylor's excuse?

The male shooter made an attempt to get to the rocky incline to the right of the car, but Will held him off with three well-placed shots. The woman directed her attention his way. Taylor revived her interest in him with resumed fire.

The male shooter scrambled back into the car and blared the horn loudly. The female left cover and ran for the car, firing off a few wild shots and throwing herself inside.

The black sedan roared forward, knocking the silver SUV rental a few feet to the side and plowing past. The sedan fishtailed, screeching up the road several yards and disappearing around a bend. The engine died.

They weren't going far. Even if they wanted to, a flat tire and a couple of holes in the gas tank were sure to slow them down.

Taylor was up and running for the stand of junipers. Will started for the SUV. If it was still functional, they'd head back for Carrizozo rather than fall into whatever trap the suits in the black sedan were planning.

"Brandt!"

He turned. Taylor reappeared, shaking his head.

"Is she hit?" Will gasped, sick at the thought. "She's not dead, is she?"

"Gone."

CHAPTER EIGHT

"**S**ignal?"

Taylor shook his head. He resisted the temptation to hurl his Black-Berry at the nearest mountaintop. "We didn't run them off. They're either blocking the road ahead or going for a better position."

"Or both."

"Or both. Either way, we can't retreat. Not without the Bionic Baby Maker."

"She's not going far." Will ejected his pistol magazine, checked the clip, reinserted the magazine. That would be his second and last clip. At a rough estimate, Taylor guessed Will probably had six, maybe seven, rounds left. He hadn't been planning to go to war. Neither of them had. He reached in his pocket, tossed Will one of his extras. It wasn't regulation, but Taylor always carried extra extras.

Will took it, slipping it in his vest pocket. "I guess that answers the question about whether she was faking labor."

"I guess. Listen, Brandt. If that car's still running, I think you should take it and head for the nearest ranger station. We need some support here. There isn't any point trying to keep this thing secret now."

"And in the meantime, you're going to do what?"

"I'm going to find Hedwig and go to ground with her until you show up with reinforcements."

"The guy who thinks Descanso Gardens is a wilderness is going to try tracking someone through Lincoln National Forest? I don't think so."

"Hey, she's no wilderness expert either. I'm the perfect choice to track her. She's going to think like me."

"Very funny. We're sticking together."

That was the way Taylor would prefer it, but honesty compelled him to speak. "We need some backup. We've got Dick and Jane ahead of us and, for all we know, Nemov coming up on our ass. Ramirez might even be out there somewhere. The situation is out of our control. We need help."

"We're sticking together."

"Would you listen to me?"

"Would you listen to *me*? I'm not leaving you out here."

What a really bad time to get choked up, but Will was glaring at him, mouth thinned to a white line and eyes so bright they were glittering. Bad timing for both of them.

"Will…"

"I'm. Not. Leaving. You. Got that?"

Taylor took a deep breath. "It's okay. I know you'll come back."

To his surprise, Will's hand closed on his shoulder and pulled him forward into a fleeting but adamant press of mouths.

"You're right. I will. Always." He released Taylor and turned away. "Let's go. It can get dark fast in the mountains."

* * * * *

"Is there any chance she *didn't* come this way?" They had been searching the tree-covered hills for half an hour with no sign of Hedwig anywhere. Now it was mostly a series of rocky downhill slopes. Where the ground wasn't rock, it was covered in golden wheat. Or something that looked like wheat but was more likely weeds. There were a few scraggly pine trees and a lot of juniper and cactus. The air was sharp and clear as a crystal bell, and every *clack* of rock on rock seemed to carry for miles.

"This is the closest thing to a trail."

Which wasn't saying much.

Taylor paused to look over his shoulder—which was when he felt the ground give way.

For a confused instant, he thought he'd misstepped, that he was falling down the hillside, and then he realized that he was falling *into* the hillside.

The ground caved in around him, dirt and rock crumbling down on him as he sank.

He seemed to hang, suspended, clawing the thick, moist dark, trying to climb back up to air and light, squinching his eyelids, spitting out soil, breathing out against the smothering shower of debris. It felt for a moment like he might fight gravity.

Then he plummeted. He landed in soft earth, though hard enough to knock the wind out of him.

He could hear Will yelling. It sounded like a long way away.

Taylor blinked a couple of times and began to rapidly take stock. Fingers, toes, hands, feet, arms, legs…everything seemed to be working. He gingerly lifted his head. A cone of light spilled down from the hole in the ceiling above his head.

A good twenty feet above his head.

"Taylor? Can you hear me? Are you okay? Can you hear me?"

Will's head appeared in the opening above.

"Brandt!"

"Jesus *Christ*. You scared the shit out of me, MacAllister."

You and me both. But Taylor refrained from saying it. Will sounded about as rattled as Taylor'd ever heard him.

"Can you move? Are you injured?"

Taylor slowly picked himself up. "I'm okay."

"Are you sure?"

"Uh, I think so." He moved into the shaft of sunlight, brushing the grit and pine needles from his clothes and hands. "Yeah, I'm fine."

"Do you see a way to climb up?"

Taylor looked around. He was forced to reluctantly admit, "No."

Will swore.

"Tell me about it. Why does this stuff always happen to me?" He thought of all the movies he'd seen where caves were filled with snakes or skeletons or bears. Occasionally treasure, true, but usually snakes, skeletons, and bears. With *his* luck? At the very least, giant spiders.

It occurred to Taylor that Will had been silent for a couple of minutes. He looked up. Will was still there, looking down at him. Taylor began to see Will's predicament.

"See, if you'd gone for help when I asked…"

"Not funny," Will said tersely.

"All right, all right." He felt around in his pockets. He was going to have bruises all over his body from falling on the junk he carried. He pulled out his pencil flashlight and shone it slowly around the walls of his prison. Rock…earth…jutting roots…a darker shadow…

He went to examine it.

"What are you doing?" Will called.

"Hang on."

That darker shadow turned out to be a slit in the wall. Taylor shone his light into it. He could feel cool air pushing against his skin.

He moved back into the ring of light. Was it fading? He couldn't tell.

"There's some kind of an opening in the wall. Maybe a tunnel."

Will was shaking his head. "No. Not a good idea."

"Really? What's your plan?"

Silence. Poor Will. Taylor sympathized. Will didn't like not being in control, and this situation was definitely out of control.

"Listen. Try and find the girl. I'll see if I can find another way out of here."

"You listen. Some of these New Mexico caves are huge. Miles long. You can't tell how big yours might be from the chamber you're standing in. And there isn't going to be any light. You won't be able to see a foot in front of you."

"I'll be able to see exactly a foot in front of me." Taylor held up his pencil flashlight.

"Seriously?"

"We don't have a lot of time here, Brandt. Our friends in the hearse could be closing in on Hedwig right now. You need to go."

"Do you have a way to mark your trail?"

Taylor held on to his patience with an effort. "I could take a leaf from Riley's book, but no. Short answer? No."

Will raked a nervous hand through his hair. "I don't like this."

"I'm not loving it either. Would you just go hurry up and find Hedwig? She's probably giving birth under a tree right now."

Will swore. "All right. But...watch yourself. Don't do anything I wouldn't do."

"You mean besides falling into an underground cave?"

"Besides that." Will stood up. "I'll be back." He disappeared from the opening.

"So you keep telling me," Taylor muttered.

* * * * *

The tunnel smelled weird. It smelled sulfurous and animal. Hopefully there was no poison gas...

Maybe the tunnel led to the center of the earth. Maybe it was the pathway to hell. Either way, it was pitch-dark and narrow—and perhaps he was even working against an upward incline. It was hard to tell in the disorienting dark. So narrow in a couple of spots that Taylor had to fight with himself to keep going. He had never been claustrophobic before, but the fear of getting trapped in this hole in the ground kept skyrocketing his pulse and turning his legs to jelly.

As lean and wiry as he was, he had to wriggle through a couple of very tight places, and he wasn't sure he could wriggle back. It was only the knowledge that Will needed him—and the belief that the cool wafts of fresh air he felt on his perspiring face meant there was an opening somewhere close by—that kept him moving.

He was surprised to find he was about as scared as he'd ever been. He was not going to like being in tight, enclosed spaces after this; that was for sure.

The flashlight beam fluttered against the slick darkness like a white moth, and a couple of times—to his frank horror—it faded out.

If the light went entirely, he wasn't sure he wouldn't break. Better not to think about it. Better to just keep moving, keep pushing and wriggling—

forget about the fact that he probably couldn't get back if his life depended on it, that he might die, wedged here beneath this fucking mountain.

There was more air against his face. He could feel...a breeze. And perhaps the pitchy blackness was fading a little?

Yes. There was light ahead. Light spilling through a jagged lightning-shaped opening.

He sped up, stumbling toward it, almost dizzy with relief.

Fresh air. Daylight. Freedom. He was embarrassingly close to hyperventilating his abject gratitude. Thank God there was no one to witness—and he sure as hell was never going to tell Will how bad it had been. How bad he had let it become in his mind.

Taylor reached the opening. It too was narrow, but it would have had to be the size of a paper cut to prevent him from getting out. He stuck his left hand and leg through and started to wriggle.

The sound of voices stopped him.

Male and female.

"I can't tell if they came this way or not," the male voice said.

Not Will.

Taylor drew hastily back. He listened.

The woman answered, but her voice was less distinct. She was farther down the hillside, already past the cave but out of his sight line.

He heard a clattering sound of falling rocks. It sounded still farther away. So where were they?

Taylor stuck his arm and leg out of the opening and began to twist. The rocks tore his shirt and scraped his skin, but that didn't matter. It was wide enough, and he was getting through.

He wriggled some more, and then he was out. Out into the amber sunlight. Yellow dust motes floated above the wheat-colored grass. And far down the hillside—much farther than he'd thought from the sound of their voices—were the man and woman from the black sedan.

CHAPTER NINE

He almost stepped on her.

Hedwig had taken shelter beneath the ragged boughs of a big juniper bush. Will spotted the white of her jeans. Probably the only white patch left.

He squatted, keeping a wary eye on her hands. She was clutching a thick, short branch, and he didn't think it was to chew on during labor. "All right. Come out of there."

"I...can't."

He controlled himself, but it wasn't easy. Every time he thought about Taylor wandering around in that underground cavern, he felt the rein he was keeping on his emotions slip. "Kelila, get your ass out of there, or I'm coming in after you. Believe me; you don't want that."

She stared back defiantly. "The baby is coming."

"We've all heard that before. Tell the baby she needs to postpone her flight."

"He. It's a boy."

"I don't care what it is." He felt a warning prickle down his scalp, that sixth sense that had kept him alive and in one piece as a marine and later in the DSS. Turning, Will spotted two dark-clad figures switchbacking down the golden hills behind him. From the way they seemed to study the ground, he didn't think they'd spotted him yet.

"Company's coming, so unless you want an audience for the delivery, you better get moving."

Kelila half crawled, half rolled out from under the bush. Will helped her to her knees.

"Don't stand up. Where the hell did you think you were going?"

"Mexico."

"On foot?"

"Plenty of people do it on foot."

"I don't think most of them are ready to drop a kid any second."

"I could make it."

He was beginning to believe she could.

He felt her stiffen as she spotted the sleek figures moving down the hill in the fading light. "You recognize them. Who are they?"

"Gretchen and Victor Hart. They work for Mikhail."

"Let me guess. Not bill collectors?"

"No. Mikhail must have found out about the baby."

"You mean it would be news to him?"

"I left when I realized I was pregnant. I didn't tell Mikhail."

Will had been helping her crawl along from bush to rock perpendicular to their pursuers, but at that he stopped. "I thought you left when you realized your life was in danger from someone highly placed in the DEA."

Kelila nodded. "Yes. That was why I knew I had to run. I had to think of my baby at that point."

"And who were you thinking of before then?"

She looked confused, throwing nervous glances at the figures still relentlessly combing the hillside blocking their way back to Taylor.

Will said, "You had a thing about Bashnakov from the time you were in high school. You apparently broke up his marriage—"

"He was widowed."

"But then before you even know you're pregnant, you start working for the DEA as an informant. Why?"

"*Why?* Because I learned my husband—my wonderful, charming, handsome husband—was a murderer and a drug dealer." Will must have looked as baffled as he felt. She spat out, "That's *not* okay!"

"I know it's not okay. Are you saying you went voluntarily to the DEA?"

"Yes." She met his eyes unswervingly. Not that that meant much. Will had met plenty of bald-faced liars in his time.

"You volunteered to act as an informant for the DEA?"

"Yes."

"And what's the name of the highly placed DEA official you believe set you up?"

"Deputy Administrator Ted Bell."

If it wasn't the truth, it was a damn good facsimile. Even Will had heard the rumors about DA Ted Bell.

She said, suddenly alarmed, "Where's your—Where's Agent MacAllister?"

"He's waiting for us. I hope." Will scanned the hills. The Harts had reached the flatland now. If they could circumnavigate them, if Will could get Kelila up the hill without being seen...

That still left the problem of Taylor.

One thing at a time. Getting up that hill unseen. That was the first thing.

And it was liable to be the last thing. They'd be sitting ducks all the way up that hillside.

He glanced at Kelila's drawn face. If ever a girl was game, it was this one.

* * * * *

Hiking down, the hills had seemed reasonably gentle. Climbing up felt like scaling Everest. Their progress was agonizingly slow. Hedwig labored ahead of him, mostly on hands and knees, panting hard. The bare stretches with only the gold-tipped grass swaying in the breeze for cover seemed miles long.

It was inevitable that they would be spotted. Will knew it, was prepared for it, but the first blast sent his heart into overdrive. Kelila let out a shriek and scuttled away.

"Get down!" Will yelled.

She was a slow-moving target, awkward as an anteater, but for some reason neither Gretchen nor Victor took the shot. In fact, all their firepower seemed to be trained on Will. Bullets chewed up the earth around him, took bites out of the sparse vegetation, nibbled at the rocks and sent them flying.

Will flattened himself to the warm soil, locked both hands around his SIG, and laid down a steady return barrage. It was only a matter of time before one of them nailed him, but he would give Kelila every possible second. He was aware of her making her spiderlike way up the slope to the left of him. Panic in slow motion.

Will changed clips.

Sorry, Taylor. Sorry, sweetheart. If it was going to end like this, Will was actually glad Taylor was safely trapped belowground, no chance of him doing anything stupid and suicidal until the danger was past.

His finger tightened on the trigger, squeezing—he was down to his last rounds.

Like a thunderclap from overhead came the loud *bang* of a .357 SIG.

Will's heart jerked with each bullet crack.

Bang. Bang. Bang.

That rapid, even staccato was as familiar, as welcome as the voice of a lover calling down the mountainside.

It was his ticket home. He turned, relying on Taylor to cover his retreat, and sprang up the hill in a couple of bounds, catching Kelila a few yards ahead and half dragging her along with him.

They reached the top. Taylor was lying in the deep grass, looking remarkably unruffled. He had that tight-jawed, implacable expression Will recognized from other tight corners, and though his eyes flicked briefly over Will, making sure he was still whole, his attention was focused on the two he had pinned down below.

"Can she make it to the car?" he asked.

"She'll make it."

"I'll cover you."

"Don't be too long about it."

"I'm right behind you."

By now Kelila had reached the end of her strength and all the panic and adrenaline in the world couldn't drive her any faster. Will put an arm around her waist and towed her along over uneven ground. A few yards from the SUV, he picked her up and carried her, his back muscles screaming protest.

Reaching the SUV at last, he tumbled her into the rear seat. Hair spilled over her face, she sprawled on the pseudo leather gasping out little moans and convulsively rubbing her belly.

Will ran around to the driver's side and slid behind the wheel. He patted frantically for the keys. *Christ.* He could have dropped them anywhere at any time...

No. There they were. He jammed them in the ignition. He had just long enough to wonder how badly the SUV had been damaged by the sedan crashing into it and then the engine roared into life.

Out of the corner of his eye he spotted Taylor cresting the hill and sprinting for the SUV.

Will reversed sharply, rolling back a few feet. He lunged across and shoved open the passenger side door. A second later Taylor jumped in, hauling the door shut behind him.

"They're right behind me. I think I winged the guy. *Go.*"

"Gretchen will kill you for that," Kelila panted.

"Gretchen wants to kill me anyway." Taylor was reloading quickly, throwing hasty looks out the side window.

Will jammed on the accelerator and the SUV shot forward. The tires spun on gravel and they bumped onto the highway. The vehicle seemed to be responding okay. Will spared a quick look at the gauges. No red lights. The left rear was dragging a little.

He gave her a little more gas and they sped round the first bend only to see the black sedan parked squarely across the narrow road.

"Shit." Will braked hard, steering into the skid, a tight hand over hand so that the SUV rocked to a halt lined up parallel a few inches from the bullet riddled sedan blocking their way.

There was a long wooded drop on the left and a steep rocky climb on the right. No way around the sedan and no way through.

"We've got to go back." Taylor gave voice to Will's thoughts.

Will nodded tightly. "Get on the floor," he ordered Kelila.

She obeyed, moving with what seemed to him clumsy, shaking slowness.

Taylor rolled down his window and scrambled to sit on the ledge, bracing himself. He thumped the roof of the SUV. "Go."

"Hang on for Christ's sake." Will reversed, yanked the wheel, and they spun out, hurtling back down the narrow road.

As they swung around the curve he saw Gretchen and Victor waiting for them. At the same moment Taylor opened fire.

Will floored it. He felt the thunk of bullets hitting the side of the SUV, heard Kelila screaming, felt the burn of glass on his neck as the side window behind him shattered.

Taylor was still firing in quick succession.

And then they were around the next bend and flying down the road back to Carrizozo.

The sound of shots faded. Gretchen was a tiny dark figure in Will's rearview, running out to the blacktop to fire final, wild shots after them.

Taylor slithered agilely back through the window and dropped heavily into the seat beside Will.

Will threw him a quick look. "Okay?"

Taylor assented. He wiped his forehead. His eyes met Will's "You?"

Will nodded. He looked in the rearview. "Everyone okay?"

No response from the backseat.

Taylor half turned, reaching down to Kelila. "You all right?"

She groaned. "I think the baby's coming."

"You always say that."

"My water broke."

Taylor returned to facing forward in his seat. "Did you hear that?"

"Roger."

"Do we try to make it back to Carrizozo or try to find a ranger station?"

"What's a ranger supposed to do?"

"What are *we* supposed to do?"

"How long before the baby comes?" Will called back to Kelila.

She was carefully picking herself up from the floor and lying on the seat. "I'm not flying anywhere till this baby comes."

"That's not what I asked you. How long till he comes?"

"It could be anytime. It could be twelve hours. It could be twelve minutes."

Taylor said suddenly, like a student recalling the answer to a tough exam question, "Are you having contractions?"

"Yes."

"How often?"

"Often enough."

Far down the road Will spied another vehicle. The first they'd seen other than the Hart's sedan. "Let's head for Carrizozo." He threw another look at Taylor who looked about as tired and disheveled as Will had ever seen him. "How *did* you get out of that cave?"

"I walked. It turned out not to be Carlsbad Caverns, after all."

"It could have been."

"Yeah, but it wasn't." Taylor sighed wearily. He ejected the magazine, removed the clip, squinted at it. "Two rounds left."

"Did you nail Victor?"

"It looked like it."

"Gretchen will kill you," Kelila offered by way of comfort.

"Been there, done that."

Will reached out to pat Taylor's thigh. The approaching car was black. An SUV. Taking the winding road very fast.

Too fast.

"What I want to know is how they found her."

"Who?" Will asked.

"Victor and Victoria. They didn't track us from Colorado. I can accept that we missed one tail. But two? No way."

"Reuben," Kelila said. "Reuben must have called Mikhail and told him about the baby. And Mikhail sent Gretchen to bring us back."

"Nanny get your gun," Taylor said. "If you knew Ramirez couldn't be trusted, why the hell did you run to him?"

"I didn't know where else to go. My parents believe all the lies the government has told about me."

"Oh right. Like the fact—"

"Trouble," Will snapped.

Taylor was instantly all attention. He observed the vehicle speeding their way. "Black SUV," he said thoughtfully. "You think it's Nemov?"

"I think I don't want to depend on coincidence." He threw back to Kelila, "Get down and hold on." Will craned his head as Taylor leaned across him to grab his shoulder strap and fasten his seatbelt.

Taylor sat back, buckling himself in. His pistol rested between his hands, relaxed and ready.

Will spared him a crooked grin. His gaze returned to the road. Tinted windows, heavy duty roof rack. Nemov. But what did the crazy bastard think he was going to do?

Wait. Had Nemov recognized them? He wouldn't expect them coming this direction.

Maybe...

There was a turnout a couple of yards ahead. Will slowed.

Taylor cast him a quick look. "What are you doing?"

"He's speeding trying to catch us. He thinks we're miles ahead. He may not even know what we're driving. Is there a map in that glove compartment?"

"I picked a map up at the motel." Taylor shook out the folds.

Will braked and they swung neatly into the turnout. Will grabbed the map, holding it up. Taylor leaned forward, keeping his head beneath the dashboard as Nemov screeched past.

Will watched the black SUV disappear around the bend.

"Go," Taylor said, sitting up. "He's going to run into that sedan in about four minutes and it won't take him long to figure out what happened."

Will hit the accelerator and they sped out of the turnout.

Neither of them spoke as they wound their way back down through the golden shimmering hills. The squeal of the tires picked up a kind of rhythm as they banked into the curves and straightened out once more.

Taylor sat half-turned to watch the road behind them, but the road remained empty.

CHAPTER TEN

Hedwig's contractions were coming faster by the time they pulled into the nearly empty parking lot of the small grouping of adobe buildings that comprised Carrizozo Indian Hospital.

"Is this place even open?" Will asked, turning off the ignition.

"It's supposed to be." Taylor double-checked the directory on his phone. "Thirteen beds. Family practice. Inpatient and outpatient."

"I need a *real* hospital," groaned Hedwig.

"This *is* a real hospital."

"You're going to kill me and the baby both."

"You couldn't find anything else?" Will asked, uneasily watching the writhing in the backseat.

"This is the closest. She keeps saying she's going to have this kid any second—"

"All right. Can you make sure they're open before we try dragging her out of the car?"

Taylor got out of the car and went up the cement walk. The heat of the day was fading, but the walls of the building still radiated warmth. Wilted flowers struggled in the baked dirt of what was optimistically intended as landscaping. It did look sort of deserted, but there was a shiny new pickup in the parking lot, as well as a very old ambulance.

He pushed through the double glass doors, and a wave of antiseptic-scented, chilled air hit him.

A plump Indian boy of about seventeen stood behind a counter. His eyes widened at the sight of Taylor. And if Taylor looked half as rough as he felt, no wonder. It had been one hell of a long day.

"Are you open?" Taylor asked.

"Yes." The kid seemed to collect himself. "If you want to sit down, I'll bring you the paperwork."

"It's not for me. I've got a woman in the parking lot who's about to give birth. Do you have a doctor on the premises?"

"My mom—that is, Dr. Cruz is over at Happy Pete's having her evening break. I can page her."

Taylor sincerely hoped Happy Pete's was not a bar. "Could you? That would be great."

"Sure, I'll—"

Whatever else the kid was about to say was lost in the jarring sounds of skidding tires, blasting horns, and breaking glass from outside. The unmistakable accompaniment of a car crash.

"It's an accident!" the kid exclaimed, coming around the counter. "It happens all the time on this corner." He ran out through the glass doors.

"Are you kidding me?" Taylor asked the empty room.

Apparently the joke was on him. He shoved open the glass doors, narrowly missing being mown down by the kid, who was already racing back, looking stricken.

"There's a guy with a gun out there!" He ran to the phone on the desk.

Taylor banged out through the entrance. He drew his weapon, keeping his pistol at low ready as he jogged down the cement walk.

"But the baby is coming. I can't walk."

"You can walk, milaya moyna. I guarantee you will find the strength. Or perhaps you wish to watch me blow a hole through the chest of this agent?"

"No, I don't want that, but—"

"I do not negotiate. Come."

"Don't get out of that car," Will ordered thickly. "Keep the doors locked."

Taylor leaned against the grainy bricks and poked his head around the rounded corner of the building. Nemov stood by their vehicle. He had one arm wrapped around Will's throat. He held a new shotgun in the other. It was pointed at Will's head.

"There you are, little man," he said, spotting Taylor. "I thought you would be here faster. Come out where I can see you."

Taylor leaned back against the wall and closed his eyes in brief prayer. He brought his weapon up and stepped out in firing stance.

"Federal agent. Drop your weapon."

Nemov seemed taken aback. He laughed. "Do you not see I have your partner?"

Taylor's eyes met Will's. Blood was running down Will's face from a cut in his hairline, but he seemed otherwise okay. Taylor flicked a quick look at their vehicle. Nemov had charged his reinforced SUV into their rental, crunching its nose into the tall brown trash Dumpsters.

Will had either gone for Nemov or been stunned just long enough for the bounty hunter to drag him out of the car. Either way, Hedwig had had the sense to lock herself in. The windows that weren't broken were firmly sealed.

"The sheriffs are on their way. Drop your weapon."

"Do you not see we have the Mexican stand—"

Taylor fired.

He had to hit Nemov at exactly the right place in the shoulder in order to paralyze his arm, and that meant grazing Will as well. He didn't want to, but he couldn't take the chance of an involuntary reflex of Nemov's fingers on that trigger. If Taylor'd stopped to weigh all the possibilities, he might not have made the shot as cleanly as he did going simply by instinct. As it was, Nemov howled his pained outrage and dropped the shotgun, which hit the asphalt and exploded, taking out the tire of their SUV.

Will stumbled free and kicked the shotgun farther away. He clamped a hand to his bloody shoulder.

"You shot me!" He was staring at Taylor in utter disbelief.

"I know. Sorry." Taylor brushed past him, slamming Nemov over the hood of the SUV. "I need your handcuffs."

Will groped one-handed, found his cuffs, and tossed them at Taylor. "You fucking *shot* me, MacAllister."

"I know, Will. I'm very sorry." He adjusted the cuffs for Nemov's massive wrists, clamped them on, and knocked him to his knees.

"I am injured," roared Nemov. "I am bleeding."

"*You*, I did mean to shoot, so just be grateful we're at a hospital."

Taylor stood as a white and gray cop car turned into the lot, lights flashing, siren screaming. It was followed by a second car with the sheriff's insignia.

The SUV door swung open. Hedwig stepped out, clutching her belly, and tottered slowly toward the walkway.

"Where are you going?" Taylor called.

"To have my baby!"

The sheriffs piled out of their cars as still another police vehicle screeched into the lot.

"This is just great," Will said.

"Hands up! Throw down your weapon!" The officer using the bullhorn wore a white cowboy hat. Clearly one of the good guys.

Taylor nodded, stooped to lay his pistol on the blacktop. He rose and locked his hands behind his head.

The sheriffs rushed forward.

* * * * *

"I still can't believe you shot me."

"I know. I'm sorry. It *is* just a flesh wound. The crack on your head needed more stitches."

"That doesn't exactly make it better." Will was scowling, although he permitted Taylor to hold his hand as he perched on the edge of Will's hospital bed. Will looked rakishly handsome with the white square of bandage on his forehead and the dark five o'clock—make that eight o'clock—shadow on his jaw.

Taylor lifted Will's hand in both of his and kissed it.

"It hurts like hell."

Taylor nuzzled Will's knuckles. He kissed each finger with a tiny, sucking kiss.

"Hmmph." Slightly mollified, Will said, "The baby's okay?"

"Small but healthy. Six pounds, nine ounces. William Taylor Hedwig."

"Christ."

Taylor laughed.

"And what did Cooper have to say?"

"Ah. Apparently Hedwig—Kelila—was telling the truth. She was working voluntarily with the DEA."

"What happened?"

"She uncovered a connection between Bashnakov and a DEA deputy administrator."

"Ted Bell."

"Yeah." Taylor was surprised. "How did you know that?"

"Kelila and I had a chat earlier."

Taylor raised his brows. "Well, around the time her contact at the DEA suffered a mysterious and fatal accident, Kelila realized she was pregnant. She decided to get out while she could. She got in touch with one of our people working in liaison with the DEA, and he put her in contact with Henry Torres. The DS was going to take on the internal investigation of the DEA, but then Torres was killed and Kelila was framed for his murder."

"So...?"

"So it turns out our new AFOD was working from Torres' notes and files to try and nail Ted Bell, which is why we were sent to retrieve Kelila. Cooper needs her as a witness. His case rests on her."

Will's face stilled. "Oh."

Taylor grimaced. "Of course he couldn't tell us that because there was obviously a leak somewhere."

"What happens to Kelila now?"

"After Cooper's got what he needs, she and the kid go into the Witness Protection Program."

"And what happens to us for going off the reservation?"

"We got her back safely; that's the main thing. Cooper's flying out tonight to get her deposition."

Will's blue eyes watched him closely. "Good. What aren't you telling me?"

"Nothing. Everything's good." Taylor took a deep breath. "You have to make your mind up about the Paris assignment. They...need an answer. Cooper's going to ask for your decision when he gets here."

Will's eyes closed then. His hand tightened on Taylor's fingers, bruising them.

"It's okay. I already know." Taylor said it so calmly, he almost believed it himself.

When Will opened his eyes, they were wet. "I..."

"You don't have to say anything." That much was the truth. He couldn't handle seeing Will tear himself up over this. "We'll be okay. It's like you said. Time flies when you're having fun."

Will pulled him forward, wrestling him into a kind of bear hug where they could hang on tight and neither had to see the other's expression. Taylor rested his face in the bare, warm curve of Will's uninjured shoulder and listened to the shuddery sounds of Will fighting his feelings. He could hear the slow, heavy pound of Will's heart, and though he was not much for poetry, he suddenly remembered lines from some forgotten time and place—all his times and places having led, it seemed, to this moment.

The bleeding to death of time in slow heart beats,

Wakeful they lie

DEAD RUN

CHAPTER ONE

There was something familiar about the man at the airline ticket counter.

Taylor studied him for a moment. Medium height…slightly stooped…medium weight…aquiline features beneath the tweed cap. Nothing unique about an old man in a raincoat. In fact, the very ordinariness of him was part of what caught Taylor's eye. It was like this old guy had taken *inconspicuous* to an art form.

"Next!" called one of the agents at the check-in desk. The couple in front of Taylor dragged their children and luggage to the next open space at the long desk. Taylor stepped forward. The serpentine line shuffled and scooted behind him.

Had he remembered the photos of Riley? Taylor double-checked quickly. No. He'd left them on the kitchen table. *Damn.* He knew how much Will missed that damn dog, and he'd meant the snapshots as a little surprise.

Oh well. If Will wanted to see Riley that much, he could always come home.

Taylor glanced up automatically as the old man ahead of him turned away from the ticket counter.

Dark eyes met his, held his gaze for an instant, then dismissed him. The back of Taylor's neck prickled. *No. No way.* It couldn't be.

But he couldn't quite ignore that feeling of recognition.

Yann Helloco.

A few days ago he'd been reading an article in *American Cop* on the history of modern terrorism in Europe. That had to be why he was suddenly seeing a long-dead Breton separatist in the first senior citizen wearing a beret who crossed his path.

Okay, not a beret, but close enough to trigger the connection.

A ticket agent at the far end opened and nodded to Taylor. "Sir."

The line behind Taylor breathed a collective sigh. One step closer to the prize.

Taylor hesitated.

"Next in line please," the ticket agent encouraged when Taylor didn't seem to be getting the hint.

Taylor groaned inwardly. He was probably wrong.

More importantly, he was on vacation. He had a plane to catch. A plane he had no intention of missing. It had been eleven months since he'd seen Will. Eleven months since they'd been together. No fucking *way* was he missing this plane.

But what if he wasn't wrong? What if by some crazy coincidence he had just seen a ghost?

Oh, what the hell.

He moved instead to the agent who had assisted Helloco, if Helloco it was. She was busily putting a little CLOSED sign at her place, with the air of someone taking her break come hell or high water.

He sized her up fast. Cute and prim in her navy blue polyester. A girl in love with the rules and regulations. He looked for her name badge. *Bridget Martinez.*

"Bridget." She did her best not to see him, but Taylor pasted on his most charming smile and pushed harder. "That guy you just gave a boarding pass to—where is he headed?"

Bridget looked as surprised as if her ticket machine had asked her to bring it back a cappuccino. "Sir?"

"Your last customer. I need his name and his flight number." Taylor already had his DSS ID out. He was keeping his voice down, trying to avoid attention, but she was backing away from the counter, shaking her head, doing her best to separate herself from whatever situation he was trying to drag her into.

"I'm sorry but we can't give out that information."

Taylor pushed his ID toward her, hoping the problem was her vision. "I'm with the Diplomatic Security Service."

Bridget stopped backing away, but her expression grew more skeptical. "I never heard of it."

"It's the law enforcement branch of the Bureau of Diplomatic Security. I'm with the State Department."

"You just said you were with the Diplomacy Service. Anyway, that's not what your *badge* says."

"The hell it doesn't." Taylor jabbed his finger at the blue and gold ring around the seal on his badge. *Department of State. Diplomatic Security Service.* "It says it right here."

Bridget didn't exactly roll her eyes, but if he thought she'd been born yesterday, he clearly had another think coming. "Anyone can have one of those made."

"Are you kidding me?"

"It doesn't even look real."

As much as Taylor hadn't wanted to start this, her obstructive attitude hardened his resolve. "Get your manager." He watched the luggage moving on the conveyor belt behind Bridget. "Did he check a bag?"

"Who?"

He smothered his exasperation. "The guy you just checked in. Do *not* let any of his luggage go through."

Bridget was looking at Taylor as though he were a nut. In fairness, working at a ticket counter in an airport probably jaded you as fast as working in law enforcement.

Bridget waved to another airline employee in a navy suit. "Mr. Yousef! Mr. Yousef, can I see you please?"

Maybe she was trying for discretion, but the overall impression was *cleanup on aisle three!* Bored passengers were staring their way, and the man who might be—but probably was not—Yann Helloco was now a quickly disappearing tan raincoat in a crowd of tan raincoats heading for the security screening lines.

Mr. Yousef, big, black, and bald, with an unexpectedly charming smile, joined Bridget at the counter. He silently examined Taylor's ID as Bridget filled him in on the details.

"This customer is trying to get personal information about another customer. He says he's a secret agent."

"What?" Taylor spared her a startled look before turning back to Yousef. "I'm with the DSS. That's a division of the Bureau of Diplomatic Security."

"Sure." Yousef spoke in a deep and melodious bass. "You're the guys who protect foreign bigwigs when they visit."

"Right." It was like the relief of finding someone who spoke English in a foreign country. "Among other things. Bridget here just processed a passenger who I believe might be wanted by Interpol." He was trying very hard not to use the *T* word.

"*Might*," Yousef repeated as the conveyor belt behind him lurched forward again.

"Please don't let that bag go through without screening it," Taylor told Bridget, who was waiting hopefully for Yousef to chop him into mincemeat. She ignored him.

"Bag? Every bag we checked is screened."

Mr. Yousef turned to Bridget, who said with a tight little smile, "I tried to tell this gentleman that the other customer didn't check any baggage."

Taylor opened his mouth, but really…bigger fish to fry. He turned to Yousef.

Yousef said, "Bridget, did you not see this agent's identification and badge?"

"Well, yes, but you can get those made anywhere. And it doesn't look real."

Mr. Yousef shook his head apologetically at Taylor. "Let's get the information Special Agent MacAllister needs."

Bridget returned to her computer and tapped the keys in quick, irritated strokes. She moved aside for Mr. Yousef, who read aloud, "Yannick Hinault. He's on his way to Paris on Delta Flight DL67 departing from Gate 57."

Yann Helloco and Yannick Hinault. Not exactly case closed but surely too similar for coincidence?

"I'm leaving my stuff with you." Taylor unloaded his suitcase and carry-on bag, ignoring Bridget's instinctive protest. "Can you call the gate and have them hold that flight? And have security meet me there."

"I can try," Yousef said. "But you better be sure this is your guy, or I wouldn't want to be in your shoes."

Taylor was already moving in that easy law enforcement lope that covered a lot of ground without giving the public the impression that there was cause for alarm. Even so he was moving way too fast for anyone in an airport, and security officers were moving to intercept him as he headed for the screening tables.

A quick survey of the lines of shoeless and coatless passengers confirmed there was no sign of Helloco or Hinault or whoever this asshole was who was already starting to interfere with Taylor's much-needed vacation.

Then the unis blocked his view. Taylor flashed his tin, doing his best to explain the situation without triggering all the alarms in the place. It was his bitter experience that getting airport security involved was usually more trouble than it was worth, but there was no way around it. It was at times like these he missed Will. Will was so much better at finessing…well, everyone.

"Are you armed, Agent MacAllister?" a short, squat guy with a face like the Great Pumpkin questioned.

Taylor shook his head. "No. I'm on my annual leave. My weapon is secured at my place of residence."

The rent-a-cops began to ask him the usual stuff: Had he been drinking? Was he on medication?

Did he *look* like a guy who had been drinking or was on medication?

In the back of his mind, Taylor could hear Will cautioning him to be cool, to play the game, so he bit back his immediate retort. He knew the ritual was partly departmental flexing of muscles and partly the fact that these jokers considered snagging a pair of nail scissors off an old lady a coup for law enforcement.

Another uniform joined the crowd surrounding Taylor. "He checks out."

"Sorry for the hassle, but we have to follow procedure," the Great Pumpkin told Taylor. "You know how it is."

"Yeah. No problem. Can we move?"

To their credit, they did hustle their asses, leading the way through a complex maze of backdoor corridors until they reached Gate 57 where, by now, flight DL67 was boarding. Taylor strode quickly through the waiting area, scanning the seats and lines of bored passengers. There was no sign of Hinault.

He began studying body types and facial structure. If Hinault was Helloco, he was one cool and clever customer, so Taylor was putting no trick in the book past him.

The airline agent behind the customer service station spoke into the microphone. "Will passenger Yannick Hinault please report to the customer service desk? Passenger Yannick Hinault, please report to the customer service desk."

Taylor moved to the edge of the waiting area and watched for anyone trying to slip away. No one came to the desk, and no one showed any interest in missing their flight.

Taylor swore inwardly. He turned to the milling security officers. The Great Pumpkin raised his arms in a *beats me* gesture.

Seriously?

Seriously?

Taylor took a couple of angry paces. What now? Nine passenger terminals were connected by a U-shaped two-level roadway. Los Angeles International Airport was one of the largest airports in the world.

He checked his iPhone. He was going to miss his flight. *Shit.* Where the hell did they even s—

"*Uncle Taylor.*" Skinny arms wrapped around Taylor's waist. Taylor spun around.

A dark-haired boy of eight or so was smiling up at him in delight. Taylor experienced one of those worlds-colliding moments as he belatedly recognized his eight-year-old nephew, Jamie.

"What are you doing here?"

He must have sounded pretty sharp because Jamie's face fell and he turned scarlet, suddenly aware of the armed and uniformed men surrounding him. He let go of Taylor and retreated.

Taylor spotted his sister, Tara, approaching. She carried her younger son Jase on her hip, and she was staring at Taylor as though an eyesore had appeared on her horizon. Looping an arm around Jamie, she pulled him close.

"Taylor? What's going on?"

Taylor said at the same moment, "Are you on this flight?"

"We're meeting James in Paris. What's happening? Is there a problem?" Her gaze traveled from Taylor to the phalanx of security officers behind him.

James MacDonald, Tara's husband, was an executive for Geo-Gulf Oil, one of the companies owned by Taylor's and Tara's stepfather. James worked and lived a large part of the year in Bahrain. Tara and the boys traveled back and forth from California.

"I don't know if there's a problem or not," Taylor told her.

"You don't *know*?"

That was the trouble being the youngest child. No matter how old you got, how good you were at your job, or what a well-known badass you turned out to be, you were always the nutty kid brother to your siblings.

Other passengers were watching them suspiciously. Taylor led Tara to the side. "I think they're going to cancel the flight, but if they don't, don't get on that plane."

"Cancel the flight?"

Taylor winced. Tara would never make a poker player.

"*Why*? What's wrong?"

"Probably nothing. But just…I don't want to take any chances."

Jase reached out and tried to grab Tara's hoop earring. She automatically shifted him to the other hip. "Taylor, you can't just drop a bomb like that and not expect any questions."

At the word *bomb,* a collective shudder went through the security people who were now watching brother and sister as much as the general boarding area.

Tara glanced back at them, did a double take, and turned to Taylor. She'd lost color. Her arms instinctively tightened around Jase. "Oh my God."

Taylor said quickly, "Nothing's been confirmed. Not even close. I'm probably way off base here. But let's not take any chances."

Tara stared at him. "You don't think you're wrong."

He admitted wearily, "I have no idea if I'm wrong. All I know for sure is I just missed my own flight."

"Where are you flying to?"

"Paris."

"You're kidding."

He shook his head. "Different flight."

Tara bit her lip, gazing at the crowded lounge area where the restless passengers were now beginning to openly share their irritation at the delay. "Maybe your guy took the other flight?"

Taylor shook his head. "He can't have boarded another Delta flight using that name. He's been flagged. Or…at least…"

"What?" Tara was watching him closely.

Taylor shook his head again. "I'm not sure. It's a long shot. I've got to go talk to these cowboys. Just wait here. They've got instructions to hold the plane."

"For how long?"

"For however long it takes. They're telling me no luggage was checked, so it's probably fine. Even so, don't board this flight."

"What are you *talking* about, don't board this flight? We can't just waste these tickets. Do you have any idea how expensive it will be to try to—"

He wasn't listening.

Was it possible that Hinault or Helloco or whoever this guy was had made him in the check-in queue?

If so, would Helloco have a backup plan? What would that backup plan be?

Will was always telling Taylor what a devious bastard he was. Okay, what would another devious bastard do in this situation? Assuming—and it was a big assumption, after all—that Taylor's imagination wasn't running away with him and that he had really seen Yann Helloco.

The more he thought about it, the more doubtful it seemed. The coincidence of the similar names and destination—Paris notwithstanding.

"We need to do a full sweep of the airport," Taylor told the Great Pumpkin.

The Great Pumpkin laughed.

"I'm not kidding around. We need to conduct a full search of all the airport terminals."

"If you're not kidding, then I want whatever the hell it is you're smoking. We can't authorize that kind of operation based on your say-so. There are *procedures*. There are *channels*."

"Fine. Let's initiate whatever those procedures are through whatever channels necessary."

The other man stared at him for a long, grim moment. "Have it your way. But you better be right."

* * * * *

He was not right.

"Better safe than sorry, sir," Taylor said to Assistant Field Office Director Cooper when he was summoned, forty-five minutes later, to the phone in Security. It was what Will would have said, for sure, in the same position. Not that Will would have gotten himself into the same position.

"That's true, MacAllister," Cooper replied. "Provided we're talking about pool safety or learning to use the crosswalk. It's not true when we're talking about the hundreds of thousands, maybe millions of dollars it would have cost to mount a full-scale search of LAX and ground all those flights you wanted grounded. I've got the FAA and TSA and Homeland Security all screaming for your head on a platter. I'm tempted to give it to them."

It was difficult, very difficult, to substitute the things he really wanted to say for a restrained, "I'm sorry, sir. I had to make a judgment call."

"*Judgment* is the last word you should be using, MacAllister. You're not even sure it was Helloco. The odds are you did *not* see Helloco. "

Taylor held his tongue. Cooper was right.

"By rights I ought to cancel your leave and drag you back here for a full inquiry, but as you clearly *need* this vacation time, we'll postpone till your return."

Taylor struggled within himself. "Thank you, sir."

Cooper hung up. Loudly.

* * * * *

"Better safe than sorry," Tara reassured him before she boarded her own much-delayed flight. "You did the right thing."

Taylor nodded. He ruffled Jamie's hair. "Be good, sport."

Jamie beamed up at him, adoring once more. It was not a generally shared view.

Hinault's flight was the one plane that had been held. Every piece of luggage in its cargo hold had been searched, but nothing had been found. Every piece of luggage matched perfectly to another irate passenger complaining about missed connections and lost hotel reservations and blown business meetings and the general inconvenience.

In fairness, Taylor had also missed his flight, and although the consensus was that he had done the only possible thing in reporting his suspicions, he could feel his lack of popularity in the apathetic effort to get him rebooked.

When he found out the next flight to Paris was not until midnight, he had to fight the urge to punch something. Ideally Yannick Hinault, but Hinault seemed to have vanished into thin air.

After he watched Tara's plane depart, Taylor found a pay phone and dialed the number of the US Embassy in Paris. Before the call went through, he remembered the time difference. It would be one o'clock in the morning. Saturday morning at that. He disconnected and redialed Will's apartment from memory. He'd be waking Will out of a sound sleep to tell him the whole story and admit that his overzealousness had cost them a full day together.

The phone rang on the other end with a perky jangle that sounded peculiarly French. The receiver picked up on the second ring, and a crisp male American accent that was definitely not Will's said, "Hello?"

CHAPTER TWO

"**H**ey, Will. Phone for you."

David Bradley's voice floated clearly through the bathroom door. Will opened the door, toweling his wet hair.

"At this hour?"

There was a suggestion of a delay before David said, "I think it's your…partner."

Shit.

Will glanced at the bedroom clock. What the hell was Taylor doing phoning when he should be in a plane winging over the Atlantic Ocean? And why the hell had David picked that phone up?

He resisted the impulse to spell all that out. It wasn't David's fault that Taylor, supremely confident in most areas, suffered from a disconcerting insecurity where Naval Lieutenant Commander David Bradley was concerned.

He went through to the front room and picked up the phone.

"Brandt here."

"It's me."

It was funny how even after all this time, his heart gave a little kick at the sound of Taylor's husky voice. Like a turbo boost. They'd been friends and partners for almost four years before unexpectedly—on Will's part, anyway—realizing that somehow along the way, affection had turned to love. "Where are you?"

He was expecting the next comment to be a question about David, though he hoped Taylor wouldn't recognize the voice as Bradley's given he'd only heard it a couple of times. Even so, Taylor was probably wondering why there was a guy in Will's apartment at one in the a.m.

But Taylor surprised him. "LAX."

"Why? Why aren't you on your way here?"

"I missed my flight."

Will swore. "Don't tell me that bastard Cooper canceled your leave again?"

"No. I screwed this up myself." Taylor proceeded to tell him about believing he'd spotted geriatric terrorist Yann Helloco from an article in *American Cop*.

When Will could wedge a word in, he asked, "Who the hell is Yann Helloco?" Anyone but Taylor and he'd figure the guy was putting in too much overtime, but if Taylor thought he'd ID'd this silver panther, that was good enough for Will.

Although he kind of wished Taylor hadn't had to go quite so Dudley Do-Right on their vacation time.

"Back in the sixties he was a member of the FLB. The Front de Libération de la Bretagne. You'd know them as the Liberation Front of Brittany."

"No, I wouldn't. I've never heard of them. The sixties? Are you kidding? I've got plenty to keep me busy with current affairs."

"They were called the smiling terrorists."

"I'm sure. I'm sure they left their victims laughing in the aisles." Will hated terrorists. Period.

"Their attacks were symbolic. No one was to be killed or injured, but then in the seventies Helloco and a few others broke and formed Finistère. Finistère didn't have the same attitude about nonviolence."

Eleven months and he's missed his goddamned plane, and for some reason he's talking to me about terrorism in the 1960s.

Will did his best to swallow his exasperation as Taylor tersely briefed him on Finistère's background and their greatest "statement," which was apparently the bombing of a Parisian museum and its collection of irreplaceable paintings by Jacques-Louis David.

Pronounced Dah-veed, but it reminded Will that Bradley was sitting on the sofa sipping his drink and trying not to listen in on Will's conversation.

He opened his mouth to address the inevitable question before Taylor had to, but Taylor was telling him—clipped tone revealing that this was the tough part—about how the plane had been delayed but no bomb had turned up and there had been no sign of Helloco.

Ouch. Taylor didn't say so, but he'd have gotten short shrift from everyone involved when this mythical bad guy failed to materialize. Reading between the lines: Taylor had exceeded his authority in spectacular fashion and was going to have to pay the price for his failed gamble. The line between hero and villain could be disconcertingly fine.

Will said comfortingly, "If that guy was who you thought he was, he's got radar. He probably pegged you for law enforcement before you ever spotted him."

"Maybe."

"He probably walked straight out of the airport and crawled back under whatever rock he's been hiding beneath."

"I guess."

Will knew that tone of old. Taylor was going to keep worrying at this like a dog with a bone.

"No? What do you think happened?"

"I think he had a contingency plan."

Because that was what Taylor would do, and nobody was better at thinking like a bad guy than Taylor. The fact that Will found that charming probably said something none too flattering about Will. "Such as?"

"He could have booked two flights."

"He couldn't use his real name. It would come up flagged."

"No, but he could book on two separate airlines as Yannick Hinault. Or he could have another alias too. Either way he could book two flights on two separate airlines, and if one flight seemed to be compromised, he could switch over to the second flight."

"Yeah, but—"

"Nobody searched other airlines. I tried, but they wouldn't do it. When Hinault or Helloco or whatever the hell his name is didn't turn up on Flight DL67, security did a haphazard sweep of the Delta terminal, found nothing and no one, and cleared the plane for takeoff."

Yep. It had gone down just as Will feared. "The problem is nobody saw him but you, and you're not sure the man you saw was Yann Helloco."

"Correct."

"Listen, you did what you could. You did the right thing. There's a chance this guy was not Yann Helloco, you know."

"I know. But the similarity of the names—"

"Sure. The names are similar."

"Not just similar. They're both Breton names."

Pretty weird coincidence, if it was a coincidence. Will didn't bother to deny it.

Taylor continued, "And why did this Hinault miss his flight? Where did he go?"

"People do miss flights, Taylor. Case in point."

"It's a big coincidence, Will. I just happen to spot a guy I think might be wanted by Interpol for the last thirty years, and that guy just happens to miss his flight?"

Will sighed, weary of the subject of Yann Helloco. "Yes, it's a big coincidence. So was your sister showing up at the airport today. Coincidences happen. They're not all sinister."

"He could be on his way to Paris right now."

"So could you." The minute it slipped out, Will regretted it. Taylor had done the right thing; Will would have done the same thing in his place. The difference being Will wouldn't recognize a terrorist from the seventies if the dude walked up and punched him in the nose. He wasn't even sure he'd recognize the legendary Carlos the Jackal, and his face had been plastered all over the news after he'd been arrested in the nineties.

"True," Taylor said without inflection.

Like Taylor hadn't taken enough shit over this? Will said quickly, "Listen, you made the right call. I just..." Too awkward to finish the thought with his former boyfriend not ten feet away, but Christ, he missed Taylor.

Even a few hours' delay seemed intolerable after all these months. Will had known the separation wasn't going to be easy, but he hadn't anticipated quite how tough it was going to get. He said instead, "Look on the bright side. If Helloco did catch a plane out of the country, good riddance. He's someone else's problem now."

If Taylor heard that, he didn't acknowledge it. "I'll be landing around eleven o'clock at Charles de Gaulle Airport. I should be at your place by—"

"I'm picking you up. We already settled this."

"Will, I can grab a cab. It's not a big deal."

"No, it's not, so enough with the cab."

"I just don't want to complicate your situation."

"What situation?"

"I don't know," Taylor said with a flash of irritability. "The situation that has David Bradley answering your phone at one in the morning."

Oh *that* situation. So much for Taylor not recognizing David's voice.

Will would have preferred to leave it at *We'll talk about it when I see you*, but the idea of Taylor spending the next ten hours thinking there was something going on between him and Bradley was not acceptable.

"David's in town for the D-day anniversary. We met for a late dinner and were coming back to my place for drinks when we got caught in the rain. I was in the shower when the phone rang." End of a lame-ass—but absolutely true—story.

"Okay."

Will said skeptically, "Okay?"

"Yeah. Okay."

There it was. One of the big reasons why Will loved Taylor. Trust was a two-way street. Will wouldn't want to be with someone who didn't trust him any more than he wanted to be with someone he couldn't trust. There had been a time when he had believed Taylor would be incapable of sustaining a long-term relationship, but Taylor had proved to be the model of fidelity, and Will had been the one who had made choices guaranteed to make any lover insecure. Yet Taylor had met the challenge with cool dignity and something pretty close to grace.

So to hell with David Bradley sitting within earshot. Will said softly into the phone, "I love you. Don't miss this plane, okay?"

Taylor's voice softened too. "Yeah. I won't."

There was more Will wanted to say, maybe would have said if he'd been on his own.

He replaced the receiver.

"How's MacAllister doing?" David asked, clearly out of politeness.

"He's fine." Will liked David. A lot. If things had been different…but they were what they were. Will was in love with Taylor and hoping they might eventually be posted to the same city again. He wasn't going to discuss their relationship with anyone but Taylor.

"Long-distance relationships are hard," David observed, as though reading Will's mind. He lifted his glass and took another sip of bourbon.

"We're working it out. But yeah, it's been tough on both of us."

"You've still got how long over here?"

"Another year at least." And that was the last thing Will wanted to think about.

Reading him accurately once again, David said, "You were saying at dinner your grandfather took part in the D-day assault during World War Two?"

Will swallowed the last of his own drink. The hot shower had relaxed him, and he was sleepy and hoping David wouldn't stay much longer. "One of them did. One grandfather was with the marines over in the Pacific and the other with the Fifth Ranger Battalion landing on Omaha Beach."

"Are you planning to attend the D-day celebration next week?"

"I hadn't thought about it."

"You should." David's warm brown eyes gazed into Will's, and Will felt that old, now uncomfortable, flare of response.

"Yeah, if Taylor's up for it."

David's gaze fell. He nodded and reached for his drink once more. "What made you give up the marines for the State Department?"

Not an easy topic for discussion. In fact, this was something Will had only discussed in depth with Taylor, and that had been early in their partnership. He was pretty sure David, being career navy, would not understand. "I did two tours of duty in Iraq. I saw a lot of people die on both sides. What I didn't see was us getting any closer to a resolution. Same in any arena of conflict in the world today. A lot of fighting, a lot of dying, but not a lot of problems getting solved."

David's expression was thoughtful.

Will said, "I guess that sounds funny coming from someone with my background. My dad was a marine too before he became a sheriff, and my brother just enlisted in the marines. I have the highest respect for the service, and I firmly believe a strong country requires a strong, well-trained, and well-supplied military. But it's my experience that diplomacy is actually the thing that ends conflict and gets problems solved in a permanent and lasting way."

David smiled. "Maybe it takes a combination of diplomacy and military might? I'll buy that. Was MacAllister in the marines as well?"

"No. Taylor joined the State Department right out of college."

"Ah. A career diplomat." David's tone was neutral. Too neutral.

Will smiled faintly. He didn't need to defend Taylor. Part of what had originally attracted him to his partner was Taylor's startlingly ruthless efficiency. Startling because Taylor actually looked sort of fragile. Fragile and sensitive. But Will had never known anyone more resilient. Physically resilient and mentally resilient. "He can be very tactful," he conceded. And that was a private joke that Taylor would have enjoyed, though Will was not about to admit he'd sat into the wee hours drinking bourbon and shooting the breeze with David Bradley if he didn't have to.

"He's a lucky guy." That was the closest they'd come all night to either of them touching on their aborted relationship. Will hoped David would leave it there because he liked David enough to try and remain friends with him.

To his relief, David swallowed the last mouthful of bourbon and said, "I guess I ought to shove off."

Will made polite noises, but he agreed. It was getting just a little too cozy in the apartment, what with hot showers and good bourbon and personal revelations.

David rose, a six-foot bear of a man with smiling eyes and a jaw of granite.

Will put his empty glass down and rose too. "It was great seeing you again, David. I mean that."

"Same here, Will. Thanks for a very enjoyable evening."

They walked to the door of the apartment. David hesitated. "Maybe I can return the hospitality and take you and MacAllister to dinner one night before I fly home?"

Will could imagine what his better half would have to say on that topic. "Sounds good to me. But technically it's Taylor's vacation. I'll see what he's got in mind."

"I know what I'd have in mind." David's smile was wry.

For an instant their gazes locked. Will broke the contact first. "'Night, David. It really was good to see you again after all this time."

David said with seeming reluctance, "Goodnight, Will."

David stepped into the hall, and Will closed the door firmly. It had been a pleasant evening, but he was glad it was over.

He glanced at the clock over the faux fireplace. Nine hours till Taylor arrived. Just nine hours to go, and then he'd be treating Taylor to a vacation he'd never forget.

CHAPTER THREE

True to his word—because he'd never be anything else—Will was waiting for him when Taylor got off the plane at Charles de Gaulle Airport.

Taylor scanned the crowd, and there he was: tall and square-shouldered and ridiculously handsome in faded Levi's and a navy T-shirt. Will's glossy brown hair fell boyishly across his forehead, and his blue eyes lit at the sight of Taylor. His face broke into a wide, white grin.

Taylor forgot his weariness and grinned back.

"You son of a gun," Will said. Or words to that effect. It wasn't the words; it was the tone.

Taylor had no idea what he answered—if he answered at all—because the next moment they were hugging.

Hugging and laughing and pounding each other on the back. So much for the famed Gallic effluence or effusion or effervescence or whatever it was. Will and Taylor were putting their fellow travelers to shame. Taylor ruffled Will's hair, and Will tried to put Taylor in a headlock.

Well, you had to do something when you'd never kissed in public.

They hugged again, not looking each other directly in the face so that any too-bright eyes could be safely ignored.

"I can't believe I'm here," Taylor said finally when Will stopped choking him and relieved him of his bags. "Jesus, you look great."

Understatement of the year. Will looked fantastic. Paris agreed with him. Taylor couldn't help feeling like he suffered by contrast. He needed a shower and a shave and a sleep. Though not as much as he needed Will.

Will growled, "I can't believe it either. I was ready to come and get you myself."

They exchanged quick, rueful looks. Twice Taylor's leave had been canceled due to pressure of work. The DSS, like every other State Department, was underfunded and understaffed.

"Hey, I'm here now."

"Yeah, you are. And you're going to have the best vacation ever."

Taylor smiled back at Will. His vacation had already improved drastically over the day before. In fact, he was only too happy to shove any thought of work and retired terrorists to the back of his mind.

They walked out of Terminal 2 to the crowded, covered parking. Taylor briefly admired Will's black and unmarked G ride, a Cadillac Escalade, the usual American-made light duty special utility vehicle that screamed Diplomatic Service to anyone paying attention.

"Did you get the memo over here on alternative fuel vehicles?"

Will snorted. "Yep." He unlocked the door for Taylor.

Taylor climbed in and closed his eyes for a moment while Will threw his bags into the back. He was so tired he felt delirious. Or maybe the giddy feeling was seeing Will again.

Will came around to the driver's seat and slid in beside Taylor.

Taylor opened his eyes and smiled at him.

Will smiled back. "Long time no see."

Taylor nodded. The laughter drained out of him. "Will."

They reached for each other again.

Will's mouth was warm and tasted familiar, and eleven months was as nothing while Will shared his breath for a couple of heartbeats. Taylor moaned, and it was only part pleasure because it hurt like hell to love anyone this much, to be whole only when that person was by your side—in your arms. Will muttered something back between fractured gasps.

They were going to leave bruises on each other, but Taylor welcomed it. Welcomed the pressure of a hard, seeking mouth, of hands that sank into muscle and bone in an attempt to hold on to what was always going to be, at most, fleeting. Will's mouth opened to his demand, and their tongues touched almost shyly after eleven months.

French kiss.

The thought made Taylor smile, and, feeling the smile, Will opened his eyes and pulled back a little. He shook his head, but it was affection, not reproof. He kissed Taylor again, kissed his upper lip, his mouth, the corner of his mouth…trying for gentleness but rapidly heating up again.

It was hard to stop once they got started. That hadn't changed.

Taylor drew back, gulping for air. Will kissed him below his jaw, trailed hot, velvety kisses down his throat to his collarbone.

"Do you think…we should…finish this somewhere more private…" Taylor panted.

"Tinted windows."

"…Still…"

Will rested against him for a moment. Taylor lowered his cheek to the top of Will's head. Will's hair was soft and smelled like herbal shampoo. For a second or two they didn't move, breathing softly, unevenly.

The alarm of the car parked next to Taylor's side chirped. Taylor jumped. Will sat up fast. Taylor automatically straightened his collar, staring at the side mirror, watching warily for whoever was headed their way.

A family of five with enough luggage and parcels for ten.

His eyes slanted toward Will. Will met his look and grinned ruefully.

"Home?"

"*Mais oui, mon ami*," Taylor agreed.

* * * * *

According to Taylor's guidebook, which he'd read cover to cover because he'd been too restless to sleep on the plane, the best time to see Paris was in the spring. From June on, tourists flooded the city, though supposedly June was still better than later in the summer. The jazz festival was in full swing—in fact, it was the season of festivals, and Parisians were celebrating everything from the French Open to Gay Pride—and the wisteria and chestnut trees were in bloom. The temperature was mild and sunny, and the sidewalk cafés were doing a brisk trade.

The spring would have been nice. So would dead of winter. Taylor was there to see Will, so much of the beauty of the city was lost on him. Not completely lost because he was aware that they were passing landmarks—

France was unquestionably beautiful—and Will was dutifully pointing out things of interest as they drove south into the heart of the city. He filled Taylor in on all the entertainment possibilities in the week ahead.

"Sounds fine to me," Taylor assured him. He really could not have cared less about seeing Notre Dame or the Louvre or Moulin Rouge or the Eiffel Tower or any museums or art galleries or parks. That didn't mean he wasn't interested in the things Will enjoyed about the city. He liked hearing Will enthuse about everything from the gendarmes on rollerblades along the Seine—in light body armor with small machine guns, no less—to watching the old men play pétanque or the children sail small wooden boats in the fountains at Jardin des Tuileries.

Will was happy in Paris, and that was good. Taylor couldn't help wishing that Will wasn't *quite* so happy, but hey…

"By the way, happy birthday." Will broke off the travelogue for a second.

Taylor's eyes widened. "Jesus. I totally forgot."

"I didn't. I've got something special planned for tonight."

Hopefully not dinner out at some fancy, overpriced restaurant. "Yeah? Does it involve silk sheets and passion oil?"

Will chuckled. "Not sure there will be any passion oil left after this afternoon."

Taylor laughed. He gazed out the window. "How far is your place from the embassy?"

"Not far. The Métro is about a four-minute walk from the apartment. You know Paris."

Actually, he didn't. Japan, Afghanistan, and a very brief stint in Haiti. So far.

Will launched off into tour guide mode again, and Taylor listened dutifully.

Will said suddenly, "This time last year you'd just been cleared for field duty. Remember?"

Like he was ever going to forget getting shot in the chest? "I remember."

"How are you feeling?"

"Huh?"

"Are you okay? That lung's not still giving you any trouble, is it?"

"What? Nah."

"Nah." Will mocked him gently. "That's right. I was forgetting bullets bounce off you, Superman."

Taylor nodded. "You have any tall buildings I can leap? Something more challenging than the Eiffel Tower?" He was trying too hard—they both were—and he fought the urge to keep talking. Since when had he and Will needed their silences filled in?

After what was starting to feel like an eternity, they arrived at Will's apartment, located on rue du Colisée.

Will unlocked the garden gate and led the way to a very pretty and newly renovated single apartment with a private entryway through the garden.

"Nice." It was nice. The living room was painted in soothing earth tones. It had high ceilings and elegant floor-to-ceiling French windows opening onto the garden and shops along the street. Next door to the old apartment building was the café where Will said he had his petit déjeuner of strong coffee and flaky croissants while he watched the world go by.

The furnishings were a mix of antiques and modern pieces: comfortable chairs in a cozy plaid, a pretty dining table, and a long, wide beige couch with fat cushions. On the opposite side of the room was an entertainment cabinet with a television and stereo.

"Three levels," Will told him. "The entryway and living room are on this floor. Bedroom and full bath on the second floor. The kitchen and half bath downstairs."

"Nice," Taylor said again because he couldn't think of anything else to say. He couldn't picture Will living in a place like this, but Will not only lived here; he loved it here.

Will switched on the stereo and the familiar, bell-clear tones of Emmylou Harris rang out in "Hard Bargain."

That helped a little, but Taylor still had the uncomfortable feeling he was a visitor here, a stranger. Not a feeling he enjoyed, and he forced it down. "This is really nice," he tried again, peering out the window at the garden. Lots of flowers. A bird was singing cheerfully from a small ornamental tree.

"Wait until you see the bedroom." Will's voice was husky. He wrapped his arms around Taylor, pulling him back against his own muscular length. Taylor gave himself up to it, tilting his head back, shivering a little as Will kissed the ticklish underside of his jaw and his throat and the curve of the side of his throat.

Will whispered, "You want to take some of these clothes off?"

"I guess I can spare my socks."

Will laughed, and Taylor turned in his arms to face him. Will's hands slipped under Taylor's blazer, warm through the thin cotton of Taylor's shirt as he pulled him closer still.

Taylor could feel the hardness of Will's erection straining against his own. He angled his head in search of a kiss. Oddly, this time when their lips met, it was a little more tentative than it had been in the airport parking lot.

Taylor's tongue traced the familiar shape of Will's teeth, and Will smiled, speaking against his open mouth. "Wanna make love?"

So formal? Since when?

Taylor batted his lashes, camping. "Why, I thought you'd never ask."

"I don't think I've thought of anything else for eleven months."

"Must make for some interesting paperwork."

"Especially after some of those phone calls." Will was giving him an odd look. "Christ. You are…" He shook his head, words seeming to fail him.

Taylor wasn't sure if that was a good thing or not. In fact, he could feel his cheeks warming. He'd had to do something to keep Will's attention across six thousand miles, but Will could be disappointingly conventional sometimes.

No. Not disappointing. More like…disconcerting.

He refused to give in to insecurity and suggested throatily, "Inventive?"

"Worth every penny of my long-distance phone bill, that's for sure."

"I hope you didn't try to expense those calls."

"Mm." Will rocked gently, insinuatingly against Taylor's hardness, and Taylor closed his eyes, savoring the warmth, the strength, the desire there. Will's mutter gave words to his own thought. "God, you feel good. And you smell good too."

"Yeah right. I need a shave." Taylor smiled, opening his eyes again. "And a shower."

Will's murmur was protest. "You'd just have to shower again afterward." He half walked, half danced Taylor toward the sofa.

"True." Taylor let himself be maneuvered backward, sparing a quick look as they tumbled to the cushions. They narrowly missed knocking over the pretty oval coffee table. Taylor started to laugh, his breath whooshing out as Will landed half on top of him.

"*Ow*. No, it's okay. I didn't need that testicle anyway."

"You've got more balls than anyone I ever knew," Will agreed.

Taylor laughed again, but he quieted at Will's expression. "What?"

"What do you want?" Will asked softly, intently. His eyes seemed to track every movement of Taylor's mouth.

Taylor licked his lips. "I want you. I want to fuck you." In fact, he *needed* to fuck Will. Needed to feel like Will was his, that Will belonged to him, that he could control…something. Even if just for a few minutes.

Will's grave face creased into his familiar smile. "Okay. Whatever you want. I want it too."

It hadn't always been that way, but Taylor wasn't about to argue.

They shifted around, sofa springs squeaking, and Will nearly knocked the coffee table over again as he shoved it aside to get whatever he needed from upstairs. His footsteps pounded up the little staircase, then receded.

Come to think of it, why weren't they doing this in the bedroom? Too much performance pressure on both of them? This way they still had the illusion of spontaneity. Whatever. It didn't matter. They would negotiate the curves.

But they both were trying too hard. Trying too hard to prove eleven months had made no difference at all. That everything was the same as it had always been.

Taylor wriggled out of his clothes in a couple of agile moves and waited patiently, resting on his side, head propped on his hand.

Will's footsteps pounded back down the stairs. Taylor laughed as Will's shirt preceded him into the room, floating down to land on the footstool. Will appeared a second later, grinning but seeming self-conscious.

"Take it off, take it ahhhlll off," Taylor ordered in his best German accent.

Will laughed, but that had been the extent of his striptease. He undressed in quick, neat moves beneath Taylor's smiling gaze.

Will's body was the epitome of lithe strength and masculine beauty. It was a pleasure just to watch him.

He joined Taylor on the sofa, stretching out beside him.

"Hello, handsome." Taylor's cock thrust playfully against Will's.

Will's mouth quirked. "Hello."

"*En garde*. That's French for *I want to fuck*."

"*Touché*. That's French for *me too*." Will's oil-slick hands found Taylor, and he made a fist, pumping Taylor's cock with quick strokes.

Taylor caught his breath, closing his eyes. "God, Will."

"Let me. I like to touch you."

Like Taylor was going to object to anything Will chose to do to him?

He was almost in pain by the time Will finished with him. With heavy, languid eyes he watched Will twist, sliding slippery fingers into his own ass, preparing himself with the little bottle of lubricant he'd brought down.

Nothing fancy. No passion oil, nothing scented or flavored or exotic. That was Taylor's thing, not Will's. Will was all about speed and efficiency and proper safety measures—which sounded dull but somehow wasn't when that eager care was being exerted on your behalf.

Will turned onto his side, and Taylor settled snugly behind him. The sofa was not nearly as large as it had appeared at first glance, but it really didn't matter. They had managed this in tighter places, hotter places, wetter places…

Taylor took himself in hand, guiding the head of his cock to the shadowy center of Will's sleek buttocks. He pushed in, slow, slowly…

"How's that?" His voice sounded strained to his own ears.

"Beautiful. Come on, sweetheart."

Slowly, sweetly…oh, that felt good. Like nothing in the world. Always good, but so much better with Will. It never ceased to amaze Taylor that Will let him do this. That Will *wanted* him to do this. But he did. He was making deep, encouraging sounds, pushing back strongly in response to Taylor's tentative thrusts.

"How do you want it, Will?"

"Whatever you want, Tay. It's all good."

That had certainly been true once upon a time. Taylor pushed a little harder, though still careful, still measuring his strokes.

When he'd pictured this, he'd envisioned something frantic and hurried, maybe taking each other in an elevator, a stairwell, pounding each other into the nearest wall, but the reality was he *needed* to be gentle. Will was tight as a virgin. Not for Will the lonely self-pleasuring of dildos and plugs.

But Will was being just as gentle, just as careful in his way, craning his head for the occasional awkward kiss, stroking Taylor where he could reach him, taking time to tell Taylor how good everything he was doing felt.

Not as cautious as they'd be with a new lover, but conscientious with each other in a way they'd never bothered with before.

Will reached behind, clumsily cupped Taylor's face, giving a shiver as Taylor sucked his fingers.

Taylor stroked Will's tanned, muscular chest. He tried to time his thrusts, fighting to keep urgent need from spilling over and ending it all too soon. But Jesus, that fierce clench of muscle sliding up his cock…

"More," Will urged. "More, Tay. Come on."

Taylor groaned. He couldn't have resisted that plea even if he'd wanted to. The heat and smell and taste of Will were driving him to overload. He had to let go or implode. He began to thrust quick and hard.

"That's it. Yeah, that's the way," Will's hoarse voice spurred him on. Will's sleek body labored beneath him as they raced toward the finish, and now there wasn't a hope in hell of stopping that train.

From a distance he could hear Will's moans, feel that moist velvet clutch dragging against his cock. He buried his face on the back of Will's head, breathing in Will's scent, soft hair against his face, damp skin against his lips. He was going to leave new bruises, his fingers digging into Will's muscles like he was hanging on for dear life.

He felt the wildness uncoil inside him, blazing through his nerves and muscles, pressure building, expanding, filling… Yes, there it was…

Taylor cried out, and he was coming, coming hard in hot jets of salty cream. Filling Will, marking Will, making Will his again. He felt that orgasm rolling through Will like a wave.

Distantly he was aware of Will turning his face into the sofa cushions and howling with his release. Taylor held him more tightly, wanting to cushion and reassure, but somehow it was Will cradling him and Taylor clinging as he sank down heavily, exhausted, into the embrace.

Emmylou continued to sing over their ragged breaths.

Will drew soothing caresses up and down his spine. The summer breeze through the window tickled their hair, cooled their damp, flushed bodies.

"What *will* the neighbors think?" Taylor managed finally.

Will gusted out a little laugh and kissed him.

Taylor dozed. Maybe they both dozed. If so, Will must have woken first, half suffocated under Taylor's weight, because Taylor came to with kisses, warm and wet on his eyelids, the bridge of his nose, the corner of his mouth.

"The bed will be more comfortable." Will's voice was heated against his ear.

Taylor nodded, disinclined to move. He nuzzled Will's chest, tasted the stickiness there.

Will's breath caught. "Come on. You need real sleep."

He sat up, dislodging Taylor.

Taylor sat up too, rubbing his head. He mumbled, "You're going to have to get these cushions cleaned."

"I don't know." Will's voice sounded too loud in the hazy sunshine. "I was thinking it was time for a change of decor. I like the loved-in look."

Taylor studied Will from under his eyelashes. Despite the sex—nice sex it was too—they were still just a little out of sync. Not much, just a fraction of a second off-beat. No big deal. They'd get it back. They—Will—needed to stop trying so much. He reached out to brush Will's hair out of his eyes.

Will moved his head away, stood, and hauled Taylor to his feet. "Did you sleep at all on the plane?"

"Not that I recall." Taylor swayed, putting a hand to the base of his spine. "I don't know if my back will ever be the same."

"Same here." Will rubbed his ass, clowning.

Taylor spluttered a laugh, letting Will steer him up the stairs to the bedroom, one of Will's hands locked on his hip, the other on his shoulder. He had a quick impression of inlaid wood, creamy walls, creamy bedding, sheer veils over a view of the garden and the roofs of other buildings. Nice but not Will's style. The apartment came furnished.

Will said, "*Voilà.* Clean sheets. Just for you."

"I ought to call Tara," Taylor mumbled, dropping face-first into the cool linen.

"Just what a fella likes to hear after a bout of vigorous lovemaking."

"My sister, you ass."

"That's probably worse."

The mattress dipped as Will flopped down on the bed beside Taylor. They rolled into each other's arms.

From somewhere a long way off, Will's deep voice said something.

Taylor murmured encouragingly and promptly fell asleep in the middle of Will's answer.

* * * * *

They dined at a fancy, overpriced restaurant called L'Ambrosie.

A sleep and a shower had gone a long way to reviving Taylor. He was all for leaving the car and walking to the Métro when Will suggested it. On foot was clearly the way to see Paris, and he enjoyed the brief walk and even the Métro ride.

Will looked especially handsome and more sophisticated than usual in dark trousers, dark silk T-shirt, and a charcoal blazer. Not that Will wasn't always a snappy dresser, but this was something more. Something uncomfortably close to elegant. He was wearing his hair a little differently too. It had to be the cut. Nothing obvious but somehow a little sharper, a little more fashionable. He looked good. He looked great. Like someone out of a magazine. Taylor was getting irritated with himself for noticing every minuscule change. Eleven freaking months in a foreign country. Of course there would be some changes. What the hell did he expect?

Every time his eyes met Will's, Will smiled. Smiled with real pleasure as though seeing Taylor a few feet from him was the best sight in the world. And *that* was all that mattered.

From the Métro it was another short walk to the restaurant. L'Ambrosie was a seventeenth-century town house in the picturesque Place des Vosges, the oldest and reportedly most beautiful square in Paris. The restaurant was also beautiful—and formal. Warm lighting from a sparkling chandelier bathed the parquet floors, chinoiserie carpets, and honey-hued walls brightened with oil paintings and rich tapestries. The tables were covered in creamy linen, and the chairs were plum or gold velvet. There was an abundance of candles and roses and tall mirrors.

Every single table in the place was filled. Great. Taylor had been hoping for quiet and intimate. In fact, he'd been hoping for dinner at Will's place and an early night.

But it was what it was, so he needed to make the most of it. He scanned the menu and nearly dropped it on the elegant flower arrangement. "Jesus, Will. *Eighty-six euros* for hors d'oeuvres? If we order wine and dessert, this meal is going to set you back a grand or more."

"Simmer down. I've been planning this meal. I want this night to be special."

"Sure. We can mark it down as the night we officially went into debt."

Will's smile faded a little. "Would you knock it off, MacAllister? I'm trying to do something nice for you."

Taylor knew better than to say it, but the words popped out anyway. "You must have one hell of a guilty conscience."

Now Will was no longer smiling. His eyebrows made one dark, uncompromising line as he scanned the menu. He said curtly, "The langoustines in curry appetizer are supposed to be phenomenal. The langoustines melt in your mouth. So I've heard."

Langoustines being just a fancy word for *lobster*. Taylor swallowed that comment and said instead, "You come here often?"

"Of course not. I was here once before for an embassy dinner."

"How are the steaks?"

Will's head shot up. "*Steak*? You're the guy who always wants to experiment and try something new, but suddenly you're going to come to Paris and eat *steak*?"

"Jeez, Will—"

"What happened to trying not to eat red meat?"

"What the hell are we arguing about?" Taylor asked softly.

Will's hard gaze fell. He shook his head. "Sorry."

Taylor studied Will's downbent head, caught his own somber expression in one of the long mirrors across the room. They looked more like two guys saying good-bye than enjoying a reunion dinner.

He took a deep breath and then let it out silently. "You pick the wine and appetizers, okay? I'll pick the dessert."

Will looked up and smiled. "Okay. It's a deal."

The food was good. Not the best meal Taylor had ever had in his life and not, in his opinion, worth the money—other than after the last eleven months he would have been willing to pay anything for dinner with Will again—but well-prepared and nicely presented. They started with piping hot *gougères*, a cheesy puff pastry fresh from the oven, and ended with a delectably light chocolate tart. Will chose, as he frequently did, sea bass, and Taylor went for the chicken stuffed with morel mushrooms and white cream sauce. They drank a good deal of very nice wine and relaxed a little further with each sip.

Will raised his glass. "Happy birthday, Taylor." His eyes were dark with affection and more—much more—so that Taylor's face warmed and he forgot all about the price tag of the meal.

They toasted, crystal glasses chiming with silvery sweetness.

Taylor said slowly, "You know, this is another anniversary as well."

Will's look was inquiring.

"It was five years ago yesterday that we were first partnered."

Will's smile was very white in the candlelight. "There are marriages that don't last that long."

They sipped their wine, both thinking.

Taylor tried to keep his tone casual, but it needed to be asked. "Has your RSO given any indication whether they'll want to extend your stay?"

He could read the reluctance to answer in Will's face. Will expelled a long breath. "I haven't accepted."

"Yet."

"I haven't accepted," Will repeated. "That's not a decision I'm going to make without talking to you."

Taylor nodded noncommittally.

"I don't want to stay. But…"

"But we both knew it was a possibility.'

"Yes. We did."

"And that's kind of the object here. To move up the ladder."

Will stared at him. "It is. Yeah. But not at the expense of everything else. Not at the expense of us."

Taylor hoped his laugh didn't sound as bitter as it felt. "I think I can simplify the choice for you. I've got my next posting as well."

Will's dark brows drew together. "Shit. Overseas?"

Taylor nodded. "It's an RSO position. Like we thought."

"Congratulations," Will said without enthusiasm. "Not France obviously. Where?"

"Iraq."

CHAPTER FOUR

"No. No fucking way."

"Will—"

"No. You are not taking a goddamned posting in Iraq." Will didn't care that diners at the next table were glancing their way. *Iraq?* And the way Taylor popped out with it like…*ain't no big deal.* The hell it wasn't.

He watched Taylor strive for patience. "Look, we both knew I was eventually going to be posted overseas."

"Not to Iraq."

"Oh for chrissake. Iraq is where they need people."

"You said you'd resign if they tried to send you overseas."

Taylor's jaw dropped.

Will flushed. He knew he was being unreasonable but…Iraq? The highest casualties in the DSS were in Iraq. Will had been stationed in Iraq when he was in the marines. It was a goddamned hellhole, and he couldn't bear to think of Taylor there.

Taylor had that dangerous glint in his eyes. He said with ominous patience, "When I said I'd resign, it was because I didn't think we could survive a long-distance relationship, but since we're *in* a long-distance relationship, what the fuck is my excuse for not taking a promotion?"

"What about us?"

"What *about* us?" There was no give in Taylor, no softening. Stone-faced, he said, "I'll be there two years, which is about how long you'll be here in Paris. Perfect timing, if you ask me."

"Two years minimum. They'll ask you stay on. You said it yourself; they need people there."

"How about I get through the first two years before we worry about it? For all you know you'll be here in Paris for however long I end up in Iraq."

"I already said I'd turn down the extended tour of duty if you asked."

"No, you didn't. And I wouldn't ask."

That was the truth. As much as Taylor had not wanted Will to go, he'd had the strength of will, the discipline to resist asking him to stay. Will, on the other hand, had already misplayed his cards by ordering Taylor not to take a posting he probably didn't want anyway, resulting in Taylor, well-known for being one of the world's most stubborn sons of bitches, now being set on going.

"What about our house?"

Taylor was looking at him like Will was an idiot. "If you want me to keep the house, I'll rent it out."

"What about Riley?"

Taylor nearly strangled over that one. "Riley? Your *dog*? You want me to turn down a posting so I can babysit your dog for a couple of years?"

He was making it worse with every word out of his mouth, but Will couldn't seem to stop himself. "You know what I mean. We have a life. We have a home."

Taylor leaned back in his chair, calm again. "Maybe someday. But we also have jobs. And right now those jobs are in conflict with these other things."

"Is this payback because I took the Paris posting?"

Mistake. What was new? He watched Taylor's temper spike, although Taylor managed a comparatively restrained, "I'm going to forget you said that."

Will shut up before he said something that had Taylor walking out of the restaurant. This was not at all how he had pictured their first night together. He'd wanted everything to be perfect for Taylor. Taylor deserved that, deserved to be spoiled after the way Cooper had been running him ragged for a year.

Will tried a different tack. "Listen, it's not that I'm putting my career over yours."

"No?"

"If this posting was anywhere else in the world, I'd be glad for you." Come to think of it, no, he wouldn't. He hated the idea of Taylor taking a posting anywhere—part of what made his own posting bearable was the thought of Taylor and the home they would eventually share and the life they would eventually build—but Iraq was definitely the worst. The idea of Taylor in Iraq terrified him. He'd lost too many friends in Iraq. Seen too many people he cared for crippled and maimed. "I was in Iraq."

"In the marines. I know."

"It's not…healthy."

Taylor's lip curled. "No? I heard it was just like Paris only they like Americans better."

"You've already been—" Will stopped as Taylor's expression went glacial. "Think about how you'd feel," he said instead.

"I wouldn't be happy, but I wouldn't assume that you'd be killed if I wasn't there watching your back every second. Thanks for the vote of confidence."

"That's not what I mean." Although, yeah, it kind of was. Taylor was smart and strong and dauntingly efficient in a fight, but he lacked a normal sense of self-preservation. He just didn't seem to understand how terrifyingly mortal he was.

Taylor said, "I still can't figure out how my getting shot is somehow more traumatic for you than me."

This time Will shut up for real.

They finished their meal, Will paid out half his life savings, and in silence they left the restaurant.

It was a short walk to the Métro station, a pleasant evening to be out, and they fell into step with the automatic ease of long partnership.

All along the cobblestone streets, the windows of fashionable cafés, galleries, and boutiques were ablaze with life and light. The elegant stone mansions of Place des Vosges—with their steeply slanted blue slate roofs and ornate facades—always seemed to Will to belong to another world, another time, as in fact they did. The square had been the center of aristocratic life in the seventeenth century.

They walked on, not speaking, though their footsteps stayed in time as they passed the center park lined with rows of shaped chestnut trees where sleepy songbirds offered a final chorus in the face of encroaching shadows.

The curved teardrop lamps winked on, casting artful shadows across the splashing fountains and the large equestrian statue of Louis XIII that dated back to the 1800s. This was the second statue of Louis. The first statue had been destroyed during the Revolution.

That was part of what Will found fascinating about France. He'd never been a big history buff—that was more Taylor's line—but you couldn't be in France and not be conscious of its history. The past was everywhere. It echoed off the cobblestones and architecture. They didn't tear down and rebuild here like they did in the States. The same old buildings changed hands over centuries—*centuries*—new paint, new furnishings, and another new start, another new beginning.

He'd wanted to share some of this with Taylor, the one guy he knew who would understand and appreciate all that Will was just discovering— hell, the executions of Louis XVI and Marie Antoinette had taken place in the square right in front of the Hôtel de Crillon, which was next to the American Embassy. Incredible. But Taylor had been edgy and slightly remote since he'd stepped off the plane. He kept making those little distancing jokes when Will was trying to be serious.

Now, of course, he was angry. And rightly so. Will had handled things like a jackass. But couldn't Taylor see it was because Will cared? How many times was Will supposed to calmly stand by while Taylor was beaten or shot or blown up? Taylor was a good agent, one of the best, but he wasn't a soldier. He didn't have a clue what Iraq was going to be like.

Such violence seemed unimaginable on this warm summer evening. Will watched children racing across the grass, their parents strolling more sedately behind.

A little girl shrieked, "Maman, vous ne pouvez pas m'attraper!"

Smiling, Will glanced at Taylor, but Taylor was staring straight ahead, frowning a little, his expression preoccupied as when he was trying to find a new angle on a difficult case.

No, not the evening Will had planned at all. He'd really screwed this up. He'd meant for this to be such a special birthday for Taylor, a real holiday—which God knew Taylor needed—and a chance to fortify their rela-tionship.

He tried to think of something neutral to say.

"Can we...table this for now?" Taylor stopped walking. "I can feel lonely at home. I didn't have to come six thousand miles to not talk to you."

Will stared. Taylor's jaw was clenched, his expression pugnacious, but his eyes gave him away. Grateful for the reprieve, Will pulled him into his arms, and Taylor hugged him right back in that fierce, bony embrace.

Will said, "The last thing I want to do is fight with you. I just..."

"I know."

"I don't know if you do, Taylor. I know it makes you mad when it seems like I'm... I just don't want to lose you."

"You won't. I promise." Taylor pulled away, as though self-conscious even though these were the streets of Paris and open displays of affection were hardly unheard of.

They shoved their hands into their pockets and walked, elbows and shoulders brushing, on toward the Métro.

Taylor asked lightly, "So what did you get me for my birthday?"

"You know that pony you always wanted? I hope you left plenty of room in your suitcase."

Taylor chuckled, and Will smiled back. Everything was okay. They just needed a little time to regain their footing.

Everything was fine.

* * * * *

Back at the apartment Will told himself to go slowly, but Taylor's body was so warm, so welcoming, he pushed right inside, Taylor taking him eas-ily despite the fact that it had been so long.

An unhappy thought occurred to Will, but he dismissed it. If Taylor was fooling around, he'd say so. There was no one more direct than Taylor. Will remembered some of the late-night phone conversations they'd had where Taylor had described in colorful detail what he was doing to himself, the naughty toys he was using. Will had figured at least part of it was brag-gadocio or Taylor simply teasing him, but he should have known better than anyone that Taylor had a wild streak. Will's comfortable assumption that the more exotic stuff was all safely in the past was apparently wrong—the real shock was that he found himself unbearably turned on by the idea of Taylor really wearing anal beads and butt plugs on his days off as he swore he had in preparation for this holiday.

Crazy, beautiful little freak.

Taylor arched back, and Will lifted his head to nuzzle Taylor's chest, suckling on the tiny point of a flat masculine nipple. Taylor made a small, desperate sound, and Will smiled. Something about that, about having Will's hot mouth on his nipples, made Taylor crazy. He could practically get off on that alone. Sexuality was such a weird thing.

Will smiled as he gently teethed the tiny point. Taylor's man titties. One of his more endearing kinks. Taylor whimpered.

"Good?" Will murmured, feeling Taylor's heartbeat thundering against his face. The best, if Taylor's responses were anything to go by.

Taylor nodded, without the breath to answer.

Will chuckled, licking and teasing until Taylor was squirming on top of him, his breathing deepening to gasps.

"Wait. I'm going to lose it."

Will obligingly waited, relaxing back into the pillows and bedding. "Eleven months is too long." He gave a little teasing rock of his hips, and Taylor cried out, shuddering.

"Damn it, Will."

"Sorry." He wasn't, of course. It was beautiful to see Taylor like this, racked and helpless, beautiful to know he could do this to him. Sometimes all that sexual experience of Taylor's was a little daunting. Comforting to know he did have a little control.

"I want it to last."

Will nodded gravely, but his sense of humor was getting the better of him—that and the fact that he was enjoying his moment of power. Anyway, it was asking a lot to expect him to hold motionless for long while he was buried to his balls in Taylor's taut, perfect ass.

"Anytime, MacAllister."

"Will you just—" Taylor moaned as Will hefted his hips, his thighs rubbing against damp skin and soft hair and that stretched and molten center of heat.

Now *that* had been a mistake because it just felt too good to stop, especially when Taylor pushed instinctively back. Will's tenuous control unraveled, and he began to thrust, hard and fast, pounding into Taylor. He could hear Taylor's soft cries as from a great distance, and the naked, helpless sounds goaded him on. There was no one who could strip control from him like Taylor—even when Taylor was the one with his legs spread and his ass split like a peach ripe for plundering.

This was probably more like a rutting heat than making love, but sometimes that was the thing you needed. Something plain and uncomplicated.

He rose up and bit Taylor's shoulder because he couldn't help himself, and Taylor made one of those acquiescent noises. Those wordless sounds really got to Will, melted away the remnants of his control—the *shreds* of his control more like it. He thrust again and again, his body responding to those subtle, knowing movements from Taylor, and then Taylor was coming, uncorked and shooting white foam like a shaken bottle of champagne. His climax set off a chain reaction in Will, and Will pumped it right into him, wanting Taylor wet and soaked with his spunk. Primitive stuff, probably, but Taylor never seemed to mind.

Spent with his own coming, he slumped on Will's chest. Will wrapped an arm around him and finished his own performance with a final twitchy spurt or two.

Taylor's back rose and fell more slowly. He expelled a long, long, contented sigh. Will kissed his damp face.

"Crazy," Taylor muttered.

"Look who's talking." Will kissed him again.

His cock softened and he withdrew, gathering Taylor closer still. The moonlight streaming through the sheer draperies revealed Taylor smiling, boneless and peaceful in Will's embrace. The most dangerous man Will knew rested sweetly in his arms, trusting him with his love as he trusted Will to guard his life. It was beyond precious. Life, love, was made up of fragile moments like these. Fragile as Paris moonlight.

* * * * *

Will woke to the scent of fresh coffee and the jangle of the telephone.

The phone stopped as sharply as it had started, and he heard Taylor's quiet voice downstairs.

For a few seconds Will gave in to the simple pleasure of that. Of just... that. Taylor in the next room answering his phone.

Yeah, it was the simple things. Will smiled wryly at himself. Apparently he was one of them. But after the horrific dreams he'd had the night before—dreams of Taylor dead or dying, where in the best-case scenario he had only been missing a couple of limbs—the normalcy felt blessed. Not that Will considered himself religious, but he knew about counting your blessings.

Taylor's voice stopped and the TV went on, the sound drifting up the staircase. Will could hear the excited voice of a newscaster.

"Le potentiel pour le désastre est énorme..."

What the hell?

Will was groping for underwear or pajama bottoms or bathrobe or *any* damned thing when Taylor appeared in the bedroom doorway. He wore jeans and nothing else. His hair was a little longer than he usually wore it. It curled slightly at the back of his neck. His eyes were as green as Paris in the springtime.

"You better come downstairs and take a look at this, Brandt."

"What's going on?"

Taylor didn't answer, already on his way back down to the ground floor. Will found his jeans, yanked them on, and ran downstairs.

Taylor was perched on the arm of the sofa, scowling at the television set. Will stared at the TV. A female reporter in a white trench coat was speaking rapidly into her microphone as she turned from the camera to point. The Eiffel Tower stood in the background.

His written French was not great, but after a year of immersion, Will could make out the simple ribbon of information at the bottom of the screen. *Eiffel Tower evacuated in bomb scare.*

Taylor's grim voice confirmed his own thought. "We've got trouble."

CHAPTER FIVE

"**W**hat the hell?" Will wiped his eyes and peered blearily at the TV screen.

"You're being recalled to duty." Taylor handed him a cup of coffee. "And so am I."

Will looked up sharply. "You're flying back to the States?"

Taylor shook his head. "I've been requisitioned by your RSO. Someone notified the media who then notified the police that a bomb had been planted in the Eiffel Tower."

"So? It's not the first time that's happened. Why would we be recalled to duty?" Will took a noisy sip of coffee before adding, "Especially you."

"Because of the group claiming responsibility."

"Which is?"

"Finistère."

Will looked blank.

"Finistère," Taylor repeated.

"Gesundheit."

Taylor swallowed his impatience. Nice to know Will hung on his every word. "The violent offshoot of the FLB."

"The FLB?"

"Jesus, Will. Were you so busy enjoying your boys' night out with Bradley you didn't pay attention to a damn thing I said?"

Will lowered his coffee cup so fast some of the liquid splashed onto the pale hook rug. "What the hell are you yelling at me for? And what the hell does *that* mean? *Boys' night out?* If you think something happened, why don't you ask?"

Given how fast Will shot back, he must have been waiting for the question. The truth was, Taylor didn't have to ask. He knew damn well Will wouldn't fool around—and if he did, he'd have relieved his guilty conscience within twenty minutes of Taylor's plane touching down. Will wouldn't fool around. He wasn't built like that. Which didn't mean that Taylor didn't find the idea of Will and David Bradley sitting around till the wee hours, smoking cigars and drinking brandy—or doing whatever the fuck it was they did—annoying as hell. But he hadn't intended to admit it.

So he sidestepped. "The Front de libération de la Bretagne."

"I know what the FLB is," Will snapped back. He might even have been telling the truth. He looked irritated enough. "That wasn't an actual question. Or if it was, the question was, are you shitting me? Why the hell would the Breton Liberation Front resurface now?"

Taylor opened his mouth, but before he could speak, Will added, "Nothing happened with David."

I know that. At least that was what Taylor intended to say. But somehow the words that came out were, "Not because he didn't want it to."

Will's face tightened. "What am I supposed to say to that? *Nothing. Happened.* Nothing will ever happen. It doesn't matter what he wants. You and I are together."

Why had he started this? Why had he let those stupid, stupid words fly out of his big, flapping mouth? Now that he'd gone this far, he didn't know how to stop. Taylor said curtly, "What do you want?"

"What do you mean, what do *I* want? I just said—"

Knowing he was being a fool, knowing he was being unfair, hot-faced but stubborn, Taylor persisted. He just couldn't seem to stop even though all his instincts were telling him to shut the hell up. "You said it didn't matter what David wanted because we're together. You didn't say what *you* wanted."

Will stared at him with utter disbelief. "Am I really supposed to answer that? What do you think I want? I want you." He added bitterly, "Who *wouldn't* want you? Seeing you're so sweet-tempered and understanding."

Taylor turned sharply and went to look out the window at butterflies dancing over the garden. He could feel Will's fierce gaze boring a hole between his shoulder blades. He reached absently to squeeze the back of his neck; the muscles were rigid with tension. He needed to apologize, but more importantly he needed to explain why he was being such a jerk. The problem was, Taylor wasn't sure he could explain. The problem was him, not Will. He knew that. They both knew that.

He was still trying to think what to say when Will said neutrally, "So I guess this proves that you really did see Yanni or whatever his name is at LAX?"

Relieved, Taylor turned. "It would be one hell of a coincidence that he just happened to be trying to get on a plane for Paris the same week his old gang suddenly reemerges and decides to blow up the Eiffel Tower."

"True."

"Yeah, so anyway, your boss wants me to check in."

Will's grin was tentative. "Sort of like old times."

Taylor dredged up an answering smile. "Sort of."

The awkwardness was fading as they slipped back into their familiar working roles. The moment to apologize was also passing, but on the whole Taylor thought it might be best to let it go, to just pretend the last five minutes had never happened. He'd been in the wrong. Will hadn't deserved that treatment. Never again. Taylor made a vow to himself. Never again would he treat Will like that. From now on his insecurities were his own problem. His alone.

He said, "You want the shower first and I'll go grab coffee and croissants next door?"

"You go ahead," Will replied. "I've got breakfast under control."

Taylor nodded and headed for the stairs.

* * * * *

The American Embassy was located at 2 avenue Gabriel, centrally positioned between the Champs-Élysées and Châtelet, a major station of the Paris Métro, on the city's right bank. They drove, but Will was right. The embassy was close enough to Châtelet that they could have walked.

From the outside, the embassy looked like any other official building in Paris. An elegant four stories of creamy stone and black wrought iron bars over bulletproof windows.

Inside the chancery, it looked like every other American embassy Taylor had been in—maybe with better art. Once they cleared the gates guarded by marines, they passed through a gracious entryway with a grand staircase of marble leading to the formal reception area which then led into the nicely appointed ambassador's office. Will and Taylor did not go to the ambassador's office, however.

They continued up through standard-issue embassy office-building-bland decor. The carpets were crimson, the walls off-white beige. Benjamin Franklin, Thomas Jefferson, and other Founding Fathers looked benignly down on them from their gilt frames on various landings.

Paris was America's first diplomatic mission, and her first envoys had included Franklin, Jefferson, John Adams, and James Madison. No question that as DSS postings went, Paris was a very cool gig and Will had been lucky to get it. Taylor was proud of him. Not so crazy about the transatlantic commute, but yeah, he was proud of Will and had been since Will had been offered the posting. And if he hadn't made that clear, he needed to do that.

They went into the DSS office, and laconic *Mornings* were exchanged.

It was easy to see that Will was right at home here, liked and respected by his colleagues. Taylor would have expected nothing less. It was still a little tough realizing exactly how well Will fit in. Initially after Will's promotion they had kidded themselves that they might eventually work together again, but deep down they'd both known the chances of that were slim to none.

Anyway they had more important things to worry about now. Terrorism, even when not specifically directed at US citizens, was the number one priority of the Regional Security Office. Will made brief introductions while everyone waited for their boss, RSO Stone, to get out of her meeting with the ambassador. They drank office coffee, every bit as bad in Paris as it was anywhere else, and Taylor answered questions about budget restrictions and cutbacks in the States.

The Diplomatic Service staff was made up of five diplomatic security special agents, an Engineering Services Office, the Marine Security Guard Detachment, Local Guard Force, the Pass and Identification Section, and the Foreign Service National Investigations Section. It was a pretty good-sized department. They'd had about a quarter that size staff in Haiti.

Forty-five minutes later, Will's Regional Security Officer arrived. She was around forty, cool, and pretty as any Hitchcock blonde, with a surprisingly deep voice.

"Welcome aboard, MacAllister. Sorry to disrupt your vacation plans." Alice Stone had a firm handshake and a quirky smile.

"Happy to help however I can, ma'am. But how is a bomb threat at the Eiffel Tower DSS jurisdiction?"

"Good question." She accepted a cup of the awful coffee with a nod. "Thanks, Arthur. Helloco came in on a US plane despite the fact that we—you, to be precise, Agent MacAllister—identified him. We could have intercepted him but failed to do so. Surely I don't need to spell out how embarrassing that is for all of us?" She looked at her team. There was a general clearing of throats and tugging on collars, although no one in that room was responsible.

Will said, "Then Helloco has been positively ID'd as the bomber?"

Stone gave her quirky smile. "As a matter of fact, no. As a matter of fact, no bomb has been found yet, although the tower is still being searched by police. However, the French paper *Ouest-France* received a communiqué claiming to be from Finistère, and we are all in agreement that Helloco's attempted boarding of a Paris-bound flight in Los Angeles is too much of a coincidence to be overlooked."

Stone didn't spell out who *we* were. The Ambassador? The French authorities? The American president? Or her little team of five—now six—special agents?

The most junior member of the team, a buff, blond boy named Arthur, said, "Ma'am, I'm still not following—"

"Our primary mission," Stone cut across, "is to protect our citizens abroad. Finistère is the violently militant wing of the FLB. They are also anti-American, which gives us a vested interest. It's peak tourist season in the City of Lights, gentlemen. American citizens are everywhere you look. Which means they are everywhere Finistère looks."

"What's our protocol?" Taylor asked. Will shot him an approving look.

"To start with, we're going to do what should have been done in Los Angeles and get a positive ID on Helloco. Brandt, when we're done here, get

MacAllister kitted out, then head over to Prefecture of Police. They can't wait to show him their pretty picture books."

Will nodded.

"MacAllister, I've spoken to your AFOD, and you're on temporary duty with us till further notice. You'll be comped your lost vacation time."

Taylor nodded.

"Okay. LAPD has provided us with the intel on Yannick Hinault, who may or may not be Yann Helloco. Hinault is sixty-seven and currently lives in Burbank. According to his paperwork, he's a French national born in Alsace who immigrated to the States—legally—in December of '72. He married an American citizen, Angelina Duff. She passed away in April of this year. No children, no known next of kin."

"That timeline works for our boy," Taylor said. "If Hinault is Helloco—"

"Exactly. *If.* The only visual ID that LAPD was able to provide was driver license and passport photos." Stone handed off a stack of papers. As the stack circled around to him, Taylor took one and studied the enlarged copy of a driver license photo.

He reluctantly shook his head. "I don't think this is the same guy." He looked at the enlargement of the passport photo. "They look a lot alike but… no."

Stone's blue eyes considered him. "Noted."

"What about fingerprints?"

"Hinault's fingerprints don't match Helloco's."

Taylor nodded. He felt Will's gaze. Their eyes met. Maybe he *had* got it wrong. Maybe the return of Finistère *was* a coincidence. Weirder things had happened.

Stone continued, "According to Hinault's records, he worked as a gardener until 1999. No brushes with the law, not even a parking ticket. Interestingly, this would have been his first trip home to France in forty-two years."

"What would bring him home now?" Will asked.

"That's the question on everyone's mind." Stone placed her hands on her trim hips. "That, and whether Hinault is, in fact, Helloco." She shrugged.

"LAPD is working to get a search warrant for Hinault's home. Once they've got access, we should know more."

"Can't *we* execute a warrant?" Will asked. "He's a terror suspect."

"Not yet he's not. The only thing we know for sure that Yannick Hinault is guilty of is looking like a lot of elderly Frenchmen—and missing his flight. So far neither of those things is a crime."

One of the older agents said, "It's not a lot to go on."

"No, it's not, but if our job was easy, they'd let the FBI do it. Anyway, that's the extent of information we have on Hinault. By all accounts he was a quiet man who kept to himself and was liked by his neighbors—and as suspicious as that sounds, sometimes a cigar is just a cigar. Brandt, you and MacAllister get over to our friends at *police nationale* and see if we can match Helloco to MacAllister's airport ID. The rest of you listen up."

"Yes, ma'am." Will jerked his head, and Taylor followed him out of the office and downstairs to the armory vault.

"How'd you land Firearms Officer?"

Will merely grinned.

Taylor shook his head in resignation as Will opened the vault. "Does Stone know she's got the kid in charge of the candy store?"

"No, and don't tell her." Will led the way inside the vault lined with everything from shotguns to a grenade launcher.

"Chocolate or vanilla?" He held up a Colt SMG submachine gun.

"Do you have something black in a size nine?"

Will said in an oily French accent, "I know just zee thing for monsieur." He selected a SIG Sauer P229R DAK and handed it over. "What do you think? It's got a lighter, smoother pull than you're used to."

Taylor assumed a firing stance, squinting through the rear sight, focusing on the front sight post. He nodded. "Yeah. She'll do."

Will handed over a magazine. Taylor slapped the magazine into the grip and pulled the slide.

"Here."

Taylor glanced up. Will held up a shoulder holster like a tailor offering a beautifully cut sports jacket. Taylor snorted but stepped forward and let

Will slip the leather straps over his shoulder. Taylor slid the pistol into the sheath and put the second magazine Will passed to him into the carrier. He let his arms hang at his side.

"How's that?" Will handed over another magazine.

Taylor slid the third magazine in for balance and adjusted the front straps. Will adjusted the rear. Taylor practiced reaching for the butt of his pistol. "Yeah. That's good."

Will slid his arms around Taylor, pulling him close for an instant. "How's this?"

Taylor's smile was twisted. He tipped his head back, trying to see Will's face. Will craned his head, and their mouths met in a quick, hard kiss. "Good," Taylor said gruffly.

* * * * *

Paris police headquarters was located in the heart of the city in a huge old nineteenth-century building. Inside the building was a network of information and command rooms coordinating the different divisions of the national police, including public order, traffic, general security, public transport safety, and regional coordination and management of calls on the police's *17* emergency line.

Were they not now technically on the job, Taylor would have requested that Will exert his legendary charm to get Taylor a courtesy tour of the place. But they were on the job—as was everyone else in the old building, threats against *Tour Eiffel* being viewed with the utmost seriousness.

Will's police contact, Inspector Suzanne Bonnet, was trim, dark-haired, and all business. She probably had to be, given that cute little snub nose and the surplus of freckles. After the exchange of pleasantries, Taylor once again ran through the story of how he happened to spot a legendary and supposedly dead French terrorist from the seventies in a busy Los Angeles airport.

He was promptly provided with books of mug shots and more bad coffee. Will and Bonnet chatted while Taylor scanned the pages quickly. Pages and pages and pages of people at what was often the darkest hour of their lives.

Nobody looked good in a mug shot.

The general public was uneasy with the concept of racial profiling—Taylor wasn't crazy about it himself—but there was no question that people ran to ethnic types. There was a lot of character in these faces, a lot of high cheekbones and aquiline profiles, dark eyes, and olive complexions. Not so many round and heavy faces as in the States.

Bonnet was saying to Will, "Do you think you and your partner will work together again after this post in Paris?"

"I hope so." Will probably said it for Taylor's benefit. He sounded grim.

Taylor inwardly shook his head. Even Will, a master of self-deception when he needed to be, had to know they weren't going to be teamed again.

But if it made him feel better about everything to think it was a possibility, okay.

One of the faces Taylor was contemplating finally registered. A long, lean face staring cynically from the pages of all the other glowering or despairing faces.

"Here's our guy."

Bonnet rose from behind her desk and came to study the page and photo Taylor indicated. She gave him what she probably hoped was a steely look. "You are sure, monsieur?"

Taylor assented.

"You have a very good eye. This photo was taken over thirty years ago."

"It's him."

"It is Yann Helloco, yes." Bonnet turned to Will as he joined them. "Unfortunately it does not prove a great deal."

"How do you figure that?" Will asked.

"If we had a photo of Helloco as he would be today, that would indicate…something, perhaps, but we have only these historical photos. And it is from the historical photos that your friend made the identification, yes? In fact, he may have seen this very photo."

Taylor shook his head. "No."

"Even so."

"Even so *what*?" Will demanded.

"She's right," Taylor said. "My identifying a mug shot of Helloco doesn't prove that the guy I saw in LAX was the guy in this photo."

"If it helps at all," Bonnet said, "I believe that the man you saw *was* Yann Helloco."

"Thanks."

Will said, "So where do we go from here?"

Bonnet shrugged, a graceful and distinctly French gesture. "We will cast our nets and see what we catch. If Helloco is in this country, he will most likely attempt to contact his old compatriots."

"And you have those people under surveillance?"

"Two of his former colleagues are in prison. Two are dead. One is missing."

That simplified everything, didn't it?

"Well then?" Will said.

Bonnet made a little face.

"What is it you're not telling us?" Taylor asked.

"We found no bomb at the Eiffel Tower. That is good news, of course. But…"

But it was also the bad news. It decidedly reduced the urgency in trying to find Helloco.

"What's the story on our guy?" Will questioned.

"Helloco was born in Brest in 1945. His artistic career began at the *École nationale supérieure des beaux arts*, where he studied painting. He had a promising career which he abandoned for activism in the sixties. He joined the FLB and was instrumental in the formation of the Breton Revolutionary Army. However, in 1969 he became impatient with the methods of his fellow revolutionaries and broke with his old compatriots to form Finistère."

"Meaning *land's end*," Taylor told Will.

"True," Bonnet said. "It is also the *département* in Brittany where Helloco was born."

"Does he have any family still living there?" Will asked.

Bonnet shook her head. "Helloco's parents are deceased. He has a sister living in Ireland. There was a brother, but he's deceased. No one else. There was a rumor he married a fellow revolutionary, Marie Laroche."

"Where's she?" Will spoke before Taylor.

"We are searching for her now. Laroche was released from prison last year. She seems to have…how do you say? Fallen through the cracks."

Will asked, "Why was everyone convinced Helloco was dead?"

"Looking back, it was perhaps a foolish mistake, but remember that in the 1970s forensic science did not play the role in law enforcement it does today. We simply did not have the resources we now do."

"Yeah, but even so. Isn't it unusually suspicious when the subject of a national manhunt turns up conveniently dead?"

If Bonnet was offended, she hid it well. "But you see there was no suspicion of this house or this family. It was only as investigators began to sift through the rubble that they pieced together the clues that led them to conclude the victim *was* Yann Helloco."

"So who *was* the victim?" Taylor inquired.

Bonnet made another one of those little faces. "We don't know for sure, but we now believe the body belonged to the estate gardener, Guillaume Durand."

"Was Durand tied to the movement?"

"There is no indication of that."

"Let's recap." Arms folded, Will leaned against Bonnet's cluttered desk. "Basically we've got nothing. No bomb, no bomber, no former girlfriend of the bomber, and no Yannick Hinault, who may or may not be linked to all of the above. Does that sound about right?"

"Correct," Inspector Bonnet said.

"*Très* fucking *bien*!" said Will.

CHAPTER SIX

"Trial run?" Will suggested.

Taylor's bleak gaze met his.

They were having coffee and complimentary lemon shortbread at Nespresso on the Champs-Élysées. The coffee break had been Will's idea. He wanted to talk the case over with Taylor where no one would overhear them. Not that there was really much of a "case." Which was undoubtedly one reason Taylor was looking so morose.

"I know that look. What's on your mind?" Will dunked his shortbread in his coffee.

"Assuming I did see Helloco at LAX, what would bring a sixty-something terrorist out of retirement? What's the incentive for this guy to rise from the dead?"

"World events?"

"What world events? The FLB and Finistère were fighting for Breton sovereignty. What's happened in recent world events that affects Breton sovereignty? When was the last time anyone on the planet gave a shit about Breton's sovereignty?"

"Presumably the Bretons do."

Taylor pulled a face. "Well, there is that."

"Look, if you think you saw this guy, then that's good enough for me. So let's start from the position that Helloco is alive and has returned to France for some reason. Maybe it has something to do with the death of his wife."

"Whose wife?"

"Hinault's wife. The other thing we're taking for granted is that Hinault and Helloco are one and the same, right?"

"The photos aren't the same. Nothing about Hinault clicks with what we know about Helloco."

It wasn't like Taylor to give up so easily. Will frowned at him. "Come on. Out of all the hundreds of people standing around you at LAX, you just happen to notice a guy who looks like this Helloco and who promptly vanishes right before an inactive revolutionary group pops up again. I mean, I know life is full of coincidences, but that's too much for me to swallow." He reached for the shortbread that Taylor absently slid his way. "Bonnet believes you. There's just not a hell of a lot she can do about it right now. But she believes you."

"Why was there no bomb in the Eiffel Tower?"

"I don't know, but I can't say I'm sorry about it."

"No. Of course not. But…why?"

"It happens more often than you'd think. There was a similar scare back in September of last year. The world is full of nuts."

"True. But why bring attention to themselves?"

"What? That's what these nuts do. That's what it's all about."

Taylor leaned back in the large leather chair, frowning as he gazed into the distance. "No. That doesn't make sense."

"What are you talking about?"

Taylor lifted his cup and drank, still thinking. Studying him, Will felt a surge of affection. This felt *right*. Working together again, being together again. This was how it was meant to be between them. This was what they needed.

Taylor said slowly, "If Finistère is back, if they've regrouped and they're planning to resume their terror tactics, why wasn't there a bomb in the Eiffel Tower?"

"Trial run," Will said again.

Taylor shook his head. "No. First of all, what would they be testing? As you say, there have been enough bomb scares on that site that they would already have a good idea of how the police would respond. Secondly, why would they tip anyone off to what they might be up to? And thirdly, they wouldn't announce their return with a dud. That's not how groups like that operate. They'd want to come back with a bang."

True. True. And true. "Okay. Agreed. So what's going on?"

Taylor frowned into space again. He sipped his coffee. Finally he put the cup down. "Someone wants us to think Finistère is back."

Will gasped. "That is absolutely astoundingly brilliant, Holmes."

Taylor curled his lip. "And it's *not* Finistère."

* * * * *

David called the embassy while Will was following up on Hinault's passport.

"Hey there," Will said warmly when he heard David's voice.

Maybe too warmly? He threw a guilty look at the door of his cubicle, expecting Taylor to walk in any moment. He was currently meeting with Stone, sharing his new theory that Yann Helloco had not arisen from the dead after all.

David's deep voice was equally warm. "I was wondering if you and MacAllister would like to join me for dinner tonight?"

Will hesitated a fraction too long.

"No?" David's disappointment was just obvious enough to be flattering without actually applying any pressure. "I'd suggest another evening, but I'm going to be busy the rest of my stay with the D-day memorial events."

"Taylor's sister is in town, and I think he mentioned trying to get together with her tonight."

"Any chance of switching evenings?" David suggested.

"No harm in asking." Although Will wasn't absolutely convinced of that.

"Why don't you check with your better half and give me a call back at my hotel?"

"I'll do that."

"Great. There's a place in the Latin Quarter called *La Boussole*. Everyone keeps telling me I've got to eat there. "

"I've heard of it," Will said. "I'll let you know."

"You've heard of what?" Taylor walked through the doorway as Will set down the handset. Taylor was skimming the folder he held, and it was a miracle he didn't fall over one of the chairs on his way toward Will's desk.

Will mentally squared his shoulders. "A place called La Boussole in the Latin Quarter. David invited us to dinner tonight."

Head still bent, Taylor asked absently, "David who?"

"Bradley."

Taylor looked up from the file and snorted.

Pretty much the reaction Will expected, but it still irked him. "What's that mean?"

"Oh, I dunno," Taylor drawled. "*Awkward*?"

"Why is it awkward? It's natural he'd want to get together. We've worked together. We're... He's an American in Paris."

"I saw the film, Will. I don't need the review."

That was Taylor being deliberately offensive. Which meant he was feeling insecure. Will yanked back his temper with an effort. "Okay. Then the answer's *no thanks*?"

"Tara wants to get together with us, remember?"

"So the answer is no thanks, or maybe we can switch and have dinner with Tara tomorrow night?"

Taylor drew a sharp breath and then let it out slowly. He said with zero inflection, "If you want to have dinner with Bradley, we'll have dinner with him."

Were they going to argue over this too? Will didn't particularly want to have dinner with David. He liked David, yes, but he could think of few things less comfortable than the three of them having dinner. The truth was he'd be happiest if he and Taylor could spend every moment—including dinner—alone together.

How come the world didn't work like that?

"No. The invitation was very casual. An afterthought, really. We'll have dinner with your sister tonight like we planned."

Taylor didn't have a lot of tells, but Will knew them all. He caught the infinitesimal relaxing of Taylor's shoulders, recognized the way his lashes swept down, hiding his eyes—the way the hard line of his mouth softened and went boyish—just for an instant.

"But how about this," Will continued. "How about the rest of your stay it's just us? Okay? There've already been too many inroads on our time together."

The surprised pleasure of the smile Taylor gave him made the discomfort of calling David back a small price to pay.

* * * * *

"I like this soap," Taylor informed him when Will popped the shower door to join him in the creamy citrus-scented steam. They were late getting ready for dinner with Tara and James, but neither felt like rushing.

"I thought you would." Will slid his hands up Taylor's slippery torso and pulled him close. "I bought it with you in mind."

"Oh yeah?" Taylor was grinning, shower drops clinging to the tips of his long eyelashes. He looked happy and contented, pliable in Will's hands as Will backed him toward the white tiled wall. "What else did you have in mind?"

"I think it's going to have to wait till after dinner." All the same, Will bent his head and pressed his mouth to Taylor's shoulder. He tried to avoid looking at the mangled skin from the bullet scar on the right side of Taylor's chest—not because Taylor minded the scars, but because Will did.

Taylor tasted like wet skin and French soap. Will wanted to inhale him. He wanted to fuck him into next week. He had to remind himself they were already late. Taylor wasn't helping. His warm breath gusted against Will's ear. His hands rested on Will's shoulders, kneading tight muscles with his long, strong fingers.

He murmured, "Why are you so tense?"

Will's arms instinctively closed around Taylor's slick, lean body, holding him tight for a moment.

Taylor laughed. "Will?" He stilled. He pushed back, tossing his wet hair and scrutinizing Will. "What's wrong?"

Will shook his head. He even managed a sheepish smile. "Nothing. Don't mind me." His gaze automatically dropped to Taylor's scarred chest. Not as bad as he remembered. The scars were fading, silvering beneath the scrollwork of fine black hair.

"Will," Taylor said again, only this time he sounded weary.

"I just have a bad feeling," Will admitted. "You asked. I'm telling you. I've got a bad feeling in my gut every time I think of you going to I—"

"Goddamn it." Taylor's face was sharp with anger. "Don't tell me that. Don't say that." He let go of Will, pounding the tile above Will's head with his right hand. "We weren't going to talk about this!"

Will shook his head. He grabbed the soap and began to lather up.

Taylor continued to stand there, water running down his face and chest in rivulets.

"You want me to lie?" Will snapped.

"I want you to shut the fuck up about it!"

For an instant they glared at each other while the warm, soft water beat down around them.

I'm going to lose him if I don't stop this. But what could he say? He wasn't going to lie. Every time he thought about the future, about Taylor flying off to Iraq, that cold, sick crawling started in his guts. Will didn't believe in premonition, but what the hell else could you call it?

Taylor shook his head fiercely, turned and shoved open the shower door. He slammed it shut behind him, and it bounced open again.

Will reached out and closed the door quietly. He expelled a long breath, closing his eyes and letting the water wash over him.

When he finally stepped out of the shower, Taylor was shaving. A white bath towel was slung around his hips; his wet hair was slicked neatly back from his face. His eyes slanted to Will, but he said nothing, running the electric razor over his cheek. The angry buzz made it impossible to talk, anyway. Will grabbed his toothbrush and the toothpaste and got very busy filling his mouth with white foam.

Taylor flicked off the razor and walked out.

They had themselves back under control by the time they left for the restaurant, falling automatically back into the safety of their working partnership, talking of their case, such as it was, and avoiding anything liable to trigger another of those bewildering clashes.

And the clashes *were* bewildering. They'd never argued so much in the entire course of their partnership. Nor after they'd become lovers. Now, when they should have been making every moment count, they couldn't seem to get through more than a few hours without an explosion.

They couldn't afford this, couldn't afford to waste this time together. Likely neither of them would have a shot at leave for another year.

On the Métro, Will kept finding himself watching Taylor. Every once in a while Taylor would give him an odd, cool look in return. For the first time Will could remember, he didn't know what to say to the person he would have said knew and understood him better than anyone else in the world.

It was a lonely feeling.

Tara had selected the restaurant. L'Arpège, specializing in vegetarian and seafood dishes, was another very well-known Michelin three-star eatery—although it was probably grounds for an international incident calling it an *eatery*. It was a small, unassuming building across the road from the Musée Rodin.

Will held the door for Taylor, and Taylor went in, scanning the packed tables. Apparently disposable income was still alive and well in this part of the world.

The decor was simple and modern. Etched glass, polished steel, pearwood paneling, a few bold strokes of color and surprising objets d'art like large squash rather than flower arrangements on the tables.

Tara and James were already seated. Tara waved when she spotted them.

"Wow. Why so serious?" she asked as Will and Taylor seated themselves. "Is there some kind of national emergency we should know about?"

Will liked Tara. She was smart, funny, candid, and generally easygoing. Much like her little brother. She was also quite beautiful with long dark hair and those wide, exotic bronze-green eyes she shared with Taylor and the rest of the MacAllister clan.

Taylor didn't look at Will. "Our leave has been rescinded."

Tara looked from Taylor to Will. "What? They can't do that!"

James said, "It's the American government, hon. They can do anything they want." James was a nice guy; at least that was Will's impression. He didn't know him well, but according to Taylor he was intelligent, capable, ambitious, and openly adored Tara. Will could see that open adoration every time James looked at Tara.

"Where are the kids?" Taylor asked.

"The hotel has a babysitting service."

Taylor looked disapproving, and Tara rolled her eyes. "You can tell me how to raise my kids once you've started raising your own," she said without heat.

James cleared his throat, and Tara's cheeks got a little pink. Taylor changed the subject without missing a beat, bringing Tara up to speed on the man he had chased through the airport in Los Angeles.

They briefly discussed the case before the waiter arrived, and then there was a lengthy question-and-answer session that Will could have done without. At last they ordered and went back to debating what would bring a man like Helloco out of hiding after forty years.

"The woman, of course," Tara said. "*Cherchez la femme*, like they say over here. He's come back for his ex-lover."

"If that was the case, why'd he wait all these years?" Will asked.

"Why'd he marry someone else?" Taylor put in.

"Maybe he had to."

"Why would he?"

Tara looked at her brother and shook her head. "For his cover."

"Then why'd he wait forty-something years to come back? Why come back at all?"

"Because he never forgot the woman he truly loved."

Taylor put a hand to his stomach. "I feel sick," he complained.

"How do you put up with him?" Tara asked Will.

"He grows on you," Will admitted.

Their meals arrived at last, perfectly prepared and artistically arranged as one would expect given the prices of the place. The chef's specialty was vegetables, and Will listened patiently, occasionally exchanging tolerant glances with James while Taylor and Tara raved on and on, both of them part-time vegetarians. Then it was his and Taylor's turn to be patient while James and Tara, who referred to themselves as foodies, went on at great and exasperating length about tasting menus and amuse-bouches and nose and palate and dégustation.

Will regarded Taylor, and Taylor gave him a droll look. Will tried not to laugh. Once again he felt one of those rushes of...well, love.

Yes, love. Of course, love. Whatever was wrong between them, they needed to work it out because what they had together was just too good to lose.

"How long are you staying in Paris, Will?" Tara asked somewhere between the departure of the *aiguillettes de homard* and the arrival of mustard ice cream on a tomato gazpacho.

Taylor was looking at him, brows raised in polite inquiry. "Another two years at least, right?"

"Oh, that's a long time." Tara was giving her brother a commiserating look.

Taylor shrugged.

To his amazement Will heard himself say, "I'll resign right now, this week, if you will too."

Tara gave a startled squeak. Taylor was staring at Will in disbelief—and not thrilled disbelief either. "Say what?" he said.

"You heard me. I'm willing to resign if you are."

"Quit?"

"What would you do if you didn't work for the State Department?" James asked.

"Good question," Taylor said. "Any ideas, Will?"

As confounded as he was to have proposed such a thing, Will now found himself arguing its merits. "It's a dangerous world. We've got plenty of marketable skills."

"I'm not resigning. And neither are you."

Tara said, "I thought you liked your job, Will?"

"I do. I can always get another *job*."

His cell phone went off, thus delaying the impending explosion from Taylor. Taylor waited, steam all but pouring from his ears, as Will took the call.

Alice Stone's terse voice ordered them to the Denfert-Rochereau Métro station. "We've got another bomb threat. This time Finistère is claiming they've rigged the Paris catacombs to blow. We need some kind of token American presence on the scene. I'm sending Arthur and Han as well. They'll meet you there."

Will disconnected. "We've got to go," he told Taylor.

Taylor nodded crisply, all business again.

"Why? What's going on?" Tara looked from one to the other of them.

"Hopefully nothing," Will told her. "But do us a favor and steer clear of the Paris catacombs tonight."

Taylor's attempt to leave money was impatiently waved off by James.

They walked out of the restaurant, heading briskly for the Métro. Will brought Taylor up to speed.

"What the hell are *we* supposed to do?" Taylor inquired. "We don't even speak French. Well, I don't."

"Moral support? I'm not sure. Here's the problem we're all facing. There's no definitive map of the complete catacombs. We're talking nearly two hundred miles of labyrinth. The tour of the catacombs that most people go on is just a fraction of the actual maze of underground tunnels. There are secret entrances and passageways all over the city that can be accessed through the sewers or Métro tunnels. There are even manholes that lead into the catacombs."

"Great."

Will was mindful that Taylor wasn't too keen on enclosed spaces after falling into an underground cave during their pursuit of a fugitive in New Mexico.

"Hey."

Taylor looked at him in inquiry.

"Are you going to be okay?"

Taylor's face changed. "No, Will. I'm going to go home and wait for you because I'm afraid of the dark. And then I'm going to call my boss and resign because my boyfriend thinks there's a chance I might get killed in the line of duty one day. Maybe I'll just give up going outside altogether. I mean, a plane might fall on me. Or a bird might crap on me."

"Can we *not* fight about this?" Will requested. "Because we need to be focused. This might be another false alarm or it might not."

Taylor gave him a narrow look and then nodded.

They weren't speaking when they reached the catacombs, but they weren't arguing either, so…win.

Most Parisians didn't bother to visit the famous catacombs any more than most Californians visited Hollywood. Will had been once, mostly because of the grandfather who had been stationed in France during World War II. His granddad had talked about the Resistance using the tunnels—ironically at the same time the occupying Germans were building a bunker in another section.

Will had found his one visit unsettling. The tour was relatively short—a hundred and thirty steps down, eighty-three steps up, and a mere mile-and-a-half-long maze of obscure galleries and narrow corridors all made of bones, the skulls and femurs arranged in romantically macabre designs set off with graveyard urns and funerary statuary. Rusted gates blocked access to passages deemed unsafe or unnavigable for tours.

Creepy, in a word.

And all the sniffer dogs and cops and military police in riot gear and special units and all the flashing lights and radios and loudspeakers blasting their warnings and instructions didn't appreciably reduce the creep factor.

Everyone was edgier because of the false alarm earlier that day. Opinion was divided as to whether that upped or reduced chances that this was the real thing. Special Agent Arthur was of the opinion it reduced chances. Special Agent Han was of the opinion it upped them. Taylor had not vouchsafed an opinion. He had that innocent, interested look he always wore when he was about to kiss off every moment of training and all thought of self-preservation and go flying faster than a speeding bullet into the most dangerous situation he could find.

Will gave Taylor a grim look that Taylor didn't even notice; he was too busy checking out and comparing the arsenal the French cops were wearing. Never happier than when anticipating all hell breaking loose, that was Taylor.

"Some vacation for your partner," Arthur said. "And the thing of it is, it's not even a DSS operation."

Will nodded. What kind of luck had put Taylor in a line at LAX in time to see and recognize Helloco? It was like fate. Not good fate. Fate with a capital *F*. Or maybe something else with a capital *F*.

"We're going in now," Taylor said, coming over to speak to them. "It looks like I'm with the guys in the big Plexiglas helmets. You're going with the Foreign Legion."

"Those are gendarmes."

"I know. I'm kidding." Taylor peered at him through the strobe-lit dark. He rammed the hard edge of his shoulder into Will's in a gesture of solidarity—or maybe just *snap out of it!*

"Helloco's not going to be down there waiting for us in these tunnels."

"Good by me. We'll finish up here and go find some joint that serves beer and nachos and then go back to your place." Taylor was being summoned. He nodded to Arthur, gave Will a crisp, "Watch your back."

"MacAllister."

Taylor turned.

"Keep your head down."

Taylor gave him a thumbs-up.

* * * * *

The sign at the entrance of the catacombs read *Arrête, c'est ici l'empire de la Mort*. Stop, this is the empire of Death.

The creak of body armor, the thud of riot boots, the jingle of dog tags, and the dying gurgle of a hidden aqueduct were the only sounds as Will and the gendarmes descended a narrow spiral stairwell.

The ghostly lighting was dispelled by the white-hot lights of the police torches flitting across the walls of carefully arranged bones. Wet glistened and dripped from the ceiling that was only about six feet high. Will had to stoop to keep from braining himself. In some areas the limestone domes had been reinforced to keep sections of the cavern from collapsing.

"I always wanted to see this place," Arthur said under his breath to Will.

Gee, how nice that someone was having a good time. For Will it brought back way too many memories of patrolling IED Alley.

Damp gravel crunched underfoot. A radio crackled. Overhead the water continued its *drip-drip-drip* to the ground. They moved slowly, meticulously, room-by-room, searching for explosives but finding nothing.

The next tunnel made a ninety-degree turn to the right and then, a short way on, to the left. More yellowed, cracked skulls gazing with empty eye sockets into the abyss.

The rich, the poor, the great, and the humble, all stacked like firewood, like bricks in a wall.

Sixty million Frenchmen can't be wrong.

In fact, there were only supposed to be six million interred in the tunnels; even that number was unfathomable—three times the number of those living in the city above.

The commander whispered into his radio, "Espace libre. Déplacement à la prochaine section."

They shuffled on a few yards. The dogs whined, tugged at their leads, and they moved to investigate another of the many tunnel offshoots. In the parts of the catacomb not open to the public, the bones were not arranged in designs. They were not arranged at all. They were simply dumped like Pick-up Sticks. To cross some of those galleries meant crawling over the scattered bones. Will told himself it was just like climbing over rocks.

He wondered how Taylor was doing. This was a very tight fit. Many of the tunnels were not even eight feet across. Usually no more than two hundred sightseers were permitted in the catacombs at one time. There had to be double that many law enforcement officers moving through the shadowy passages now.

"How far do you think we've traveled?" Arthur whispered.

Will shook his head. He checked his watch and was startled to see they'd been underground for over two hours. It really didn't feel anything like that long, but this was tiring, painstaking, and stressful work. They had to check every possible hiding place, every indentation in the earth, every mound of bones, and every bit of debris that looked a little too artistically placed.

The smell was strange. Mold, damp earth, something funky—not death, or at least the smell of death that Will knew—and the chill was pervasive.

Another hour went by. Then another.

The patrol began to be convinced there was nothing here. No bombs. No Helloco. Not even the usual kids hoping to party undiscovered by the catacomb security.

In Iraq rarely a day had gone by that they didn't come across a lollipop, and the patrols had consisted of hours poking and prodding every suspicious-looking lump or dip in the ground. IEDs were the second greatest threat to Americans in Iraq. Will still had nightmares about those truffle hunts.

Now here he was in Paris hunting for explosives again.

And so was Taylor.

Up ahead a radio crackled, and an urgent voice said something in French that Will couldn't follow.

"Did you get that?" he asked Arthur. Arthur had a better grasp of the language.

"I think they're saying they've found something."

"*Who* found something?"

Arthur shook his head. It was impossible to hear over the voices speaking excitedly in front of them. Everyone had stopped walking. One of the sniffer dogs suddenly sat back on its haunches and let out a long, bloodcurdling howl.

"What the hell?" Will looked at Arthur. Arthur's face was pallid and alarmed in the faded light.

Arthur shook his head quickly.

In all his experience in Iraq, Will had never seen a sniffer dog react like that.

The thought no sooner registered than the ground began to shake. Bones clacked as they spilled like dominoes; people began to shout. Sand and water and bits of rock rained down from above.

"What's happening, Brandt?" yelled Arthur.

"Retreat!" Will ordered. "Fall back now."

The men behind them began to go back. The last thing Will saw before the lights went out was a grinning, hollow-eyed skull caught in the glare of his flashlight.

CHAPTER SEVEN

Taylor must have paced a hundred miles of hospital linoleum before the gray-faced doctor appeared at the end of the long hallway. It seemed the longest walk of Taylor's life even though the doctor met him halfway.

"How is he?" Despite his effort, his voice shook. Of all the scenarios he had pictured, this one had been comfortably missing from Taylor's imaginings. Will was too practical, too careful—and yet here he stood as Will had stood too many times before. It was ludicrous. It was impossible, but here it was.

"You are the partner of Monsieur Brandt?"

Taylor nodded, dry-mouthed, dry-eyed, heart banging away like it was going to snap its brackets, bracing himself for it. For the first time he understood why Will maybe felt he couldn't go through it all again.

The doctor smiled briefly at whatever he read in Taylor's expression. "*Non, non, monsieur.* Your friend, your partner, he will recover. He is not greatly injured. Shock and concussion, this is the extent of his injuries. A very lucky young man."

The relief that washed through Taylor left him weak. If there had been something to grab, to lean on, he'd have reached for it. As it was, he stood there, trying to hide the fact that he wasn't quite steady. In the background he could hear the hospital intercom and a calm voice summoning help for another emergency in a long night of catastrophes.

"Can I see him?"

"Non, je regrette ce n'est pas possible." It was the same in every language.

Taylor wasn't above pleading. "Just for a minute. I won't disturb him." He swallowed. "I just need to see for myself."

With so many more gravely injured, so many crises to deal with, the doctor didn't have time for this. The expression that crossed his face was a mix of impatience and reluctant sympathy. "Two minutes, monsieur. No more."

Taylor nodded. Belatedly he remembered his manners. "Thank you."

The doctor waved him on. Taylor passed the nurse's station. They looked doubtfully at the doctor who again waved Taylor on, and then at last Taylor was standing beside Will's hospital bed.

He barely registered the monitors, the IVs, the medical paraphernalia. He saw only Will, who looked like the fallen hero in a movie: bare-chested and pale. One of his hands was taped. There was a square white dressing on the side of his head. Not nearly the extent of repair work Taylor had been expecting. They hadn't even had to shave much of Will's hair. There was a scrape along his jaw and a bruise along his eyebrow.

He was caught between the desire to cry and to strangle Will. "Jesus, Brandt," Taylor whispered. "You bastard. Why'd you have to do that?"

Will slept peacefully on. His long black lashes never stirred.

Taylor stayed as long as the nurses allowed. He wasn't doing anyone any good, including Will, but it was impossible to leave voluntarily. He stood leaning against the wall, watching Will sleep as closely as if he were going to be tested on how many breaths Will took in a minute.

They'd been lucky. Not everyone was that lucky. Arthur was still in surgery the last Taylor had heard, and the rumor was that two gendarmes had died in the collapse of the tunnel. Now the emergency services of the city were scrambling to make sense of the disaster.

When Taylor finally returned to Will's apartment, he found a dozen messages from Tara on the answering machine, each terser than the last, indicating her escalating alarm.

It was past five in the morning, but she'd ordered them to call her regardless of the hour.

She answered on the first ring. Taylor debriefed her in clipped sentences.

"It's all over the news. You should see the footage. It looks like a sink-hole swallowed a section of the city above where you all were. But *you're* all right?" Tara insisted at the end of his succinct accounting.

"Yes."

"Thank God. And Will is going to be all right?"

He was very tired. The words stuck in his throat. All he could manage was a grunt.

"Were you able to see him?"

Taylor pried out another assent.

"That's good." When he didn't respond, she asked experimentally, "Does anyone there know about your relationship?"

"No. At least…not at the embassy. We kept it under wraps so we could continue working together. And then…"

Tara possessed a few diplomatic skills herself. "Don't worry. Everyone knows you're close. You were spending your vacation together. And the bond between partners is a TV cliché."

Taylor confirmed wearily. Should he call Will's family? He didn't know. They'd never really discussed it. Taylor was the one with the penchant for winding up on the critical list. He wasn't even sure Will had told his father and brother about their relationship. Definitely not the way to break it to them.

"According to the news, two police officers were killed. Why do people *do* things like this?"

"I don't know." He'd stopped wondering long ago. His was not to reason why. "I just wish you and the kids weren't in Paris right now."

"I wish *you* weren't in Paris right now," Tara retorted. "I've paid you enough hospital visits to last me a lifetime. Anyway, we're only here for a couple of days, and we're not big on tourist attractions."

"Keep it that way. The word is, the last message was definitely anticapitalist and anti-American."

"So what else is new? Isn't hating Americans de rigueur? It's like adding salt to a dish. No terrorist mission is complete without it."

"You're starting to sound like me."

Tara laughed. "That's what James says. Speaking of which, he's signaling me to get off the phone so you can get some sleep."

"Yeah. I'm beat. Tara, remember what I said about staying away from places Americans usually go. Skip the Louvre. No Euro Disney. No—"

"Roger wilco, little brother. We'll stick to our *Parisian's Guide to Paris*. Okay?"

"Okay." Taylor yawned so widely he had to wiggle his jaw to realign it. "Night."

"Bonne nuit, mon enfant."

"And enough with the little brother stuff."

Tara was laughing as she rang off.

Taylor went upstairs and stared at the neatly made bed. As tired as he was, the thought of facing that empty expanse of sheet and blanket was too much right then. Every time he closed his eyes, he saw again Will buried beneath that tumble of rock and earth and bone. *Bone.* Like a premade grave.

He pulled off his stained, torn shirt and tossed it into the trash. He was filthy and his hands were a mess. He'd been part of the panicked rescue effort that had attempted to dig into the collapsed cavern before emergency services had arrived. One thing for the French, they had top-notch disaster services. But then it was a city that had suffered a lot of grief in its two thousand or more years.

Taylor ran a quick, hot shower, closing his mind to the memory of a few hours earlier and that stupid, pointless quarrel with Will. The cuts and scrapes on his hands stung, but that was just proof he was still alive. Alive and lucky.

He turned off the taps and dried himself. Reminders of Will were everywhere, from the damp towel draped over the laundry basket to a glop of spilled hair gel.

Downstairs he made coffee and poured a healthy splash of Will's bourbon into it. He got Will's laptop out and started it up, hacking into Will's accounts without trouble. He knew all Will's password variations, as Will knew his.

Once he was on the net, though, Taylor found himself at a loss. Where did he go from here? The only lead they had was Helloco, and that trail was cold any way you looked at it.

He typed Helloco's name into the search engine. Pages and pages of results flashed up. Everything from a Wikipedia page to a number of books and documentaries. Yet Taylor had never heard of Helloco until he'd read that article in *American Cop*.

But then, as terrorists went, Helloco was relatively small potatoes. Especially in a country like France, which had a long and intimate acquaintance with terror—starting with their own bloody revolution. The French had suffered years of attacks by Algerian independence fighters and were currently coping with the ongoing threat posed by Islamist extremists. So a few car bombs and the loss of one small museum thanks to the acting out of a handful of disgruntled Bretons probably fell more under the heading of Significant Irritation than Terror.

Taylor read the translated Wikipedia article on Helloco, wondering who maintained the page. It was a regurgitation of Helloco's political "manifesto" and an account of how he'd destroyed his various targets. The article wasn't flattering, exactly, but it wasn't critical either. There was very little information about Helloco's early years, which made Taylor suspicious as to whether Helloco or someone close to him monitored the account.

One thing Taylor had learned in the DSS was that criminals great and small tended to share one characteristic: an oversized ego. Maybe that was one of the requisites for believing what you wanted was more important than the rights of others.

He followed the links on the Wikipedia article to the other members of Finistère—they also had Wikipedia pages, but the information on Gabriel Besson, Jean-Louis Roland, Paul Jacquard, Brice Didier, and Marie Laroche was even sketchier than the information on Helloco.

Taylor rubbed his eyes and drank more coffee. None of this connected in any way with Yannick Hinault.

Had LAPD managed to come up with a warrant to search Hinault's home yet?

Taylor resumed his search. Wikipedia even had a stub article—if you could call it that—on the gardener who had died when the explosives Yann Helloco was preparing for a new political "statement" had blown up the country house where members of Finistère were hiding out. Guillaume Durand had been twenty-four years old with no apparent political leanings nor any particular ambitions when he died. Just an ordinary young man.

Yet someone had thought it worth starting a Wikipedia page on him. Was that significant or not?

The police on two continents would be doing their job. He needed a different angle. A fresh angle. He clicked back to Helloco's page and pondered the minimal personal information.

Before Helloco had turned to activism, he'd studied art. According to both Wikipedia and Inspector Bonnet, Helloco's work had shown great promise. *Il a eu une passion grande pour la peinture et l'art*, according to the nameless Wikipedia author.

Maybe that was the angle they needed?

One thing stood out. Finistère had never been a major political movement, and it had not been a large organization. The membership had extended beyond Besson, Roland, Jacquard, Didier, Laroche, and Helloco, but those six had formed the nucleus, the body of the snake—and Helloco had been the snake's head. Besson and Roland were still serving prison sentences. Jacquard and Didier were dead. Laroche was…a chick. So even if Helloco was back from the dead, there wasn't much of an organization to resurrect.

In fact, the idea of these remaining senior citizens racing around Paris and planting bombs was just, well, *incroyable*, as they said here.

So what the hell was going on?

Why was it important to someone to make it look like Helloco was still alive and that Finistère was back in action?

Taylor clicked on one of the Helloco links leading to *École nationale supérieure des beaux arts*. His lips parted. What the…? He copied the introductory paragraph, pasted it into Babel Fish, and pressed Translate.

Associated in various ways with New Realism, the artists of such international political movements encouraged a do-it-yourself aesthetic and valued simplicity over complexity. Painters such as Helloco included a strong current of anticommercialism and an anti-art sensibility in their work, disparaging the conventional market-driven art world in favor of an artist-centered creative practice.

Yeah. Whatever. That still didn't explain why every damn painting Helloco did was of a graveyard or a grave.

* * * * *

"There's been a development," RSO Stone informed Taylor when he crawled groggily out of an exhausted sleep three hours later to answer the shrilling phone. "Get over to the Prefecture of Police ASAP. Inspector Bonnet is waiting for you."

"What's up?"

"Bonnet will fill you in." Stone was uncharacteristically curt.

"How's Arthur?" Taylor knew how Will was because he'd called the hospital before he'd stretched out on the sofa for a quick nap and had been reassured Monsieur Brandt was "comfortable" and had even regained consciousness briefly. Taylor had left instructions with anyone who would talk to him to call regarding any change.

Stone said, "Arthur will make it. They couldn't save his arm."

Shit.

Taylor said, "I'm on my way to see Bonnet."

Stone clicked off.

Taylor stumbled upstairs to borrow a clean shirt from Will and get changed. Nine minutes later he was in Will's Cadillac Escalade, negotiating Paris midmorning traffic. He arrived eventually at the Prefecture of Police shaken but unharmed—and dead set on using public transportation for the rest of his stay anytime possible.

The mood at police headquarters was much darker than the previous day. Taylor found his way to Inspector Bonnet's office. She had bags under her red-rimmed eyes—but then so did he.

"I was sorry to hear about your colleagues," Taylor said after the initial greetings.

Bonnet dipped her head. "Yes. Two good men. Two good officers. It is a tragedy for the entire city." She managed a tired smile. "I was happy to hear that William is recovering."

Taylor nodded.

She said, "You have been friends a long time?"

"Five years now. We were partners in the States." Funny how it felt longer. As though he'd always known Will, as though Will had always been part of his life.

Bonnet smiled wanly. "Yes. I know. He was looking very much forward to your trip." To Taylor's relief, she briskly changed the subject. "We have had a break in our case. Marie Laroche has been discovered living in a commune twelve kilometers from Fontainebleau."

"Is Helloco with her?"

"*Non.* However, you may ask her of his whereabouts yourself. It is the wish of your director that you accompany us to interrogate her."

"Fine by me. Let's go." Taylor hooked a thumb over his shoulder.

Go they did, sirens screaming. Taylor was tempted to cover his eyes until they were safely out of the city proper. At the best, driving in Paris felt like playing bumper cars with very angry children. At the worst, it seemed to him that everyone in the city had a death wish—and very low insurance premiums. Funny that he hadn't been nervous with Will behind the wheel. In fact, he barely remembered anything of their drives together other than Will.

The other police officers and Bonnet mostly discussed the tragedy in the catacombs. Bonnet translated their conversation for Taylor's benefit. He learned that, ironically, the explosives had been set well away from the central passageway. Whatever had set them off—an unlucky rat?—the resulting blast need not have had lethal consequences. Unfortunately the catacombs were not the most stable of structures, and the underground blowout had set up a devastating chain reaction.

Taylor suggested, "It's possible then that Finistère did not intend anyone to be harmed by the explosion?"

"That is unlikely given the mission of Finistère."

"If they have a mission."

Bonnet's eyes met his.

"Has anyone questioned the former members of Finistère?"

"That is being done now. We have officers on their way to Fleury-Mérogis Prison to interrogate the remaining members of the organization. We will see what they have to say." She gave another of those graceful shrugs.

With that, Taylor had to be content.

* * * * *

The farmhouse had been built before the French Revolution, and Laroche looked like she could have been living there since the first stones of the foundations were laid. The years—and prison—had not been kind to her. The photos Taylor had seen had been of a slender blonde girl who consciously or unconsciously played up a startling resemblance to Brigitte Bardot. Any trace of that girl was long gone. Somewhere along her travels—or travails—she'd picked up a piratical scar across her left eye. But even without the disfiguring furrow, she looked more like someone who'd be at home sitting in front of a guillotine shrieking for more heads than the chic little revolutionary she'd once been.

Although Marie spoke some English, the interrogation took place in French with Bonnet quickly translating the rapid-fire exchanges.

"Finistère disbanded after Yann's death. Finistère had nothing to do with yesterday's attack. This is what she says."

"This is what they all say," Taylor retorted. "Ask her where Helloco is now."

"She insists Yann died in the explosion," Bonnet told Taylor after she asked his million-dollar question and got Marie's plugged-nickel answer. "Whoever this man is that you saw in the airport, he is not Helloco."

"I bet. Ask her if she knows Yannick Hinault."

Bonnet asked the question.

Marie shook her head.

Taylor said, "Tell her I believe that Hinault is Helloco."

Bonnet repeated his words. Marie's expression was contemptuous. *"Porc stupide!"* She rattled off a short and clearly to-the-point sentence.

Bonnet looked mildly apologetic. "Marie says she is in better position to know if her lover is dead than you."

"Then how does she explain how some forty years ago the only body in that blown-up country house in Sarthe belonged to Guillaume Durand, the gardener?"

Bonnet relayed the request. Marie gave Taylor a long, strange look before she responded. Her answer seemed to excite the other two police officers. Bonnet looked doubtful.

"What did she say?"

Bonnet replied, "She says that *both* Yann and the gardener died that day. She says she, Roland, and Didier removed Helloco's body after the explosion. They did this to try to keep us, the police, from discovering that the estate in Sarthe was used as a safe house."

Marie continued to stare at him with her basalt gaze. Taylor said, "What did they do with Helloco's body?"

Bonnet inquired, and Marie answered shortly. Bonnet shook her head. "She says they buried it in the woods."

"What woods?"

"The woods surrounding the estate. I think she is lying. The woods were searched repeatedly, and this grave would have been discovered."

Watching their faces, Marie added something else and gave a harsh smoker's laugh.

Bonnet said, "She says they hid the grave too well for us to find. I do not believe her."

Taylor wasn't convinced one way or the other. Marie might be lying. She didn't display the obvious giveaways of looking into space or changing vocal pitch or fidgeting, but prison was a great training ground. Even FACS, or micro expressions, were open to multiple interpretations. And on the other side of the coin, Bonnet was naturally defensive on behalf of her colleagues. Even in the most closely conducted investigations, mistakes were made.

"It's easy enough to prove. She can take us to the gravesite, and you can run a DNA sampling on whatever's left of him."

Maybe Marie could guess the direction the investigation was going to go because she interjected another string of French.

"She says it was too long ago and the grave was concealed too well. She could never find it now."

"She'll never know until she tries."

Bonnet translated for Marie, who folded her arms and stared fixedly into space.

Taylor said, "Throw her wrinkled butt in jail and ask her again in forty-eight hours."

His tone must have made his feelings clear. Marie glared at him. Bonnet stifled a stern smile. "You are what they call a hard-ass, Agent MacAllister, *oui*?"

"Me?" Taylor raised his brows. "I'm a pussycat. Go on. Tell her she's headed back to prison."

"But you realize we cannot jail her for such an infraction as you suggest? There is the parole violation, *oui*, but we do not really have anything to link her to—"

"Charge her as an accessory—or whatever you call it over here—to last night's attack on the catacombs."

Bonnet frowned. "*I* cannot make such allegations. We have already investigated, and as she has informed us, there is proof that she possesses an alibi for all of yesterday. She does not appear to have received any visitors—"

"Somebody from Finistère claimed responsibility, and according to her, she's the only remaining member of Finistère still on the loose. Remind her of that. You have that guilty-until-proven-innocent thing, right?"

Bonnet said tartly, "*Oui*, but we prefer to arrest and charge the correct people, Agent MacAllister." All the same she turned to Laroche and began to speak.

Laroche folded her arms and stared stubbornly out the window at the blue-green blur of the distant forest. However, Taylor—or the memory of the atrocity the night before—prevailed, and Laroche was duly arrested and bundled into a police car that preceded them back to town.

* * * * *

It was six o'clock that evening before Taylor was at last able to get over to the hospital. He'd tried calling twice during the day, but once he'd been informed Will was sleeping, and the second time the doctor had been with Will. So it did nothing to improve his temper when he finally walked into Will's hospital room only to find Naval Lieutenant Commander David Bradley sitting beside Will's bed with a big, fat grin on his face.

Taylor checked in the doorway.

Will looked up. His eyes lit and he smiled. "Hey. Where've you been all day?"

"Trying to figure out who dropped a crypt on you." He smiled without warmth at Bradley, who had stood at his entrance.

Bradley said, "Can I talk to you, MacAllister?"

Taylor looked from Bradley's strained face to Will, who was still smiling and holding a hand out in greeting.

"Can it wait?" Taylor moved toward the bed, but Bradley intercepted him.

"No."

Taylor opened his mouth, but the message in Bradley's eyes was urgent.

"MacAllister? Where the hell are you two going?" Will complained as they stepped into the hall.

"Back in a minute, Will," Bradley said.

"What's going on?" Taylor demanded. He'd only met Bradley once before, but he wasn't an easy guy to forget, being very big and very handsome. He had thick brown hair and warm brown eyes. When off duty he sported a beard, but he was not off duty now, and he looked offensively impressive in his uniform. Taylor hated that he had to look up to meet the other man's gaze.

Bradley's ham-sized hand closed around Taylor's biceps, and he forcibly shifted him a few feet down the hall and out of earshot of the room.

Taylor freed himself. He was now thoroughly alarmed and thoroughly angry. "What the hell's going on?"

"Shut up and listen." Bradley kept his voice low.

Taylor's apprehension ratcheted up another notch. "Say it. Whatever it is."

"Will is…a little confused."

He'd been thinking subdural hematoma or spinal injuries or… He didn't know what he'd been thinking, but all of it had been terrifying and terminal. His abject relief that it was none of these things, nothing serious at all, apparently, mutated to fury. He shoved Bradley.

"*Confused?* What does that mean? Jesus, I thought—why the fuck did you—"

It was like shoving an elephant. Bradley barely shifted, didn't seem to notice, in fact—which was even more infuriating. He cut across Taylor's angry outburst with a crisp, "I mean he doesn't remember that you two are together."

Taylor froze. "What?"

"He doesn't remember the last year or so. Or at least his memories are sketchy. He doesn't remember that you have a relationship beyond work." Bradley added, "And friendship."

Taylor's mouth opened. "I… What?"

"There's more. And, from your perspective, worse."

David. He knew what was coming. His heart was pounding so loudly he almost couldn't make out Bradley's voice, but he knew what he was saying, could read his expression and his lips.

"He thinks he and I are still dating," Bradley told him.

CHAPTER EIGHT

"**W**hat was that about?" Will asked when David returned to the room. "Where's MacAllister?"

"Using the head." David took the chair next to the bed and smiled into his eyes.

"Yeah? Then give me a kiss before he gets back." Not that Will felt like kissing. His head ached like a son of a bitch, he felt vaguely nauseated, and for someone who had apparently spent fourteen hours in bed, very, very tired. And then there were the giant moth holes in his memory. But there was something troubling in David's gaze. Almost a trace of sadness.

"I don't think your doctor would—"

"Shaddup," Will growled.

David leaned over, smiling, and their mouths brushed. That was better. Nice. Familiar.

"Sorry to interrupt," Taylor said from the doorway, and David jumped and sat up as straight as if he were undergoing a military inspection. Or possibly a rectal exam, given the extreme discomfort of his expression.

"Didn't anyone ever teach you to knock," Will drawled.

Speaking of expressions, Taylor looked ghastly. His face was bone white, his eyes shadowed and red-rimmed. He looked sick. Will's memory flickered. Something about Taylor being ill. Nearly dying? It worried him. He needed to hurry up and remember. But Taylor must be okay now because he was working again. According to Stone he'd been out all day chasing leads to last night's terrorist attack. So he had to be okay, right?

Why couldn't he remember this stuff?

Taylor still stood in the doorway. Since when did he wait for an invitation?

"You okay?" Will asked.

"Great." Taylor came in and took the room's other chair. He gave David a baleful look, and David looked guilty. What. The. Hell. It wasn't Will's imagination. There were more currents running through this room than the entire Pacific.

"How are *you* feeling?" Taylor turned to Will.

"Like someone dropped a piano on me."

A familiar if faint gleam lit Taylor's gaze. "Maybe you tried to sing for them."

"Nah. I know better by now."

"What's that?" David asked, watching them.

"Will can't sing," said Taylor, who *really* couldn't sing. "His dog howls every time he tries."

That reminded Will of something. "If I'm posted here in France, where's Riley?"

"I've got him."

Will nodded. That made sense. Taylor was the closest thing he had to family in the Southland. "How did it go today? How's the investigation coming?"

Taylor made an iffy motion. Will's gaze sharpened. "You sure you're okay? Your hand's shaking."

Taylor gave him a wan smile. "Long day."

"I bet." He didn't like the idea of Taylor out there on his own. Talk about lousy luck. For both of them. "Some vacation."

"Yeah."

Will said slowly, "You're staying with me?"

A muscle jumped in Taylor's jaw. "Right."

Will turned to David. "And you're here for the D-day anniversary celebration, but you're not staying with me."

David's expression was as blank as Taylor's. "Right."

Will's head was starting to pound again. "And how long have I been posted in Paris?"

Taylor's tone was hard to describe. He was looking at David, not Will. "I guess you're supposed to remember all this on your own."

"It's a simple question," Will said irritably. He closed his eyes. By now the throbbing in his head was making his stomach roil. "I thought amnesia was just something they made up for the movies."

"Me too." Taylor sounded a little bitter.

"We ought to let Will get some rest," David said. His chair scraped back.

"You care if I sit with you awhile, Will?" Taylor's tone was very casual.

"Yeah, stay," Will reassured, not bothering to open his eyes. He knew how he'd felt when Taylor had been…

When Taylor had been what? It was there for a moment. The image of Taylor in a hospital bed looking like death warmed over. Had Taylor been *shot*? Where the hell had Will been that he let Taylor get shot?

Already the memory was slipping away. He knew he should pursue it, get this nailed down, but he was just too damned tired.

"Can I trust you?" David was saying. It was supposed to be a joke obviously, but there was an undernote of seriousness.

"Further than I can trust you." There was zero humor in Taylor's reply.

Will didn't catch David's response. Maybe just as well. The two guys he cared most for hated each other's guts. That was a problem. But it was a problem he just didn't have the energy for right then…

* * * * *

Will was having a very weird dream about Taylor. Not the first time. He'd had dreams about Taylor since they'd been partnered. It was only natural. Taylor was disturbingly attractive. More, he was sexy. *Sex on legs* as Will's granddad would have said—though not about another man, God knew.

But this was definitely a weirder dream than usual. Taylor was lying naked next to him, and Will was feeding small, shiny globes of the world into Taylor's exquisite ass. A little rope of them, each globe just a bit larger than the one before it, though not large enough for Will to make out what part of the hemisphere he was looking at. Not that that was the point. The point was that Taylor was moaning and squirming and begging Will for more each time Will pushed one of the smooth little balls into his pink little hole.

Will woke embarrassed and excited and aware that he'd come messily in his sleep. He remembered at once where he was, that there had been a terrorist attack on the catacombs, and that he'd been caught in an explosion with…wait. No. That was where the memories came to a shrieking stop.

Retrace his steps.

He'd been dreaming about Taylor. *Okay, skip that part.*

Taylor was in France.

Will stared at the empty chair beside the bed. Before the disappointment could sink in, he realized Taylor was in the room after all.

He stood at the hospital window, and he was gazing out at the starry night. He was rubbing the back of his neck, and there was a tired slump to his shoulders that somehow hurt Will's heart.

If something was really wrong, Taylor would tell him. He wouldn't keep anything from him, surely.

"So we're not partnered anymore?" Will was still having trouble adjusting to that idea. He'd been shocked when Stone had brought him up to speed during her brief visit that afternoon. Of course they couldn't stay partnered forever, but…

Taylor turned quickly and came back to the bed, pulling the chair around and straddling it. "No."

"But you're still posted in LA?"

"For now."

"For now?" Will considered this uneasily. "You've been offered another posting?"

Taylor nodded, but instead of elaborating, he said quietly, "Do you really not remember, Will?"

Now there was a dumb question. "Why the hell would I fake something like this?" He regretted his sharpness at once as Taylor shook his head. He looked exhausted, drained. He looked like Will felt.

"What's the last thing you do remember?"

Will squinted, trying to look back into the past. "It's not like that," he tried to explain. "It's not like my memories break off. I remembered my name and what year it is and who's president. I remembered being posted over here, sort of, and I remember we were talking on the phone. I remember all kinds of stuff, but it's all blurred together and the gaps are…big."

"And I'm one of them."

Will couldn't take the look on Taylor's face. The naked hurt. He was embarrassed for Taylor, and at the same time he ached for him. "That's not true. Of course I remember you, Tay."

Tay? Since when did he call Taylor Tay? What kind of a sappy nickname was that?

Taylor was giving him a funny look, and no wonder, but the nurse chose that moment to swan in and tell Taylor in her painstaking English that visiting hours were over.

Taylor turned on the charm—he could be charming when he wanted to be, despite rumors to the contrary—and she allowed him another half hour.

"Merci, mademoiselle."

Will found Taylor's awkward French sort of cute, and so, clearly, did the nurse. She spent a few seconds flirting with him. The French flirted as naturally as they breathed.

When she'd departed on rubber soles, Will said, "Tell me about the investigation. What were you doing today?" Even as he asked, he was wondering exactly why Taylor was involved in a Paris RSO investigation when he was supposed to be on vacation.

"We're not supposed to try to jog your memory."

Will said exasperatedly, "How are you jogging my memory by telling me about stuff I never knew?"

To which Taylor snapped back, "How should *I* know how this works?"

That was more like the Taylor he knew. Will grinned at him and Taylor scowled, but his ire was already fading. He proceeded to tell Will the whole crazy story from the start, which no one else had bothered to do, either because they were trying not to overexcite him or they thought he remembered.

"You tried to get them to ground all the planes at LAX?" Will felt winded just thinking about it.

"Not *all* the planes."

He even sounded offended, as though such an idea would never have crossed his mind. Will started to laugh, and after a second Taylor joined in. "You're a nut," Will commented. "I've always said so."

Taylor rolled his eyes like Will was flattering him outrageously, and an image flashed into Will's mind of the two of them standing on a mountaintop somewhere…the High Sierras?

"You're a nut, MacAllister. Did I ever tell you that?"

"A girl never gets tired of hearing it."

When was that? When the hell would they have gone camping? Taylor hated camping.

The next instant the vision was gone. Taylor was talking about what he'd learned about this Yann Helloco who might or might not be Yannick Hinault.

"I think he's got a death wish. All he painted were graveyards and graves. Tell me that's not seriously disturbed."

"I won't argue that with you. This is a guy who thinks planting car bombs and blowing up museums is part of the dialogue for change."

"At least no one was crippled or killed when they blew up the museum."

Will narrowed his eyes. There it was again. That glimmer of memory. He'd been on the phone talking to Taylor about the destruction of the museum and its collection of paintings by Jacques-Louis David, and David—his David—had been on the sofa listening. And there was some reason he didn't want Taylor to know David was there.

Or was it David who couldn't know that he and Taylor were…

Wait.

He and Taylor were what?

A picture flooded his mind of himself licking Taylor's nipples, of Taylor whimpering his name, pleading for more. *Christ.* It was so real he could taste Taylor's skin, feel the flushed heat radiating off him, the touching dampness of his underarms and groin—

"Man, you have a funny expression on your face," Taylor remarked.

Will jerked back to reality. Taylor's expression was curious. Will felt hot and uncomfortable as though his astonishing thoughts were running above him like a CNN Chyron. *Brandt wants to fuck MacAllister.*

He must have hit his head harder than he thought.

Okay. Focus on the job. That always helped in the past when he got to thinking undisciplined thoughts about his partner.

"So you think Helloco returned for this ex-girlfriend of his?"

"Do *I* think that? No. That was Tara."

"Tara?" Will put a hand to his head. It was starting to throb again. "Right. Tara."

Focus.

"So why do you think Helloco came back after all these years?"

Taylor said, "I'm not sure he *is* back."

"You know what," Will said as kindly as he could. "My head's pounding like a son of a bitch. I don't think I'm going to be a lot of help tonight."

Taylor was already on his feet. "Right. I should have left ten minutes ago anyway." He hesitated. "You're supposed to be getting out of here tomorrow. Do you want me to pick you up?"

"David will—"

Taylor flinched. What was going on there? "Sure. Of course. I'll talk to you tomorrow."

He was at the door before Will could say good night, and now that the moment came, Will was dismayed at how much he didn't want Taylor to go. Especially not looking like that.

Will called his name. Taylor turned in inquiry.

"You didn't say where your next posting is."

Voice and face were expressionless as Taylor answered, "Didn't I? Iraq."

"Iraq?" Will was surprised the monitors didn't sound the alarm, because he was pretty sure his heart stopped.

It made sense, of course. They needed good people in Iraq. Taylor was one of the best. And he was overdue an overseas position. And this would be a promotion for him, and he'd earned it.

Yeah, it made perfect sense.

But Will had lost some close friends in Iraq. He didn't want to risk losing another. Particularly not Taylor, the best friend he'd ever had. He loved Taylor like another brother. Like…

His head was pounding so badly he wondered if he should ring for help. He spoke over the thump. "Did you accept?"

"Not officially."

"But you're going to?"

Taylor hesitated. "Yeah," he said finally. "I'm going to go."

There was nothing left to say after that. Will listened to the soft, steady footfall of Taylor's steps disappearing down the corridor.

CHAPTER NINE

For the nth time, Taylor was reading over the brief and inglorious history of Yann Helloco. Portrait of a Terrorist. There weren't a lot of details on Helloco's history, but what there were didn't seem to hint at the course his life would take.

His family was small and poor but not so poor that they did without the essentials. Père Helloco was a schoolteacher. There was no mention of what Mère Helloco did. It didn't sound like political activism had been a strong force in their family life.

Helloco's siblings did not appear to be famous for anything other than being Helloco's siblings. The sister had married and was still living in Ireland. The brother had been living in the States but had died in 2010.

Taylor made a note to follow up on the brother. It was a stretch, but there wasn't much else to go on.

Helloco had shown artistic promise early on and had earned a scholarship to the prestigious *École nationale supérieure des beaux arts*. It seemed to be in art school that Helloco had become involved in Breton nationalism. He hung around with a couple of other art students from Brittany—Gabriel Besson and Paul Jacquard—who eventually provided introduction to the FLB. Through the FLB he had met the sex-kitten radical Marie Laroche. Again there were not a lot of details on their relationship, but rumors persisted that they had married.

Taylor made another note.

Eventually Helloco became impatient with the FLB's methods and broke with the larger organization to form Finistère. Besson, Jacquard, and, of course, Laroche went with him. Finistère. As anarchist organizations went, Finistère achieved so-so results. There were two failed attempts at robbing banks and the successful but mostly pointless destruction of the museum in Bagnols-sur-Cèze. They were mostly known—and hated—for a car bombing that had killed an elderly couple and a young mother pregnant with her second child.

A few months after blowing up the museum and its millions of dollars' worth of paintings by Jacques-Louis David—who had been one step from a terrorist himself, in Taylor's opinion—Finistère leadership had retreated to the country home of wealthy, politically sympathetic friends in Sarthe. As far as anyone could determine, Helloco had been concocting more bombs when something had gone wrong and he'd blown up himself, the house, and the gardener.

Considering how often Helloco's experiments with explosives went wrong, Taylor wondered if the destruction of the museum in Bagnols-sur-Cèze had been an accident. The organization had needed financing and had failed at robbing banks. Maybe they had turned their attention to robbing museums, only to fail there as well. It made more sense than blowing up a small, obscure museum off the beaten track.

Following the death of Helloco, the rest of Finistère had escaped mostly unscathed but hadn't survived long without their mastermind. Didier died in a shootout with police. Jacquard had driven his car into a brick wall while attempting to evade capture. Laroche, Besson, and Roland had eventually been tracked down and arrested.

And that was pretty much that. Taylor scratched his nose, considering his notes. Not many leads to pursue. As cold cases went, this one was giving him frostbite.

Outside Will's cubicle in the embassy DSS office, Taylor could hear the quiet murmur of voices on the phone and the ordinary office equipment sounds. It could have been any DSS office in the world. But then that was the point.

His gaze moved to the framed photo of him and Will on Will's desk. It had been taken right after they'd won the West Coast Regional competitive shooting championship. An unobjectionable picture of a couple of buddies sharing a moment of triumph.

Maybe deep down Will secretly wished that was what they had remained.

Because Taylor really had trouble believing Will could have forgotten everything between them without some considerable effort. If he didn't remember, then he didn't *want* to remember. That was the conclusion Taylor kept coming back to.

Will hadn't been forced to take this Paris gig. That had been his choice. Knowing it meant the end of their working partnership, he'd still opted for promotion and Paris.

Slow down.

Now he was letting his insecurity and frustration get the better of him. Will loved him. Taylor believed that. He *knew* that.

That didn't change the fact that they hadn't stopped arguing from the moment Taylor had landed. And what were they fighting about all the time? Taylor wasn't sure. Will probably wasn't any clearer.

Regardless, it didn't bode well for the future. A future that Will apparently preferred to pretend didn't exist—

There was a knock on the cubicle doorframe. Taylor glanced up from his dark thoughts.

RSO Stone looked as tired as Taylor felt. "We finally heard back from LAPD. They searched Hinault's home. They've discovered a safe box with five passports in five different names."

"Passport fraud. Right up our alley."

"It is. There's more. Hinault may actually be Yves Helloco."

"*Yves* Helloco?" Taylor was already scanning his notes, verifying.

Stone said, "You heard right. Yves Helloco. Yann's brother."

Taylor sat back in his chair. "I thought the brother was deceased?"

"He is. Or let me put it this way. *One* of the Helloco brothers is deceased. We're not exactly sure which one yet. The Hinault passport photo matches up to the brother. A couple of the other passport photos appear to be Yann Helloco appropriately aged."

"There's no indication that the brother had any criminal background— or showed any sign of political activism."

"It remains unclear whether Yves willfully participated in passport fraud. It's possible he was the victim of identity theft perpetrated by his brother."

"Or…" A crazy thought took hold of Taylor. "Are they sure they know who was living in Burbank?"

Stone's smile was a shadow of her old one. "Good call, MacAllister. Neighbors identified *both* Helloco brothers as being Yannick Hinault."

All at once Taylor's mood improved considerably. "Now we're getting somewhere."

"Yes, but let's not get ahead of ourselves. The only thing we really know for certain is *one* of these Helloco brothers is deceased and one of them is in Paris."

"Fingerprints will settle it one way or the other."

"True, but this isn't TV. We're not going to get lab results on the forensic evidence within twenty-four hours, and unfortunately there's a time element here. The French police just notified us that they received another communiqué from Finistère this morning. Finistère is claiming the explosion in the catacombs was just the beginning and that within forty-eight hours they will make a political statement that the world will never forget—and punctuate it in blood."

Taylor started to speak, but the phone on Will's desk rang.

Stone nodded dismissingly. "Go ahead and take that. Find me what you can on the brother. And I mean I need that information yesterday."

Taylor picked up the phone as she departed. "MacAllister."

"Does that offer to give me a lift home from the hospital still stand?" Will asked, and Taylor's heart gave a start of pleasure. Stupid, but there it was.

He answered automatically, "Of course." Then couldn't help asking, "What happened to Bradley?"

"It turns out he's tied up in meetings all day for this anniversary celebration on the sixth."

"That's tomorrow."

"Is it? I guess I lost a day."

He'd nearly lost a lot more than a day. "Okay. When are you being released?"

"Actually…I've just been sprung."

"Now?"

Will said immediately, "I can always grab a taxi if you can't get away."

"No way." Taylor clicked out of the program he was using and turned off the computer. "I'm on my way."

* * * * *

"You must already be driving like a native if you made it this fast," Will said a short while later as Taylor unlocked the passenger door and ushered him inside. Taylor threw Will's carryall into the back and jumped in behind the wheel.

Will grunted as he eased himself down in the seat. Taylor spared him a quick look.

"How are you feeling?"

"Fine."

Taylor's mouth twitched at the staunchness of that. Will looked pale, and he was moving slowly, but he seemed pretty much like his normal self. "Yeah? How's the memory?"

"Still spotty." Will sounded uncharacteristically grouchy. Amnesia, even partial amnesia, had to be hell for a control freak.

"Maybe being home will help."

"Maybe." Will gazed moodily out the window as Taylor maneuvered away from the curbside. "You seem to be keeping busy. I thought I'd s—"

"What?"

"Nothing. What's the latest?"

Taylor filled him in on Arthur's progress, which didn't cheer Will up any, and then he brought up the news that Helloco's brother had possibly aided him in passport fraud. "Either that or he was a victim of identity theft. I'm leaning toward willing accomplice myself."

"That's because you're naturally devious."

Taylor curled his lip. Deep down was that really what Will thought?

"It's a joke." Will was watching him.

"Sure."

"It's a *joke*."

Taylor obligingly grinned. "Now *I* took it as a compliment."

Will made a politely disbelieving noise.

"Anyway, Finistère seems to have phoned the national police this morning to warn them that within forty-eight hours they'll leave the world a political message no one will ever forget."

"They're going to close Euro Disney during the peak of tourist season?"

Taylor snorted. "Maybe. The part I don't follow is Helloco's brother didn't display any political awareness according to anything I've read so far. I'm not sure why he'd be part of this."

"People change."

Taylor had no response to that.

"Maybe he doesn't realize he's a party to it." Will shrugged and then winced.

"I guess that's possible. Anyway, I'm supposed to focus on investigating Yves Helloco. Stone thinks he's the key. I think she might be right."

"What about the girlfriend? Laroche?"

"She was hanging tough last I heard from Bonnet."

They reached rue du Colisée, and Taylor parked outside the front of the apartment building.

Will went slowly into the house. Taylor grabbed Will's carryall and then paused to take a look at one of the tires that seemed low. Deciding the tire was fine, he continued inside.

As he entered the living room, he heard one of the floorboards on the stairs to the bedroom squeak.

A vision of the bedroom as he'd left it that morning flashed into his brain.

Shit.

He'd been in a hurry and had intended on straightening up that afternoon before Will got home.

He flew up the stairs two at a time. Will stood in the doorway surveying the room. He glanced over his shoulder as Taylor reached the landing.

"Make yourself at home, MacAllister." His voice was teasing, but Taylor could see a trace of unease in his eyes.

"Sorry. I meant to tidy up." He scooted past Will, snatching up the still-damp bath towel lying over the foot of the bed. "I was running late this morning."

"I see that." Will took in the coffee cup on the nightstand, the unmade bed, the open suitcase with Taylor's belongings spilling out. Taylor was fairly neat. There was nothing out of line in any of this for a house guest—unless the guest was using his host's room as his own. Then it might look like someone was taking a few liberties.

"No problem," Will said slowly, his gaze returning, as though magnetized, to the rumpled bed.

Despite all the resolutions Taylor had made over the past twelve hours, that was the breaking point. He tossed the towel aside. "Jesus, Will. How the hell can you *not* remember?"

Will watched him warily. "Remember what?"

"*This.*" Taylor crossed the room, locked hands on Will's shoulders, and pressed his mouth to Will's.

For a couple of fraught heartbeats, Will did nothing. In fact, he was so still he might not have been breathing.

Then a ripple went through him like someone had thrown a lever. He heaved Taylor off. "What the fuck are you doing?"

It had been a risk. Even so, Will's furious rejection stunned him. Taylor cried, "What do you think I'm doing?"

"Are you *crazy*?"

Will's obvious shock, shock verging on horror, sobered Taylor fast. "Look, I'm sorry. I shouldn't have done that. But Will…" His voice trailed with all that he wanted to, needed to—and didn't dare—say.

Will's colorless face worked. "What are you telling me? You're telling me that we're…that we've…that you and I…?" Will stared at Taylor's suitcase, and Taylor followed his gaze to the perfectly blameless tumble of boxers and socks that in this context somehow managed to look sordid.

"You have to remember!" Taylor protested, and despite his very best effort, he was getting angry. Will wasn't hurting him on purpose, but he *was* hurting him. Again and again, and Taylor was getting good and goddamned sick of it. "If you don't remember, it's because you don't *want* to remember."

"I don't remember because it wouldn't happen. I wouldn't let it happen."

"And why is that?"

"Because it would be the worst fucking idea ever. Because we're partners. Because you're not someone who—" Will stopped.

Taylor's face must have given away the things he'd have killed to hide from Will at that second.

"I don't mean that." Will spoke quickly. "I mean, *you're* not interested in settling down. You've never been interested in a relationship that lasted longer than a month or so."

"I'm not the one who—" Taylor swallowed the rest of it. No, he wasn't going to do that. This was bad enough without recriminations.

Will wasn't listening. "We agreed a long time ago we'd never risk… We'd never…because of…of this." He waved roughly at the bedroom window looking out over the rooftops of Paris. "Because of me being stationed here and you heading out for Iraq. It's a fucking disaster of an idea."

"You think I'm lying?"

He could see that brought Will up short. Watched the wheels slowly, belatedly turning behind Will's blue eyes. Will put a hand to his mouth as though checking for damage done to him by Taylor's kiss. "No," Will said finally. "You're not lying. You wouldn't lie."

"But?"

Will shook his head like someone surfacing from deep water. "What about David?"

It was like taking a punch to the heart. Not that it wasn't a reasonable question. Will had come to and found Bradley sitting by his bedside like a devoted suitor. According to his last memories of Bradley, they were still involved, and Taylor knew Will had really liked the other man, that they had been on the verge of getting serious when Taylor had been shot. So it was a fair enough question even though Taylor thought it might kill him.

"I don't know," he said when he could find his voice. "I guess that's something you and Bradley still have to work out."

He turned away, but Will took the steps needed to grab his shoulder. "No way, buddy boy. You opened this can of worms. You're not walking out of here now."

Taylor slid out from under his hold. He cried, *"What the hell do you want from me, Will?"*

His pain was too raw, too transparent. Will stared at him. "I don't know," he admitted. "I guess I need to understand."

"What is there to understand?" *Jesus fucking Christ,* in a minute he was going to be crying. After this, Iraq would be a Sunday picnic. "I'm telling you the truth. It's been you and me for over a year, Will. Ever since I got sh—" He stopped.

Will looked paper white, his eyes black. Taylor remembered that Will had nearly died. That Will was supposed to remember on his own. That however hard it was on him, it had to be harder on Will. He struggled for control, for Will's sake. "I don't know what to say to you. If you don't want to believe me, then I guess that's the answer."

Will's expression changed as though he was suddenly seeing Taylor, seeing him clearly for the first time since they'd walked into the bedroom. "I'm not doing this to hurt you."

Taylor made a sound intended to be a laugh. "Good to know."

Will was working for control too, trying to meet him halfway, and Taylor tried to take comfort from that, but he couldn't seem to get past the sick hollowness that had opened up inside him following Will's instinctive *"What about David?"*

"If we're together, why am I in Paris and you're getting ready to ship out to Iraq?"

"Good question," Taylor said. The steadiness of his voice came as a surprise. "Best question, as a matter of fact."

"And what's the answer?"

"Maybe you just hit on the answer. Maybe this is the answer."

Will sat down heavily on the side of the bed. "I don't know what the hell you're talking about."

Taylor stared at Will's bent head, his drawn profile. "It means I don't know the answer to your question. I didn't want this separation. Paris was your choice. And maybe the fact that you've blocked out any memory of us as anything but friends and partners is the answer. Maybe that's how you wish it was." He let his breath out quietly. "In which case, that's how it is."

Will continued to stare at his boots.

Taylor became aware that the phone was ringing downstairs. That it had been ringing for some time.

He wished he could make it easier for Will. He wished he could make it easier for himself. But like he'd said…it was what it was.

Taylor turned and went downstairs.

CHAPTER TEN

Will leaned forward, clutching his head. He felt like, if he didn't hang on to it, it was liable to fall right off his shoulders, roll across the room, and bounce down the stairs to the living room where he could now hear Taylor's admirably calm voice speaking on the phone.

Now things were beginning to make sense.

In a completely insane way.

From the moment he'd regained consciousness, he'd known something was wrong; something vital was missing. Beyond the obvious gaps in his memory had been an uneasy awareness that something crucial was being overlooked. Now he understood why David had been nonplussed and then a little awkward when Will had greeted him. And Taylor...

Will's heart felt like it was shriveling as he remembered Taylor's now obvious pain and confusion the night before. *The night before?* How about five minutes ago?

Poor bastard.

But what the hell had they been thinking? Knowing the score? Knowing the way the world—their world—worked?

They? What had Will been thinking? For God's sake. *Taylor?* Taylor, who had the sexual restraint of a young gazelle? Taylor, who changed boyfriends like he changed shirts. Who was on record as saying he believed sexual monogamy was a myth and gay men should reject the romantic mirages and sexual mores of heterosexuals. *That* Taylor?

Yeah, that Taylor—who was also smart and strong and unfailingly courageous and loyal to the death. Who had absorbed every hard, hurtful bullet Will had fired and somehow managed not to shoot back.

Whatever this mess was, Taylor sure as hell hadn't gotten into it on his own.

In fact, if Will was going to be absolutely honest with himself, and this seemed like the time for it, when Taylor had walked over and pressed his warm, soft mouth to Will's…for one dizzy moment all Will had been able to think of was the forbidden thrill of Taylor's lips touching his. He couldn't think of a kiss in his entire life that had electrified him like that one.

No wonder he kept having those odd dreams about Taylor.

This wasn't Taylor's fault.

Not his fault alone, anyway, and there was no excuse for Will sitting here leaving Taylor to carry the can for him.

He rose from the mattress and made himself walk downstairs. As he reached the ground floor, he could hear Taylor.

"But you could get me in to see her, right? You could pull strings?"

To Will's great relief, he sounded normal, ordinary. The earth, which had been drunkenly careening like a skipping stone across the universe, suddenly righted itself. If they could just get through the next few hours, next few days, it would all work itself out. No matter what else was going on here, they were still friends and they were still partners, and that was what really counted.

Merci beaucoup," Taylor said in his cracked French. "I'll see you there." He put the phone down and raised his gaze to Will's—he must have heard Will coming down the stairs. He said in that same calm, unhurried voice, "Are you okay here on your own for a few hours? I've got to get back to work. Bonnet wrangled an interview with Marie Laroche. She's suddenly decided she wants to talk."

"I'm fine," Will replied in the same tone. "But I'll go with you."

"I don't think that's such a good idea. Anyway, you're still officially on sick leave."

"We're too shorthanded for me to sit here on my butt thinking about stuff I don't want to think about anyway. Besides which, as you pointed out, there's a time factor here."

Taylor gnawed on his lip, trying to decide—like he really thought he was going to keep Will out of this?

"We're wasting time we don't have," Will observed.

Taylor's eyes met his, veered away. Taylor gave a curt nod. "Have it your way, Brandt."

"I intend to," said Will.

* * * * *

Marie Laroche looked, in Will's opinion, like a scary grandma. She had a gravelly smoker's voice and tattooed eyeliner. She looked like she cut her hair herself—with the hatchet she used to decapitate chickens. But she had a deep, surprisingly engaging laugh. She sounded like a woman who had once laughed often and easily.

She was not laughing much that afternoon. None of them were. She took the cigarettes and coffee with a mutter of thanks, lit up, and blew a thoughtful stream of smoke at the soundproof ceiling with the mounted security cameras. She began to speak.

Bonnet translated briskly, "You wish to know about Yann Helloco. Well? Ask your questions. I am Yann's wife."

"Is that true?" Will asked Bonnet.

Bonnet shrugged. For the French, shrugging wasn't merely a gesture. It was its own language. That particular shrug meant *It remains to be seen, but we're checking on it.*

"Why have you changed your mind about talking to us?" Taylor asked.

Bonnet translated and then relayed the answer. "I'm too old to go back to prison. The things that once fired my heart no longer warm me."

Will and Taylor exchanged looks. Will raised his eyebrows.

Taylor asked, "Is Helloco alive?"

"Je ne sais pas."

They didn't need a translator for that.

"Did Helloco die in Sarthe?"

Marie seemed to struggle with that one. She said at last, spitting it out for the recorder, "*Non.*"

Bonnet and Will looked at each other, well-satisfied. "Tell us what happened?" Bonnet asked.

The story that Marie told unfolded in bits and pieces between long drags on her cigarette and sips of cold coffee.

For some time Yann had been growing less and less invested in the movement. He grew not only cynical about the chances of Breton sovereignty but what Breton sovereignty might ultimately mean. One night he went so far as to say he believed all governments were the same and that Brittany would fare no better under home rule than under French imperialism. This attitude led to increasing tensions within the group. There was even talk of ousting Yann as leader.

Matters grew worse after they blew up the museum in Bagnols-sur-Cèze.

At this point in the recital Marie's story got a little vague.

"Did they mean to blow up the museum?" Taylor asked Bonnet. "Or did they plan to rob it?"

Bonnet translated, and Marie looked alarmed. There was a quick volley of French, and then Bonnet said, "Marie says they did not intend to destroy the paintings. The idea was to close the museum to make a political statement."

"Did she answer my question? Was the plan to rob the museum?"

Bonnet's eyebrows rose. She repeated the question. Marie shook her head vehemently.

"Okay. Go on."

Marie went on. After the affair at the museum went so wrong, Yann was even more disenchanted and began to talk about leaving the movement completely and going underground. He and Marie discussed fleeing the country and hiding out in some part of the world where their faces were not so well-known—and from where they could not be extradited. Unfortunately they both had significant media presence even back in those days when there had been no Internet. Marie in particular, being very photogenic, had had her picture splashed everywhere, including appearances in *Hara Kiri* and *Paris Match*. They were forced to conclude that it would be impossible for them to make their escape together. They discussed the option of a separate escape, then living apart for a time, and finally reuniting in six months or so. But this wasn't a serious plan. Or at least Marie didn't think so.

After the museum, things were very hot for the group, and they gratefully accepted the offer to stay at the country home of some wealthy supporters of the movement. It was during the stay in Sarthe that everything changed.

It seemed to Will that this part of the story was not so easy for Marie. She had been brusque and businesslike, but now her eyes grew watery and her mouth trembled. She puffed impatiently on her cigarette.

The group had been staying in the country for about a week. One afternoon Marie, Didier, and Roland went to purchase supplies. They returned in time to see the house catch fire. They rushed inside and found the body of a man they believed, at first glance, to be Yann. But examination proved it was the gardener in Yann's clothes and wearing Yann's wedding ring. He had been bludgeoned.

It was obvious at once to Marie what her husband had done. He had faked his own death in order to leave Finistère. In doing so he had abandoned her and murdered Guillaume Durand who, unluckily for him, bore a strong resemblance to the reluctant revolutionary.

Once she understood her husband's purpose, Marie did her best to ensure his plan succeeded. She persuaded the other two to augment the fire and make sure Durand was burned beyond recognition

"Why would you?" Will was skeptical. "After what he did to you. Abandoning you? Why would you try to help him?"

Bonnet translated, and Marie turned her pitch-black gaze his way. Bonnet reported her flat, quiet words. "You would not understand. You are a man and cannot understand love as a woman does. I would have done *anything* for him. I would have killed Durand myself if Yann had required it. I saw that he had to escape, and I did my best to ensure his escape would be successful."

Taylor said sardonically, "If you love something, set it free." To Bonnet, he said, "If that's true, why has she changed her mind now?"

Bonnet asked the question in French. It was fascinating to see Marie's expression change, grow dark and bitter.

"She says all these years she believed Yann made the only choice he could, that he left her out of desperation, and that he's been as lonely as she has. But if he has returned home at last yet has made no attempt to see her, she is no longer willing to protect him at the expense of her own freedom."

Will commented, "If it doesn't come back, hunt it down and kill it."

Taylor's laugh was short. "Ask her why they targeted the museum in Bagnols-sur-Cèze?"

Bonnet looked skeptical, but she recited the question.

Marie looked confused. She said something to Bonnet, who said, "They wished to make a political statement."

"In Bagnols-sur-Cèze? It's out in the middle of nowhere. How would blowing up a small, mostly unknown museum make a statement?"

"She doesn't understand the question."

"She understands all right." Taylor studied Marie. Will knew that expression very well. Taylor keeping a suspicious watch on the mouse hole.

"What are you thinking?" Will asked him.

"Not sure."

Will said to Bonnet, "If Helloco lost interest in the movement, why is he back targeting American tourists and French landmarks?"

More back and forth. "She says she doesn't know."

After that, the interview was not as productive. Marie denied knowing where Helloco was—or whether he was alive at all—what his motives might be, and whether his brother was knowingly involved in passport fraud.

"Are there any final questions?" Bonnet looked from Taylor to Will.

Will shook his head. It was clear to him that Marie had been, at best, hedging for the last fifteen minutes. They'd got all they were going to get out of her.

Taylor said suddenly, "Why did Helloco only paint graveyards?"

Marie seemed surprised by the question. "Yann was interested in the existential flux and flow."

"What the hell does that mean?" Taylor turned to Will, who shrugged.

"For Yann, art was a philosophical problem," Bonnet supplied from Marie.

"And death was the answer?"

The look Marie delivered relegated Taylor to the category of philistine. Or possibly pill bug.

"There's one graveyard he seems to paint over and over. Which one is it, and why is he so fascinated by it?"

Marie replied that Helloco mostly painted Père Lachaise Cemetery.

Will and Taylor turned to Bonnet, who explained, "It's the largest cemetery in Paris. Certainly one of the most visited cemeteries in the world. It is also said to be one of the most haunted."

"Jim Morrison is buried there," Will said.

"I kind of doubt that was a big factor for Helloco."

"It is where Yann wishes to be buried," Marie replied with finality.

* * * * *

"Helloco came back here for a specific reason," Will said as they headed back to the embassy. "And it wasn't any sentimental journey."

"Agreed."

Will eyed Taylor curiously. "Any idea what?"

"Working on it." Taylor was frowning at the road ahead, but Will suspected the problem wasn't the relatively light Parisian traffic.

"What is it about that museum in Bagnols-sur-Cèze that bothers you?"

"Hm?" Taylor shook off his preoccupation. "It doesn't make sense as a political target. It was a small, obscure museum. The only reason I can see it being targeted is it would have been easy to hit. Which doesn't change the fact that hitting it would be politically meaningless."

"Who knows what something means or doesn't mean to fanatics like Finistère."

"I'm starting to wonder how much of a fanatic Helloco was."

Maybe Helloco had tired of terrorism, but his girlfriend—wife, whatever she'd been—was a fanatic through and through. Even in her loyalty to Helloco. Not that Will couldn't, on one level, understand. Laroche was wrong about that, wrong about men not understanding love.

Anyway, most of the romantic poems and songs and paintings in the world were by men, so what was she talking about?

She'd just hitched her wagon to the wrong star. Helloco hadn't deserved that unswerving loyalty. He'd been willing to abandon her for his own safety—hell, he'd been willing to blow up the house of the people giving them shelter and murder a man. Abandonment had been the least of his sins.

The problem with love was you didn't always get to choose who you loved.

And sometimes the people you loved didn't love you back.

He glanced at Taylor. All through that interrogation—in fact ever since they'd left Will's apartment—he'd seemed withdrawn. Polite, professional, pleasant—and about as distant as you could get and still be in the same room. Or car.

"Look," Will said abruptly, awkwardly. "I just want to say—"

"I know. It's easier if you don't." Taylor glanced his way, and he seemed so cool, so composed that Will felt foolish for bringing it up again. Especially when they were supposed to be on the job.

But he had to—wanted to—say it anyway. "There isn't anyone who means more to me than you."

Taylor said in the same calm voice, "Will, if you say you still want to be friends, so help me God I'm going to shove your teeth down your throat."

CHAPTER ELEVEN

They were not speaking.

They had not spoken since Taylor had threatened to punch Will. He was a little ashamed of that, but Jesus, Will could be an insensitive bastard.

Work was the best refuge, and there was a mountain of it. Taylor was diligently researching everything he could find on Yves Helloco and not letting himself think about anything else—like the fact that Will was sitting in his cubicle talking to David Bradley on the phone.

He'd nearly walked in on the conversation but had caught a low-voiced and apologetic "So if I said anything out of line..." in time to back out the door again.

He'd nearly fallen over the fax machine in his haste, but he thought he'd got out without Will seeing him. That was the main thing. For his own sake, not Will's. If he could salvage some of his pride, that would be something. At this point it might be the only thing.

So...Yves Helloco. Yann's older brother. Schoolteacher. By all accounts—not that there were many—a quiet, law-abiding man who was sympathetic to the aims of his politically active sibling but not motivated to join the cause. A normal citizen, in other words.

Something Taylor hadn't paid much attention to in his earlier info gathering were casual mentions that the Hellocos had been a close-knit family. It was an open-ended term people used to describe everything from cousins marrying cousins in Arkansas to anyone still speaking to their relatives by the time the holidays were over. Now Taylor considered it from the perspective of the mix-and-match passports in Hinault's possession.

Yves had been married and living in Los Angeles at the time of Yann's death. He had traveled to Brittany with his wife for his brother's memorial service and gone back to the States two days later. Taylor frowned over that date. Not a lot of time to visit the family. He lifted a pile and began searching for another printout of Helloco's passport records. Unfortunately, back in the seventies there had been no biometrics with which to track passport use. Even with biometrics, it was still possible to scam the system, especially in the case of imposters, people who closely resembled the owners of the stolen passports they were using. It was primitive but effective, where there was a strong family resemblance.

That was Taylor's hypothesis. That Yves had handed his passport over to Yann, and Yann, posing as Yves, had flown home to the States with Yves' wife.

Which meant Yves would have returned home a short time later using a different passport. Not Yann's obviously. No, he'd have used Yannick Hinault's.

Because there was no Yannick Hinault.

And instead of tracking Yves' movements, Taylor needed to track Yannick Hinault.

He rose from Special Agent Arthur's desk and the computer he was borrowing and started for Will's cubicle. However, a glance across the dividers and desks showed Will in Stone's office with the door closed.

What was that about?

Of course it could be about anything. There was no reason for that instant sinking in Taylor's stomach. He was too much on edge, that was the trouble. Waiting for the next bomb to drop—figuratively, not literally. At least he hoped so.

He went back to Arthur's desk. He'd have liked to bounce his theory off Will like they used to do, but maybe the timing wasn't so great, come to think of it. Picking up the phone, he began the laborious process of negotiating his way through the circuits to the Prefecture of Police and his new good buddy Inspector Bonnet.

Inspector Bonnet was a little—actually *beaucoup*—busy, but once she understood what Taylor was requesting, she agreed to do the background research.

"You understand this does not change the fact that regardless of who we are dealing with, this man has made a threat most grave against this nation? And that we have less than forty-eight hours to deduce what he intends, and stop him."

"Depending on who we're dealing with, maybe not," Taylor said.

"I'm not following, Agent MacAllister."

"If we're dealing with Yves Helloco, all bets are off. We don't know enough about him to predict what he might or might not do. It's possible he went off the deep end after the death of his wife and brother. But if we're dealing with Yann Helloco, then I think we do have enough information and history on him to make an informed guess about what he's up to now."

"And that is what?"

"I have a theory, but I'd rather not make a fool of myself until I've got a little more to go on."

"Very well, but it may take some time to collect the information you wish."

"I just want to know if this guy, Yannick Hinault, ever existed. I don't believe he did. I think Hinault was a false identity, an alias used by Yves Helloco to return home after he'd sent his kid brother ahead with his wife."

"How would Yves, a schoolteacher, know how to procure forged documents?"

"I don't think Yves set it up. I think Yann set it up. There have always been links between terrorists and organized crime. I think Yann planned the whole thing out ahead of time and then enlisted Yves' cooperation."

"Why would Yann not use the Hinault passport if that's the case?"

"The risk of discovery was higher with the Hinault passport. Yves' identity was real, and traveling with the wife made it all the more legitimate-seeming. The Hinault passport was a little trickier, but Yves' chances of succeeding were much higher, especially since they could use his real photo."

Bonnet's sigh was just audible. "I'm confused, but I suppose it is not so important. I'll see if I can find the confirmation you require."

"Thanks. I mean, *merci*." Taylor's gaze was on Stone's door. He automatically replaced the handset as Stone entered the main office, followed by Will. Something was up. Something major. Will stood behind her, arms folded, looking uncharacteristically somber.

"If I can have your attention," Stone said. Her voice was even, but it carried. The other agents pushed their chairs back or hastily ended their phone conversations.

Taylor stepped out of the cubicle and leaned against the wall. He was directly across from Will, but after a brief, uncomfortable tangling of gazes, they both avoided each other's eyes.

Stone was saying, "As you're all aware, the annual D-day anniversary celebration has been one of several potential blips on our radar as a possible target for Finistère. Given their virulent anti-American sentiments, it's not a stretch to believe whatever this target is, it's something that will hit home for US citizens as well as the French. Brandt has spent the afternoon on that angle, and he's come up with what I believe is a pretty strong indicator that Normandy is where we need to focus our preventive efforts."

Even given the strain between them, it was startling that Will hadn't talked any of this over with him. Taylor looked at Will, but Will was gazing fixedly at Stone.

Of course. Forgetting all the rest of it, Will would be uncomfortable talking to Taylor about this particular supposition because of David Bradley's involvement in the D-day memorial. Will believed Bradley was in peril, and he was acting fast while trying not to rub it in Taylor's face.

Or something like that. It didn't really matter because Will had it wrong. Taylor was almost certain. *Almost.* Not so certain that he wanted to propose his theory without a little more supporting evidence.

Stone nodded to Will, and Will stepped forward.

"Thanks to MacAllister's groundwork on the history behind the founding of Finistère, I got the idea to focus on the Front de libération de la Bretagne. FLB was Finistère's parent group. One of the things I discovered was that Breton nationalism became largely discredited through its collaboration with the Nazis during World War Two. And a couple of its founding members were sentenced for treason."

Taylor could see that *aha!* moment radiate through the room.

Stone said, "I think the connection between the FLB and tomorrow's events scheduled to take place in Normandy is pretty clear. D-day was an Allied effort. It will take place on French soil, but there will be plenty of

Americans on hand, which I believe makes it an ideal target for Finistère both from a symbolic and a practical standpoint."

"From a practical standpoint, it's a logistical nightmare," Will put in. "I've been talking to some of the brass involved, and it's going to be tough to achieve any kind of security perimeter."

"Correct," Stone said. "I've alerted the Ministry of Defense and the Ministry of the Interior. The National Gendarmerie is policing the memorial service, and they'll be expanding their onsite presence in response to the increased threat."

"We need to be there," Will stated. His very quiet was convincing.

There was a murmur of agreement from the remaining agents. Stone nodded. "That's my thought."

Don't say it.

Don't do it.

This was where Taylor had come in. Sticking his nose in where it wasn't wanted. Maybe even wasn't needed. If he was right, it wasn't going to do anyone any harm to muster out the DSS tomorrow. Two-thirds of RSOs in France would have been attending the service anyway. Will and Taylor would have gone in honor of Will's grandfather, who'd taken part in the landings.

No need to volunteer his own wild theory, and it was sure as hell going to look wild in comparison to Will's. He didn't want to challenge Will anyway. Things were bad enough between them without it looking like Taylor resented David Bradley so much he was willing to risk the lives of hundreds of Americans.

Keep your damn mouth shut.

The phone was ringing at Arthur's desk. All he had to do was turn and answer it, and he could decide later how much to tell Will. If anything.

"I think the D-day memorial is a dodge."

Every head in the room turned Taylor's way. He steeled himself and forged on. "I think we were meant to hit on the anniversary ceremony as Finistère's target. I think Helloco deliberately dropped those bread crumbs for us to gobble up."

"Bullshit."

Stone looked startled at Will's flat response, but she didn't caution him. "What's your theory, MacAllister?"

"First, there is no Finistère. Finistère is defunct. There's one man, and he's acting on his own. I don't believe his motivation is political."

Will demanded, "Then what is it?"

Taylor sidestepped. "Second, how come all at once Helloco has started playing guessing games? Up until now he's always said exactly where he was going to strike. But suddenly he's playing coy. Why?"

"He doesn't want us to stop him," one of the other agents said.

"I don't think so. I think he wanted us to stay busy trying to figure out where this big attack was going to happen. If he just named the site, we're liable to start wondering exactly what else he might be up to. But think about it. Where else *would* this strike take place? What other major newsworthy event is going on this week that involves Americans and the French?"

Will was shaking his head. "You're overthinking this."

"I don't think I am. Here's another thing. Why is Helloco suddenly so anti-American? He's been living in the States for forty years. And living comfortably enough, it sounds like."

Stone said, "That's pretty shaky, MacAllister. We have no way of knowing what might have triggered Helloco's return."

"You think you know." Will was watching Taylor with hard, unfriendly eyes.

"According to Helloco's wife—ex-wife? Whatever—Helloco had lost interest in the movement. He didn't care anymore. He said all governments were equally corrupt. He just wanted out. And he was willing to commit murder to get out."

Will said, "Again, this is bullshit. You're speculating. You have no idea what Helloco thinks or feels after all this time."

"Well, I know one thing, Brandt. I know Finistère is not, and never was, the FLB. And the connections you're trying to draw between collaborations with the Nazis that took place before Helloco was even born are totally bogus."

Will's face tightened. "Okay, Monsieur Poirot. What's your theory? What's his target? You keep avoiding that question. What do you think he's after? Why do *you* think Helloco's back?"

The phone was ringing on Arthur's desk again.

Taylor tried to picture excusing himself to answer it. Or maybe he could just decline to answer on the grounds he was going to look like he'd been hitting Will's bourbon.

"I think he's here to recover a cache of paintings by Jacques-Louis David which he liberated and then hid when Finistère bombed a small museum in Bagnols-sur-Cèze."

It could have gone worse.

No one laughed. Even Will was silent, eyes narrowed in that way he had when something struck him out of the blue. Taylor offered his reasoning, such as it was, and Stone heard him out all the way to the end without interrupting.

She said at last, "It's an ingenious idea, but you don't really have anything more to support it than Brandt does his theory. Yet you believe he's drawing his conclusions based on circumstantial evidence."

That was pretty much what Taylor had expected, which was why he hadn't wanted to broach his theory till he had more proof.

Oh, and he had a gut feeling, but he wasn't about to offer *that* into evidence. Especially after the *Monsieur Poirot* crack.

"I think the wife knows. I think that's why she finally turned on him. She knows he's back for the paintings, not for her. But she was part of that robbery and the destruction of that museum, and while the original statute of limitations has expired, the possession of stolen art is a separate offense. She gave us what she could without incriminating herself."

Stone made a small musing sound. "You make a good case. But so does Brandt. The bottom line is I'd rather be wrong and see Helloco get away with a couple of million dollars in French art than be wrong and see innocent Americans injured or killed."

"I understand." He didn't look at Will.

To Taylor's surprise, Stone added, "However, since you *do* make a good case, and since you're technically on vacation, and since the gendarmes, the national police, *and* the military have all been alerted and will be involved in protecting the Normandy site, if you'd like to follow up on your theory and start looking for those paintings, I'm not going to stop you."

That was a lot more than Taylor had hoped for. "Thank you, ma'am."

"Coordinate your efforts with the French police. We want to build relations, not risk them."

"Yes, ma'am." He glanced at Will. Will stared back at him without an ounce of emotion. No question that Will considered it his priority to make sure David Bradley was safe.

That answered that. Had there really been a question?

Once more the phone was ringing on Arthur's desk. Taylor thanked Stone again and went to answer it.

Inspector Bonnet said, "Good news, Agent MacAllister. At least, if it is not good news, it is the news you expected. There is no such person as Yannick Hinault."

CHAPTER TWELVE

Will turned to RSO Stone. "If you don't mind, ma'am, I'd like to stick with MacAllister while he's pursuing his hunch."

Stone looked taken aback. "I'm confused. Normandy was *your* call, Brandt."

"I know. But here's the thing: MacAllister's got an instinct for crime like nobody I've ever known. There might be something to this idea of his."

"I realize that. That's why I've given him permission to investigate."

"He doesn't know the city. He doesn't speak the language." Will could see Stone thought he was being an ass, but he plowed ahead. "You said yourself we've got more than enough manpower assigned to the D-day ceremony. I think MacAllister could use some backup. Whether he realizes it or not."

"You're serious?" Stone's blue gaze rested on his face for a moment. "You *are* serious." He could see her weighing it. "Brandt, I can't believe what I'm about to say, but seeing that you shouldn't be here anyway since you haven't been cleared for duty, if you choose to spend your sick leave tagging along with MacAllister, that's up to you. Maybe you can keep him from triggering an international incident."

Will's smile was lopsided. "Thank you, ma'am."

"For the record, I think you're both wrong, but..." Stone shrugged. She had bigger fish to fry.

Will found Taylor in Arthur's cubicle, surrounded by framed photos of Arthur's parents and girlfriend. Taylor was on the phone, his voice quiet but urgent.

"I don't care. Don't attend the ceremony." He was silent for a moment. "I know. I know all that." Another silence. "I know that too. Just…humor me on this. You said you'd steer clear of any places American tourists might go. Well, Normandy counts." He listened. "Thank you. I'll let you know." Then his face changed, and his tone with it. "He's fine… Yeah… I'll tell him you were asking… Yeah. Me too."

Taylor dropped the handset into the cradle and noticed Will standing in the doorway. "Hey." Face and voice were neutral.

"Hey," Will returned. Now face-to-face with Taylor, things were a little different. If Taylor's expression had been any blanker, Will would have been getting the No Internet Connection message. "Tara?"

Taylor nodded.

"So you're not one hundred percent sure about this idea of yours?"

Taylor's face tightened. "I'm not one hundred percent sure, no. And I'm not taking a chance with my family."

"Okay. Okay. I'm not here to argue with you. I just got the okay from Stone. I'm working the art theft angle with you."

Taylor's expression came to life then. He looked less thrilled than Will might have expected. "Why would you be? Your theory is—"

There were plenty of things Will could have replied. He cut straight to the chase. "Because we're partners."

Taylor's eyes flickered. "Yeah, only we're not. Remember?"

"You know what I mean. It doesn't have anything to do with where we're posted. We're a team."

Taylor looked away. A muscle in his jaw moved. His eyes rose to meet Will's. "Are we? Where does David Bradley fit in?"

It must have cost him to say that aloud.

In the main room the other agents were making plans for traveling to the coast. Will stepped away from the door. He kept his voice low. "My memory might be shaky on certain points, but I meant what I said in the car. Nobody means more to me than you do. So if I'm going to have to choose who I'm watching over for the next forty-eight hours, I'm watching you."

Taylor gave him an unblinking look. Then he smiled. It was an odd smile. "That's because you believe me about the stolen paintings. If you thought the threat to Bradley was—"

"This is going to come as a shock to you, MacAllister, but you're often wrong. About a lot of things."

Taylor's gaze dropped. He shrugged, clearly unconvinced on that point.

Will let it go. This wasn't the time. When it was all over, they were going to have a serious and uninterrupted talk. As crazy as this whole amnesia thing was, it had allowed him to see their situation from the outside looking in. And what he saw was pretty damned alarming.

Right now they had other things—even if not more important things—to deal with. "So what's our next move?"

Taylor hesitated. "We've got a few hours. Grab some dinner, I guess? Make a plan?"

Now that Will thought about it, he hadn't eaten since that morning. Maybe that persistent yawning emptiness inside him was just hunger. He nodded agreement.

As they walked down the grand marble staircase on their way out of the embassy, Taylor quickly caught him up on recent events.

"But Hinault *did* exist," Will objected. "He lived in Burbank. He was married and owned a business."

"He existed in the States, yes."

"Helloco lived forty-something years under a false identity?"

"Yep."

"With his brother?"

"It kind of looks that way."

"So Yves and Yves' wife must have been complicit too."

"Yes. A regular family affair."

"How does that help us?"

"I don't know that it does. It eliminates some of the possibilities, though."

And it raised some.

Neither of them had much to say on the drive to Will's place. Taylor had to concentrate on his driving—the Parisian evening traffic was a lot trickier to negotiate—and by then Will was starting to feel all his bumps and bruises. He was very tired. In fact, there was nothing he'd have liked more than to go to bed, pull the covers over his head, and wake up with his reality—whatever it was—restored to him.

He was increasingly impatient with the sensation of groping in the dark for his memories. Amnesia struck him as weak and gutless. He hadn't chosen it, but he was still angry with himself for giving in to it. The doctors had described his condition as retrograde or declarative memory loss, a kind of posttraumatic amnesia most likely resulting from a combination of shock and head injury, and likely to be mostly temporary.

Already things were starting to come back to Will in unsettling lurches. While he'd been working on his own that afternoon, he'd remembered stocking up on bottles of French beer because Taylor liked trying different beers. He'd remembered buying soft Egyptian cotton sheets for his bed— for Taylor. The memory had dried his mouth, but he'd recognized it for the truth. And he remembered that he had bought a small, expensive possible birthday gift—or possible something else gift—that was currently sitting at the bottom of his underwear drawer. And the memory of *that* had reached out and grabbed him by the throat, nearly throttling him.

So whether he remembered or not, whether he thought it was a good idea or not, he and Taylor were most definitely romantically involved. He trusted himself enough to know he wouldn't have made that choice lightly or carelessly. He'd known what he was doing, and that meant he needed to show Taylor he honored that commitment.

As for Taylor... He'd been through hell during the past twenty-four hours. Will had put him through hell. The memory of Taylor's stricken expression when Will shoved him away wasn't something Will was going to forget anytime soon, amnesia or no amnesia, and it was one reason he was determined to stick to Taylor like glue. No way was he letting Taylor walk into potential trouble because his mind was distracted or because he simply didn't care enough to be careful. The very possibility of that sent Will's heart into thunderous overdrive.

For all his stubborn resilience, sometimes Taylor took things too much to heart.

Still preoccupied with their separate reflections, they reached Will's apartment and went inside. In unspoken accord, they went downstairs to the kitchen and started to put a meal together. They didn't speak—didn't need to—and Will found the familiar rhythm of being together like this soothing. It brought back good memories of winding down after other operations.

As far as Will recalled, they'd never cooked beef bourguignon together, but the old mind meld seemed to be working again. Will cubed the stewing beef while Taylor chopped the vegetables.

"Where do you think the paintings are hidden?" Will asked while the oil heated in the pan.

Taylor didn't hesitate, so he must have been giving it some thought. "Père Lachaise Cemetery."

"Because Helloco kept painting it?"

"Because it's huge and crowded with lots of tombs and crypts and nooks and crannies. Lots of great potential hiding places." Taylor scraped the vegetables from the cutting board into the heavy skillet. "And, yeah, because Helloco kept painting it. He was obsessed with the place. That's got to mean something."

"You really believe the bomb threats were all about setting up this giant diversion so he could retrieve the paintings?"

"I do. I'm guessing Helloco already has buyers lined up because transporting the paintings would be complicated and dangerous."

"Nothing he ever shied from before."

Taylor considered that. "True."

Will poured enough wine and bouillon to cover the meat and vegetables. "Why do you think he came back now?" He covered the pan. The dish would need to simmer about three hours, but that was no problem. Taylor was adamant that they didn't want to show up at the graveyard until well past closing hours.

"I don't know. Maybe he needed the money. He must have always intended to at some point. Maybe he knew it was now or never. He's not getting any younger." Taylor drank from his bottle of beer. He flicked a drop from his full lower lip, and Will found himself mesmerized by that unconsciously sexy gesture.

"Yeah. Well." Will filled a glass with water. He'd have preferred wine or, better yet, bourbon, but his brains were scrambled enough. "And our plan is what? We're going to stroll around the cemetery until we spot Helloco with his trusty spade?"

Taylor laughed. Will's heart lightened. It felt like it had been a very long time since he'd heard Taylor laugh.

"No. I've got a list of the gravesites we need to check out."

"Aren't there something like seventy thousand graves?"

"Seventy-something plots. Over three hundred thousand graves."

"Please tell me you narrowed the list?"

Taylor's eyes tilted. He seemed to be thoroughly enjoying his private joke. "Don't worry. We're only going to be checking out the graves marked *Hinault.*"

* * * * *

Chopin's grave was alight with flowers and burning candles. Bright moonlight illuminated the downbent head of Music atop the pale pedestal and gilded the composer's profile within the stone medallion beneath the statue. The profusion of red roses ringing the tomb rustled in an invisible breeze.

"Wait. I think maybe we're going the wrong way." Taylor stopped walking. The moonlight also delineated his features as he studied the map he'd purchased from the florist shop outside the walled city of the dead.

Will peered over Taylor's shoulder. The night air smelled of Taylor's— actually Will's—soap, damp earth, and sycamores.

"We have to go back." Taylor folded the map again.

"Don't think I'm criticizing, but—"

"We're not lost."

"Okay. But if—"

"This way," Taylor said briskly, turning back the way they had come. Will followed.

Taylor was a little in the lead as they started up two sets of stairs, turned right toward the intersection of small chapels, and turned right again onto avenue Laterale du sud. They took the steps of avenue Transversale #1 briskly, the pound of their boots in perfect time as they moved—straight to a dead end.

Taylor swore.

They stared up at the towering obelisk to the right.

The gravesites at Père Lachaise encompassed everything from simple, unadorned headstones to towering monuments like the obelisk puncturing the heavy canopy of stars above them. There were statues too numerous to count, fenced plots, and even elaborate minichapels dedicated to the memory of a well-known person or family, and all of it crammed together in an architectural hodgepodge. Many of the moss-covered tombs provided perfect hiding places, roughly the size and shape of phone booths, with just enough space for a mourner—or a shooter.

One hundred acres of potential ambush, in Will's opinion. The cemetery—or park, if you had a taste for the macabre—was enclosed by a massive wall, its maze of dirt and gray cobblestone paths lined with five thousand and more chestnut and sycamore trees. There was no rhyme or reason to the layout as far as Will could see.

A motion to the left, and they both drew their pistols.

A pale cat walked delicately across the top of a headstone and vanished with a flick of its tail.

Both men relaxed. They'd already noted the strange number of cats prowling the grounds.

"Back," Taylor said tersely.

They retraced their footsteps. Scattered flower petals whispered against the cobblestones, blew like grave dust across the grass. Overhead, the stars glittered in the midnight vault of sky. The same stars that had watched over the cemetery for centuries.

"It seems like you still have feelings for Bradley," Taylor said suddenly.

Will threw him a quick look, but there was a conspicuous lack of lighting along the avenues and boulevards of Père Lachaise.

Taylor's tone was neutral. Will kept his tone neutral too. "I like him, sure."

"It's got to be more than that. If you can remember being with him but not me."

"I don't know why my brain made that jump," Will said honestly. "I'm sorry for the hurt that caused you. "

"This way." Taylor turned and headed up a small stone staircase. At the top of the steps was a large urn. The plaque underneath it read HINAULT. Taylor sighed. "What do you think?"

"I still think we're looking for a tomb or a chapel."

"Agreed."

Over the course of the long evening, they had eliminated thirty of the forty-three possible sites labeled *Hinault*. That still left a busy night ahead of them.

Will said, "On the plus side, this place must have changed a lot in forty-something years. Helloco is probably as lost as we are."

"Unless he's on his way to Normandy," Taylor said darkly.

"No."

"We don't know that for sure."

"You've got good instincts, MacAllister. I'm going with you."

Taylor huffed a breath—a sure sign he was on edge. Will reached out and hooked an arm around his neck, pulling him close in a rough hug. And God, it felt good—right—to hold Taylor. Even that briefly. Even feeling Taylor's instant tension and instinctive drawing back.

Will said against his ear, "I don't know why this happened to us, but we'll get through it. I swear to you."

Taylor freed himself, turning his back to Will. Will watched the quick rise and fall of his broad shoulders in the pale moonlight.

Will took mercy on him. "Are you sure the police know we're here? It feels like we're the only people in this entire damned labyrinth."

"They know. Somewhere out there we're supposed to have some backup."

"Where to next?"

Taylor turned. "I could tear this list in half and we could split up. We'd cover a lot more ground that way."

"We don't do so well on our own."

Taylor snorted. "Give it a rest, Brandt. I know you're sorry. I'm not blaming you. Let's just get through this. Then we'll see where we are."

Will nodded. They both stiffened at the distinct sound of a muffled *bang* drifting through the wall of trees.

"Explosives," Will identified.

"Where? Where did that come from?"

"North." Will pointed. They were already running, gaining speed, separating as they headed for the sound and the hint of smoke that still drifted on the night breeze.

Taylor ran like a deer, with a fine disregard for low fences and graves alike. Will tore after him, but he'd never been quite as fast as Taylor and he was slower now, thanks to his assorted injuries. His head pounded with each footfall as he sprinted around the gravestones and statues that seemed to rise in his path like pop-up targets in a training course.

As Taylor pulled farther ahead—vaulting the obstacles Will veered around—Will put on more speed, swearing under his breath. It was like watching Riley jetting after a cat. He'd need fucking wings to catch him.

He watched Taylor scramble over a short wall and disappear. A sudden dread filled him.

The wall was carved with a long row of ornate, smiling skulls.

Memory opened up beneath his feet, and once again Will was in the catacombs feeling the earth tremble, the roar of the ceiling giving way, the screams of the men around him as the lights went out. His final vision: the black and cavernous smile of a yellowed, cracked skull.

And his only thought—his final thought: *Taylor.*

A distant and unmistakable *pop* bounced off the limestone and marble. Adrenaline flashed through his veins, and Will hurdled over the low wall of skulls and shot across the wet stretch of grass. His feet thudded on the damp earth.

He crossed another cobblestone walk and faced another city block of tall sepulchers and tombs. The silence was eerie. Where the hell was the cemetery security or the police who were to provide backup?

Heart thundering, Will pulled his weapon. He wound his way through the monuments, sticking closely to cover until he came to a short set of steps leading down to a small crypt. From behind the shed-sized building came the grating scrape of stone on stone.

Will pressed back against the wall, stole a quick look around the corner. His heart stopped.

Taylor lay facedown on the walkway in front of a comparatively plain square of limestone, about the size of a large sofa. An elderly man dressed in black was busily using a crowbar to pry open the face of the tomb.

As Will stared, Taylor stirred and tried to push up. The elderly man turned, made an exasperated sound, and raised his crowbar to bring it down on Taylor's head.

"Don't do it." Will stepped out from behind cover and brought his weapon up.

The man stared at him. He threw the crowbar away. It clanged on the stone and rolled away. The man raised his hands over his head.

Will spared a quick look. "MacAllister?"

Taylor muttered something, sounding reassuringly alive and pissed off.

"Are you okay?" Now there was a silly question. But somehow it was the only one that mattered.

Helloco soundlessly stepped back into the concealing shadows.

"Don't take another step," Will warned him, half his attention still on Taylor, who made another clumsy attempt to push up.

Will stepped forward, locking a hand in Taylor's collar and dragging him out of range of Helloco's feet or reach. It wasn't easy to do and still keep his pistol trained on Helloco. Helloco remained still and watchful.

"Come on, MacAllister. Get it together."

Taylor muttered something that might have been assent or just obscene.

Will kept his gaze on Helloco. The moonlight silhouetted the old man's aquiline features and the silver of his hair. He never said a word, his black eyes as hollow and unrevealing as any death's head.

"Turn around. Lock your hands behind your head," Will ordered.

The old man didn't move.

"Do it."

"Shit…" Taylor bit off the rest as he made it to his knees, using one hand to balance and the other to grab for the black wrought iron fencing of a nearby tomb.

Will ignored him, but Helloco either misread him or figured he had one chance and one chance only, because he suddenly snatched at his waistband and brought up a gleaming and efficient-looking Beretta.

Will shot him.

The *bang* of his SIG Sauer crashed through the forest of stone and iron, reverberating around the monuments and statuary.

It wasn't possible to miss at that range. Helloco clutched his chest, staggered back, and fell over the tomb. Taylor snapped upright, turning to Will and then the fallen Helloco in shock.

"Jesus."

"He was armed." And Taylor had been perfectly positioned to get caught in the crossfire. No way was Will taking chances with that. He stepped around the tomb and looked down. The pistol lay a few inches from Helloco's outstretched fingers. The center of his chest glistened in a pool of spreading darkness. Helloco's eyes were wide open. They stared fixedly up at the moon. Will watched him for a few seconds.

"He's dead?" Taylor leaned on the tomb, peering blearily over. He closed his eyes for a moment. "Yeah, he's dead."

"Are you okay? What the hell happened?"

Taylor folded slowly onto the tomb. He rested his head in his hands. His voice was subdued. "I think I tripped."

Will, trying gently to examine the lump rising out of Taylor's hairline, paused. "You *tripped*?"

Taylor's response was terse.

"*You* tripped?"

"Shut up, Brandt."

"You're like a cat. I've never seen you tri—"

"Shut *up,* Brandt."

Voices were coming toward them, drifting on the night air. Will tore his gaze from Taylor's bent head in time to spot the circles of flashlight beams bouncing through the trees.

"Better late than never," Will muttered.

Taylor raised his head and peered nearsightedly into the gloom. "I don't see them."

"They're on their way. Just relax."

Yeah. Right. It was like telling a jack-in-the-box to settle down. Taylor clambered to his feet and swayed. Will reached to steady him. "Would you sit still? You could have a concussion for all you know."

Taylor's heavy eyes popped open. He leaned forward, studying Will's face intently. "Wait. Wait…"

"What is it? What's the matter?"

Taylor's jaw dropped. He peered closely. "Do I know you? Who are you again?"

Will couldn't help the laugh that escaped him. He grabbed Taylor and pressed a hard, hungry kiss against his startled mouth.

There wasn't time for more. Within a minute or two the French police had reached them, and the questions began. Will and Taylor were separated and asked to give their individual account of events while the side door of the tomb was dragged open the rest of the way.

Whistles and exclamations followed the discovery of the contents of the tomb. Will and Taylor joined the circle around the opening as a heavy, square bundle wrapped in canvas and rope was lifted out.

Brief discussion followed as to whether they should wait for museum officials. *Hell no!* seemed to be the same in every language. The canvas was carefully ripped and laid wide to reveal the portrait of a smiling woman in an elaborate powdered wig and the rich robes of a long-ago empire.

Merveilleux! Fantastique!

And Will had to agree.

"You realize now we're never going to know what it was that brought Helloco out of hiding?" Taylor muttered when they were finally waved off in dismissal. "We're never going to know why he left Finistère. We're never going to know if he was having a three-way with his brother's wife. We're never going to know—"

Will had a vision of Taylor trying to push to his feet directly in the line of fire between himself and Helloco. He interrupted mildly, "I can live with that."

He looked back. Taylor had stopped at the fenced monument next to the tomb where Helloco had hidden the five paintings. "What's up?"

"Look at this."

Will obligingly walked the few steps back and looked—and then looked more closely.

Beneath the bronze medallion of a man's profile were four stone placards. One of the placards bore the name *Jacques-Louis David.*

"Could that be a coincidence?" Taylor couldn't seem to tear his gaze away.

And studying his profile, Will said, "I don't believe in coincidence." He added, "Not anymore."

* * * * *

The Eiffel Tower was gilded in pink-gold sunlight by the time they finished their phone calls.

Will listened to Taylor reassuring his sister with the usual white lies. "No, no one was injured. I mean, besides Helloco. I don't know why. You know the news; they've got to say something, right?"

Will, lying on the bed and staring out the window at the sunrise, rolled his eyes.

"If you want to go ahead and attend the D-day ceremony, sure. No, Will and I have plans." Taylor looked over his shoulder at Will.

Will nodded.

They had plans all right. Plans Taylor didn't even know about yet.

"Sound him out," Stone had said when Will had spoken to her a few minutes earlier. "He's a little unorthodox, but he's got imagination. He'd be a good man to have on our team, and we've got an opening."

If nothing else it was vindication for Taylor. He'd gone out on a limb, but in the end he'd been proved right. So now he had another option. They both did.

Stone hadn't been the first call Will had made. The first call had been to David. Will felt like he owed him that. The last few days probably hadn't been much easier on David than they had on Taylor.

"You don't have to apologize for anything," David had said, once Will had gotten past the excuse of relating the news about Helloco and the confirmation that the D-day events could proceed as planned. "I'm glad for you both."

Yeah. Well, that was why Will liked David so much. Why at one time he'd thought it might be him and David.

But as things stood, Will was never going to forget Taylor's face when Will had inadvertently blurted out, "What about David?" Taylor had looked less hurt getting shot in the chest. Will was going to make that up to him.

So he'd apologized to David, and he got off the phone as soon as possible, and as soon as he disconnected, he'd gone to Taylor, burying his face in Taylor's hair for a moment. Taylor had looked surprised and wary, but then he'd relaxed, giving Will a friendly little shove and ordering him to call Stone.

Taylor finally said good-bye to his sister. Will held the duvet up, and Taylor slid between the sheets, lithe and brown from the Southern California sun. He moaned his relief as he sank into the pillows.

"We're officially back on leave," Will informed him.

"Thank you Jesus." Taylor closed his eyes and then opened them. "You never said. When exactly did you get your memory back?"

Will rolled onto his side, facing him. He had never been so grateful for a good mattress, clean sheets, and the superior quality of European painkillers.

"Not long after you went bounding off like a stag running from a forest fire." He carefully brushed the hair from Taylor's bruised forehead. Taylor winced but didn't object. "What gets into your brain?"

Taylor's eyelashes flickered a couple of times and lowered. "Hm?"

Will continued to stroke his hair. "I thought we were a team? Why didn't you wait for me?"

Taylor sighed but didn't answer.

"Are you falling asleep?"

"A little…" Taylor's lashes didn't stir.

Will smiled faintly. "Well, don't fall asleep until you hear me out."

Taylor's eyes opened at that. "It's okay, Will. Y—"

"Shut up," Will said gently.

Taylor shut up.

"I don't know why my brain selected the memories it did, but I can tell you this much: it wasn't because I don't care enough about you. I think maybe it's the other way around."

"I don't care enough about you?"

Will sighed. "How hard did you hit your head tonight? No. I mean maybe I care too much about you."

Taylor's eyes narrowed. "What's that mean?"

"Pretty much what I was always afraid of from the start. If I ever let go…" Will had to stop.

Taylor pushed up on his elbow. "I don't understand. *What?*"

"It's not complicated," Will said finally. "If something happens to you, it's going to happen to both of us. Because I'm not going to survive losing you. You see what I mean?"

Taylor was silent. Finally he eased back to the pillows. "That. Okay. Fair enough. Same here."

"I have something for you."

A smiled flickered across Taylor's lips. "Are you sure in your weakened condition—or my weakened condition—"

"You've got a one-track mind."

"Like you're not headed the same direction?" But Will had left the bed and was at his dresser, rifling through his undershorts. Taylor sounded rueful. "Maybe you're not."

Will found the small blue velvet box and tossed it to the bed.

Taylor caught it one-handed as he sat up. He stared down at the box. His gaze lifted to Will's. He looked a little pale. "What's this?"

Will came back to bed and slid in beside him. "Cuff links. What do you think it is?"

"We never…"

"I know. We should have. We sure as hell should have before I left for Paris. I was going to give it to you for your birthday. But we kept… I don't know. The time wasn't right. The thing about Iraq threw me."

Taylor's gazed as if fascinated at the small box. A muscle moved in his jaw.

"So here's the thing." Will cleared his throat. "I didn't handle this right the first time, and I'm probably not going to handle it right this time. I don't want you to take the posting in Iraq. Not because I think something bad will happen to you. Because I think something bad will happen to me. I think we'll have to wait more years to be together, and we've waited long enough already."

"We were at this point once before, you know?" Taylor was smiling, but something in that little twist of lips hurt Will's heart.

"I know. I wasn't expecting…Paris. I let my ambition get in the way of us. That was my mistake. But this…" Will nodded at the blue box. "This is my way of trying to show you that nothing has changed for me. It never will. And I'm tired of waiting. Life is too short. So…"

"So?"

"I meant what I said at dinner the other night. I want to resign. I want you to resign."

Taylor closed his eyes. "Will…"

"No, listen to me. I've thought about this. I've been thinking about it for a while, to tell the truth. I want us to go into business together. I want us to start our own global security consulting business. We could do it. You know we could. We're the best at what we do."

"That's enough of a reason to give up both our—"

"We could be partners again. Partners in every way."

Taylor was silent so long Will's heart grew cold.

Finally Taylor's lashes lifted. He studied Will gravely. "Are you sure, Brandt? You sure you know what you're saying?"

"I know what I'm saying."

Taylor sat up, knees touching Will's. He handed the box to Will. Will took it back slowly.

Taylor held out his left hand. It was a man's hand. Nicely shaped, strong, steady. Understanding dawned in Will. He flipped open the lid of the box. The ring glinted brightly. A plain platinum band—platinum mixed with a small percentage of lead from the bullet that had hit Taylor slightly over a year ago. The bullet that might have ended everything—but somehow had meant a new beginning for them.

Smiling a little self-consciously, Will took Taylor's hand in his.

KICK
START

CHAPTER ONE

One minute everything was fine. The next minute the job was going south. Fast.

The limousine with Dragomirov hurtled toward the mouth of the alley where Taylor waited. Not unprepared—Taylor was never unprepared—but unsuspecting. Taylor would be occupied watching for threats to Dragomirov. It would not occur to him that Dragomirov was now a threat to *him*.

So Will reacted, he responded to the threat to Taylor. That's what partners did, right? Even as Will dropped down onto the top of the limousine, he was mentally justifying his decision to Taylor—justifying it because before he ever hit the roof, he knew he had made a mistake.

Problem Number One: There was nothing to hang onto. Had the car windows been rolled down…maybe. But the windows were not rolled down, and Will began to slide. The instant the limo braked or turned the corner, he was going to go flying—at thirty-plus miles an hour. Problem Number Two: Problem Number One was moot, because even if Will didn't go flying, which he *would* do any minute now, he had no way of stopping the vehicle. And Problem Number Three: If he did survive, MacAllister was going to kill him.

The rush of garbage-scented air blasted against his face, blurring his vision. The alley was nicer than some alleys in Los Angeles, meaning there were no bums to run over. Orange and green and purple graffiti bled into a long smear of chain link fence topped by coils of barbed wire, old brick walls and metal roll up doors. A couple of phone poles with sagging lines flew by, interspersed with several dumpsters. The alley opening—and the busy cross street beyond—was coming up fast. With only seconds to spare, Will wrapped his arms around his head and rolled, launching himself at a fast-approaching blue dumpster.

He missed.

There was a sickening moment of flying through thin—very thin—air, and then he crash-landed on a mountain of cardboard boxes and black and white garbage bags.

It wasn't like in the movies. Will landed hard and heavily, the bags giving way, the boxes not so much. It hurt. It hurt a lot. But without the boxes and bags, he'd probably have been killed. He reflected on that for a stunned second or two while he listened to the screech of tires fading into the distance, the pound of approaching footsteps.

"Brandt?" Taylor splashed through a puddle and skidded to a stop. He sounded winded, though the entire alleyway was only a block long. "Will?"

Will opened his eyes as Taylor bent over him. Taylor's eyes were black in his white face, his jaw set. Ready for the worst.

"Right here," Will said.

Life came back to Taylor's face. "Oh, you bastard. Don't *do* that to me!" He expelled a long, shaken breath, and began to check Will over with swift, anxious hands. "What the *hell* was that supposed to be?"

Will gave a weak laugh and raised his head. "Everything still attached?"

"Shut up. Don't move."

"I'm fine." Will waved him off. "I'm fine! *Oww!*" Yeah, *fine* was possibly overstating the situation. But he was alive and, miraculously, he seemed to be in one piece. One black and blue piece, probably. "Shit." Painfully, he crawled out of the stinking, slimy nest of garbage. Taylor moved to help him, removing a shoebox that had gotten stuck on Will's elbow. Will climbed—and it did feel like a climb—to his feet.

"Jesus Christ, Brandt. You want to explain to me what you thought you were doing?" Taylor, sounding much more like his normal ornery self, punched him in the shoulder, and Will toppled back into the trash bags.

"Goddamn it," Will said slowly and with feeling.

"Sorry," Taylor muttered, hauling him out of the garbage bags once more. He brushed eggshells off Will's shoulder. "But what just happened? Explain to me. *Why* would you act like somebody in a goddamned *movie*?"

Will shook his head.

"Dragomirov tears out of here like a bat out of hell. *With you on the roof of his car.* His asshole driver nearly runs me over—"

"We've been laid off."

"What?"

"Fired. Without the severance package, I'm guessing." Will brushed orange peelings and what looked like—and pray to God was—raspberry jelly from the front of his leather jacket. The seat of his Levi's felt soaked with something he hoped wasn't caustic. Or toxic.

Taylor looked stunned. "What are you talking about? After ten days? What the hell happened?"

It was a fair question. Will was trying to figure that one out himself. "Gretchen Hart is what happened."

"Who?"

"Gretchen Hart. New Mexico. Two years ago?" Will prodded. "You remember Victor and Victoria?"

Taylor blinked. "Yeah, but...are you telling me...? What *are* you telling me?"

"Gretchen Hart apparently now works for Glukhov. She walked into that meeting, recognized me, and gave Dragomirov her version of what happened in New Mexico."

"Which was what?"

"Pretty close to the truth," Will admitted.

Taylor opened his mouth but couldn't seem to find the words. Will knew the feeling. He said wearily, "As predicted, Dragomirov doesn't like feds. A lot. Even ex-feds. So we're off the case. I guess he thought we were trying to set him up in some kind of sting operation."

"What sting? We're doing low level security work. Mall cops could have handled this gig."

"I never said Dragomirov was a genius."

Taylor was silent. Then he said, "How the hell would that bitch recognize you?"

Will shook his head.

Taylor's face screwed up in anger. "Fuck!" He turned and kicked a white and blue, half-deflated child's ball that had rolled out of the pile of trash bags. The ball shot to the left, bounced off a green brick wall and landed on the pitted pavement with a flat, angry smack.

Will said nothing. What could he say? Taylor had not wanted to take this job in the first place. But they had needed the money and Will had talked him into it. End result: they had put in ten days, working a bodyguard detail for a guy who, though maybe not a crook, was certainly a scumball—and they would not be getting paid for the privilege.

He opened his mouth to apologize, but no. He was already on defense over the Paris thing; not smart to further weaken his position. Anyway, he wasn't going to apologize for being a realist. They were not in a position to pick and choose clients. How was he supposed to have known their arch-nemesis would show up? He hadn't realized they *had* an arch-nemesis until he'd watched Gretchen Hart freeze in recognition and then morph into the Borg Queen.

Taylor turned back to face him, fists planted on his narrow hips, eyes glinting the same shade as a Mojave Green. "Fuckin' A. What now?"

"Find a new client, I guess. Shower. Sleep." They were short on sleep these days. It wasn't helping.

Taylor bit back whatever he started to say. This unusual restraint was almost worse than hearing him voice his feelings.

"Look," Will said. "I couldn't predict this. Nobody could predict this. We're independent contractors now, and sometimes things are going to go wrong."

"Does that mean sometimes they're going to go right?" Taylor inquired. "Because so far...not so much."

Now it was Will's turn to hold his tongue. He said shortly, "We're done here, let's grab our gear and get the hell out of Dodge."

* * * * *

"I'm going to talk to Richard," Taylor said, breaking the silence of their drive back to Ventura.

Will shifted painfully in the passenger seat. His tailbone felt bruised. Along with his ego. "About?"

Taylor didn't answer. He didn't have to. "Richard" was Richard Lamprell, owner of Geo-Gulf Oil and Taylor's stepdad. Taylor's parents had divorced when he was in junior high, and his mother had remarried a multimillionaire. A fact which always seemed to make Taylor uncomfortable, and never more so than when Richard had offered to lend them the start-up capital for their security consulting business after they'd left the DSS.

Taylor had turned the offer down flat. Knowing his feelings on the subject, Will hated that Taylor was now having to rethink his position. He hated that his own initial reaction was relief. Anyway, it was only his initial reaction because he did not want them beholden to anyone, even family.

"No. We're okay. We'll work it out," he said.

Taylor's hands whitened on the steering wheel. "No, we're not okay, Brandt. We're taking jobs we don't want to take because we can't pay our bills—and then we can't pay our bills anyway. We're not okay."

"Throwing money at a problem is not a solution."

"It sure as shit is, if the problem is you don't have enough money."

"I don't want to be in hock to Richard. Nothing against Richard. I don't want to owe anybody. I don't want to be obligated."

Taylor gave a short laugh. He glanced away from the shifting parking lot that doubled as the 101 Freeway. "Really? Because we're already sixty grand worth of obligated to our mutual credit card companies. At twenty percent interest. Unless you plan on cashing out our retirement funds next, we're out of resources. Which means we're out of options."

"MacAllister. Taylor—"

"We could try and get our old jobs back, I guess," Taylor added tersely. "It won't be Paris, of course, given that you already turned that posting down for both of us."

There it was again. Fucking Paris. Right on schedule.

"Christ. Enough with Paris." Will couldn't help the edge in his voice. In fact, he didn't want to help it. He was tired, in pain, and sick of feeling guilty over a decision he had made with the best possible intentions.

"I guess so," Taylor said. "I guess you had enough. I didn't get a choice."

"Did you want that posting?" Will snapped. "Because if you did, if you do, I will talk to Alice Stone myself. I will move heaven and earth to get you your job and that goddamned posting back."

"Not the point, Brandt," Taylor said coolly. "The point is, you didn't give me a say. You didn't tell me Stone wanted to offer a posting, that maybe we could have worked together in France. You—"

Will broke in, "Are you telling me you would have made a different choice?"

"I don't know."

"The hell." Will stared at Taylor's profile for a long moment before turning to scowl out the side window. Office buildings and restaurants and billboards and busy side streets slid past while he tried to deal with that.

"Not about us. Obviously." Taylor's voice softened briefly. "But you hustled me into this freelance gig, and we don't have the assets or the contacts or the experience."

Will started to protest, but Taylor cut across. "We're experienced field agents, sure. We're not experienced business owners. We're not even experienced office managers. We're sinking. We rushed into this and we did it for all the wrong reasons."

What Taylor meant was, Will had rushed *him* into it for the wrong reasons. Not true. Not fair. Not even close.

Was it?

"I did it because I wanted us to start our life together. Our real life together. I wanted us to have control of our future. Of our fate."

"You did it because..." Taylor didn't finish the thought. But, again, he didn't have to. They could usually read each other's minds.

Will let it go. If he answered Taylor now, it would not go well. They were both tired and frustrated and, yes, worried. He put his head back and let Taylor take his aggressions out on the other drivers crowding into the sluggish river of metal and glass.

He didn't sleep, but maybe he did doze because the next time he opened his eyes they were pulling into Taylor's driveway and the security gate was rolling shut behind them.

Actually, it was Will's driveway too. He'd been living with Taylor in this small beach community since his return from Paris last summer. The house, an original Craftsman bungalow they had been restoring in their free time—back when they still had free time—was large and comfortable. The street was quiet and felt secluded; old but lovingly maintained homes beneath venerable shade trees.

"I'd burn those jeans if I were you," was Taylor's only comment as they went into the house.

In the bathroom, Will examined himself in the long mirror over the sink counter. His torso and the back of his thighs were mottled with bruises and contusions. His hands were scraped, his left knee swelling.

He turned the shower on full blast, cranked up the heat to just short of scalding, and stepped under the stinging spray. After a few minutes, and a lot of soap and water, he was both cleaner and calmer.

True, things were not going strictly according to plan. Maybe they needed to adjust their plans. Or maybe it was their expectations they needed to adjust? It was a tough time to start a business, naturally there would be challenges, a few setbacks. Regardless of what Taylor thought, or didn't think, they did have the experience and the qualifications to make a success of this business. They just needed to give it time.

Will turned off the water, toweled down, and shaved. He dressed in a pair of soft jeans and an even softer gray T-shirt that read: *To err is human, to forgive divine. Neither of which is Marine Corps policy.*

He found Taylor in the kitchen, drinking coffee and reading *American COP*. He must have used the guest bathroom because he had showered too, and had changed into faded jeans and an olive T-shirt that made his eyes look greener than ever. He needed a haircut and a shave, but he was still the best looking guy Will knew. Even if Will did want to strangle him sometimes.

The smell of coffee and toast warmed the kitchen. The washer was rumbling peaceably in the laundry room. Riley lay on the rug in front of the stove. He thumped his tail in welcome. Taylor glanced up, offered a crooked smile, tossed the magazine aside. "Coffee?"

Something eased inside Will. He'd been mentally arguing with Taylor all the time he'd been in the shower, but the residue of frustration and irritation drained away. They were home. They were whole. They were together. That had to count for a lot.

Will shook his head to the coffee. He was still wired from ten days worth of endless cups of lousy coffee. He was looking forward to eventually sleeping.

He sat down at the table across from Taylor. Taylor gazed back at him steadily.

"I was thinking. Since the job is a bust, maybe I'll drive up north and see Grant while he's home on leave." Will's kid brother had dropped out of college to join the marines. Grant was currently home in Oregon on a ten-day leave. Will had wanted to make the trek north, but the protection detail had come up. Now Will's dance card was suddenly empty, so why not take advantage?

Taylor nodded.

Will took a deep breath, expelled it, and said, "If you want to talk to Richard, go ahead. It's up to you."

"I *don't* want to." Taylor sounded tired too, and more conciliatory. "I don't think we have a lot of choice here, Will. We've sunk just about everything we have into this venture. We can't pull out without losing it all, but to make a success of it, we'd need to invest more. We need money. We need the right equipment. We need an assistant. Hell, we need an office."

"I don't agree. We don't need an office. We don't need an assistant."

"Will." Taylor stopped. He ran both hands through his damp hair, clearly trying to restrain himself, which put Will's temper on edge again. *"You're* the one who said it. If we want to attract the kind of clients we originally talked about, high-end clients—if we want to run a *global* security consulting business—we've got to *look* the part. We've got to seem like we could handle that kind of job. An answering machine and a website aren't going to cut it."

Developing the kind of image Taylor was talking about wasn't going to be in their budget, with or without a loan from the folks. They'd need Richard's help just to get out from under their credit cards. Will was willing to take that hit to his ego because it was Taylor's credit score at risk too.

When the hell had they turned into guys who worried about their credit scores?

"Look. Here's how I see it. We can make due without an office or support staff. At least for a while. Till we're on our feet. But you're the one who has to ask for the cash. You're the one who thinks we're not going to make it."

Taylor opened his mouth to protest, but that *was* the truth and they both knew it.

"So it's up to you," Will concluded. "You figure out how much you can bear to be into Richard for, and I'll go along with your decision."

Taylor thought it over and then nodded. "Okay. Fair enough."

Probably. Will absently rubbed his freshly shaved jaw. "Your mom and Richard are in Bahrain now. Does that mean you're planning to fly out to talk to them?"

"Well, there's this newfangled invention called the telephone. I thought maybe I'd give that a try first."

Will smiled reluctantly. "If you think you can make the case for that size loan long distance."

"I think Richard will give us the money."

"Okay." Was it that simple? Maybe it was. Lamprell seemed pretty generous with his family, and unlike his siblings, Taylor had never asked his multimillionaire stepdaddy for anything. Maybe he'd racked up some credits for being the fiscally sound stepkid. Maybe no business plans or pie charts of the economic trends within the security industry would be needed.

The ancient washer jogged into its spin cycle filling the silence between them. Taylor said slowly, "That doesn't mean I have to go to Oregon with you. If you want to head home on your own, that's okay. I've got plenty to keep me busy here."

It was tempting. God, it was tempting. With everything going on between them—the unexpected tensions of learning to live together at the same time they were trying to get this business off the ground, the blow up after Taylor had discovered that RSO Stone would have offered him a posting in Paris if Will hadn't informed her they were resigning… Yes, it was very tempting to snatch an opportunity to get away, to put a little space between himself and Taylor who was riding his ass relentlessly—and not in a good way—to give himself some breathing room. Just a very little space for a very little time.

Because as much as Will loved Taylor, as much as he hated the thought of being separated from him for even a day, yes, he could use a break. *Needed* a break maybe.

Especially given the situation at home. Home in Oregon, not home in Ventura. Home in Oregon, Will's sexual orientation was not widely known. In fact, *nobody* knew except for his father. Yeah, that had been an awkward conversation—not that you could exactly call the gruff assertion that he was not ever going to be "settling down," exactly a conversation. He wasn't even sure his brother knew he was gay. And sure as hell nobody knew about Taylor.

And Will would have been happy to keep it that way. Which would be impossible if Taylor chose to ride shotgun on this trip.

He looked at Taylor. Taylor looked back at him. He was smiling faintly, a complicated sort of smile. There was complete understanding there, and a little friendly mockery, and something else.

What?

What was that emotion lurking in the back of Taylor's gaze?

Will stared, and he felt a funny dip in his chest. His heart sank.

That look in Taylor's eyes...was that the beginning of disappointment? Maybe...disillusion?

No.

No, he could take Taylor chewing on his last nerve from now to eternity before he could take one second of Taylor feeling disappointed or disillusioned with him.

"What? Are you serious? Hell, yeah, I want you to come!" Will said it with such conviction, he almost believed it himself.

CHAPTER TWO

"So Gretchen Hart now works for Glukhov." *Jeeeezus* the relief of stretching out in his own bed. Taylor arched luxuriously and felt his spine unkink for the first time in ten godawful days. Thank God. Thank *God* it was over. Even if they had spent almost two weeks working for a scumbag like Dragomirov for free.

Through the open bathroom door he could hear the taps running, see Will brushing his teeth. Will scowled at his mirrored reflection, his thoughts seemingly a million miles away. He was bare-chested, his skin tawny and smooth against the pale blue flannel sleep pants. Tawny and smooth where he wasn't bruised and contused. Will had been lucky today. They both had. Just a few inches either way and it could have been all over.

Anxiety, an increasingly common sensation, gnawed at his guts. Or maybe he was getting an ulcer. Except he couldn't afford to get an ulcer. Neither of them could afford to get sick or injured. Not without health insurance.

When the hell had they turned into guys who worried about their health insurance?

Will spat toothpaste into the sink, scooped up a couple of mouthfuls of water, rinsed. He turned off the taps, scrubbed his face with Taylor's towel.

Always Taylor's towel. Never his own.

Taylor sighed.

"You say something?" Will turned the light out in the bathroom and crossed through the moonlit bedroom to the bed. He was limping a little. Even in the gloom, Taylor could tell.

He swallowed the things he wanted to say, unproductive things that would not be conducive to a peaceful night's rest, saying instead, "I said I wonder how that came about? Gretchen working for Glukhov."

The mattress dipped as Will climbed into bed. Will eased himself down with a long, heartfelt sigh. His shoulder brushed Taylor's. He tiredly patted Taylor's thigh. "God, I'm beat."

"You want a backrub?" Taylor asked. He prayed Will would say no because he didn't think he had the strength to sit up.

"I don't think I can turn over."

Taylor snorted. "You want a front rub?"

"I don't think I can get it up to save my life."

"Me neither," Taylor admitted.

"What?" Will raised his head and peered into Taylor's face, breathing minty fresh over him. "Oh, sweetheart! *No.* Are you sick?" He clumsily felt Taylor's forehead, and Taylor started to laugh.

"Jackass."

Will laughed too and dropped back on his pillows. He groaned. "I don't think there's a part of my body that doesn't hurt."

Taylor was silent and then, against his will, he started to laugh.

"What?" Will asked, amused.

"You. James Bond. On the roof of that car." He couldn't help it. All at once it was funny. Not funny at the time. But now? He was going to be giggling any second.

Will started to laugh too. "Christ. I must have been crazy."

"No argument."

"What the hell was I thinking?"

"That was your expression. What the hell was I thinking?"

"It's the kind of thing you'd do."

"*I* wouldn't miss the dumpster."

"You might not have missed it. Or you might have plowed your head through the lid."

For a couple of seconds they leaned against each other laughing. That was relief, more than anything. Not just the relief that Will hadn't been killed or seriously hurt; the relief from the nervous strain of two weeks playing bodyguard to the kind of dirtball they'd spent most of their law enforcement careers trying to put away.

"Gretchen Hart," Will said finally, reminiscently. "Of all the gin joints in all the towns in all the world..."

"Yeah. Well, I guess with Bashnakov in prison, she had to find a new mob boss."

"Neither Glukhov nor Dragomirov are mob bosses."

"Close enough."

"Taylor." Clearly Will didn't have the energy to take it further, but felt the point needed to be made.

"All right," Taylor said. He didn't have the energy to argue either. He and Will were arguing too much these days. It was starting to feel like Paris all over again.

He really did not want to think about Paris.

Will followed his thoughts though, because after several long minutes of silence, he said quietly, "About earlier."

"Don't listen to me. I was just pissed off."

"Yeah, but it's the *why* you're pissed off that I need to listen to."

Taylor sighed. "I don't know, Will."

"You do, yeah."

Taylor moved his head in negation.

"We have to keep talking to each other, Taylor. Even if we think we're not going to like what the other has to say."

"I know that." But in all fairness, this was not something either of them was very good at. Sometimes their efforts at talking things out only made things worse.

"Are you saying you wouldn't do anything within your power to protect me?"

Taylor snorted. "From what? Too many croissants? Paris drivers?"

"Come on, Tay. I'm serious."

Tay. Yes, he was serious. Taylor said, "You know exactly what I'm saying, Will. Would I take a bullet for you? Yes. What I would not do is take away your right to choose your own course."

"All right. All right. I know." Will rolled onto his side, facing Taylor, although it was too dark to read each other's expressions. "I was wrong not to tell you about the possibility—because that's all it was, a *possibility*—of the Paris posting. I know it was wrong. I said I was sorry. I've said it three times now."

"But you keep doing this shit, Will. 'Acting in my best interests.' Like you don't trust me to know what I want or need. How many times are we going to have this conversation?"

"This is the last time. Paris...everything got so messed up. We were both off balance, okay? I admit I wasn't thinking straight. So, yes, I did rush you into making a decision without letting you have all the facts. And I know it wasn't fair or the right thing to do."

Taylor sighed.

Will felt for, found Taylor's left hand, his fingers tracing the platinum band on Taylor's ring finger. "Do you regret the choice you made?"

"No." That was emotion talking, not logic, because Taylor did regret the way they had launched themselves into this new endeavor without proper preparation and only the sketchiest of plans. And Taylor was supposed to be the impulsive one! This was totally unlike Will, which was probably what bothered Taylor the most about it. He couldn't help believing that Will's primary motivation had been to prevent him from taking the post in Iraq—or something equally asinine and high-handed.

Will leaned forward, his mouth finding Taylor's in a soft, apologetic kiss. His mouth was warm, his taste familiar. "I won't try to excuse it. It's just...this is all still new to me. I didn't expect it to be like this. Not with anyone. So good I'm terrified it can't be for real, that it can't last."

Of course that melted Taylor's heart. He felt the same way. All the time. But "it" wasn't *that* new, that was part of the problem. They had been partnered five years now, and officially a couple for almost two. Though, granted, one of those years they'd spent apart. Still.

He said sternly, "It can't happen again, Will." He was dead serious. The realization startled him. At one point, he had believed nothing could split them up, nothing could change his feelings for Will. But now they had been together long enough that he understood there were things that no relationship could survive. Lack of respect was one of them.

"It's not going to happen again." Will covered his mouth and Taylor surrendered. It was an earnest and uninhibited effort, but though pleasurable, they just didn't have the energy. Will fell asleep mid-nuzzle. Taylor a rueful sigh later.

They slept late the next morning. Sunlight was crawling sheepishly across the white coverlet when Taylor opened his eyes. He turned his head, studied Will's face. That contrast of dark stubble and long eyelashes always did something to him. Will looked disarmingly unguarded and boyish in sleep, and Taylor smiled.

If they were traveling north today, they needed to get moving. But first things first. There had not been enough time these last couple of weeks for the essentials, the essentials being...taking good and proper care of each other. Maybe he wasn't good at talking things out, maybe he didn't have experience at long-term relationships—his own parents' marriage should have put him off the idea of commitment for good. But this much he did know. You had to pay attention and you had to take care of each other in the little ways as well as the big.

He ducked under the sheet and set about waking Will the best way he knew how—with a warm and willing mouth and a bone-melting rhythm.

Proof of how exhausted Will was, it took several long seconds before he even stirred, but at last he began to twitch and sigh under Taylor's expert attentions. Finally, he made a small sleepy sound and shuddered, starting to move instinctively, hips pushing, cock thrusting. Taylor sucked harder, applying lips, tongue, even the suggestion of teeth, using his considerable knowledge to give Will maximum pleasure.

Will groaned, heartfelt and inarticulate.

Taylor's heart seemed to beat in time to the pulse of Will's cock, tasting the salty pre-cum. He knew what Will was feeling, knew how to make it just the way Will wanted, sucking hard, then softly, then harder still. Sweet and soft, then hard and fierce, then so soft again, so tender. Tugging him along, *Come on, sweetheart, this way...*

Will tossed in the sheets like he was delirious, but it was the best kind of suffering, and Taylor could feel the exact moment that tingle started at the root of Will's cock, exquisite sensation unfurling, flowering through nerves and muscles, tissue and bone, that dizzy delight blooming in his bloodstream.

"Oh my *God*!" Will choked out.

And there it was, the blood-hot spurt of his release, and Taylor only too happy to take it from him, to swallow it down, the spill of all that tension and worry and aggravation. Relieved and relaxed by the best medicine of all. That would be love, not sex, though sex was a vital ingredient.

Afterwards, he rested his head on Will's thigh, breathing in the sharp, pungent smell of sex mingled with bare skin and spring rain-scented laundry soap.

Will's fingers tangled in his hair, whether in caress or just the need for contact. "Hey, what about you?" He spoke with what was clearly an effort.

"I'm good," Taylor said. And it was true.

"**D**id you feed Riley?" Will asked. They had showered and dressed and were making breakfast. This was the first time they'd had a chance to have breakfast in their own kitchen for nearly a month, and if Taylor never saw another breakfast burrito or Egg McMuffin, he'd die a happy man.

He assented, catching the whole grain waffles with his plate as they flew out of the toaster.

Will glanced his way, smiled. "Nice catch."

Taylor grunted, carrying the plate to the counter and taking the lid off the butter dish.

"Orange juice?" Will asked.

"Just coffee." He buttered the waffles. Spread grape jelly over Will's, almond butter over his own.

"You having sugar today?"

"I guess. Why not. It's our weekend."

Will sweetened Taylor's coffee appropriately and carried the blue earthenware mugs to the table. He sat down at his place.

Taylor finished slathering the waffles and delivered the plates to the table.

"You sure you don't want any of these sausages?" Will paused, his fork poised above the plate.

"Nah."

"They're turkey."

"I know."

Will shook his head over such foolishness and proceeded to eat all the turkey links before Taylor could wise up and change his mind.

Taylor smiled inwardly. This was what he'd wanted when he had pushed Will to move in with him. Just this. Just being together. Not that they weren't together most of the time anyway, but there was something about waking up with Will, puttering around the kitchen as they made coffee, talked—or not—ate breakfast, worked out their plans for the day, that was different, special, better than how it had been before. It felt so right. For the first time in his life, Taylor felt...content.

Mostly.

There was a knot in his stomach every time he thought of having to go to Richard for money. Even if Richard had been his own dad, which he wasn't, Taylor would not have liked asking for a loan. He almost wished he hadn't suggested it. But they had to have money. They couldn't go on like this. All that had to happen was one of them getting injured for real, and they'd be finished. CLOSED FOR BUSINESS. Permanently.

As it was, they were losing their shirts, and half killing themselves for the pleasure. They were exhausted, their nerves were frayed, and they hadn't had sex—fucked—in two weeks.

"If we can be on the road by noon, we'll be in Mist Bend by suppertime tomorrow," Will said.

Taylor nodded, cut his waffle in quarters, speared one of the quarters.

"I figure we'll just take our time, enjoy the sights. No rush. No pressure. It's not like we've got an assignment to hurry back for."

"Right." Not exactly a positive, but Taylor chose not to point that out. Diplomacy in action.

Will finished off the last turkey link and turned his attention to his waffles. "You'll like it up there. It's not that far from the ocean, and it's quiet and peaceful. There are a couple of good restaurants and a movie theater in town."

When was the last time they'd had a chance to watch a film in a theater? Taylor couldn't remember. "Dinner and a movie sounds great."

"I think so. The fishing is still pretty good in the fall. November is good for Chinook salmon and summer steelhead. In fact, trout, salmon, and steelhead are year round. We can fish all we want and sleep late on the mornings we don't fish. I was thinking we'd stay up there for three or four days. How's that sound?"

Well, it sorta sounded like Will was trying to talk himself into the idea. Trying to convince them both that this trip was going to be great.

"Fine by me." Taylor took a mouthful of coffee. He set his mug down and said, "But are you sure you wouldn't prefer to break the news to your kid brother on your own?"

Will stared at him. "What news?"

"That you're pitching for the other team."

Will took a moment before he said, "I'm not sure that Grant doesn't already know."

"If you're not sure, then no, he doesn't know." Not if Grant was anything like Will.

Another silence. Sometimes it was like panning for gold. At last, Will said, "Grant's shipping out overseas. I don't know when I'm going to see him again. I would like him to know you. At least meet you. So, the answer to your question is no. But it might get awkward for you. I don't know. If it is, we'll stay in town."

"No worries. I've got a thick hide."

There was a little sparkle in Will's eyes as he said gravely, "You know, I seem to recall you've got one or two...sensitive spots."

Taylor's mouth quirked.

"There's the back of your knees, the inside of your elbows..."

Taylor noisily slurped his coffee.

"And that thing you like me to do to your nip—"

"*Okay*, Brandt! Enough."

Will laughed.

When breakfast was over, they washed up, put the trash out, packed. It didn't take them long. They were used to traveling and traveling light, so it was just a matter of throwing a couple of changes of clothing in their bags, dumping the perishables from the fridge, and finding their much neglected fishing rods.

They stowed their gear in the back of Will's Toyota Land Cruiser, gave Riley—uneasily watching their preparations—permission to come aboard, and were on the road by half past noon to the accompaniment of Emmylou Harris.

The CD was an old one. *Luxury Liner*. An album Will had played a lot when they had first been partnered, and Emmylou's bell-clear voice was familiar and sort of comforting even when she was singing about love lost forever.

Making believe that you still love me

It's leaving me alone and so blue

They didn't talk much; both of them had a lot on their minds, but the quiet was relaxed and easy, and they knew and were used to each other's silences.

Taylor took the first stretch of driving. He knew Will was still stiff and sore from his *Starsky and Hutch* routine the day before. It was a long drive, and it would be even longer for Will.

"What do you plan on saying to Richard?" Will broke the silence of the last one hundred miles.

"I haven't worked it out yet."

"But you seem pretty sure he'll cough up the cash."

Taylor nodded.

"He seemed like an okay guy, the one time I met him." Will sounded thoughtful.

"Yeah. He'll give us the money, don't worry."

"I'm not worried." He could feel Will watching him. Will added after a minute, "So long as you're still okay with this. Because if you're not—"

"I'm fine with it, Will." He knew he should explain, but he hated to talk about this stuff, about anything to do with his dad. Will knew the bare bones, of course. That Taylor's parents had split up because Taylor's college professor dad was a drunk and, in Taylor's mom's opinion, a complete loser. His mom had made sure to marry for success the next time around.

He didn't blame her for that. And he didn't blame Richard for being everything his own dad wasn't—couldn't—be. But if there was any other way, he wouldn't be calling Richard for help. No drama. He just...wouldn't.

They stopped for gas outside of Stockton. Will jammed the pump nozzle into the Land Cruiser and took Riley for a walk while Taylor went inside the mini-mart and stocked up on coffee, bottled water, peanuts and granola bars. He rounded a disheveled- looking magazine stand, frowsy covers featuring buxom women, muscle-bound hunks, and souped-up cars all fluttering in the blast from the glass door air curtains, and came face to face with a burly guy in a black leather jacket and mirrored sunglasses.

Different breed, but same species as himself.

The skin on the back of Taylor's neck prickled. They eyed each other for a moment, the other man cradling his pretzels and blue slushy. Taylor nodded curtly, stepped around him.

The other man stuck to the back of the store while Taylor paid for his purchases; Taylor could see him in the round mirror behind the cashier. Not skulking exactly, but certainly keeping in the background.

Taylor gathered up the coffees and the bag of snacks, strolling out through the glass door. There was a black Porsche parked at the front curb. California plates. 2GRR313. He memorized it, carrying the coffees and bag to the Land Cruiser.

Will was across the road, throwing a ball to Riley in a dirt lot. Unhurriedly, Taylor unlocked the Land Cruiser, set the bag inside. He paid for the gas, replaced the pump nozzle. He opened the back hatch, found his bag, found his SIG within the bag, and tucked it in the waistband of his Levi's. It nestled reassuringly in the small of his back.

Still no sign of the convenience store's other customer. Taylor walked around, opened the driver's door, got behind the wheel, and started the Land Cruiser's engine. He idled for a second or two, waiting, but when there was no sign of his quarry, he pulled away from the pump and drove across the road.

Will whistled to Riley and came to meet him.

Riley leaped onto the backseat, panting cheerfully. Will slammed the door behind him, opened the passenger seat door and said, "Did you want me to drive?"

"No. Get in."

Will got in, buckled up, saying mildly, "National emergency?"

"I think maybe we're being followed."

"You're kidding." Will studied his profile. "You're not kidding."

"No." Taylor put the Land Cruiser into drive. "Did you happen to notice that black Porsche behind us on the five?"

"You think we're being followed by a guy in a Porsche? That's not exactly inconspicuous."

"I don't think he's the inconspicuous type."

Will studied the mini-mart as they drove past. "I don't see the driver anywhere."

Taylor lifted a shoulder.

"Okay," Will said, declining to argue with what Taylor was not bothering to articulate. He opened the glove compartment and pulled out a map. Very old school in these matters, Will. "You want me to find us a back road?"

Taylor nodded, watching the rearview. The mini-mart door opened and the man in black stepped out, looking after them. "He's on the move."

"I see him."

Taylor glanced at Will. "They had wasabi peas in the mini-mart."

Will was watching his side mirror. "Well, then it's all for the best."

"They're probably a million years old."

"Just makes them more of a delicacy right? Are you packing?"

"Yep." Taylor said ruefully, "I'm probably paranoid. He still hasn't pulled out of the driveway."

"Take a left up here on Bannerman Road."

Taylor took a left on Bannerman. Will navigated the next few miles of back roads and then they were back on the Interstate. Taylor put the pedal to the metal.

"No sign of Mr. Black," reported Will after a time as they flew past cattle ranches and the occasional billboard.

"I guess I'm just edgy," said Taylor.

"Maybe. What put you on edge?"

"Just a feeling in my gut. He knew me."

"Did you recognize him?"

"No."

"Okay." Will didn't bother to argue or point out all the obvious non-alarming possibilities. He trusted Taylor's instinct. "You want to get a motel for the night or drive on through?"

"Up to you."

"Let's drive."

Taylor nodded.

The sun was setting, the sky turning a hectic orange and indigo, the golden California hills fading into anonymous brown and gray shadows.

There was no sign of Mr. Black on the road behind them. No sign that anyone was paying any particular attention to them, and now both Taylor and Will were keeping an eye out for patterns in the traffic around them.

"I'm surprised Gretchen would recognize you," Taylor said abruptly. He kept circling back to this. It bothered him. It especially bothered him because *he'd* mostly forgotten about Gretchen.

"Maybe she has a good memory for faces."

"Maybe. Did you recognize her?"

"I did when she started screaming."

"But you must get that a lot?"

Will briefly turned his gaze to Taylor. "Ha."

Taylor smirked, but returned to his line of thought. "I've got a pretty good memory for faces, but I don't think I'd be able to pick Gretchen out of a lineup. Not if I didn't know I was looking for her."

"I can tell you this, she was as surprised to see me, as I was to see her."

Taylor mulled that over. "Okay. So running into her was random." He didn't like coincidences.

"I think so."

"The fact that she recognized you? That means she did some checking up on us after New Mexico."

"It's possible. Hedwig did say Gretchen was a girl who held onto a grudge."

"I wonder if losing us our jobs will be enough for her."

Will looked his way again. "You think she might come after us?"

"It's been known to happen." Taylor's thoughts shied away from the memory of Alexandra Sugimori. He'd made his share of enemies through the years, and his experience was that enemies had long memories.

"You think Gretchen sent someone after us?"

"Not very likely, is it?"

"No." Will added, "But maybe we should do a little checking up on Gretchen when we get back to L.A."

"That's my thought."

"While we're at it, maybe we should find out if Bashnakov is still in prison."

Taylor's gaze met Will's grim one.

Will glanced over his shoulder and studied the road for a long moment. "If someone was back there, I think we've lost them."

"Yeah."

Will reached over and squeezed Taylor's shoulder. "Don't you worry, sweetheart, I'll find you someone else you can shoot."

Surveillance Report
Case #3433BR
Subjects: Brandt, William and MacAllister,
Taylor
Investigator: Schwierskott
November 13, 2013 (Wednesday)
7:00 a.m.:
Investigator arrives at the residence of Taylor
MacAllister and William Brandt located at 1041
Cornwall Lane in Ventura, CA 93001. Investigator
observes no vehicles are present at the
residence and establishes stationary vehicle
surveillance with a view of the driveway of the
residence.

8:00 a.m.:
NO ACTIVITY

9:00 a.m.:
NO ACTIVITY

10:00 a.m.:
NO ACTIVITY

11:00 a.m.:
NO ACTIVITY

11:28 a.m.:
Investigator observes the side security
gate of the MacAllister residence open.
Investigator observes a blue 2010 Toyota Land
Cruiser (California License Plate 2GNH635:
currently registered to William Brandt exit the
driveway of the residence and depart the area.

Investigator observes Mr. MacAllister (Caucasian male, 33 years old, shaved, black hair) is driving the vehicle. Mr. Brandt (Caucasian male, 31 years old, shaved, brown hair) is a passenger in the vehicle. Subjects appear relaxed and unhurried. Investigator initiates mobile surveillance of the vehicle.

3:13 p.m.:
Investigator observes the blue 2010 Toyota Land Cruiser enter the parking lot designated for the El Dorado 76 located at 8 Mile Road in Stockton CA 95209 and pull up in front of the gas pumps. Investigator observes Mr. Brandt exit the vehicle with a German shepherd dog and cross the street to a deserted lot to play fetch. Investigator observes Mr. MacAllister exit the vehicle and enter the mini-mart. Investigator initiates stationary vehicle surveillance with a view of the entrance/exit of the building and the deserted lot.

3:27 p.m.:
Investigator observes Mr. MacAllister exit the mini-mart carrying two cups and a brown paper bag and proceed to the blue 2010 Toyota Land Cruiser. Investigator observes Mr. MacAllister pay for gas and enter the vehicle. Investigator observes Mr. MacAllister pull across the street. Investigator observes Mr. Brandt and dog enter the vehicle.
3:30 p.m.:
Investigator observes Mr. MacAllister driving away at a speed estimated in excess of 70 miles

per hour. Investigator was unable to pursue due to the arrival of a big rig truck which pinned in investigator's vehicle.

3:35 p.m.:
Investigator is forced to terminate surveillance.

CHAPTER THREE

It was raining.

More of a mist than actual rain, but it was most definitely wet, and Will spared a moment's regret for Taylor who did not like rain or the cold. Then they topped the rise, and the house seemed to materialize before them. Will experienced an almost painful sensation of time standing still. He could have been a kid of seventeen again, driving home in his truck after football practice.

"Wow," Taylor said, beside him. "Your dad built that himself?"

The house was constructed of lathe turned hand-peeled logs. It was a rambling, two- story ranch-style, with a long front deck and a wide covered back porch. The front gable dormer windows offered the always breath-taking view of the surrounding mountains and pine forest. Smoke wisped from the fireplace, ghostly against the dark trees and darker mountains. The many windows reflected the smoky purple sunset.

Will answered, "When he got out of the marines, yeah. My dad and my Uncle Grant and my Uncle John."

"It's beautiful. Really beautiful."

Growing up, Will had taken *home* for granted, but seeing the place through Taylor's eyes, he realized it *was* beautiful. Just looking at it gave him a lump in his throat.

He grinned. "Relieved?"

"Hell, yeah. This looks like there might even be indoor plumbing."

"There is, but we only use it for special occasions."

"No worries," Taylor said. "A real man can hold it."

Will laughed. He'd teased Taylor about the place being a log cabin. Or maybe subconsciously he'd made it sound worse than it was to discourage Taylor from coming. He hoped that wasn't true, but there was no denying he could feel himself tensing now that the moment of truth was upon them.

Riley stood on the backseat, tail wagging furiously, tags jingling. Will glanced back at him. "You know where you are, don't you?" Will asked him. "You recognize this place."

Riley licked his chops.

Will drove up the hill and parked in front of the double garages beneath the open deck at the front of the house. He turned off the engine, cutting Emmylou off. The silence was instant and profound. Just the ticking of the falling rain.

He could feel Taylor looking at him and he wished—and was immediately ashamed—that he could have made this trip alone. Or arrived first. Something. He'd told his dad he was bringing Taylor, but he'd left it at that, and now he wished he'd given more of a clue as to what that really meant. He should have prepared them, his dad and Grant, for this.

Not least because he was liable to dump Taylor in an embarrassing situation.

And yet at the same time he was glad Taylor was here. He *wanted* Taylor to meet his family. Wanted Taylor to see where he'd grown up. So he unsnapped his seatbelt, turned to Taylor, and smiled. It was probably a grim sort of smile because Taylor studied him and then said, "If you want me to be your fishing buddy this weekend, I can do that."

Will felt his face redden. "I hope you're kidding, MacAllister."

Taylor didn't answer, just kept watching him with those enigmatic green eyes.

"Hell no, I don't want that!"

"Okay."

"I *don't* want that. I'm not in the goddamned closet!"

"You are up here, Brandt."

It was a jolt to hear it. In particular, a jolt to hear it from Taylor. Will said, "Look, I want my dad and my brother to know...you. Us. I'm not going to pretend we're anything but what we are. And I appreciate what you're offering in an unconditional support kind of way, but I don't want that from you."

"Okay."

"I mean, I want support, yeah. I *don't* want you thinking you need to support me by encouraging me to be gutless."

Taylor said again, mildly, "Okay." He glanced over his shoulder. "Incoming. Six o'clock."

Will ignored that, reaching over, locking his hand on the back of Taylor's neck. He drew Taylor forward for a quick, hard kiss.

The next minute Will was out of the SUV, raising a hand in greeting to his father and brother, who were walking down the wide fieldstone path to meet them. He opened the passenger door so Riley could jump down. Riley immediately sprang away to greet Roxie, his sister. Roxie greeted him by trying to chew his face, her tail wagging as furiously as Riley's.

Will was aware, as always, of Taylor in his peripheral vision, taking his time getting out of the SUV, giving Will time to go ahead and do his meet and greet. He strode up the hillside to meet his dad.

"Son." Bill Brandt was in his early sixties. They were the same height, but his father was a little heavier and a lot grayer since the last time Will had seen him. Even his dad's mustache was iron gray.

"Pop," he said gruffly.

"Welcome home, William." His father's big, muscular arms closed around him and they embraced briefly but tightly. Will shut his eyes for an instant. That was something you just didn't outgrow—the pleasure of getting a hug from your dad.

He smiled over his dad's shoulder at his brother Grant. The family resemblance was striking between all the Brandts: dark hair, blue eyes, wide shoulders and long legs. Their trademark, his Uncle John used to joke. The trademark of the Brandt men anyway. There weren't any Brandt daughters. Not in two generations.

"Hey you," Will said to Grant. He stepped back from his dad who was smiling that crooked grin that Will knew was the mirror of his own.

Bill Brandt bellowed, "Roxie, will you knock it off!" before turning to Will once more. "How was your trip?"

Will didn't have a chance to answer because Grant was pounding his back in greeting, and Will was trying not to wince as Grant's affectionate blows landed on his assorted bruises.

"It's about time, *monsieur!*" Grant was laughing. It had been over a year since Will had seen him last. Grant was twenty-five now, a little shorter and a little stockier than his big brother, pumped to physical peak from basic training, but really not so different from the enthusiastic kid Will had helped move into his college dorm what seemed like such a short time ago.

Will thumped Grant in return. "So it's true. The Corps will take anybody now!" He turned to Taylor, who had joined them. "This is Taylor." He added self-consciously, "My partner." But then it belatedly occurred to him that "partner" could be taken a couple of different ways. They would all be correct, of course. He should have figured out ahead of time how he would make this introduction, but the fact was, he hadn't wanted to think about it. Had postponed thinking about it.

His dad put his big, work-roughened hand out to Taylor. "Nice to meet you, Taylor."

"Sir," Taylor said, shaking hands.

Bill Brand studied Taylor shrewdly for a second or two. His navy eyes crinkled in his tanned face. He smiled. "Call me Bill, son."

Will's heart lifted as his dad's gaze met his own. Yes, it was okay. His dad knew, understood. He grinned at Taylor, feeling a surge of possessive pride in him. Why wouldn't his dad approve? MacAllister was everything a prospective father-in-law ought to wish for. Smart, strong, and an excellent shot.

Taylor offered a half smile in return, looking uncharacteristically serious. Almost grave. Will had been so busy worrying about his father and brother's reactions, he hadn't really stopped to consider whether Taylor might find this a little stressful. He wanted to put his arm around him, reassure him, show his solidarity, but not only did he not know how Taylor would feel about being hugged openly—they were sparing in their public demonstrations of affection—his own family wasn't much for physical gestures of affection either.

"Taylor? So you were in the marines?" Grant asked, glancing from Will to Taylor.

"Huh?" Will said. But then memory clicked into place. Hell. Grant was thinking of Bob Taylor. Which was pretty damned disconcerting given that Grant had been a kid when Will and Bob—

Will's thoughts broke off as Taylor glanced his way curiously, offering his hand to Grant. "Sorry. Wrong Taylor."

"Friend of mine from the Corps," Will said by way of explanation.

"Aw. Too bad," Grant said, Grant not being the most tactful member of the Brandt clan. He shook Taylor's hand anyway.

"Taylor's my partner, you knucklehead," Will said. This time he meant the other kind of partner. Or maybe he didn't. Even *he* wasn't sure anymore. He just knew he didn't want Taylor, fresh from the David Bradley debacle, wondering about Bob Taylor.

"Oh. *MacAllister*," Grant said. "The DSS one. Will said you like to fish. I thought you liked deep sea fishing, though."

"I like fishing period."

Taylor's amused gaze met Will's, and Will opened his mouth, but was this the right moment for a dramatic announcement? His father had the rear door of the SUV open and he was handing their fishing poles to Grant who was saying, "You came to the right place for fishing. Best fishing in the state. In the country."

Taylor gave a laugh under his breath and went to grab his bag, and Will followed suit.

They went up the fieldstone walk, everyone talking at once, and even so, their voices sounding small in the vast emptiness of the surrounding silence of trees and mountains and endless sky. The damp air was cold and smelled of distant snow, pine trees and woodsmoke.

"It's beautiful," Taylor said, staring at the snowcapped peaks. "Do you get snow this time of year?"

"Sometimes. Not usually," Bill said. "It's not going to snow in the next day or two."

"How did you like San Diego?" Will asked Grant, who had completed his training at Camp Pendleton.

"I'd have liked it better if you hadn't been in France."

"Yeah, I get that a lot," Will said, his eyes meeting Taylor's.

Taylor gave a derisive shake of his head.

They walked up the log steps on the east side of the house and trooped inside the enormous front room with its hand-hewn cathedral ceiling. Golden evening poured through the wall of picture windows, bathing the log ceiling rafters and tall fieldstone fireplace in a warm light. Colorful Indian rugs covered the floors. The furniture was comfortable and man-sized. A fire glowed in the fireplace grate and the house smelled of something good cooking. Chili, probably.

Which always gave Taylor indigestion. Chili and salsa.

A slender, bald-headed, bearded man sat at the rough-carved dining table. He nodded politely in greeting, his brown eyes watchful.

"And if anyone asks, that's your cousin Dennis," Bill said.

Will, who knew perfectly well he didn't have a Cousin Dennis, said, "Is someone liable to ask?"

His father shrugged. "You never know."

"Got it." Will met Taylor's gaze. Taylor raised his eyebrows.

"So," Bill went on, "we've got a full house this weekend. Dennis is in the loft, but we can—"

"Taylor's fine with me."

"I figured," Bill said easily. "Supper's ready. You may as well give Taylor the grand tour, and then we can sit down to eat. Grant, since when do you leave fishing poles in the living room?"

Grant was making his protests as Will led the way through the open kitchen, past the large downstairs bathroom, which they'd be sharing with Grant, down the hall lined with family photos to his bedroom on the north side of the house.

The room looked mostly unchanged. The posters and sports pennants were gone along with the school books and scattered dirty clothes. The handmade navy blue quilt was the same one Will had slept beneath growing up.

"Double bed," Will said. "It's a good thing you're such a little guy."

"So funny," Taylor returned, dropping his bag on the floor beside the bed. "So what's the deal with Cousin Dennis?"

Will grimaced. "Occasionally Pop provides a way station for...uh..."

Taylor's eyes widened. "For...uh...what? Who? Witness Protection?"

"Whom. Whom would be, yeah, people entering WITSEC."

Taylor stared at him. "Seems a funny thing never to have mentioned before, Brandt."

Will shrugged. "It never came up. Anyway, it won't be for long. Usually overnight. The longest was a week."

"Great. So Dennis is a bad guy?"

"Probably. Generally."

Taylor laughed. "Okay. And who's Bob Taylor?"

"Just a friend." Will sighed.

"Mmhm." Taylor studied the framed photo of Will's mother on the dresser. "A friend like David Bradley or a friend like Alice Stone?"

"Immaterial. Irrelevant."

Taylor glanced back at him and raised his eyebrows. "I...see."

"You nut." Will grabbed a fistful of Taylor's shirt and hauled him in for a quick but comprehensive kiss.

When he lifted his mouth from Taylor's, they were both smiling. Will looked over Taylor's shoulder in time to see Grant standing in the doorway, Grant's wide grin fading into a look of horror. His stricken gaze met Will's and he stepped back into the hall.

"Whoa." Will released Taylor so suddenly, Taylor staggered back and sat down on the edge of the bed. "Hang on. *Grant*?"

"Hell," Taylor muttered. "That didn't take long."

"Be right back."

If Taylor replied, Will missed it. He sprinted down the hall after Grant, catching up to him as Grant's bedroom door was closing.

"Hey. Grant." Will turned the knob and stepped inside Grant's room. Grant turned like he was at bay. "You need to listen to me."

"What the hell, William." Grant's face was pale. His eyes still looked stricken. "What the fuck? What. The. Fuck. You were *kissing* him."

"He's my partner."

"I thought you meant you worked together!"

"We do work together. But we're also—"

"But he's married! He's wearing a wedding ring."

It surprised Will that Grant had noticed. He wasn't always so observant. "He's wearing *my* ring."

Grant shook his head, repudiating this. "I don't believe this. You're saying you're a *homo*? There's no way!"

This was going pretty much the way Will had feared any time he'd pictured this scenario. The fact that his father had taken Taylor's presence so calmly had lulled him into a false sense of security. Grant's reaction was the normal and expected one. Or at least the expected one.

Will should have been a lot more careful about kissing Taylor.

Except…no. Why *should* he have to be careful about kissing the guy he planned on spending the rest of his life with? No, what he should have done was communicate the real state of affairs before he ever made this trip. Or at least before he dragged Taylor along on such a trip.

"Hell," he muttered. "We should have had this talk a long time ago."

"*What* talk? The talk where you tell me you're a queer? You're a fag? You're a goddamned—"

"Okay," Will cut in. He kept his voice quiet, but it took effort. "You can cut that shit out now. Yes, I'm gay. You're going to have to deal with it."

"Since when? Since *him*? Since MacAllister?"

"Since forever. Taylor doesn't have anything to do with me being gay."

"The hell he doesn't. He's your *partner*, isn't he?"

"Yes. But I was gay long be—"

"That's bullshit, Will. You aren't gay. You weren't gay in high school. You weren't gay in college. You were going to marry Madonna Agnelli. You *should* have married her."

Will hung onto his patience. "No, I shouldn't have. Because I *am* gay. And the reason I stopped dating Madonna was I figured that out. Look, I'm sorry this is such a shock to you, but—"

"Does Pop know?"

"Yes." Will reflected on the last three minutes and revised. "I'm assuming Pop knows."

"You *assume*? I wouldn't assume, William. This is so...I can't believe it. This is a goddamned *nightmare*."

Will said wearily, "Grant, I realize this news is a shock, and I guess I didn't handle breaking it to you right. Okay? But—"

"I don't want to hear it." Grant actually put his hands up like he was going to cover his ears. He stopped himself, but clearly it was his desire.

"Oh for chrissake."

"No." Grant's chin jutted out defiantly. "I don't want to hear it. I don't know why you would do this, but I'm not going to be a part of it."

"I'm not asking you to be a *part* of it. I'm asking you to not be an ass about it."

Grant glared at him. "I can't believe you'd bring *him* here."

Will said in warning, "Grant, you can think what you like, but you don't say one goddamned thing to MacAllister, you got that? Not a word. You're my brother and I love you. That isn't going to change, even if you are a jackass. But if you give MacAllister *any* grief, we're going to have a serious disagreement."

Grant opened his mouth, but changed his mind.

"Good choice," Will told him, and walked out.

"**A**ny regrets about leaving the DSS?" Bill asked, passing the basket of cornbread to Taylor.

Will winced inwardly, but Taylor caught his eye and winked. "Nah," Taylor said. "We were ready for a change. This way we get to be our own bosses and take vacation when we need it."

"Like now," Will said.

"And you boys are working as private eyes or what exactly?"

That was the question, wasn't it? The ongoing debate between them.

"Mercenaries?" Cousin Dennis said, showing his first interest in the suppertime conversation. It was easy to forget about Cousin Dennis. He sort of blended into the oak paneling.

"Global security consultants," Will said.

Taylor gave Cousin Dennis a narrow look. "Definitely not mercenaries." He did not like mercenaries in any way, shape or form. They'd had a few arguments on the topic over the years. Will had friends who'd moved from the military to mercenary work for companies like Blackwater. He saw it as a viable option. Not for himself, but for a certain kind of guy, yeah.

Taylor, not so much, and Will smiled inwardly at his tone. He caught Grant's scowl, and his amusement faded. He was stupid not to have foreseen Grant's reaction to his coming out, but Will hadn't spent a lot of time with Grant over the last decade. The fact was, he didn't really know the adult Grant all that well. It was a sad thought.

"There's good money in mercenary work," Cousin Dennis said, showing an unexpected streak of stubbornness.

"It's not just about money," Taylor said.

"Not that we have anything against money," Will said cheerfully. He nudged Taylor's boot under the table.

Taylor's mouth quirked but he went back to eating his chili.

"Nothing wrong with a steady paycheck," Bill said. "But a man has to be able to look himself in the eye every morning."

"What does that mean?" Cousin Dennis said. "You can look at yourself in the mirror or you can look someone in the eye, but how do you look yourself in the eye?"

"Eat your cornbread and shut up, Cousin Dennis," Bill said pleasantly, and Taylor laughed.

"Anybody want another beer?" Will asked, rising.

"I will," Cousin Dennis said. Taylor nodded. Will's father shook his head.

Grant said suddenly, "Jem Dooley got released from prison last week."

"Let's not ruin a good meal talking about the Dooleys," Bill said in a tone Will remembered well from his youth.

"Have you heard from him?" Will asked his father, frowning.

"Nope. And I don't expect to."

Will had gone to school with Jem Dooley, with all the Dooleys. No-accounts and troublemakers pretty much summed them up. Jem had taken his no-account status to a whole new level when he'd tried to rob a local gas station and ended up killing the owner when the man had opened fire on him. Bill Brandt had been the Columbia County Sheriff at the time, and it had been his job to track Jem to Deer Island and arrest him. It had not endeared the Brandts to the Dooleys. Not that they had ever been neighborly exactly. But after Jem went to prison, it had felt more like the Hatfields and the McCoys. No one had been killed, but it had come close a couple of times.

Jem had sworn to seek revenge on Bill Brandt once he got out of prison, but he'd had his sentence extended twice for committing assault and battery on fellow inmates, so Will had started thinking Jem would spend his entire life behind bars.

Will continued his trip out to the kitchen to get the beer. He could hear Cousin Dennis asking, "Who are the Dooleys?"

He sounded like an easterner to Will. Not Jersey. Not New York. Maybe Connecticut? Maryland? Not a tough guy. Definitely not a tough guy. A smart-mouth. A too-smart-for-his-own-good guy. Maybe an accountant or a business owner who'd made the mistake of hooking up with the wrong partner. It happened.

"A local family with more than their share of bad luck," Bill said with finality. "Taylor, son, you don't have to stand on ceremony. Have some more chili."

"Here you go." Will tossed the plastic bottle of Tums to Taylor, who was already in bed and looking very much at home. Taylor popped the lid and shook two tablets out. He grimaced, chewed the orange tablets, and set the bottle on the bedside table.

"What do you think of Cousin Dennis?" he asked.

It was nearly midnight and everyone had retired for the evening. In fact, Grant had turned in not long after dinner, claiming he wanted to get an early start fishing the next morning. It was disappointing that Grant was being such an ass, but Will was hopeful once he'd had a little time to think things through, he'd come around.

Or maybe he wouldn't.

Painful to think, but it was possible.

Will shrugged. "Seems harmless enough. Hopefully the marshals will yank him out of here tomorrow." He opened the cedar chest at the foot of the bed and pulled out a heavy wool Indian print blanket. The blanket smelled of camphor and wood and something he couldn't quite place but that reminded him of his boyhood. Liniment? His first aftershave?

"He's no wise guy, but he's no innocent bystander either," Taylor commented.

"He's also not our problem." Will shook out the red zigzagged folds and let the blanket drift down and settle over the bed. "You warm enough?"

"Sure."

"You want a pair of wool socks?"

"Nah."

"It gets cold in this house at night." Will pulled an extra pair of socks out of his suitcase and dangled them enticingly. "Pop doesn't run the heater."

"Thanks, but they make my feet sweat."

Will went around to the side of the bed, pulled the blankets back and slid between the blue flannel sheets. "My, this is cozy."

Taylor laughed. At home they shared a king-sized bed, so this was definitely a tighter fit. "If I wasn't your boyfriend before, I would be now."

Will snorted. He reached over and turned off the lamp.

The darkness was instant and all encompassing. For a few moments they lay quietly, simply absorbing the depth and silence of night in the forest.

"That is one beautiful moon," Taylor remarked as the window slowly filled with bright silver light.

"Yeah. Nice." Will turned his head on the pillow, trying to make out Taylor's features in the uncertain light. "So what do you mean you're not going fishing tomorrow? I thought that was the plan. You love fishing."

"I do, yeah. But I don't want to break Grant's heart."

Will said tersely, "Grant is going to have to adjust."

"Sure. And tomorrow you can break that news to him." Taylor yawned, wiggled his jaw. "Anyway, there's plenty of time for you and me to go fishing, right?"

"Yep. What are you going to do then?"

"I'll find something to keep me busy."

"Don't wander off into the woods."

Taylor spluttered. "Right, because going for a long hike by myself in the woods is the first thing I'd think of to amuse myself."

"I know, but you can't do the other thing all day. You'll go blind."

Taylor started to laugh.

Will's feet brushed Taylor's and he jumped. "Christ, MacAllister. Your feet are like popsicles!"

"You'll take care of that."

Will did his best, folding Taylor's feet between his own and rubbing them.

Taylor, who was extremely ticklish, gave a little gasp. Actually, it was kind of a squeak. *Almost* a squeal.

"That was manly," Will muttered, trying not to laugh.

Taylor started to respond, but there was a heavy thump against the wall, as though someone had kicked it or thrown a boot at it.

"Are you *kidding* me?" Taylor lunged up and whumped the wall back, hard. Will winced, but Taylor was in the right. Grant was pushing his luck.

Taylor flopped back and gave that little irritated huff he made when he was nervous or worried.

"Hey." Will wrapped his arm around Taylor's bony shoulders and tugged him still closer. "I'm going to have another talk with him, don't worry."

"I know."

"He's my only brother. Please don't kill him."

"I won't touch him. I won't touch a hair of his backwoods head."

Will grinned fiercely into the darkness and pressed a kiss on top of Taylor's city boy head.

They lay in companionable, warm silence.

"What's funny?" Taylor mumbled.

"Hm?"

"I can feel you smiling."

"Just thinking."

"About?"

"You."

"What about me?"

"I don't know. Something about you being here now. All those years I used to lie here and think about…I don't know."

Taylor tilted his face up, as though listening for what Will wasn't putting into words. "What?"

"The usual stuff, I guess."

"Homework? Football? Girls?"

"Yeah." Will added softly, "And boys."

Taylor gave a little shiver, and Will squeezed him tighter. "See. I knew you'd be cold."

"*Cold*? The opposite. Do you think—?" He rocked his hips insinuatingly against Will's.

"No! I sure as hell don't. With Grant's ear pressed to the wall?"

After a pause, Taylor said, "I hope you're kidding."

"I'm kidding. But we *can't*. You know that. We've got to—"

He floundered, and it was Taylor who drawled, "Slow their ascent so they don't get the bends?"

Will laughed, but he couldn't deny—and probably hadn't been able to hide—that instinctive surge of panic. Panic at the very idea. He was ashamed of it, but there was no denying the idea of having sex within earshot of any member of his family was more alarming than exciting.

Taylor snorted. "Relax. Your virtue is safe with me."

Will groaned softly. "It's only a couple of days. If it helps, I'd feel the same if you were a woman."

"Uh, no, Brandt. Actually, that doesn't help. *At all*." But Taylor was laughing, and Will began to laugh too.

After a bit Taylor said, "It wasn't easy for you, was it? Growing up here. Small towns, small minds. You had it tougher than I did."

"It was okay," Will said, uncomfortable with Taylor's sudden sympathy. "It was tougher being the son of the local sheriff."

"Yeah?"

"Yeah. Every so often some asshole, usually one of the Dooleys, would accuse me of being a narc. You know how kids are."

"A *narc*," Taylor's tone was derisive. "I bet. But you were the big varsity guy, right? Quarterback of your high school football team, then the big college star, then the marines."

"I did okay," Will admitted. "It was probably tougher for Grant."

Taylor said unexpectedly, "Probably, yeah."

Will thought that over, frowning into the darkness. After a time Taylor turned his face into Will's shoulder and began to snore softly.

CHAPTER FOUR

"**Y**ou sure you don't want to come?" Will's voice murmured warmly against his ear.

Taylor's eyes popped open.

Will corrected hastily, huskily, "Fishing, I mean."

Taylor expelled a heavy sigh. He shook his head, burying his face in his pillow once more. It was still dark. The flannel sheets were soft and warm and smelled pleasantly of soap and Will. It felt good, very good, to stretch out after a night of sharing a too small bed.

"I'm fine," he mumbled.

"I'll leave you the keys to my Land Cruiser in case you want to drive into town."

"'Kay."

"We should be back by lunch."

Taylor nodded, smothered a yawn in the pillow, and promptly fell back asleep.

The next time he woke, really woke, the sun was shining brightly and his cell phone, when he focused blearily on its screen, informed him it was nine thirty. That was sleeping in very late for him. He must have needed the rest. He smothered another huge yawn and spent a few moments listening to the birds outside and Riley barking somewhere in the distance.

Someone had made coffee. He could smell the encouraging aroma drifting from down the hall, and the thought of a hot cup and something to eat that wouldn't give him heartburn got him out of bed. He paused by Will's desk to check out Will's high school yearbooks, smiling faintly at photos of

Will with uncharacteristically long hair and a very square jaw the rest of his face hadn't quite grown into. The same old grin though.

Yeah, Will would have been quite a heartbreaker in high school.

Taylor hoped this fishing trip was mending some of the frayed feelings between Will and the kid. That had gone about as well as Taylor had expected. But he felt a little sorry for Grant. Finding out his idolized big brother was a faggot had clearly rocked his world on its axis.

Taylor sighed, closed the yearbook, and headed for the bathroom.

A shower and a shave later, he wandered into the kitchen to find Cousin Dennis eating eggs and bacon.

"There's plenty of food in the fridge," Cousin Dennis told him.

Taylor nodded, pouring himself a cup of coffee. Bahrain was eleven hours ahead, which meant it was after eight at night there. He needed to call Richard before it got any later. He took his coffee and his phone out onto the long log deck behind the house.

The air was cool and smelled damp and pine-scented, with just a hint of the ocean on the breeze. Several yards from the house, he spotted a doe grazing in the meadow. That peaceful scene wouldn't last long once the dogs spotted her.

He dialed 973 for Bahrain and negotiated his way through the usual obstacle course of telecommunications, then household and support staff, until he reached his mother—the very person he did not want to speak to right then.

"Taylor, sweetie. Is that you?" He could hear the instant alarm, the fear that he was the subject of the call and not the one making it. He mentally resolved to be better about phoning.

"Yep, it's me. Hi, Mom."

"What's wrong?"

"Nothing's wrong, Mom. I just needed to speak to Richard."

"Has something happened? You're not injured again?"

"No. I'm fine. I'm great. Really."

"I was afraid it was Will again." Will being the usual bearer of bad news.

"Nope, it's me. I was just hoping to talk to Richard, if he's home this evening."

"He's at his club, sweetie. Is it something I can help you with?"

"Not really. What time does he usually get back? Do you think he could give me a call?"

"Of course, sweetie. He'd be happy to."

He gave her the number and, like a fool, mentioned they were staying with Will's dad.

"Then it's official?" Her voice shot up with excitement. "You boys have set a date?" She hadn't always been this thrilled with his sexuality. In fact, she had been very uncomfortable and unhappy when he'd tried to come out in college. But as society and her social circle had adjusted their attitudes, her feelings had changed. Now she seemed to believe having a gay son was a kind of cultural coup.

"Uh…not exactly. I mean, it's official, yes. But we're not…we haven't really made any plans."

She launched into a spate of unneeded advice and unwanted opinions, and he remembered why he didn't call very often.

He finally managed to disconnect, her admonishing to *please* not get shot again ringing in his ears.

Damn. So nothing was solved and he'd have to wait for Richard's call, assuming Richard didn't arrive home too drunk and tired to phone.

He drank his coffee and ruminated. So okay. Next on the agenda, he wanted information on Mr. Black, the driver of the Porsche they had spotted in Stockton.

In the DSS this kind of information had been right at his fingertips, but now days…not so easy. California had strict laws about allowing civilians access to DMV records. Once upon a time anyone could run a license plate, but now release of personal information was restricted by the Information Practices Act of 1977 and the federal Driver's Privacy Protection Act of 1994. Any request for information meant the subject was notified of the request. These laws provided excellent protection for citizens but they were a PIA if you were a global security consultant who needed info fast and didn't want to spook his subject.

Granted, there were private firms who could provide that info given time and money, but if someone was gunning for them, Taylor didn't want to waste time on figuring that out. They still had contacts at the California DMV. He and Will tried not to tap their old associates because—unlike on TV—getting someone to circumvent the system too many times resulted in reprimands and loss of employment. Not the way to treat a friend.

He was probably paranoid, but he couldn't shake the feeling that running into Mr. Black hadn't been coincidence. Mr. Black hadn't been surprised to run into him, no, he'd been *uncomfortable*. Uncomfortable because he hadn't wanted to be spotted by Taylor. Because he was following them? That's how it looked from Taylor's perspective.

He dialed the California Department of Motor Vehicles in Ventura and asked for Ms. Euphonia Jones. He was still on hold when Cousin Dennis ran out onto the deck.

"Someone's coming!" Cousin Dennis looked pale and wild-eyed.

Taylor disconnected. "Okay. Well—"

"A white pickup is coming down the road!"

The dogs barking from the front of the house seemed to confirm this intelligence.

Taylor swore inwardly, and led the way back inside. How the hell was Cousin Dennis suddenly *his* problem? "Is this the first vehicle that's shown up since you arrived?"

"No. You showed up."

Taylor drew a long breath and mentally counted to…three. "Who is it you think is coming after you?"

Cousin Dennis stared at him, silent and stricken.

"Hell." Taylor went to the window and gazed out. A white pickup was indeed traveling at a fair clip down the dirt road, bouncing over potholes and rivulets.

No way would Bill Brandt have left Cousin Dennis here on his own if he'd thought there was a chance in hell of anyone coming after him.

On the other hand, Cousin Dennis was in WITSEC for a reason.

"Is there a cellar or a basement in this house?"

"A cellar. Yeah. They use it as a safe room."

"Get down there and lock yourself in." Taylor brushed past Cousin Dennis on his way to Will's bedroom. He dug his SIG Sauer out of his bag and returned to the front room where Cousin Dennis was still standing paralyzed.

Taylor jostled his arm. "Hey. Snap out of it."

Cousin Dennis blinked at him.

"I don't know what your story is, but I can tell you that nobody is sending a hit squad after you in the form of a couple of yahoos in a beat-up pickup truck. All the same, get your ass in that cellar and don't come out until I give you the all clear."

Cousin Dennis seemed to have to work to unstick first one foot then the other, but at last he pulled free of his inertia and disappeared down the hall. Taylor jammed his pistol in the back band of his jeans and strolled out onto the front deck watching as the white pickup jounced to a stop on the hillside below. Riley and Roxie trotted up the steps to stand beside him. They had stopped barking and were watching the pickup truck with evident anticipation.

Three guys, who looked like extras from *Duck Dynasty*, were crammed in the cab of the rumbling truck, apparently getting the lay of the land. Blake Shelton's "Mine Would Be You" blasted off the surrounding mountains, and several empty beer bottles, rolling around in the bed of the truck, clinked cheerfully.

"Wow," muttered Taylor, and Riley wagged his tail as though in agreement.

Taylor lifted a hand in greeting.

One of the yahoos, dressed in woodland camo—complete with matching bandana—crawled out of the truck window and jumped to the ground.

"Is Brandt here?" he yelled. He was a big man. Some of it was muscle, some of it was flab, a lot of it was hair. Long black hair and long black beard. Altogether, it amounted to a sizeable and sturdy form.

Taylor relaxed. Not that he had really thought this was some country cousin branch of the mob come hunting Cousin Dennis, but life could be weird.

He called back, "Nope. Anything I can do for you?"

"Who are you?"

"Who wants to know?"

The guy said impatiently, "*I* want to know."

I'm Larry; this is my brother Darryl, and this is my other brother Darryl. Taylor bit back an inappropriate smile. First rule of visiting the in-laws: No laughing at the local wild life.

"And you are—?"

"Going to kick your ass if you don't tell me what I want to know!" The big man drew himself up as though readying for battle.

Really? Taylor sighed. The weary sound carried in the sharp, crystalline air and Larry looked a little discomfited.

He recovered though, cheered on by the other two in the cab who were calling instructions to him, though unintelligible over the music and the truck engine. He bristled. "You a cop?"

"Something like that." Actually, that was no longer true, and Taylor was startled to realize it.

But it was certainly true in spirit, and Larry bought it. He deflated a little, glancing back at the truck and his snarling kinfolk. Whatever messages of hope and comfort they were delivering seemed to inspire him. He yelled, "You tell Brandt that the Dooleys are looking for him."

Taylor put a hand to his ear. "Sorry. I missed that. Who?"

"The Dooleys."

"The...?"

"DOOLEYS," roared Larry.

"Right. Got it." Taylor leaned comfortably on the railing, smiling down at Larry who looked more and more baffled. "I'll let 'em know."

Larry stared at him a moment longer and then climbed awkwardly, heavily back through the truck window. He was not built for climbing in and out of truck windows, and the endeavor revealed more glimpses of fish-white anatomy than Taylor wanted to see before breakfast.

When Larry was once more packed inside the sardine can, the truck pulled away in a wide arc, sending stones and beer bottles flying.

Blake Shelton's voice faded mournfully into the distance.

"I need a lot more coffee if this is the way the day is going," Taylor told the dogs. He went back into the house.

It took him about half a minute to find the cellar and less than a second to ascertain that Cousin Dennis was not in it.

"Dennis?" Taylor called.

No reply.

"Yo, Dennis. The coast is clear."

Nothing. The dogs looked at him with interest. Riley cocking his head, Roxie flicking her ears and looking around helpfully.

"What the hell?" His voice sounded loud in the silence.

Dogs on his heels, Taylor conducted a swift but thorough search, striding from room to room, checking showers, bathtubs, closets, looking under beds. Cousin Dennis was nowhere in the house.

"No. Fucking. Way."

But yes. Way. Cousin Dennis was gone.

Movement outside the small square window to his left had Taylor crossing the loft and staring out at the green meadow and a tiny figure in jeans and a plaid shirt making for the treeline of the forest of pines carpeting the mountains.

"*Why*? Why would you do that, you dumbass?"

It was a rhetorical question seeing that Cousin Dennis was too far away to hear—and getting farther by the minute.

Taylor pushed away from the window and tore downstairs, managing to avoid falling over the dogs who thought this was the start of a terrific new game.

Near the bottom of the stairs, he grabbed the railing and vaulted, landing lightly and running for the back of the house. He banged out through the door and jumped down from the deck to the soft, damp earth below.

Dennis was now a speck in the distance. Where did he think he was going? Did he have a plan or was he just running blind? Taylor whistled, the high, sharp sound cutting through the cool November air, but if Dennis heard, he gave no sign. The dogs began to circle Taylor, thrilled at whatever this was.

"You've gotta be kidding."

If it was a joke, the joke was on him. Taylor took off after Dennis, the dogs loping alongside. His feet pounded the soft earth, the air was sweet and clear. Also thinner than he was used to and he had to work a little harder to get up to full speed. Dennis had a good head start, but Taylor wasn't worried. He figured he was in a hell of a lot better shape. He set his pace and quickly closed the distance between them, but not in time to keep Dennis from reaching the trees and vanishing in the green and blue shadows.

Oh no you don't, you bastard. Taylor slowed, stopped and reached for Riley, grabbing his collar and looking into Riley's golden-brown eyes. "Find him, Riley. Go get him. Go get him, Riley!"

Riley was no police dog, but this was a game Will and Taylor played with him, and he gave Taylor a happy, hopeful look and darted ahead after Dennis.

Roxie followed, tongue lolling, as though she was laughing at them both.

Of course Riley was probably looking for Will, but maybe he would stumble over Dennis while he was at it.

Taylor, bringing up the rear, ducked under the pine branches, and stopped. He braced his hands on his thighs, catching his breath and listening. He straightened, wiped his damp face on his flannel sleeve and listened harder. The trees seemed to swallow all sound.

No. Not all sound. A couple of yards ahead, he could hear the dogs crashing through the undergrowth—and beyond that, something that sounded like a moose charging through the brush. Of course, maybe it *was* a moose. Did they have moose in Oregon?

Hopefully not. He'd seen moose in museums and those suckers were huge. He *really* did not want to run into a moose.

Or a bear.

Taylor began to move again, this time angling to the east of where he estimated Dennis was headed.

"Dennis, it's MacAllister," he called. "Stop running. It's all clear."

The thrashing sounds stopped.

"Dennis? You hear me? It's okay. You can come back to the house."

Taylor kept working his way forward, clambering over a fallen tree, avoiding a patch of something that looked suspiciously like poison ivy. Somewhere to his distant right he could hear the dogs. Whatever they were chasing now it wasn't Dennis.

It wasn't Dennis because Dennis was close by. Taylor could sense him, even if he couldn't see him yet. He stopped walking, scanning the gloom.

"Dennis?"

What the hell was this guy so afraid of?

A bird suddenly burst out of the brush, wings flapping, twittering its distress call. Taylor jumped. There was movement to his left. He half turned and something swung out of the darkness and slammed into his head.

Gusts of dog breath and a rough, warm tongue frantically licking his face…

Taylor opened his eyes and pushed away Riley, who ducked under his arm and resumed efforts at resuscitation.

Taylor swore thickly. "Okay, Riley. I'm okay…"

Mostly. His face hurt like hell. His nose felt like it had exploded and there was warm, coppery, salty sludge slipping down the back of his throat. He gagged at the taste of his own blood, rolling onto his side and spitting it out into the pine needles. "God *damn* it."

He cautiously felt his nose. Was it broken? His lip was definitely split. He looked at his hand, focusing blearily on the red smearing his fingers. "Jesus. That's just great."

How long had he been out? Not more than a minute or two, surely? Plenty of time for Cousin Dennis to make himself scarce. And what the hell was the guy's problem? Even if he hadn't recognized Taylor before he swung at him, he had to know after he knocked him down.

Taylor spread his palms and pushed up onto his knees. He reached for the nearest tree trunk and hauled himself to his feet. Roxie sat a few feet away, watching him curiously. Riley was much more agitated about recent events and kept dancing in front of Taylor like he was trying to encourage him to take action.

The only action Taylor was taking was going back to the house to call Will to let him know his father's asshole charge had flipped out and made a run for the hills.

Not. His. Problem.

He wiped his sleeve against his still trickling nose, studied the gory results grimly, and started walking back to the house.

The sun felt good. He was cold from lying on the damp ground, cold from the shock of getting knocked out. Not that he was unused to physical punishment. Taylor knew he wasn't badly hurt—although he was going to be seriously pissed off if his nose *was* broken—but his head thumped unpleasantly, his face throbbed, his heart was racketing around in his chest in a sick mix of shock and pain and adrenaline. It was not a good start to his day off.

And, as he crossed the meadow and drew close to the Brandt house, his day got abruptly worse.

Will's SUV was gone.

He broke into a slow and painful jog, although he wasn't sure why he was running. The Land Cruiser was not there. It wasn't a trick of the light or a problem with his eyes. The Toyota was missing.

He came to a stop where it had been parked, breathing hard, staring stupidly at the tracks in the drying soil.

"I don't believe it."

But he did. As much as he'd have liked to tell himself he was dreaming, the drops of blood landing on the ground next to his boots seemed to indicate otherwise. He wiped his nose again, turned away and continued up the hill, up the stairs, and let himself into the house.

Inside, it was hushed and quiet. Empty.

Taylor walked back to Will's bedroom. Will's keys were no longer lying on top of the bureau.

He was finishing his phone call to the Sheriff's Department when the Brandts returned, noisily trooping in, flushed with sun and wind, smelling of fish and river water, talking at the top of their voices and sending the jagged pain behind his eyes spiking.

"Hey, you're here," Will greeted him in evident surprise. "I thought you'd gone into t—" He stopped, took a closer look. "What the hell happened to you?"

"Your Cousin Dennis."

"What are you talking about? What happened?" Will dropped his knapsack and went to Taylor. He put his hands on either side of Taylor's face, tilting his head back. "He *punched* you?"

"Not exactly."

"*What* exactly?"

Bill Brandt said in a hard voice, "Where is Dennis?"

"Gone."

"Gone?" He got it from all three of them at the same time. They could have started their own barber shop quartet. Well, trio.

Taylor focused his ire on Grant, who was looking at him like he'd crawled out from under a bush. Technically, he *had*, but that expression didn't exactly warm him to Will's kid brother. Under the heat of his return glare, Grant reddened.

Taylor said, "Yes. Gone. Long story short. He's on the run."

Of course, no way were the Brandts going to accept the *Reader's Digest* version, and Taylor had to go back and give the whole embarrassing play by play.

"Jeb and Tobe Dooley were here?" Bill's face was thunderous.

Jeb and Tobe. Will had grown up in *Deliverance*, USA.

"There were three of them. I didn't catch their first names," Taylor said.

"You didn't think you should keep an eye on Cousin Dennis?" Grant said. "You just left him to walk out?"

"Hey," Will growled, turning to face his brother.

"You two knock it off," Bill said. "I've gotta call Clary Bennett at the Marshal's Service."

"Bill, I reported Will's car stolen to the Sheriff's Department," Taylor said.

"Oh great! Why would you do that?" Grant demanded.

"Because my car's been stolen!" Will said.

"It didn't occur to him that Cousin Dennis has to fly under the radar?"

"Since when are you an expert on witness protection? It looks to me like Cousin Dennis has decided to take his chances in the no-fly zone."

"You done with that phone, son?" Bill asked Taylor, ignoring the debate in the background.

Taylor nodded and handed over the phone. He picked up the chunk of towel-wrapped ice and placed it gingerly against the bridge of his nose.

"You okay?" Will asked.

Taylor nodded.

Grant made a sound of repugnance and walked out of the kitchen.

Will turned, as though to go after him. "Forget about it," Taylor said.

"I don't think I want to forget about it."

"Can you boys give me a minute?" Bill asked, with a clear effort at patience.

Taylor jumped off the counter where he had been sitting, and led the way to the living room. Will followed.

"*Are* you okay?" Will asked, as Taylor lowered himself to the long leather couch.

"I think the asshole broke my nose."

Will leaned in, frowning. Taylor fended him off. "Careful."

"Hold still..."

"Don't touch it. It's still bleeding."

"I see that. You have to put pressure on the bleeding point." Will delicately used his thumb and forefinger to pinch the tip of Taylor's nose. "Like that. I don't think it's broken."

Taylor brushed his hand away. "It didn't use to wiggle so much."

"I've seen a lot of broken noses, MacAllister. Your nose is still in one piece."

Taylor huffed his irritation.

Will soothed, "It's still a very handsome nose."

Pinching his nostrils shut, Taylor said indistinctly, "Go to hell, Brandt."

"I'm serious." But he was smiling.

Taylor shook his head. His pride hurt worse than his nose.

Will moved closer, nuzzled his ear and murmured, "Yeah it is. And you're going to have a beautiful pair of black eyes to go with it."

Taylor closed his eyes and sighed.

CHAPTER FIVE

"Not your fault," Will said for the third time. It went over as well as it had the previous two.

Taylor gave him a bleak look. "Explain to me how losing Cousin Dennis was not my fault? It happened on my watch. Under my fucking nose." He touched the nose in question cautiously.

"To start with, he wasn't your responsibility. Secondly, he's supposed to be here voluntarily, so of course you weren't expecting him to rabbit."

His father was still talking to his contact at the Marshal's Service. Will could hear his deep, calm voice floating from the kitchen, though the words were not clear. Not that there was any mystery about his report.

Taylor gazed bleakly into space. "We have to find him."

"What?" Will did a double take. "No, we sure as hell do not. Why would we want to? If the asshole wants to leave the program, that's his choice."

"He stole your car."

"I want my car back, but the Marshals Service can worry about Cousin Dennis."

Taylor continued to scowl. His bruises were starting to show now. He was definitely going to have a couple of black eyes to go with that split lip. If they'd been at home, Will would have pulled him down to his lap and rubbed his head for him. Taylor reminded him of a cat, the way he liked being stroked and caressed. But here in his father's house, Will couldn't—

His internal reflections broke off. What kind of stupid thought was that? He couldn't what? Show sympathy? Show affection? Show love? To a man he was as good as married to?

"Hey." He rested a hand on Taylor's shoulder, giving him a gentle tug. "Lie down. I'll rub your head for you."

"Huh? No." Taylor looked genuinely startled. The flip side of Will's first reaction, because at home, Taylor wouldn't think twice about surrendering himself to Will's care.

"Yeah." Will gave him another tug. "I've been punched in the face. Don't try to tell me you don't feel like hell, because I know you do."

"I'm fine, Brandt." Taylor threw an instinctive look at the hallway down which Grant had disappeared.

Will tightened his grip. "I said come here."

After an uncertain moment, Taylor caved in, stretching out on the couch and resting his head in Will's lap. He closed his eyes with a little sigh.

Will gazed down at Taylor's battered face with a rush of tenderness. Blood crusted his nostrils and his lip was swelling. He looked both disreputable and defenseless.

"You'd better not be laughing at me," Taylor muttered, not opening his eyes.

"I'm laughing *with* you," Will assured him. He touched Taylor's soft, dark hair lightly, and Taylor shivered. "What we *should* do is stop laughing and take you into town to get someone at Urgent Care to take a look at you. You could have a concussion."

"I'm fine."

"Sure you are."

"I've been concussed a million times. I'd know if I was concussed."

"A million times," Will marveled. "Well, that explains a few things."

Taylor laughed.

Will's dad said from the doorway, "Clary says Dennis is on his own from here on out." Both Will and Taylor jumped. Taylor sat up straight and Will scooted over, both of them moving apart as fast as if they'd been caught with their pants down.

Bill studied them, opened his mouth, then turned away as the phone in the kitchen began to ring again.

After a strained moment, Taylor said, "I wonder what the story is on Cousin Dennis?"

"Why?"

"Just the way he freaked out today."

Will said carefully, "People freak out for different reasons. It doesn't always mean…"

"True."

"I guess it's reasonable somebody in Witness Protection would be jumpy."

"I guess."

"Do you have a different theory?"

Taylor moved his head in negation.

From the other room, Bill called, "Will, that was Jack Hardy at Mist Bend PD. They found your SUV."

Will rose and went into the kitchen. "That didn't take long. Where?"

"Parked behind the feed store on Main Street. The keys were left in the ignition. It looks like Cousin Dennis may have grabbed the CC Rider to Willow Creek."

"Well, he's out of your hair anyway," Will said.

"Looks that way. Jack says you can pick up your vehicle anytime. Why don't you ask Grant to give you a lift into Mist Bend?"

Will thought it over. Cousin Dennis had clearly left of his own free will, so there wasn't any reason for the police or sheriffs to hang onto Will's vehicle. He wasn't going to press charges and it wasn't like it was a crime scene. "I'll do that. Maybe I'll show Taylor around town. Buy him lunch."

His father's blue eyes met his. Bill's mouth twitched. "I'd say he earned lunch," he agreed.

"Hey," Will called to Taylor in the other room. "You feel like driving into town for some lunch? We can pick up my car."

"Sure," Taylor called back. "I'll just go put on a clean shirt."

Will went looking for Grant. He found him in the den watching Classic Global Wrestling. Grant must have seen Will out of the corner of his eye, but he didn't look away from the TV.

"The police in Mist Bend located my SUV," Will said. "You mind giving me and Taylor a lift into town?"

"Sure," Grant said. He pointed the remote at the TV and the screen flicked off.

Will studied his brother's profile. Not including the exchange in the kitchen, Grant had been polite but distant all morning. He had relaxed a little when their dad had started reminiscing about past fishing trips, but whatever rapport had been gained was lost the minute they got back to the house and found Taylor on the phone.

They needed to talk. Really talk. But Will wasn't sure what to say. What more *was* there to say really? Wasn't the ball kind of in Grant's court now? If Grant needed time to come to terms with learning Will was gay, okay. Talking wasn't going to speed the process any. Not that Will could see. Frankly he didn't want to talk to his kid brother about his relationship with Taylor anymore than he'd have wanted to talk about any other romantic relationship with him. The whole subject was uncomfortable.

But…it hurt. He loved Grant. He'd been delighted when he'd realized they were going to have this unexpected time together before Grant went overseas. Now it looked like his brother was going to spend his entire visit hiding out watching TV and sleeping.

"So…about five minutes?" Will said.

"I'm ready now," Grant said. "I'll meet you outside."

Will nodded and continued down the hall to his bedroom. Taylor was tucking a black flannel shirt into his jeans. He glanced up at Will's entrance.

"Everything okay?"

"Of course," Will replied.

Taylor eyed him a moment longer, and then finished dressing.

* * * * *

Taylor, not always the most sociable creature on God's green earth, made an effort on the twenty-minute trip to Mist Bend. The three of them were wedged in the front of Grant's Toyota pickup, with Will acting as a buffer in the middle. Taylor's lean thigh pressed against Will's, his hard shoulder pushed into Will's.

"Did you play football too, Grant?" Taylor asked.

"Yep." Grant replied curtly.

"He was All Stars in high school," Will said.

"Impressive," Taylor said.

"Big deal. You were voted Most Valuable Player how many years?"

"Yeah, but—" Will's words were cut off as Grant turned the CD player on full blast.

Gotta keep your head up and move along move along

Gotta keep your head calm and carry on carry on

Will reached over and turned the volume down to the non-head-exploding range.

Grant scowled, gaze still locked on the winding road.

"Lifehouse, right?" Will identified. A band and a song he was very familiar with after the long drive to Oregon. "Taylor likes them too."

Grant reached over and punched the button for a new CD. "Sorry. I'm actually kind of tired of them."

There was a short silence while the CD player noisily shuffled through its selections.

The Fray came on. Another of Taylor's favorites. Will opened his mouth, but he felt Taylor's elbow dig into his ribs.

Yeah, maybe not.

Taylor said, "What did you think of Cousin Dennis, Grant? Did you have any time to form an opinion?"

Grant shrugged. "He seemed okay. I didn't pay a lot of attention to him."

Will said, "Do you know what his story was? Did Pop say?"

Grant shook his head. "Something to do with getting on the wrong side of the owner of a private club in South Florida."

Will could practically hear the calculator whirring between Taylor's ears, but it didn't take a genius to work this out. South Florida had been a mob stomping ground since the days of Al Capone and Meyer Lansky. So it was pretty much what Will had figured. Cousin Dennis had got on the bad side of some good fellas.

Mist Bend looked just like Will remembered. Old houses and small family businesses. The area had been first settled in 1874. It had started out as a farming community, but its main industry these days was logging. There was little to convince the next generation to stay put and invest, and nothing to attract tourists. In Will's opinion, it was the perfect place to retire one day. Except now of course, his retirement plans would be contingent on what Taylor wanted.

He gave Taylor a sideways look. Meeting it, Taylor raised his eyebrows. And Will shook his head, smiling faintly.

Grant dropped them off in front of the police station on Bridge Street. It was a small, square brick building with bullet-proof windows, cement flower planters, and a flag pole positioned in the single square of lawn.

Taylor climbed out of the truck, then Will. He leaned into the cab. "I'm just going to say hi to Jack Hardy and grab my keys. Why don't you join us for a beer?"

"Thanks. I've got to get back," Grant said, looking straight ahead.

"To do what? Watch wrestling? Come on, Grant. You can spare time for one beer."

Grant faced him, his expression tight. "No, I can't, William."

"Suit yourself." Will slammed the cab door shut a lot harder than he had to.

Grant gunned the motor and roared away down the wide, mostly empty street. Will stared after him.

"Okay, I admit it," Taylor said, behind him. "I should have stayed home this trip. My being here is complicating the situation."

"The hell," Will exclaimed. And though he had privately thought the same thing before they left for Oregon, Grant's rude and mule-headed behavior had completely changed his mind. He turned on Taylor. "I want you here. You belong here."

"Sure," Taylor said. "But I just—"

"I don't. Come on."

Will led the way up the cement walk. Despite the bullet-proof glass, the entrance was an ordinary swinging glass door. He pushed through.

"Holy shit," said a heavy-set bald man of about thirty, rising from the desk in a glass fronted office. "Is that *the* Will Brandt?"

"Jack Hardy, is that you?" Will returned. "*You're* Chief of Police now? Didn't anyone else want the job?"

"No. Nobody else wanted the job. Why would they? It's a lousy job." Jack shook Will's hand.

"This is my partner, Taylor MacAllister." This time Will didn't care what interpretation Jack or anybody else put on *partner*. He was getting good and goddamned sick of worrying about how other people felt about his personal and private life. "Jack and I went to high school together about a hundred years ago."

"Nice to meet you, Jack." Taylor offered his hand.

"High school? We played *football* together. Took the Lumberjacks all the way to the state championships twice. Those were the days. Our current team's on a ten-game losing streak." Jack pointed to a series of framed photographs of the Mist Bend Lumberjacks in action. "This guy was the best quarterback we've had in twenty years." He shook Taylor's hand. "You another fed?"

"Used to be."

"We're flying solo now," Will said.

"No shit? You left the DSS?"

"We decided to go into business for ourselves. Security consulting."

"Security consulting? What's that entail?"

"Anything it needs to," Taylor said, and they all laughed.

"I hear that," Jack said. He handed Will's keys over. "Your vehicle's in the parking lot out back. Your dad said you're not pressing charges?"

"No. I forgot I told my cousin he could borrow my SUV if he needed to."

Jack guffawed. "Another one of the crazy Brandt cousins, is that the story?"

"That's the story."

"Have it your way." Jack's fair, plump face grew serious. "You know Jem Dooley is out?"

"Yeah. Seems he dropped by this morning to say hi."

"Anybody else and I'd say it was all bluster, but I'm not so sure about Jem. There was always something not quite right about that guy."

"He just got out of prison. It's hard to believe he'd risk going back this soon." Will asked Taylor, "What did you think of him?"

Taylor shrugged. "You don't have to be smart to be dangerous."

"I agree with your partner," Jack said. "I think Bill needs to keep an eye out for Jem."

* * * * *

"You want to grab some lunch now?" Will said, as he and Taylor walked out to the parking lot. "Or you want to see the sights?"

"Let's eat." Taylor's sunglasses hid most of the bruising around his eyes, but that split lip looked painful as hell. Will, still smarting in tender places from his collision with cardboard boxes and trash bags earlier in the week, felt a jab of sympathy.

"How about I take you to the place with the best selection of micro-brews in town? You can drown your sorrows."

"My only sorrow is Cousin Dennis is out of my reach."

"That's my boy." Will gave Taylor's shoulder a friendly bump with his own.

They drove to Tucker's Tavern, which was a rustic-looking building with a giant mill wheel out front and an old-fashioned painted tavern sign with a mermaid patting a dolphin. What the mermaid and dolphin had to do with anything, Will had never understood, but the sign had hung there as long as he could remember.

He held the front door for Taylor and followed him inside. It was dark and quiet, except for a radio playing from a back room. The tables and bar were empty. A tall, curvy young woman with waist-long brown hair was wiping down tables. She smiled hello. Then her expression changed. She dropped her yellow sponge. "Oh my God. *Will Brandt?*"

Will looked closer. And closer still. His jaw dropped. "I don't believe it!"

She threaded her way through the tables, and he met her halfway, picking her up. "Madonna Agnelli?"

She was grinning, shaking back that brown-honey waterfall of hair. "Not Agnelli anymore. I married Jim Tucker." She gestured to the bar and the taps. "Home sweet home."

"Jimmy Tucker. No way!"

Madonna laughed. "That's right. Your archrival, Will."

It occurred to Will that he was still hugging her, that her long, shapely legs were wrapped around him, that they were not in college anymore, and that his boyfriend was watching their reunion with a profound and utter silence.

"Jim's a lucky guy," Will said sincerely, setting her on her feet. "You look great." He turned to Taylor. "Taylor, this is…"

"The famous Madonna," Taylor supplied.

"Right," Will said hastily, not at all sure about that expression on Taylor's face. "Madonna, this is my partner, Taylor MacAllister."

"Nice to mee—" Madonna offered a hand. Her eyes widened. "What happened to *you*?"

"I walked into a tree." Taylor shook hands.

"You're bleeding again," Will observed, frowning at the scarlet trickling from Taylor's right nostril.

Taylor touched his nose. "Damn. I am. Do you have a washroom somewhere?"

Madonna pointed out the way and Taylor excused himself.

"That's one nice-looking man. Even with his face bashed in," Madonna observed, as Taylor moved out of earshot.

Will smiled faintly. "Yeah. He is."

She tilted her head thoughtfully. "So when you say he's your partner, do you mean…?"

"I do, yeah."

She laughed without bitterness and shook her head. "Well, that answers one question."

"I bet it answers more than one question."

Madonna laughed ruefully. "Maybe it does."

Will drew a deep breath, but he didn't begin to know how to explain, and it was too late anyway, really. "You really do look fantastic, Maddy," he said instead, lamely.

"Thanks. You're still pretty gorgeous yourself, William."

"I thought you moved to Chicago?"

"I did. But my dad died two years ago—"

"I'm sorry."

"Thanks. And my mom's getting on, so I moved home. And then Jim and I started seeing each other. We got married last fall."

"I don't know why that seems so…right. He was always crazy about you."

"What about you? You work for the Secret Service?"

"Diplomatic Security. Used to. We're freelance now." Will heard the restroom door swinging open again. Funny how he never lost his awareness of where Taylor was at any given moment.

"Oh wow." Madonna was smiling reminiscently. "And Grant's in the Marines?"

"Shipping out to Afghanistan this month."

"It's so crazy. Sometimes it seems like only yesterday we were going to football games and—"

"*More* football?" Taylor inquired, joining them again.

Madonna laughed. "I bet you've heard all you can take of Will's glory days. Will's one of our hometown heroes. Sit anywhere you want, you two. I'll bring over a couple of menus."

She went out to the kitchen. Will pulled out a chair at a table near the unlit fireplace. "Okay?" he asked Taylor.

"Fine."

"You sure?"

Taylor gave him a level look.

"You can't blame me for asking. The spontaneous hemorrhaging *is* a little distracting."

Taylor snorted and then put a careful hand to his nose. "Ow."

Madonna reappeared with menus. "What can I get you two to drink?"

"What have you got in the way of microbrews?" Taylor asked.

Madonna proceeded to extol the virtues of Oregon's top three micro-breweries: McMenamins, Deschutes, and Full Sail.

Taylor opted for McMenamins' Sleepy Hollow Nut Brown. Will went for Deschutes' Cascade Ale.

Madonna said to Will, "You know Jem Dooley is out?"

"Yep."

She nodded and withdrew. Taylor said, "She's not at all how I pictured her."

"How did you picture her?" Will was trying to wrap his brain around the idea of Taylor spending a minute's thought trying to visualize his old girlfriend.

"Blonde. Cheerleader. Not too bright."

Will spluttered, *"Not too bright?"*

Taylor shrugged. "She seems smart enough though. And nice. And I bet she liked camping."

Will laughed. "She did. She was a great little camper. Good kayaker too." He really had loved her. Still did in a funny way. His heart had flipped when he'd seen her standing there. But that was how he'd finally come to terms with being gay, because as much as he'd loved Madonna, as much as they had in common, he'd finally realized he was not going to be happy or satisfied with her. Or any woman. He gazed at Taylor across the table and felt such a wave of closeness and affinity to this man who was his partner in every sense of the word, it startled him.

The object of all this feeling was frowning over the menu. "No wonder I'm starving. I haven't had anything to eat since that damn chili last night."

"You need protein," Will said. "And iron. Order a burger." Closeness and affinity aside, the part-time vegetarianism drove him nuts.

"Hell."

Will glanced up.

Taylor was feeling for his cell phone. "Richard didn't call back."

"Bahrain is how many hours ahead? Ten? Eleven?"

"Eleven." Taylor checked his cell phone. "No. He didn't call."

He chewed worriedly on his lip, and Will said, "Look, if he doesn't call we'll find another way."

Taylor threw him an impatient look, but he put his phone away, and returned to scanning the menu. Probably worried they couldn't afford more than salads.

Madonna returned with their beers, they ordered their burgers, and sat for a few companionable minutes sipping their brews.

This was good. This was what he'd wanted on those occasions Will had pictured bringing Taylor up to Mist Bend. Just this. Just being together. Showing Taylor where he'd grown up. Sharing the things he'd never had anyone to share with before.

"Maybe we should pay Jem Dooley a visit," Taylor remarked.

"And we would do that why?"

"Be proactive. Head him off at the pass?"

"It might not be heading him off. It might be stirring him up."

"He came looking for your dad this morning."

Dooley had, and Will didn't like the thought of that, but things were not always what they seemed. That was something he'd learned from growing up with his dad. Over the years, more than one ex-con had shown up to thank Bill Brandt for changing or even saving his life.

Not that it was very likely Jem Dooley had showed up to pay his respects.

But he hadn't necessarily arrived to start a war either.

"You want to piss Pop off, hunting trouble with Jem Dooley would be the way."

Taylor lifted a shoulder. "I just think it would be better dealt with while we're all here."

That struck home with Will—not least because of Taylor's automatic and unconscious identifying with his family—but the assumption that trouble was inevitable was not incontrovertibly correct. "And that's another thought Pop would not appreciate. The idea that he couldn't take care of himself."

Madonna arrived with their burgers and they chatted for a few more minutes. When she walked away, Taylor said, "Did you notice she looks like the mermaid on the sign out front?"

Will inhaled his beer and started to cough.

CHAPTER SIX

As they stepped out onto the sidewalk outside Tucker's Tavern, Will was saying, "What would you like to do now? You want to see where they filmed *Ring of*—"

Taylor missed the rest of it, his attention caught by a glimpse of a broad-shouldered figure in a black leather jacket, vanishing into the Laundromat across the street. He stopped walking.

Will glanced back and stopped too. "What's up?"

Taylor started patting his pockets, miming someone who had misplaced their phone. Head down, so that his face could not be seen, he said, "Don't turn around. I think Mr. Black is in the Laundromat."

Will did not look around, but he sounded confused as he said, "Who?"

"The guy in the Porsche who was following us up the I-5." Taylor glanced back at the tavern door. He pointed at it and said, "Can you act like you're going to get your SUV and cut around to the back of that place?"

"Okay." Will still sounded confused, but was now businesslike. "Are you carrying?"

"No."

"He might be. So watch yourself."

"Roger." Taylor turned and strode back into Tucker's Tavern.

"Hi," Madonna said, looking up from clearing their table. "Did you forget something?"

"Just wanted to say that was a great burger." Taylor stared out the window at the street outside. No sign of his quarry.

"Oh. Thanks. Glad you liked it."

…thirteen…fourteen…fifteen…sixteen…

Taylor pulled out his phone. He threw a quick, absent, "See you next time," and walked out of the tavern again, looking down at the small screen. Then he glanced across the street, waved to an imaginary Will and sprinted across.

Will met him in the doorway of the Laundromat. "He's not in here."

"He didn't come out the front. I've been watching."

"I guess he could have slipped out the back before I got around the building."

Taylor looked past him to a couple of women folding laundry and a pregnant teen in a chair by the window, reading *Seventeen* magazine.

"I sure as hell didn't mistake him for anybody in here."

"Okay. Well." Will was watching him. "What do you want to do?"

Taylor ran a frustrated hand through his hair. He looked up and down the street. There were a couple of pickup trucks, a red Corolla, a green Volkswagen, and a Jeep. No Porsche. There were a few people, women in jeans and jackets, guys in ball caps and corduroy or plaid shirt coats. No burly, bearded dude in a black leather jacket.

"You want to look for him?" Will asked.

"How the hell could he disappear in under a minute?"

"He had to have seen that you made him. He must have gone straight through the Laundromat and out the back."

Taylor appreciated that Will did not question whether Mr. Black existed at all. Nice to know one of them was certain. Maybe he *was* starting to see things. "And went where?"

"Ducked into one of the businesses on either side?" Will said briskly, "Let's have a look for him."

But there was no sign of Mr. Black in the Realty office or the pet grooming service on either side of the Laundromat. There was no sign of him in the coffee house or hardware store on either side of those businesses either. There was no sign of Mr. Black anywhere.

"There's always the chance he lives up here," Will said as they walked back to the Land Cruiser. "Maybe this is his regular Laundromat. Maybe his boxers are tumbling around on Perma Press cycle right now."

Taylor made a scornful sound.

"I don't think so either," Will agreed. "But I also don't see why anyone would be tailing us."

Will was right. It didn't make sense. It wasn't like they were working any sensitive or potentially dangerous cases. They weren't working any cases at all.

"I agree."

"So?"

"What about Gretchen Hart?" Taylor threw it out there, though he didn't really buy into the theory.

"She's had two years to set an investigator on our trail. Why would she wait until now?"

"Maybe she forgot about us until she saw you again?"

"Forgetting about us for two years doesn't jibe with instantly putting someone on our tail."

"True. I was going to get Euphonia to run his plates through the DMV, but I got sidetracked with everything else going on."

"You were going to call in a favor to run his plates?" Will looked surprised.

"Yes."

"You're that spooked?"

A little irritably, Taylor said, "I don't know if I'm spooked, but yeah, it bothers me to think this guy is following us for reasons unknown."

"You don't think there's any chance he recognized you from an old case? Or maybe from somewhere else?"

He couldn't quite read Will's expression. Taylor said cautiously, "Somewhere else *where*?"

"I don't know. Maybe socially or something?" Will's expression was even more indecipherable, given that he was, apparently, trying to be tactful.

"What does that mean?"

"Nothing. You're the first to admit you've had an active social life."

"Active social life? What is that, code for *fucked around*?"

"Hey." Will looked meaningfully—warningly—at the not entirely empty street. "I didn't realize this was suddenly a sensitive subject. I only mean—"

"I know exactly what you mean, Brandt. And no, I didn't fu-ool around so much that I wouldn't remember that guy."

"This isn't about you, MacAllister. I'm trying to think of other possibilities for someone recognizing us. I thought that was the object of this discussion."

Well, hell. Will was absolutely right. Maybe he was a little oversensitive right now. It was hard to erase the image of Will's old girlfriend with her *legs wrapped around him*, for chrissake, as she renewed their acquaintanceship.

Into his distracted silence, Will asked, "What now? What next?"

"I don't know. Maybe I *am* seeing things. I guess there could be more than one guy in a black leather jacket walking around."

"True."

Will was nothing if not honest. Taylor sighed. "What do you want to do?"

"Up to you. You want to head back to the house?"

Taylor thought of Grant, who winced practically every time he looked at him, and of Bill who, though welcoming, was still Will's dad and kinda, sorta, an inhibiting presence.

No. He did not want to go back to the house. He wanted to spend a little quiet time with Will where no one was going to talk about high school or football or the births, marriages, and deaths of people Taylor did not—and did not particularly *want*—to know.

He shook his head.

"Okay. You've now pretty much seen the sights," Will said, studying him. "We could check what's playing at the theater. You want to catch a matinee?"

"No. I don't want to catch a matinee."

"Okay. Well." Will was looking at him in a humoring kind of way. "Whatever you want. You choose, MacAllister."

"Is there a motel around here?"

"Well, there's the Black Be—" Will broke off. "A motel?"

"Yes. A motel. We haven't…" Taylor lowered his voice as they passed an elderly couple, "*been together* in two weeks."

His heart sank at the Does Not Compute look he was getting from his partner. Honestly? Was this only bothering him? How could that be? How could it not matter to Will?

But then it got worse.

"*Oh.*" Will actually blushed. Blushed! Jesus. They had to get out of Mayberry before Will turned straight again. Failing that, they had to go somewhere and fuck before Taylor's head exploded. Either head. Both heads. Take your pick. He was about as frustrated as he'd ever been in his adult life.

And dismayed that it seemed to be all his problem.

They reached the Land Cruiser and climbed inside. Will had still not said anything since that startled, *Oh.*

Taylor said, trying to sound calm and reasonable, but knowing he was failing miserably, "Brandt, Jesus. Do I have to beg? Can we *please* go somewhere and fuck?"

Will looked at him in surprise. "Hell yeah, we're going somewhere," he assured Taylor. "I'm just trying to think if there's a nicer place to take you."

Taylor started to laugh, largely with relief. For one alarming moment he'd wondered. "Not worried about the décor, Brandt. Seriously. Just find us some place where no one you knew from the good old days is going to walk in on us."

"The Black Bear Inn it is," Will said, turning the key in the ignition. As they pulled away from the curb, he said, "For the record, those weren't the good old days. These days with you, these are the good old days. Right now."

Taylor wanted to make some joke, say something to lighten the moment, but he couldn't. It meant a lot to hear Will say it. Especially here in this Will Brandt alternate universe he found himself in.

Will reached over and squeezed his thigh. He was smiling faintly.

* * * * *

A large faded statue of a black bear defended the driveway entrance to the Black Bear Inn. One of the statue's eyes had been scratched out, whether by time or teenagers, giving the bear's expression a half-blind, baleful cast.

There were two cars in the motel parking lot. A Forest Service green pickup and a late model silver sedan.

"Here's a scary thing," Will said, pulling up beneath the motel archway. "I think I recognize those vehicles."

"That *is* scary." Taylor opened the door and jumped out. "I've got this."

There followed a brief but mildly embarrassing business exchange at the front desk with a pimple-faced youth, and then Taylor climbed back into the SUV. He held the plastic card key up. "This entitles us to a lovely Continental breakfast, which I got to examine firsthand because this morning's is still sitting out on the counter."

Will shuddered.

"We're around the back. Don't run over any hobos."

"I knew this wasn't a five-star place, but I don't remember it being such a dump." Will pulled slowly around the L-shaped, one-story building. There were more cars parked behind the motel, most of them partially concealed by the wildly overgrown myrtlewood trees.

"I'm guessing the tourist trade is not how this place stays in business?"

"There is no tourist trade up here."

Will parked far beneath the boughs of the Oregon-myrtle and they walked across the cracked asphalt lot to the line of discolored blue doors. A couple of rooms down, a curtain twitched and went still.

"Here we are," Taylor said, sliding the key.

"Don't remind me," Will muttered, but his hand was a warm and welcome weight, resting in the small of Taylor's back.

The door opened to the scent of stale cigarette smoke, bleached linens, and Lysol. The lights were dim, but that was probably a blessing. Taylor had a vague impression of furniture made from plywood and orange-and-brown curtains and bedspreads. There was a faded square over the king-sized bed where a framed picture had once hung. The fact that the picture had possibly been stolen or defaced was probably the most interesting thing about the room.

The bed offered a coin-operated massage.

"Is this where you used to bring Madonna when you'd come home from college?" Taylor couldn't stop staring at the bed. There was a wrinkle across the shiny polyester spread. He glanced at Will.

Will made a face. "A couple of times, yeah."

"I gotta say. I'm both depressed and weirdly turned on by that."

Will gave a funny laugh. Their eyes met. Will grabbed Taylor's shirt and pulled him in for an unexpectedly deep and hungry kiss.

He tasted like Cascade Ale and charbroiled hamburger and himself. He tasted like home. Like everything worth having. It just didn't matter that they were standing in a seedy, run down motel. They could have been standing in a live volcano, for all Taylor cared. Will's firm mouth pushed confidently, possessively onto Taylor's, and Taylor closed his eyes and leaned into that kiss. Until Will, kisses had not meant that much to him. Just a polite preliminary. Hors d'oeuvres before dinner. But he loved to be kissed by Will, actually longed for Will's kisses.

Will groaned, the sound so heartfelt, so resounding that they both started to laugh. That was sweet too, trying to maintain contact as they shared that amused understanding.

Will pulled away enough to say, "I don't know what it is about being up here, but every time I look at you I want to throw you on your belly and fuck the daylights out of you."

Taylor snickered at the *daylights out of you* comment, but it was reassuring to hear, given that he felt the same way. "Okay," he said.

"Okay?" Will's blue eyes were hopeful but also doubtful. "It's not my turn."

They had always been respectful in their taking turns topping each other—they both liked being in control, running the show—but since striking out on their own, they were scrupulous about it. It seemed vital to their survival to preserve the balance of power between them, both inside and outside the bedroom.

"I don't mind," Taylor said, which wasn't exactly true and sounded lukewarm even to his own ears. He did want, felt the need, to possess Will. Badly. But he also wanted to give Will whatever he wanted, whatever would make Will value what they had above anything else he'd known. So he said softly, deliberately, "I want you to, Will. I think I need it."

Will's eyes widened and then went dark with something that was a mix of excitement and passion. He made another of those inarticulate sounds from deep in his chest, something between a groan and a growl. "Yeah? You *need* it?"

Taylor nodded.

Will's hands slid down Taylor's back, closing on his ass, fingers digging through the denim as he snugged Taylor's crotch to his own. Beneath the denim, Will's erection was huge. Or maybe that was his own because there was no question that it was a total turn on to see how worked up Will was getting at the idea of his complete submission. Not that Taylor didn't do his fair share of submitting, because he did. In fact, he didn't find it particularly complicated or difficult the way Will did. Only the one time, the very first time, that time in the High Sierras hot spring, had submitting to Will freaked him out.

But something about this felt different. It wasn't like he'd never said he needed Will to fuck him before. So what *was* so different here? What did Will think he was saying? What *was* he saying?

"I need you..." Didn't that go without saying? For the first time it occurred to Taylor that maybe his sexual expertise was more of a hindrance than a help, that maybe Will—occasionally—felt performance pressure? He whispered, "Whatever you want. Tell me. Show me how..." The idea of Will intimidated by anything was ridiculous and yet, no question Will was aroused by this, by Taylor asking him to take complete charge.

Will's arms locked around him, hefting him up—the image of Madonna wrapping her legs around Will flashed into Taylor's brain—and transporting him to the bed. They fell onto it. The bed knocked against the wall, and one of the mattress springs went with a resounding *boing*. Comical, but neither of them was laughing. In fact, they were both breathing hard, watching each other.

Will reached out to gently touch the bruising around Taylor's right eye. Taylor lowered his lashes. Will's fingertips feathered over his skin, a touch that seemed to whisper apology as well as tenderness.

There was a knock on the door.

Will's hand froze.

Taylor's eyes flew open. "No way."

"Housekeeping?" Will suggested. "A preemptive strike?"

"You think they have *housekeeping* here?"

The knocking came again. Quiet. Almost furtive.

Will rose from the bed, went to the window, opened the curtains a centimeter and looked out. The tension left his body. "You're not going to believe this." He glanced back at Taylor. "It's Cousin Dennis."

"*What?* He's *here*?" Taylor was off the bed and moving toward the door. "I'm going to kill him myself."

Will intercepted. "Let's hear what he has to say." He added, "Then I'll kill him for you."

CHAPTER SEVEN

"I panicked," Dennis said. "I'm sorry. It's not my fault. I saw that truck racing down the hill and I thought they were coming for me."

"Then you're an idiot," Taylor replied. "I told you at the time nobody working for the mob drives a beat-up pickup."

"Okay, look," Will began again, and as before, the other two talked right over him.

"Mob? How do you know the mob is looking for me?" Dennis stared at Taylor in alarm. Not exactly what you'd call a Fulbright Scholar, Cousin Dennis.

"Come off it," Taylor scoffed. "I sincerely doubt you've got links to, or evidence pertaining to terrorism or national security."

Will said, "Why don't we continue this—"

"And why the hell would you hit me?" Taylor added.

"I didn't realize it was you," Dennis said, "until I'd already knocked you out."

"The hell you didn't. The dogs were with me, I was calling to you. You must have heard the truck drive away."

"I told you, I *panicked.*"

"Yeah, but I don't believe you," Taylor said.

Surprised, Will said to Taylor, "What do you think was going on?"

"I don't know." Taylor glared at Dennis who shifted nervously and looked at Will. "Oh, I believe he was scared. I believe he panicked, yes. He was sure the Dooleys had come for him. But why? Why was he so sure? Nobody knows where he is." He looked at Dennis. "Right?"

"How do I know?" Dennis said. "I know they're looking for me."

"Maybe he's seen too many movies," Will said. "All I know is, we can't stand around here talking about it. Let's get back to the house. Pop needs to let his pals in the Marshals Service know that Dennis is back."

It was disappointing though. Disappointing and frustrating. Frustrating to the point of physical pain. And if Will found it painful, Taylor must be tied up in knots. Just what Will did not want, could not afford. Taylor feeling neglected and unsatisfied. Which he clearly already did. One more thing to worry about.

They left the card key on the table as they exited the room and walked out to the parking lot. They climbed into Will's Land Cruiser. With perfect timing, Emmylou Harris launched into "Together Again."

"I thought you got on the CC Rider." Taylor was clearly not going to let this go, and Will mentally braced for a very long drive.

"I snuck off again," Dennis said, sounding pleased with himself.

"Why?"

"Because..."

"Exactly," Taylor said dryly. Though exactly *what*, Will wasn't clear.

Dennis leaned forward between the two front seats. "Look, I'm not a-a secret agent. I'm not used to life on the run."

"So far it's been a morning on the run."

Will threw Taylor a look, but Taylor ignored him.

"Did you work for the Russian mob?"

"Me?" Dennis sounded genuinely bewildered. "Of course not."

"That's quite a leap," Will said to Taylor.

"The Russian mafia has taken over a lot of the criminal activity on the Gulf Coast."

"Is that true?"

Taylor nodded. To Dennis, he said, "Well?"

"Well, what? I never worked for the Russian mob. I've never worked for any Russians. Ever."

"Did you make any phone calls to anyone this morning?"

"Of course not! I'm not *crazy*."

"Where are you going with this?" Will asked.

"I don't like coincidences."

"What coincidences?"

"You run into Gretchen Hart who used to work for a Russian mobster and less than twenty-four hours later we pick up a tail. We lose the tail but then we run into Cousin Dennis here who just happens to be running from trouble in South Florida, and now suddenly the tail is back."

"Okay, slow down," Will said. "First of all, we have no proof that anyone was or is tailing us. Secondly, that would be too big of a coincidence. That somehow Dennis is connected to someone in the Russian mob who would have it in for us? Who?"

"I don't know, but I don't like this."

"What is it you don't like?"

Taylor threw Dennis a cold look. "Well, one thing I don't like is getting my nose broken."

"Your nose isn't broken," Will said. "Believe me, if your nose was broken, you'd know it."

"I did not call anyone," Dennis said. "I don't know anyone in the Russian mob to call."

Taylor ignored that. "What did you hit me with?"

Dennis looked uncomfortable. "I, uh, found a broken-off tree branch to defend myself with."

"Nice." Taylor stared straight ahead.

Will was angry about the tree branch himself. It wasn't that difficult to kill someone if you hit them hard enough in the wrong spot.

Dennis rambled on, "I don't have anyone I could call even if I wanted to. That's the point. That's why I'm back. I didn't know what to do. I realized I wasn't going to be able to make it on my own. I decided to lay low somewhere, but then I saw you two show up at the motel and I realized my best bet was to stay in the program. So I ran down and knocked on your door." He added, "I thought you were looking for me. But I guess you were just—"

Out of the corner of his eye, Will saw Taylor's forearm recoil. The back of his fist connected with Dennis's face with machine-like precision. Dennis howled and fell back.

"I knew that was coming." Will muttered.

"What was *that* for?" Dennis protested, cupping his nose.

"Nervous twitch," Taylor said, gazing out the side window as the town of Mist Bend grew smaller and smaller behind them.

* * * * *

When they arrived back at the house, Will's dad greeted his runaway houseguest without particular joy, and retreated to the kitchen to once more call Clary Bennett at the U.S. Marshals Service.

Dennis, still cupping his nose, retreated to the loft. Grant was in the den watching television again.

"You want to take a walk?" Will asked Taylor. He felt obliged to ask, although the drive and his various worries had resolved his own state of arousal. He'd been up since four, and what he most wanted was a nap. A nap with Taylor would be especially nice, but that was liable to get them both—certainly Taylor—wound up, and they had enough trouble with that already.

Taylor glanced at the clock on the bookshelf. "I'm going to try to get hold of the DMV before Euphonia leaves for the day."

"If you feel like it's important, okay. I'm going to close my eyes for half an hour."

Taylor nodded, already punching in the numbers on his cell phone.

Will headed for his bedroom. Passing the den, he spotted Grant sacked out in one of the large leather chairs, mouth agape, snoring in front of the TV. Will paused in the doorway. Grant looked like such a kid, sprawled there. It made Will's chest ache. The next time he saw Grant, Grant would no longer be a boy. The service would change him. It would change him in good ways, but... Will was going to miss this impulsive, hot-headed, sometimes irresponsible, but always good-hearted young goof. It was crazy they were wasting this time together. The whole reason Will had made this trip was to spend time with Grant. Why did Grant have to turn it into a choice between himself and Taylor?

Will hesitated, then reluctantly continued to his room.

The house had a quiet, peaceful, familiar feel to it. It reminded him of Saturday and Sunday afternoons growing up.

And the thought of Taylor here, right down the hall, made it even better. Will pulled off his boots, stretched out on his bed and was asleep in seconds.

When he opened his eyes again the room was in shadow. He could smell woodsmoke from the fireplace in the front room, and the smell of home cooking. He listened, but the only voices came from the television set in the den.

He got up, splashed water on his face, and went into the kitchen. His father was lighting the burner beneath a kettle of peeled potatoes.

"Where's Taylor?"

"I think he took the dogs for a walk."

"Taylor did?"

His father looked up. "Any reason he shouldn't?"

"No. Just that Nature and Taylor don't get along."

Bill smiled faintly. "Maybe we're winning him over. You could give him a shout. We're going to eat before too long."

Will nodded. He glanced back at the living room, but there was no one around. Grant had still been sleeping in the den when he walked past. "Grant isn't taking this well," he said.

"Your brother has to work this one out for himself."

Not exactly what Will had been hoping for.

He mulled it over and said resolutely, "You haven't said. What do *you* think?"

Bill, placing trout in an iron skillet, looked up. "About what?"

"About MacAllister. Taylor."

"He seems like a good kid."

"Kid." Will snorted.

"You're all kids to me." Bill went back to arranging the fish, but he must have felt the weight of Will's gaze. He said slowly, "I think he's a straight shooter, son. He won't let you down. Not if he's still standing."

Will thought about that *still standing* comment as he crossed the meadow to where he spotted Taylor standing motionless, watching a Cooper's hawk hunting.

His dad had unknowingly zeroed right in on Will's deepest fear. That reckless streak of Taylor's, that apparent, terrifying belief that he was impervious to harm, despite plenty of evidence to the contrary.

But he wasn't forgetting that conversation with Taylor the night before they'd left Ventura. Whatever his private anxieties—the fear that his happiness was tied to the safety and well-being of someone who didn't give a damn about his own safety and well-being—he could not afford to let any of that show. They could not have a repeat of Paris. He could not treat Taylor any differently on the job than he had when they'd first been partnered.

Or he would lose him.

As much as Taylor loved him, and Will didn't doubt that for a second, he saw now that this was Taylor's line in the sand. Why it should be so, he didn't know, but he had seen it on Taylor's face in Paris. And he'd heard it in his voice the other night.

Riley came tearing across the meadow toward him, followed by Roxie. Taylor turned, and seeing Will, smiled and started back to meet him.

"Enjoying yourself?" Will greeted him. "Sorry for sacking out like that. I must be getting old."

Taylor shrugged in a *doesn't matter* gesture, kept walking till he was face to face with Will, and Will's arms closed around him automatically. Taylor fastened his mouth on Will's, wrapped his arms around Will's shoulders. Will held him hard, absorbing all that warmth and energy and strength in one wiry, lithe body, enjoying the aggressive press of Taylor's cool mouth on his.

They broke the kiss, smiling.

"And sorry for the Black Bear Inn," Will said, holding him still tighter.

Taylor laughed. "It could have been worse. It could have been four minutes later, and then I *would* have killed Cousin Dennis."

"Pop says the marshals will be extracting Dennis on Sunday."

Taylor nodded absently, stepping back, and Will let him go reluctantly. "I got hold of Euphonia at the DMV."

"Oh yeah?"

"The black Porsche is registered to a Stuart Schwierskott. He's a private investigator. He works for Schwierskott & Associate. He's the associate. His old man owns the company."

Will took a moment to digest this. "Not a coincidence then. He was following us."

"Yep."

"And you did see him going into the Laundromat."

"Yep."

"I think we need to pay Schwierskott and his associate a visit next week."

"Yep."

They started back to the house, the dogs racing ahead. "I wonder who the hell hired them." Will said.

Taylor shook his head.

"And who the hell conducts surveillance in a Porsche?"

"A graduate of the *Magnum PI* School of Investigation?"

"I thought Magnum drove a Ferrari."

"Did he? I don't remember."

Will glanced at him. "Hey. I know we said three or four days up here, but since we're all here, Pop wants to have a Thanksgiving dinner on Sunday. Do you mind staying till Monday?"

"Nah. It's fine."

"Have I told you lately what a good boyfriend you turned out to be?"

Taylor grinned lazily. "Better than David Bradley?"

"He's not even in your weight division, sweetheart."

Taylor laughed. "Sure."

Dinner was pan-fried trout, mashed potatoes, and roasted vegetables. A staple when Will was growing up. Not that his dad had been home often to cook meals, but when he did cook, it was usually some kind of fish and vegetables. Or chili. Or lasagna. Will had learned to cook early. He didn't get much opportunity these days, but he enjoyed cooking. He enjoyed cooking for Taylor when he wasn't on one of his vegetarian streaks.

He was obscurely flattered to see Taylor eating heartily at his dad's table. Of course, Taylor usually ate like a horse. He had to fuel all that nervous energy. He had been cautious about the chili though, so it was nice to see him tucking in.

They were all eating heartily; maybe that was partly to avoid dinner table conversation. Cousin Dennis put away nearly as much food as Grant, and Grant was apparently preparing for a famine. Which wasn't far from the reality.

In an effort to reach out to his brother, Will started talking about his own tour of duty in Iraq. "The best meal was always midrats. That's where most of the socializing takes place. You've got the first crew coming off shift and the second crew coming on. It's not just that it's a hot meal—although when you're cold, tired, and being shot at, that does matter—it's also the camaraderie."

Grant said, "I think they cut midrats in Afghanistan because we're supposed to be winding down our presence there."

"Is that true? What total bullshit," Will said, and Grant nodded in complete accord. For a moment it was like old times.

Bill put in, "Food in the Corps is never just about food."

Will said, "True."

"I remember my first Marine Corps Birthday in Nam. We'd just come off the Hải Vân Pass and I was five days shy of my first year in the Corps and a whopping one month in country. We were living off two C-Rats a day and I don't recall ever getting a hot meal out there both times we were on the hill. But I do remember the 10th. It was just after noon and a lone CH-46 came flying in low and landed. A work party unloaded a small bunch of cases, and then down the ramp comes a cook in white trousers and green T-shirt, wheeling a rickety old mess hall cart with a cake on it. He just missed getting stuck in that damned red clay. We got the word to line up, and the cook started cutting pieces of cake no thicker than a slice of Wonder Bread. Every single Marine got a piece. And we each got two beers and a soda."

Grant was grinning.

Dennis said, "Sounds pretty miserable."

"Not at all," Bill replied, eyeing him without favor. "It's the essence of being a Marine. And the essence of being a Marine is what we celebrate every November 10th. Marines are the only fighting force in the world that stops a war to have a beer and wish each other a Happy Birthday."

Will laughed. "I guess the Continental Marines passed around the flagons of rum outside Philadelphia in 1776?"

"I wouldn't be surprised."

"If you're a global security firm, I guess there's a possibility you could be working out of Iraq or some other international hot spot one day?" Dennis asked.

Taylor's gaze met Will's.

"Now there's a question," Taylor said.

"I guess anything's possible," Will said evenly.

After dinner Bill suggested cards. They cleared the dishes and then sat down again at the dining room table for a game of poker. Now *that* brought back a lot of memories. Good memories.

He knew his father and brother's strategies as well as he knew his own. The real challenge came from Dennis who turned out to be quite a card sharp.

Taylor, on the other hand, was a steady but usually unlucky card player. Surprising, given how Machiavellian his thought processes could be. But no. He did not have a poker face and he did not have a poker mind.

They whiled away a relaxing and harmonious hour and then, while Bill was shuffling the next hand, Will rose.

"You want another beer?" he asked Taylor.

"Sure."

"Anybody else?"

"I guess I'll have another," Dennis chimed in. He was in a jovial mood as his stash of Honey Nut Cheerios mounted steadily.

"You'll have to get it from the fridge downstairs in the garage," Bill said. "We already drank everything upstairs at dinner."

"There isn't any downstairs either," Grant said.

Bill stared at him. "There was still a twelve-pack down there yesterday."

Grant shrugged.

"You drank the last of the beer and you didn't say a word," Bill said slowly, as though this were beyond human comprehension.

Grant's expression grew defensive. "I didn't know it was the last beer in the house."

"You damn well know you're supposed to check whether it's the last beer or not. That rule hasn't changed since you lived here."

"We were in town today, we could have picked up a couple of cases." Will caught Taylor's eye and realized too late that comment really wasn't helping.

Grant exploded. "I suppose *you* never forgot and drank the last beer, Will?"

"Not once I was your age."

"Yeah, I know, William. You're perfect in every way! Except for the fact you like to su—"

"*Grant,*" his father said in a voice the Brandt boys had only rarely heard growing up.

Grant didn't finish the thought. He glared at Taylor.

"Except for the fact I like to do what?" Will asked.

Grant was still glowering at Taylor as though this was where the real battle lay.

Will repeated quietly, "Except for the fact that I like to do what, Grant?"

Taylor gazed back at Grant calmly. He put his cards face down on the table. "Why don't you and I go on a beer run, Grant?" he asked.

"I wouldn't go anywhere with *you,*" Grant shot back.

"You're over the limit. You're sure as hell not driving yourself," Bill said.

"Can I take your car?" Taylor asked Will.

"Anything I have is yours," Will said. Including his jerk-ass brother, and if that sounded like a declaration, everybody could just get used to it. He got up, got his keys from his jacket hanging on the rack near the front door. He tossed his keys to Taylor.

Grant looked from Will to Taylor. "I said I'm not going!"

"Yeah, you are," Will said. "You drank the last beer, you need to replace it."

"I don't need to replace it tonight. And I don't need you tel—"

"Yeah. You do," Bill said with finality.

Grant stared at his father. He swallowed.

"Don't worry," Taylor said. "I won't bite."

Will knew that sardonic curve of Taylor's mouth, that not-quite-smile, and as furious as he was, he felt a flicker of sympathy for his brother.

Possibly he wasn't the only one, because as Taylor gestured politely for Grant to precede him, Cousin Dennis said, "Uh oh."

CHAPTER EIGHT

Grant buckled himself in with the air of someone about to take a trip to outer space.

"I think I remember the way," Taylor said. "But if I miss the turnoff, tell me."

Nothing.

Not that Taylor expected anything. He was only one of a number of things Grant was mad about, but he provided the focus for all that resentment and frustration. He understood that. But in order to move forward... well, they had to move forward.

He put the Land Cruiser into drive, the tires crunched over sand and stone and they bumped their way onto the dirt driveway.

The moon over the mountains and pine trees was ridiculously large and bright. He could practically see every crater and dry lake in its silver face. The stars glittered like glass shards in the cold, black night.

"You don't see stars like this in the city," Taylor commented.

"I know. I went to college in Portland. I'm not some dumb hick."

"I don't think you're a dumb hick. I grew up in Los Angeles where there's too much light even at nighttime to really see the stars."

Grant folded his arms across his chest.

Taylor chewed the inside of his cheek, thinking it over. He had to handle this right.

How old was Grant? Twenty-four? Twenty-five? Not exactly a boy. But not exactly a man either. Younger than either Taylor or Will had been at that age. At twenty-five Will had already graduated from college and was in the Marine Corps. Whereas Grant, from what Taylor knew, was a little bit of a goof-off, a little bit of a screw-up. He had waited a couple of years to enroll in college, hadn't done so hot, and was only now finally following family tradition and joining the Marines. The Marines would be good for him.

In the meantime…Grant had always looked up to Will, always admired him, and had always fallen short of the example Will set. What a pain in the ass to spend your life being compared to Hometown Hero William Brandt.

That was the first point of resentment.

The second point would be…your idolized older brother, the afore-mentioned Hometown Hero William Brandt, whom you haven't seen in a year, finally returns for a visit and drags along his new significant other. So instead of getting to spend undisturbed quality time, the last chance you'll have to spend this time for—maybe—ever, you have to watch your brother catering to this stranger who also happens to be…

Point three. A cocksucker. Or words to that effect.

There were a couple of ways Taylor could do this. If they had more time, he'd have opted for diplomacy. He hadn't joined the DSS for nothing. But the Brandt brothers did not have time. They had less than forty-eight hours to sort it out.

Taylor yanked the wheel, pulling over to the side of the road. The car bumped over rough ground onto the narrow shoulder, and rolled to a stop. He cut the engine and turned to Grant who, even in the enveloping wood-land darkness, he could feel watching him warily.

Taylor said, "You have something you want to say to me?"

"No, sir." Funny how disrespectful "sir" could sound, depending on the tone and the expression.

"Sure you do," Taylor said easily. "Let's hear it."

Grant unsnapped his seatbelt, shoved open his door and got out. "I'll walk back," he said, and slammed shut the door with all his force.

"Shit." Taylor undid his seatbelt and opened the driver's door. The night air was very cold and rich with the spicy scent of pine and earth.

He followed Grant who was moving fast, fueled by rage, and already several yards away. Grant's compact silhouette stomped up the steep in-cline. Taylor loped after him.

"Do I really scare you that much?"

Grant rounded on him. "*You* don't scare me at all."

"Then why are you running away?"

"Because Will won't like it when I kick your skinny ass from here to Portland."

Taylor chuckled.

"You think that's *funny*?"

He did, yeah. And the offended note in Grant's voice struck him as even funnier, but Taylor didn't want to escalate this any higher than necessary.

"Kind of. Don't you? What are we really fighting about?"

"We're not fighting. And we won't fight so long as you stay the fuck away from me."

"Only the problem is, we're family now. So I can only stay so far the fuck away from you."

"You're not family! You're just Will's…friend. He's not going to— you're not going to be here forever."

Ouch. Would it have been different for David Bradley? Taylor had to wonder. Bradley's military background, even his size and looks, would probably have been more palatable to Grant.

"I wouldn't bet on that. Why don't you just tell me what the problem is."

He could feel anger and frustration coming off Grant in waves. "You *know* what the problem is."

"Sure. I have a pretty good idea, but why don't we get it out in the open." Taylor gestured at the towering trees and moonlit mountains. "It doesn't get more open than this, right?"

He could feel Grant's inward struggle. At last, Grant spat out, "You're a queer."

"I don't like that word, but yep. I'm gay. And you have a problem with that."

"I don't give a fuck what you are," Grant said. "I don't care about *you*. I care about Will."

"I understand that. But Will is who he is. He didn't become gay for me. I didn't make him gay." Taylor's sense of humor sparked back into life—did Grant think he'd forced Will to watch musicals? Eat quiche?—but he squelched it. This was serious because this angry young man was Will's little brother and his feelings and opinions mattered to Will. Therefore they needed to matter to Taylor.

"He was never queer before."

"He's been queer for as long as I've known him."

Grant made a sound of fury and launched himself at Taylor.

Taylor was ready. Mostly. He had known from the minute he forced Grant to go with him, this was probably going to happen. In fact, he had been pushing Grant into it. Even so, he'd had a long and exhausting day, and as Grant piled into him like a young bull charging a red cape, he felt a flicker of alarm.

He had underestimated his own weariness and stiffness. He had also underestimated Grant, who had been taught to fight by Will.

Grant tackled him low, burying his head in Taylor's gut, wrapping his arms around Taylor's knees, and Taylor, who relied on kicks and footwork to avoid getting thrown to the ground where his lack of weight was a dangerous liability, couldn't maneuver. The wind was knocked out of him and he went down hard in the damp earth with Grant on top.

Worst case scenario. Thirty seconds in and he was about to be pinned in a double leg takedown his own sister could have avoided.

Instinct and adrenaline saved him. That and Grant's unsportsmanlike attempt to knee him in the balls. Possibly a subconscious wish to neuter him, or maybe not subconscious, but Grant's shift allowed Taylor to twist and bring his own knees up. He used his left forearm to trap both of Grant's in an arm bar. That left his right hand free. Taylor swiveled, grappling under Grant's legs, and throwing his left leg behind Grant's neck. He was trying to pin Grant face down, but Grant knew that move and yanked out, rolling away to his knees.

Taylor let his own momentum carry him to his feet, and he scrambled ungracefully up. Standing, he was no longer vulnerable. He faced Grant who was upright again as well.

He needed to prevail here. It was that simple. Partly because he would not be able to live down the embarrassment of pushing for a fight he couldn't win. Partly because with a young guy like Grant, winning was nine-tenths of the law. The law that said Might Makes Right. But he had to do it without seriously hurting Grant—and without letting Grant seriously hurt him. Because Will wouldn't forgive either of them for seriously harming the other.

Now aware of his own limitations, Taylor waited, breathing hard, for Grant to charge back in—which he did, still too angry to be cautious, throwing a powerful right punch that would have taken out a rib or a lung had it connected. Yeah, that power strike was straight out of the Will Brandt book of hand-to-hand combat. Taylor deflected, grabbed Grant's lapel and hauled him sideways while delivering a hard kick to the inner knee area of Grant's weight bearing leg. He was careful not to take out Grant's knee, but even so the strength and speed of that blow should have brought Grant down.

No such luck.

Oh, Grant was hurting, limping, but he was still on his feet, still looking for a way past Taylor's defenses.

"Come on, Kwai Chang," Grant jeered. "What else have you got?"

It was the Kwai Chang comment that did it. It sounded exactly like Will, and Taylor started to laugh, albeit breathlessly. "You little shit. Why do we have to do this? Will is *exactly* the same person you loved and respected two days ago. He hasn't changed."

"You don't get to tell me what to think." Grant crowded in on him, and Taylor realized the kid was shrewdly trying to maneuver him onto the wet grass where his footing would again be precarious.

Taylor's aggravation bubbled over. "I'm not telling you what to think. I'm pointing out what oughta be obvious even to a boneheaded jarhead like you. As far as you and Will are concerned, nothing has changed. Nothing will ever change unless *you* change it."

"Things are already different if *you're* going to be around all the time."

That note of childish grievance said it all. This was exactly what Taylor had thought, and the reason he had thought it, was he too had been the youngest kid in a family where failure was not an option and most attention and affection had come from his two older siblings. So yes, he understood the instinctive fear of being supplanted. And it would be worse for Grant.

With a woman, a girlfriend or wife like Madonna, there would be clearly defined roles and parameters. But another man…

"Sorry. I'm not going anywhere," Taylor told him. "Will and I are partners in every respect. But I'm not going to get between you. I've got a brother of my own. I know how it works. I'm not going to push in where I'm not wanted."

"You already did. You're *not* wanted."

"No. *You* don't want me. Will does. And how come his feelings don't matter?"

He couldn't read Grant's face in the darkness, but he saw his rigid figure deflate a little. "He shouldn't have done this," Grant said sulkily.

Taylor shivered. "For all I know, he agrees with you," he admitted. "But he did do it." The cold was sinking into him now, perspiration drying, muscles stiffening up. He really did not want to go another round with Grant. The morning would be hell as it was. "You know what, I don't have energy for this. I'm too tired to disable you without actually disabling you."

Grant instantly flared up. "Oh, you think you can take me?"

"I *know* I can take you." Taylor said wearily, "But it won't be quick and it won't be easy. So I'm going to go pick up a couple of six-packs of beer. If you can't handle being in the car with me, start walking and I'll pick you up on my way back."

He didn't wait to hear Grant's response, instead turning and striding back to the SUV. He had started the engine and was just rolling forward when the passenger door flew open and Grant slid in. He didn't say anything and neither did Taylor.

They bumped back onto the road. Taylor turned on the CD player and punched the button for Lifehouse.

* * * * *

It was closing time at the liquor store in Mist Bend, but there were two other customers wandering the aisles, and Taylor had the impression the elderly man behind the counter was not sorry to see him and Grant enter the store.

"Evening," Taylor nodded.

"Five minutes, boys," the old man said. He looked uneasily at the two long-haired men in camo and sunglasses, holding a low-voiced conference in front of the shelves of Bushmills and Jamieson.

Taylor gave the men a considering look—and recognized the yahoos who had got his day off to such a lousy start. The Dooleys.

He glanced at Grant, and Grant's black-browed scowl said it all.

No. He really, really, really did not have the energy for this.

"What's your dad like to drink?" he asked Grant.

Grant looked at him blankly.

"Beer," Taylor prodded. "What's your dad's favorite?"

"Kölsch."

"Kölsch?"

"Yeah. The Occidental Brewing Company in Portland has an agreement with Germany."

Taylor nodded and proceeded to the refrigeration units in the back, relieved when Grant trailed after him.

Taylor studied the racks of bottles. Grant disappeared but then reappeared with a six-pack of Deschutes River Ale. Taylor found the Kölsch, grabbed a couple of six-packs, and they returned to the cashier.

"That be it, folks?" the old man asked, ringing their purchases.

Taylor nodded.

The camo clones had finally noticed them. One of them said, "Hey, it's the Brandt kid. And that other guy."

Taylor said, "Evening, gentlemen." He handed over a twenty, keeping one eye on Grant and one eye on the Dooleys' reflections in the glass windows. Grant stared unwaveringly at the Dooleys.

Taylor took his change. "Grant?"

The Dooleys were whispering to each other and chortling at some private witticism. Grant's face turned red.

Taylor sighed inwardly. He must have been this young once, but he couldn't remember it. He said, "Are you getting that to go or are we drinking it here?"

Grant looked at him in confusion and then paid for the six-pack. By then the Dooleys were inching toward them. They smelled of tobacco, whisky, and something animal. Goat? Weird, whatever it was.

"Hey, other guy," the taller and skinnier brother said. "What's your name?"

Taylor knew better, of course, but somehow the words just popped out. "Why?" he asked. "Are you going to invite me to your birthday party?"

Grant laughed.

The tall, skinny Dooley turned red, at least on the patch of skin visible to the eye. "You got a smart mouth, mister."

"I know," Taylor said. "I keep signing up for self-help courses, but then I forget to go."

The second Dooley, shorter and squatter and browner than the first, took a couple of steps forward like a rottweiler trying to decide whether to charge. He swung his attention to Grant.

"Kid, you better tell your daddy Jem is looking for him."

Grant retorted, "He can't be looking very hard then."

Dooley's head went back as though Grant had punched him. For the first time Taylor understood the instinct that had Will wanting to clap a hand over his mouth and drag him away from trouble. His scalp tingled, and he wondered if his hair was standing on end.

He pulled open the glass door, which jingled merrily, nodded to Grant, who sauntered unhurriedly out, nodded to the man behind the counter, and nodded—levelly—to the Dooleys who were glaring after Grant.

They stowed the beer in the back of the SUV. The Dooleys were at the counter buying cigarettes and booze as Taylor sped out of the parking lot. "How many Dooleys are there?" he asked.

"Four. Not counting their mother."

"Are you sure you shouldn't count her?" Taylor watched his rearview mirror, but the road behind them was empty. "So neither of those two was Jem, I'm guessing?"

"No. Jem is bigger. A lot bigger. And he has these weird tattoos all over his face. Or he used to. They kind of make him look like a skeleton. Or maybe a wolf."

"Does he have a beard as well?"

"He didn't use to."

Taylor turned this information over as they drove out of town and started up the winding road leading back to the cabin in the woods.

No one resembling Jem had been in the truck that morning. Not unless Jem had seriously altered his appearance. As far as Taylor knew, there was no way of getting rid of tattoos like the ones Grant described.

"How long has Jem Dooley been out of prison?" Taylor asked Grant, breaking the silence of the last few miles.

"A week or so I guess."

"But he hasn't made any effort to contact your dad?"

Grant shrugged.

Maybe Bill was right. Maybe there wasn't a real threat here. Maybe there was just a lot of blustering and posturing.

Or...maybe not.

A pair of headlights that had been meandering miles back on the road behind them suddenly blazed into the back window of the SUV.

"What the hell..." Taylor pressed the gas, and the Land Cruiser sprang forward.

Grant half-turned in his seat. "They're still right on your ass."

"Are you buckled?"

Grant fumbled with his seatbelt.

Taylor floored it and the SUV raced ahead, tires squealing as they whipped around a sharp curve in the road. The lights behind them fell back but then loomed large again.

"Shit, man." Grant sounded disbelieving. "I think they're going to ram us!"

Taylor swore. The Land Cruiser had the horsepower but he couldn't risk going any faster than he already was. Even if he had been familiar with this route, this road with its hairpin turns and sudden dips wasn't made for speeding.

The Land Cruiser's headlights picked out the black outlines of tree trunks like motionless sentinels as they flew past.

"Is there anywhere I can pull over?"

There was a bang as the truck rammed their bumper and the Land Cruiser bounced forward and skidded. It was a heavy vehicle though, and Taylor was able to maintain course. Barely.

"Shit," Grant warned. "Here they come again."

There was another bang, and the Land Cruiser flew forward, fishtailing slightly. Taylor fought for control. If they went into a skid on this road, they were finished. They'd be over the edge and down the mountainside.

"Grant, is there a place coming up where I can pull over?"

"They almost went over the side that time," Grant reported.

"Is there a place I can turn off?" Taylor repeated. "Grant?"

"There's the Sawmill Road turnoff. It's about another mile on the right."

Another mile. God. Every second felt like an eternity.

Taylor risked it and punched the gas. The Land Cruiser shot ahead once more, screeching around the next two S-curves in the road.

The truck behind lagged and then lunged forward.

"Right there, where that white fence post is," Grant said suddenly. "That's the turnoff."

Fuck.

Four. Taylor tapped the brakes.

Three.

Two. He tapped the brakes again. Harder. Slowed as much as he could in hopes of avoiding a skid that he already knew there was no avoiding—

He wrenched the wheel, and turned into the inevitable spin, hand over hand, going with it, praying as the Land Cruiser hit the dirt, spraying sand and gravel, kicking across the moonlit stretch of grass and shrubs, the rough terrain grabbing at the tires, slowing…slowing…

Not a road, just a large, round turn-off or staging area. Thank God. Thank God for that much.

The Land Cruiser rocked to a hard stop, the shoulder restraint cutting into the still- sensitive scar tissue on his chest. Beside him, Grant was breathing hard. *"Christ."* He sounded exactly like Will at that moment.

"You okay?" Taylor asked him.

Grant nodded.

Taylor expelled a long breath. The SUV's engine was still running. More good news. He checked the dashboard. Green lights everywhere.

"Hang on," he muttered, and got out to check the tires.

His heart was still hammering as he walked slowly around the Land Cruiser. All four tires looked fine. The bumper had taken a beating, but it was still attached. He got back inside and buckled up.

"They tried to kill us," Grant said. He sounded like he couldn't believe it.

"Maybe."

"No maybe about it."

"If it was the Dooleys, I'm guessing drunk, stupid, and dangerous is their natural state. They could have just as easily killed themselves."

"*If* it was the Dooleys?"

"I didn't see who was driving."

"*I* did."

"Okay. Well." Taylor didn't have the energy or inclination to argue. They could easily have been killed, Grant was right about that. Malicious intent had certainly been present.

He shifted into drive and pulled slowly, cautiously back onto the now deserted road.

The rest of the trip back to the cabin went without incident. Taylor parked and they went inside only to find the lights down low and everyone but Bill apparently retired for the evening. Bill was nodding over his pipe in front of the fireplace. The dogs slept near him, Riley's feet twitching in sleep as he chased dream rabbits or deer.

As Taylor followed Grant into the room, Bill opened his eyes and straightened. The dogs lifted their heads, blinking sleepily in the firelight.

"Where is everybody?" Grant asked.

"Cousin Dennis was tuckered out from his adventures. Your brother is taking a shower."

Grant relayed the story of running into the Dooleys at the liquor store and their subsequent near mishap on the road.

"And you think it was the Dooleys?" Bill asked Taylor.

"I didn't get a license plate," Taylor admitted. "But it seems likely."

"It was them," Grant said. "Same dirty white truck. Same dirty white faces. I *know* it was them."

"All right," Bill said at last, grimly. "I believe you. I'll take it from here."

Grant stood there seemingly undecided. He looked at Taylor, looked away, looked back again. "That was good driving back there," he said grudgingly.

"Thanks. That's the advantage of a tactical driving course," Taylor admitted.

Grant turned his back. "Night, Pop."

"Night, son."

Grant departed for bed, yawning widely. Roxie rose from her place by the fireplace and trotted after him.

Bill was smiling faintly as he studied Taylor. "You look like you could use a drink."

"What I really need is sleep, I think."

"Other than the fact that you and my son both look like you were rolling around in the dirt earlier this evening, neither of you seem the worse for wear."

In the excitement of nearly being run off the road, Taylor had forgotten all about the first part of his road trip with Grant. "I don't know if we reached détente or not. We each had our say."

Bill grunted. "Grant's got a good heart, but he's as stubborn as a mule."

Taylor nodded acknowledgment. He folded his arms staring down at the fire. The movement of the flames was sinuous, almost hypnotic.

Bill took his pipe out and set it in the handmade clay ashtray beside his chair. "Something on your mind, Taylor?"

Taylor said slowly, "You seem to be taking all this pretty calmly, Bill. I mean about Will and me."

Bill took his time answering. He said at last, "One thing about being a lawman as long as I was, you learn there's no such thing as 'normal.'"

His blue eyes, so like Will's, held Taylor's gaze gravely.

Bill said, "I can't say I ever noticed Will had feelings for other boys, but when he told me he was gay, well, Will was always a level-headed kid. I knew there was no mistake about it, that it was something he'd been working through a long time."

Taylor nodded and looked back into the red-and-yellow flames dancing in the fireplace.

He heard the faint smile in Bill's voice as he said, "And it's not like I didn't know about you. From the time you and Will were first partnered, it was *MacAllister this* and *MacAllister that*. Knowing you had the same orientation, I wondered how that was going to work out. I'd think sometimes, *I hope this MacAllister feels the same way.*"

Taylor laughed. "Actually I had to talk Will into the idea. I still think he sometimes wishes…" That was further, a lot further, than he'd meant to go. His face burned hearing the echo of his words. He must be more tired than he'd realized.

Neither of them said anything as Bill knocked the tobacco out of his pipe. He said suddenly, briskly, "You're wrong about that. Will called me the night after you got hit. He said, Pop, Taylor's been shot and nobody can tell me if he's going to pull through. And then he couldn't say anything more."

Taylor cleared his throat. "Yeah, but that's just—"

But Bill shook his head. "The last time William came to me for comfort was the night his momma died. He was six years old. He may not be good at talking about how he feels, but you were number one for him practically since the day you met."

It seemed to lift a weight off him Taylor hadn't even known was there. He smiled at Bill.

"Thanks, Bill. Goodnight."

"Goodnight, son."

Surveillance Report
Case #3433BR
Subjects: Brandt, William and MacAllister,
Taylor
Investigator: Schwierskott

November 15, 2013 (Friday)
7:00 a.m.:
Investigator arrives at the residence of William
Brandt, Sr. located at 76011 Mellinger Road,
Mist Bend, OR 97064. Investigator observes
the blue 2010 Toyota Land Cruiser currently
registered to William Brandt in the driveway.
Investigator establishes stationary vehicle
surveillance with a view of the driveway of the
residence.

8:00 a.m.:
NO ACTIVITY

9:00 a.m.:
NO ACTIVITY

10:00 a.m.:
NO ACTIVITY

11:00 a.m.:
Investigator observes the blue 2010 Toyota
Land Cruiser exit the drive of the residence
and depart the area. Mr. Brandt is driving
the vehicle. Mr. MacAllister is a passenger
in the vehicle. Investigator initiates mobile
surveillance of the vehicle.

11:45 a.m.:
Investigator observes the blue 2010 Toyota Land Cruiser park on Main Street in Mist Bend, OR. Investigator observes Mr. Brandt and Mr. MacAllister walk up the street and into Tucker's Tavern. Subjects are engaged in conversation and appear cordial. Mr. MacAllister appears to have sustained facial bruising consistent with a physical assault.

1:28 p.m.:
Investigator observes Mr. Brandt and Mr. MacAllister exit Tucker's Tavern. Investigator observes Mr. Brandt and Mr. MacAllister enter the blue 2010 Toyota Land Cruiser and proceed to the Black Bear Inn on Silver Pines Road in Mist Bend. Investigator observes Mr. MacAllister enter the lobby and return nine minutes later. Investigator observes Mr. Brandt pull behind the building. Investigator initiates on foot surveillance of the vehicle.

1:45 p.m.:
Investigator observes Mr. Brandt open the door of Room 26 to an unidentified male (Caucasian, mid-forties, blond beard, balding). Investigator observes Mr. Brandt, Mr. MacAllister, and unidentified male leaving rendezvous site, driving away at a speed estimated in excess of 70 miles per hour and proceed to the residence of William Brandt, Sr. on Mellinger Road.

2:35 p.m.:
NO ACTIVITY

3:00 p.m.:
NO ACTIVITY

4:00 p.m.:
NO ACTIVITY

5:00 p.m.:
NO ACTIVITY

6:00 p.m.:
NO ACTIVITY

7:00 p.m.:
NO ACTIVITY
7:30 p.m.:
Investigator observes the blue 2010 Toyota Land
Cruiser exit the driveway of the residence
and depart the area. Investigator observes Mr.
MacAllister is driving the vehicle. An unknown
male (Caucasian, mid-twenties, shaven, brown
hair) is a passenger in the vehicle. Subjects
appear tense and unspeaking. Investigator
initiates mobile surveillance of the vehicle.

7:38 p.m.:
Due to extremely poor visibility and dangerous
driving conditions, Investigator was forced to
suspend mobile surveillance.

CHAPTER NINE

"This is the life," Will said contently.

"Yep."

Will reeled in his line, glancing back at Taylor, absently admiring both the graceful line of his lean body—even in chest waders—and the beauty of that forward cast. Taylor whisked the fly over his shoulder so that it seemed to dance in the air for an instant—the line looping lazily and straightening out behind him—then snapping his forearm to send the shining line singing out ahead.

The line hummed sweetly and the fly dropped lightly to the green water.

Yes, this was the life. Taylor was smiling at him, his dark hair falling boyishly in his eyes, and Will grinned back.

Taylor was not a big outdoors guy, not by any stretch—unless the outdoors was a warm beach somewhere—but he'd have to be blind not to appreciate the beauty of this scene, the distant, snowcapped, purple-blue mountains and the surrounding dense forest, red-gold foliage blazing in contrast to the green and gray spikes of conifers and pines. Even the white thunderheads moving in slowly from the east like airborne glaciers, were beautiful and dramatic.

"Worth getting up at four in the morning?" Will asked.

"For this? Sure."

Protection details, not so much. But they would have to make due with the work they could get until things turned around.

"Richard never called back?" Taylor would probably not have forgotten to mention it, though he'd had a lot on his mind that morning between last night's bonding exercise with Grant and nearly being run off the road by the Dooleys.

"No." One little word, but Will knew Taylor was troubled.

"We'll find another way."

Taylor didn't reply.

Will walked backwards a few steps, eye on a boulder on the far side of the river. He lifted the tip of his fishing rod, swinging the rod back and over to create the loop in the line and casting forward. The line glinted, snaking through the air and dropping down.

"Nice," Taylor observed.

"We should try salmon fishing in Alaska some day," Will said. "Supposedly there's nothing like it." Someday when they could afford to take a real vacation again. Will's stomach growled. "You getting hungry?" he called to Taylor.

"Always."

They hadn't caught much that morning, but that wasn't really the point of the exercise. Even exercise wasn't the point of this exercise. A little time to themselves, a little communing with the Great Outdoors. Mostly a little time to themselves.

Will felt a drop on his face and glanced at the slate skies overhead.

"Same here. You ready to call it a day?"

In answer, Taylor began to reel in his line.

"Thanks for this," he said.

"For what? Fishing? My pleasure."

Taylor's expression was serious. "No. For letting me come along on this trip."

"*Let you*? There was no *let you* about it. Of course you were coming on this trip." Will said it heatedly because he was unhappily aware that he had not initially wanted Taylor to come. What a dumbass he was sometimes. Now he couldn't imagine having made this trip without him. Just when he thought they couldn't get any closer, too. But somehow he felt closer to Taylor than ever.

"I like your dad," Taylor said, still serious, still following his own thoughts.

"Me too."

Taylor made an absent, amused sound. "You're lucky though. I love my parents, but I don't have that. What you have. I never did."

Will had known that for a long time. Taylor was close to his siblings and had a polite, distantly affectionate relationship with his mother. He rarely spoke about his father, but Will had the impression Taylor would have liked a closer relationship. It bothered him to picture a much younger, much more vulnerable Taylor yearning for what should have been his by right.

Families were complicated. But some people shouldn't be allowed to have kids. That was a fact.

"Grant's okay too. In his way," Taylor added.

Will laughed. "Thanks for, you know, not pulverizing him. Of course, I may pulverize him myself."

"Nah. I like him. He'll grow out of what I don't like about him."

They reeled in their lines, waded out of the water, and stood beside the Land Cruiser, stripping off their protective gear. Will wore Polypropylene long johns under his waders, but Taylor, as usual, had worn Levi's, and the cotton had acted as a magnet for the damp cold.

"God damn it," Will said. "Why will you never listen to me? You're turning blue!"

"Then the rest of me will match my balls," Taylor said tartly. He was kidding of course, except…not entirely. All at once his smile was too tight and his green eyes looked gray. Glacial.

"Huh?" Will stared at him and he had that sinking feeling again. "Wait a minute."

"Forget it. I'm joking." Taylor flashed him a brief, meaningless smile and threw his waders in the back of the SUV with the ice chest of fish. The boots clunked heavily and fell away from each other.

"Taylor." Will put a hand on his shoulder and Taylor slid out from under it.

"Let it go, Will."

"No. I'm not going to let it go." Will's hand closed on Taylor's bony shoulder, and he turned Taylor to face him. "It's been a little awkward, that's all."

"Oh, believe me, I know."

Frowning, Will regarded Taylor, taking in the flushed cheeks, the stormy eyes, the sulky mouth. Taylor was not a guy who sulked, but that was definitely an unhappy curve to his lips. Not just unhappy. Hurt.

"You're wrong," Will said. "You couldn't be more wrong." He angled his head and covered Taylor's mouth in a coaxing kiss. Taylor kissed him back reluctantly. Will deepened the kiss, and Taylor's lips parted with a tiny sigh.

It was the sigh that did it, that helpless concession, Taylor suddenly receptive and accessible and so sweet as he opened to Will, even leaning against him as though he was suddenly too tired to fight.

Which was probably true. He sure hadn't seemed to do much sleeping the night before, had even turned down Will's offer of a backrub.

Maybe that made sense now.

"You're nuts," Will said softly. "This is every bit as frustrating for me. I just don't let myself think about it, that's all." He reached down and found Taylor's waistband, undoing the metal button, popping the rivets of his fly… *pop…pop…pop…*

"How do you mana…" Taylor's voice gave out as Will pushed his hand in, worked his way through the front of Taylor's boxers, meeting his cock halfway.

Yes. Beautiful. Velvet skin stretched taut over that tensile thrusting hardness. He could only spare a brief caress, reaching further for those painful, much-neglected balls. He cradled the plush, fragile sacks in his palm.

Taylor sagged back against the side of the SUV, arching a little, moaning, "Will…" Stricken and beautiful, eyes shut, trembling, making those small sounds as Will petted and stroked him, occasionally jumping as Will pinched his thigh or butt cheek.

This was crazy. A forest ranger could be watching them right now. Another fisherman could drive up any second—with a carload of kids. And his mother. And the family minister. But no way could Will stop now. He flexed his hand, pressed his thumb to the hot entrance between Taylor's butt cheeks, and Taylor gasped, shuddered.

"What do you want, sweetheart?" Will's voice was rough with excitement and longing.

"Whatever you want, Will."

Christ almighty. Hearing those soft, submissive words, Will's cock went so rigid so fast he nearly did himself a permanent injury. Sheer crazy fantasy because there was no one less submissive than Taylor. When he handed over control it was on a strictly limited basis, and even then Will always had a suspicion Taylor was secretly directing the action.

"I'm going to fuck you," Will said.

Taylor shivered, started shoving at his Levi's. Will turned him to face the SUV, yanked his jeans down, yanked his boxers down. And Taylor leaned against the side of the car, docile, pants around his ankles, goose bumps on the pale perfect globes of his ass. Waiting for whatever Will was going to do to him. Beautiful. Taylor rested his forehead on his bent arm, and the nape of his neck looked boyish.

Will swallowed dryly, shoved down the clinging long johns, taking himself in hand, pressing against Taylor. The exquisite sensation as the head of his cock pressed against the hot bull's-eye of Taylor's body... Taylor whimpered.

Will stopped. "*Hell*. Hold on..."

Taylor's head jerked up. "What. The. Hell. *Now*?" he asked, sounding anything but submissive.

"Hold *on*," Will said desperately. He yanked open the driver's door, crawled inside, rifling through the glove compartment until he found the small pink bottle. "Got it."

"My cock is about to freeze to the side of this fucking car, Brandt!"

"I said *hold on*," Will said, ducking back out of the car. He held up the sample-sized baby lotion.

"Oh my God." Taylor's head flopped down on his arm again. His shoulders shook. Will couldn't tell if he was laughing or crying. Either way, Will was damned well going to have him. He slicked himself thickly, briskly with pink-smelling lotion, and pressed against Taylor again, guiding himself. Taylor's body offered token resistance, Will pushed, and he was in, enveloped in that warm, suede grip.

Taylor made a small, satisfied sound—a sound of almost heartfelt relief—and pushed back. Will braced his hands on either side of Taylor. *Whoa.* Taylor was right. The car was like a block of ice. He gathered Taylor close, wrapping him in his arms, holding him tight against the warmth of his own body. He turned so that he was leaning against the SUV and Taylor was leaning back against him. Taylor folded his arms over Will's, so they were melded tight all the length of their bodies.

Will thrust tentatively, and Taylor let his head fall back on Will's shoulder. "Oh, God, Will."

"Good?"

"Don't stop. Please God. Don't stop."

"I won't. I won't."

They'd caught the rhythm now, sliding into it like a runner hitting his stride, only two runners, a relay team, working together. Will thrusting, Taylor pushing back. The paced themselves, picked up speed, and then they were running full out. Will lifted Taylor a little, changed his angle, and felt that jolt roll right up Taylor's spine and hit the back of his skull. The sound Taylor made that time was a sound there was no faking, a broken sob of something way beyond pleasure or even delight.

Will did it again, aimed for the sweet spot, and felt Taylor jump in his arms and give another breathless sob. "*Will.*"

"Oh you do like that," Will muttered. But then they both liked that.

Third time was the charm. Taylor arched in his arms and went rigid like he was having a seizure, and then he was coming in a hot, sticky mess, shooting white across the wet grass and wild flowers. Over his shoulder Will could see a buck several yards away staring at them in astonishment.

Taylor went boneless in his arms, hanging onto the band of Will's arms like he needed Will's support to stay on his feet. Will kissed the damp side of his face, thrusting faster, moving to short strokes. He felt flecks of wet hitting his skin. It was raining now, really raining. He thrust harder, straining to get there, to reach the finish line, stretching out for it. And there it was. The road rising up to meet him and he was home. Homecoming. It was never sweeter.

He hung onto Taylor as release rippled through him, so sharp, so bright, so intense it blinded him for a few seconds. Reaction nearly made his knees give way. He and Taylor clung to each other, which was all that saved him from sitting down in the mud. The rain peppered down harder and harder. Will opened his eyes and Taylor was smiling at him, looking more warmed and relaxed than he had in days, maybe weeks—despite the fact that his hair was plastered to his head, his skin shining.

Will opened his mouth. He wasn't sure what he was going to say, but two rifle shots, clear as the crack of doom, echoed through the valley, ringing off the mountains and rolling away into silence.

Hunters.

It could easily be hunters.

But it wasn't. He could feel it in his bones, in that sick coldness pooling in his gut. That was instinct. The same instinct that had Taylor moving away from him, alert, tense, trying to place the direction of the shots in relation to the house.

"Is the house over those hills?" asked Taylor, watching Will.

Will nodded, already getting behind the wheel. His legs were shaking, whether from recent sex or fear, he wasn't sure. Taylor ran around the front of the SUV and jumped in beside him. "My SIG is in my knapsack."

"My backup piece is in the glove compartment."

Handguns against a rifle. Those were not good odds.

The SUV bumped and bounced over the rough terrain as Will headed for the dirt road that led out of the valley. Taylor was on his cell phone to the Columbia County Sheriff's Department.

"It could be a hunter," Will said for the sake of argument, but Taylor did not relay this info.

He disconnected and said, "Your dad might not even be at the house. He was going to drive into Mist Bend for groceries for the Thanksgiving dinner tomorrow, remember?"

Will nodded grimly. The thought of Grant there on his own was not a lot more comforting.

"You want me to try and contact the Marshal's Service?" Taylor asked.

"By the time you get through, we'll be there," Will said. He realized that until that moment it hadn't crossed his mind that this could be anything but Jem Dooley seeking vengeance. But of course Taylor was right. It was even odds that this attack—if attack it was—had to do with Cousin Dennis.

And the idea of Grant trying to deal with mob hit men was even more terrifying than the idea of Grant squaring off against Jem Dooley.

Will stomped on the accelerator and the Land Cruiser slammed onto the road. Taylor had dragged his knapsack into the front and was checking his weapon. He opened the glove compartment and pulled out Will's backup weapon. His calm focus steadied Will. This was what they did. This was who they were. And the fact that this time it was personal—family—was beside the point.

It didn't feel beside the point. It felt like the longest drive of his life. The car smelled of sex and rain and fish. Will was sure he would never forget the scent of these seemingly endless miles.

Suddenly the elastic band of road snapped and they were racing up over the final rise.

He didn't see the red Corolla until it was almost too late. It came flying over the top of the hill and nearly crashed into them. Will jerked the wheel left, the Corolla careened right, skidded off the dirt road and went out of control down the hillside. It shredded the brush and crashed into an oak tree.

"What the hell was that?" Taylor said.

Good question. Will shook his head and pulled off the road into the grass. Taylor passed him his SIG. They got out into the rain. There was no movement inside the Corolla. Steam rose from the crumpled hood.

Will turned. He could see his father's house in the valley below. There were no lights, but smoke drifted from the fireplace chimney, pale against the stormy skies. He heard the crack of a rifle coming from the direction of the house, but at first couldn't place where the shooter was. Then he located Grant hunkered down on the back deck with a carbine.

At the same time he heard the sound of another vehicle racing up the road toward them. Will identified the angry lug of a truck engine in need of a tune-up before he spotted the white pickup hurtling their way.

Out of the corner of his eye he saw Taylor dropping down in a speed kneeling position. He stepped out into the road and brought his weapon up.

The pickup crested the hill. Will got a good look at the three men wedged inside the truck cab at about the same instant they got a good look at him. The truck swerved wildly, tried to complete a 360 and drove off the side of the hill. The pickup rolled once and slid on its cab to a stop at the bottom of the road.

Taylor rose, lowering his pistol. "What is this, some kind of demolition derby?"

"Let's find out," Will said. "I'll take the pickup. You take the Corolla?"

Taylor frowned, staring down at the upside down truck. The engine was still running, tires spinning. Shouts and curses floated from the cab. "You sure you don't need a hand?"

Will gestured to Grant running from the house, carbine in hand. "Under control."

Taylor nodded and turned, jogging down the hillside to the smashed Corolla.

Will started down the road to the pickup. The Dooleys, bloodied but largely unhurt, were crawling from the wreckage of their truck when Will reached them. He reached in and turned off the engine. A small arsenal of weapons lay scattered around the cab.

As Grant jogged up, Will said, "You okay?"

"Sure. Luckily none of these jerk-offs can shoot straight."

That seemed to touch a sore spot and the Dooleys began snarling obscenities again.

"I'm going to sue you!" Tobe shouted at Will. At least Will thought it was Tobe. He'd gone to school with Tobe, but it was hard to keep all the facial hair and camo straight. Every one of them looked about a decade older than their natural years.

"That ought to be an interesting court case," Will replied. To Grant, he said, "Do me a favor and start collecting these guns and knives and whatever else they've got stashed in there." He turned back to the Dooleys. "I want you all prone—that means face down—on the ground. Hands locked behind your head. Do it now."

"We're injured," protested Vin, who was, true enough, bleeding profusely from a cut on his scalp.

"All the more reason to lie down and stop moving around. Help is on the way."

He'd already picked up the distant wail of sirens through the wash of rain. "Where's Pop?" he asked Grant.

Grant, holding a Bowie knife as long as his forearm, said, "Pop's not even here. Cousin Dennis is hiding in the safe room."

"What happened?"

"Nothing. They drove up and started firing at the house."

"That's not exactly nothing."

"I mean, nothing happened to start it," Grant said. "They pulled up and started shooting."

"What the hell is the matter with you?" Will asked Tobe. Tobe screwed his face up and spat at him. Given his position and the direction of the wind, it was a strategic error.

Will shook his head and turned his attention back to Grant. "How much damage did they do?"

"Probably took ten years off Cousin Dennis's life." Grant grinned. "They knocked out some windows and that globe lamp that belonged to Grandma Mills. That's about it. They turned tail the minute I started firing back."

Will studied the men lying in the mud. They were using their clasped hands to shelter their sodden heads from the rain. Three more bedraggled and miserable specimens he'd rarely seen. Tobe, Hal—who had somehow managed to hang onto his sunglasses—and Vin. No Jem.

"Where's Jem?" Will asked. "Did he put you up to this?" The three men stared at him sullenly.

"You do realize you crossed a line, right? You don't get off this time with a fine or community service?"

They stared back at him with silent loathing. Maybe stupidity wasn't a crime, but it sure played a role in plenty of crimes. The scary thought was that Jem was—had always been—the brains of this outfit.

"Fine. You want to share the rap with your brother, go right ahead. But Jem is going straight back to prison for this. Maybe you can share a cell. Wouldn't that be cozy?"

Tobe snarled, "No it wouldn't and no Jem ain't. 'Coz he's gone."

"What do you mean, he's gone?"

"What I said. He's gone."

"Where did he go?"

"Wherever he wanted to."

Hal lifted his head. His sunglasses were askew. He said, "Jem left last week. That's how much you know about anything."

"He can't leave the area without violating his parole."

Hal shrugged, then winced, rubbing at his shoulder.

"If he left last week, what was all this?" Will asked. "All this driving around, raising hell, claiming Jem was coming for revenge?"

Hal and Tobe stared sullenly at him. Vin stared down at the mud.

Will gave a disbelieving laugh. "You're saying this was all *your* idea?"

Well, *idea* was probably an exaggeration.

Taylor whistled sharply from up the hill, and Will turned at once. "Grant, if any one of them moves, shoot him," he instructed, and switch-backed up the road at a brisk jog.

"My pleasure," Grant called from behind him, which started the Dooleys snarling and swearing again.

Will topped the hill and looked down the gully. The driver of the red Corolla leaned against the side of his car, talking to Taylor. Taylor turned as Will approached.

"Look who it is," Taylor told him.

"Who?" As far as Will knew, the driver, a big man in a black leather jacket, was a stranger to him. He was taller than himself or Taylor. Beefy but well-groomed with one of those geometrically precise beards that nobody besides actors and male models bothered with. There was a cut above his eye where the airbag must have caught him, but otherwise he seemed unhurt.

"I keep telling you, I didn't have anything to do with this," he said as Will reached them. Will's boots skidded a little on the wet weeds. He steadied himself on the hood of the car.

"You do," Taylor agreed. "But you've yet to convince me."

"Who the hell are you?" Will asked.

Brown eyes met Will's briefly. "I was parked in the trees over there when that truckload of rednecks arrived and started shooting up the place."

"That doesn't answer my question. And those trees where you were parked are private property. So who are you and what were you doing parked over there?"

"Nothing. I was taking a little rest stop."

"Resting on your way to where?"

"Look, I don't know why you're hassling me. I had nothing to do with anything that happened here. Those hillbillies opened fire and I tried to leave the area as quickly as possible. *You almost* crashed into *me*."

"You didn't think about maybe calling for help?" Will asked. "Your only thought was to flee the scene?"

"I figured help was on the way."

"That's convenient."

"What happened to the Porsche?" Taylor asked.

The man blinked. He looked from Will to Taylor. His expression changed. "Hey, wait a minute. It's not what you think," he said quickly.

Taylor said, "I think you're a PI by the name of Stuart Schwierskott and you've been hired to run surveillance on us."

Rain pattered down on the ground around them.

"Okay, it is what you think," Schwierskott admitted. "But listen, you can read my reports. I don't have anything on you. I'm no threat to you."

No threat to them? Did he think they were going to shoot him? Who did he think they were?

"What is it you think there would be to have on us?" Will asked.

"I don't understand the question."

"You understand *my* question. Who hired you?" Taylor asked.

"I don't know," Schwierskott said, a little desperately. "That's the truth. I don't know who hired our firm, and I don't know what they hoped to uncover."

"There isn't anything to uncover."

"I want to see these reports," Taylor said.

"Go ahead. Be my guest. My notes are in my briefcase on the front seat."

Taylor yanked open the car door, lifted out the briefcase, and set it on the hood of the car. He shuffled through the sheets of notes, glancing over the reports, frowning.

"Well?" Will asked.

Taylor rifled through the papers again. He raised his head and stared at Schwierskott in disbelief. "Are you supposed to be for real? People are paying you for this? Listen to this, Brandt. *Due to extremely poor visibility and dangerous driving conditions, Investigator was forced to suspend mobile surveillance.* This is last night when Grant and I went on our beer run." He turned to Schwierskott. "You got lost, didn't you?"

Schwierskott looked uncomfortable. He didn't answer.

"I don't think he was even here for half the stuff he's reporting."

Taylor looked at Will, and Will said, "Okay. He's not good at his job. Is that really the p—"

"Well, it's one point. Schwierskott & Associate is a big firm. A big, profitable firm. If they can make it, we sure as hell can."

"You're PIs?" Schwierskott asked.

"You don't know?" Taylor questioned. "You're running surveillance on us and you don't know what we do for a living?"

"We're not PIs," Will said.

"I know you both left the DSS at the same time and under mysterious circumstances," Schwierskott said. "Which in my book translates to you getting canned."

"Oh, your book," Taylor said. "Let's read another page out of that, shall we? Investigator is forced to terminate surveillance when German shepherd dogs pursue him through woods."

"Mysterious circumstances? There was nothing mysterious about it," Will said.

"I want to know who hired you," Taylor said again.

"First of all, that's privileged information. Secondly, like I keep telling you, we *don't* know."

"Bullshit."

"I'm telling you the truth. We were hired by a third party. We're supposed to observe and report until further notice. That's it."

"What third party?"

"I don't—"

"*Tell* him," Will said to Schwierskott. "Unless you want to spend the rest of the day on this fucking hillside, tell him."

Schwierskott scowled. "We were hired by a representative of the legal firm of Gently, Fallis & Landreth."

"What? They're ambulance chasers," Taylor said, and now he looked as confused as Will felt.

"I already told you they were hired as a go-between."

Taylor chewed his lip, thinking it over.

"This guy is a dead end," Will told Taylor. "When we get back to L.A. we'll contact Gently, Fallis & Landreth. See what we can find out then."

Taylor nodded. "Okay."

Schwierskott swallowed. "What about me?"

"What about him?" Will asked Taylor.

"Personally, I'd look for another line of work," Taylor said. "I don't think you got one thing in this report correct. Maybe the part where the dogs chased you."

Schwierskott said, "But wait. I'm doing you a favor, right?"

"I don't see it that way," Will said. He nodded at Taylor. "I guarantee you *he* doesn't see it that way."

"No. Look. You don't have to mention any of this, do you? When you talk to my old—my boss. I've been cooperative, haven't I?"

"Is that what you call this?"

"I'm just trying to earn a living. I'm one of the good guys."

"Actually, we're the good guys," Will told him. "You're someone who spends his time digging through other people's garbage cans."

"Wait a minute," Taylor said.

Will waited. Schwierskott looked both uneasy and hopeful. Taylor said slowly, "So if we don't mention having this conversation with you, if we don't share any of the events of the last few days with your boss, you'll turn these reports in as is?"

"Yes. Yes," Schwierskott said eagerly. "I'm happy to help. We'll call it a professional courtesy. Where you're concerned, I see nothing. I know nothing."

"That last shouldn't be hard to sell."

"He's a witness to the Dooleys shooting up my father's house," Will said.

"I know, but it's not like he's going to be needed to prove the case against the Dooleys."

"That's not the point."

Taylor drew him aside. "I know this goes against the grain, but hear me out."

"Go on."

"This gives us an advantage, Brandt. Whoever is watching us doesn't have to know that we know he's out there. And meanwhile, Stuart's feeding him—or her—wrong information."

Will grunted.

"You see where I'm going with this?"

Yes. He saw exactly where Taylor was going. Will didn't like it, but Taylor had a point. After a moment he nodded curtly.

Schwierskott let out a long breath. "Excellent. You won't regret this, boys!"

"I already regret it," Will said, but Taylor winked at him, and he sighed.

* * * * *

Taylor said sleepily, "I'm still not sure I get it. The Dooleys were waiting for Jem to come back and even the score, but when he finally got out of prison, he didn't want to have anything to do with his loser family either. So Jem takes off, and Jethro and the rest of the clan are left with nothing. All those years of threats and warnings and predictions of what was going to happen when their big brother got out of prison turned out to be nothing but hot air?"

"Something like that," Will said.

It was nearly midnight. They were lying in the too-small bed in Will's old room, warm and comfortable, wrapped in each other's arms. The Dooleys had been arrested and carted off by the Sheriff's Department, Stuart Schwierskott was on his way back to L.A., and the Marshals Service had decided Bill Brandt's Home for Wayward Fugitives was getting a little too much attention these days and had pulled Cousin Dennis out and sent him on the next leg of his journey.

Tomorrow they would celebrate Thanksgiving. The first Thanksgiving Will had made it home for in a couple of years. Maybe it wasn't the actual official holiday, but what mattered was he would be with his family. All of his family, old and new. He smiled at the thought. He had a lot to be thankful for this year.

"So they were just…keeping up appearances?" Taylor was still thinking aloud.

"I guess."

"Jem never was a threat?"

"Nope."

Taylor yawned widely, belatedly smothering his exhalation in Will's shoulder. Will absently kissed the top of his head. He smiled to himself. Taylor smelled like Dial soap, which was the soap Will's father had bought as long as Will could remember. The deodorant soap smell was strangely sexy on Taylor.

Grant had stopped by his room while Taylor had been taking his bath, and they'd talked for a minute.

Grant's face had worked. "He's okay, Will. I see he's a good guy. And I see how he feels about you. I just…can't understand it. It doesn't make sense. It doesn't seem right to me. It doesn't seem natural. I can't help it."

"Okay," Will had said at last, wearily. "I guess I can't fight that."

"But…" Grant sucked in a deep breath. "But I'm glad you have him. I'm glad you found somebody and you're happy."

It was less than Will wanted, but by then more than he'd hoped for. "Thanks. Thank you, Grant."

"You're my brother," Grant said more steadily. "I want whatever you want. I love you."

"I love you too."

He wasn't sure if they'd ever said the words out loud before. They'd always taken love for granted. But it wasn't something you could—or should—take for granted.

"You okay?" Will asked Taylor softly.

"Hm?"

Will ran his hand under Taylor's sweatshirt, stroking his back. "Not feeling neglected or anything now?"

He felt the curve of Taylor's smile. "I'm okay."

Will closed his eyes.

Taylor's cell phone rang. Taylor jumped as though he'd been electrified and scrambled for his phone. He cleared his throat, swiped the screen. "Hi Richard. Thanks for returning my call."

Will listened to Taylor's half of the conversation, stroking Taylor's back. He could feel Taylor's heart pounding, and though Taylor sounded careful and calm as he explained their plans and business strategy, Will knew him well enough to recognize the nervousness beneath that even tone.

Taylor hated this and Will hated that Taylor found himself in this position. That they were both in this position. He ran his hand down Taylor's back and he could feel the hint of dampness between Taylor's shoulder blades.

Then Taylor said gruffly, "One hundred and fifty thousand dollars," and Will sat up too.

"What?" he whispered. He hoped he'd heard that wrong. He knew he hadn't.

Taylor ignored him. He listened to the tiny voice on the other side of the world for what seemed like a very long time.

"That's very generous," he said at last, and his voice cracked, making him sound about fifteen years younger. "But no. We appreciate it, but no, there's no reason why you shouldn't at least earn some kind of a percentage.

We look at this as an investment not a—" He listened again. "I know, but family or not, we wouldn't feel right."

Will reached over and squeezed Taylor's rock hard shoulders.

"That's…"

More silence.

"Thank you. That's…"

Taylor sucked in a sharp breath. "All right. Of course. Thank you, Richard. I'll keep an eye out for the papers…yes…I appreciate it…love to Mom…"

Taylor clicked off. He fell back on his pillow. Will took the phone out of his unresisting hand.

"You got the money," he said, still not quite believing it.

"I will have, within a week or so. But we're paying him back, Will. Every cent. With interest. I don't care what he says. We're not…"

"Absolutely," Will tried to reassure him. "I agree. It's just a loan."

"I can't…"

"We're on the same page."

Taylor let out a long sigh.

A hundred and fifty grand. Will felt winded just thinking about it. The possibilities of it. They could pay off their credit cards. They could hire someone to answer their phone. They could buy the proper equipment. They could go after the big jobs. The lucrative jobs.

They were in business.

They were in debt.

He could feel Taylor thinking it over, absorbing it as well.

He said at last, "Taylor?"

"Hm?" No trace of sleepiness in Taylor's voice now.

"Was I wrong?"

"Which time?"

But Will was serious. "I gambled everything on us striking out on our own, starting this new business. I risked everything. For both of us. I didn't give you a choice, not really. I just shoved it through, made it happen, and now...if I'm wrong..."

Taylor raised his head, peering through the darkness. "Hey."

"You were right to be angry. You were right about all of it. If I've fucked this up, it's going to take us years to dig ourselves out."

Taylor rolled onto his side. He ran his hand slowly up and down Will's arm. "This isn't like you."

"What does that tell you, right there?"

Taylor made a sound of amusement. "That you usually think you're right. And a lot of the time you are."

"And a lot of the time I'm not."

"True. But I pick up the slack there, so we're okay."

Will just shook his head.

They listened to the rain tick-ticking against the window panes. Nothing but rain ahead in the next few days' forecast. It was going to be a damn long drive to L.A. on Monday.

"Will, listen." Taylor sighed. "Maybe I haven't been entirely fair. Or honest. Yes, I was pissed off at being hustled into making decisions I wasn't ready to make, but the fact is, this *is* what I ultimately wanted. I did want us to be together, I did want us to start our life. I said from the start I wanted us to live together and work together, and I wanted it to happen as soon as it was feasible. Where we differed was on when that would be feasible. But ultimately the goal was always the same."

"That difference might mean success or failure."

"We're not going to fail."

"You can't know that for sure."

"Yeah, I can. I do." Taylor said it with calm certainty. "We're not going to fail. I don't think it's going to be easy, but we're not going to fail."

"And why is that?"

"Because it doesn't matter if we fail."

"What?" Will raised his head off the pillow.

"This was never about making a bunch of money or winning Businessman of the Year. If we're not successful at this, we'll be successful at something else."

"You're going a little too Zen master for me now, MacAllister. Ten minutes ago you were shaking at the idea of being in debt to your stepfather."

"The main thing, the important thing to both of us, is what we already have. We're together. And as long as we're together, we're okay. And if we're okay, then really everything is okay."

Will was silent for a moment. He said at last, "That's beautiful, Tay."

Taylor lay back again and settled his head on the pillow. "Thank you."

"You realize if we can't make this business work, we'll be in hock to Richard for the rest of our natural lives?"

"Yes, I do."

"This venture of ours really does have to succeed."

"Yes, it really does." Taylor added for good measure, "Really."

Will started to laugh.

"Really," Taylor said.

Surveillance Report
Case #3433BR
Subjects: Brandt, William and MacAllister,
Taylor
Investigator: Schwierskott
November 16, 2013 (Saturday)

7:00 a.m.:
Investigator arrives at the residence of William
Brandt, Sr. located at 76011 Mellinger Road,
Mist Bend, OR 97064. Investigator observes
the blue 2010 Toyota Land Cruiser currently
registered to William Brandt in the driveway.
Investigator establishes stationary vehicle
surveillance with a view of the driveway of the
residence.

8:00 a.m.:
NO ACTIVITY

9:00 a.m.:
NO ACTIVITY

10:00 a.m.:
NO ACTIVITY

11:00 a.m.:
NO ACTIVITY

12:00 a.m.:
NO ACTIVITY

1:00 p.m.:
NO ACTIVITY

2:00 p.m.:
NO ACTIVITY

3:00 p.m.:
NO ACTIVITY

4:00 p.m.:
NO ACTIVITY

5:00 p.m.:
NO ACTIVITY

6:00 p.m.:
NO ACTIVITY

7:00 p.m.:
NO ACTIVITY

8:00 p.m.:
NO ACTIVITY

9:00 p.m.:
NO ACTIVITY

10:00 p.m.:
NO ACTIVITY

11:00 p.m.:
NO ACTIVITY

12:00 p.m.:
Investigator terminates surveillance and
departs the area.

BLINDSIDE

To Marilyn, because *of course*.

"What is that feeling when you're driving away from people and they recede on the plain till you see their specks dispersing? It's the too-huge world vaulting us, and it's goodbye. But we lean forward to the next crazy venture beneath the skies."

Jack Kerouac, *On the Road*

PROLOGUE

TWO CHRISTMASES AGO

The walkie-talkie crackled, and Taylor said, "Romeo to Base."

Romeo? Will, who had been blowing on his hands to warm them, spluttered a laugh and picked up his walkie-talkie. "Base."

"Refresh my memory. Whose idea was this again? Over."

Will grimaced, looked up at the stars burning bright and cold in the black night sky of the Mojave Desert. Not another light for miles out here. Nothing but Joshua trees and sand and the sharp cutout ridge of distant mountains. "Not sure now."

"Yeah, that's what I thought. Yours."

"Thanks for not saying I told you so."

Taylor's wicked laugh rustled across the six chilly miles of empty airwaves and Will's lips twitched in instinctive response. "That is one nasty laugh, buddy boy. I could get a search warrant based on that laugh."

"Base, standby." Taylor was suddenly all business.

Will waited, his eyes scanning the darkness. Nothing moved in the sky or on the ground. He caught motion out of the corner of his eye. A shooting star. He smiled faintly. Taylor was not much for the great outdoors.

At the same time Taylor, sounding relaxed again, said, "Go ahead, Base."

"You were saying?" Will replied. It was only the two of them out here, after all.

"I was saying, this is one hell of a way to spend our last Christmas Eve."

Will was terse because he wasn't enjoying freezing his ass off any more than Taylor was—and because this was a sensitive subject. "It's not our last Christmas Eve."

The following silence stretched long enough to start sweat prickling on Will's hairline. He had accepted the posting in Paris despite knowing Taylor's feelings—and the strain it would put on their relationship. After a couple of months of delays, on January 1st, he'd finally be shipping out for a two-year tour of duty in the City of Lights.

And what happened at the end of that two years was anybody's guess.

"If I do take the assignment in Paris, it doesn't mean we're not still together."

"Other than the six thousand miles between us."

"Five thousand six hundred and sixty-one miles."

"But who's counting."

Will knew what he wanted to happen at the end of that two years. And he was confident it was what Taylor wanted too.

But two years was a long time.

And Taylor was a guy with little patience and a lot of options.

"Copy that," Taylor said at last. "Doesn't change the fact that we're currently one step up from snipers."

Will started breathing again. "Not if we don't shoot anybody."

Taylor said darkly, "That depends on how much longer we're stuck out here."

Will peered at the luminous dial of his watch. "I make it half an hour."

He could feel Taylor's sigh, though the walkie-talkie remained silent. Taylor hated this op for a dozen reasons, starting with the fact that it was their last *not*-last Christmas Eve for the foreseeable future and ending with the fact that any half-awake civilian with a radio and a pair of binoculars could have handled this. They were simply providing backup for the backup.

"I'll make it up to you, Romeo," Will said suddenly, surprising himself. "Next Christmas will be different."

"Roger so far." There was a smile in Taylor's voice. "Should we switch to a secure channel?"

In one short week, phone calls would be all Will had to keep him warm at night.

Not for the first time he wondered if he was mistaking stubbornness for smart choices. Because if this promotion ended up costing him Taylor—

But no. It wouldn't. Taylor understood. Taylor had ambitions too. It would be okay. They would be okay. And he would make it up to Taylor. He really would. Starting now.

"Affirmative," he said gruffly. Why the hell not? It was just them and the coyotes, and any smart coyote was safely curled in his den, dreaming of rabbits and the spring.

"Yeah?" Taylor sounded alert and interested.

Will realized with blinding clarity that there was no going wrong with this; anything he said would, at the least, make Taylor laugh. But Taylor wouldn't laugh. Will knew that too. Realized that however awkward he was at verbalizing…stuff, the very attempt would mean something to Taylor. Taylor, who spent more than his fair share of time putting it all on the line. Phone lines included.

"Yeah," Will said boldly. "That's right, Romeo. They don't call me Roger Wilco for nothing."

THREE HOURS LATER

"Roger Wilco?" Taylor started to laugh.

"I don't recall hearing any objections," Will said mildly. "Then or now."

"No, and you won't." Taylor stretched luxuriously against the tumbled stack of pillows and grinned at him. In the soft lamplight he looked young and happy. No shadows in his eyes tonight.

Will leaned across to the bedstand, picked up the bottle of bourbon Taylor had given him for Christmas, and topped up the two tumblers. He handed one glass to Taylor.

Taylor held it up thoughtfully, watching the light catch and flash in the two fingers of red-brown liquid. "You trying to get me drunk, William?"

"I shorely am," Will drawled. Not drunk enough to ruin Christmas morning for either of them, just drunk enough to keep Taylor in that agreeably pliable and affectionate mood his rare boozing triggered.

Taylor laughed again and clinked it against Will's. "Merry Christmas." He sucked in a soft breath, said steadily, "And here's to Paris."

"Merry Christmas," Will said. He took a swallow, set his glass aside and leaned down to kiss Taylor. He whispered, "And here's to us."

CHAPTER ONE

The razor-sharp edge between Before and After. That's what haunted Will.

That split second between the moment when all options were still on the table, when there were still infinite possibilities as to how it could all play out, and the moment when the choice was made and consequences rolled out with the inevitability of high tide.

He hadn't seen it coming. That was part of it. He'd been blindsided.

And the thing was, it had started out as a perfectly ordinary evening. No indication of what lay ahead. In fact, the ordinariness of it was what made it perfect.

"Why don't we celebrate?" he'd said.

Not quite five o'clock, it was nearly dark as they crossed the wooden bridge. The damp twilight smelled of car exhaust, Mexican food, and maybe, distantly, the ocean. Colorful lights blinked and twinkled in the ragged black silhouettes of the surrounding trees. In the manmade hollow beside the Spanish-style strip mall, the miniature golf course was decorated for the holidays with fake snow and leafy garland. It looked like Santa's Village. Quaint, cute, commercialized.

Will didn't mind. He sort of liked the holidays, even if they typically worked straight through them. People tended to be in a better mood around the holidays, and people in better moods were a good thing in their line of work. Less bullets. More bonuses.

Taylor answered, "Sure. What did you have in mind?"

"A couple of steaks. A couple of drinks. An early night." He wiggled his eyebrows suggestively.

Taylor's "Okay" was said absently. He probably couldn't have read Will's expression in the dusk anyway, but he was no longer looking at Will. He was staring ahead at their office, the last space in the mall, where a blond man in a leather jacket was exiting through a glass door that read *American Eagle.*

"He changed his mind," Will commented, following Taylor's gaze. "He doesn't want to know she's cheating."

Taylor made a dismissive sound. They didn't do cheating spouses. They weren't PIs. They were security consultants, and as of this afternoon's successful landing of the Webster Fidelity account, they were moving into the big leagues just like they'd been talking about since they'd left the Diplomatic Security Service to strike out on their own three months earlier.

The man in the leather jacket hesitated for a moment, aimlessly jingling the keys in his pockets, and then started toward the bridge. Technically, there was parking in the mall, but the hair salon at the opposite end guaranteed that there was rarely any available space. Will and Taylor always parked on the street.

Anyway, it was just as well this guy was bailing. Securing the Webster account solidified the fact that they were understaffed. Not as understaffed as they had been two weeks earlier when Will had persuaded Euphonia Jones to quit her job at the DMV and come work for them. But for the first time ever, they did not need another client.

As though reading his mind, Taylor said, "Maybe he's dropping off his résumé."

Probably not. Nothing about that slender, slightly aimless figure gave off a law-enforcement vibe.

"So. Outback? Black Angus?" Will returned to more important matters. "Aloha Steakhouse?"

"Aloha," Taylor said. No surprise there. He did not like chain restaurants. Well, and after Paris, neither did Will.

The blond man had reached the head of the bridge and was starting toward them. His aftershave, a distinctive and disagreeable blend of musk and patchouli—what was that? Obsession?—reached them first. Taylor checked mid-stride.

The man also seemed to lose step and waver, peering forward as though trying to see through the gloom. He said doubtfully, "Taylor?"

And in a voice Will had never heard out of him before, Taylor said, *"Ashe?"*

He sounded—well, the cliché would be he sounded like he'd seen a ghost. But actually, he sounded like he *was* a ghost. The ghost of his former younger self. Taylor's husky voice sounded lighter and uncertain, and there was just the suggestion of a boyish crack. It startled Will.

Taylor and Ashe strode toward each other, and hugged—or rather, half hugged, half collided—before stepping back to have a look at each other. Or at least as good a look as they could get in the wavering shadows of the Christmas lights.

"Taylor. It *is* you," Ashe said. "I was thinking it couldn't be. That it had to be some other Taylor MacAllister."

"Jesus. How long has it been? What are you doing here?" Taylor was already turning to Will, making the introductions. "Will, this is Ashe Dekker. Ashe is an old friend of mine."

Will shook Dekker's hand. "Nice to meet you." There wasn't much he could add to that because until that moment, he'd never heard of Ashe Dekker.

Taylor was still talking. "Ashe, meet Will Brandt. Will's my partner. We worked together at DS."

"Sure," Dekker said. "How're you doing, Will?" His grip was firm, though his hand was ice cold.

"Great." Will studied Dekker curiously—and felt his interest returned.

Dekker was a good-looking guy. Average height, slim, with carefully groomed stubble and the kind of shaggy haircut that actually costs a fortune. His clothes were casual and expensive: designer jeans, leather jacket, alligator skin Western boots. Will didn't think much of guys who wore cowboy boots as a fashion statement, but he was willing to make an exception for a pal of Taylor's.

"Taylor and I were at UCLA together," Dekker said.

"Right," Will said. So this was a very old friend, predating any of Taylor's other old friends—not that Will had met so many of them, and not that Taylor had so many of them. "What brings you to our neck of the woods?"

Dekker gave a self-conscious laugh. "To be honest, I was hoping to hire you. Hire American Eagle, that is."

Taylor said, "You need security consulting services?"

"I'm not exactly sure what I need," Dekker said. "But I think someone's trying to kill me."

Euphonia was locking the front door when they arrived at the office, Ashe Dekker in tow.

"That's okay, we'll lock up," Will told her.

"The painters are coming at eight. I was going to run home, have dinner, and come back." Euphonia—Nee to her friends—was a petite black woman with a mop of bronze-gold curls and wide brown eyes. For years she had been their go-to girl at the DMV, so it had been a surprise, when they finally met in person, to discover she really *was* a girl. She was only in her twenties.

Regardless, she was a paragon of efficiency and ingenuity, and within the first week they had promoted her from receptionist to office manager. Not that that meant a whole hell of a lot, given there were only the three of them employed at American Eagle.

"They've got an access code," Will said. "You don't need to drive out here again."

Euphonia smiled the smile of a woman who was going to do exactly what she thought best. She glanced past Will, spotted Dekker, and said in surprise, "Oh, you changed your mind?"

Dekker grimaced. "Yeah. Sorry for being so mysterious." He said to Taylor, "I was here earlier. I, er, declined to fill out any paperwork."

"That's okay. Let's hear your story first," Taylor said.

"Thanks, Nee. Is your car on the street?" Will asked Euphonia.

She sighed. "No, Agent Brandt. My vehicle is located in the lot as ordered."

"Good. And we're not feds anymore."

"Uh-huh. You can take a boy out of the agency, but can you take agency out of a boy?"

They were still trying to come up with an answer to that as Euphonia swept out into the damp night, the brisk *click* of her heels fading quickly.

"She's been waiting to use that line on us," Taylor commented, resting his hip on the edge of Euphonia's terrifyingly neat desk.

"I know." Will ripped the plastic off one of the waiting room's two brand-new chairs, saying to Dekker, "Have a seat, Ashe."

"I'm sure I freaked her out," Dekker confessed, taking the chair Will indicated. "I couldn't stop pacing up and down."

"She used to work for the DMV. She's freak-proof." Taylor absently picked up a paperweight shaped like a crumpled 1040 application, raised his brows, and replaced it.

Dekker watched him. In fact, Dekker seemed to have trouble taking his eyes off Taylor. Not that Will blamed him. With his black hair, burnished green eyes, and elegant bone structure Taylor was probably Will's favorite thing to look at.

Maybe Dekker was comparing the college kid with the man. Maybe he was wondering about that striking single strand of silver in Taylor's hair—a souvenir of his shooting almost two years ago now. Maybe he was looking at the wedding ring on Taylor's left hand and wondering exactly what "partner" meant.

If it was the last, good, because Taylor was definitely off-limits to Ashe Dekker.

Now that he could see Dekker in the light, Will reconsidered his original impression. The guy was attractive, true. He had that kind of bad-boy sexy vibe that Will found annoying, but that appealed to some people—Taylor maybe? His features were a little too sharp, his eyes a little too narrow, his mouth a little too thin. He looked quite a bit older than Taylor, but that could be because he was also—appeared to Will, anyway—a drinker. That slight puffiness around his pale blue eyes, the tiny broken capillaries on the tip of his otherwise perfect nose? Taylor's dad was a drinker, so alcohol abuse was not a trait he found endearing. Although everybody had their exceptions to the rule.

It was hard picturing this guy being close to Taylor. Close enough that a decade later he felt he could call on him when he was in trouble.

Maybe that was more about Taylor than their friendship, because one thing about MacAllister: he was loyal. He was also not what you'd call a naturally gregarious guy. He had friends, of course, a few good men, as the saying went. And for the most part, those were relationships that stretched back years.

Will tuned back in to hear Dekker saying, "I've been living in Europe a while now. Anyway, after my mother passed, I came back to sell the beach house and found a bunch of squatters had moved in."

"*Squatters*," Will repeated, glancing automatically at Taylor.

"Right. They call themselves a family, but if they are, it's more like the Mansons than the Brady Bunch."

Squatters? That was the threat? That was what had driven Dekker to reach across time and tap Taylor? Will couldn't help thinking it was kind of a flimsy excuse. Or were they now supposed to be in the trash removal business?

"What did you do?" Taylor's attention was still focused on Dekker.

"I went through all the legal steps. Posted a three-day notice, filed an unlawful detainer, made sure they were served—"

"Made sure *who* was served?" Taylor interrupted. He was not the stickler for details Will was, but he liked his facts straight.

"A guy by the name of Mike Zamarion seemed to be the head man. His was the name I used for the lawsuit. He never responded, so I got a default judgment."

"This has been going on for a while, I take it?" Will asked.

"It's been going on for about six months."

Will nodded.

Taylor said, "Then what happened?"

"I took that judgment to the sheriff's department, but when the deputies went out to the beach house, everyone was gone. Their stuff was still there, though, so I figured they were hanging around, watching the place, waiting for a chance to come back."

"Probably," Will said. He was starting to wonder why Dekker had had second thoughts about asking for their help. Since he didn't seem to realize this was not the kind of service they provided, it couldn't be that. But he *had* changed his mind about hiring them. He had been in the process of leaving their office without giving Euphonia his contact info. If the traffic had been just a little worse, they'd have missed him and that would have been that.

Of all the nights for smooth sailing on the 101.

"The deputies went ahead and changed the locks, although I guess technically, they were only supposed to post a five-day notice. If you can believe that bullshit. I hired a company to clean out the place—which the assholes had trashed—and to dump their junk."

"Ah." Taylor glanced at Will. "Problematical."

"Yep."

In California, the laws concerning squatters vs. trespassers were a little more complicated than in some other parts of the country. Trespassing was a criminal charge and much simpler to resolve, whereas, depending on a variety of factors, squatters actually had rights and protections. Even after a formal eviction, dumping or destroying a squatter's belongings could lead to legal problems for the property owner.

Plus, it was a shitty thing to do.

Granted, so was squatting in most cases.

"Well, I know that now," Dekker agreed, "because Zamarion came back demanding I hand over their personal property, and when I told them everything had been carted to the dump, they threatened to burn down the house, which they tried to do a week later."

"Are you sure—" Taylor was, by nature, a skeptic. It was one of the things Will liked about him.

"I'm sure," Dekker said with finality. "According to the fire department, it looked like arson."

This was getting better and better.

"Sounds to me like a case for the sheriff's department," Will said. Maybe working in conjunction with the fire department investigators. Maybe not. *Looked like arson* wasn't exactly conclusive. What none of this sounded like was a case for a global security consulting firm.

Taylor directed an unreadable look his way.

Dekker said, "That's what I thought too. Except the sheriff's department says there's nothing they can do. Even after someone ran me off the road a couple of nights ago."

"Wait a minute. Back up." That was Taylor. "You went to the sheriff's department with an arson report? And told them about threats made by—"

"Zamarion. Like I said, he's the ringleader. He claimed he'd been paying property taxes for the past two years and had a legal right to the house. He said he hadn't received the eviction notice and that it had been illegal to change the locks and dump their belongings."

Which, if this Zamarion guy was telling the truth, was correct.

Will said, "Ashe, I know you're not going to want to hear it, but this is a civil matter, not a criminal one."

That time the look Taylor threw him was one of impatience. But Will was just telling it like it was. Clearly, the sheriffs weren't impressed by the arson report, assuming there had been one. This whole thing was a mess and a matter for the courts. It sure as hell wasn't something they needed to be involved in—although if someone really *had* tried to kill Dekker...

"*Did* Zamarion pay the property taxes?" Taylor questioned.

"Yes, but so did I. The way it works, his payments were applied to *future* bills, but there won't be any future bills because I always pay my taxes. The fact that he's paid toward the property taxes complicates my selling the house. It's the craziest situation."

"You said Zamarion made threats," Will said. "What kind of threats exactly?"

"The kind you take seriously." Dekker's blue eyes grew glittery with emotion. "He came to the house and told me, in front of witnesses, he'd see me dead before he'd let me force him and his so-called family out."

"That's a criminal threat. If he made it in front of witnesses, you can—"

"Take him to court?" Dekker's laugh was bitter. "Sure. If the sheriffs can find him. He's a transient. He doesn't have a legal residence. He's using my house as his mailing address. *And* if I can persuade the painters to testify—that's another big if right there since their own legal status is questionable. In the meantime, Zamarion is going to keep on trying to kill me."

Taylor chewed his lip, said, "Do you have proof that the person who tried to run you off the road was Zamarion?"

"You mean like a convenient snapshot of the license plate number? Hell no! *I nearly went off a cliff.* There wasn't time to grab my cell phone and start snapping photos!"

"Okay." Taylor was calm, his voice neutral. "How are you so sure Zamarion was the other driver?"

"Of course he was! Who else? He had just threatened to kill me the day before! That's not a coincidence."

Taylor opened his mouth, but Will cut in. "MacAllister. Can I have a word?"

"Sure." Taylor's tone was easy, but the look he gave Will was direct and uncompromising. Clearly, his mind was already made up.

Well, he could just unmake it.

They went through the reception area door, crossed the hall, navigating ladders and cans of paint, and stepped into the boudoir-pink room that would ultimately be Will's office. Their building space had previously belonged to a bridal shop, and the walls were painted in delicate shades of peach and pink. Pastel wallpaper borders featured parasols (*why parasols?*) and wedding cakes and lovebirds nibbling gold bands. None of which projected the appropriate YOUR SAFETY IS IN OUR HANDS! vibe—or even, in Will's view, a reassuring preview of marriage.

They were hoping to have the renovations finished before the end of the year, but the holidays turned out to be an unexpectedly busy time for contractors. Most of the work at American Eagle was having to be done after-hours—and at a premium price.

Will closed the door to his office. He kept his voice low. "Okay, listen. Dekker is a friend, and I understand that you want to help him, but this is *clearly* a case for the sheriffs."

"Sure," Taylor replied. "That doesn't mean we can't take a look around, ask a few questions."

Will didn't trust that reasonable tone. "Yes. If that's all you're talking about. Because we've got to be realistic. You know as well as I do, we're not in a position to take on another client."

Taylor shrugged dismissively. "If you don't want to take Ashe on as a client, that's okay with me. I wasn't planning on billing him. I'll handle this as a favor. In my spare time."

This was exactly what Will had feared. Taylor had not only already made his mind up, he was busily working out the details before they could even finish identifying what those details might be.

He tried very hard to keep his exasperation from showing. "*What* spare time? You don't have spare time. Neither of us do."

"What's your point, Will?" Taylor rested his hand on his canted hip, and studied him with cool, green eyes.

That—in fairness, unconsciously—cocky posture, that skeptical *really?* stare, were the reason so many people longed to punch Taylor five seconds after meeting him. It wasn't really who Taylor was. Or rather, yeah, the confidence, the cynicism, were facets of his personality, but not the main facets, and not traits he typically turned on Will.

Obviously, this was a unique case, and Will needed to respect that. Which he was *trying* to do.

He said, "All I'm saying is, doesn't it make more sense—isn't it better for all of us—if we direct Dekker back to the sheriff's department? And if you don't feel like that's enough, we can refer him to another—"

Taylor cut him off. "Uh-uh. We're not referring him anywhere. Ashe came to *me*."

"I know that. That's why I'm saying—"

"I gave Ashe my word that if he ever needed help, I'd be there. I didn't say, if you ever need help, I can refer you to someone. I promised *I'd* be there for him."

"I get that." Will did. It would be unreasonable to be irritated with Taylor for making those kinds of promises years before they'd ever met. He *wasn't* irritated, and he definitely wasn't jealous—he didn't think—but Christ, Taylor could be so bullheaded.

"Do you?" There it was. That hint of cynical smile. "Because that's not what I'm hearing."

"What you're hearing is me trying to work out what's going to be best for *all* of us. We're not bodyguards—"

"We've handled plenty of protection details, so don't give me that. What's your real beef?"

"My real beef is not two hours ago we landed the kind of job we've been hunting since we left the DS, and we both know we don't actually have the manpower to carry it off."

"So we're going to be stretched thin. We should be used to that by now."

"*So*, taking on another job—one that's liable to be as time-consuming and distracting as this one sounds—is not smart." He shook his head.

"It'll take a day. Two at most."

"You're dreaming."

"The hell. You think I can't handle tracking down this Zamarion guy?"

"Of course I don't think that. But come on, you know what this is going to be. Chasing smoke in the wind."

"I know."

"Then you admit it's not an efficient use of our resources."

Taylor opened his mouth, and Will added, "And while we're on the topic of resources, I thought you were frantic to pay Richard back? Just this morning you said again how much you didn't want to be in debt to him. Which is all the more reason not to take on a pro-bono gig that's liable to jeopardize the first job we've had that might allow us to start paying off that debt."

Everything Will was saying was true, so it was maddening to have Taylor keep looking at him with that skeptical expression like...*what*? What did think was really motivating Will?

"I see," Taylor drawled. "If David Bradley came to us for help, you'd just give him the name of a good local firm and send him on his way?"

Will felt himself change color. "It's not the same situation. David is— *was*—"

He stopped, realizing he was wading into quicksand.

Brows arched in pointed inquiry, Taylor said mildly, "David is—
was—?"

"David is *our* friend—"

"He's no friend of mine."

"He's not someone from my distant past asking for a favor. And any-
way, I'd have to tell David the same thing I'm telling you now. We don't have
the resources to handle this."

"Bullshit."

Somehow the quietness of that was more jarring than if Taylor had
shouted at him. "If David Fucking Bradley came through that door, asking
for your help, you'd move heaven and earth to give it to him. We both know
it. And guess what? I understand that. I even respect it. Which is why I ex-
pect you to understand and respect my position. I'm not asking you to put
in extra hours. I'll handle this on my own. And I'll make damn sure that it
doesn't interfere with the Webster Fidelity job. Okay? Fair enough?"

No, it was not okay, it was not fair. It was foolish and impractical. But
after Taylor invoked David's name, what else could Will say? No way in hell
could he risk arguing with Taylor about David, and clearly that's where this
conversation was headed.

Will said curtly, "Fair enough."

Taylor nodded, yanked open the door, and they walked in silence back
into the front office. They found Ashe scrutinizing a stack of framed pho-
tos. He looked up with an expression of hope mixed with wariness, and set
aside a seven-year-old picture of Will accepting his marksmanship qualifi-
cation badge.

"Okay," Taylor told him. "We talked it over. We're taking your case."

"You are?" Ashe threw a quick, doubtful look at Will.

"Yes," Will said.

Ashe still seemed unsure. "If this isn't the kind of thing you do—"

"We do whatever needs doing," Taylor said.

"It's our company's slogan," Will said sardonically. "We're going to
get it printed on coffee mugs."

Taylor gave him an unamused look before saying to Dekker, "Where are you staying?"

"The beach house. Carpinteria."

"Okay, I'll drive up first thing tomorrow and take a look around. You can fill me in on the rest of the story. We'll start there and see where it leads us."

"That's... I don't know what to say. Thank you," Dekker said, with another of those slightly ill-at-ease glances at Will. "Thank you both."

He did seem thankful. But Will couldn't help thinking Dekker also seemed more scared than when he'd first walked into their office.

CHAPTER TWO

Will was not happy.

Even after two Knob Creek bourbons and ordering Aloha Steakhouse's legendary prime rib Menehune cut, he remained stern-mouthed and steely eyed, and, in the normal course of things, that would have bothered the hell out of Taylor. In this case… Well, in this case, Brandt needed to suck it up.

Taylor sighed mentally, gazing out the wall of windows overlooking the moonlit ocean. The restaurant was one of their favorite places. The food was good, the drinks were good, and the beachy decor with its high ceilings, polished wood, and marine-themed art was usually as relaxing as a walk on the beach.

Not so much tonight.

This was not exactly the celebration Will had wanted, and Taylor was sorry about that. But a promise was a promise, and if anyone ought to understand that, it was Will. He was the most honorable guy Taylor had ever known.

He swallowed the last of his Aloha Amber Ale. He was sticking to beer tonight, not wanting to risk an alcohol-infused argument when they got home—he recognized the precariousness of his own mood. He should never have brought up David Bradley. Will, still appalled by the hurt he'd unconsciously inflicted in Paris, was bound to think that's what this was about. But it was nothing to do with Bradley. This was about one thing and one thing only: keeping his promise to Ashe.

And yeah, Will was right. Taylor had made that promise in a different life. Will was right that the timing was not good. Well, that went without saying. There was no good time for bad things to happen. Will was also right that they were already stretched too thin and they couldn't—could *not* under any circumstances—afford to jeopardize the Webster account.

And finally, Will was right that Ashe was not being completely candid with them.

That was something he'd brought up after the first round of drinks. They'd been making carefully neutral conversation over the fried calamari, and Will had said suddenly, "Maybe I'd feel better about the situation if I didn't have the feeling your boy Dekker is hiding something."

Until Will put it into words, Taylor hadn't acknowledged his own reservations. And even then he said, "Yeah, well, he's probably a little embarrassed. No guy likes to feel like he can't take care of himself. I'm guessing the sheriffs weren't particularly diplomatic."

"He was definitely vague about the arson report."

"That doesn't mean someone didn't try to burn down his place."

Will hmmed and sipped his bourbon. Eventually, he said, "How did he find us?"

"We're in the Yellow Pages. We're on the web. We're running ads in *Ventura Life* magazine. I would hope people could find us."

"That's not what I mean. How did he know American Eagle is you?"

"Us."

"Us. It's not like we're running ads under our names."

Taylor said, "We're not hiding our identities either. Anyone who looks up our website is going to see our About Us section. It's reasonable that our names might be popping up in Google searches."

"Maybe." Will still sounded dissatisfied.

Taylor again considered Ashe's nervousness, came up with, "After all, it's been a long time. Maybe he wasn't completely comfortable coming to us."

"Coming to you." It was said dispassionately, but point made.

"Still."

Will's comments confirmed his own gut feeling that there was more to Ashe's story. But then Ashe had always been a little...evasive.

He said slowly, watching Will's face, "What are you thinking?"

"Nothing," Will said. "I'm just making observations as they occur to me."

They were both a little paranoid after Oregon.

Maybe with good reason. A few weeks earlier they had visited Will's father for Thanksgiving—now *there* was a homecoming for the history books—and discovered they were being tailed by a not-very-efficient PI by the name of Stuart Schwierskott.

Schwierskott swore he did not know who had hired Schwierskott & Associate to conduct surveillance on them—or rather he insisted he had been hired by a legal firm acting as a middleman—and despite their best efforts, Will and Taylor had not been successful in finding out who wanted to keep tabs on them.

It seemed pretty unlikely Ashe could be connected to any of that. For one thing, he claimed his troubles had begun months ago, and that was something that could be easily verified.

Besides, Ashe was genuinely afraid; that had been plain to Taylor. And really, that was all that mattered. Ashe needed help, and Taylor owed him that much.

Their meals came, and within a few bites of meltingly tender black & bleu filet mignon, Taylor's mood lifted. Will stopped looking quite so bleak and ordered a third round of drinks.

They were halfway through their dinners when Will said thoughtfully, "He doesn't really seem like your type."

"What's my type?"

"Me," Will said promptly, and Taylor gave a little huff.

But Will was smiling at him, teasing, though maybe a bit tentative— they had come way too close to really arguing earlier. Taylor smiled back. After all, it was perfectly true. And Will, with his chiseled, square-jawed handsomeness—alert and amused blue eyes, boyish sweep of glossy brown hair—was about as far from Ashe's edgy, sensual, and slightly dissolute appeal as it got.

"Maybe we were just friends," Taylor suggested.

"No. Not the way he looked at you." Will shook his head. Started to say ruefully, "And..."

Taylor glanced at him. "And?"

"There was a note in your voice."

"A note in *my* voice?"

What did that mean? Was Will jealous? No. Will knew perfectly well he came first for Taylor and had from practically the minute they'd been teamed. Will had never doubted Taylor's feelings for him, just his ability to keep his pants zipped in the face of temptation. To mix a metaphor or two.

Anyway, he didn't want to dwell on old resentments. Not everything could be resolved. Sometimes you just had to let go of the hurt and move on.

Will said, still smiling, still rueful, but *something* was going on there, "You sounded *very* happy to see him."

"Well, yeah. Sure." He *had* been glad to see Ashe. Ashe had been a little wild, a little reckless back in the day. Taylor had wondered and even worried a bit about him over the years. Maybe not as much as he should have, but he had been very glad to see Ashe was okay.

He circled back to the safer ground of Will's earlier comment. "Anyway, he's not my type. Now. But it was college. I didn't have a type."

"Sure you did."

Taylor's smile twisted, but okay. Maybe. "He was different. I was different." He shrugged.

"What happened?"

It was a fair question, given that Ashe was sort of their client, but Will had never shown any interest in Taylor's romantic attachments before. In fact, he'd always been studiously *not* interested.

Taylor said, "It wasn't like you and Madonna. We weren't childhood sweethearts."

"Yeowch."

"Just sayin'. It only lasted a year. There weren't any plans for a future together. I knew I'd be going into the DS."

"What was Ashe planning to do after college?"

"He hadn't decided. I was four years ahead of him."

Will's brows rose. "You're kidding. I thought for sure he was older than you."

"Nope. Anyway, I graduated, went into the DS as planned, and that was that. My first posting abroad was Japan."

No further explanations needed. Will knew all about Japan. Come to think of it, given the messy nature of some of his romantic entanglements, no wonder Will didn't want to know more than he already did.

Will said, "I see. How did the pledge of eternal fealty come about?" His tone was light, but yeah, there was a faint edge.

Taylor controlled his impatience. He wasn't enjoying this, but he did not want secrets between himself and Will. Even if the truth was liable to confirm some of Will's misgivings. "Ashe wasn't out before he met me. I mean, neither of us were. Officially. But he hadn't ever been with anyone. He was…emotionally vulnerable in a way I wasn't." Taylor met Will's bright and curious gaze. "I did care for him, but I wasn't in love. He was."

Painfully so. He didn't like remembering. Even now.

"I see."

Taylor said—he needed Will to understand this, "It wasn't just something I said. I meant it. About being there for him if he ever needed me."

"I know you did," Will said. "You never say anything you don't mean."

Well, that was maybe an exaggeration, but it was true he didn't make promises carelessly.

They turned their attention back to their meals. To Taylor's relief, when Will spoke again, he was back to business.

"You know, we probably need to think about bringing a cyber security expert on board sooner rather than later. All the top firms offer cyber security now."

Truth. Gone were the days when firewalls and antivirus software could keep a company's secrets safe. In their technically reliant society, cybersecurity risk was growing exponentially, driven by global connectivity and usage of cloud services to store sensitive data. Increasingly sophisticated cyber criminals meant the risk to organizations, both large and small, was steadily on the rise. While there were no national laws overseeing data breach disclosure, every state had their own data breach laws, with California leading the way since 2003. If they were really going to be a world-class contender, they were going to have to take a serious look at providing cyber security.

Frankly, something Taylor had zero interest in.

He didn't say that, of course. What would be the point? They were all in now. No turning back. Not professionally. Not personally.

He said instead, "Who do we know looking to make a career change?"

"Let me think. Lousy hours, lousy pay, lousy benefits. Who wouldn't jump at that?"

Taylor grinned because they had both jumped at that.

Will met his eyes, smiled in wry acknowledgment. "I don't know, but the market is only going to get more competitive for prospective employers. We should put feelers out."

A tiring thought. Taylor nodded, his thoughts circling back to their meeting that day. "Webster's IT team manager got pretty defensive at the suggestion that cyber security should be its own department."

"Predictable."

"Nobody wants to think the threat could come from within, but that's the truth."

"Yep."

Will's cell rang. He checked it, and his face went blank. Of course, that very lack of expression was a tell to someone who knew him as well as Taylor.

"Who's that?" Taylor asked, just to turn the knife a little.

"No one important." Will put his cell down and met Taylor's gaze steadily.

Taylor's grin was crooked. "I guess Bradley's back from parts unknown?"

"Probably."

Taylor let it go. It wasn't Will's fault that his ex-boyfriend couldn't seem to come to terms with Will having moved on. Or at least, it wasn't completely Will's fault.

Riley, Will's German shepherd, was beside himself with joy when they finally walked through the Craftsman bungalow Taylor had restored with periodic help from Will.

"Hey, Riley. Hey, boy," Will said wearily. It had been a long-ass day. And tomorrow looked to be even longer.

They shrugged out of their jackets as the dog ran circles around them, whining his complaints about the hours they were keeping. It turned out their work schedule was hard on the whole family.

"I'm going to take him for a walk on the beach," Will announced.

Taylor, sorting through the mail, looked up, studying him. Will's attention was on Riley, and his expression seemed remote.

And honestly? Taylor didn't have the energy to deal with it. Assuming there was anything going on there besides fatigue.

"Sure. Watch yourself."

Will nodded, hesitated, then called to Riley, who slid magic-carpet style on the hallway rug in his hurry to get out the front door.

Taylor went back to sorting the mail, absently listening to the front door close, Will's deep voice checking Riley's enthusiasm, the jingle of Riley's tags, and Will's footsteps growing fainter.

There wasn't much of interest in the day's post. Not even many bills, thanks to the loan from Richard. There were a couple of Christmas-card-shaped envelopes, one from his insurance company and one with David Bradley's return address.

Taylor scowled at Bradley's machine-precise cursive, propped the envelope against the coffee machine, where Will couldn't miss it, and turned his attention to their phone messages. Not much excitement there either—mostly those annoying "Hello? Hello?" spam calls.

No question life was quieter now that they were civilians. But that wasn't a bad thing. In fact, knowing odds were good they'd both live to make old bones was one of the best things about their sudden career change. And landing the Webster Fidelity account was a huge coup. It was the kind of thing they had been talking about since they'd opened shop.

So why this sense of almost…letdown?

He shook off the feeling impatiently. He was just tired. They both were. Plus, red meat did not really agree with him, and they were eating a lot of red meat lately. Will gravitated to meat and potatoes when he was stressed. And yes, they were stressed. They'd be stupid not to be. Although

Will was equally energized. Will had really wanted the Webster Fidelity account, and he'd worked his ass off to land it. He'd been jubilant today. Whereas Taylor...

Well, naturally he was jubilant too. He just wasn't used to feeling out of his element, and he'd definitely felt out of his element at that afternoon's meeting.

Besides which, if he'd wanted to work in the corporate world, he'd have taken his stepfather Richard up on one of his many offers to join the family firm.

But what was the use in thinking like this? Taylor shook off his reflections. The main thing he had wanted was for him and Will to be working together again, so what did it matter what the job was?

It didn't.

He washed up the breakfast dishes left in the sink, showered, tossed a load of laundry into the washing machine. Will and Riley were still not back by the time Taylor finally climbed into bed. He stretched out on the king-size mattress with a groan of relief. His body was not designed to sit on its ass all day in a conference-room chair.

Absently, he listened to the wet *thump* of the washer, staring at the ceiling, considering Ashe's sudden reappearance.

It *was* odd.

Will was right about that. But Ashe had always been a little odd. Or maybe odd wasn't the right word.

Okay, yeah, odd. And impulsive. And kind of careless. Easy to see how he had made a bad situation worse with Mike Zamarion and his crew.

But Ashe was also smart, funny, good company, and surprisingly easygoing. Most of the time. The sex had been *crazy good*. Sometimes just crazy. But mostly really good. Their twelve-hour marathon of goodbye sex had been the best in Taylor's life—up to the point of Will.

Of course, that was first love for you. Mostly on Ashe's part, but Taylor *had* loved him. In his way. Admittedly, back then, his way had been pretty self-serving. So what? They had been two horny young college guys. Nobody had plighted their troth or anything.

What had Ashe been doing living in Europe?

Taylor hoped he was not making the wrong choice by insisting they could handle Ashe's case and still deliver for Webster Fidelity. He did not want to let Will down.

Will.

That was another point of concern.

Will had definitely not warmed to Ashe. He was not jealous by nature, even if he did suffer the occasional flash of insecurity when it came to Taylor's sexual past. It had to be his concerns about Taylor's decision to take on additional work when they were already stretched so thin. A legit worry. It was Taylor's responsibility to make sure Will's qualms remained unrealized.

They were in a good place right now—it had taken effort to get there—and he did not want to jeopardize that. However, not to hold on to old grudges, but Jesus, didn't he deserve some room to maneuver, given how much latitude he'd given Will over good old Lt. Commander David Bradley? Not to mention a few other missteps by his partner that he was doing his best to forget?

But maybe he was anticipating problems where there weren't any. There was every possibility he'd get Ashe's situation sorted out within a day. Certainly, before the end of the week. If there was one thing more than a decade in the DSS had taught him, it was that most problems were solved through communication. Diplomacy in Action.

He blinked sleepily against the increasing weight of his eyelids.

First thing he was going to do was find out for sure whether there really was an arson report...

He came awake when the mattress dipped beneath Will's weight. The room and hallway beyond were in total darkness, the gap in the curtains offering a glimpse of stars and Will's pale outline easing down beside him.

Taylor mumbled, "What time is it?"

"Shh," Will soothed. "Still plenty of nighttime."

Good news because sleep was in short supply these days. Even so, he was coming back to alertness, aware that it was much later, that Will had been gone hours.

Will must have had a lot to think about that evening, must have put in several miles of sandy contemplation. Or he'd been making phone calls he didn't want Taylor to overhear.

"Everything okay?"

"Everything's good." Will kissed him. It was a soft kiss. Tender. Almost apologetic. Was Will sorry for being gone so long or for the things he had been thinking while he'd been gone so long?

"You sure?" Taylor put his hand against Will's cheek—Will's eyes were a gleam in the shadows.

"I'm sure." Will kissed him again, and Taylor responded with quick, ready hunger—there were more important things than sleep, after all.

The rough velvet of their jaws rubbed against each other, the butterfly flutter of eyelashes brushing eyelashes, the warm bump of noses and mouths…and other things.

"Sorry," Will whispered. "Sorry for being a jerk this evening."

Taylor moved his head in negation. "No. You were right. It wasn't only my decision."

"A promise is a promise."

True. But.

"Yeah, and I promise I'll get Ashe's problems wrapped up ASAP."

Taylor felt Will's mouth curve, maybe in a smile, maybe in acknowledgment, maybe thinking the joke was on Taylor. Will kissed him again, promised, "We'll work it out together. He's my client too."

That was the Will he knew and loved. Taylor's heart expanded with gratitude at being met more than halfway. He nodded.

Their mouths gentled, lingered, tasting—Will was peppermint-flavored with bourbon undertones—taking a moment to savor what they had. It had taken them long enough to get here.

Will traced Taylor's mouth with his fingertips, slowly traced his cheekbones, his eyebrows, not exploration, more a slow and thoughtful confirmation. Taylor could feel each fleeting caress after Will moved on. Was that what they meant by cell memory? Because every cell in his body recognized Will's touch; could not imagine any circumstance where he would not know Will from anyone else, everyone else. Even the first day they'd met, he'd had a sense of discovery, a feeling that this was what—who—he'd been waiting for.

Not that he'd *waited*—clearly—which was occasionally part of the problem for Will.

He nipped Will's finger, and felt Will's smile. Will whispered, "I really do love you." There had been a time when he had struggled with saying the words aloud.

"I had an idea you might."

But Will was serious, even earnest. "Don't ever think I take you for granted."

Until that moment, the thought had never occurred to Taylor, but okay.

Will lowered his head, and they kissed again. Taylor shoved up the soft cotton folds of Will's Henley to stroke the hard, muscular planes of Will's naked back, slid down over Will's hips to the opening in his sleep pants, arrowing in on soft skin, hard muscle. Will groaned, reciprocating, tugging at the band of Taylor's boxers, dragging them down, stopping as Taylor's gulp of pleasure turned to protest when elastic band met rigid cock.

Will muttered breathless apology, still plucking clumsily at the thin cotton, and Taylor started to laugh, lifting up, allowing for less perilous access. The heady scents of body-heated flannel and imminent sex rose with him. The bedclothes floated up, ghostlike, as Will laughed too, breathlessly, wriggling to free himself from his pajama bottoms, which he did in a couple of desperate heaves.

They landed back in each other's arms, their cocks rigid and swollen, and the laughter dried as they humped against each other, hips grinding, backs laboring, shivering and shoving against each other in that desperate struggle for release.

Always the same, always different.

Their mouths fastened once more, the kiss deeper, hotter, tongues twining, suddenly starving for each other, eating each other alive.

Taylor arched into Will's thrust, and they found their rhythm—practice made perfect—push-me-pull-you-ing into each other's touch, feverish with the need for connection, urgent with the necessity for the most intimate of intimacies.

Will groaned against his ear, a hot, moist gust of pained delight. Taylor pulled him closer, arms wrapping tight, licking Will's throat, nibbling beneath his chin, moaning half-hearted remonstrance when Will sucked him back on the side of his neck, hard, wet suction that would leave a mark for sure.

Bodies writhing, cocks rubbing, muscular chests pushing against each other, moving together with the ease of practice, sex not any less pleasurable for being a familiar and reliable source of comfort and release. Will nuzzled velvety kisses against Taylor's throat, bent his head to tongue Taylor's nipples, reached down and took Taylor's wet-slick cock in his hand. It didn't take more than a stroke or two before Taylor arched, seeming to light up, his body taut and trembling, crying out.

"*Jesus.* Will..."

"Christ, *Tay*," Will groaned from deep in his chest, and sudden wet warmth spread between them.

Taylor closed his eyes, feeling that pulse of warm seed spilling from him, waves of sweet, soft relief washing away the earlier tension and strain.

They lay there for a few moments, shattered, dazed, not minding the hot stickiness gluing them together. Just one of the things that glued them together. When they stopped twitching and trembling, they shifted a little, getting more comfortable, still cradling each other as they tumbled into their separate dreams.

CHAPTER THREE

"In addition to increasing employee accountability, we've encouraged our staff members to consciously foster an environment of loss prevention..."

Was there anything more boring than department-head meetings?

Will resisted the temptation to look at his phone as yet another Webster Fidelity manager rose to defend at length why their department did not need some outsider analyzing their security risk and offering unnecessary advice.

The fact that CEO Harvey Reid had kicked off this already very long meeting by reassuring everyone present that American Eagle was not out to "get" anyone, that they were being hired as a preventative measure and solely in an effort to keep up with changing times, seemed to have no effect on "the team."

It didn't help that Taylor had not made the meeting.

In fairness, Will hadn't thought he would. He appreciated that Taylor *wanted* to be there.

But Taylor's absence underscored the fact that American Eagle had two consultants and WF had five locations, from San Diego to Yreka, each needing to be personally visited and assessed for possible security threats so that separate and specific contingency protocols could be created—oh, and that Harvey Reid wanted it all done before Webster Fidelity closed for the week between Christmas and New Year's.

Maybe they shouldn't have gone into the Private Eye biz after all, because when Will considered the list of services they ostensibly offered their clients, he felt a kind of alarm he had never experienced either in the Marines or in the DSS.

Whose bright idea had this been again?

Oh, right. His.

Also in the column of things he was not thrilled about was the realization that he was going to have his work cut out acting as a buffer between Taylor and Todd Kohl, WF's pompous and pugnacious head of security.

Kohl was in his forties, short, pudgy, with thinning red hair which he tried to disguise by sweeping it forward in a swoop of bangs that looked like a donkey's forelock. His favorite things in life appeared to be his impressive-sounding gun collection—wasn't that a weird thing to mention when first being introduced?—and hunting monster elk. He had never served in the military, and seemed a little defensive about it. In fact, Kohl seemed a little defensive about everything, starting with why CEO Harvey Reid had felt it necessary to hire American Eagle.

Kohl and Taylor were going to be oil and water. Or maybe oil and firewater. Maybe it was just as well Taylor was missing this meeting.

It was clear there would be plenty of other interminable meetings ahead.

Will's phone vibrated on the wooden conference table like a *knock-knock-Fate-calling!* moment, and ten pairs of disapproving eyes turned their laser beams his way. Thinking—hoping—it might be Taylor, Will reached for his cell and saw David's contact profile photo flash up.

His gut twisted in nervous response, which just the thought of David gave him after Paris. Not David's fault, but the memory of what Taylor had suffered during those forty-eight hours half killed Will. Remembering Taylor's mocking smile at dinner the night before—and the sight of that Christmas card strategically positioned against the coffee maker…oh, hell no.

He did not have the energy for that.

He rose, nodding apologetically to Reid, and stepped into the hallway. The truth was this meeting was for Webster Fidelity employees, to give them a chance to vent their frustrations and fears. He probably shouldn't have been present anyway.

On the elevator ride to the lobby, he checked his messages, but other than the now two messages from David, there was nothing of interest. Meaning no word from Taylor yet.

What part of *keep me posted* did Taylor not understand?

Will reached the lobby, nodded at the portly security guard, who promptly sucked in his belly, and went out through the revolving glass door—which, by the way, needed to be changed out for a ballistic-resistant high-security revolving door.

It was a gray day. The air felt dull and heavy, tainted with smog and car exhaust. A couple of strands of wan white Christmas lights spanned the width of the street, and that was about it for striking a festive note. Spring Street, in the heart of Los Angeles's financial district, was known as the Wall Street of the West with good reason. It was also a historic district with over ten buildings designated Historic-Cultural Monuments by the Los Angeles Cultural Heritage Commission. A lot of the original Beaux Arts facades remained virtually intact, making the district a popular shooting location for production companies filming period pieces. There were no film crews present that day, but a number of Asian tourists with cameras and a walking tour led by a guy in a fedora passed him as he phoned David back.

David picked up within two rings. "Will, good to hear from you." David greeted him in that deep, sexy growl of a voice. "How are you?"

"Good," Will said. "Actually, great. Sorry it took so long to get back to you, David."

"It's a busy time of year. How's your better half?"

That was David having a little joke because he did not consider Taylor to be Will's better half. Not in any way, shape, or form. They all knew he believed Will had made a serious mistake in choosing Taylor over him. And as much as Will liked David, that made it hard to stay friends.

It was a shame too, because Will shared interests with David that he didn't share with Taylor—and since when was there a law that a gay man couldn't have a close same-sex friend?

"Taylor's fine." Will remembered Taylor was currently in Carpinteria with his college boyfriend, and suddenly couldn't think of anything to add.

David chuckled, a warm, friendly sound. "That's a little terse. I won't ask. How's the new business venture?"

David was a perceptive guy. Maybe too perceptive. Will admitted, "Things are different in the private sector, but we're figuring it out."

"I don't doubt that for a minute. We should catch up one of these days. In fact, that's why I called. I'm having a little Christmas party this weekend—just a few good friends, nothing extravagant—and if you and MacAllister don't have any plans, I'd love you to come. You could spend the night. The guest room is ready and waiting."

Uh, yeah. That room was going to have a long wait, because this get-together was never going to happen. Will could imagine Taylor's reaction to learning of David's invitation. His ears rang just thinking about it.

"It sounds like fun," he said regretfully. "Unfortunately—well, no, actually, fortunately—we just landed a huge contract, and we're going to be working right through the holidays."

David responded, and Will heard the disappointment but not the words because all at once he registered a silver Honda Accord parked across the street. The driver held a pair of binoculars, and the binoculars were trained in Will's direction.

His first thought was this might be some security threat to Webster Fidelity, but even as the possibility formed, he remembered noting a silver Honda Accord following him off the freeway and onto Spring Street.

Granted, Honda Accords were one of the most popular cars in LA County, but Will was trained to recognize potential vehicle surveillance, and while he was a few months out of practice, he wasn't *that* much out of practice.

Nor was it the first time he'd been tailed in the past month, though it was definitely not Stuart Schwierskott behind those field glasses. It might be another operative from Schwierskott & Associate.

"If you ever need to talk," David was saying.

"Thanks, David." Will was no longer listening. "Have a Merry Christmas." He disconnected, turned, and went back inside Webster Fidelity.

Through the tinted glass windows, he observed the driver of the Honda Accord for a few seconds. There was too much traffic and street activity to get a good look, but he had the impression the driver was male, middle-aged, and probably Caucasian. Frankly, not much of a guess given that middle-aged Caucasian males dominated the security industry.

He didn't want to leap to conclusions. This guy was not necessarily a pro. Even if he was, there were plenty of people inside and outside this building. Will was not by default the target of surveillance. In fact, a nondescript guy in a nondescript car was not by default conducting surveillance, even if he was holding a pair of binoculars. He could be another tourist, a location scout, a jealous boyfriend.

If he could get a look at the car's license plates—

In the midst of this thought, the driver of the Honda Accord pulled away from the curb and merged into the flow of late morning traffic.

The meeting with Webster Fidelity's department heads was followed by another, briefer but equally dull meeting with an alphabet soup of top-tier executives, which was followed by lunch with Todd Kohl, head of security.

And if all that wasn't enough of a recipe for indigestion, all Will had heard from Taylor since he'd left for Ashe's Carpinteria beach house that morning were a couple of cryptic messages promising to keep Will updated. Updates promising updates were not actually updates, in case MacAllister didn't know it.

Anyway, Kohl's ego had taken a bruising over the hiring of American Eagle. Webster Fidelity did not have an actual Chief Security Officer—that role would be taken on at least temporarily by American Eagle—and Will spent a fair bit of time and money on a nice lunch and a lot of schmoozing.

Midway through the meal he realized there were going to be a lot of lunches like this in his future, and nearly lost his appetite.

Kohl was never going to be their ally, but not having him as an enemy would be a good thing. Will wasn't sure he had achieved that objective by the time he and Kohl walked out of Nick and Stef's Steakhouse, but détente had to start somewhere.

By four o'clock he was on the freeway headed back to Ventura, trying to decide whether to phone Taylor or not—and feeling aggravated over his uncertainty—when he noticed a silver Honda Accord lurking several cars back.

"Are you for real?" Will muttered, eyes on his rearview mirror.

He amused himself for a few miles by speeding up and slowing down, and each time, the Honda surged forward or fell back, always preserving a safe distance behind a wall of cars that made it impossible to make out the driver or license plates. Of course, it was always possible this manoeuvring was not maneuvering at all, was merely coincidence, but that was not very likely.

Will considered getting off the freeway and then getting back on just to be sure he wasn't letting his imagination run away with him, but if he did, the tail would almost certainly know he had been made, and Will would lose whatever element of surprise he had.

Assuming he had any.

He thought it over and then, instead of phoning Taylor, phoned Stuart Schwierskott.

A few weeks earlier, Schwierskott & Associate, a Southland private investigation company, had been hired to conduct surveillance on him and Taylor. Schwierskott had followed them to Oregon, though Taylor had made him almost immediately.

In return for their keeping quiet about his botching the job, Schwierskott had told them everything he knew about who had hired him, which turned out to be pretty much *nada* because Schwierskott & Associate had been hired by a third party, Gently, Fallis & Landreth, a legal firm better known for their schlocky TV ads than their ethics.

Will had tried to get someone from Gently, Fallis & Landreth to roll over on their client, but with no luck. It just wasn't as easy to get results without the weight of the federal government behind them.

Besides, as the weeks passed with no further threat manifesting—not even signs of continued surveillance—he and Taylor had been inclined to dismiss the incident as a case of mistaken identity.

It wasn't like they didn't have plenty of other things vying for their attention.

Anyway, Schwierskott, the associate in Schwierskott & Associate, owed them for not letting his old man know he'd faked most, if not all, of his surveillance reports, and Will decided to call in that marker.

"Schwierskott," said the voice on the other end.

"Hey, Stuart, remember me? Will Brandt?"

"*Brandt?*" Schwierskott's voice shot up an octave. "What are you calling me *here* for?"

"I don't have your home number."

"My…" Schwierskott's breathing sounded like someone starting to hyperventilate. "Why are you calling me at *all*? I thought we had an agreement!"

"We do," Will assured him. "So long as you continue to cooperate."

"Cooperate how? Continued cooperation wasn't the agreement."

"It is now. Who at S&A is currently handling the surveillance on us?"

Schwierskott gulped audibly. "No one!"

"Eh'nt!"

"W-w-what was that?"

"That was the Wrong Answer buzzer," Will said. "Try again."

"It's true," protested Schwierskott.

"Stuart, I hate to threaten a forty-year-old man with telling his father on him—"

"I told you the truth. They yanked the account from us."

"Who did?" Will asked.

"Gently, Fallis & Landreth. They cancelled their contract about a week ago. They were upset about what they called our lack of results."

Will considered this grimly, watching the Honda Accord speed up to match his unconscious acceleration. Usually it was MacAllister who didn't trust coincidences. In Will's experience, coincidence happened. But really, what were the odds here?

"Who's the contact person over at Gently, Fallis & Landreth?"

Schwierskott said indignantly, "How should I know? I never dealt with them. That's front-office stuff."

"Wait a minute," Will said. "You're telling me you got back from Oregon and you didn't have *any* curiosity about what was actually going on? And you call yourself a PI?"

"Uh, I call myself a *private investigator*," Schwierskott said huffily. "And maybe I'm not comfortable sharing that information with you."

"I don't know why not. I don't care what you call yourself."

"Hardy har har."

"Look, Stuart," Will said, "I'm asking for a favor. Professional courtesy, remember? There's something hinky going on here, and by now you must know that yourself."

Schwierskott was silent.

"If they're no longer your client—"

"Dina Shey," Schwierskott answered abruptly. "She's who you want to talk to. But be prepared. She is a *frosty* bitch."

"Thank you," Will said, and he meant it sincerely. "I appreciate it."

"Sure you do."

Will glanced again at the Honda's miniature reflection. *Objects in mirror are closer than they appear. No* lie.

He said slowly, "Stuart, do you do any freelancing?"

"*Me?*" Schwierskott sounded startled. "Uh, well, yeah. I *could*. Sure. Sure, I do."

Will considered. He was taking a chance. Schwierskott was kind of a screw-up, and even if he wasn't—even if Oregon had been a fluke—MacAllister was liable to lose his shit if he ever found out about this.

Schwierskott was saying quickly, eagerly, "You want me to follow up with Shey? I could take a run at her. I'd be—"

"No," Will cut him off. "No, I'll handle that angle. This is something else—and you'll deal directly with me and only me. Got that? Don't call the office. I'll give you my personal cell number."

"Okay, sure." Schwierskott sounded less certain. "This isn't some kind of shadow op, is it?"

Will managed not to hoot at the idea of bringing Schwierskott in on something like that. "No. This is not some kind of shadow op. This is a completely routine investigation. *Rockford* 101. But it's potentially sensitive. It requires discretion."

"My middle name," Schwierskott assured him.

This was probably a mistake. He was probably going to regret it. He was *definitely* going to regret it if MacAllister ever learned of it.

Will ignored the little warning voice in the back of his head. He said, "I need a complete background check on a guy named Ashe Dekker."

CHAPTER FOUR

He had forgotten the house until it rose out of the mist like something remembered from a dream.

Nestled among the avocado orchards in the Carpinteria foothills, the Mediterranean-style mansion offered endless blue ocean vistas and inspirational glimpses of sun-gilded mountains. Not the kind of place you expected to be overrun with squatters, although the library, exercise room, and master bedroom sauna must have made a nice change for them.

There was a tall iron gate at the bottom of the grapevine-covered hillside, but it was standing wide open when Taylor passed through just before eight o'clock.

He drove up to the wide empty courtyard, got out. Though he could see the ocean, the air felt dry and warm, winter sunlight edging everything in gold. Bees hummed industriously in the yucca and scarlet bougainvillea trailing down the stucco walls.

Taylor spotted Ashe sauntering down the wide, shallow, blue-tiled steps, red coffee mug in hand, and raised a hand in greeting.

Ashe wore some kind of embroidered white tunic shirt and something alarmingly like harem pants. "Morning!" he called.

Taylor called back, "Morning."

"Still punctual as ever." Ashe reached him, handed the mug to Taylor. "How was your drive?"

"Quick and easy. Thanks." He eyed Ashe thoughtfully. Ashe's blond hair was mussed, and there were gray shadows under his eyes. Rough night? Taylor raised the mug, sipped, and felt his eyebrows hit his skull. "Wow. What's in there?"

"Tequila, Kahlua, coffee." Ashe grinned. "Like we drank back in college."

Taylor gave a short laugh. "Uh, yeah, I don't really do Mexican coffee for breakfast these days."

"Ah, come on. Live a little." Ashe nodded toward the giant urns and columns. "Did you want to come inside? Or is this supposed to be strictly business?"

Huh?

"Sure. In a minute. Can I take a look at where the fire started?" Taylor took another swallow of Mexican coffee, decided *better not,* and followed Ashe, who was already striding down the drive toward the three-car garage.

"I take it there's no live-in staff or caretaker now?"

"No."

Taylor didn't see any sign of security cameras or sensors. "What about a security system?"

"No. Mom didn't like them. She believed the security company would use their cameras to spy on her." Ashe grinned at Taylor, and Taylor grinned back because he remembered Ashe's mother had been a character.

He also remembered that Ashe had been very close to his father, and that his father had died Ashe's first year at UCLA. He remembered holding Ashe after he got the terrible news, and going to the funeral with him. Things he had not thought about in ages.

He said, "But the gates would have been locked?"

"I have no idea." Ashe's lip curled in scornful amusement. "You think you're going to look for fingerprints or signs of a break-in two years later?"

"No. But just for my own information, I'd like to understand how they got access to the house. And how they managed to live here for two years without, apparently, raising any alarms."

"Zamarion's story was that my mother invited him to live here as a guest before she passed away."

Okay. Not trespassing so much as a holdover tenant situation? That would definitely make it a case for the courts. At least this piece of it.

"Any possibility that's true?" He couldn't quite read Ashe's expression.

Ashe stopped walking. "No. Zero. Mom was terrified of guys like Zamarion."

"Guys like Zamarion?"

"Hippies."

"*Ah.*" Taylor said, "Was Zamarion able to produce any kind of documentation to support his claim?"

"Of course not." Ashe's harsh laugh ricocheted off the pale stucco walls and brick. He glanced at Taylor's coffee mug. "You're not going to drink that, are you?"

"Better if I don't." Taylor smiled apologetically, handed the steaming mug to Ashe, who made a face, then took a swallow.

"Hair of the dog." Ashe continued walking.

"Right."

Ashe's lashes flicked up. He smiled with his old charm. "Uh-oh. You've got your big brother face on."

Taylor opened his mouth, but Ashe abruptly returned to the topic at hand. "*Oh.* Get this. Zamarion tried to claim Mom intended to leave the house to him."

Taylor frowned. "Was there a will?"

Ashe flushed, said darkly, "There *was* a will!"

"What does that mean?"

"That the will disappeared by the time I got here."

"Wouldn't your mother's lawyer have a copy?"

"No."

"But—"

"You think I'm lying?" Ashe demanded. "That's beautiful."

"Hey, I'm just trying to get the facts straight. I'm on your side. But I can be of more help if I know exactly what we're dealing with. So even if you have information that you think strengthens Zamarion's case or weakens yours, it'll be better if you tell me up front."

Ashe snapped, "He broke into my mother's house after she died, turned the place into a rathole, and lived here with his derelict friends until I came home and discovered what had happened. That's the whole story."

"Okay, Ashe," Taylor said, his tone conciliatory. "I'm sorry if I upset you."

Some of the hurt drained from Ashe's face. His gaze, a much paler, cooler shade of blue than Will's, fell. He nodded, sighed. "I get that you have to ask these questions, but I'm tired of nobody believing me. I can't understand why everyone is willing to give so much leeway to a lowlife like Zamarion. I thought if anyone would know I was telling the truth, it would be you."

Ouch.

"I'm sorry," Taylor said again. "I really am."

And he really was, but he also couldn't help remembering that, at least in the old days, Ashe and the truth enjoyed what one might call an open relationship.

They had reached the back of the three-car garage. A good portion of the terracotta walls was scorched and blackened. Taylor squatted down to better examine the burn marks. Modern stucco was naturally fire resistant, which could explain the lack of any significant damage. A couple of empty yards of stone drive separated the back of the garage from the thick stone perimeter walls where winter brown vines formed a dense net. The vines showed no signs of having caught fire.

Ashe said, "The firefighters figure they used a couple of wooden crates to climb over the wall, then stuffed the crates with gasoline-soaked rags and set them on fire. It was drizzling off and on that night, but even so, if I hadn't come home early, the whole structure could have gone up in flames, including the house."

Taylor nodded thoughtfully. "Did you say an arson report was filed?"

"No."

"No, you didn't say, or no, an arson report wasn't filed?"

Ashe seemed to have trouble meeting his eyes. "There was no arson report."

"*Why?*"

"I asked them—convinced the fire department not to request an arson investigator because I wasn't going to make an insurance claim anyway."

"Why would you do that?"

"Because I was afraid!"

Taylor hung on to his patience. "Afraid of what?"

"I was afraid—I knew—I'd come under suspicion."

Now they were getting somewhere. Maybe not a place Taylor wanted to find himself, but somewhere. He kept his tone even. "Why would that be?"

"Because the house is underwater. It's mortgaged to the hilt, and it only appraised for two thirds of the amount owed on it. Put that together with the problems I'm having with these squatters, and someone—the sheriff's department—is liable to think I decided to burn my way out of a bad financial situation."

Taylor was silent.

Ashe must have read his silence as condemnation. "And before you ask, *no*, I didn't try to set my house on fire. Jesus. I get that you have to be objective in your line of work, Taylor, but you *know* me."

Yes. Yes, he did. Or had at one time. But one of the brutal lessons of law enforcement was discovering that no one could completely know another person. Hell, you couldn't even know for sure what you yourself might do in every single possible scenario. For better or for worse, people—even the people you thought you knew best—could surprise you.

You could surprise yourself.

"Okay." Taylor sighed. "Let's go inside, and you can tell me everything you know about Mike Zamarion."

As it turned out, they didn't talk much about Mike Zamarion.

Partly that was because it seemed all Ashe knew was that Zamarion was a "scary dude" trying to steal his house. Partly that was because Ashe had a second—or more likely a third—Mexican coffee.

"Did I get it wrong?" Ashe asked. "I got the feeling you and Brandt are together, but you're the only one wearing a wedding ring."

By then they had adjourned to the library, where Ashe was rifling through desk drawers in search of whatever documents he seemed to think would help prove his case to Taylor.

It was a room Taylor remembered disconcertingly well because he and Ashe had once fucked on what appeared to be the very same black and scarlet Persian rug lying before the field stone fireplace.

Fun times. His back twinged just thinking about it.

Anyway, it was a wide, comfortable room paneled in golden oak. There were several tall, arched windows overlooking the garden of cacti and succulents, and a couple of ceiling-high bookshelves at either end of the room. Not that many bookshelves and not that many books for a room known as *the library.* But Taylor recalled none of the Dekkers were much for reading. For sure Ashe's amusements ran in a more sporty direction: tennis, swimming, sex. His parents had made good use of their memberships to the nearby racquet and polo clubs. They'd enjoyed less athletic activities too. Drinking, gambling, driving too fast. Those last three had been the combination that ended Ashe's father.

"We're not married," Taylor answered. Engaged sounded pretentious—and it wasn't like he and Will had set a date—but they were certainly committed to each other. Will had given him a ring. He *felt* married to Will. Maybe he should just give Will a ring and they could call it done?

Although maybe there was something to be said for formalizing that commitment.

Or maybe it said something that they *couldn't* seem to get around to formalizing their commitment?

Nah. It was more about the expense and hassle. The very idea of trying to organize a wedding was daunting, and he knew Will felt the same. Assumed he did. Since he hadn't pushed the idea either.

He compromised with, "But we're together."

"I see."

Probably not. This wasn't something Taylor usually gave a lot of thought. He figured one of these days, when the time was right—when they *had* some time—he and Will would make it official.

He said, "What about you? Anybody special?"

Ashe stopped digging through the desk drawers for a moment. His smile was twisted. "I wondered if you were ever going to ask. Yeah, I have someone. His name's Josip. We've been together five years. Off and on."

"Same as Will and me." Well, not the off-and-on part. He and Will had been apart, yes, but never in their hearts. Corny as it sounded, he really believed that.

"Where's Josip now?"

"He couldn't get a travel visa."

Hm.

"Where are you living in Europe? What do you do now?" Taylor asked.

"Croatia. I'm a director."

"Director of?" He was thinking in terms of corporations, financial institutions, his new reality. A reality dominated by Webster Fidelity.

"Films. Movies. I direct films. I make movies."

He couldn't understand why Ashe's eyes were suddenly bright and glittery, why he so abruptly sounded upset. "I had no idea. Wow. Good for you."

Ashe said bitterly, "You don't remember I was studying film in college? Do you remember *anything*? Do you *ever* think of me?"

"Well, of-of course," Taylor was so startled, he actually—to his chagrin—stammered a little. "Of course I remember. Of course I think of you sometimes. I always hoped you were doing well, that you were happy and… things were good."

"But you couldn't be bothered to find out for yourself?"

What. The. Hell?

He said helplessly, "Ashe…"

Ashe laughed, shook his head. "I'm being an ass. Don't mind me. You were my first love, so obviously it had an impact."

"It had an impact on me too," Taylor said. "It's not like I was—am—so much older than you. I know I was sometimes oblivious. Maybe self-centered—"

"Insensitive, overbearing."

Taylor fell silent.

"I'm kidding," Ashe said quickly. "You were a kid. We were both kids. I don't hold a grudge. I just wish it had meant more to you. You were one of the most important relationships in my life. I wish it had been that for you too. But that's not realistic. I know."

"It was an important relationship in my life as well. *You* were important to me. I was glad to see you last night, and I'm glad for the chance to help. I'm…sorry for any hurt I caused. Hopefully, helping you out now makes up for some of that."

"No good deed goes unpunished," Ashe said. "Can you just forget I said all that? You're right about the Mexican coffees for breakfast. They're a bad idea."

Taylor refrained from comment, said instead, "Okay, well, I think I'll go check in with the sheriff's department. See what they can tell me."

Ashe had gone back to searching the desk. "Don't believe—" He broke off, saying, "Hey, look what I found!" and lifted out a Ruger LCP. "This was my dad's."

Taylor was not afraid of guns, not even after being shot, but something in the way Ashe handled that piece prickled the hair on the back of his neck.

He said without emotion, "I'm surprised your squatters left it."

Ashe, still examining the pocket pistol, shrugged. "Missed it, I guess. They didn't steal as much as you might think. That's the funny part. But I guess that's because Zamarion thought—thinks—he's going to get it all anyway."

He weighed the Ruger for a moment and then aimed it at Taylor's face. His hand wasn't quite steady. He smiled.

Time seemed to stop. Taylor could hear the wind moaning down the chimney, hear the clock ticking across the room, hear his heart thumping hard and steady in his ears.

"Remember teaching me to shoot?" Ashe said.

"I remember," Taylor said. His mouth was dry, spitting the words out like bits of gravel. "We used to practice at the Beverly Hills Gun Club. Could you not point that at me?"

"It's not loaded."

Yeah, actually, that fucking gun was loaded. When you knew weapons as well as Taylor did, you could tell just from the heft of someone picking up a piece. It was loaded all right. But he knew with sickening certainty that if he said so, Ashe would fire at him just to prove a point.

He said in a flat, no-nonsense voice, "Put the gun down, Ashe."

Ashe shrugged, lowered the Ruger. "Sorry. I didn't mean to scare you."

Taylor resisted the desire to relieve his feelings by punching Ashe in his vacuous, glassy-eyed face. He said, "I was shot in the line of duty a couple of years ago. It…leaves an aftertaste."

Ashe whistled. "You're kidding. I'm really sorry. What was that like?"

"I don't remember much about it," Taylor lied, "but it's not an experience I want to repeat."

"No, I guess not. Obviously, I didn't know."

Until that very moment, Taylor had taken it for granted Ashe *didn't* know, but something in the way he said it made him wonder.

Maybe Will had been right to question how Ashe had known where to find them. Maybe Ashe had been keeping track of Taylor through the years. It seemed unlikely, but some people did that—tracked their exes through social media, kept tabs through friends of friends. Clearly, Ashe had some unresolved feelings toward him, so maybe.

If that was the case, Ashe pointing a gun at him hadn't merely been a dick move, it had been sadistic.

"Sure." Taylor headed for the door, saying, "I'll let myself out."

Ashe followed. "You'll keep me informed, right?"

"You bet."

They walked down the long, tiled hall, out through the wood and iron door. The sunlight was almost blindingly bright, the air sweet. A seagull sat on the edge of one of tall blue urns, cranking its head this way and that, the better to see them.

Ashe said, "I don't think I even thanked you for this, for trying to help me."

"It's okay."

Taylor started down the wide front steps. From behind him, Ashe called, "I hate being here alone at night. I'm always afraid they're going to come back. Like the Manson family."

There was a grim thought. Taylor turned back to face him.

Ashe said, "But then that's the same reason I don't dare leave. In case they're waiting for a chance to move back in."

"I'll try to locate Zamarion today," Taylor promised. "I'm pretty sure we'll manage to work something out."

"You were never short on confidence," Ashe agreed.

Taylor grimaced. "No. I just knew how to fake it."

Ashe shook his head. Blurted, "You know, you could come back here tonight. If you wanted."

Taylor hesitated. Ashe's fear touched him, but he didn't want to come back to this house. It wasn't just having a gun pointed at him or Ashe's drinking or his troubling passive-aggressive comments. He wanted to see Will, talk to Will, get Will's take on the situation. He wanted to sleep in Will's arms, listen to the reassuring beat of Will's heart, and take a moment to appreciate how very lucky they were. How lucky *he* was.

At the same time, the whole point of this was to help Ashe. And if Ashe was truly afraid?

But then Ashe made it easy for him. "One last night together. For old times' sake?" His smile was sort of sly, sort of hopeful.

Taylor said, "What about Josip?"

"I won't tell Will if you don't tell Josip."

Taylor smiled, shook his head. "Thanks. But I think we better let our last goodbye stand."

Ashe laughed. "It was a record breaker. Wasn't it?"

Taylor smiled again, continued down the steps.

Ashe called after him, "If you change your mind, you know where to find me."

* * * * *

Ashe was right about one thing.

Down at the Carpinteria sheriff's station, they did indeed think Mr. Dekker had, at the very least, toyed with burning down his mother's house for the insurance money.

The interesting part was nobody blamed him.

"It's a hell of a situation," Lt. Don Capaldi told Taylor. "He needs money, but because of this lowlife loser, he can't sell the house."

Capaldi was a genial-looking fiftysomething with thinning gray hair, a neatly trimmed mustache, and warm brown eyes behind wire-rimmed glasses.

"How is it that Zamarion and the others managed to take possession of that house without anyone noticing?"

"We did notice," Capaldi said. "The whole valley noticed. But he and his girlfriends had been living there with the old lady for several months before she passed away. Zamarion claimed she was leaving the house to him, that it was in her will."

This was at odds with Ashe's story, but Taylor was not entirely surprised. It had seemed unlikely a tribe of hippies could have moved into that house and lived there for two years without anyone noticing.

"What about the will?" Taylor asked.

"There is no will." Capaldi smiled grimly at Taylor's expression. "Exactly. Mrs. Dekker died intestate. It seems like there had been some rift with her son, which is why, I guess, it took him so long to come back. If his trust fund hadn't run out, I don't know that he would have come back at all. I don't know that he'd have cared about the house or who lived there. But now he needs to sell the place, and Zamarion is standing in the way."

Hell. It was all starting to add up.

Or was it?

"But since there's no will, wouldn't the house automatically go to Ashe?"

"Yes. Correct. Well, technically, the estate is in probate, but it's all going to go to Dekker. The main asset is the house, from what I understand. If Zamarion still had possession of the property, it might be more complicated, but rightly or wrongly, he and his family were evicted." Capaldi cleared his throat. "Anyway, the most he can do is sue for wrongful eviction and destruction of private property, but I can tell you that he's not likely to find a sympathetic jury in Carpinteria."

"But you said Zamarion is standing in the way of Ashe selling the house."

"That's right. Because when you sell a house, you have to declare if there are any liens or claims against it. Well, Zamarion is claiming that there *was* a will naming him as the sole beneficiary, that Dekker destroyed it, but that he, Zamarion, has a copy of one of the original drafts. He's supposed to have hired some shyster lawyer to stop any attempt to sell the house. That's the rumor anyway."

"I…see."

"I don't know if it's true. And of course, I'm no lawyer. But I sincerely doubt anyone or anything is going to court. Zamarion is just a nuisance."

"Just a nuisance? Then you don't think he tried to run Dekker off Toro Canyon Road?"

Capaldi sighed. "I don't know if he did or not. Zamarion is an unsavory customer. But we can't do a whole hell of a lot with a single pair of skid marks and no witnesses."

* * * * *

It was after eleven in the evening when he finally made it home.

The kitchen light was on, the house otherwise dark and silent. Well, not entirely silent. Riley came to greet him, tags jangling, tail wagging.

"Hey, Riley." Taylor knelt, murmuring to the dog.

No sign of Will, though. Which was to say, there was every sign that Will was home but had already gone to bed.

Well, not *already*, because it *was* late, but not that late. Usually they tried to stay up for each other. Usually they came in together.

Taylor considered the rather heavy silence as he patted Riley.

If Will was really that beat, he didn't want to wake him, but it was disappointing. He had wanted to talk over the day with him, talk over the things he had learned, the things he was still trying to figure out, the things that worried him. A lot of things were worrying him.

But Will had probably had a tiring day himself—made more tiring by the fact that Taylor hadn't been there to shoulder his half of it.

He was guiltily conscious that, as weird and frustrating as his day had been, he was sort of relieved he hadn't had to sit through another round of meetings at Webster Fidelity.

Was Will sleeping? Because the house had a listening quality to it.

No. Will would not be lying there...what? Sulking because Taylor hadn't made it to any of the day's meetings? Because he hadn't made it home for dinner?

He moved quietly around the house, poured himself a glass of water, drank it, checked the fridge for something to eat, tried to decide between a bowl of granola and an English muffin, and gave up.

He turned off the stove light, picked his way down the pitch-black hall—nearly falling over Riley, who thought this was a great start to a new game—and felt his way through the dark and deadly silent bedroom to the bathroom.

Inside the bathroom, he relieved himself, washed his hands, brushed his teeth, turned on the shower, and stepped into the humid warmth.

All at once he was very tired and feeling...let down.

Not a good day.

Sure, he'd had worse, but still. Not a good day.

And if Will really was lying in that room pretending to sleep, nursing some unknown resentment like a goddamned adolescent, the day was about to get worse. For both of them.

But no.

Will was not a goddamned adolescent. He was the guy carrying the can while Taylor was busy doing whatever the hell he imagined he was doing. He was no longer sure of anything. Beyond the fact that Ashe was probably—*probably?*—emotionally unstable and lying about pretty much everything.

He braced his hands on the white subway tile, hung his head, letting the hot water sluice over his head and shoulders, slowly inhaling, slowly exhaling.

Distantly, he heard the *pop* of the shower door, felt a gust of cool air.

The heft of an erection smacked against his buttocks, jarring him from his hazy thoughts. Taylor growled low in his throat—warning, not protest. He didn't resist, didn't fight when he was pushed flat against the slick, warm tiles, pushed so hard, his heels came off the floor.

Hard, soapy flesh and wet, wiry hair ground against his ass.

Will's hand fastened on his shoulder, holding him in place, and his mouth traced the down bent line of his neck, kissing his flushed, wet skin. Taylor made another sound, softer, comforting. Will buried his face in Taylor's wet hair, not speaking, seemingly just breathing him in, and Taylor lowered his head, shivering, when Will kissed the nape of his neck.

He closed his eyes, conscious of the intimate smell of Will's soap, the heat radiating between them, the tension of Will's hard, muscular body pressing into him. Will's left hand still gripped his shoulder as Will reached down to knuckle wide Taylor's butt cheeks.

Taylor swallowed, muscles tensing as something slick and stringy—shampoo?—drizzled down his crack. The flick of fingernail against his hole sparked red lights behind his eyelids, flared along his nerves.

"Tay..." Will's voice was tense and low, somehow working its way beneath Taylor's skin, into every nerve, every cell, and Taylor's breath hitched, sped up, waiting for the moment when Will's cock pushed into him, and all the while Will's hot mouth brushed the back of his neck, lingered, nuzzling the sensitive spot behind his ear.

"Here," he whispered, so softly, the word was almost lost beneath the rush of water. Anticipation sparked a thrill in the pit of his belly.

Funny how he had never liked this until Will. Never let anyone do what he let Will do, never gave what he instinctively offered Will.

Why was Will hesitating? What was he waiting for?

Taylor's hands flexed against the tiles, his cock filled and hardened. He pushed back, restless, longing. "Yeah, come on, Will. Let's do it." He bent his right leg, canted his hips, and the snub head of Will's cock poked, poked, shoved in, filling him with that familiar pressure, that intimate burn.

Taylor took in a lungful of moist, steamy air, dizzyingly conscious of Will's powerful body covering his, Will's hot breath against the back of his neck, his own harsh breath misting against the wall of the shower.

That sensation of being penetrated, filled, united... Was sex ever just about sex?

Will gasped, "Yeah?"

"Yeah. Come on." Taylor moved again, impatient.

Will drew back, pushed into him, each thrust scraping across Taylor's nerves, sending them vibrating like a tuning fork. He groaned, wanting... what? More? Always more.

Will's hand slid across his soapy skin, wrapped around his cock, and Taylor bit his lip, pushing into that solicitous grip, let his head fall back, resting on Will's shoulder. Will's knuckles banged the tiles, found the rhythm. His hips pounded Taylor's buttocks.

Taylor shook down to his bones, the hard weight filling his ass, the frantic heat of Will's hand, slightly off-kilter as he bounced off the wall. The showerhead rained down on him, and Taylor gasped, drowning in sensation as a tingling, explosive energy gathered at the base of his spine.

Will's grunts sounded desperate, wounded, against his ear. They wavered on the edge, teetering, and then Will let go of him for an instant, his hand closed around Taylor's balls, teased, tugged, and Taylor felt a kind of ferocious detonation, like triggering a mechanism. They plummeted into the desperate freefall of release.

Taylor was still shuddering, his asshole clenching and unclenching at the fierce pleasure of orgasm, smashed against the streaky tiles as Will shook against him, as they spiraled back to sanity together. It seemed to take great effort to lift his lashes. He stared down at their bare feet, at suds and spunk swirling around their toes, spilling down the drain.

CHAPTER FIVE

Taylor was shouting from down the hall, "Brandt, do you have *any* idea where my goddamned briefcase is?"

Will expelled a much put-upon breath, threw his head back, yelled, "It's at the office. I've been using it."

Silence but for the ominous *tick-tick-tick* of rain over the sink window.

Today's drive to Encinitas was going to be a bitch.

Taylor appeared in the kitchen doorway, wearing jeans and a still un-buttoned white shirt that offered an enticing view of ridged abdominals, cut pectorals, and taut nipples. How was it he could want to strangle Taylor one minute and go dry-mouthed with desire the next?

"Damn it. I was even there last night."

It took a second for the words to register. When they did, Will felt al-most shaken with the mix of relief and guilt that washed through him. "You were at the office last night?"

"Yeah. For a few hours. Do we have another briefcase somewhere?"

"My old one's at the office too. Sit down and have some breakfast, MacAllister."

Taylor considered, sighed, headed for the coffee machine.

Will glanced at him, glanced away. He had already been feeling ashamed about the night before. He didn't think he'd hurt Taylor—Taylor was as resilient as a jack-in-the-box when it came to sex—but Will had been rougher than he was comfortable with in the cold light of day. Especially knowing in his heart that a lot of his aggression had been fueled as much by frustration as lust.

Taylor hadn't seemed to mind a little roughness. But Taylor wouldn't recognize he was out of his depth if the fucking ocean closed over his head. Will was disgusted with himself for giving in to feelings that had nothing to do with love and everything to do with control.

Why the hell hadn't it occurred to him that Taylor had gone to the office? It was the most obvious explanation. Why had he leaped to such a dramatic and dumbass conclusion? In fact, he hadn't even reached a conclusion. It had all been speculation and suspicion over one too many glasses of bourbon.

He studied Taylor's downturned face. "How are you feeling this morning?"

Taylor blew on his coffee. "Hm?" He glanced up. Winked. "Fine."

Will's face warmed. His heart felt heavy. What a way to treat a guy you loved more than life. A guy you trusted *with* your life.

Taylor must have misread his expression. He said, "Sorry about yesterday. How did the meetings at WF go?"

"Like you'd expect." Will shook his head. "Kohl, the head of security, is going to be a never-ending thorn in our side."

Taylor's lip curled. "The guy who introduced himself by showing you his gun collection software app?"

"That's the one."

Taylor hid a smile in his coffee mug.

Will said, "Do you feel like we suddenly grew up and had to get real jobs?"

Taylor's laugh was wry. "Yeah. I do."

Will sighed. "Are you going to be able to drive down to the Encinitas site with me?"

Taylor's smiled faded. He looked apologetic. "I've got a lead on Zamarion. I feel like I need to follow through on it. He's a guy who moves around a lot."

"Okay."

"I'm sorry, Will. I'm trying to get this wrapped up as fast as I can." Taylor was up from the table again, going to the counter to shake granola into a bowl.

"I know. How's the case coming?"

Will watched curiously as Taylor got milk out of the fridge, poured it into the bowl, carried the bowl to the table, and sat down.

Knowing him as he did, Will couldn't help thinking Taylor was considering how much to tell him. It didn't do a lot to soothe his unease.

He waited as Taylor dug his spoon into the cereal, stirred the oat clusters around, and said finally, "You were right. Ashe wasn't being completely honest with us."

Will resisted temptation, saying only, "How so?"

"Well, to start with, Zamarion probably did have permission to live on the estate. There's even a possibility Ashe's mom intended leaving the property to him."

Now that was news. "You're kidding."

Taylor gave a brief shake of his head. "No. Ashe and his mother were estranged. I haven't been able to discover the details. Whatever her intentions may have been, there doesn't seem to be a will, so Ashe legally inherits everything."

"That sounds pretty cut-and-dried."

"As far as it goes."

"Sounds far enough to me. So why isn't that case closed? It's going to end up in court, right?"

"Maybe. I'm not even sure there's enough doubt to warrant a lawsuit."

"Is there enough to warrant our continued involvement?"

"I think there is. I think, putting aside missing wills and squatters' rights and a whole lot of hearsay evidence, Ashe is genuinely terrified. Of who or what, I'm not quite clear on."

"Zamarion would be the obvious answer."

Taylor frowned. "Yeah, presumably. He sounds like a rough customer. But I talked to the lieutenant at the sheriff's station in Carpinteria. He didn't come right out and say it, but it was obvious he thinks Ashe lied about someone trying to force him off the road. And about chickening out of setting fire to his own garage for the insurance money."

"Fan-fucking-tastic," Will muttered. "And we're still involved in this clusterfuck *why* again?"

"Because none of that changes the fact that I promised to help him. He *needs* help."

"Christ almighty, Taylor. How the hell much do you think you owe this guy?"

"I think I owe him keeping my word when I give it."

"Even if he's lying to you?"

"Yes. Even then."

This wasn't really coming as a surprise to Will, but it was still exasperating. "Great. Okay. How long do you plan to spend trying to figure out what's keeping your old pal up at night? Because I can handle Encinitas on my own, but after that we've got four more locations all over the state and eight days to complete those surveys. I can't do it on my own."

"I know that."

"So?"

Taylor said, "I'm asking for twenty-four hours. Forty-eight at the most. If I can't get this wrapped up by Friday, then I'll tell Ashe we're out."

That was fair. And yet... Will regarded him for a long moment. He shook his head. "I don't like it," he said. "What is it you're not telling me?"

Taylor hesitated.

"You don't like this any more than I do." Will was sure of it now. "What's going on?"

Taylor said reluctantly, "Ashe pulled a gun on me yesterday."

"He did what?"

Taylor winced. "Cool it, Brandt. He was fooling around."

"Fooling around with a goddamned gun?" Will was sputtering with rage, and Riley scrambled out from under the table to see where the threat was.

"He claimed the pistol wasn't loaded."

That really didn't make it any better, as Taylor, of all people, ought to know, and Will proceeded to share his thoughts on the matter.

"Jesus Christ, Brandt. You think I don't know all that?" Taylor snapped when Will finally had to stop for breath.

"I don't get it," Will said. "What the hell hold does this asshole have over you?"

That, as he should have known, didn't go over well.

"I already *told* you what *hold* this asshole has over me," Taylor shot back. His face was white, his eyes greener than a pit viper. "And if you don't believe me, you can go to hell. What hold do you *think* he has, Brandt? You think I'm starting up again with my college fuck buddy because I just don't have enough assholes in my life?"

Two things were immediately clear to Will. First, Taylor had a few residual resentments of his own. Secondly, Taylor was every bit as uneasy and worried about this situation as he was.

"You're right," Will said at once. "That was out of line."

"It sure as hell was. When I think of the bullshit—" Taylor swallowed the rest of it so fast, he made a choking sound.

But Will knew what he'd been about to say, and his face turned as red as Taylor's was white. "I apologize," he said. "I didn't—I really didn't mean what you thought I meant."

"Oh, the hell you didn't."

"Taylor, I don't want to fight with you."

"Then let's not." Taylor rose, picking up his cereal bowl, and carried it to the sink. He turned the taps in a brief blast of water, and said without turning around, "I'll see you tonight."

"Will you keep me posted today? I don't mean a couple of phone messages—"

It seemed that once again he had said the wrong thing. Taylor swung away from the sink. "If you're not happy with phone messages, take your damned cell off Do Not Disturb. *Comprende?*"

Will put his hands up in a Don't Shoot gesture.

Taylor gave him a final glare and stalked out of the kitchen. Riley wagged his tail, watching him, then turned to Will.

Will said, "Tell me the truth. Is my head still there?"

Riley grinned, tongue lolling.

* * * * *

The news wasn't a whole hell of a lot better at the office.

"What in the name of God is *that*?" Will stared in horror at the gold-painted…bird? covering most of the lobby wall.

Euphonia said doubtfully, "It's our logo, right? The American eagle?"

"That's not an eagle. It's a…a chicken. A giant golden chicken." Or maybe a vampire bat? No, a bat would have ears. Maybe a dragon? He couldn't seem to tear his gaze from the menacing-eyed monster swooping down from the ceiling, talons stretched toward prospective clients.

"It might be a little overwhelming," Euphonia agreed diplomatically.

"A *little*? It's the whole wall." Will shook his head. "We were better off with the lovebirds and parasols. Get the painters back in here. They've got to fix that. If MacAllister sees it, he'll hunt them down one by one and shoot them."

Euphonia smirked, but was back to business a moment later. "Is Agent MacAllister coming in today?"

"I doubt it."

"Because these were delivered first thing this morning." With an apologetic look, she handed over two identical, fat, official-looking envelopes with the return address of US District Court, Central District of California, Western Division.

Subpoenas.

Great. Because life wasn't complicated enough right now.

Will retired to his office, now a restful shade of cloudy blue-gray, and opened the envelope. Inside was a subpoena to appear at deposition.

Well, well. It looked like Mikhail Bashnakov—The Technician—was finally going to face justice.

That had been a long time coming. So long, in fact, Will had almost forgotten the court case was still pending.

He wondered if he and Taylor would be seeing Kelila Hedwig in a courtroom someday soon.

The good news was they did not need to appear until after the New Year, so in theory, it would not interfere with completing the surveys for Webster Fidelity. They could enjoy their holidays in peace.

Yeah, right. Webster Fidelity had them on an electronic leash, and that's how it would be from now on.

He picked up the phone to call Taylor, then decided this news could wait. Instead, he tossed the subpoenas in his desk drawer, told Euphonia he'd probably not be back that day, and headed out for Encinitas.

Rain poured down, flooding the freeway. In the distance, streaks of flashing light turned the pewter-edged clouds a bruised black and purple.

Will kept an eye out for the silver Honda Accord—for any sign of a tail—on the four-hour drive to the Webster Fidelity jobsite, but there was no indication he was being followed. And as sure as he'd been the day before, he found himself now wondering if he really had simply made too much of a coincidence.

There was no word yet from Stuart Schwierskott, so he tried phoning Dina Shey at Gently, Fallis & Landreth again. To his surprise, his call was put through.

"Dina Shey," stated a cool, melodious voice.

"Ms. Shey, nice to finally speak. This is Will Brandt, one of the men you hired Schwierskott & Associate to run surveillance on."

Shey didn't miss a beat. "I would say what a surprise, Mr. Brandt, but given that you've left us thirteen messages over the past weeks, I'd be lying. What can I do for you?"

"You can start by telling me who hired you to hire Schwierskott & Associate."

"You're a former federal agent, Mr. Brandt. I'm sure you've heard the term attorney-client privilege before."

"You've presumably passed the bar, Ms. Shey, so I'm sure you've heard that if a client initiates a communication with a lawyer for the purpose of committing a crime, the attorney-client privilege typically doesn't apply.

Likewise, the State of California allows attorneys to disclose information learned from a client that will prevent death or serious injury."

She chuckled with apparent good humor. "Rule 3-100B Confidential Information of a Client: A member of the bar *may, but is not required* to reveal confidential information relating to the representation of a client to the extent that the member reasonably believes the disclosure is necessary to prevent a criminal act that the member reasonably believes is likely to result in death of, or substantial bodily harm to, an individual.

"Do you have any proof that my client—currently unknown to you— is planning a criminal act likely to result in death of, or substantial bodily harm to, yourself or another individual?"

"No. I don't have any proof."

"I didn't think so. Well, it was lovely chatting—"

Will said quickly, "Ms. Shey, I don't know you, but you'd have to be a special kind of cold-blooded not to care if your actions, or lack of action, resulted in real harm to someone else. I'm asking, as one human being to another, is that who you are?"

Shey was silent.

"Maybe you don't know it, but you're on the side of the bad guys," Will said. "Is that really where you want to be?"

Another stretch of silence. Then, "Do you realize what you're asking?" There was no humor in Shey's voice now. "I could lose my license."

"I'm not asking for anything more than a name. That's it. I just want to be sure that I or my partner aren't going to get shot walking out to our car one night."

"I have no idea."

He expected her to hang up—he thought she intended to hang up—but she stayed on the line.

After a long pause, she said, "My client asked that surveillance be terminated. Which is what I instructed Schwierskott & Associate to do."

"Did your client request that you initiate surveillance through another firm?"

"No. My client determined that you and Mr. MacAllister no longer posed a threat."

"Posed a *threat...*"

"Correct. And that is all the information I'm willing to share. You and your partner can walk to and from your cars in safety. No one is following you."

She hung up.

He stopped for gas and a restroom break in Carlsbad, and sure enough, when he walked out of the mini mart, he spotted a silver Honda Accord parked on the other side of the lot.

Will pretended not to see the car, making a production of checking his coffee and adjusting his sunglasses. As soon as he got in his Toyota Land Cruiser, he yanked open the glove compartment, grabbed his compact binoculars, and turned them toward the Honda Accord.

Despite the rivulets of rain trickling down his windshield, he had a perfect view of the Honda slinking out of the lot. He studied the rear license plate. "6 Golf Tango X-ray 534," read Will. "Got you, you son of a bitch."

He pulled out from the pumps, parked beside the tire air station, and phoned the office.

"American Eagle," Euphonia greeted him pleasantly. "How may I direct your call?"

"Nee, who at the DMV owes you a favor?"

"Here we go." She sighed. "Is this why you hired me?"

"You know why we hired you. Come on, I'm serious."

"Who *doesn't* owe me a favor?" Euphonia retorted.

"I need someone to run a California license plate. And, if at all possible, I need it fast."

"Plate number?"

"6 Golf Tango X-ray 534."

Euphonia repeated, "6 Golf Tango X-ray 534?"

"Correct."

"I'll see what I can do." She hung up.

It took four hours to complete his survey of the Webster Fidelity jobsite. By then it was three o'clock, Will was starving, and he stopped for a late lunch at a little pub called the Regal Seagull.

He was drenched in the quick jog from vehicle to building. Shoving through the glass door outlined in Christmas lights, he heard the blast of "All I Want for Christmas is You," and it was *Hark! I bring you not-so-great tidings*. Lt. Commander David Bradley sat on his own at a table near the bar.

Maybe it shouldn't have come as such a surprise, the way his luck was going. Encinitas was about half an hour from San Diego, and San Diego was home to several Navy, Marine Corps, and Coast Guard bases.

David glanced up from the menu, spotted Will, and his face lit up. He half rose. "Will!"

What could Will do? Frankly, he was irritated with a situation in which he felt guilty just engaging in the normal, courteous social behavior. Of course, he was glad to see David. He *liked* David. He went over to the table, and they hugged hello.

"This is a surprise," Will said.

"You can say that again. What are you doing down here? Why didn't you let me know you'd be in the area?"

David was a big, handsome moose of a guy. Six-plus feet of well-toned muscle. He had a silky dark beard, smiling brown eyes, and a deep voice that still gave Will a little tingle at the base of his spine.

Will said, "Webster Fidelity is a client. I'm down here doing a security survey for them."

David looked puzzled, but then his face cleared. "Right. The global security consulting business. How's that working out?"

"Business is good," Will said, with about as much enthusiasm as he could summon after a day of interviewing employees, analyzing assets, and making a preliminary identification of what security measures had to be highest priority.

David's smile was sympathetic. "This was MacAllister's plan?"

"This is all on me," Will said. "I dragged Taylor into it."

"Well, come and join me," David invited. "Unless you're meeting clients?"

"God no," Will said. "About the clients, I mean. Yes to lunch. I need a burger and a beer."

He got them both within a matter of minutes, along with David's easy, and frankly charming, company. They were of a similar temperament, which Will had always considered one of the strengths of their relationship, but that day he couldn't help wondering if he and David weren't maybe too much alike. Would they maybe have bored each other eventually? Taylor could be mercurial, mulish, and downright maddening, but no question, life with him would never be dull.

David had been overseas at CFNK at Busan Naval Base, and they talked about his trip and the current precarious situation with North Korea. Will finished his burger, declined a second beer, admitted he should be heading home, and his cell phone rang.

Taylor.

Christ, it was like he had a built-in sensor where David was concerned.

"Hey."

"Hey," Will said, relieved to hear no hint of the morning's ire in Taylor's voice. "What's up?"

"I just had a phone call with Mike Zamarion. He says he wants to talk to me."

"That's a good sign. Maybe this will be cleared up by the end of the week."

Taylor gave a funny laugh. "Or maybe not. He's asking me to bring twenty grand and meet him on Carpinteria State Beach at seven o'clock at lifeguard tower number eleven."

"That's not going to happen," Will said.

"I'm not bringing twenty grand, no, but I do want to hear what he has to say."

"What makes you think he'll tell you anything if you don't have the money?"

"My knowledge of human nature?"

"Try again."

"I think he wants to talk. He's an opportunist, sure, but just from the hints he dropped, this is a guy with a story to tell."

Will checked his watch. "Look, I'll do my best to get back in time to go with you. I'm still in Encinitas." He glanced at David, who was watching attentively, and realized, awkward or not, he could not risk this looking like anything but the accidental meeting it was. "I ran into David when I stopped for lunch."

"Of course you did," Taylor said. "Well, don't let me rush you, but it would be nice to have some backup."

"You're damn right I'm going to back you up," Will said. "If you have to leave before I get back to the office, I'll meet you at the beach. You said lifeguard tower eleven?"

Taylor said briskly, "Be there or be square," and hung up.

Will reached for his wallet and rose. "Sorry. I've got to go."

"Lunch is on me," David said. "I had no idea MacAllister was so insecure." His expression was sympathetic.

Will felt a flash of irritation. "This isn't anything to do with that."

"No? I have to say, from my end, it kind of sounds that way."

It occurred to Will that the moment had come to draw a line in the sand. He liked David a lot, but he loved Taylor.

"He isn't insecure, generally speaking. But in fairness to him, you haven't made any secret of the fact that you'd like to get back together. That you think it's a possibility."

"In fairness to me, I can't make that happen without cooperation on your part."

"That's true. But we both know—all three of us know—that what you and I almost had together was something we both thought might be serious."

David stopped smiling. "Yes," he said. "I believe we had something special together. But I'd have to be deaf, dumb, and blind not to realize that you and MacAllister have something pretty special too. I don't think there's any getting in the middle of that, and I wouldn't try. I'd like to stay friends, but if you don't think MacAllister can handle it—"

"I think he can handle it, so long as he's confident everyone's on the same page."

David raised his brows but said nothing.

Will said quietly, "I hurt him in Paris. That can't ever happen again."

"You can't be blamed for what happened in Paris. Nor is there a likelihood of those circumstances ever being replicated."

"He doesn't blame me. He knows none of it was deliberate or even in my control. But the pain I inflicted? *Never* again. So long as I have the power to prevent it, nothing will hurt him like that again."

David's dark brows rose. "That's very admirable. I don't know how realistic it is. People do hurt each other. But I can see you mean every word. I only hope MacAllister appreciates what he has in you."

Will's mouth curved without humor. "One thing he wouldn't appreciate is me telling you any of this, and it's the last time I discuss him with you. But I feel it's only right to let you know that if I did offer mixed signals or seemed divided in my feelings, that was a mistake. I know exactly who and what I want, and that's Taylor and our life together."

"Message received loud and clear."

Will nodded. "Thanks for lunch."

"My pleasure," David said. His smile was rueful. "Next time we'll try to arrange it so MacAllister can join us."

His cell phone rang while he was merging onto the I-5 N. Traffic was always a snarling mess this time of the afternoon, and the heavy rain made it that much worse. Will was starting to fret he would never make it back to Ventura, let alone reach the office before Taylor left.

Ordinarily, that wouldn't have been cause for sweat beading his hairline or warming his underarms, but he'd had a sense of foreboding ever since Ashe Dekker walked into their office, and it was a feeling that grew stronger by the day, stronger by the hour.

AMERICAN EAGLE appeared on his screen. He pressed to accept.

"Nee. Anything yet?"

Euphonia said crisply, "License Number: 6 Golf Tango X-ray 534. Make: Honda Accord. Registered Owner: Anne or Michael Zamarion, 3000 Foothill Road, Carpinteria, California."

Will blinked, stared unseeingly at the gleaming roadblock of cars in front of him. "Say again?"

Enunciating clearly, she repeated, "The car is owned by a Michael Zamarion."

CHAPTER SIX

"I thought you'd call last night," Ashe said. His laugh was strained. "Hell, I thought for sure you'd come by."

He pushed away from the front door frame, walking down the long hall, bare feet soundless on the distressed hickory wood floor. Taylor stepped out of the rain, followed him, conscious that he was leaving wet boot marks on the hardwood floors.

"I didn't have anything to report last night."

Ashe threw a bleak look over his shoulder. "That's not what I mean and you know it."

Taylor smothered a sigh. "Ashe."

"Forget it. It's just lonely here." He glanced back again, but now he was smiling. "It's haunted, you know. The house. Lots of ghosts. Including yours."

Taylor quelled his rising impatience. "Ashe, we need to talk."

"Sure. Did you want coffee?"

"Coffee would be great. But just coffee. I've got a lot to do today."

Ashe shivered. "Is it cold in here, or is it just me?"

Now that he mentioned it, it *was* cold. It felt like a window was open somewhere and a rainy wind was blowing through the house.

"It's December. Even in California, that's cold," Taylor said.

Ashe said nothing, so he probably had not been referencing the weather. Taylor followed him into the long airy kitchen with its vaulted ceiling and incredible views of the fog-shrouded ocean.

"Do you still take sugar?" Ashe asked, pouring coffee into red mugs.

"No. Not usually."

Taylor was not one for beating around the bush, but he was finding this difficult. Not just awkward—painful. He watched Ashe going through the motions. Maybe not drunk, but clearly hungover.

What would Will do? Will would get it over with.

Taylor decided to get it over with. He said, "Part of the trouble I'm having in locating Zamarion is his legal address was changed to this one almost three years ago."

Ashe didn't respond.

Taylor tried to keep any hint of accusation out of his voice. "I don't understand why you lied to me. I spoke to Lt. Capaldi at the sheriff's station, and he said Zamarion was living here while your mother was alive. A bunch of squatters didn't invade this house after it was left empty. Zamarion, his wife, a friend, and the friend's baby were already living here. They were maintaining the house and garden for your mom in return for room and board. And it seems like they even took care of your mom once she got sick."

"That's their story!" Ashe glared at him.

"Sure, but it seems to be corroborated pretty thoroughly. I talked to a lot of people yesterday. Friends of your mom, neighbors, the mailman, the kid who delivered her groceries, the lady who did her nails at the beauty salon—"

"I didn't ask you to do any of that!"

Taylor hung on to his restraint. "I'm not completely sure what you *are* asking me to do."

Ashe cried, "Did you bother to notice that Zamarion has a prison record, or were you too busy investigating me?"

"Yes. I noticed he's got form, including a conviction for manslaughter."

"What does that tell you?"

"That he can be a violent guy."

"Exactly! That is exactly right!"

"*Ashe.*" Taylor stopped. Tried for a reasonable tone. "He did his time, and there's no indication that he's been in any trouble with the law since. I don't know what happened regarding your mother's will. It's clear you don't think Zamarion has any right to this property. And I guess that's understandable. But unless the two of you can reach some agreement, it seems like that's a fight that has to be made through the courts. From what I heard yesterday, there doesn't seem to be any doubt you would win that battle."

"Yes! That's what I said. So why are you lecturing me?"

Taylor sighed. "Because being angry about Zamarion coming for your inheritance doesn't give you the right to harass him or try to set him up."

Ashe scowled. "I don't know what you're talking about."

"Don't you?"

"No!" But Ashe seemed to have trouble meeting his eyes.

"Here's what I think. I think you're in a hurry to sell this property. I think you want to get back to Josip and making movies. Zamarion is standing in the way of that. And I think you decided the best way to deal with a 'lowlife' like him was turn the law on him by accusing him of things like threatening to kill you, trying to run you off the road, and setting fire to this house. He's already got a record *and* a reputation." Taylor shrugged.

"You are *so* wrong."

"Honestly? Nothing would make me happier. I don't like feeling manipulated. Or used."

Ashe gaped. "*Used?*"

"Yes. You presented me with a portrait of a bad guy, told me you were afraid for your life, and set me loose. I think you hoped I'd eliminate your problem for you."

This was the part that most troubled Taylor. The suspicion that Ashe had thought Taylor might push Zamarion into doing something that landed him back in prison—or worse.

Ashe's hands were shaking. He dropped the coffeepot, which shattered, spilling glass and coffee over the counter and floor.

He screamed, "I am *afraid* for my life!"

The dripping silence following that shriek was almost as loud as the scream itself. As protests went, it was pretty convincing.

"*Yes*, I'm trying to fight fire with fire, you're right. And I'm sorry if you feel used." Ashe's eyes filled with tears, and his voice got choky. "But for fuck's sake, Taylor, you're the only person I know who could deal with something like this. Maybe he didn't try to set fire to the house, but he did try to run me off the road. He *did* threaten to kill me. Not once. *Three times.* He is *going* to kill me. But he's smart. He's been through the system. He knows how it works. He knows how to play it. So no one believes me. Even you don't believe me. I don't know what else to do. *I don't want to die.*"

Taylor wavered. He had walked into that house convinced he was being manipulated, but now he wasn't so sure. Ashe was frightened to the point of near hysteria. He wasn't faking it. He also wasn't denying he had lied again and again.

Now what?

The thought must have been there on his face to read because Ashe said hopelessly, "Taylor, if you won't help me, I'm dead. It's that simple."

Maybe it was that simple. Probably not. He kept coming back to the heart of the matter: he had promised to be there if Ashe ever needed him, and it was pretty damn clear that Ashe needed *someone.* Taylor seemed to be it.

He watched Ashe cry, mopping feebly with a paper towel at the coffee dripping off the counter onto the floor. Ashe shook his head hopelessly, wiped his face on his shoulder, mopped at the coffee some more.

"All right," Taylor said grimly. "I have a lead on Zamarion. I'll try to talk to him. If that doesn't work... I don't know. One thing at a time."

"Thank you. Thank you, Taylor." Ashe dropped the sodden paper towel on the floor, came to him, put his arms around him, and Taylor stood motionless. He felt sorry for Ashe. He was also repelled by him. Not an attractive combo. He let Ashe hug him, then carefully disengaged, trying not to look like he was backing away.

"Okay. It'll be okay. I'll let you know what happens. In the meantime, stick close to home. And don't be afraid to call the sheriff's if something spooks you."

"I won't. And I have my father's pistol."

Taylor's heart sank.

"Right. But you don't want to pull a weapon unless you're prepared to use it."

"Don't worry. I'll use it," Ashe said. "When the time comes."

It took Taylor all morning and part of the afternoon to locate Mike Zamarion.

He finally tracked him down through his former parole officer from a youthful felony assault and battery conviction, which led to the parents of Anne Zamarion, which led finally to Anne herself.

"Who are you?" Anne questioned when Taylor finally managed to get through to her at the North Hollywood art supply store she managed.

"My name's Taylor MacAllister. I've been hired by Ashe Dekker to see if some agreement can't be reached with Mike over the house on Foothill Road in Carpinteria."

"What agreement?" demanded Anne.

"That's what I'd like to figure out. It's better for everyone if this can be resolved without the expense and stress of a court case, don't you think?"

Silence on the other end.

"What did you say your name was?" Anne asked.

"Taylor MacAllister. My company was hired by Ashe to see if some compromise can't be worked out."

"Taylor…MacAllister?"

"That's right."

"I'll have Mike call you back." She disconnected.

Taylor was doubtful about ever hearing voluntarily from Mike, but about an hour later, as he was sitting in a North Hollywood Starbucks, drinking coffee, watching the rain bounce off the green umbrellas on the small patio, and wondering if there was any other fucking Christmas song besides Mariah Carey's "All I Want for Christmas is You," his phone rang.

The profile of Unknown Caller popped up.

"MacAllister."

A raspy voice said, "This is Mike Zamarion. I hear you're trying to find me."

"I am," Taylor said. "Can we meet?"

"Not so fast. What is it you want?"

"Just to talk. Ashe hired me to see if there was maybe a friendly way to resolve this situation."

Zamarion laughed. There was a lot of ambient noise in the background, like he was on a cell phone while driving. "I doubt that!"

"What is it you doubt?"

"A peaceful resolution."

Taylor asked patiently, "Why's that?"

"Because your boyfriend is a fucking sociopath, in case you didn't know it."

Taylor didn't answer. He'd had a number of enlightening phone conversations that day. Zamarion's former parole officer actually thought pretty highly of him. She believed that Zamarion was a victim of environment, bad temper, and bad luck. He was apparently, among other things, a talented artist, and had things gone a different way, could have had a very different life.

Which kind of went without saying.

Anne Zamarion's parents also seemed to believe that, despite a fondness for booze and broads (Taylor's words, not theirs), Mike was a good-hearted, talented guy that Fate just seemed to have it in for. They believed Mike's manslaughter conviction was a great injustice.

Taylor, liking to know who and what he was dealing with, had read the court case, and wasn't convinced. He thought Zamarion was probably smarter than the average bear, but also probably more prone to violence.

Zamarion said, "He destroyed that will, you know. Alice wanted me and the girls to have the house. He didn't care until he ran out of money. He sure as hell never cared about Alice."

"Families are complicated." Taylor had good reason to know.

Zamarion snorted. "Greed isn't. He wants what he wants, and he doesn't care who he has to hurt to get it. Which you—" He broke off.

"Okay. How do we resolve this? Because let's be honest. You're not going to get that house. You can make life difficult for Ashe, and maybe that's your goal, but you strike me as a practical guy. Maybe we can reach some arrangement which actually brings benefit to you and your family."

Zamarion began to laugh. It was kind of unnerving. "Are you for real?"

"Yes."

"You really don't have a fucking clue, do you?"

"Suppose you fill me in?"

"Not a fucking clue."

Taylor opened his mouth, but he was suddenly aware that he *didn't* have a fucking clue. Something was going on here that he didn't understand.

The windy silence between them stretched, and then, startlingly, Zamarion hung up.

"What the hell?" Taylor stared at his phone.

He thumbed through his Recents, found Unknown Caller, and tried phoning back. The cell rang and rang.

Nobody home.

He thought about calling Will—that was his default—but Will had enough on his plate today. No point rubbing in the fact that the partner who should have been sharing the drudgery of that survey was busy wasting time they didn't have.

He thought about ordering a sandwich to-go, wondered what the hell he should get Will for Christmas, considered his quickly dwindling options for getting hold of Mike Zamarion.

His cell rang. Unknown Caller was back.

"Bad connection?" Taylor asked.

"You have no idea." Zamarion's voice dipped.

"What?"

"If you want to know what's really going on, bring twenty grand in cash to lifeguard tower eleven on Carpinteria State Beach. If you're not there by seven o'clock, don't bother showing up at all. This is your one and only chance."

"You're dream—"

Zamarion disconnected again.

"*Shit.*" Taylor glared at his cell screen and saw that while he had been speaking to Zamarion, Ashe had phoned.

He muttered his exasperation, checked his messages.

Ashe's recorded voice sounded contrite. "Hi, Taylor. I should never have involved you in this. Can we just forget the whole thing? Don't try to contact Zamarion. It's not worth it. I don't want to live with knowing something happened to you because of me." He gulped audibly. "Let's just... Consider yourself fired, okay? And...why don't you come by for a drink tonight. For old times' sake. Say seven o'clock?"

Taylor groaned. Behind the long counter, the baristas eyed him doubtfully. Taylor put his hand up in a don't-mind-me gesture, and phoned Will.

Whereupon his day went from bad to worse.

Lunch with David Bradley? *Seriously?*

Not that Will was lying. Will did not lie. Even when it might have made life easier for both of them. But of all the fucking gin joints in all the fucking world, did he really have to walk into a restaurant where goddamned Lt. Commander David Bradley happened to be eating lunch? It wasn't even lunchtime!

Was the universe trying to tell them something?

To make it worse, Will had sounded so guilty and nervous and apologetic.

Was that how Taylor made him feel? Was *he* the bad guy here? Because he really, honestly hadn't thought there was a bad guy, just bad luck.

It kind of took the heart out of him, thinking that maybe Will was starting to feel beaten down and misjudged. Especially since Taylor had been thinking he was doing such a good job of letting go of the past. God. The last thing he wanted was for them to start that kind of bitchy, barbed interaction so many couples seemed to devolve into.

Was that where they were headed?

Maybe once he'd sorted out Ashe's problems, and the gauntlet of Webster Fidelity was behind them, he and Will could sit down and just...talk. Like they used to. Before they'd left the DS. Before everything got so complicated.

Before it was too late.

* * * * *

Will called as Taylor was leaving the office.

"I'm ten minutes out. Don't leave without me."

"Meet me there. I can't afford to be late."

Will said urgently, "No. Taylor, no. Listen to me. I heard from Stuart Schwierskott a little while ago. Ashe Dekker is not who you think he is. He's not the guy you used to know."

"I'm not the guy he used to know either." Taylor lowered his phone to greet Euphonia, who was trotting across the rain-slick bridge. "You're supposed to be parking in the lot, Nee."

Euphonia, returning to the office to make sure all signs of the godawful gold duck on the lobby wall were eradicated before another sunrise, called cheerfully, "Good night, Agent MacAllister."

He raised the phone to his ear to hear Will saying, "...not to mention he's got expensive habits."

"Schwierskott? What are you talking about? Why are we suddenly working with Schwierskott?"

"You're not *listening* to me," Will cried.

Taylor, remembering his reflections earlier that afternoon, stopped walking. He said quietly, "I'm listening."

Rain pattered on the leaves overhead. There was a short in the Christmas lights strung around the miniature golf course, and the windmill and pagoda appeared and disappeared in red-green lightning flashes.

"Taylor, he's setting you up. This is a trap." Will sounded as out of breath as if he was running on foot from San Diego.

Taylor looked skyward. "Who? Zamarion?"

"No!"

"Ashe. Right. Of course." He controlled his restiveness.

"Yes, Ashe. He's in hock up to his eyeballs with gambling debts."

Taylor was silent. He'd known—suspected—that Ashe was so desperate for money, he was willing to lie, cheat, and steal from Zamarion in order to sell that house. But it wasn't likely Zamarion would be complicit in that, so how did it fit with Taylor meeting him on the beach in less than thirty minutes?

Besides, Ashe had told him not to meet with Zamarion.

"Don't worry, Brandt. I won't turn my back—"

"*No,*" Will said. "You still don't understand. I think Ashe hired Zamarion to kill us."

"*What?* That's crazy."

"No. Hear me out. The Russian mafia is huge in Croatia. You know that. You're the one always talking about the Russians and organized crime. And you know who has a finger in that cabbage roll? Mikhail Bashnakov."

"I know, Will…"

Will was still talking, stumbling over his words in his hurry to get it all out, and that desperate haste was unexpectedly convincing. Maybe more convincing than his words. "He's coming up for trial. Bashnakov. We're being deposed in January. What do you want to bet he's trying to eliminate loose ends? Witnesses? I think he called in a marker with Dekker. I think Dekker hired Zamarion to take us out. Remember when we ran into Gretchen Hart before we went to Oregon? I think that's the connection."

"The actual witness is Hedwig. Bashnakov wouldn't bother—"

"*We're* witnesses to the attempt to take Hedwig out."

"They weren't trying to take her out. They were trying to take her baby."

"And *then* take her out."

"We don't know that for sure."

"The hell we don't."

Was Will having a nervous breakdown? Because this was the most far-fetched, Machiavellian… Well, actually, it sounded like the kind of scenario Taylor would come up with. Russian crime was something he knew a little about. Except this scenario didn't hold together.

He said firmly, "I'm not saying you're wrong about Bashnakov wanting us out of the way, but Ashe working with Zamarion? It makes zero sense. What does Zamarion have to gain?"

"Money. Of course."

"But if that's the case, why's he asking me for twenty thousand dollars?"

"You think these assholes wouldn't double-cross each other? Or even triple-cross each other?"

No, he didn't think that.

Taylor said, "Either way, we need to hear what Zamarion has to say. Correct?"

A pause—because they both knew that was correct.

"Wait for me," Will said. "Do you hear me, MacAllister? Whether you're right or I'm right, Zamarion isn't going anywhere. *Wait.*"

True. Whether Zamarion was waiting for a payoff or an ambush, he would not leave because they showed up five minutes late.

"And counting," Taylor said tersely.

* * * * *

There was no sign of Zamarion on the rainswept beach.

No sign of anyone.

The seaside sentinel of lifeguard tower eleven stretched up, a tall and boxy silhouette against a sagging sky.

The wet sand was cool and slippery beneath their feet as they approached, pistols at low ready, from opposite ends of the long, vacant beach. In front of them, white-capped waves crashed against the shore with a sharp *crack* and withdrew, shushing. The rain tasted briny. Taylor blinked the blur from his vision.

He reached the bottom of the tower first. Will joined him, saying, "Maybe I guessed wrong."

"About?"

"Zamarion being willing to wait." Will sounded rueful.

"No." Taylor believed Zamarion had wanted to talk. And he'd wanted the money more than he'd wanted to talk.

Or maybe it was Taylor who had it wrong, and Zamarion was lying in the hills with an infrared scope, waiting to pick them off.

No. He could already have tried that a dozen times over, starting with their disembarking from their vehicle in the parking lot.

Taylor glanced around the mounds of soft, wet sand, switched his pocket flashlight on. The white beam illuminated a kaleidoscope pattern of footsteps. Rain puddled in the deeper footsteps, and in one pair of indentations pooled something much darker than rain.

He felt a kind of internal slump. Since he'd climbed into Will's SUV, he'd been trying to convince himself Will was jumping at shadows, that people didn't change that much…

"Will."

Will turned, followed Taylor's gaze, and turned his flashlight beam in the direction of Taylor's. They looked at each other. Taylor glanced up at the boarded face of the lighthouse tower.

Will grunted, aimed his flashlight at the bottom step, at the water splash of darkness. He let out a soft sigh.

"Cover me," Taylor said, and Will stepped to the side, resting both hands on the railing, aiming his SIG Sauer P229 at the doorway.

They already knew this precaution was unnecessary.

Taylor sprinted up the stairs, crossed the balcony in two steps, pushed open the cracked door. His flashlight beam picked out a motionless form facedown on the floor. He had a quick impression of shaggy silver hair, bulky shoulders, and a black-leather clad back with a wet and glistening hole in the center.

Funny how without ever meeting Zamarion, he had managed to form a picture of him. The truth was older—much older—heavier, and carrying a lot more wear and tear.

Taylor stepped back from the doorway and called down to Will. "He's dead. Phone the sheriffs."

* * * * *

The rain had stopped when they finally pulled up in the courtyard of 3000 Foothill Road. Every light in the house appeared to be blazing, though it was after midnight.

Taylor and Will had spent a long time talking to the sheriffs—and a long time not talking to the sheriffs. Will was not happy with the not-talking part, but he had acquiesced to Taylor.

"I want to speak to him first, that's all," Taylor said.

"You can't get him out of this. You understand that, right?" The concern in Will's gaze was all for Taylor. He hadn't wanted Ashe as a client to start with.

"If he did this, I don't want to get him out of it."

"*If* he did it?" Will questioned. "Do you have an alternate theory?"

No. He did not have an alternate theory. And he was the guy known for coming up with alternate theories.

Will did not approve of keeping things from law enforcement, but he followed Taylor's lead and kept his answers brief and largely uninformative, and for that Taylor was grateful.

He was less grateful that Will had hired Stuart Schwierskott to investigate Ashe, but he had listened in silence as Will had told him everything Schwierskott had learned about their former client. And hey, kudos to Schwierskott who, while not great at fieldwork, turned out to know his way around an intelligence report.

The most disturbing piece of information Schwierskott had uncovered was that Ashe's boyfriend, Josip Marić—a low-level drug dealer—had died falling off the balcony of their Zagreb penthouse, a suspected mob hit.

Gee, no wonder he'd had trouble getting that travel visa. Being dead would cramp anyone's travel plans.

If Taylor had been a guy prone to freaking out, that news would have freaked him out. But it also explained why Ashe was so terrified.

"I don't think you should go in there on your own," Will said as they studied the brightly lit windows.

"He has nothing to gain by harming me now."

"Maybe he doesn't know that. Maybe he still thinks his main worry is Bashnakov. He never struck me as the most rational guy."

"He's not stupid."

Will made an if-you-say-so sound. He said, "He's got a thing about you. That worries me. There's a reason he was tapped by Bashnakov."

"He was tapped because he owes the Russians millions."

"You know what I mean."

Yes, he knew. And yes, Ashe did seem to bear him a considerable grudge. Although likely his main motivation had been self-preservation.

"I think there's less chance of it all going sideways if I talk to him on my own. If I can make him see the advantage of being first through the door—"

Will was shaking his head. "He's not going to roll over on Bashnakov. Anyway, he won't have had personal dealings with The Technician. You know how it works."

"I know." Taylor reached for the door handle, stopping when Will grabbed his arm.

"Be careful in there," Will growled. "I mean it. Don't give him the benefit of the doubt—" Taylor cut him off with a kiss, and got out of the SUV.

Ashe did not answer Taylor's knock or the doorbell.

With a sinking feeling, Taylor tried the door, and it swung open on well-oiled hinges.

"Ashe?"

No answer.

The unlocked door could mean a lot of things, including the fact that Ashe had asked him to stop by for drinks and a little bit of Auld Lang Syne earlier that evening. It did not have to mean what he feared: that finding himself cornered, Ashe chose the easy way out.

Not that it would be easy for Ashe. He had a strong sense of self-preservation. As indicated by recent events.

Taylor glanced back at Will's Toyota Land Cruiser. The clouds had parted, and the full moon shone, bathing the courtyard in eerie silver light. He couldn't see Will inside the vehicle, but he raised his hand in reassurance, and stepped inside the tiled hall.

Once inside, he pulled his weapon and proceeded down the corridor.

Despite its grand facade and 3.5 million price tag, the house proper was not even four thousand square feet. It took him less than three minutes to conduct a rudimentary search for Ashe.

There was plenty of indication he was around somewhere. An empty tequila bottle sitting on the kitchen counter, the washing machine sudsing through its cold-clean cycle, the television in the family room blasting out a local newscast.

"The body of a gunshot victim was discovered this evening by two private investigators, in a lifeguard station on Carpinteria State Beach. The victim, whose identity is being withheld pending notification of next of kin…"

The back door to the outdoor covered veranda stood open. Taylor went out, walked down the steps leading to the pool yard, and found Ashe sitting next to the burning fire pit. He was hunched forward, holding his father's Ruger, staring at the fire.

He didn't look up at Taylor's approach, but he said, "That could have gone better."

He sounded calm. Even a little wry.

Taylor's heart stopped skipping in dread. He holstered his weapon. "Why didn't you tell me what was really going on?"

Ashe laughed. "Really? How do you think that conversation would have gone? Hey, long time no see. If I don't want to wind up like my boyfriend, I'm going to have to arrange for you and your boyfriend to have a little accident."

Taylor sat down across from him. "But you know what I do for a living. You must have realized I had the contacts and resources to help you."

Ashe gaped at him. "You can't— Taylor, wake up. You're so goddamned… I don't know. *Impervious.*"

"I don't follow."

"Oh, I know. You really just don't get it. You can't touch people like Bashnakov. You don't bring people like that to *trial.* You don't put people like that in *jail.*"

"What do you think this is about, if not that?"

Ashe looked at him without comprehension, firelight flickering in his eyes.

"Hell, yes, you put them in jail," Taylor said. "No one is above the law."

"You and the Boy Scout." Ashe's voice wobbled. "You think you're living in a movie where the good guys rush in at the last minute and save the day. You think *you're* the good guys."

"We're sure as hell not the bad guys. We're the guys who are going to help put Bashnakov away. And if you want to make sure Bashnakov *stays* in jail, give yourself up and cooperate—"

Ashe jumped up, walking agitatedly up and down along the pool. He waved the pistol in Taylor's direction. Maybe more in illustration than threat, but Taylor tensed, pulse quickening. Guns had a way of going off.

"This is why I didn't tell you. Because *that's* your idea of a solution. Cooperate with the feds! Are you *kidding* me?"

"Okay," Taylor said quickly, reassuringly. "Fair enough. I can't be right all the time."

"No, you sure as shit can't. But you think you can. You always did."

"I promise you, I really don't. Ashe, come on. Sit down and let's talk."

Ashe laughed unsteadily.

"I'm on your side."

"Yeah, we'll see about that," Ashe muttered. He stared down at the pistol in his hand.

Taylor continued to try and coax him to sit again. "Why don't you give me your side. Tell me what happened tonight?"

Ashe glared. "Well, what happened tonight is you didn't tell me you were going to meet Mike, even though I specifically told you *not* to. So I didn't know until it was too late. If the asshole had just stuck to the plan, everything would have been okay. He'd have gotten his share of the money from the sale of the house, and *nobody* would have put two and two together."

"Because you were known enemies."

"Exactly! But no. He had to try and back out."

Taylor kept hoping he was going to hear some extenuating circumstances, but with every word, Ashe was confirming the worst-case scenario: a cold-blooded murder plot.

"And that was just greed. He wanted more money." Ashe added, "And gutlessness. He was also gutless. He was afraid there would be some big investigation if two ex-feds got killed."

Right. Because Will would have to go too. It was a two-for-one deal. The thought of Will dying because of...because of *what*? Why? Because this selfish little shit thought everyone else was expendable? Jesus. He had been sorry for Ashe, guilty about Ashe, but now he was close to hating Ashe.

Still, he kept his voice even, unemotional. "He was probably right."

"Yeah, well…" Ashe abruptly pointed the pistol at Taylor. "That doesn't mean you get off scot-free. This is partly your fault."

Taylor sat up straighter. He said with the calm of long experience— granted not this particular experience, "You can make the argument you killed Zamarion in self-defense. If you shoot me, it's murder one, and Bash- nakov will be the least of your worries."

"Maybe it's worth it." Ashe's voice wavered. "Maybe—"

"Maybe I'll blow your head off if you don't put the gun down," Will said.

Will stood in the shadows on the other side of the pool near the stone staircase. Pretty much invisible, though Taylor knew him well enough to discern his outline among the silhouettes of rock and plants.

Ashe threw a frantic look over his shoulder but did not lower the pistol. "You can't stop me. I'll—"

No. Goddamn it. No, Will.

"Will, stand down," Taylor called.

Will ignored him. "Lower your weapon, Ashe. I won't ask nicely again."

For such a reasonable guy, Will could be so goddamned intractable sometimes.

Ashe turned tearful eyes toward Taylor. "You couldn't even come alone. Even now, even after everything, you couldn't even give me that."

Taylor said desperately, "Ashe, I'll sit here with you as long as you want. Just you and me. Will's going back to the car. Aren't you, Will?"

"Not a chance in hell," Will said.

Ashe sucked in a sharp breath. His hand wobbled, the pistol glinting in the firelight.

"Ashe, listen to me," Taylor was speaking quickly, urgently. "There are things you want to say, and I want to hear them. Let's talk. There's no hurry here. No one's coming. It's just us."

Jesus, he sounded like someone on a terrible TV cop show. *You don't want to do this!* But Ashe *didn't* want to do it. And if Will would just back off and give them space, let Taylor handle this…

"Sure," Ashe said bitterly. "Just us. You and me and *him*. The time for talking was ten years ago, so don't pretend you give a shit now. You walked away and never looked back. The only reason you care now is him. You're worried about him."

"No, I'm—"

Ashe swung the Ruger in Will's direction, and Taylor launched himself forward. Ashe caught the movement, swung the pistol back toward Taylor, and Taylor heard the loud report of Will's SIG Sauer P229.

Ashe staggered back, fired skyward, and fell into the pool.

"No no no no…" Taylor ran to the ledge of natural rock. "No." He stared across the choppy water. "Jesus Christ, Will. I said I *had* this. I said…" He was suddenly, abruptly, out of breath, feeling very weird, almost light-headed as he stared at Ashe floating facedown, not moving. An inky cloud unfurled lazily around Ashe's head.

"He was going to shoot you." Will stood on the other side of the pool, pistol still trained on Ashe's bobbing body.

"He wasn't going to shoot!"

Will's icy calm shattered. He shouted, "He *did* fucking shoot. At *you*."

Taylor shook his head and dived into the pool.

CHAPTER SEVEN

You had to wonder at whatever data insights and advertising algorithms determined who got what catalogs in the mail.

Like *Occupant* receiving a brochure for Christmas in Hawaii.

Why?

Just...why?

What did people even *do* in Hawaii for the holidays?

Will scowled at the colorful cover of a happy, laughing couple running on white sand and splashing in turquoise water. First of all, despite the background sandcastle with the star on top, that did not look like Christmas. Secondly, that couple was just goddamned annoying in their airbrushed perfection. Thirdly...

"And when this is over, you owe me a real vacation," Taylor said, precariously balanced in the window. "We'll call it a honeymoon."

Will's heart seemed to shrivel within the cage of his ribs.

A lifetime ago.

Eighteen months, if you wanted to get technical. But a long eighteen months, and the longest stretch had been the grueling last eight days.

Was Christmas in Hawaii something Taylor would like?

Was Christmas anywhere, *anything* something Taylor would like?

For an instant Will was back at Ashe Dekker's house in Carpinteria, watching Taylor working over Dekker's drenched, bloodstained body, shivering in the winter air and cursing as he tried to resurrect him.

And then, when it was clear nothing could be done, Taylor had stumbled to his feet, fighting Will's efforts to take him into his arms.

"I told you to wait in the car!"

"I'm not your goddamned chauffeur. Lucky for you."

"I had this. I had it under control."

"Oh yeah, it was going great if your goal was to be dead by Christmas."

"You had to push him. Couldn't let me handle it. Couldn't trust me—"

"That's rich coming from you. I told you that first night I didn't want to take this job. That I thought it was a mistake. Where was your trust? You brushed me off. You kept me out of the loop. You just assumed I was jealous."

"You were jealous. Because you don't trust me."

They had argued before. That was a given. But not like that. Never like that. They had nearly come to blows. Will's brain hurt from the things they had said to each other. His heart felt bruised.

Of course, it was a different story once the sheriffs and emergency services had arrived. Taylor had been stone-cold and completely professional. He had come to persuade his friend and client to surrender himself to the authorities. Dekker, drunk and terrified, had panicked and turned his weapon—the weapon used to murder Mike Zamarion earlier the same evening, as it turned out—on Taylor. Taylor's partner had come to his aid, and Dekker had been killed.

It was the truth, but it probably didn't hurt their credibility that the victim had a 0.15 blood alcohol level and his fingerprints on a murder weapon.

Will blinked away the memories.

Anyway. Hawaii had to beat what they usually did for the holidays, which was work their asses off.

In fact, the last time Will could remember one of them taking Christmas off was a year ago when he'd had the flu. He'd been hoping to fly home from Paris to surprise Taylor, but that plan had gone down the drain with half a box of Fervex.

They *needed* a break. And here they were, unexpectedly free for the holidays, having managed to complete the surveys for Webster Fidelity in record time. Partly that was because they had worked nonstop—mostly apart from each other—after the disaster of Ashe Dekker. Partly that was because

Euphonia had turned out to be a genius at organizing and interpreting their scribbled and sometimes chaotic notes and less than pristine surveys. Nee was very good, even scary good, at calling the clients and worming out the information needed to fill in the blanks.

Sure, Will could head back to Oregon for Christmas, give Taylor some space. But they had been giving each other a lot of space this last week—had barely seen each other—and things weren't getting better. No. The strain and silence were only solidifying. And Hawaii was everything Taylor loved: sun, sand, water, and plenty of comfortable alternatives to camping.

Will frowned at the framed photo of a smiling Taylor that sat on his desk. Not many smiles out of Taylor these days.

No. Not true. Taylor smiled all the time. If the curve of lips, the crease of cheek, the flash of teeth equaled a smile. Taylor was brisk and cheerful—and hard as a slammed-shut door. But the sunlit unguarded happiness of the photo? That smile hadn't been seen in what felt like a long time.

Not since Ashe Dekker. Goddamn him.

Yeah, maybe it wasn't such a bad idea. They had to do something for the holidays, after all, and sitting around in a silent house that suddenly felt too small for both of them? No. Maybe if they could get away, take a real vacation like Will had been promising forever, maybe talk things out? Maybe then they could get back to normal…

"Hawaii?" Taylor said skeptically when Will broached the idea that evening.

Will had almost lost his nerve after Taylor's indifferent response to Japanese takeout from his favorite restaurant. It was possible he hadn't even noticed. His conversation, per usual—their new usual—had revolved strictly around work.

Which was ironic, given how little enthusiasm either of them had for the job these days.

That wasn't the worst of it. They hadn't touched each other, beyond an inadvertent brush of hands or arms, since the night Ashe Dekker died. That quick, warm brush of Taylor's mouth before he had gone to talk to Dekker.

Taylor hadn't wanted to hear what Will had to say then—and he didn't want to hear it now.

They had never been great at talking about their feelings, but until recently they hadn't stopped trying.

And once they stopped trying…

"We can afford to take a little break," Will said.

Taylor pushed his plate aside. "We took a little break for Thanksgiving."

"I mean a real break."

Taylor shrugged. "Thanksgiving with your family. Seemed like a real break to me."

It was hard when he was like this. Hard to say the things Will knew he needed to say.

"I know. I mean…" Will took a breath. "I think maybe it would do us good to get away after…everything."

Taylor's green eyes met his, direct and unblinking, like the stare of an unfriendly cat.

"I would like to take you on a real vacation," Will said. "Like I've been promising for…"

Years.

Since before Paris. Since before the High Sierras. Since before Taylor had been shot and everything had changed forever.

"I appreciate the thought," Taylor said. "But we're busy now, and I don't want to waste money we don't have."

Finances remained a touchy subject given that they were still in hock to Taylor's stepfather. Not that Richard gave a damn about the money—he spent that amount and more on charity dinners—but Taylor did.

"Business is as slow as it's going to get. It's the holidays. Plus, I talked to Stuart Schwierskott about covering for us if something does come up."

"*Schwierskott?* You're serious?"

"Yes. I'm serious. He's looking to make a change."

"From bad to worse?"

Will let that go. "We're not going to never take a break again, and we need some kind of coverage, so why not give him a shot? It's only a couple of days." Lately Will had gotten into the habit of not arguing when Taylor shot him down. He didn't want to risk the fragile balance between them. But there were worse things than arguing.

"Will…"

"We need some time together," Will said. "We need to *talk—*"

Taylor said with unexpected, almost shocking fierceness, "*What the fuck do you think there is to say, Brandt?*"

Will stared, silent and stricken in the face of that restrained fury.

Taylor glared at him, then rose and went to the window to stare out at the night-shrouded garden.

Will watched him, his heart beating unpleasantly hard in his chest. He had not seen that coming, had not anticipated Taylor's…what the hell *was* that even? Had never expected to see Taylor looking at him like he hated him. He almost couldn't think past it.

His gaze dropped to Taylor's left hand, spotted the glint of platinum. Taylor was still wearing his ring. So okay. That was a relief. It wasn't over. Not yet. Maybe that would change in the next five minutes. He was afraid to speak. He had no idea what to say. He was never going to regret any decision that kept Taylor alive and in one piece. And even if he *did* regret it, he would make the same decision every time. Period. He wasn't going to lie about it.

Taylor reached up and squeezed the back of his neck. He let out a long sigh, and turned back to Will. "I know what you're saying, and I'm working through it, Will. Okay?"

"Since when do we work through things alone?" Will added bitterly, "Or am I what you're working through?"

Something flickered in Taylor's eyes. *Bingo.* The pain of recognition was beyond anything Will had experienced. Maybe even worse than the night he'd thought Taylor was going to die.

His mouth was so dry, he thought the words would turn to dust before he got them out. "Are you leaving me?"

Taylor's face twisted. He shook his head. "No."

And now it was Will turning away.

Taylor came back to the table, dragged his chair out, and sat down. He rubbed his forehead. "I'm not leaving. I'm not… I'm still…" He stopped and tried again, and the fact that he was trying again was a good sign, right?

"I can't help feeling the way I feel. I'm not saying it's fair. I know it's not."

Will nodded, expelled a breath, turned back to face Taylor.

"Okay," he said wearily. "Where do we go from here?"

They locked gazes—once upon a time and not so long ago, they had known everything the other was thinking just by looking into each other's eyes.

Taylor grimaced, offered a curl of his mouth that was not quite a smile.

"I guess we head to Hawaii for Christmas."

* * * * *

A Santa in a red and yellow Hawaiian shirt and shades was Alo-ho-ho-hoing everyone passing through Kahului Airport on Maui.

It turned out Christmas in Hawaii was not an original idea, and the small airport was packed with holidaymakers in shorts and Santa hats. Even so, it was only a brief wait for their rental car, and then they were on the road to Kihei and the Pineapple Inn.

They'd had a couple of drinks on the not-quite-six-hour flight, and the lush scenery—luminous and sparkling from recent rain—was genuinely breathtaking, so their collective mood was cheerier than when they'd boarded at LAX that morning. Taylor, face partially hidden behind his aviators, looked…maybe not relaxed, but less rigid than he had in a week. The damp breeze through the Jeep windows whipped some color into his face, and Will began to feel a little more confident about insisting they needed to get away.

The inn turned out to be cozy, quaint, and very small—a total of four guest rooms and a little cottage—which was not a problem for two guys pretty sick of humanity at the moment. It was about a twenty-minute walk to the ocean, but that was also okay. They were surrounded by a sprawling tropical garden complete with fountains, pool, and hot tub, and, most importantly, given Taylor's precarious mood, the whole setup was relatively affordable.

Taylor nodded in approval at their room, unexpectedly soothing with lots of verdant light streaming through all the windows, dark-wood furnishings, and classic Hawaiian leaf-patterned linens. A private lanai faced seaward, offering a stunning view of palm-tree-framed ocean.

They unpacked with their typical quick efficiency—maybe less talkative than usual, but then there was no job to discuss. Or rather, the job was to get their relationship back on track. In a funny way, Will was reminded of that camping trip from hell in the High Sierras. The trip that had changed everything between them.

Or rather, the trip that was supposed to fix everything that had changed between them.

That was the hope here, and Taylor must have shared it too because he had agreed to this impromptu vacation, just as he had agreed to camping in the mountains. At least this time they were somewhere warm and comfortable and to Taylor's liking.

At least Will hoped it was to his liking.

"What do you think?" he asked as Taylor sat down on the foot of the bed, pulled off his sunglasses, and pinched the bridge of his nose.

Taylor glanced up. "Nice. Very nice."

"What would you like to do first? Grab something to eat? Check out the beach?"

Taylor gave a funny half-laugh. "Honestly? More than anything I'd like to sleep."

They had not been sleeping much. Over the past few days, there had been a lot of lying still and controlling breathing so as not to disturb the other. Funny how you could know someone so well, you could tell the difference between their real sleep and their fake sleep.

"We're on vacation," Will said. "We're allowed to sleep. Let's sleep."

"Are you sure? Because we've only got—"

"I think we'll enjoy the rest of our time a lot more if we get some rest." Will sat down on the bed. All at once he was so tired, he couldn't see straight. As if it had taken all his strength to get them here. He let himself fall back on the fern and cactus print comforter, folded his arms behind his head. He closed his eyes.

After a moment, he felt the mattress give as Taylor rose, heard Taylor's boots hitting the carpet, felt the mattress dip again. He opened his eyes.

Taylor lay beside him, as straight and neatly contained as a stone effigy, and once again Will thought that he'd shoot a hundred Ashe Dekkers before he'd let anything happen to Taylor, whether Taylor ever forgave him or not.

For a moment they lay still and silent, their breathing even and regular. The sliding doors to the lanai were open, and the whisper of draperies, the rustle of the palm trees was peaceful. The breeze was a little moist, scented with exotic flowers. It did not smell like home, but it was nice.

Once, and not that long ago, Will would have turned to Taylor and kissed him, and regardless of how tired they were... But he didn't quite dare. In fact, as much as he wanted to put his arm around Taylor, he didn't quite dare that either. These days it was like Taylor had a force field around him, and Will was standing outside, looking in.

He was so afraid of making matters worse, he did nothing, which was probably guaranteed to make matters worse.

It was just that he was so painfully aware of the, well, error of his ways. For two years he had been taking things for granted. Everything from dismissing Taylor's insecurities about David to turning down the Paris posting without discussing it with his partner first. And yes, he had realized he was being kind of high-handed about stuff, but he had excused his behavior because he was sincerely trying to do the right thing for both of them. But however much he loved Taylor—more than his own life, that was the truth— and however much he wanted to take care of Taylor, keep him out of harm's way, he didn't have the right to make some of the choices he'd made without talking it out with the person most affected by these decisions.

It was kind of ironic that this epiphany should be brought about by the one decision he didn't second-guess, wouldn't take back even if he could— the decision to put Ashe Dekker down. Regardless of what Taylor thought, Dekker had been about to kill him. Will had zero doubts.

He could understand and sympathize why Taylor had doubts, why Taylor didn't want to believe his old friend had been willing to murder him, but Will? No regrets.

It didn't mean he was *happy* about it, for God's sake. He felt sick every time he remembered.

And sicker still on the nights he dreamed he fired too late.

If they could just talk like they used to…

That was the main thing he hoped for from this trip. If they could just manage to open the lines of communication again, that would be a start.

In the midst of these grim thoughts, Taylor shifted onto his side and put his arm around Will's chest.

Taylor didn't say anything, didn't put his head on Will's chest as he once would have done, but just that simple gesture closed Will's throat, made his heart expand with emotion—not least gratitude.

They were a little groggy but definitely more relaxed at dinner. They found a place on the beach called Mama's Fish House, with decor vaguely reminiscent of Aloha Steakhouse—lots of wood and bright-blue accents. They drank Bali Hais and Mai Tais and Scorpions—the kind of thing they ordinarily never touched   and got a little plastered. Taylor ordered the grilled Ahi baked in banana leaf, and Will got South Pacific salmon with caramelized onions, chili pepper, and avocado. They ate, drank, and watched the sun go down over the ocean.

They did not talk much, but the silence between them was friendlier than it had been of late.

"We should have done this a long time ago," Will said, and Taylor smiled faintly because they both knew all the reasons they couldn't have done this before. Maybe they shouldn't be doing it now since it meant leaving Schwierskott—their newest employee—and Euphonia to deal with anything that might crop up. But maybe Santa would bring them an absence of trouble for Christmas.

After their leisurely meal, they agreed they were both too much the worse for wear and phoned an Uber to take them back to their hotel.

Once back in their room, there was an unexpected awkwardness about what to do next.

Will began, "Did you want to—" He was thinking along the lines of *go for a walk in the moonlight,* but Taylor looked so instantly and totally blank, the words died in his throat.

His expression was probably a reveal, because Taylor said quickly, awkwardly, "Whatever you want."

Which was clearly *not* how he felt.

"We could try out the hot tub," Will said desperately, and Taylor leaped at that.

And, in fact, the hot tub turned out to be a great idea. The air was cool and balmy, the tub deliciously, bone-meltingly hot, and they had its frothy, steaming waters all to themselves. The lush garden and twinkling stars gave the night a magical feel.

Nothing like that hot spring in the High Sierras, where they had first made love.

Could you call that making love? Maybe not.

"What would you like to do tomorrow?" Will asked. "You want to go on a whale watch? Take a helicopter tour?"

Taylor murmured, "You've been reading the guidebook."

"Whatever you want to do, I'm up for it," Will said. "You want to go surfing? The big winter waves are supposed to be great for experienced surfers."

Taylor raised his brows. "Do you surf? Because that would be news."

"Well, no. But I wouldn't mind having drinks and watching *you* surf."

Taylor was silent for a moment. He said, "Nah. Big-wave surfing is out of my league these days. Besides, we should choose something we can both enjoy."

"Hey, there's nothing not to enjoy about sitting on the beach, drinking Mai Tais."

Another pause before Taylor said almost gently, "Will, you don't have to try so hard. I'm not convalescent."

He didn't mean it as a slap, that was obvious, but it still stung.

Will said, "No, but you're not happy."

"Are you?"

Will's heart was pounding so hard, he wondered if it was going to explode. He had known they had to talk, he wanted to talk, but not this soon. Not before they had a chance—he had a chance—to remind Taylor of everything that was right between them.

"At the moment? No."

Taylor's shadow nodded as though this confirmed his thoughts.

Having admitted that much, Will couldn't think of another thing to say. Or rather, he could only think of one thing, and he was afraid that if he said it, it would mean the end of everything.

The words came out anyway.

"You don't want to believe it, but he was going to shoot you."

Taylor turned his profile to him.

Will said harshly, "But even if he wasn't, you'd have made the same choice."

"Only I didn't. I didn't pull my weapon."

"I don't mean to protect yourself. I mean to protect me. If our positions were reversed, you'd have made the same call."

"As usual, you're thinking you know b—"

Will burst out, "You shot *me*, MacAllister. You shot someone you loved when you believed you had to, so I know you'd have shot him in my position."

Taylor gave that little huff that indicated unwilling acknowledgment.

The minutes ticked by and Taylor didn't reply, so maybe Will was wrong about that.

Taylor finally said, "Is there a Plan B?"

"What?" Will asked blankly.

"For tomorrow. Did you have a Plan B for how we spend tomorrow?"

Will's heart started beating again. He had been expecting annihilation, but it seemed he had cut the blue wire after all.

"We drive to Hana. It's supposed to be spectacular. Rain forest and waterfalls and ocean views. It takes about three hours if you drive straight through, but if you do it right, there are all kinds of hiking trails and places to swim and roadside stands. We could make it an all-day trip."

Christ. He really *was* beginning to sound like the guidebook.

"Okay," Taylor said. "Sure. If that's what you want."

What I want? More than anything, I'd like my best friend, partner, lover back.

Instead, Will said lightly, "Your wish is my command," and Taylor's mouth curved politely.

Excruciating. Since when did they have this kind of trouble talking to each other?

Neither spoke for a time. Taylor tipped his head back, watching the stars, and Will watched him out of the corner of his eye.

After a time, Taylor commented dreamily, "Hey, a shooting star."

"Aren't you supposed to make a wish?"

Taylor closed his eyes. Opened them. He continued to stare at the sky.

CHAPTER EIGHT

The next day—two days before Christmas—they spent the morning and afternoon driving the road to Hana, which turned out to be a 64.4-mile-long very windy, narrow highway through lush tropical rainforest with passes over fifty-nine bridges—many of which were only wide enough for one lane of traffic.

Hours of wind in their hair and sun on their faces. Hours of nothing to do but drive and think and be. They stopped a few times to take photos, to hike up to see waterfalls, to buy iced coconut water and snacks at roadside stands. They didn't talk much, but they shared smiles, helped each other across tricky patches of terrain, shared bites of their shrimp and pineapple and garlic hot dog and red bananas and hot Kona coffee over ice cream.

Anyway, it was a great day. The best Taylor had in what seemed like months. He felt almost normal. It helped that Will had quit watching him like he expected him to detonate at any moment. Better yet, Will had stopped looking so drawn and weary. The shadows around his eyes were fading, the hard line of his mouth softening. Will had needed this trip.

Maybe they both had. Maybe Will was right about that.

In Hana they swam at Red Sand Beach and lunched at the Hana Farms fruit stand and restaurant, which, they agreed, served the best fish tacos either had ever had. They were watching cars zipping along the road when a red Ferrari went roaring past, driven by a guy in sunglasses, Hawaiian shirt, and old-school *Magnum PI*-style mustache.

They shared a sardonic glance, and then grinned because maybe the mind meld was rusty, but it was still working.

Taylor used his chopsticks to steal a slice of glazed bell pepper from Will's plate.

Will's mouth quirked, he fended off another foray of Taylor's chopsticks, and said, "Do you think we made a mistake?"

"Which possible mistake are we talking about?"

"The global security consulting business."

It was almost a relief to hear Will put it into words. "Yes. I do."

Will snorted. "Just say what you think. Don't worry about my feelings."

"I think we made a mistake."

Will sighed. "Me too. It bores the hell out of me. From meeting clients to asset control."

"Me too. I was thinking it didn't matter what we did as long as we did it together."

"But it does," Will agreed.

"It does, yeah. I don't know what we can do about it, though. It's going to take two years to pay Richard back even with Webster Fidelity."

"There's no way we can get our old jobs back. And even if we could..."

"We wouldn't be working together. We'd be repartnered."

Will was watching him carefully. "Does that still matter to you?"

"What?" Taylor frowned. "What do you mean? Of course it matters to me. That was the whole point."

"It was before. But now?"

Taylor froze. "Now? Are you saying it doesn't matter to *you*?"

"It matters, yes. But if we're not..."

"If we're not what?"

Will seemed to gather himself. He said stoically, "If we're not going to be together, maybe it's not the obstacle we're thinking it is."

The impact of Will's words was weirdly similar to being shot. It was hard to get his breath, he felt cold all the way through, and the pain was incredible.

Taylor said unemotionally, "Good point."

Will swallowed, gave a little *okay then* nod, stared out the open window.

They were quiet and careful, almost gentle with each other the rest of the day.

They had dinner at...well, really, what did it matter? One of the big hotels overlooking one of the big beaches. The food was great, the scenery beautiful, and Taylor felt numb to the bone. The way he had felt all afternoon after he realized Will wanted out.

Not that he blamed him.

He had not listened to Will's concerns over Ashe. He had put Will in a position where he'd had to shoot to protect him—and Will was having nightmares about that. No surprise. So was Taylor.

He could have gotten Will killed.

No wonder Will was done.

Not that he hadn't made mistakes too, but even after Paris, even after David Bradley, even after the pursuit of Webster Fidelity when they didn't have the resources to pull it off, Taylor hadn't been ready to throw in the towel.

It had been such a good start to the day. Such a great morning. He'd started thinking they might find their way home. But by lunch, Will had made it clear there was no going back.

"Are you okay?" Will asked over their after-dinner drinks. "You haven't said anything in twenty minutes."

Taylor pulled himself together, smiled, said, "I think I need some air. Maybe I'll walk on the beach for a little bit. I can get a cab back to the inn."

If anything, Will looked more concerned. "You want some company?"

Not really. And at the same time, yes, desperately, because if these were the last few days of being together, being a couple, then Taylor wanted every minute. Even if it made it harder in the end.

Honestly, what could be harder than what they were facing?

Taylor shrugged. "Sure."

They paid their bill, left the restaurant, and walked down a long, sandy flight of stairs to the beach. It looked mostly deserted. A few distant couples with the same idea—or probably, a better idea. The night was cold, the coldest night yet, and Taylor was wishing Will would put his arm around him.

He almost missed a step, realizing that Will might never put his arm around him again. Will's hand shot out, grabbing Taylor's arm, steadying him.

"You didn't have that much to drink." There was a teasing note in his voice.

Taylor laughed. At least, he tried to make the pain blocking his throat sound like a laugh.

Once again, he could see Will looking at him, trying to read him, could feel Will's concern, his kindness. Because even if they weren't going to be together, Will would never stop caring about him. They would always be friends. Witness good old Lt. Commander David Bradley.

Who now had a good shot at having all his dreams come true.

They reached the soft, sandy floor of the beach, and Taylor strode off. Will followed. They walked just out of reach of the waves. It was chillier by the water, but the chill was better than the numbness.

He walked toward the huge silver moon, walked and walked and walked, and then finally sat down in the sand. It still felt warm from the sunny day.

Will sat beside him, shoulder brushing Taylor's.

They said nothing, just watched the inky flood and retreat of glittery water against glittery shore.

There was so much Taylor wanted to say, but he didn't know where to start, and what was the point now?

He could feel Will watching him. He turned to meet Will's gaze. The moonlight threw everything into stark relief, making Will's eyes look black and fathomless.

"What?" Taylor asked.

Will looked out toward the waves. His mouth curved, but there was no humor.

When he didn't answer, Taylor said, "You're going to think it's funny. Until today, I didn't realize you'd given up on us."

"I don't think it's funny." Will glanced at him. "And I would never give up on us. Except…"

"Except you have."

"No." There was pain in Will's voice. "What do you think this trip was about?" He drew an oddly shaky breath. "But."

"But what?"

"Do you really think you'll ever forgive me?" Will's voice was quiet. "Don't you think this is always going to be between us?"

Initially, all Taylor heard was, *This is always going to be between us.* Then the first part of Will's words sank in.

Honestly, regardless of anything else, he could not have Will go on thinking that Taylor blamed him for Ashe.

"No, Will. Jesus." Taylor looked at him, shook his head, pained at the idea. "No, I don't think that. There isn't— That isn't— Forgiveness isn't in this, isn't part of this—"

Will nodded, turned again to stare at the restless tumble of waves, as though Taylor's stumbling inability to explain confirmed something for him. Taylor heard his words through Will's ears and tried again, tried harder.

"Because there isn't anything to forgive, Will. You said it yourself. I'd have made the same choice. It wasn't even a choice, I guess. It was instinct. I know that. And if it had been the other way around, I'd probably have had the same...instinct."

No probably about it. Will had called it last night in the hot tub.

That didn't mean it didn't hurt, that it hadn't been a shock. They were no strangers to violence, but it was still a gut punch, thinking about it, remembering that terrible moment. He still heard that shot in his dreams.

Will asked huskily, "But?"

"There isn't any but."

"Yeah, only there is. And I get it. You can't help the way you feel."

Yes, he had said that, and it was true. And it was easy to see why Will didn't understand. "I also said I wasn't...that I'm still..."

Had he said it, though? He had said he wasn't leaving. He had said he didn't blame Will. At least, he thought he had. Had he said in plain English that he was still emotionally invested in *them*? That, for better or for worse, when it came to Will, even wholesale slaughter probably wouldn't shake the depth of his feelings?

Maybe not in so many words.

Maybe not in any words.

Taylor struggled with himself and finally managed to confess the truth. "I'm trying to come to terms with it. I ignored my own instincts—and yours—and insisted we take Ashe as our client. I pushed going to the house that night. I'm not forgetting. You tried to talk me out of it. I insisted we had to give him a chance to give himself up. You didn't want to."

Will broke in, "It's not that I didn't trust you. I know you think that."

Taylor couldn't help grimacing because yeah. That was true. He did believe that.

Will said, adamant, "It isn't that. I know I've made mistakes, that mistake, before. But that night... I love you. I can't— It's not in me to stand aside. I *did* try. But, Taylor, that night you'd have made the same call. I *know* you would have."

"Maybe." Honesty compelled Taylor to say, "Probably." He would not have let Will walk in there alone in the first place. That was the truth.

Will let out a little breath, like that was a bigger concession than he'd hoped for.

Taylor's thoughts were running on a separate track. "It wasn't that I was blind to the signs. But it's not easy thinking that for all those years, Ashe hated me; hated me so much, he was willing to kill me."

Will put a hand on his shoulder, gripped hard. "I'm sorry, Tay."

"I know."

"So sorry. About all of it."

Taylor nodded. Said again, "I know." Adding a moment later, "Me *and* you. That's the thing I can't forget. I dragged you into it and almost got you killed."

That was the part that made it hard to sleep, to eat, to think. He hadn't managed to help Ashe—Ashe was dead—and he'd nearly got Will killed too.

"You didn't drag me into anything."

"The hell, Will. Of course I did."

"Like I haven't dragged you into things? Christ."

"Okay, that's fair," Taylor admitted.

Will groaned. "I know. Believe me, I know. I swear to God, Taylor, if you could give me another chance… I *have* changed. I know you don't see it, but I have. That day I ran into David, I told him his friendship wasn't worth losing you."

It was probably childish that that concession meant so much.

"Is that true?" Taylor tried to read Will's face.

"Yes. It is. I'm sorry it took me so long to realize what I was doing."

Taylor, starting to feel uncomfortable, said, "It's not like I ever thought you were—"

"I would never cheat on you. Never. Never betray you."

Taylor really wasn't *that* insecure. Will knew that, right? "I know that. I never thought that. You don't have to choose—"

"There isn't any choice," Will interrupted. "That's what I'm trying to say. There never has been. It's *you*. It's always going to be you. And yeah, because of the way I feel about you, I am always going to try to protect you, but I swear to God, I'm past trying to make your choices for you. These last few days…" Will swallowed. "Knowing you probably can't forgive…"

"Will, listen to me. It's not that. I feel like I failed. Everybody. I failed Ashe. I failed you——"

Will sounded almost shocked. "What are you talking about? You never failed anyone in your life."

"I did, though. And I'm trying to work through it. I know I've been withdrawn and moody and… I'm trying. But I'm so goddamned…"

"What?"

Taylor shook his head.

"Angry?"

Taylor drew a long breath, let it out slowly. "Depressed. I guess."

"*Depressed?*" Will sounded like he'd never heard the word before, and he probably never had. Not from Taylor, anyway. Neither of them was prone to overanalyzing—or any analyzing of—their feelings. Hell, when had they ever had the luxury of time to even consider what they might be feeling?

"You mean like… Why didn't you say something? Why wouldn't you let me help?" Will tried to pull him into his arms, but Taylor, feeling like a fool, resisted.

"Right. Because my feelings are your problem too?"

Will peered at him closely. "Hell, yes, your feelings are my problem. Aren't my feelings your problem?"

Taylor let out a shaky breath. "Yeah. I guess so."

"I knew you weren't okay. I knew you weren't sleeping, weren't eating—"

"Neither were you."

"But I thought you were grieving. I killed your friend."

Taylor rested his face in his hands. "If I hadn't— If I could have—"

"Stop," Will said. "Sweetheart, you know better."

That soft *sweetheart* melted him. Taylor turned to Will, and Will wrapped his arms around him, pulled him close.

Taylor said, words muffled against Will's chest, "I just feel like I could have—should have—"

Coulda, shoulda, woulda.

"*None* of this is on you," Will said fiercely. "*You* sure as hell aren't to blame for what happened." He rested his face against Taylor's hair.

Taylor closed his eyes and gave in to the luxury of leaning on Will. "That's the thing, though. I was so sure this was a chance to make up for the past. To set things straight. I didn't handle it well, back in college. He cared so much, and I was just…glad to be starting my real life."

"Christ, MacAllister. You were both kids. What were you supposed to do?"

Taylor shook his head. Not in answer to Will. He was lost in his own thoughts. "Neither of us was really out…"

Will said, "I know. Of course not." Will got it. Taylor had been planning for a career in the Bureau of Diplomatic Security, and back then there were no gay federal agents. Or, more exactly, there were no *out* federal agents. It was a different world. The only people who thought things hadn't really changed were the people who hadn't lived through the old days.

He raised his face to meet Will's gaze. "And it was partly because of that, our friendship meaning so much."

"Yeah." The understanding in Will's blue gaze was both painful and a relief, because Will did absolutely understand everything Taylor was saying—and not saying.

"I did care for him."

"I know you did," Will reassured.

"He cried like it was the end of the world." It had shaken Taylor, those hot tears and shuddering sobs. Ashe had sounded like his heart was breaking. And Taylor had all but fled. Then he'd followed that relationship up with the affair with Inori.

No wonder he'd so often been accused of being emotionally unavailable. That had been his MO. Until Will.

Will sighed, as though Taylor's pain was a weight on his heart.

"And there was nothing I could say except...if he ever needed me, I'd be there for him."

"And you were. You tried to be. He made bad choices. And the worst choice was thinking he could pay off his gambling debts by handing us over to Mikhail Bashnakov."

Taylor nodded. "Yes. But it's still..."

"Shocking. Painful. Depressing," Will agreed. "Yeah. I see that. I'm sorry." He held Taylor still more tightly, and Taylor rested his face in the curve of Will's neck. Will bent his head, said softly against Taylor's ear, "I'm sorry it turned out the way it did. But I'm not sorry we're both here tonight. I'm never going to be sorry for that."

Taylor whispered, "No. Me neither."

The rain-scented breeze of island flowers, the soft, cool cotton of freshly laundered sheets, the lazy *click* of a digital clock beside the bed, the faint *tap-tapping* of old plumbing. Bliss.

When Taylor finally opened his eyes the next morning, Will said, "What if we make that ring of yours for real?"

Taylor blinked at the ceiling, blinked at Will, said rustily, "It is for real."

Will was smiling, but his blue eyes were grave. "I mean official. Legal."

Was Will asking what he seemed to be asking? Taylor said slowly, "You want to get married in Hawaii?"

"Well, we're here."

He was clearly kidding—and yet, clearly not kidding.

Okay, it was understood they would one day marry. They had never discussed the logistics, but Will knew Taylor well enough to be confident Taylor didn't want a big fuss any more than he did.

Will said, "Did you know gay marriage has been legal in Hawaii since 2013?"

"I did not know that, no." Taylor tilted his head, studying him. "What's the rush?"

Will laughed. "*Rush?* We've been together five years."

"Uh, I don't think we can count the time we weren't actually *together* as together."

"I think it all counts. It all goes into me knowing I want to spend the rest of my life with you." Will drew in a breath. "And I'm thinking you feel the same."

Like there was any question of that?

Taylor smiled, all his tenderness and affection right there in his face—but maybe a little exasperation too, because even though this was one of the nicest things Will had ever said to him, it was a case of *it's the thought that counts.* Taylor had lived through the weddings of two siblings, and if Will imagined it was possible to pull off a spur-of-the-moment wedding, he was hitting the Mai Tais again.

"Okay. Agreed. But."

"But?"

"For starters, I don't know how you think we're going to arrange a wedding in three d—"

Will interrupted, "I spent the morning phoning around, and I found a company that will marry us before lunch."

Taylor's heart jumped. *"Today?"*

"Yep, today. If you want to go for it. It's $325 for a licensed minister, beach permit and insurance, a decorative certificate of marriage, and two fresh-flower leis." He added, as though all those parasols and lovebirds had suddenly made him an expert, "The hard part about pulling off a wedding is arranging the venue. This entire island is a venue."

"You're serious."

"I am. I'm serious. If you want them to take photos using our phones, it's another two hundred dollars."

"Another two hundred." Taylor sat up, shoving the hair out of his eyes. "Okay. Right."

"No frills, obviously, but—"

"We're not frilly guys." Taylor was starting to laugh. "Are you— Are you sure you know what you're saying? Because I will *not* take kindly to being left at the altar."

"No altar. Are we going for it or not?"

Taylor hesitated.

Will said softly, "I'm not pushing you. This is up to you. Say the word, and I'll make the phone call. They said they'd hold that slot open for thirty more minutes."

For a long moment they held each other's gazes.

Their love, their relationship, was not perfect. It was complicated, occasionally messy, sometimes even confusing, and probably always would be. But it was the real deal. The *for better or worse, in sickness and in health, till death do us part* deal. Theirs was a partnership in every sense of the word.

Will's voice was deep, a little husky, as he said, "Will you marry me, Taylor?"

Taylor laughed, a shaky, breathless laugh. He shoved the blankets aside and jumped out of bed. "Which beach?" He held his hand out to Will. "And who's driving?"

EPILOGUE

It was raining.

Not hard, more mist than rain, but wet enough to keep the sun and surf crowd away. Now and then during the very brief ceremony, the sun peered through silver-edged clouds, smiled briefly, and faded out. The aqua surf hit the white sand in regular, leisurely heartbeats, and occasionally the grooms' words were lost in the pound of waves and the cries of gulls.

"I, William, take thee, Taylor, to be my lawfully wedded husband, to have and to hold from this day forward, for better, for worse, for richer, for poorer, in sickness and in health, to love and to cherish, till death us do part."

Will slipped the platinum band—platinum mixed with a small percentage of lead from the bullet that had changed everything—onto Taylor's ring finger. His hands were warm, his fingers steady, and his eyes smiled into Taylor's.

Then it was Taylor's turn.

"I, Taylor, take thee, William, to be my lawfully wedded husband, to have and to hold from this day forward, for better, for worse, for richer, for poorer, in sickness and in health, to love and to cherish, till death us do part."

Taylor reached into his shirt pocket and pulled out a ring: a chrome and box elder band with a line of laser-carved pine trees. He met Will's astonished gaze, slid the ring on Will's left hand, and winked.

The damp wind tasted salty, but there were no tears. They were not men who cried easily or often, and surely not for happiness. The only moment of self-consciousness was as they each placed a wedding lei over the other's head. The leis were made of ti leaves, wound with tiny, fragrant white tuberoses, and they were beautiful and festive. There were a couple of laughs, a muttered comment from Taylor, a few more *clicks* of phone cameras, and at last a kiss, so careful, so tender.

Afterward they had lunch at another of the big hotels, where they were serenaded by Christmas carolers clad in Hawaiian shirts. Will ordered champagne, Taylor ordered some kind of cake made with pineapple, cinnamon, and nutmeg and frosted with cream-cheese frosting and toasted coconut.

"You had a ring all ready to go," Will teased, nudging Taylor's booted foot with his own.

Taylor laughed and shook his head. "Yes and no. That was your Christmas gift. I picked it up yesterday at that little shop in Hana before we stopped for lunch." His mouth twisted. "I thought it was time you wore a ring too. Of course, half an hour later you were telling me you were leaving me."

"Not what I said. Never. And not what I meant. *Ever.*" Will spoke without heat, was even smiling a little. They were past the misunderstandings and miscommunications. Maybe there was something to the idea of a formal commitment. "From this day forward, buddy boy."

Taylor said, "I guess we're going to catch hell from pretty much everyone for running off and getting married like this."

"Probably."

They smiled at each other.

Later, Taylor said thoughtfully, "What *are* we going to do about American Eagle?"

"I've been considering that. What do you think about splitting off the global security consultant side of the business from the other side of the business? We could promote Euphonia to project manager and let Schwierskott handle the meet-and-greet stuff. He's pretty good at it."

"Uh, what other side of the business?" Taylor inquired.

"Private investigations."

"Private... You want us to become PIs?"

"Well, think about it. What's in our wheelhouse?"

Taylor opened his mouth, and Will said quickly, "Investigating. Investigating is what we're good at. We're field agents. We're not analysts. I believe it's a natural fit for us."

"Do you?"

"I do." Will smirked. "No pun intended."

Taylor's mouth twisted. He said, "Hm. It's going to be hard getting a letter of recommendation from our last client."

Will winced. "Will you consider the idea, at least?"

"Yes." Taylor relented. "Actually, I kind of like the idea."

"Do you?"

"I do." Taylor's turn to smirk.

Will said, "I thought you would."

"But we're not moving to Hawaii, Brandt. And you're not buying a Ferrari."

Will snorted. "Deal."

And much, much later that night in their hotel room, Will held up his left hand and said, "You know, I like the etched pine trees."

Taylor said, "It reminded me of—"

"Me too," Will said gruffly. "It reminds me of where we've been and where we're going."

"Which is hopefully not camping."

Will leaned over to kiss him. He whispered, "Which is together. Forever."

AUTHOR'S NOTE

Dear Reader,

It's hard to say goodbye to characters I love as much—and for as long—as Will and Taylor. I think it's one reason I kept delaying this book.

The journey of Taylor MacAllister and Will Brandt began in April 2008 when Loose Id published *Dangerous Ground*. The stories were intended to be quick, fun, episodic adventures, and I believe I've kept that promise. The boys have had a good long run, and it's certain they will continue their adventures long after you turn the final page. Thank you for sharing the ride.

Thank you to Keren. Thank you to Kevin.

ABOUT THE AUTHOR

Author of over sixty titles of classic Male/Male fiction featuring twisty mystery, kickass adventure, and unapologetic man-on-man romance, JOSH LANYON'S work has been translated into twelve languages. Her FBI thriller *Fair Game* was the first Male/Male title to be published by Harlequin Mondadori, then the largest romance publisher in Italy. *Stranger on the Shore* (Harper Collins Italia) was the first M/M title to be published in print. In 2016 *Fatal Shadows* placed #5 in Japan's annual Boy Love novel list (the first and only title by a foreign author to place on the list). The Adrien English series was awarded the All Time Favorite Couple by the Goodreads M/M Romance Group. In 2019, *Fatal Shadows* became the first LGBTQ mobile game created by Moments: Choose Your Story.

She is an Eppie Award winner, a four-time Lambda Literary Award finalist (twice for Gay Mystery), An Edgar nominee, and the first ever recipient of the Goodreads All Time Favorite M/M Author award.

Josh is married and lives in Southern California.

Find other Josh Lanyon titles at www.joshlanyon.com, and follow Josh on Twitter, Facebook, Goodreads, Instagram and Tumblr.

For extras and exclusives, join Josh on Patreon.

ALSO BY JOSH LANYON

NOVELS

The ADRIEN ENGLISH Mysteries
Fatal Shadows • A Dangerous Thing • The Hell You Say
Death of a Pirate King • The Dark Tide
So This is Christmas • Stranger Things Have Happened

The HOLMES & MORIARITY Mysteries
Somebody Killed His Editor • All She Wrote
The Boy with the Painful Tattoo • In Other Words...Murder

The ALL'S FAIR Series
Fair Game • Fair Play • Fair Chance

The ART OF MURDER Series
The Mermaid Murders •The Monet Murders
The Magician Murders • The Monuments Men Murders

The SECRETS AND SCRABBLE Series
Murder at Pirate's Cove

OTHER NOVELS
The Ghost Wore Yellow Socks
Mexican Heat (with Laura Baumbach)
Strange Fortune • Come Unto These Yellow Sands
This Rough Magic • Stranger on the Shore • Winter Kill
Murder in Pastel • Jefferson Blythe, Esquire
The Curse of the Blue Scarab • Murder Takes the High Road
Séance on a Summer's Night
The Ghost Had an Early Check-Out

NOVELLAS
The DANGEROUS GROUND Series
Dangerous Ground • Old Poison • Blood Heat
Dead Run • Kick Start • Blind Side

The I SPY Series
I Spy Something Bloody • I Spy Something Wicked
I Spy Something Christmas

The IN A DARK WOOD Series
In a Dark Wood • The Parting Glass

The DARK HORSE Series
The Dark Horse • The White Knight

The DOYLE & SPAIN Series
Snowball in Hell

The HAUNTED HEART Series
Haunted Heart Winter

The XOXO FILES Series
Mummie Dearest

OTHER NOVELLAS
Cards on the Table • The Dark Farewell •The Darkling Thrush
The Dickens with Love • Don't Look Back • A Ghost of a Chance
Lovers and Other Strangers • Out of the Blue
A Vintage Affair • Lone Star (in Men Under the Mistletoe)
Green Glass Beads (in Irregulars) • Blood Red Butterfly
Everything I Know • Baby, It's Cold • A Case of Christmas
Murder Between the Pages • Slay Ride

SHORT STORIES

A Limited Engagement • The French Have a Word for It
In Sunshine or In Shadow • Until We Meet Once More
Icecapade (in His for the Holidays) • Perfect Day
Heart Trouble • In Plain Sight • Wedding Favors
Wizard's Moon • Fade to Black • Night Watch
Plenty of Fish • The Boy Next Door
Halloween is Murder

COLLECTIONS

Stories (Vol. 1) • Sweet Spot (the Petit Morts)
Merry Christmas, Darling (Holiday Codas)
Christmas Waltz (Holiday Codas 2)
I Spy...Three Novellas
Point Blank (Five Dangerous Ground Novellas)
Dark Horse, White Knight (Two Novellas)
The Adrien English Mysteries
The Adrien English Mysteries 2